D0935351

Graves
without
Crosses

Graves without Crosses

Arved Viirlaid

Translated from the Estonian
by Ilse Lehiste

With a preface by
The Rt. Hon. John G. Diefenbaker

Clarke, Irwin & Company Limited
Toronto/Vancouver/1972

© 1972 by Clarke, Irwin & Company Limited

ISBN 0-7720-0525-7

No part of this publication may be repro-
duced or transmitted in any form or by any
means, electronic or mechanical, including
photocopy, recording, or any information
storage and retrieval system now known or to
be invented, without permission in writing
from the publisher, except by a reviewer who
wishes to quote brief passages in connection
with a review written for inclusion in a
magazine, newspaper or broadcast.

1 2 3 4 5   JD   76 75 74 73 72
Printed in Canada

PREFACE

Graves without Crosses describes, simply, eloquently and dramatically, the sufferings of a group of people who are all too representative of millions still living under the yoke of Communist dictatorship.

Although this book is a reminder that history reveals freedom dies when people take it for granted, yet everywhere in the world there are many who take for granted the right to speak, the right to worship and the right to go about their daily occupations without fear of arbitrary arrest. Indeed there are many who take for granted all the priceless privileges of freedom and are careless about preserving them.

The author has done well to emphasize the need for everyone to show by action and not by words alone a greater appreciation of freedom and a determination to guard it more vigilantly than ever before.

JOHN G. DIEFENBAKER

House of Commons
Ottawa
April 1972

Man's spirit will grow in victory as well
as in defeat, even in humiliation, as long
as he defends noble ideals.

(A. Viirlaid, *Year of Storms*, 1949)

CONTENTS

To my people

Graves without Crosses

CHARACTERS
(in order of appearance):

Taavi Raudoja, Taavi of Piskujõe, lieutenant, former member of the
   Estonian regiment in Finland
Hilda, a war orphan, living at the farm of Hiie
Aadu Mustkivi, a deaf-mute, living at the farm of Hiie
Linda Raudoja, Linda of Piskujõe, Taavi's mother
Osvald Roik, Osvald of Hiie, Hiie's hired man, partisan
Eduard Tähn, Eedi of Piibu, partisan
Ferdinand (Värdi) Uba, former lawyer, partisan
Mart of Liiskaku, partisan
Leonard (Leo) Kibuviir, partisan
Marta Laane, Marta of Roosi, former girl friend of Taavi
Ignas Tammela, Ignas of Hiie, former district elder
Krõõt Tammela, Krõõt of Hiie, Ignas' wife
Ilme Raudoja, Ilme of Hiie, their daughter, Taavi's wife
Tõmm Tammela, Tõmm of Hiie, son of Ignas and Krõõt
Lembit, Lembit of Hiie, son of Ilme and Taavi
Selma of Kuuse, Taavi's former schoolmate
Uuno of Kuuse, Selma's brother
Heino Roode   )
Joakim Lompus   )
Vello Kasar   )
Jaan Meos   ) former members of the Estonian regiment
Manivald Pihu   ) in Finland
Jüri Paarkukk   )
Richard (Riks) Kullerkann)
Ruudi Ugur   )
Arno Ting, Taavi's former schoolmate
Liisa Ting, his wife
Mihkel Tümatõnu, Mihkel of Lepiku, Taavi's former schoolmate, mem-
   ber of the Estonian Corps in the Red Army
Mrs. Inga, a member of the underground
Leida Soolepp, her assistant
Paul, a boatman
Arthur, his helper
Anton Tümatõnu, Anton of Lepiku, farmer
Luise, Luise of Lepiku, his wife
Siim of Kruusiaugu, a forest ranger
August of Roosi, Marta's father, a district messenger
Ebehard (Reku) Kõhva, Reku of Võllamäe
Jaak of Võllamäe, Reku's father, farmer
Leena of Võllamäe, Reku's mother
Juhan of Matsu, farmer
Meeta, Meeta of Matsu, his wife

1

Lonni)
Ella) their twin daughters
Paavel of Kadapiku, farmer
Sessi, his wife
Endel, their son
Evald, a former soldier
Jaan Holde, Chairman of the Executive Committee
Captain, interrogator of the NKVD
Lieutenant, interpreter of the NKVD
Tõnis   )
Johannes)
Hendrik) Taavi's cellmates in the NKVD prison
Valter   )
Kuusk, a political commissar in the NKVD prison
Evald's uncle, a farmer
Eedi's mother
Eedi's father
Michael Turban, new Chairman of the Executive Committee of Kalgina
Peetal Rause, the militiaman
Captain Jonnkoppel, the leader of partisans
Peeter of Valba, partisan
A male nurse, in prison
Hilja, Ilme's infant daughter, born in prison
A woman interrogator
Elli, Ilme's cellmate
Director of the prison
Tiit Kalmre, former schoolmate of Taavi, demobilized soldier of the
   Red Army
Red Army lieutenant, commander of the terror squad
Captain Kasinski, the boss of the district NKVD cell

2

Estonians belong to the Finno-Ugrian group of people who settled on the shores of the Baltic Sea more than 4000 years ago.

Although all the Baltic nations lost their freedom after a long fight against the German crusaders and other invaders in the thirteenth century, they each struggled to maintain strong cultural and national identities in the face of foreign oppression. Three of the five Baltic nations managed to survive the seven dark centuries and gain their independence with the onset of the First World War and the Russian Revolution.

After just two decades of self-rule the Republic of Estonia was overrun by Soviet Russia in 1940. (The Molotov-Ribbentrop Pact had placed Estonia in the Soviets' sphere.) A year later, war ended the honeymoon between Stalin and Hitler and the Baltic was occupied by the German forces. During both occupations a number of young Estonian men escaped across the forty-mile-wide gulf to Finland to join the Finnish army. They were mostly high school graduates and university students who could not bend themselves to the Nazi or Soviet régimes.

Most of these Estonian volunteers did not, however, stay in Finland until the end of the war. After the Soviet offensive had reached the Estonian border in January 1944, a strong urge to return home, to help defend it against the brutal invader, made itself felt. The Finns found themselves compelled to comply and "the Finnish boys"—as people at home called them—returned to Estonia in August 1944.

Two months later more than half were dead—killed in action against the Red Army or in some instances against the Nazis. Those who remained were hunted by the Russian occupation forces and their secret police.

Our story begins. . . .

PART ONE

I

The village seemed to be slumbering in the golden peace of the autumn afternoon. After the recent rains, the moss-covered roofs were green as in spring, although birches in the pastures were already dropping faded yellow leaves, and maples blazed here and there like red flames against the forest of dark firs.

It was the beginning of October 1944. It was the season when, formerly, threshing machines used to hum from early morning to late night, grain was carried to barns, and potato loads were rolled to storage. These used to be the days of great labours and due rewards, busy days, satisfying days.

A young man was leaning on the moss-covered stick fence and looking toward the village. He enjoyed the late warm light with all his being. His glance took in the farms, the fields and the village road, which, flanked by stone fences, spreading trees and telephone poles, seemed to lead straight into the sun. The fields of Metsaoti were wide, but the village itself kept close to the forest, as if the houses dreaded the excessive openness of the fields. Even the Võllamäe farm, at the far edge of the village where the road faded in the distance, had grown some lush young pines to shelter itself from the wind. The storms must have reached even these secluded backlands—there was hardly a place left anywhere in Estonia that had not been branded by the recent events.

Taavi Raudoja climbed the fence, threw his three-pronged fork over his shoulder and started walking along the cattle track toward the village. Up to now everything had been simpler than he had expected. He fancied he was returning from the outlying woodlands of the Hiie farm, where he had been forking the last haycocks into the barn. It didn't matter that the haymaking season was several months past. Right here the specially cultivated corn of Kadapiku was bent and broken into the dirt, and the windblown shocks of rye of the Lepiku farm were already sprouting—the work had been done as fast and as ill or well as the war had permitted.

The village road was the same as Taavi remembered it from previous autumns: it smelled of cattle, of ripe grain, turnips and morning glories that grew behind the Hiie barn. Only some fresh car tracks seemed ominous, since one had hardly ever seen any car tracks here before; but the white flock of chickens was encouraging, as they walked slowly home to Matsu, picking at something on the roadside. The old sickly dog of Lepiku acted familiar, barking a couple of times and then trotting off between the faggot pile and the raspberry bushes. The weather would turn bad soon—the dog was chewing on some broad blades of grass. Yes, all of Metsaoti was unchanged. There were no ruins, no fields trampled by battles. No red flags were flying to announce the advent of the new order. Yet still Taavi felt an emanating presence, something that filled the village road with an anguish that could somehow be sensed physically.

Although the open gate of the Hiie farm admonished Taavi to be careful, his heart began to beat with excitement when he stepped into the farm road. It was good he hadn't met any of the village people until he could discuss future plans with his wife and his father-in-law.

A young, suntanned, barelegged girl was standing beside the barn, a man's heavy sweater over her cotton dress, a bright-eyed shepherd dog at her side.

"Hello, Hilda! So it's you!"

"Hello! Yes, it's me," the girl answered seriously. "But I don't see how you would know me."

"What are you prattling about?" Taavi laughed. "Look here, even Pontus recognizes me!" He pointed to the dog that was wagging its tail, jumping up and down, and yelping with joy.

Suddenly he felt embarrassed. He passed his hand over his stubbly chin and smoothed the sides of his faded homespun coat, which was ridiculously short for him.

Perplexity and joy mixed with fear flashed in the large blue eyes of the girl, but her face remained unchanged.

"Why, it's you!"

And as if she was still not sure, she took a quick step toward the man and touched his arm. "You came—you came back! It's not good at all that you have come. . . ." She stopped short and turned around.

"Wait a minute!" Taavi did not understand. "Where are the others?"

"In the fields. Aadu is somewhere around or in the house. I'll tell them that—you've come back."

"Go and tell them, Hilda. Is Lembit in the fields too?"

"Your son isn't at home," the girl replied and went quickly away. But then she ran back to Taavi. "I think you'd better go up to the hayloft."

"Do the Russians come here too?"

"All the time. There are several camps at Kalgina. People have been driven out of their houses at the estate. Go upstairs; Aadu's bed is right next to the trap door. Get some rest, while I call your mother."

"My mother is here at Hiie?" Taavi was surprised. "Is Ilme also in the fields?"

"Your wife isn't at home," replied Hilda and was gone. Taavi was not sure whether he had seen right, but it seemed that the girl's eyes were shiny with tears. But she might have run for no reason at all; she always ran that way, with her head bent down and her thick hair flying behind, matching the colour of the autumn fields.

The constant dangers of the long flight had made Taavi cautious. He climbed up to the hayloft and sat down on the bed of old Aadu Mustkivi to wait for the workers from the field. The dirty pillowcase and the sheepskin which had been thrown over the bed added the smells of sweat and tobacco to the aroma of the fresh hay.

The deaf-mute Aadu and the orphan Hilda had both found shelter on the Hiie farm. The farmer, Ignas, had picked up the half-frozen girl after a destructive air raid on Tallinn. Since that time she had been living at Hiie, the only survivor of her whole family. Aadu he remembered from his childhood, when the pauper had been making his rounds from farm to farm, and cruel urchins had made fun of him on the highways. Then, however, Ignas had been elected district elder, and because of the dignity of his office he stopped the begging rounds of the old man by giving him a home.

Taavi had sat only a few moments when he heard the shuffling steps of the deaf-mute and the thumping of his heavy juniper-wood stick. Aadu came straight to the ladder. Taavi looked around, baffled. There was no doubt that the old man would become panicky and fall off the ladder, seeing his bearded chin, high boots, army pants, and generally unfamiliar appearance. Taavi could do no better than climb up the stacked hay underneath the roof of the barn.

At that moment he heard the noise of an approaching car from the direction of Võllamäe. Before the grey, bearded face of Aadu and his head of long, white hair had emerged from the trap door, the vehicle turned into the Hiie farmyard. All at once the whole yard was full of loud Russian clamour. Sharp, commanding words were addressed to old Aadu, who was just pulling himself up into the hayloft. The deaf-mute calmly groped toward his bed. Taavi saw that he wore the same long black coat as years ago, and shoes of untanned leather which gave off a pungent smell.

The loud talk of the Russians seemed to be aimed at the hayloft. As far as Taavi could make out, the old man they had seen on the ladder was considered suspicious, and they demanded that he come down right away. They banged against the wall and shook the ladder, but this did not disturb the deaf-mute in the least. He fumbled in his pockets for his pipe and lay down on his bed, puffing contentedly at the empty pipe.

Somebody babbled downstairs in Estonian, in a drunken voice which sounded familiar to Taavi.

Then someone began climbing the ladder. Taavi pulled his heavy German army Luger from his pocket and sidled farther back under the rafters. Aadu got up, as if sensing something. But when he saw the broad ruddy face of the Russian in the trap door, he raised his hands in terror and backed up toward the hay, making guttural sounds.

The Russian, gun in hand, shouted orders.

"Aa-ao-ah! Rra-rrah!" the deaf-mute rasped, clutching the sharp clover with his thin bony hands. The old man wished to escape by climbing up the stacked hay, but his limbs, paralysed with fear, refused to obey.

Taavi unfastened the safety catch on his gun. Then he saw the Russian raise his gun, too. Without realizing what he was doing, Taavi aimed squarely into the face of the soldier.

Another loud argument broke out in the yard. In addition to the Russian clamour, women's voices were heard: the people had arrived from the field. The soldier up on the ladder cursed and brandished his pistol. A woman spoke commandingly in Russian. That voice, too, sounded very familiar to Taavi, but he was unable to identify the speaker. Yet he gathered that the woman spoke about the deaf-mute and tried to drive the Russians away.

9

"You should know, old man, that there's no vodka here," she angrily told somebody in Estonian. "You've already got yourself so drunk that you can hardly stand up. Shame on you! Go to Matsu; Juhan will have some beer left. All right, I'll come along myself."

The soldier disappeared from the trap door, rattling the ladder. A long discussion was carried on outside, and a woman's deep, energetic voice argued violently, now in Russian, now in Estonian. Then a sub-machine gun rattled. The bullets ran through the boards of the wooden gables, scattering splinters and dust into the darkness of the loft. Car doors slammed, the motor began to cough, and the noisy party drove away.

Aadu rushed to his bed, pulled the sheepskin over his face, and lay down. He kept emitting his excited sounds, and his limbs twitched.

Taavi slid down from the haystack. Down in the yard were his mother, the hired man Osvald Roik and the dog Pontus, ears pricked up. None of the Hiie family were there. His mother embraced Taavi without words, and tears flowed over her wrinkled cheeks. Osvald, too, did not say a word, but just clenched Taavi's extended hand with his big, powerful fist.

"Come, have something to eat," the mother said. "They won't be back today; Marta will take care of that."

"Damn those swine, shooting all through the barn!" The hired man spat.

When Linda had given Osvald and Hilda some work orders, she took her son to the farmyard. Absent-mindedly Taavi gazed at the windlass of the well, the newly painted fence, the wide windows of the house and the late dahlias underneath. On the other side of the yard, in front of the old threshing floor with its moss-covered roof and the chamber that had been converted into a chicken house, the climbing roses lay broken down by the wind.

"Sit down and rest," the mother said, when they had reached the living room. "You're tired. Even your face looks worn, like skin and bones. Do you have any tobacco? No. Wait, I'll see if Ignas has left some."

While his mother hustled toward the back room, Taavi sat down on the long, carved wooden bench, somewhat dazed and quite weary. Thoughts and emotions rose to the surface of his mind and broke the calm of his exhaustion. What did all this mean? Why was his mother, mistress of the small Piskujõe farm, giving orders here as if she were at home? Where were the Hiie people? Where were his wife and son?

Suddenly something in the large room perturbed him. The curtain moved quietly in front of the open window. Dishes sparkled in the dark recesses of the buffet. In the corner stood Lembit's huge wooden horse, waiting for a new owner, as the boy had outgrown the playing age. Even the picture of the President was hanging in its old place. Everything was the same, but life itself was gone. Taavi stood up and walked on the striped rug around the table. He met and recognized a few familiar things from his own apartment, which his wife had taken along to the country. But even these seemed strange.

The mother returned with a box of tobacco.

"Are you alone?" she asked.

"No. There are five of us," Taavi answered. "The others stayed in the Hiie barn."

"When Hilda goes to let the cattle in, she can call them."

"Yes. Only . . . one of them is wounded," Taavi said. "Just a little scratch, well bandaged, that will heal soon. We happened this way and I thought—where else should I go looking for help? One of the men is from Tenise."

"Who? Mart of Liiskaku? Must be one of the Johannes' sons. Did you look for me at home?"

"I came straight here. I'd thought of going home—it would be safer there in the woods—but I just happened to look at the village and kept on coming."

"Well, I'm keeping two farms now." His mother smiled. "I'm really putting on the dog in my old age." Her thin face had aged even more during the last few months, and heavy dark rings of weariness shaded her eyes. She came quite close to her son. "They went away, Ilme and all."

"So," Taavi drawled, making himself a cigarette from the country tobacco and betraying no emotion. "To Germany?"

"Ignas wanted to go to Sweden. But it was late already. Who knows where they ended up?"

"Which way did they go?"

"They went by way of Pärnu. Ignas kept thinking so long, and Ilme was against going—like that—without you. Lembit started crying at the last minute, saying he wouldn't go without Daddy. He just clung to my skirt and wouldn't go. Krõõt objected too. But Tõmm said he'd go all alone—and so they went. I am here taking care of the stock. I even brought my own cow and my sheep to Hiie."

She invited her son to the kitchen and got busy at the stove. Taavi sat down at the well-scrubbed wooden dining table and blew rings of smoke thoughtfully.

"I see that Osvald is back already."

"For about a week," Linda answered. "He went home first, but didn't stay. He just changed clothes and was off. He says there are bigger woods around here. Well, nobody knows what will happen or what will become of any of us. There's been no bloodshed in our village or at Harukurgu, but they are great at smashing and shooting things up. At Ilmaotsa they are said to have burned and killed. At Kalgina they shot old Toomas Kuuse right in the middle of his rye field, and at Ahtama they broke windows and attacked women. Here and there fighting seems to be still going on. Every night we hear shooting, and the day before yesterday we saw the glow of a big fire in the southwest. What's going to come of it all?"

"It'll go on from where it stopped in 1941."

"My God! But they say the English are in Tallinn."

"Is that so?" Taavi became excited. "Who did you get that from?

What are they doing in Tallinn?"

"That's what people ask. Maybe they are keeping an eye on the Russians, so they won't oppress the people. Old August Roosi, too. . . ."

"That drunkard! Just now he was hobnobbing with the Russians here under the hayloft door."

"He says we'll get the republic back soon."

"Ah, that's nonsense, Mother, as long as the Russians are here."

"But on Sunday they held a prayer meeting in the old chapel at Harukurgu. It isn't prohibited any more. Drunken soldiers had been dancing and carousing in the place, but nobody came to disturb the meeting."

Linda placed the food in front of her son. Taavi smiled to himself: people were so inventive when looking for consolation.

"Eat now! Look, Osvald and Hilda are back from the cellar. I've got to go. I'll send Hilda to pass the word to the men."

Taavi wolfed down the food. He had not seen such an omelet for years. He cut another slice of sourdough bread, spread it with butter and cottage cheese mixed with caraway seed, and emptied half a pitcher of creamy sweet milk.

Having finished his meal, he walked about the rooms and saw how the Hiie family had left things on their departure. His return home had not turned out as he had imagined. Here it was—the farm started by their grandfathers, all the little things that added up to a wealthy household: the fields, the livestock, the beehives, the garden, the grain in the storage bins and the corn in the fields. They had left everything behind; only the people had departed on the horse-drawn wagon, with empty hands and aching hearts.

Walking through the darkening rooms and looking out through the windows into the farmyard, the garden, and at the village road, Taavi felt that he had somehow delayed too long. It was foolish of him not to have joined those friends of his that night they left. They had invited him along, and the boat was waiting. But he had been exhausted by the battles, and the thought of his family had held him back. And—why deny it?—he had believed in a miracle. Now he was here, alone in the abandoned house. Not a letter, not a greeting had been left for him, as if Taavi Raudoja in his soldier's boots had been a totally forgotten figure from the past.

He looked up at the somewhat gloomy, firm face of the President in the picture on the wall. No—he pressed his fist against the thick oaken table—no, he would *not* admit defeat.

When he entered the farmyard, Taavi could smell the heated steam bath: the sharp odour of the hot stones and the sweetish scent of lye. His mother had sent Aadu to heat the bath for them. Taavi clutched the cool handle of the pistol in his pocket. He felt as if his father, who had been murdered in 1941 by the Communists, was standing right beside him with his hand on his shoulder, saying, "Look, son, I don't want you with me yet, for you have much to do. You are still young and strong.

12

I will call you when you become weary."

The fir forests of Piskujõe loomed dark behind the pastures, stretching to Tenise, Verisoo and Ilmaotsa. The reddening orb of the sun sank behind the jagged treetops into the black depths of the woods.

Old Aadu Mustkivi greeted everyone with a dignified handshake when, after gobbling a sandwich and drinking some warm milk, they went to the steam bath.

"He accepts you as ours." Osvald laughed. He was a red-faced giant, with square shoulders and angular limbs. He towered above the other five. Only a blond string bean of a boy came close to his height. He had innocent blue eyes and the first traces of a beard on his chin, and the fellows called him Eedi of Piibu. He had a speech defect, so that a stranger often could not make out what he said. The wounded man— Ferdinand Uba—was hardly taller than a shepherd boy. He seemed the oldest of them all, close to forty. He wore glasses, his face was pale and drawn, and he had narrow shoulders, so slumped that he appeared hunchbacked. The others seemed to Osvald like real fighting men, who had already been through fire and lightning and would not shrink from it in the future.

The sauna was hot.

"Aadu wants to give us a real baptism." The hired man of Hiie grinned.

"It would be nice if we could dip ourselves into something cold afterwards," Ferdinand said.

"The river is about a hundred metres across the pasture."

"What the devil, how could I get there with this leg of mine? I can hardly limp along with a stick," the hunchback muttered angrily. When the others hurried to go through the rituals of the steam bath, he remained in the front room to wash himself by the light of a candle. His thigh was heavily bandaged.

Taavi climbed in front of the opening where the steam was gushing forth. Let it scald off all hopeless thoughts and dark portents. The long high bench was full of men; he wasn't alone. In the front room, in the pockets of the clothes they had obtained from forest farms, every man had a trusty little weapon. And their army rifles were hidden in the woods.

The leafy birch twigs swished in the hot steam, as the men worked over their bodies with dogged persistence. They puffed, grunted and groaned with pleasure. Streams of sweat ran from their bodies, and Osvald kept pouring bucketfuls of water on the hot, crackling stones.

"Old Ignas left us a real first-rate bath! Aah! Turn on the heat like at Stalingrad! That's it, brother!" he shouted.

"W-wouldn't it be f-fun, if Ivan h-happened b-by just n-now," Eedi stuttered.

"Don't worry," Osvald answered. "Hilda is a smart girl. She'll pipe up right away when she hears a noise. I told her I'd marry her when she grows up, if she keeps a good lookout. But they won't dare come here, into the woods, after dark."

"I remember that when we were hiding in the forests as partisans, one Saturday night we went to a steam bath near Kohila," Mart of Liiskaku said. He had a long, sharp nose, and tattooed blood group symbols showed from under his hairy arm. "Well, it was a nice Saturday night, we drank some Saku beer, took a thorough steam bath, swam in the river to cool off, and afterwards danced with the girls on the village green till morning. Next day we found out that because of the noise, the Black Hundred had avoided our village, turned in at the next village and swept it clear of all the men. The revel saved our skins. Who would have thought that the 'bandits' were celebrating a wedding on the village green!"

Leonard Kibuviir, a fellow with thick lips and wily eyes, raised his head, where a shiny bald spot was surrounded by a crown of black hair.

"You know, that gives me an idea," he said. "We should get such powerful papers that we could get out of the woods and among people. If you don't have a paper in your pocket with plenty of seals on it, they'll shoot you so full of lead that even worms won't eat you. And, worst of all, one can't get close to a woman like that."

"N-now he star-t-ts ta-talking a-bout w-women again," said Eedi.

"Why not?" Leonard laughed and spat across the room. "I'm a baptized and confirmed man!"

"It's very simple to get an identity card now," Osvald said. "I got me one from the county house—just a piece of paper with your name, date of birth, and place of residence. They even used the old county seal on it. I told the chairman of the executive committee that nobody would be fool enough to be impressed by this piece of paper—to show to a Russian, you've got to have several pages of seals and signatures. He just laughed and said that it was only temporary anyway."

"You can't expect them to hand out a Soviet passport to anyone who jumps out of the bush." Leonard stated the obvious truth as if he were the only one who knew it.

"What kind of a beast is your chairman of the executive committee?" Taavi inquired.

"Looks like any ordinary Christian. An Estonian from the other side of Lake Peipsi. A close-mouthed and tired fellow. He had a five-pointed star on his breast, but made a better impression on me than I would have expected."

"They have to cater to the people."

"Why should they try to cater to the likes of us? You, complete with your hair and guts, will just make a good tooth filling for Stalin," Osvald remarked. "Shall we throw another bucketful of water on the stones?"

"Do-don't squ-squeeze th-the soul ou-out!" Eedi complained helplessly.

"Stop whimpering!" Leonard scoffed. "There you are, crooked like a dog's flea, with your nose between a crack in the wall! I've told you how we used to bathe in Finland."

"I'm m-more u-used to oth-other wa-ways of ba-bathing; if you'd b-been on th-the East-tern f-front, you'd kno-know."

"Oo-ooh! Why didn't you come to Syväri? I told you to. But you were still wet behind the ears, when I was already doing distant reconnaissance. Don't forget, I took part in the Winter War and came back with the Erna group!"

"You're quite a man," Osvald admitted. "I never got any farther than the Eastern battalions, and they were about to kill me right there, the devils!"

"Eastern battalions, legions, bah! Why didn't you jump across to Finland?"

Osvald threw another bucketful of water on the stones. "I'm sort of a big-bodied fellow, not used to jumping," he answered. "Later I had a company of boys; no jumpers among these either."

The men drifted toward the front room to wash.

"The time is past when there are Finland fighters, legionnaires, border guards or national guardsmen," Taavi said. "Now there are only beaten Estonian soldiers, who refuse to accept defeat, for their spirit has not yet been crushed."

"And won't be either!" Osvald retorted. "They can cut off my head, but the spirit—well!" He grinned. "And right now I still have the head." He hung the lantern on a hook in the centre of the room. "Does every man have a bucket?" he asked, filling his own with cold water from the tub and pouring it over his shoulders.

"Hey, what about going to the river?" Taavi shouted. Without waiting for an answer, he jerked the door open and ran across the pasture to the river, the others at his heels, bare feet thumping. Their eyes soon became used to the darkness outside, for the sky was covered with stars, and a faint afterglow of the sunset lingered in the west.

Taavi was the first to plunge, head first, from the heap of stones on the bank into the black waters of the river. He swam a few circles around the deep pool before his overheated body began to feel the chill.

They raced back to the sauna like a bunch of playful youngsters, and Osvald threw several more bucketfuls of water over the heated stones.

Ferdinand, or Värdi, as he was called, opened the door. Rubbing his unruly hair with a towel, he did not show a trace of the high spirits of the others. He was small and bent, and his movements were sudden and jerky.

"The mistress came to ask when we'd be ready. Dinner is waiting," he growled.

When the others followed him to the front room, he was just pulling on his clothes. The clothes were old and filthy, and their smell made him spit.

"Wait," Taavi called. "Here's a clean shirt for you from my mother. She found something for every man."

While the others thanked him for the clean underwear, Värdi accepted the shirt with the same disgruntled expression with which he began pulling off his ragged and greasy army shirt.

"Is your leg bothering you?" Taavi asked.

"No, that doesn't matter," the hunchback mumbled. "The bandage is all right, and I kept the water from it." He chewed each word, his narrow chin pushed forward.

"Say, can you make it alone all right? Let me help you," Osvald offered. "That leg is no joke; you've got to take care of it. If it gets real bad, why, all you can do is tie a rope around your neck."

"Ah, leave me alone. I'll be all right," Värdi answered and turned his back toward the others, leaning on the water barrel for support. He fumbled there until he got his trousers and boots on. Then he took his crutch-like stick from the corner, folded his coat under his arm and limped out in pain.

"A strange character," Osvald whispered to Taavi. "Where does a fellow like that hail from?"

"Who knows for sure? We picked him up in the woods. His leg was shot through. I remembered his face from Finland. We had been in the same front sector in the winter. We met around Tartu, too. Wait, I'll go and take him to the house. It's dark, and he doesn't know the way."

Värdi had not got very far from the sauna yet. He was sitting under a birch tree in the pasture.

"I was afraid you might not find your way to the house," Taavi said. "With that bad leg of yours."

"Damn it, I am not a baby," Värdi snarled, "Go and tell the other men to hurry up. All that yakking and giggling—like children. Got any tobacco? Oh, Lord, you're naked; obviously you can't be carrying tobacco around! Say—say, what about tomorrow?"

"We'll see. We'll leave you here as planned."

"I don't care where I'll rot, but the others—what about the others?"

"Don't worry about the others."

"Ah, the devil! You're grown-up men, but you act like kindergarten kids! You probably don't even realize what has happened to us."

Returning to the bath, Taavi found the other fellows quietly washing. Värdi would not have had any reason to reproach them right now. Each was wrapped in his own thoughts, trying to find some path in the thickets of the future.

Old Aadu was sitting on a bench, eating soup from his earthenware bowl. He held a huge wooden spoon, which he manipulated calmly and imperturbably, putting the food behind his beard with contented smacks. From time to time his left hand broke bread or swept over his wrinkled forehead. He was bothered by the hot steam rising from the bowl and by the white wisps of hair which kept falling over his eyes.

Linda had set the table in the kitchen, and was waiting for the men to come for supper. The cows had been milked and tied to their stalls

16

in the barn, and Hilda was putting away the milk pails. Right now she was no doubt standing idly outside, listening for suspicious sounds in the night. She was a great help now at Hiie. Without her, Linda would have got nowhere trying to keep the big farm going. And Osvald was a help too. Now at least the livestock was properly cared for, even though their labour was hardly adequate to work the fields.

Strangely enough, Linda felt no great joy this time at the coming of her son. Seeing him alive and well, tears of joy had risen to her eyes, but she knew that soon they might turn to tears of sorrow. The question overwhelmed her: What would become of him now?

Aadu finished eating, carefully licked his spoon, bent his head, and clasped his hands in prayer. This was also a sign to the mistress that he did not want any more food. Otherwise he would have made a restless noise and moved his empty bowl. He got up with the slowness of a very old man, placed his spoon on a cupboard, and shuffled out, his legs stiff from sitting.

What if she were to keep her son right there, just as she was going to keep that friend of his with a crippled leg, hiding him in haylofts and barn corners? Or perhaps he could go to the county house and try to talk himself clear? The chairman of the committee was said to be a friendly man. If Linda should go herself and beg for him. . . . Taavi had fled to Finland to get away from the Germans. He was no criminal or Fascist! It was hard to look at him now—so thin and worn out. Coming back from Finland he had been cleanly dressed, and proud like a general. The whole house and yard had been full of fun and laughter. Now he was wearing old rags, borrowed from God knows where, his hair full of hayseed and moss, boots muddy like a ditchdigger's. Perhaps she would go to the county house to see what she could find out. A general amnesty was said to have been proclaimed. But at Kalgina old Toomas Kuuse had been shot in his rye field at high noon. No, one could not expect mercy. One would only humiliate oneself by futile begging.

Hilda came in. Her movements had become awkward and restlessness had come into her eyes since Taavi's arrival.

"I took blankets up to the attic for them," she said.

"That's good," Linda answered. "They should be coming soon."

"Yes, but I have been thinking. The sauna is closest to the woods. They could sleep up in the attic there," the girl said quickly. "If I myself slept in the storage barn, I could hear everything that. . . ."

Then someone knocked on the door.

Both women were startled, as if caught committing a crime, although the knocking was quiet and modest. When the door was opened, a woman was standing there, a bright scarf over her black hair, hands in the pockets of a heavy overcoat.

"You, Marta! What is it?"

"Could I . . . speak to Taavi?" the visitor asked.

"Come on in. They are in the bath right now—Taavi and Osvald. I'll go tell them that. . . ."

"Oh, thanks. I can wait. No, I won't come in. Is Taavi all right?"

17

"Nothing wrong with him; all the limbs are whole, thank God," Linda answered, scanning Marta's face in the light that fell from the kitchen. What was the matter with the woman? Her breast was heaving, as if she had been running hard for a long distance.

"I'll go and tell Taavi," his mother said, and started toward the bath. All the way across the pasture she had a queer feeling in her legs. All kinds of stories were told about Marta and her marriage to old Laane, who had been arrested in 1941. What was Marta doing here at home? All through the German occupation she had been living off her husband's wealth in Tallinn and had had dealings with German officers.

Linda met the men halfway out.

"What's up, Mother?" Taavi asked. His shirt was open to let him cool off from the heat of the bath.

"I came to tell you that Marta wants to speak with you," his mother replied quietly. "She is at the house. I thought it might not be good for the men to be seen, since she is working at the county house. But she just happened to be here this afternoon when you came and—it turned out all right with the Russians."

"She really has a nose for men," Osvald mumbled. "Well, can't say a word against her looks. She wears furs and pearls and smells like a. . . ."

"Like giving you heart failure after a hot bath." Leonard laughed.

Taavi paid no attention to Osvald's jeering. He knew that the feelings of the hired men of Hiie toward Marta of Roosi were of a completely different kind. Maybe he was still in the habit of going over to Roosi and sitting around in the yard as before.

Taavi was pleased at the prospect of meeting Marta.

The woman's handshake was warm and strong, so that Taavi felt the rings on her fingers. They walked out of the gate toward Roosi and Võllamäe.

"So you are home now. Planning to stay?" Taavi asked.

"Who knows. I thought I'd rest my nerves some."

"You probably need it." Taavi's remark had a double meaning.

"The last weeks in Tallinn were terrible."

When Marta had described the fall of Tallinn and her return to Kalgina, they walked in silence. But this silence was tense and somewhat embarrassed.

"A fine evening," Taavi remarked finally.

Now Marta burst into laughter, shattering the reserve which the years had built up between them. "Fine," she said, in her pleasant, deep voice. "Very fine indeed," she repeated, and her voice sounded somehow sad and full of remorse.

They sat on the old stone fence, and Marta asked, "Tell me honestly, what are you planning to do? I know there were no pleasant surprises waiting for you when you came out of the woods."

Taavi began silently groping in his pockets for tobacco.

"Take this, I have some cigarettes," said Marta offering her cigarette case and matches. "Why, you're trembling! Take my coat. After a bath like that! Take it!"

18

Without waiting for an answer, she exchanged the coat on Taavi's shoulders for her own heavy overcoat. Taavi sensed the warmth of her body and the smell of her perfume that lingered in the coat. It disturbed and bothered him.

"I was thinking of you all day today," Marta confessed. "Strange, as if I had had a premonition. I just walked over to Hiie this afternoon for no reason at all, and there you were."

She breathed deeply and excitedly. Even her voice sounded excited. From the fields behind them rose the smell of ripe grain and wet earth. The road in front smelled bitter with lime.

"You know,"—Marta took Taavi's arm—"don't think that I am a fool. I'm not a schoolgirl any more, but after you came I felt such a joy in my heart that I ran around in the woods like crazy. I went to the foot of the Koolu hills behind Võllamäe. Remember? Where we sat once in winter. Remember?"

Taavi made a defensive move, so that Marta withdrew her hand.

"It was a beautiful winter, wasn't it? I've thought of it so often. Those were the happiest days of my life," Marta whispered.

"Well, there was really nothing, I mean, nothing really happened." Taavi threw his cigarette away with an abrupt gesture.

The woman leaned heavily against the stone fence, Taavi's coat around her shoulders. "We sat in the snow all day," she continued. "You were heaping up fir branches for me to sit on. You were afraid that I would catch a cold. You fool, I was burning in your arms!"

Taavi got up and took a few steps.

"Isn't it funny, how all that comes back? What foolishness! We were children. We did not even know how to play. But these memories are wonderful to me." She jumped up, knocking a stone from the fence. "Well, and now you are here again, left behind like a child. With a cruel face, exhausted by battles and worn out by wanderings in the forests . . . a bandit!" She burst into laughter again. "What are we going to do with you now? I don't know, and you don't seem to care very much. You're just glad that your son is out of danger and that your wife has left you."

"Marta!"

"Don't be angry. That's how I feel. I cannot understand—a woman who loves her husband. I did not love my husband, I did not even like him. But when he was arrested I almost went crazy. I went from office to office, I did not sleep a wink, I carried parcels to the jail until they wouldn't accept them any more. Yes, I even begged them to send me with him."

"That was a completely different situation."

"All right. That's none of my business. Say, are you planning to go to Tallinn or to stay here in the country?"

"Maybe I'll go to the seashore," Taavi answered coolly.

Marta bowed her head and dug her heel into the road. "So," she said. "Are you going after them?"

"I won't be able to go to Germany any more, but. . . ."

19

"Do you think you can still get somewhere else?" Marta asked ironically. "Listen," she said, grabbing his sleeve again. "We are at least friends, aren't we? I would like to help you."

"That's fine," Taavi answered. His voice was indifferent, and he did not seem to expect much.

"You know, in the attic of the county house I found a box full of old Soviet passports, the ones that the Germans made the people turn in. I just got the idea that somebody who is hard up for a passport might have some use for them now."

This was really a splendid idea. Taavi thought immediately of his comrades.

They walked toward the Võllamäe and Roosi farms. The big trees at the roadside rustled softly, and a grey mist rose over the fields from the Verisoo moor. Hoarfrost could be expected for the morning. A feeble glow of light showed far on the horizon in the direction of Kalgina, and from Harukurgu trailed the drawling songs of Russian soldiers.

"Let's change coats now," Taavi suggested.

"Isn't my coat good enough for you?"

"Too good, that's the trouble. What do you think? A hungry wolf like me comes out of the woods and smells the warmth of a human being, and a woman to boot. . . . That can drive you crazy," Taavi replied, teasing her.

"I didn't notice anything of the sort," Marta answered. Her voice expressed challenge and suppressed joy. Exchanging the coat for her overcoat, she squeezed Taavi's wrist quickly and passionately.

The same little devil, the man decided. They walked to the Roosi farm in silence. Across the road, the dog of the Võllamäe farm began to bark furiously, forcing them to hide between the storage barn and lilac bushes of Roosi. At any rate, Marta pulled Taavi there by the hand, clinging to him, out of breath.

"Where do you have the passports?" Taavi asked.

"Shh!" she whispered.

"That dog won't stop for a good while. Go and get the passports and let's go back."

Marta went. Taavi followed her brisk walk with his eyes. Then the door squeaked, and Marta vanished into the house. Taavi leaned his back against the barn wall and waited. The Võllamäe dog continued to bark and growl. Other dogs answered him in the distance. Taavi thought he recognized the powerful wolf's howl of Pontus of Hiie. Then he heard somebody walking in the Võllamäe courtyard. Somebody was talking, too.

Taavi leaned out from behind the house. No, these were not Russians. He recognized the coarse cough and spitting of the farmer, Jaak.

"Wonder which one it is today, the girl or the old man?"

"None of the damned Russians seems to be around," someone answered. "It must be the girl, then. Maybe she found somebody to warm her back again."

"Or maybe she brought herself some Germans from town."

The men moved away, and even the dog calmed down.

Taavi spat, as if he had inadvertently got something dirty in his mouth. Who could trust that Marta? Maybe she really had brought a lover along and was hiding him in the woods. Maybe they had just kept making love and missed the last boat.

Marta returned soon after. She carried under her arm a little package wrapped in brown paper, and handed it to Taavi.

"Perhaps you'll find something suitable," she said.

"I'll surely find something."

"So you'll go across?"

"If I can, of course. The fight is over for this time."

"Be careful! I have heard that the roads are patrolled, and whoever looks in the least suspicious is arrested." Her smile was very melancholy and tired. "Maybe we'll meet again some time. Farewell and—so long!"

"So long, and thanks!"

"You have no reason to thank me," the woman muttered. She slipped her hand from Taavi's palm and turned toward the house. Her walk was very slow and tired.

Taavi, however, marched back toward Hiie with his chin up and with a springy step. The stones crumbled under his army boots, and the dog of Võllamäe began barking with renewed vigour. Taavi was holding the package of Soviet passports in his hands, and he had a hard time holding back a cheerful whistle. Bright stars flickered in the autumn sky above the forests which embraced the whole horizon, and the breath of the ripe fields engulfed him. The forest thickets stretched out their protective arms around him, and he felt clean and strong.

A single splinter of a falling star left a long bright trail in the sky and fell into the woods of Ilmaotsa.

II

The following evening, when the outsiders who had assembled at the Hiie farm—Linda of Piskujõe, the hired man Osvald, old Aadu Mustkivi, the orphan Hilda and the wounded Värdi—were sitting at the supper table, a squeaky wagon turned from the village road into the farmyard. Suddenly the angry barking of Pontus gave way to joyous yelping.

"Well, now," Osvald said and got up.

All the others followed him except Aadu, who regarded the movements of the others from his corner of the table with restless concern. A horse snorted, voices were heard, and Pontus yelped deliriously. They met the newcomers at the door.

"Holy heavens!" Linda exclaimed. "The Hiie folks are back! Hilda, Hilda, light the lantern quickly; they can't see in the dark yard."

"They'll be all right. There's nothing to see anyway," Krõõt, the mistress of the Hiie farm, answered. "Their eyes are used to the dark, and they only have to unharness the horse. You are all still alive?"

"Oh, never mind about us now. . . ."

"Wait, I'll go and help the master," Osvald blurted.

"Yes, go and send Ignas in," Krõõt ordered. "My limbs are so shaken from sitting on that wagon, I can hardly move." Krõõt leaned on a heavy stick of fresh alder wood, but even so Ilme was supporting her. Lembit walked in at their heels, wearing a new peaked cap and his winter overcoat.

Nobody said much at first. Those in the house were too surprised to speak. Only Värdi mumbled a greeting, and the newcomers took off their overcoats and wraps. Hilda's eyes were glued to Ilme. In her mind she saw Taavi, how he had stood at the gate last night, and her eyes suddenly filled with tears. Lembit ran out and carried some lighter packages in from the wagon, and Linda brought more food to the table.

"You just go ahead," Krõõt said, sat down on a chair close to the stove, heavy and tired, and began rubbing her swollen legs. "Are the animals all well?" she inquired.

She was a woman of medium build, much heavier than Linda, with dark eyes and dark hair that showed very little grey. There was not much left to remind one of the curly-headed, dancing and sparkling young bride whom Ignas had brought home from a faraway county. She had changed completely since then. She was stern and spoke little, was deliberate and respectable.

Her daughter Ilme, though the mother of a sturdy youngster, still had the face and movements of a young girl.

Soon Ignas and Tõmm came in. Both were tall, strong men, and yet no one would have taken them for father and son from their appearance. Tõmm had inherited his father's build but his mother's looks and girlhood disposition. Tõmm was the life of every company he joined.

Today both men were silent and gloomy, their cheeks pale and their eyes sunken. The father began lighting his pipe with a live coal from the fireplace, and Tõmm threw himself down on the bench behind Värdi's back.

"You're from strange parts?" he asked Värdi.

"Still farther."

"So. From the woods?"

"From the woods."

Silence reigned in the room. It seemed as if the newcomers felt strange in their own home. Even Lembit's voice did not sound joyous and lusty. He called Pontus, picked up a candle, and looked over a thing or two in the dark rooms which he had been worrying about during the long trip, but all the toys and books seemed to be left peacefully alone, even his double-bladed pocketknife with its bone handle. The Russians hadn't got around to their farm yet, as grandfather had feared on the way back.

Aadu closed his eyes, moved his lips saying his after-dinner prayer, and got up to carry away the dishes. His face and eyes were still bright with childish joy at the return of the Hiie people. Passing by Lembit, he stroked the boy's light curls tenderly with his gnarled hand. This was a

22

surprise to everybody, especially to Lembit himself. His wide-open eyes followed the old man.

"What's new at home?" Ignas asked.

"Ah, here. . . ." Linda was searching for words. Her movements had become unsure. The same tension showed in Hilda's behaviour. She hustled between the kitchen and the pantry as if under some compulsion. "You brought your souls back alive," the mistress of Piskujōe observed.

"Our souls, yes, but I wonder how long we can keep them," Ignas mumbled, pipe in mouth. "Now many a man has to give up his soul on the road. It was lucky that there were two of us."

"Are they that bad?" Värdi growled. "I thought they only killed in the woods."

"They killed any way they could in Pärnu," Tōmm replied viciously. "It was a sea of flames when we left. We had to lie low at Uncle's place for a week."

Again the work was done in silence and thoughts were stifled. Why should tired people waste words, if they have nothing good to report? Hilda's eyes flashed and her mouth opened, but she, too, kept quiet. Lembit sat down on the logs in front of the stove and held his arms around Pontus' neck. Ilme went around the rooms making beds and unpacking clothes. Osvald entered, his eyes on the floor, and gloom on his face in place of his usual broad grin.

"Those accursed beasts, what a nag they have given you to pull your wagon! That's not a horse any more; it can hardly stand up on its legs! You can't even sell it for the skin, it's so beaten up and full of scars!"

"That's nothing, the wagon is no better," Tōmm exploded. "They took the whole business—horse, wagon and. . . ." He stood up, and his dark eyes glinted angrily in his young face. "If I had had a rock in my hand, I tell you, I would have hit them with it!"

"Tōmm!" his mother warned.

"Come, now, what's the use of blowing your top like that," his father said, soothingly. "We kept our lives, and that's enough for this turn."

Tōmm shrugged. "Sure, we kept our lives—what a wonderful outcome! We should have been in Sweden a long time ago. Now we are caught! Now we are in their hands, and that's that! But I tell you, they won't catch me. I won't give myself up!"

"Don't, if you don't want to," his father answered. "You've grown to a man's size. If your bones hold up and you use your head, nobody will try to tell you what to do. But give it some thought first. Don't kick about for nothing. No good ever comes out of beating against thin air."

"Here we were thinking and thinking at home, until it was too late and no place to go. If you'd paid any attention to my words then, we'd now be in Sweden."

"Please, Tōmm, don't talk that way," Ilme begged. "Listen to Father."

"I've listened enough," Tōmm burst out. His eyes glistened, as if he were ready to burst into tears. "See what came out of that listening! We didn't even get to Germany!"

"What's wrong with being here?" Osvald retorted. "The house is full of men."

"Just right for Ivan to come and pluck."

As suddenly as the talk had filled the room, it stopped. The returned travellers began to eat quietly, but no one showed much appetite.

All at once Hilda, who was standing behind Ilme, broke the silence. "Taavi is back!"

"Taavi!" Ilme exclaimed, dropping her fork to the floor.

"Taavi!" the others echoed.

"Where is Daddy?" Lembit demanded, jumping up from the table.

"Taavi *was* here," Linda said.

The Hiie family looked at one another, confused. What had happened here during their absence? Hilda was crying. Tears were running down her cheeks, and her large childlike eyes looked at Ilme, full of anguish. Her lips moved, but she was unable to speak.

"It's really stupid the way things have turned out," Taavi's mother said. Her eyes, too, became moist against her will.

"Tell me, what about him?" Ilme was frightened. "Has something happened to him? Where did he go? When was he here?"

"Grandmother, where is Daddy? Grandmother!"

Linda smiled weakly.

"There's nothing wrong with him. He's well, like a fish in water. Really funny clothes he had got himself in the woods. Look, his friend is here now—wounded. Taavi left to go after you."

Now it had been said.

"To Pärnu?" Ilme asked.

"No, he was going to Tallinn first, hoping to get across the bay some-how—his old familiar way," Osvald replied.

"Stupid," Tõmm remarked. "There's no way out any more."

"Who knows? He's got across before," Ignas retorted, as if to challenge his son.

"Poor Taavi," Krõõt lamented. "He comes home, can't find anybody."

"That really stunned him at first," Linda said. "I was scared to tell him. He didn't stay long, just slept the night. They came last night and left this morning."

"This morning!" Ilme exclaimed. Her flaming cheeks proclaimed her agitation. "This morning!" she repeated, looking at her curly-headed son, who was listening to the talk of his elders, his dark eyes big and restless.

"Well, if those Russians hadn't. . . ," Tõmm mumbled, angry again.

"We would have been home last night," his mother finished calmly. "But it was not up to us. Now is a time when nothing is up to us any more."

"But what's going to happen now? What did he say? What were his plans?" Ilme inquired. Everybody had forgotten about the food, even though they had eaten but little.

"He was glad you had got away, that's all," Taavi's mother replied.

"There was no use, then, of the war or anything," Ilme lamented.

"That cannot be true! You, Father, say that isn't true! What do you think, Tōmm? Or you, Osvald?"

"They won't stay here for long," Tōmm muttered darkly.

"What do you think?" Ilme turned to Värdi. "You are Taavi's friend. What do the Finnish boys say?"

Värdi shrugged his narrow shoulders. His brow was wrinkled as always.

"What do I think?" He seemed to bite off his words. "Cripples have no voice any more. We came back like a flock of homing pigeons to their nest. No one gave much thought to anything. Now we begin to realize that some things should have been done differently. We could have prepared ourselves for this present predicament."

"Your homecoming sort of flopped," Osvald remarked.

"Regardless of how it turned out, the fact remains: we came!" Värdi stretched himself haughtily.

"The men deserve a great deal of respect," Ignas acknowledged. "Nobody can say a slighting word about them, regardless of where they are now—some lucky ones beyond the sea, others here, anguished in body and soul. If we hadn't had our men to stand up against them at Narva and elsewhere, this Sodom would have come upon us last winter."

"What's the difference? What was that reprieve good for?" Ilme asked impatiently. "Taavi would have been in Finland."

"Who can tell? We are no prophets! What do we know about life here, now?" Ignas demanded. "We only saw how they ravaged around Pärnu. The first thing we'll have to consider is whether we can't somehow keep alive here. Let's see tomorrow what is in the fields that can be gathered. We are in the middle of big forests here. If we keep our ears open to what's going on outside, we can find shelter in the woods if really necessary."

"What shelter can the woods give when winter is coming?" Krōōt sighed.

"It'll be like the times when they shot my husband," Linda mourned.

"But what's going to happen to Daddy?" Lembit asked. "I don't want to live without Daddy any more. All those Russians and Kirghiz. . . . What are they going to do to Daddy?"

"Don't worry, Lembit." Osvald comforted him. "Your Daddy isn't afraid of those slickers."

"Come along, traveller. Grandmother will put you to bed," Linda said. "Or do you want your other granny?"

"It's all the same to me." Lembit shrugged. "Mother, do you think Daddy will be home tomorrow?"

"Perhaps." Ilme smiled. "Let's hope so."

"You all hope, but you don't believe," Lembit said wisely. "But I believe quite firmly that Father will be home in the morning."

The adults looked at one another, shaken. They realized suddenly that what the child said was true. They did not have his simple faith. Silently, they began to get ready for the night.

"That's a fine youngster my friend has," Värdi muttered through his teeth and leaned his head on the table. Yes, his own daughter might have been that old. . . .

"Are you planning to come to sleep today?" Osvald asked.

"Mh? Yes, sure," Värdi answered.

By mid-morning Ignas was ready to go to the county house. All morning he, Osvald and Tõmm had been puttering around the yard, the stable and the toolshed, and had been figuring how to get things back in shape. The chores had been neglected for so long that they all demanded attention at the same time, and old Ignas really had to use his head.

"What are we to do with that fellow from town?" he asked. "He doesn't look as if he would make a good farmhand. He's a lawyer, you said, didn't you? I didn't know there were any lawyers who would keep their mouths shut so well."

"He can't dish out his statutes and paragraphs here," Osvald said. "At least he doesn't whimper, and he talks like a real front-line soldier."

"I guess we'll have to keep him," Ignas conceded.

"I think so, Farmer. Where could we drive him? Let him get well first. . . ."

"But what if we get in trouble because of him?" Tõmm put in. "I'm sure he's got no papers."

"You don't have any either," his father remarked.

"I'm not even going to apply for them!"

"I'll get them for you myself. Then they won't have any grounds for complaint. You never fought in the army. That you walked around with a gun in the Home Guard won't matter. And maybe we can just keep it from them that at the end you were stationed by Narva. Or perhaps you can say that the Germans forced you to go along."

Tõmm burst out laughing.

"You seem to be feeling secure again, Dad, now that you're back on your own plot of land. But you won't fool either yourself or me with your big talk. Your land isn't secure at all now, and there's nothing we can do to change that. When we were routed so miserably at the front, it suddenly dawned on me that only on the other side of the sea would we be safe."

"But now we are caught in their way. Now we've got to watch out that they won't step on us."

"Go ahead and put my name down, then. But I don't think any good will come of it."

"If you don't want to register, nobody will make you. But this state of affairs can last for a long time."

"No more than a couple of months," Tõmm asserted positively. "Then they'll be fighting with the Americans and the British in Berlin."

"Not that soon, they won't. They're still busy mopping up the Germans on the islands here," Osvald observed.

"The Allies won't fight them without the Germans. Who else should they put on the Eastern Front? I am sure that when they've got rid of

Hitler, the Germans will just carry on against the Russians, with this one difference—the Allies will support them from air and sea."

"If you were in charge you'd make it really simple." Ignas smiled. "The Germans are human too; they can't keep it up much longer, tired and defeated as they are."

"You don't really think they'd have trouble mopping up those ragamuffins!" Tõmm was indignant. "It's a disgrace that we let such a horde descend on us."

"Yes, such a horde. That's the trouble—the horde is too big. Those bastards multiply so fast. I don't believe that the millions that were killed off will leave an empty place anywhere in Russia. But here the land is waste," said Osvald.

"Well, then,"—Tõmm shrugged his shoulders—"let's just admit that we're done for. The Russians will drown us. Period."

"We've got to see how we can keep going for the time being," Ignas retorted. "Why do you always have to flare up like brush fire? The war is still going on. Let's wait and see how it ends. I don't think they'll leave Ivan sitting on our necks like this. Some kind of a change is bound to come. If the British are already in Tallinn, they'll see what's going on. They aren't blind. They'll do something. Wait—I'll go to the county house. Maybe I'll pick up some news."

Tõmm merely shrugged and turned his back on the others, as he often did of late. His peace of mind was gone completely, and despair gnawed at him steadily from dawn to dusk.

At noon, Linda left Hiie, taking her cow along.

"Aren't you afraid to live all by yourself near the woods?" Krõõt asked.

"Should I be afraid in my own home?" Linda replied, with gentle irony. She would be glad to be back at Piskujõe. When she was seized with fresh anguish about her son, she could go to the grave of her husband. It was good to talk to Andres there under the peaceful ancient firs.

Lembit had a thousand things to do in the yard, the fields, the garden and the pasture—things that had to be attended to in haste. He had been away from home so long! What a joy to run around again with Pontus! The dog did not leave him for an instant. He watched the boy's doings, tilting his head to one side. Occasionally he jumped up and placed his paws on the boy's shoulders, so that both fell down and rolled on the ground with playful clamour. Everything seemed unchanged to Lembit, from old Aadu to the little black ram who had nevertheless grown a good deal in the meantime and had begun to show a real fighting spirit. Only Mother was sad and seemed to be as tired in the morning as she had been at night. This was on account of Father, and it put a check on Lembit's high spirits. During the last couple of years, ever since he had begun to remember things and fit them into some kind of a coherent picture of his world, he had seen his father only on rare oc-

27

casions. He therefore remembered him only in connection with bright, vivid moments, and in the course of time his father became almost a legendary figure to him. All the heroes that his grandmothers or his mother talked about had traits of his father and they all looked like him.

Ilme was having a difficult time. The more the day progressed the more she regretted that she had not joined the others in the fields. It had been her father's advice that she should take care of things at the house and rest a little from the hardships of their futile journey. She had thought his advice good. But today she was sure it would have been better for her to be working outside along with the others. She was not very tired or exhausted any more. Was she disappointed and frustrated because of their unsuccessful journey? Returning from the coast she had felt relieved they had not made it across—because of the thought that Taavi might still be in Estonia. She had felt it, strongly and clearly, and she had not been mistaken.

She was doing the family washing, but she did not get much done in a day. Her eyes kept scanning the village road leading to Võllamäe, as if she were expecting someone. Or they kept following her son around in the yard, as if she ought to look after the youngster now with particular care. How long would he be able to continue this careless play? Lembit should have got away across the sea! Here he would have to go to school soon. What joy can a mother have sending her son to a school where all truths are distorted into lies, where the home is scorned, and the history of the people torn down?

Ilme felt a tightness in her chest. She did not have enough air, bending over the washbasin. Taavi had left for Tallinn the previous morning. Only a few hours had separated them. These hours might mean that seas and countries could come between them, lifelong uncertainty, even the separating wall of death. Maybe she could catch up with Taavi before that wall could rise. Why not go to Tallinn and look for him? This was not so absurd as it seemed. He'd probably stop by at their own apartment, where a former schoolmate was living now, or spend the night with some people they both knew.

Ilme straightened herself. Suddenly she felt hot, and every muscle in her body sensed the tenseness brought on by her hurried thoughts. It would be foolish to waste any more time. She ran to the farmyard and called out for Lembit.

The boy came running from the pasture, where he had been playing with Pontus. He had succeeded in getting himself dirty all over—after all, he'd been working in the fields, too, and it wouldn't do to have clean hands and knees as if it had been Sunday. And he had somehow managed to get a few scratches.

"Mother, Uncle Värdi promised to make me a bow! You know, Mother," Lembit whispered suddenly, "I think that there's something not quite right with Uncle Värdi's leg. He says he fell and sprained it, but I think it was the Russians. Uncle Värdi's leg has been shot clean through."

"Maybe it was the Germans," Mother suggested.

"The Germans," Lembit considered. "Could be, but I still think it was the Russians this time."

Ilme bent down to the boy.

"What would you say, Lembit, if we were to go to Tallinn? Right away, maybe tomorrow morning, to look for Daddy? Wouldn't you like to?"

"Yes, Mother!" Lembit shrieked, and threw his arms around Ilme's neck.

Now Ilme and Lembit were both full of feverish eagerness. Soon everybody on the farm knew about their plan. The others were less enthusiastic and weighed soberly the chances of success. Krööt doubted whether any good would come of it. This was no time for travelling, especially for a young woman, when all the roads were filled with the violence of a hostile army. Ignas was still at the county house. One should first wait for news. It seemed an almost impossible task to Krööt to take a child by the hand and go out into the world looking for Daddy. Who said that Taavi went to the capital, anyway? Perhaps he went directly to the coast, or took refuge in the woods. Why should Taavi have gone to Tallinn, knowing that it was full of Russians?

Tõmm made Ilme's plans look altogether ridiculous, even though Osvald defended the young woman's initiative.

Only Hilda caught fire from Ilme's enthusiasm, and her joy was no less than that of Lembit. But when Ilme invited Hilda to come along to her native city the girl turned pale with fright.

"No, no," she whispered with trembling lips and turned quickly away.

When Ignas walked back home later in the evening, he was worried and downcast, even though he put on a more cheerful mien at the gate so that inside the yard nobody could tell that he was troubled. Nothing special at the county house—just that everyone had to go in person and get his name listed. And no one should breathe to anyone that he had planned to get out of the country. It would be better to say that the Germans forced you to go along, tried to make you go to Germany, and that you escaped from them at the last moment.

In private he said to Osvald, however, "Seems as though they want to get us really trussed up this time—and soon. As if I didn't catch on! How come everything is suddenly so rosy, all is supposed to be forgiven, nobody will be hurt? Just imagine, they even play the Estonian national anthem and all our other songs over the radio. Cunning devils! But their first question is: What did you do during the German occupation? No, no, they can't fool me. They just smile at first—I know that kind of smile—and then. . . ."

"Do you think, Farmer, that it will get tough again?"

"If no help arrives from the outside, then it will get tougher than before. Right now it's the army. They loot and burn, that's all. But I am afraid of what will come after the army."

"I, for one, won't place my head on the block for them," Osvald said, firmly setting his jaw. His high cheekbones showed in his square face, when he turned his glance toward the woods.

"We'll see. Nobody is going to take it like a lamb." The farmer of Hiie spat on the ground.

To Ilme's surprise, her father was all for her plans. They discussed them at night in the back chamber.

"I had the same idea myself," Ignas said.

"Really?" Ilme was pleased. "I don't know whether it will help any or not, but I want to do it for my own peace of mind."

"That's the way I feel about it. Only—it won't be easy to go now. It's a long distance to the railway station. They say that some trains are running already—army trains—but I am worried about the highway. And money is another problem. They tell the people to bring their German money to the county house, but they give nothing in return. You know, I figure that if you should happen to find Taavi, you should both try to get across the sea."

"That's what Taavi was planning to do."

"Yes. He may be crossing over right now. I wouldn't be surprised at anything he might do. He has such spirit that he manages to do things that others don't dare dream about. But he might be in a much worse place."

"Don't, now. . . ."

"No, I'm just talking, for I wouldn't be surprised at anything. He's young and a little too careless. Who knows, perhaps that is just the right thing in times like these. He may succeed, and a person who doesn't try has nothing to hope for anyway. It would be good if you could see Taavi and talk to him. That's all I am hoping for."

Ilme sighed. She knew her father, who had lived on the same farm all his life, and whose hopes and beliefs were different from those of Taavi, whose father had seen much of the world on his adventurous travels. In Pärnu, when they had been about to take leave of their native soil, her father had been greatly troubled. He had not hesitated or shown his helplessness in any way, but Ilme had felt instinctively that her father's heart was somehow torn, and that he could not possibly just stick his hands in his pockets and walk away whistling. Now it was her father who was talking about hope!

"You all hope, but you don't believe." Ilme recalled the words of her son. The boy must have picked it up from someone. And suddenly Ilme decided not only to hope, but also to believe.

III

"So you've decided to go home?" Taavi asked his companion.

"That's my intention," Mart answered, a little dejectedly, but firmly. The four of them were standing at the crossroads close to the county house of Kalgina, where they had come two by two, so that their movements would attract less attention. Even so, they attracted the gazes of foreign soldiers in a column which was just passing by. Most of the faces were hostile and suspicious, especially those of the officers, who seemed to notice their German and Finnish army boots.

"Good-bye then,"—Taavi squeezed Mart's hand—"and take care of yourself. Let's hope we'll get together again some day."

"A good journey to you, Lieutenant! So long!"

Mart began to walk down the road alongside the rattling Russian supply columns and the other three stared after him. But something strange happened where the road turned. Their departing companion was helped into a mud-covered truck. He waved uncertainly to them from his seat among the grey figures of the soldiers, and then disappeared behind a group of pine trees.

"Lo-lo-looks as if-if they kid-na-napped him," Eedi of Piibu said with surprise.

"They want to win over the people by a show of kindness, that's all."

They turned their steps toward the railway station. Taavi knew the district and he led the way. He had been to Piskujõe before they left and had exchanged the miserable rags he had received from a forest farm for one of his own half-worn suits. It felt strange and unfamiliar to be dressed in civilian clothes again. He could not get rid of the feeling that he was about to lose some item of clothing.

There was not much traffic on the highway. Only Russian army vehicles rushed by. Farm people were busy in their fields on both sides of the road. But often they passed a farm where the empty buildings and abandoned fields mourned in mute silence. No battles had been fought here, but everyone who had eyes to see could notice the imprint of war.

A tree had been felled across the highway before a bridge where soldiers, armed with submachine guns, demanded papers. Taavi presented the Soviet passport he had received from Marta the evening before. The soldier with the most medals on his chest scrutinized it page by page, while the other, his gun in readiness, watched Taavi's every move. With deliberate slowness Taavi put his hands in his pocket. It was idle bluffing; he knew well enough that they had left all their arms, well-oiled, in Osvald's care at Hiie. The soldier gave his passport back and saluted, which was the signal for him to move on.

"Spassibo," Taavi said. Such encounters were a good opportunity to practise self-control. Foolish fellows, he was not the kind of bandit who would try to shoot them in broad daylight in the middle of an army encampment. All around the towering manor, the hedges and bushes of the garden were teeming with the grey-green military mass.

At the checkpoint across the river Taavi was not asked to show his papers, although the soldiers watched him with the same suspicion. What seemed to arrest their attention particularly was the food parcel which Taavi had received from his mother and was carrying in his hand.

A third checkpoint was on the road which led directly to the railway station through a quiet section of the small town. They did not ask for papers here, either, for a black limousine was standing at the control post, and the passengers were engaged in a noisy conversation with the guards. When Taavi offered his passport, an officer waved him on.

Arriving at the station, Taavi and his companions sat down on a bench near the tracks and absent-mindedly watched the people who had already spent half a day there waiting for the train. Many of them looked just like themselves—homeless people, who had dared to come out of the woods into the open, whose eyes betrayed fear when they saw Red Army men carrying boxes of ammunition. The station-master assured them that the train would be there in the next hour or two. There was no fixed schedule, and no tickets were sold. The trains ran by order of the military authorities and according to their needs.

Leonard and Eedi had found another occasion to squabble. They were sitting at some distance from Taavi, but their quarrelsome voices reached him clearly. Leonard was boasting again about his Finnish army, which according to him had been the only real thing. Eedi of Piibu, excited and flushed, was replying vigorously. He was no elocutionist, but several years of practice had made even him a master at army lingo.

Then the train arrived. It was a long, mixed train, and the few passenger cars were crammed full. Taavi and his two companions moved toward the rear of the train, hoping to find a place in some boxcar.

"S-say, wh-wh-what's up, f-for th-the L-Lord's s-sake? T-this is a pr-prison t-train," Eedi of Piibu exclaimed.

It was true. More than half of the long train was made up of stinking old boxcars, their narrow window slits barred with barbed wire, against which were pressed thin, bearded faces.

"Germans," Leonard hazarded.

"Aren't th-they hu-hu-human beings, too?" Eedi still bore a grudge toward his companion. "To-together w-we had to b-bite th-the d-dust. That ma-makes us one and th-the sa-sa-same."

"Don't come too close; they'll nab you, too!"

"Damn it, those are our own boys," Leonard said with a shudder.

They stopped short, wordless. All at once it seemed strange that they were still free, as if something were not quite in order. Right here, only a few steps away from them, guarded by the barbed wire and locked doors of the cars, were their own blood brothers, beginning their long journey east.

"Let's see; maybe we'll find somebody we know," Taavi said. His face had turned drawn and grim. They moved on along the side of the train.

"Let's not go too far; maybe the train will leave." Leonard hesitated.

"So w-what? If we sh-should be left be-behind, w-w-what's the hu-hurry?" Eedi mumbled angrily.

The doors of some of the cars were opened. Behind the wide doors there were men—sitting, and standing, men of every age and in every possible kind of clothing. German and Estonian words were heard from the hot, smelly interiors of the cars. Smoke mingled with the stench; cigarettes made from country tobacco wrapped in newspaper were passed from one bearded mouth to another. There were wounded men, and coatless men in soiled shirts.

"Where did they capture you?" Taavi asked.

"Near Haapsalu. Many of us are from Suursoo. The women soldiers smoked us out, damn their hides. But we left plenty of them on the turf of the moor, their rear ends sticking up toward Stalin's sun!" One of the prisoners said it with a kind of grim joy. His face was dirty like that of a blacksmith's apprentice.

"What's new on the outside?" a high voice asked. "Are they still holding out in Saaremaa?"

"Are there any Finland fighters among you?" Leonard shouted in turn. "*Perkele!* Hell, yes!" someone shouted. But before further questions could be asked and answered, the door was slammed shut and the guards drove them away.

Then Taavi wiped with his hand over his eyes, as if he had been wakened from a dream. That thin, besmudged face behind the barbed wire!

"Don't you recognize me any more?" asked a familiar voice.

"I just don't seem to recall," Taavi muttered. "Well, I'll be damned! It's Uuno!" The joy of recognition did not last long. Their most recent meeting had taken place only a short while ago. Taavi had happened to see him among the remnants of a shattered border defence regiment. Uuno had been tired and exhausted, and he had admonished Taavi to make sure to leave in time along with the Germans. Now he was here.

"How did this happen? How come you stayed behind?"

"God knows. Luck didn't hold out. When I had got a good night's sleep after that rout, I got angry and turned around. Had a few more rounds and—now we sing a new tune. I guess they'll send me to the eastern paradise for ten years. Tell my parents, if you should see them."

"Yes, sure." Taavi was suddenly embarrassed. Should he tell his friend that the Russians had murdered his father in the meantime? No, it would be a deadly sin to give this news as a farewell message to a man on his way to Siberia. "Certainly, I'll tell them. I'm just coming from home, though. I'll go and see your sister in Tallinn."

"Yes, please do. I am in good health and I'm tough. I'll try to pull through. It won't be too long."

Leonard cursed under his breath.

Uuno was pulled down from the window by his comrades, and new bearded faces appeared with new questions.

They found room in a half-empty boxcar fitted out with an iron stove and wooden benches. They sat gloomily in the corner and were silent, letting their eyes glide over the passing melancholy landscape. It became clearer and clearer to them that they lived now in a completely new era, in a totally strange and unfamiliar situation, and that the events were carrying them along like this prison train in which they were travelling. Their yesterday—their battles and defeats—that was their real inheritance, and they could not simply leave it behind by putting on civilian dress. Changing their worn army clothes in forest farms and thickets, they had assumed a new acting part, but they were very bad actors.

Their fellow passengers were silent, too. Some of them were country people, some disappointed city dwellers returning from the coast, some soldiers of yesterday like themselves, struggling with their own minds and memories. Even the least expressive face was still showing incredulous astonishment at what had taken place. Yet combined with this was a sense of objective contemplation and philosophical calm. The worst had now happened. The first contacts with the new order had been made and the prevailing disorder presented possibilities. There just might be a loophole somewhere, and one might squeeze through.

Tallinn had not changed much since Taavi had seen it last, half an hour before the Russians had moved in. Life was somehow struggling along again in the city after the initial apathy and confusion. People went about their errands, although their steps lacked energy and their eyes revealed hopeless resignation.

Taavi set a time when he and his companions would meet again, and went to deliver Uuno's message.

Selma, Uuno's sister, opened the door herself.

"Hello! It's great to find you home!"

"Hello, Taavi!" Selma exclaimed, stunned. "How on earth did you get here?"

The young woman seized his hands, excited and happy, squeezing his wrists, as if to make sure that the visitor was flesh and blood. "Please come in. You know, I'm still department head in the office as before, and my work starts at nine. I'll call the boss and tell him that I'll be late. We have still the same old order and our own people. Please excuse me for a moment! Sit down right there. Nobody will disturb you. My aunt is leaving for the bank right away. Please feel at home!"

Taavi sat down on the couch and stretched his legs comfortably. Look how well people still lived even in this day and age! Well, her aunt had been quite wealthy and was probably still well off, and Selma herself had a good job. They had known each other for a long, long time, almost since they were children, and their relationship was strangely close, like that of a brother and sister. Selma was a year older than Taavi, but she had always been boyishly frank and sincere. Taavi knew no other girl, except his own wife, with whom he could get along as well as with Selma. If he hadn't experienced it, Taavi would not have believed that a man and a woman could be such good friends. He had been especially surprised at Selma's genuine joy at Taavi's marriage. In the years that had passed since then, he had come to treat her more and more like a sister.

Selma returned with coffee and cakes. She was already dressed, wearing a simple brown dress. She was not beautiful, but rather attractive and slender, small and homey.

"How quickly you do things!" Taavi marvelled.

"We have to fulfil our five-year plans." Selma laughed. She poured Taavi some coffee and sat down on a high chair facing him. "I don't reach up high enough to see otherwise," she explained. She had strong white teeth. "Hurry up now and tell me how come you are still alive. It's been a couple of years since I last saw you. You've grown thinner, and older, too."

"You are exactly the same as before. You'll never grow old."

"I'm unmarried, that's why. Eat something now. I baked every bit of it myself, and you used to like my cooking."

"Say, why haven't you got married? You would have made a good wife."

"You're noticing it too late." Selma smiled.

"Are you married, then?" Taavi was startled.

"Not I, but you," Selma retorted. "Speak up now, man, speak! I'm about to die with impatience. What's new at home? You're coming from there, aren't you? Ah, I don't know what to ask first. Two years—how should I know where to begin? You yourself have been halfway around the world, from one army to another. I heard you are an officer now. What are your future plans?"

Taavi told in a few words what had happened.

"I was delirious with joy when you all came back from Finland. And now everything is finished."

"Not everything, but much."

"Are you going after Ilme and your son?"

"I'll try."

"It's wonderful that your family managed to escape. Now your hands are free, and one can get by where the road is too narrow for many. It's too bad about your boys—I suppose most of those who are still alive stayed behind in the country."

"Most of those who are still alive," Taavi repeated.

"In Tallinn they are hunting them down already."

"That was to be expected."

"Yes, every night they round up some of them. By the way, is your passport all right?"

Taavi produced it.

"Where did you get that?" Selma marvelled. "That isn't yours!"

"Looks a bit unfamiliar and the name is different, too, but it will have to do. It's a Soviet passport. What else can you wish for? I got it from Marta."

"Marta of Roosi?" Selma asked. Her sidelong glance was inquisitive and cool. "She gets into all kinds of business."

"You don't seem to like her very much."

"Like her? She is none of my business. But I tell you as a friend— watch out. You were away from Estonia for a long while, and you don't know what she has been up to in the meantime. It is not fitting for me to tell you. I'm not that old yet that I enjoy spreading gossip. What's she doing now, that you ran into her?"

"She's working in the county house at Kalgina."

Selma whistled and then burst into laughter. She laughed long and then stopped abruptly.

"She must be a smarter woman than she appears to be. She seems to know how to keep herself above water. And who can say that she wasn't spying for the Russians, when she was carousing here with Litzmann's men and high German officers? She must be smart for she usually gets what she wants. I know her from our school days. A woman who has been married twice. . . ."

"Twice?"

"I suppose only very few people know that. The second one was a German." Selma observed Taavi from under slightly raised eyebrows, when the latter gave a start. "Does that mean anything to you?" she smiled.

"No, what could it mean to me? I was just thinking that Marta must be quite a serpent," Taavi murmured.

"So it seems," Selma agreed.

"What happened to her second husband, then?"

"Went the same way the first one did."

"Was he arrested? How come? Did it happen recently?"

"No, Marta got fed up with him before the Russians came. He was arrested by the Germans themselves."

"I didn't know that."

"Not many people do. And that must be the main reason why Marta disappeared so quickly and is now hiding out there among the woods."

"That's quite some news! Thanks for the warning."

"You're welcome. I thought it wouldn't hurt you to know, even though you'll hardly be likely to have anything to do with her. Would you like some more coffee?"

Taavi thanked her and began lighting his pipe. He had deliberately kept his bad news to the last, but now, while the clock moved on, it became more and more difficult.

"Stay a little longer," Selma begged, noticing the restlessness in his eyes. "I have time, and I have so many more questions to ask. If you leave now, God knows when I'll see you again. Are you going straight to the coast?"

"I can't go without making some contacts first. The coasts are empty. There's nobody there waiting for me."

"I don't know much about these things, but I suppose the coasts aren't empty any more. They must be swarming with Russians. Otherwise everyone would leave the country. But now the going days are over. I have met acquaintances who have returned from the coast. They couldn't make it."

"Yes, the best time for leaving is over. I saw many empty farms on my way here. Nothing but a starving dog or two."

"It's sad for the country during these hopeless days. I was expecting news from Uno, but there's nothing to wait for any more, I suppose. Have you heard anything about the fate of the border defence regiments?"

Slowly Taavi put his pipe away. Now he had to say it.

"I met Uno," he said calmly. "As a matter of fact, I've met him twice during the short time I've been back in Estonia."

"Really?" Selma uttered a short cry. "And you didn't tell me before! Where is he now?" She jumped up, squeezing the edge of the table with both hands, as if she were preparing herself for the blow.

"That's why I came to see you right away when I arrived in Tallinn."

"Is he dead?"

"No, Selma. He isn't even wounded. He's in pretty good health. I saw him last night—on a prison train."

"So he was taken prisoner?" Selma asked quietly.

"Yes, somewhere around Haapsalu. The train pulled in at the depot here last night and was supposed to move on to Kiviöli. Maybe they won't take them out of Estonia so soon. Uuno asked me to say hallo to you to tell you not to worry about him."

"That's just like him," Selma said fondly. "Do you think—you know, if I ran—I might still get to see him?"

"I think you might. Take some food, and if you have some warm clothes maybe you can give them to him. We have to prepare ourselves now for such leave-takings. There are bound to be more."

"Yes, Taavi," Selma said quietly. "There will be more."

Taavi arose and took Selma's hand. Her small hand was still and warm.

"I have some bad news for you. Don't tell Uuno. It might be better for him not to know."

"Has something happened to my parents?" Selma asked.

"Yes, to your father."

"Is he dead?" Selma swallowed.

"Yes. The Russians shot him."

Selma pressed Taavi's wrist. Her glance was turned toward the floor, and she clenched her teeth. Taavi stroked her hair with his hand.

"How did that happen?" The woman raised her grey eyes.

"In the middle of his rye field. They had just been passing by and. . . . He's been buried a week."

"Beasts!" Selma muttered. Her low voice expressed anger, disdain and torment. Taavi marvelled how well the girl could keep herself under control.

"I suppose I'll have to go to the country, then, for a time. I don't know how well my mother and sister can take care of things by themselves. Excuse me now, Taavi, please; I have to get a few things together for Uuno. You brought me sad news, but it could have been even worse. And I'm glad you are well yourself. Thanks for everything! I won't hold you any longer, for we both are in a hurry. Come and see me as often as you can. At least come and say good-bye, when you go. And if there is anything I can do for you. . . . Wait, do you have any money?"

"What money?"

"Our current money—rubles."

"No. How could I have any, and what could I use it for anyway? I got some from Mother at home, and that's all I'll need for some time."

"Take this!"

"Put that back right away!"

"I wouldn't dream of it. Please! We haven't got paid yet, but they advanced us some on our salary. They distributed bread, too—for free, up to now. Take it. Don't be silly!"

Taavi put the money in his pocket with the revolting feeling that he had been paid for his news.

IV

Soon after leaving Selma's apartment Taavi ran into a former comrade, Roode, whom he remembered from his days in military school in Finland. Heino Roode, a medical student and a year younger than Taavi, greeted him from a distance with a broad smile and an energetic wave.

"You've really got yourself dressed up. I hardly recognized you."

"And you are still wearing the old army boots, as if there were nothing to fear."

"They give your step a firmer feeling. And besides, every man is wearing them here. Most men don't have any others, and if you're an Estonian you are suspect anyway, even if you were to put on angels' wings. What are you doing? Are you looking for 'chances' too?" There was a shade of irony in his voice.

"I just arrived in Tallinn a couple of hours ago."

"So you're still a greenhorn and don't know a thing. Yes, everybody is hunting for chances here. Every man has several possibilities in his back pocket. Only trouble is that the men with all these big chances haven't gone anywhere yet."

"Why not?"

"It's all pure hogwash. The sea is closed."

"Don't tell me that. The sea is not a door you can shut and keep locked. It's a bit wider than that."

"Be careful! I am afraid that some spies have been smuggled in, and that's why things can't get off the ground. Have you looked for a job? Oh, of course, you haven't got around to it yet. Get a job first thing, and then you'll have time to look around when you have papers in your pocket. I've got it arranged at the university so that I don't have to fear conscription."

"Isn't that dangerous?"

"Dangerous? It's dangerous everywhere. I might just be able to talk myself out. I escaped to Finland when the Germans were after me."

"Have you been knocked on the head in the meantime or what?" Taavi was stunned. "What are some of the other boys doing? How many of them have you met?"

"Oh, about a score of boys from the military school, not to speak of others. They have their headquarters on King Street, in the cooperative. You can always find some of them there. And you can't even walk down Viru Street without meeting one. Jaan Meos and Lieutenant Pihu are heading the cooperative."

38

"So Pihu has stayed behind? Litzmann's former aide-de-camp!"

"Yes. Coming from Finland, he went to the government offices to see his old friends and to apologize for having left so suddenly. They had been hopping mad, but couldn't do a thing, since Hitler himself had proclaimed amnesty for everyone who returned."

"I remember his fancy getup when he returned from Finland. He looked like a city slicker, but you can't say a word against the man as a fighter."

"Well, the cooperative has twenty-five carpenters right now. Not one of them has held a plane in his hand, and the lowest rank is second lieutenant."

"Sounds like a decent place. And all are free from mobilization."

"Yes. Oh, our guys are getting away with stranger stuff yet. Do you know who is deputy to the port director of Tallinn? Little Tõnn! Lembit Uduse shifts rails at the Central Station, Jüri Kinga attends a driving school.

"And, just imagine, that squirt Endel Krass got away from Saue just in time. They wanted to make a militiaman out of him. He struggled against it with all his might, told them that his past was too shady for such a job. Finally, when nothing else helped, he blurted out in anger that he'd fought against the Communists in the Wehrmacht, in the S.S., and in the Finnish army, so how could he put on the red armband now? The chairman of the executive committee just laughed at all his arguments and said that all past sins were now forgotten and forgiven. Endel answered that he was not a confirmed Communist yet, was not even close to it. Even that didn't help. So the poor man fled to the coast as fast as he could."

The story made Taavi laugh too.

"Yes," Roode continued, "at present all doors are open, all kinds of possibilities are there for the asking. The new unoiled Soviet machine is in desperate need of trained personnel. You'll notice that yourself when you look around. You can pick any job you want right now. Nobody will even ask whether you can read and write."

"Our men aren't biting on that, are they?"

"Some have already bitten off more than they can chew. Voss has already been twice to the NKVD."

"What the devil!"

"That's why it's so easy to get a three-month passport right now. The screening and sieving will come later. They've got us where they want us, and they have plenty of time. Yes, Voss said after he'd been there for the first time that he'd never been treated so well. Rather than being with the NKVD, it had seemed like a visit to his best friends. Cigarettes, sensible conversation, and—just picture it—even coffee and liqueurs! Voss didn't deny anything—his presence in the Finnish army or with the Germans. Everybody showed deep understanding, as if they realized that Voss had had no other choice."

"How smooth they can be, these devils! Wonder where they learned these kinds of tricks?"

"The NKVD is a very refined institution. After the second visit Voss did not have so much to say."

"And after the third?"

"The man is as silent as the grave."

They walked back and forth in front of the girls' commercial high school. A militiaman in a brand-new uniform directed traffic at the corner of Freedom Square. His movements were still unsure and his gestures awkward, but he wore white gloves and broad epaulets. Occasional streetcars rattled down the street as usual, but all motorcars were of a military type. From a distance one could hear raucous Soviet propaganda blaring forth from loudspeakers around the Public Market.

"Well, I'll see you later at the cooperative," Heino Roode said, and offered Taavi his hand in parting. "Look around and take in a whiff of the air of the new world. It's not healthy, but it won't kill you off right away."

Hardly had Roode left and Taavi turned his steps toward the centre of the city when he met another acquaintance in front of St. John's Church. He recognized the fat man from far away, as the latter approached with his swaying gait.

"*Perkele!*" Lompus the cook shouted with a shrill voice, as if he had caught Taavi in the chow line for a second time. "Men from our regiment can't take a step without bumping into one another."

He pushed his cap back on his head and brushed his sleeve over his fat, sweaty face. The other fleshy paw he pushed into Taavi's palm. Then he stood, arms akimbo, with protruding stomach, as if he had been standing guard behind his soup kettle, and scrutinized Taavi with his small grey eyes.

"Where're you coming from?"

"From the woods; where else?"

"From the woods." Lompus laughed scornfully. "Where else? What did you do there that long? And now, of course, you're looking for a chance like everybody else. Man, you're even supposed to be an officer, but you're so dense that you sleep around in haystacks while the best time is passing by, and then you jump up like somebody had stuck you and come to Tallinn, saying, I want to get across the bay now! Where's your good sense? The Russians aren't such monsters that they'd eat you right away, hair and guts and all. The likes of us are hard to digest. Listen, I haven't got much time. What are you doing now? Are you also in that cooperative?"

"I haven't got there yet. I only arrived this morning."

"Don't even poke your nose in there," Lompus said with a disdainful gesture. "So you just arrived this morning? They hold conferences there. *Perkele*, looking at each other won't help anybody at this stage of the game. It's a fine time—a heck of a fine time—if you're a man and know how to get around.

"Do you really want to get across?" he asked abruptly, stepping close to Taavi and grabbing his lapel.

"That's a foolish question. Just show me the way."

"Give me your hand," Lompus said. "Do you have any money or valuables? Well, if you don't, we'll get by. But keep your mouth shut. We have only room for one more in the boat."

Taavi gave him a sharp look.

"Are you telling the truth?"

"*Perkele*, have I ever lied before?" Lompus was offended. "Remember, when I shut the cover on the soup kettle in the army, nobody got a drop, even if the hunger wails could be heard all the way to head-quarters. I live close by, on Tatari Street." He mentioned the name of a well-known statesman. "We're going in his boat. The old man himself is in a safer place. I'm not foolish enough to sleep in his apartment at night, but sometimes I go to catch a nap there in the daytime, when I've been off on a longer trip. Otherwise I sleep every night in a different place. Say, come along!"

He pulled Taavi by the sleeve.

"Give me a few more details; I can't take the plunge blind," Taavi demanded.

"*Perkele*, don't forget, it's the last place in our boat. If that's not good enough for you, say so right away. Anyone would be glad to grab the chance. But I just happen to have a little more respect for you than for anybody else. Or don't you believe in our statesmen any more? Are you crazy or something? I can't draw you a map here in the street of the place where the boat is standing, half a kilometre to the east of this particular coastal village. Tomorrow the trucks are leaving for Kiviõli—fire depart-ment trucks. They are taking the people out. There's so much to arrange and get done. I can't be everywhere myself at the same time."

They had reached the front of another big secondary school building, where horse-drawn carriages stood for hire, as they did before the war. Lompus did not take the first one, but moved on to the third. The owner gave him a familiar nod.

"Take us directly to the loading station in the back of the consumers' cooperative, and make it quick!" Lompus whispered directions to the old man. "Get in," he told Taavi.

The horse trotted off. Taavi was amazed—everything seemed to fall into his lap by itself, without exertion or trouble. He really had an incredible amount of luck.

"But listen, I have two other men with me," Taavi said to Lompus. The latter nudged him to keep quiet, grimacing and pointing at the back of the coachman.

"Here, have a smoke! They're German cigarettes, but it's hard to get hold of any decent ones. Even the Russians esteem them and go to the free market to buy them at black-market prices. I got a few thousand recently, and now I don't have to worry."

"You've really settled down to this new kind of living," Taavi re-marked, noticing the fine shoes Lompus was wearing and the excellent material of the trousers which showed under his tight grey raincoat.

Lompus giggled. "I told you so. Right now the water is muddy and full of fish. You can pull a lot of them out if you know how."

"This is it. Turn in right here," he shouted to the coachman. "Come on, let's lift these sacks of sugar on the carriage," he whispered to Taavi. "There's no way to get oil and gasoline except by barter. I have to take a couple of trips this afternoon. The fuel is already in the boat, but the bills haven't been settled yet. Can't leave any stink behind, you know. We have to pay a heaping good price for everything, for we want to keep the boat running back and forth after our first trip. Wait here!"

He ran, puffing, around the corner of the house and returned a few moments later with a haggard, dark-complexioned man. They stood a while discussing something. Lompus laughed, slapped the other one on the back and offered him a cigarette. Then, standing in the corner behind boxes of merchandise and keeping a close lookout so that no strange eyes could see their transaction, he pulled a fat wallet from his pocket and counted a considerable number of Russian bills into the man's hand.

The men then carried three big grey sacks to the carriage. They were quite heavy, so that the former army cook was out of breath and had to wipe the perspiration off his face. Leaving the yard, Lompus looked nervously around, but soon enough his broad, oily face regained its satisfied smile.

"The Russians are stupid. They are easy to handle, but our own Communists are real devils. They just might get wind of it. Or someone might stumble on it and get envious. Right now everyone seems to be still quite stupefied. Nobody thinks of spying or informing on anyone."

They were already expected at their destination, for as soon as the coachman stopped his horse in a narrow side street, the gate was opened and nimble hands reached for one of the sacks. Taavi and Lompus took the other one and carried it across the yard into the woodshed.

When he entered the shed Taavi was astonished to find himself in a room filled with sacks and boxes of merchandise. Oh yes, he remembered —business and markets were supposed to be free again. What startled Taavi most, however, was the five-pointed red star on the chest of the other man carrying the sack.

It was already afternoon, when Taavi got away from his companion and turned his steps toward the cooperative on King Street. Now he had a little time to take a look at the city. No startling changes seemed to have taken place since the previous occupation. The pictures and slogans in the store windows had changed, but the red colour in the background had remained the same as in German times. The loud-speakers on each street corner were new. They blared old and new Soviet songs and music, mixed with propaganda slogans. The Red Army was surging mightily westward, and this inspired the announcers with increased enthusiasm and loudness. The people remained unmoved: Estonians went about silent and gloomy, leaving the impression that they were inanimate puppets kept in motion merely by habit.

The Soviet soldiers were more lively, not to mention a few tattered

Russian women, who had already managed to make their way to this westernmost corner of their huge territory. They were noisy and happy, and clapped their hands in wonder at the store windows, which two occupations had actually left quite empty. Their fellow-countrywomen in uniform, however, marched with a careless soldier's step behind a female officer, with rifles slung across their shoulders and self-confidence showing on their robust faces.

Near the Viru Gate, Taavi met three of his former comrades, who were engaged in a lively conversation. They all had high army boots, and one was still wearing the blue-grey trousers of the Finnish army. Taavi wanted to pass them on the other side of the street—what stupidity and recklessness it was to act like that in the midst of all these Russians! But he was noticed, and someone called his name. That too! He was quite angry when he approached his comrades.

"Where are you going with that long undertaker's face?" he was asked.

"To your funeral," Taavi answered sarcastically. "The way you are carrying on, it won't be long. Has Stalin's sun got you all so hot already that your brains have turned soft? Don't ever call me by name again, if you can't do it quietly."

"Do you think everybody knows you?"

"Maybe not everybody, but a few are enough. Elmo was taken prisoner at Valamu, and he had Mannerheim's proclamation on him, of course. And Sulev was killed on the same spot, with a list of Finnish military school graduates in his pocket. And they were not the only ones. You know, of course, that Voss is being interrogated by the NKVD. Soon they'll have the names of every single one of us. And yet when you run into friends you raise your hands and holler names across the street at the top of your voices. How far do you expect to get that way?"

"You probably just got out of the woods." Tall Vello Kasar laughed, hurt. "Don't make a mountain out of a molehill! We aren't children any more, you know."

"My first impression is that you're just a bunch of boys trying to play Indians according to the book," Taavi insisted.

"We are more careful and better organized than you can imagine," Vello replied.

"Let's hope to God that you are. And tell the men you see that they should at least exchange their Finnish army things for something else. It's safer to walk around in underpants. Even the German field grey is less dangerous. Mind my words—we'll be the first to be pulled on the carpet, and can expect no mercy. You can excuse yourself that you were forcibly conscripted into the German army, but there's no excuse for the Finnish army, and the fact that you volunteered to come back to Estonia to fight against the Communists makes it a deadly sin."

"Do you think I don't realize that?"

"You may realize it, but some others may not."

After parting from the others, Taavi and Vello Kasar turned in under an archway, and Vello pressed a doorbell button. The round boyish face of Jaan Meos appeared behind one of the doors.

43

"Hello, men," he said, and offered his hand to both of them after he had closed the door. "Is anybody else coming?"

"I don't think so. I'll see the other guys tonight," Vello said.

They entered the smoke-filled room. Two men were sitting at a table playing chess.

"Hallo, hallo!" Lieutenant Pihu shouted vivaciously and jumped up to shake Taavi's hand. "Nice to see a new face once in a while. Where're you coming from? I heard you'd been in the fight at Valamu."

He spoke quickly, and his blue eyes sparkled joyfully. He made his next chess move standing up, tugged at his short black moustache, and asked new questions.

The other man—Jüri Paarkukk—was only a little over twenty years old. He gave Taavi a searching, strained look and shook his hand energetically. They had fought together at Valamu, and Jüri had lost his glasses in the battle. His near-sightedness made him even less talkative than he had been before, and he concentrated again on his chess game, wrinkling his forehead.

Lieutenant Manivald Pihu, the former disloyal head of the Estonian bodyguard of the German Commissioner General, however, was talkative. He accompanied his speech with lively, fidgety gestures. He had a compulsion to do several things at the same time, and if he had nothing else to occupy his hands, he tugged at his moustache. His map case had formerly been full of pictures of women, and even while issuing battle directions he had glanced at movie stars' legs. He had a great weakness for women's pictures, and women, too. The chief duty of his orderly in Finland had been to cut out pictures of nudes from various magazines and cover with them the walls of his temporary quarters.

"What are you up to now?" he asked Taavi.

"Same as everyone else," Taavi replied.

"That doesn't say a thing. Here every man is in such a hurry that his skin and his shadow have a hard time keeping up with him, and yet they come back every time with disappointed faces and start hunting for other openings. Why are you all kicking around like this?"

"What are your own plans?"

"My own plans. . . . Check again? Wait a minute, I can't play with you like that! Oh, there's nothing the matter with me. I'm having a big time living with my wife after a long while, with nothing to do but look around. Boys, hide behind the back of a woman. That's the safest place right now."

"The Russians will clean up behind those backs soon enough," Jüri growled.

"And what are your plans?" Taavi asked him.

"My plans?" Jüri drawled, keeping his attention on the chessmen. "Checkmate!" he said quietly, and straightened himself up. "I am going to try to get out. My parents and sister have gone to Germany. They only left a letter on the table." He took another look at the chessboard and then leaned back, contented. "I'll keep looking around. Maybe the sea is still open somewhere. In the meantime I have a regular job and my

44

papers are in order. I have even had a vacation already—I got a few days off from work to take care of personal business." He smiled.

"You don't seem to be in a hurry either," Taavi turned to Jaan Meos. "I heard that you have organized a cooperative of workers or something."

"That's more my uncle's business, but now it is turning out to be a real boon when they are starting their forced conscriptions again. I think we'll have to get out, if at all possible. Some of our men are out on the northern coast," Jaan added. "Travelling conditions are getting worse every day, and therefore it would be good to get something done soon. Before winter comes, anyway."

"I just got fresh news from the North," Vello said. "Lieutenant Ojala, our battalion commander, has sent a contact man."

"Why didn't you say that right away?" Jaan exclaimed, and his eyes shone with childlike joy.

"He has already left, but the boat is coming back. I'm leaving for the coast tomorrow morning to get a clearer picture."

"So the thing is finally moving again," Jaan said, rejoicing.

"Don't celebrate too early," Pihu warned. "I've heard that kind of empty shouting here all too often."

They sat down and discussed the problems of getting across. Taavi did not bring up the chance mentioned by Lompus. There was only place for one, and it would be senseless to let his comrades get excited about that. He talked briefly about his recent adventures and about the atrocities of the Russians in the countryside.

Vello Kasar and Manivald Pihu were the first to leave.

"The work was easy today." Pihu laughed.

"Soon we'll have some real work," Jaan promised.

"Chess would be good enough for me, especially since I take a licking every time. So long, men!"

Jaan, who went out to see them off, was gone for quite a long while. To the surprise of Taavi and Jüri they all returned together with a new man.

"We caught him in the street. He was walking back and forth in front of the door, but didn't dare come in," Vello explained. "And he's got important news that will knock you flat on the floor."

"Riks, it's you!" Taavi shouted, welcoming the newcomer. Richard Kullerkann, a perpetual student, who had been the life of every party and who had never yet lost his sense of humour even in the most adverse of circumstances, stretched out his hand with a sickly grimace. His hand was slack and cold. He sank on a chair, wiped his glasses, and fingered his collar as if he were choking. The others gathered around him.

"Speak up," Jaan Meos demanded. His boyish face had become serious and worried. Manivald Pihu walked around the group with quick steps.

"Voss has been taken in again this morning," Riks said dejectedly. "And Mats Luukas was arrested last night."

With trembling fingers, he began rolling himself a cigarette.

45

"Isn't Voss back yet?" Jaan asked. "He was only kept a couple of hours before."

"Voss' mother ran to my wife, crying," Riks muttered. "I left home then, for I didn't know what. . . ."

All were silent. It was as if a black shadow had fallen over the room. Pihu stopped at the table and lifted the chessmen around. Then he resumed his quick walk around the others.

"Well, they've got him now," he said carelessly.

"And what about Luukas?" Taavi inquired.

Riks lighted his cigarette and wiped his glasses again. Now everybody noticed that his handkerchief was bloody. There was nothing peculiar about that. He might have had a simple nosebleed, but it disturbed the others that Riks was obviously trying to hide his handkerchief from them.

"Mats, yes, he. . . . There was a roundup, as there is every night now," he stuttered. "I don't know what they found suspicious about him, but they took him away."

"His papers were not in order," Pihu ventured. "What else could it have been?"

"No, they searched the place thoroughly."

"Then somebody must have informed on him," Jüri said darkly.

"Maybe." Riks' chin trembled. "If they got the list of the Finnish military school graduates, they'll start rounding up all of us."

"Do you really think they don't already know the names?" Taavi said. "No, they've known every name for a long time."

"How . . . how do you know?" Riks was frightened and stared at him with glassy eyes. "Tell me, how do you know?"

"No mystery! Men have fallen or been taken prisoner in a Finnish officer's uniform. I don't believe that everyone was circumspect enough to destroy his documents beforehand. I tend to believe that they have known the whole roster of the military school since the very beginning," Taavi said calmly. "And besides, the NKVD knows how to make its victims talk."

Richard Kullerkann crouched, on hearing these words, and his shoulders and hands shook as if he had been in high fever. Taavi could not understand how a man could change so much in such a short time. Something was seriously wrong. Men like Riks should be put in a boat and sent off at the first possibility.

"When the chances open up, perhaps we can put you in the boat." Vello Kasar expressed Taavi's thought.

"Me?" Riks was startled, looking from one man to the other. "Me?" he repeated and laughed nervously. "Thank you, boys, but I'll be done for pretty soon anyway."

"Don't talk nonsense," Pihu scolded. "Don't let these small matters get you so beside yourself. What's the trouble with you? Seems like you've got a head on your shoulders. Can't you handle the Russians now, the dirty bums?"

Riks groaned. "The circle is getting tighter," he said, and again stretched his collar. "Yesterday Mats, Voss today—and who tomorrow?

Speak up, men. Who will it be tomorrow? Who tonight?" He raised his red-rimmed, sleepless eyes.

"Take hold of yourself," Taavi counselled quietly. "This is only the beginning. We have to hold out to the end."

"The beginning, the beginning," Riks mocked and jumped up. "Go to the devil with your beginning! This began in the fall of 1939. Beginning! This is the end," he shouted wildly, his temples bursting with red veins. "This is the end! The beginning of the end!"

He fell back on the chair and covered his sobbing face with his hands.

Taavi rang the bell at the familiar door, which only recently had borne a card with his own name.

Mrs. Ting opened the door.

"We were expecting you," she said, taking hold of Taavi's shoulders in a cheerful greeting. She was a couple of years older than the young man, had a tendency to put on weight, and overflowed with exuberance. "I warmed your dinner so many times that I finally had to feed it to Arno."

"That's the way women are," Arno put in from behind her back. "What is about to be spoiled is quickly saved from the garbage by feeding it to the husband. Hallo, now, you old so-and-so!" he said, shaking Taavi's hand and scrutinizing him from head to toe. "Can't complain much about your looks, except that you seem to be catching up with me in age."

"Ten years won't be so hard to catch up with," Taavi answered. "Run a couple of months through the woods, and the difference is all gone. It's harder to make up for that tummy of yours. It will probably take a lot of loving care before mine reaches the generous proportions of yours."

"But life is a lot warmer this way. And if they should take me to Siberia, I'll have a full breadbasket of my own."

"Aren't you afraid that it might be difficult to keep it filled out there?"

"Quit that banter," the woman said. "Come in, Taavi!" She disappeared into the kitchen.

"Don't, Liisa," Taavi called out after her, but the woman wrinkled her nose at him, laughing, and began to rattle the dishes.

"Where are my two companions?" Taavi asked, entering the living room.

"They had no time to stay put," Arno replied. "They went out right after they arrived this morning. I had already left for work, so I didn't even get to see them."

"I came out of the woods with them. One is a Finland fighter, the other is from the Legion. So they're out gadding around? Leonard said he wanted to see his girl friends—I suppose he has more than one—so he can fix up his friend, too. How are you getting along? Well, it surely makes me envious to look at you two—living like a couple of turtle-doves in a cosy nest."

Liisa arrived with the dinner.

"I was in such a hurry, and I was afraid that now you are telling Arno everything and I don't get to hear it. My goodness, have you already told him everything?"

"You missed every bit of it."

Taavi ate and talked, spicing his adventures with a humour which surprised even himself. Liisa's cheerfulness and the comfortable surroundings had made everything else seem far away, as if he had read it in a book. Or did he feel light-hearted because he knew that the following afternoon he would be riding on a fire department truck toward the coast?

Reaching the point where he had to talk about his family, Taavi's account became serious. Liisa stroked Taavi's hand in a motherly way.

"Poor Ilme, going away like that with the child at her side!" she said. "It is a strange and hard world. She won't have it easy. Of course you have to go after her right away. She needs her husband's help and support. And what would your life be like without them?"

After dinner Liisa ordered Taavi to take a nap on the couch. Taavi did not argue and took off his coat and shoes. "I'll just lie down for a while. I won't fall asleep," he promised. But slumber overtook him while he was still uttering the last words.

"Falls asleep as if he'd been mowed down," Arno said wryly.

"Wake, awake, the night is flying; the guardsmen on the hills are crying!" somebody yelled in his ear and shook him. "We'll have to give him our 'Moses' treatment. He won't come to life otherwise!"

Taavi braced himself and rubbed his eyes.

"Don't sleep the rest of your life away," Leonard warned in a jolly mood. "The boat is about to leave."

Taavi jumped up.

"What boat?" he asked, startled. "What time is it? What do you know about the boat? Say, what boat are you talking about?" He looked alternately at Leonard and Eedi, not comprehending anything. "Did you meet Lompus or what?"

"No," said Leonard mysteriously. "I contacted a woman."

"You promised you'd go and see your girl friends," Taavi reminded him.

"Who do you think I am?" Leonard measured both his companions with a disgusted look. "More important things are at stake now than chasing the tail of a petticoat! This woman I'm talking about has accomplished more than all three of us put together. She has helped men across all the time. She only got out of the Battery prison when the Germans left."

"Sit down now and let's talk it over," Taavi suggested. "It will pay to deal with that kind of a woman, I don't doubt that. Does she have any free space in her boat?"

"That de-depends on ho-how bi-big a bo-boat she'll ge-get," Eedi of Piibu said.

"Doesn't she have one yet?"

"It's a safe bet and as sure as if I showed you the boat," Leonard insisted. "This woman has seen all kinds of weather, and she has more experience and better connections than anybody else. Do you think that somebody will stop you on a street corner and say, 'My dear fellow, everything is ready, let's go!' No, if you hear that, you can count on being fooled, for nobody but a real idiot will talk like that. And you must be a bigger fool yet if you believe that kind of hogwash. You have to make your own connections, run around and hunt until you are blue in the face."

"I'm going to the coast tomorrow afternoon," said Taavi.

"To lo-look a-r-round or what?"

"No, to go across. An offer walked up to me on a street corner, as you said before."

"Who was the crazy fool?"

"I can't tell you any details now, for they say there's only place for one. But it won't hurt for you to come along and take a look with your own eyes. If we're left behind, we're left behind, but at least our minds will be more at ease. We have shared dark days together. Let's face together whatever comes."

V

The following afternoon Taavi stood at the corner of Pärnu Avenue before the appointed time and waited for Lompus. He carried his mother's food parcel under his arm. The faded collar of his raincoat was turned up, and he had pushed his hands deep into its stretched pockets. The weather was cold and damp, and the waiting was unpleasant. At a short distance from him Leonard and Eedi walked back and forth, shivering, for their clothing was even less adequate.

"Excuse me, do I see right?" somebody suddenly asked.

Taavi looked up and froze. A young man in the uniform of the Red Army stood in front of him. The face was so unfamiliar that Taavi could not tell who it was, even when they shook hands in greeting.

"Don't you recognize me any more?" The haggard face with black eye sockets convulsed in a wry smile.

"It's you, Mihkel of Lepiku!" Taavi recognized his neighbour, the young farmer who had been conscripted into the Red Army in 1941. "How did you get here? Are you going home on furlough, or what?"

"Furlough. . . ." The other one spit and began to cough, out of breath. His face turned quite blue when he coughed, and his thin back shook in the army overcoat which exuded the familiar Russian smell. Taavi saw him spit a large mouthful of blood into the gutter.

"Damn it, you're in a bad way!"

"Do you think that anybody is well who returns from that hell? But tell me . . ."—he grabbed Taavi violently by the sleeve—"tell me how they're doing at home. Are my old folks still alive?" His eyes gleamed.

"A few days ago they were still all right. I passed by your gate."

"You passed by my gate," Mihkel muttered, full of emotion. "The gate of Lepiku! And the chickens were walking in the yard, weren't they? Was the dog still alive?"

"Yes, he was."

"God bless you! And you are a free man. Hell, I wish this war would come to an end. How I wish we could go home at last. For three and a half years I've fought against lice, hunger and death. Now home is so close you can almost smell it, but. . . ."

"Where are you going, then?"

"Tomorrow they're sending us to Saaremaa. Today the hospital orderlies looked at my tongue and patted my back muscles—and I was pronounced fit. I'd been lying in bed for months."

"Did you get wounded?"

"Just a little hole, but it was slow in mending. The holes the Germans shoot are always slow in mending," he said looking around, as if he were saying something sinful. Then he took Taavi by the lapel and whispered: "I've lost my appetite for all that. For the war. For the whole mess. But Saaremaa is the last stretch. Then we'll have peace."

"But if we have to go to Germany? They are mobilizing like hell in the country."

"You don't say!" Mihkel was upset and began to cough with new vigour. "Lieutenant-General Pärn himself has said that we won't be sent outside Estonia's borders. Say, you are not a Communist, are you?" he whispered, looking askance at Taavi. "Of course not. Don't think I am, either. I am now only a rag. That's true; only a rag that's been pulled through the Russian slop, but. . . ." He stopped, embarrassed.

"Would you like to leave Estonia?" Taavi asked, surprising even himself. It was a simple question, asked in an ordinary tone.

The effect upon his former neighbour was shattering. For a long time he stuttered something incomprehensible. The momentary surprise that had flashed in his eyes gave way quickly to hopeless, numb fear. Coughing, he reached for Taavi's hand and rushed off.

"So long! Say hallo to my mother and father if you happen to go by home." His voice was suddenly strange. He turned away and hurried off. His knees seemed to be giving way under him.

Taavi looked after him with sorrow and amazement. So this was what was left of Mihkel of Lepiku, who had formerly been so full of fun and high spirits, and who was a couple of years younger than he!

Taavi checked his watch. Lompus was already fifteen minutes late. Of course, there was nothing extraordinary about that. Unexpected delays could be counted upon when such things were being arranged. The main thing was that the final outcome should be successful. It would be madness to stay in the country. If they had turned Mihkel, an innocent young fellow, into such a human ruin in three years, what would they do to him—a convinced anti-Communist, an officer in the Finnish army, who according to Soviet law would merit the death penalty many times over? No, the time left for him would be very short.

50

Half an hour. Lompus did not show up.

Leonard walked past him.

"Is he laying an egg somewhere?" he asked. "What did the Russian want?"

"He was an acquaintance from back home. He's in the Estonian Corps now."

"What does he think of this mess?"

"Oh, he. . . . It didn't occur to me to ask so suddenly. He lives in a strange world."

Another fifteen minutes went by. Taavi lit his pipe and began to curse impatiently under his breath. He uttered his curses in time with the march that blared out from the loudspeaker on the corner, and walked back and forth with quick steps.

Lompus arrived exactly an hour late. Taavi saw him from afar across the market and hurried to meet him. The cook raised his fleshy hand in a Nazi-style greeting.

"Have you asked what the cigarettes are selling for?" he inquired, pointing toward the nearest table, where, for an outrageous price, one could buy cigarettes, candy and sweets that had been left behind by the retreating Germans. "The prices will surely rise some more. I'll have to save my supplies till then. But now there's not much money in circulation and the rubles are worth more," he calculated.

"How is it?" Taavi demanded harshly.

"Miserable," Lompus said and made a gloomy face.

"What does that mean? Aren't things turning out as they were supposed to?"

"No, no, we can't go today. The drivers, damn their hides, lost their nerve. One wailed that he has a wife and children, and asked for more money. Where should I get that money from? As a cook I have eaten good tidbits all my life, but that does not mean I can make gold. And you don't have any money either, do you?"

"How could I?" Taavi answered darkly.

"There's nothing to be done." Lompus shrugged his shoulders. "Don't worry, we already have the boat and the fuel. A day more or less won't make any difference."

"Couldn't we go to the coast on foot?" Taavi asked. "Where is that boat of yours?"

"How could we go on foot with that crowd, like a bunch of pilgrims? And it isn't that close."

"How far is it?"

"Don't ask too much. If you should get caught the others would be stuck too, and the coasts are swarming with Russians anyway."

"Old comrade from Finland—don't you trust me?" Taavi was hurt.

"Don't speak nonsense! Remember that the lives of an important statesman and some high officers are at stake. I've told you too much already. Let's just say good-bye now. The weather is miserable today."

"Wait, where shall I meet you?"

"Well, I have to run around quite a bit. I have no fixed address. Let's meet tomorrow morning at ten in the same place. Perhaps I'll know something by then. Where are you staying?"

Taavi mentioned his former address, where Arno and Liisa were now living, and Lompus promised to come by there in a couple of hours.

"So long, then!" he shouted in Finnish.

"So long," Taavi muttered. He was feeling low—not from the bad news, since that could be expected, but from that futile waiting in the cold. Lompus, always in a hustle, had not even apologized for being late. Nor had he given any cogent reasons for it.

"Never mind, we have another iron in the fire," Leonard said carelessly, turning his collar down when they began to move on.

Taavi recalled suddenly the little woodshed, where they had carried the sacks they had brought from the consumers' cooperative yesterday, and the five-pointed red star on the coat of one of the men.

Taavi waited in vain for Lompus that afternoon, and the following morning he approached the meeting-place with a somewhat unpleasant feeling. Just so the boat wouldn't leave without him. If a man should turn up who offered Lompus a gold watch or some table silver, his chance to leave the country might be lost for good. On meeting Lompus he would talk it over and make sure. Crooked dealings had no place in such matters.

But there was no chance to talk things over. He waited for an hour and a half without any results, and then turned toward King Street, cursing quietly under his breath. One chance was gone. He had been led around by his nose, and for half a day he had been used as a handyman. Taavi Raudoja wouldn't forget that. Next time he met Lompus, he'd at least give him a black eye or a bloody nose.

In the green-papered "committee room" of the cooperative he found the other men—Pihu and Paarkukk bending over their chess table, Vello Kasar nervously smoking his cigarette. A new man was pacing back and forth in the room—Ruudi Ugur, one of Admiral Pitka's liaison men among the Finland fighters. He was a typical young Estonian—straight and expressionless features, slightly protruding cheekbones, hair that was neither light nor dark.

"Nice to see you," Taavi said. "Where did you leave the old man?"

"He came back from Canada to finish the war, not to take a vacation. Besides, you can't carry such a stubborn specimen to Tallinn in your pants' pocket," Ugur answered. Not a shade of a smile appeared on his motionless face. Taavi had never seen him laugh. Only a quickly disappearing grin had sometimes lurked in the corners of his mouth.

"What are you doing here, Vello?" Taavi asked. "You were supposed to go to the coast today. Has something gone wrong?" He looked from one serious face to the other.

"Several things are wrong," Jaan Meos said.

"Those devils, they didn't let us out of Tallinn." Vello Kasar cursed and extinguished his cigarette in the ashtray with an abrupt gesture.

"The roads are heavily patrolled. Anyone who comes in is caught in a trap."

"So they want to screen all of Tallinn first?"

"Looks that way. They are busy every night, and those who have no papers are done for. We didn't expect that the highways would be so tightly sealed. If I didn't speak Russian so fluently, God knows how it might have turned out. We saved our skins in exchange for a pack of cigarettes. We'll try again tonight, taking some out-of-the-way roads across Lasnamäe. We would have tried today, but I thought we should give the men here a warning, otherwise someone could really wind up in a mess. If you have an identity card, a job certificate, and travelling orders, then you can go, and nobody will interfere."

"Don't go at night," Lieutenant Pihu warned them. "You won't get far."

"No, there's no use trying at night," Ruudi Ugur agreed. "It's likely you'll get arrested, or, even worse, the patrol might shoot you on sight. I've travelled around in the country. I know what it's like."

"And besides that, we just pronounced a death sentence," Jaan Meos added.

"On whom?" Taavi asked.

"One of the worst swine imaginable is among our Finland boys. It's the duty of every Finland fighter, and especially every officer, to make this traitor harmless at the first opportunity."

"Who is he?"

"Joakim Lompus," Jaan said.

Taavi felt as if somebody had given him a slap in the face.

"Joakim Lompus?" he repeated.

"Speak up, Ruudi!" Jaan commanded.

"Lompus handed over some twenty young Legion boys to the Russians when he came out of the woods, to get clean papers for himself," Ruudi said with a motionless face.

A moment of silence ensued.

"Is there positive proof?" Taavi demanded sternly.

"I wasn't there myself, but my information is trustworthy," Ruudi answered calmly. "In addition he has already performed all kinds of other tricks, taking advantage of the trust and loyalty of our boys. He has arranged for non-existent boats to go across the sea, and has cheated men out of their gold rings and revolvers."

"And has he arranged a boat for a well-known statesman?" Taavi inquired with growing disgust.

"You seem to have some firsthand experience with him yourself," Manivald Pihu said ironically from behind his chessmen, and everybody looked at Taavi with interest. The myopic eyes of Jüri Paarkukk were narrow and searching.

"The damned s.o.b.," Taavi swore. "Half a day I helped him carry sacks around, my heart aflutter with fond expectations!"

Manivald Pihu burst out laughing, and Jaan Meos excitedly grabbed Taavi's sleeve.

"Do you know where he is? Let's go and silence him right away, before the NKVD closes in on us!" he said with flashing eyes.

"He didn't show up for the last meeting," Taavi replied.

"Lompus is no fool. He'd be wary once he has got into that kind of a game," Ruudi Ugur reasoned.

"I don't doubt that there are small-time crooks among us, but that such a scoundrel could have been in Finland with us is beyond my comprehension. I haven't used a knife on a human being yet, but it seems that the time has come," Taavi said keeping his eyes on the floor.

"Go ahead if you have a chance; the sentence has been passed," Ruudi said quietly. "The life and honour of every one of us is at stake."

"The situation is going to the devil in a hurry," Taavi said to himself on leaving his comrades. He looked carefully both ways when he stepped into the street, as he had been advised, and then turned his steps toward the nearest militia station.

Getting a new passport proved to be as simple as his friends had reported. No suspicious questions were asked, not even what he had been doing during the German occupation. The clerks were young girls, and the queues were long.

"Your former documents, please," the girl said.

Taavi produced the red-covered Soviet passport he had got from Marta, and gave a street address at random.

"I don't know how long I'll stay there, though," he said, hesitating.

"When you change your residence, please register at the nearest station. This document is temporary anyway. You are lucky that you managed to keep your Soviet passport."

Taavi received a white slip of paper and left. They had not paid any attention to the strange-looking photo in his passport. Now he was Elmar Remmelgas, a year younger than he actually was.

Feeling more secure, he went directly to another militia station and got a similar paper in his own name for the *Ausweis* that the Germans had issued him. After that he went to the central office of the state railroads and asked about a job.

"Please see the chief of personnel," a youth in a railroad uniform told him. "Third door on the right."

Taavi knocked and entered the room. Two young girls were sitting at a huge desk. One of them had just placed her poorly stockinged legs on the table and was arranging her underwear.

"Excuse me," Taavi stuttered.

"Please come in, comrade." the other girl smiled amiably and turned toward Taavi, while the first one pulled her legs quickly under the table.

Taavi was undecided. The girl who had addressed him continued to put polish on her fingernails, not disturbed in the least by his entrance. She was stout and carelessly dressed. Her blonde hair was cut short, and she spoke Estonian with a stiff Russian accent. The other girl was busily arranging some papers in front of her, blushing.

"I wanted to see the head of the personnel department," Taavi began.

"What can I do for you, comrade?" the chubby girl asked. "I am the head of the personnel department." She looked Taavi over from head to foot.

"I wanted to ask for a job on the railway."

"How old are you, comrade? Twenty-eight. Mmm. Are you married? Mmm. We have plenty of vacancies. Did you want a job at the Tallinn terminal?"

"Yes. I live in Tallinn. I don't care what kind of a job."

"Give your name and address to this comrade. And go then to the Tallinn terminal and find out what kind of a job they'll give you. Then come back here and we'll issue you your papers."

"Couldn't you issue me the certificate right away?"

"We don't know to what kind of a job you will be assigned."

"They'll at least let me shift the rails, I'm sure. To be truthful, I couldn't start working for about a week anyway. I have to take care of some personal matters. Moved all my stuff to the country from the Germans."

"Come back in a week, then."

"Yes, but I need the certificate now. When they check papers they always ask where you are working. If you don't have any papers, you are in trouble. I am a conscientious Soviet citizen. I don't want to cause extra trouble for the authorities. Please, comrade, maybe you could issue the certificate immediately? Here's my Soviet passport and my temporary identity card."

The girl took both documents and gave Taavi another searching look. When Taavi smiled, she lowered her eyes coquettishly. Then she discussed something with the other girl in rapid Russian, which Taavi with his meagre store of Russian phrases could not comprehend. It seemed to him that the girl was willing to do him a favour, but the complication lay in red tape. She spoke and gesticulated, adjusted the gaudy cotton dress on her swelling breasts, and sighed.

"It's within your power, comrade," Taavi told her convincingly. "I'll certainly go to work next week. I'm sure you are an understanding lady." He smiled.

The word "lady" had a decisive influence on the official from Russia.

"Estonian men are wonderful," she said, flattered. Taavi had to complete a questionnaire, and when he left the office of the head of the personnel department, he had the desired paper in his pocket, complete with proper stamps and signatures. An unknown Elmar Remmelgas had become a new Soviet citizen and a labourer at the Tallinn terminal of the state railways.

The little room was quickly filled with smoke. Even Inga, the woman Leonard had been talking about, smoked incessantly. The expression on her sallow face was too stern to be feminine.

An interesting party had gathered. "A fine mouthful for the Russians," Leonard Kibuviir said. Most of them were young men. Many were still wearing the trousers and boots they had worn in their last battle, and they had German or Finnish army stamps on their underwear. They were sitting on chairs, on the floor, and on pillows taken from the couch, their expectant faces looking up to a small woman with faded hair, about thirty-five years of age.

"We have had more luck these last two days than anybody dared expect. We have a boat now," the woman said. "And this morning the men drove to the coast with a motor. At present we have sixteen men. Please don't mention it to anyone else, for I don't want to leave anybody behind, disappointed."

"Has it been planned that the boat will come back?" Taavi asked. "There are a lot of Finland fellows here, at least fifty that I know of, looking for a chance to get across."

"I don't know whether the skipper of the boat wants to take the risk," the woman answered. "He's my colleague from the Battery prison. We were arrested together by the Germans. I don't know how good his nerve is. His family was already in Finland when he was arrested, and he is probably longing to be with his wife and children. But if there's a man among yourselves who is willing to come back, that's something else again. The boat couldn't serve a better purpose."

"I'm sure that such a man will be found," asserted Ruudi Ugur, who was the only representative of the gang from the cooperative. "In that case I wouldn't go on the first trip."

"Now," Inga said matter-of-factly, "let's see how much money we have, for I promised to pay the rest of the price for the motor today. And I'll have to get fuel too."

She placed her rings on the table.

"Your engagement ring and your wedding ring!" the young girl sitting next to her exclaimed. Her name was Leida Soolepp, and they were meeting in her apartment. She wavered. Then she took off her own rings.

"Lives are more precious than memories," Inga said calmly, with a melancholy smile in her blue eyes. Leonard had told Taavi a little about the life and the past of this remarkable woman. She had lost her husband in the summer of 1941, when the Russians had arrested him, and her daughter and mother had perished in the air raids the previous March.

The men searched the empty pockets of their borrowed clothes. Two gave their wrist watches, one a wedding ring, some a few rubles. Taavi gave the small amount he had received from Selma upon his arrival in Tallinn. Everybody could see that this was not enough to save so many lives.

Another girl, the roommate of Leida Soolepp, brought a silver spoon she had been given on her baptism. "I also have a length of dress material," she said with an embarrassed smile.

"All that is not quite enough," Inga said wistfully, fingering expertly the revolver which someone had placed on the table. "A beautiful thing, this Belgian FN. I had a similar one in my pocket when they arrested me. I was lucky not to use it. Yes, that's not enough. We are too poor." She smiled.

The men searched their memories for things they could add to the small treasure on the table. One promised a length of suiting, another a pair of half-worn shoes—and that was all.

"Let's see what we can do. I'll keep these things. I have a fairly new fur coat and a few trinkets. I was bombed out in March, you know." She swallowed and sucked at her cigarette. "All right, I'll give my fur coat. Perhaps I'll get something else to wear."

"We should attack a Russian. Their arms are full of robbed wrist watches up to their elbows," Leonard said sardonically.

"Yes, I saw one yesterday tearing a ring from a woman," Ruudi remarked. "The woman was too scared to scream. She seemed quite glad that she got away so easily."

"One of them asked me for the correct time today," one of the men growled. "I know them already. If he'd been alone, I'd have struck the time of the day right between his eyes. When you come from the station, they line up to ask you for the correct time, and yet you can hear them ticking all over."

"Let's hurry up now," Inga said matter-of-factly. "It will be evening soon, and I have to see several people for oil and gasoline. We'll meet tomorrow. Maybe Paul will be back from the coast by then. They went on bicycles. We don't have much time, for the noose around our necks is being pulled tighter every day. And please be extremely careful. Let's leave gradually, one by one, and when you come back tomorrow, some of you come a couple of hours earlier, so we won't attract attention."

She addressed one of the young men. "You are welcome to stay here for the night, if you don't have a place to go. And if any one of you has a problem—if you're hungry or if you don't have a place to sleep—just speak up without false shame. We'll do what we can to fix you up. We have to be like one big family, and I am the mother of all of you."

Taavi was worried where he should spend the night. He had misgivings about staying with Arno and Liisa. After all, he had given his address to Lompus, and it was better to be careful than sorry. Staying with Leonard's friends was out of the question; there were two of them already, Leonard and Eedi. He did not dare go to any of his former comrades, for they were all under suspicion. Nobody could be sure that Lompus was not already betraying his Finnish companions instead of the boys from the Legion, should he have got himself into another tight spot. The NKVD was insatiable. Taavi did not quite trust the cooperative on King Street, either. They were too careless there in his opinion.

He said good-bye to his companions and went to Selma's apartment.

Selma had got over the recent shock. She seized Taavi's hand and gave it a hearty squeeze.

"It's great that you came," she exclaimed.

"I'll tell you my trouble first thing," Taavi said. "Can you put me up for the night?"

"Why not, you silly boy?"

She took Taavi to the dining room and began to set the table.

"You came at the right time, but my dinner isn't much to brag about. First, there's nothing to cook, and second, when I come home from work I don't feel like spending much time on food. But I'll see if I can find something special for you."

"Don't go to any trouble because of me. I should tell the people where I spent last night where I am. But it isn't that important. Let them think that I left the country. Tell me now, did you get to see Uuno?"

"Yes, I did. I got to see him twice. They did not even stop me from talking with him. When the people were deported to Siberia in 1941, they wouldn't let their relatives close enough for even a last look."

"They have nothing to hide any more. We are completely in their hands now."

"That's what they seem to think, the simpletons," Selma said with such conviction to the contrary that it made even Taavi's heart lighter. "We talked everything over. We even settled all our childhood quarrels. I took warm underwear to him later and as much food as I had and could carry. They were sent away that same evening."

"You don't know where?"

"No. I asked the guards, but they didn't know a thing. I heard that a similar train had been standing at Ülemiste yesterday, mostly full of German prisoners-of-war, but that a few Estonian partisans had been there in civilian clothes. How are your affairs getting along? I have been quite worried about you."

"Oh, don't worry. There's nothing the matter with me. The limbs are all whole and I haven't got a ticket to Siberia yet either."

"If a man is already dead or on the train, then he is beyond help. Perhaps I might still be of some help to you, though. Have you found a chance to go to Finland?"

"I've had foggy opportunities every day. That seems to be the only thing you hear when you walk down the streets here in Tallinn. Everybody seems to have gone crazy about that. After one chance is lost, you begin to believe in the next."

"Don't tell me any details, Taavi. It's best not to know. Eat now, and I'll make up your bed."

Taavi slept without dreams on the wide couch in the living room. He had become accustomed to the noises which had disturbed his first night in town: the sudden jerks and stops of heavy, rumbling trucks, and the rapid bursts of submachinegun fire. In the haystacks in the woods it had been quiet; only the wind had rustled in the bushes or the birch trees. It seemed to him that it was safer and more secure to sleep in the woods.

When he visited Liisa the following morning, he learned that he had again done the right thing, as if guided by a guardian spirit. There had been a roundup at night in the part of town where Liisa lived. No, the hand of Lompus had not been in it—the roundup had been the standard hunt for Germans and Nazis, arranged now in this district, now in another, which provided a pretext for loading on the truck every suspicious-looking, sleepy person who did not have papers with the required number of stamps.

"It was a blessing you were away," Liisa stuttered. Her usually glowing cheeks were quite white and transparent.

VI

The following day they met again in Inga's apartment, as they had planned. A man was sitting at the table next to her. His face was unshaven, and his clothes were dirty and greasy. He was called Paul, and he had just arrived from the coast.

"The thing is clicking," he said with a gruff voice. "Only the boat is too small for all of us."

"How many do you think it will carry?" Inga asked.

"No more than ten. If the weather is calm, maybe twelve, but no more than that, or we'll go directly down to Neptune. And the autumn weather is unpredictable."

Silence reigned in the room. The men smoked quietly and looked gloomily at the floor and into the corners. Four of them had to stay behind, perhaps even six. This ruined their hopeful mood, and brought bad thoughts. Those who the day before had not even had any money to contribute toward the cost of the fuel, felt that they had forfeited their right to express any opinion.

"That's tough," Inga said heavily and let her glance glide over the waiting men. "Whom could we leave behind? They are all soldiers. Death sentences are waiting for all of them in the Soviet courts. . . . We'll do this," she decided—"the women will stay behind."

Linda Soolepp sprang up.

"I won't stay behind! I've sacrificed everything to arrange this trip! Why don't the men look out for themselves, if they are men?"

"No, that won't do," somebody mumbled. "Who of us would be so ungrateful? You have shared your last crumbs of bread with us and have given us shelter."

"There's no ingratitude involved," Inga said. "We have to figure soberly and impartially. I have heard of plenty of cases where people were left to their fate on the shore, because they did not have enough gold, and the boat left half empty. Yes, the crew risked their lives and deserved something for that, but that women and little children were left on the shore because they didn't have the full price of the passage in gold—that stinks! Linda, dear, don't get excited. The men go first this time."

"No, I won't stay." Linda burst out crying.

"Don't behave like a child," Inga admonished her. "When Paul comes back with the boat, we'll follow them."

"I won't come back," the man said. "My life is worth something too. I have a family. Nobody can force me to come. I've learned what it's like in the prison. I have had enough of that."

"Then you'll send the boat back with someone else, if your own hide is too precious," Inga said sternly. She stood up. Red spots showed on her pale cheeks. "It seems I'll have to accompany you to the coast myself, and take the Browning along to keep order among you. I hope my word will have some weight. I don't know the names of some of you—I have deliberately avoided learning them—but I know each one well enough, and I know what kind of a fate is in store for you."

"I won't stay behind," Linda insisted, eyes wet with tears.

Paul looked gloomily under the edge of the table in front of him.

"Don't cry now, I'll come back for you. I know the shores and—all right, I'll come," he muttered through half-clenched teeth.

"Thank you very much," Inga said with frank simplicity. "We'll meet on the coast tomorrow night. I got a small car to carry the fuel. Come closer now, all of you. I'll tell you exactly how to get there." On the table in front of her was a map of the northern coast and a pencilled sketch. "We'll divide the men into two groups, for we can use two roads. You'll have to move alone or in pairs, and without any baggage. Especially near the coast you'll have to take village roads and shortcuts through the woods. I'll point out to you the places where Russians are stationed, as far as my information goes."

The men formed a circle around the table. She spoke briefly and clearly, and displayed great experience and firmness.

"I recommend that you start out this evening, so nobody will be late and you can leave tomorrow night," she said in conclusion.

"Won't you try to go along too?" Ruudi asked.

"I'll go with the last boat."

"Who says which will be the last? I was thinking that I would volunteer to stay behind, at least for this trip."

"Have you got a girl or what?"

"No, but I have about twenty men, and I'm trying to trace down old Admiral Pitka. If you would leave the boat under my orders after this trip. . . ."

"No!" Linda shouted, scared anew. "Then there will be men only again, and we'll have to stay behind for ever."

"I'm happy to hear about your plans," Inga said calmly, "and I'll be pleased to have you stay to help me. But the boat would be overloaded even without you, so your staying would not mean an additional passage for someone else. And besides. . . ."

The shrill sound of the doorbell interrupted her and froze everybody to their seats. The bell rang twice; one long ring, one short.

"That must be one of us," Inga said with composure. She stepped to the window and looked down into the street. "There are no Russians to be seen. Will you open the door, Linda?"

The new arrival was a youth with a flushed, perspiring face. He was startled in his turn when he entered, and mumbled a greeting. He remained standing at the door.

"You, Arthur?" Inga was amazed. "What has happened? Why did you leave the shore?"

"It's lucky I got away," the youth answered. He looked from one person to the next. "The shore is positively filthy with Russians."

"What are you talking about?" The captain of the boat jumped up. "When I left, there weren't any around."

"Go and see for yourself. They started pouring in right after you left. Could I get a glass of water? My throat is parched."

He emptied the glass with a gulp and wiped his perspiring forehead.

"Did you manage to tuck away the boat in a safe place?" Paul asked excitedly.

"How could I, when they descended on me so suddenly? I was just fixing the bow—it was leaking a little when the waves hit—when suddenly there was a damn commotion all around."

"Stupid, where were your eyes and ears?" Paul was furious. "And why did you run like a scared rabbit? Why didn't you wait until they left, or take the boat somewhere else?"

"Don't be naïve," the boy answered. "It's easy to criticize from here. We've lost the boat, for they don't seem to have any intention of leaving. They began setting up their artillery and digging trenches right there. It's not just one or two. There are any number of them. All the roads and villages are swarming. They ordered me out of the boat and hauled it up on the shore. I had a hard time keeping the bicycle. I had to hold on to it by sheer force. I thought they'd shoot me when I got on it, but they finally let me go."

Paul swore and rubbed his huge fists together. "I'd break your neck right here if it would be of any help. A brand new motor and a good boat! Where was your good sense? Why didn't you crank it up, whoosh away, and send the Russians to the devil in a shower of foam? Hell fire!"

He pounced his head with his fists as if he had a terrible headache.

Inga stood, defeated. She was limp and pale. Suddenly her eyes flashed with a peculiar gleam.

"We must get the boat back, cost what it may," she said firmly.

The eyes of the men centred on her. Taavi Raudoja felt an irrepressible desire to laugh out loud. In the few short days he had spent in Tallinn he had seen so many former comrades put their faith in chances to get away and had heard their talk until his own suspicious mind had come to hope and believe in those chances too. And yet all had turned out to be mere castles in the air. This woman was right. They had to get that boat back in spite of fate, cost what it may. Now every man was giving full rein to his ingenuity. Couldn't they recover the boat by force? Were the Russians really so numerous? Perhaps they had moved away from the coast? The men split up in groups, and their discussion became so loud that Inga had to quiet them down.

"I have a plan," she said. "I don't know if it will work, but we'll have to try. We must trick the Russians out of the boat and bring it to a different place. I have connections over there and I know the shore well. That part will be simple. The question is how to get close to the boat and who should do it."

61

"I want to take a look at it myself," Paul threatened. "I can't get over it otherwise. You can't trust young boys with a man's job. We've found that out." He glowered at the young man who had returned from the coast, and his swarthy unshaven face was dark like a cloud. "But there should be somebody with me who can speak Russian better than I."

"I figured I'd go myself," Inga said.

"You—yourself? All right."

"Does anybody have any connections with the port authorities in Tallinn?"

"What for?" Ruudi Ugur asked. "One of our men is assistant to the director."

Inga stood up and said cheerfully, "That's wonderful. Go and look him up right away and get a paper from him, in Russian, with huge stamps on it, saying that our boat must be brought from such and such a place to the harbour in Tallinn."

"That is really an excellent idea," Taavi Raudoja agreed. An urge to act surged through him. "Couldn't I go along to bring the boat back? It might not be so fitting for ladies."

"Do you speak Russian?"

"A couple of words."

"That is not enough. My Russian is quite fluent, and besides I look pretty good in old overalls and rubber boots. I have acted the part of a fishwife before. Paul and I will go. I don't know exactly where we could take the boat. We'll be back in a couple of days, and then all will be clear. We have to provide ourselves with knives. We can't use any other weapons. Maybe the Russians will dispatch a few men to accompany us. How many could we handle?" she asked Paul calmly.

"Count at least two for my share," the man growled.

"Then we'll manage, for they won't send more than three."

Three days had passed since the departure of Inga and her companion, the skipper. It was time to expect them back, if everything had gone as planned. The mood of the men waiting for the boat became tense and restless. The girls, in whose apartment they met, were nervous and gloomy. They begged the men not to come so often, for that would certainly attract attention. Everyone realized that fact and was aware of the seriousness of the situation, but it was hard to wait calmly. It was a matter of life and death.

On the afternoon of the third day Taavi sat in the green room of the cooperative.

"There'll be bad news," said Jaan Meos.

"Wait a little. Maybe something will turn up," said Lieutenant Pihu from behind the chessboard. "'Well, what's so wrong now? Voss is free again and plays soccer in the 'Dynamo.' And Mats Luukas is free too; they arrested him by mistake."

"How do you know that they arrested him by mistake?" Taavi inquired. He, too, was restless today. "Have you seen him?"

"Now you are getting that way too," Pihu exclaimed, scoffing.

"Yes, you haven't seen either one of them," Jaan continued. "I met Voss this morning. The man has changed a lot. His face is thin like a shadow. He just said hallo and ran along as quickly as he could. Maybe he does play soccer—he is one of the best of those that were left—maybe that's why they spared him. But we had better keep away from him. He got married after coming back from Finland. He has a young wife, and I'm afraid he'll be quite soft soon."

"Has anyone seen Mats Luukas since his arrest?" Jüri Paarkukk asked.

"Riks should be coming soon. They are good friends; Riks might know," Jaan said.

"Any news from Vello?" Taavi asked.

"No, there is no news of any kind from the coast," Jaan replied. "Any man who leaves Tallinn just disappears."

Somebody rang the doorbell.

"Some fellow or other. Riks won't be here so soon."

But it *was* Richard Kullerkann. He wore the same funereal expression as before, and after greetings he sat down, as if standing were strenuous for him. But sitting down, he seemed to collapse altogether. "What are you doing here? Playing chess!" he exclaimed, as if noticing it for the first time.

"Have you seen Mats?"

"No!" All of a sudden Riks stood up. "I haven't, and I don't want to see him."

"We might find out something."

"Don't you know well enough what it's like!" Riks' voice had a cutting edge. "I came to tell you not to invite me here any more. I won't come here any more!" he shouted and raised his hand, pointing to the chess players. "What are you sitting here for? Do something. Run, look around, act! Everything has changed! You fools! You aren't tied down yet. You're still free. What the devil are you sitting here for?" He stopped short; his eyes focused on a spot on the wall in a fixed stare. His eyes bulged behind his glasses, and a disorderly strand of thin hair fell over his forehead. Then he swept his hand over his face and started retreating toward the door, his gaze still fixed on the same spot.

The others followed his stare. There was nothing on the wall except a large iron nail.

"What are you staring at?" Pihu asked.

"Go to the devil!" Riks yelled and tried to run out of the room. Taavi, who was standing near the door, grabbed him by the sleeve.

Riks jerked his arm loose, ready to strike out. His eyes were wild.

"Riks!" Taavi exclaimed.

The man swayed back and forth and reeled back to his chair.

"Men, brothers," he muttered, looking from one to the other, as if for help. "I'm afraid I'm going crazy."

"So it seems," Manivald Pihu agreed calmly. Riks jumped up again and stared at him, his eyes almost bulging through the glasses from tension.

63

"You damned filthy toad!" he screamed. "You damned. . . ." He ran forward, panting for breath, and swept the chessmen off the table.

Jüri Paarkukk rose quietly, gave him a silent scowl, and then grabbed him by the coat.

"You too!" Riks shouted, throwing the chessmen he felt under his hand into his comrade's face.

Jüri did not utter a word. He was a strong, broad-shouldered young man, with big angular wrists. He quickly took off Riks' glasses, put them on the table, and holding his opponent by the lapels of his coat, shook the man back and forth like an empty bag. Kullerkann fell on his chair.

"Don't attack your own side!" Jüri panted.

This time Riks did not cry, as might have been expected from his feverish, rasping breathing. His eyes flashed, swollen and red, but his face was sunken and grey. He looked at Taavi imploringly, when Taavi stepped to him.

"Say, man, tell me, what's wrong with you?" Taavi said, placing his hand on his friend's shoulder.

Riks pulled his shoulder down, as if it hurt.

"I have nothing to tell," he muttered.

"We're all old friends here. Maybe we could help?"

"Nobody can help me," Riks hissed back. "I see you can't even help yourselves. How then could you help me? Go somewhere, wherever you please, but get away from these rooms. Go, where nobody will know or find you. If you like your bones beaten to pulp, if you like to sell out each other—I don't know, maybe you do—then stay. Your death won't be glorious; don't expect that. They won't let you die proud and defiant like you think. Your last hours will be made uglier than you can imagine. I can't keep this up much longer, I am not as young as you."

"I can't understand," Manivald Pihu said. "What nightmares are you having? What's the trouble with you? What's the trouble with any of us right now? The situation has changed since 1941; everyone can see that. It's Allied influence, I'm sure. Let's not start painting devils on the wall, before we have a clear picture of the situation. And if it turns out like the devil, I just can't believe that men like us couldn't get out of the country. Let's take it calmly!"

Riks looked at him with a bitter, scoffing grimace. He did not speak any more but walked up to the table and started taking off his coat. His movements betrayed pain. Realization began to dawn on the men.

Then Riks took off his shirt. When he stood naked to the waist, and turned around in front of his friends, everyone was silent from the shock of what he saw. The man's whole body was blue and swollen from beatings. Long bloody stripes ran closely together over his back and shoulders.

"Take it calmly!" It was Riks' turn to scoff from between clenched teeth.

"What the devil does this mean?" cried Manivald Pihu.

"NKVD!" Taavi muttered. A terrible hush had descended upon the room. Riks was busy with his clothes and Jaan helped him as though he were a little child. Manivald Pihu looked on the table in front of him and absent-mindedly lifted the disordered chessmen. Paarkukk frowned at Riks, as if he were still considering him a potential assailant. The noise of the street and the rumble of heavy military vehicles suddenly seemed much closer in the little back room.

"Tell us, how did all this happen?" Taavi demanded. "Have you betrayed anyone?"

"There's nothing to tell," Riks said harshly. "I happened to fall into their hands—and here I am. Don't ask any foolishness! Your turn will come, sooner than you may think. Right now I'm getting it for old sins. I hope they never get to the Finnish affair.

"An old enemy of mine looked me up. He knows me through and through, and he's now in the NKVD. The Estonian Communists themselves are the most fiendish. The Russians don't know what's what. Organization is still completely lacking, although they are recruiting units and moving them here as fast as they can. But I am in a hellish spot because of that acquaintance. He hasn't forgotten anything during his three years' absence. Who can guarantee that I won't give them your names and addresses even tonight, and that tomorrow I won't walk like a shadow after those whose addresses I don't know today? That's why I say: Go, run, do something. I can't. I have a sick wife and small children. And you invite me here. You entrust your plans to me—to me, a leper!" He crouched on the chair, motionless, gesticulating with one nervous hand. "Maybe now after I leave, you'll decide to kill me. That would be all right. Then I couldn't betray you. I wouldn't consider it a crime, even. It's better that one should fall for all, since all of us are too few right now to save even one!"

"Do you know how much they have found out about us?"

"Right now probably very little," Riks answered. "I don't know, of course, what others have revealed and what they have been questioned about. I must have been on their list for years."

"Do they still have their lists?"

"I guess so. But as I said: the setup is just being organized. I'll go now."

"Where are you going?" Manivald Pihu jumped up. "You're going to betray us!" he shouted.

"Stupid!" Riks said quickly and absent-mindedly. Then he turned to Jaan. "Can you give me a couple of sheets of paper? I have to write some letters—some official business."

"Right now?"

"Yes, right away. It's late already."

"Come to the office. There's nobody there just now. Do you want stamps too?"

"Yes, please. Let's say good-bye now, brothers. I won't have time to come by here any more." He pressed everyone's hand with a peculiar solemnity and left. Jaan accompanied him to the small office of the cooperative.

"What are we going to do with him?" Pihu asked. His smiling

65

superiority and recklessness were gone. He walked back and forth in the room and puffed at his cigarette.

"We must try to send him away, before it's too late," Taavi said firmly.

"But when the man won't leave his wife and children?"

"Then all together."

"When the NKVD are keeping their eyes on them, it won't be so simple to go with the whole family."

"Come, now, the house can't be surrounded yet!" Taavi said with conviction. "I think he'll have to leave the nest right now or never."

"His wife is sick," Jaan reminded them returning.

"How sick is she?"

"She won't stand hardship and transportation. I've seen her myself."

Taavi was annoyed.

"For goodness' sake, there must be some way for him to get out! We can't leave the situation as it is!"

"No, we can't," Jüri Paarkukk added resolutely from behind the table. But when the glances of the others turned toward him, he did not say anything more.

For a long time they talked, argued and made plans. Finally they stood by Taavi's proposition. Riks must leave immediately in Taavi's stead, and the wife and children must be sent somewhere to relatives or friends, to the country, as far away as possible, if she could not stand the trip in the boat. Taavi, however, was convinced that he would be able to get Leonard and Eedi to yield their places in favour of Riks' wife and children.

But when Jaan went to get Riks, he had already left. Two envelopes were lying on the table, one closed, the other open. The closed envelope was addressed to Riks' wife.

With a premonition, Jaan Meos pulled the letter from the open envelope. Having read a few lines, he rushed downstairs, calling out loud for Riks, although he knew the foolhardiness of his act. The alley was empty. He ran into the street, colliding with passers-by, crossed the square to the city hall and ran then down to the ancient Viru Gate. Riks was gone. Jaan turned back with hopeless steps. There was a turmoil of emotions in his soul, which made it hard for him to restrain himself from plunging his fist into the face of every Russian soldier whom he encountered.

"Riks is gone, and he won't be back, ever!" Jaan said when he returned. "A man less from our number."

"What are you talking about?" Pihu exclaimed.

For an answer, Jaan Meos read aloud the fine lines of Richard Kullerkann, beautifully written, even though they betrayed haste:

Dear comrades-in-arms:

With this letter I am saying good-bye to every one of you, and I wish for you tireless energy and superhuman will to continue our common fight. I am old and tired, and I am afraid that I might betray our noble aims to save my family. Therefore I am taking my

66

leave while the road is still open. I thank you all as a friend and brother—but I cannot accept the chance to escape, leaving my sick wife with two small children in the clutches of the NKVD. Our house is being watched, and it is impossible to leave. I have not betrayed anyone. I know the NKVD too well and I warn every one of you: betrayal will not save any of you.

Please send the other letter to my wife. I know it will break her heart, but she will still have the children, and I have no other choice. I will get over it with the help of the Almighty. This is the right way.

God save our people and our fatherland!

When Jaan Meos finished, silence reigned in the room. Taavi felt as if something rustling had run over his temples. His glance touched the nail on the wall, which Riks had been scrutinizing before. Then his glance fell on Jüri Paarkukk's angular wrists, which recently had held Riks by his coat lapels, and now were supporting his chin, which was hidden by his palms. Manivald Pihu looked at his watch, as if he were trying to fix the fateful hour in his memory.

"Couldn't we catch him yet—find him somewhere?"

"I ran all the way down to Viru Street already. How far could we go? Maybe he didn't even go that far."

"He was afraid the spirit might leave him," Pihu remarked, the joke of his words contradicted by his motionless face. "But I'll say, he's a man of honour! A damned fine man of honour. I take my hat off to him!"

The rest of Taavi's afternoon was full of gloomy thoughts and premonitions for there was still no news from the coast. The girls in the little apartment were frantic with despair. Taavi left them and went to see Arno and Liisa—simply for a diversion, and also to keep these good people from becoming too convinced that he had actually succeeded in his much-discussed enterprise. Taavi himself began to doubt that anything would come of it, sitting in Tallinn like that. Would it not be better to go to the coast himself? But he had no connections, and he knew that the coasts were mostly empty.

"Where have you been?" Liisa asked with motherly joy and tenderness. "Why, you're still here!"

"Seems that it won't be so easy to get out," Taavi answered. When he hung his coat in the hall he suddenly regretted having come. But he did not want to bother Selma, either, with his low spirits. It was miserable not to have a place of one's own where one could go when evening came.

"Somebody has been here a couple of times every day, looking for you," Liisa whispered.

"Looking for me? Who the devil?"

Liisa put her hand over her mouth and whispered:

"She is waiting for you now in the living room."

"Who?" Taavi was dumbfounded.

"A lady. She says she knows you well and is very anxious to see you. Go in. I'll find something for you to eat. Arno hasn't come home yet."

Taavi entered the living room, flustered. The daughter of August Roosi, Mrs. Marta Laane, was sitting on the couch.

"Taavi!" she exclaimed and ran to meet him.

"You!" Taavi muttered in surprise. "How did you get here?"

Marta laughed. "I took a leave of absence, and I've been in Tallinn now for three days. But it was impossible to get hold of you. I've walked all over town and been here every day. I almost lost hope and began to think you'd left for the coast. But here you are!"

"What do you want of me, then?"

"I'm planning to leave the country with you."

"Excellent," Taavi mocked. "Do you have an opening then?"

"What does that mean?"

"If you don't even know that, how do you expect to get across? Now everybody has openings and if even those with the best openings don't get out, how do you expect to make it without one? An opening is an opportunity to go. Can't you see that?"

"You're in a terrible mood."

"There's no reason to rejoice. Quite apart from everything else, there's too much noise outside all the time. My ears are hurting from the loud-speakers."

Marta sat down, still unable to suppress her joy. Taavi measured her with a grim glance. The woman was conspicuously well-dressed, considering the times. She wore expensive silk stockings, and was showing off her rings and her broad golden bracelet. Marta was wearing the passage price for several men, Taavi decided. That might come in handy one of these days. He was able to look at many things now from a very practical point of view.

He sat down on a chair on the other side of the table.

"Take these; my cigarettes are better," Marta said, when she saw Taavi groping for his pipe.

"Thanks. What? American cigarettes? Where did you get those?" Taavi was amazed.

"Don't forget that the United States are our allies now. Our party bosses have all kinds of good things from the New World."

"Those fools!"

But Taavi smoked the cigarette with enjoyment. He seemed to forget his situation for a while. Suddenly his thoughts moved from the cigarette to the place of their origin. All kinds of rumours were circulating about a British control commission, which was supposed to watch over the welfare of the people like benevolent guardian angels. Almost everyone insisted that an acquaintance had met them personally. Taavi placed the two differing worlds side by side in his mind, and he did not doubt for a moment that a conflict between the two was inevitable.

"Do you like it?" Marta referred to the cigarette. "They seemed awfully strong to me at first. Tell me now, where do you stay at night?"

"Nowhere in particular. Now here, now there, as it happens," Taavi answered.

"Wouldn't you like to stay at my place? My big apartment is still empty. They'll soon put Russians in there, of course. They have already been there to look over the rooms. You won't find a safer place anywhere."

Taavi hesitated, but did not refuse outright.

"Oh, it's only a couple of nights now," he said. "I won't be staying here much longer, anyway. Besides, what would it look like if I stayed in your apartment?"

"You are not a schoolboy," Marta laughed. "Or are you scared of me? No, be sure to come. I have provided myself with some food and supplies too. I would like to take care of you a little—for the sake of our old friendship, if nothing else."

Taavi began to have misgivings when they reached the door of Marta's apartment. Wasn't it a little reckless to come here, where so many Germans had been going in and out such a short time ago? The house was large, and some of the inhabitants were sure to know about and disapprove of Marta's way of life.

"Here we are," the woman said, pulling him into the darkened hallway. "It wouldn't be bad at all living here, but they won't allow that any more. I don't know what to do with my furniture—I guess I'll try to sell it. This is all that is left from the time I was married. I moved here after my husband was arrested. I couldn't stand living in our own house after that. And it was nationalized anyway. It was a fairly large apartment house. Sometime I may be able to live off the rents, when I'm old and all these occupations are over."

She took Taavi into the living room and invited him to sit down on the large sofa. The room was not big, but comfortable, and full of indications of former wealth. A lighting fixture made of carved wood hung from the ceiling. The artist had employed motifs from Estonian folk art. It was massive and big, and the room seemed too small for it. The living room seemed too small also for the oil painting in a heavy gilt frame on the wall above the sofa, and for the bookcase with glass doors, where disorderly heaps of volumes were piled up in confusion.

"I checked the books in a hurry," Marta explained. "I removed the banned literature and took it to the basement. I packed up the radio, too. I haven't had time to take it away yet. I was surprised to find everything just as I had left it. The superintendent only asked what I was going to do with the apartment and who would be living in it. They have the same statute again; nine square metres of floor space per occupant. Sit down and smoke; the cigarettes are here. I'll go and make some coffee."

Marta slipped quickly into the kitchen, and Taavi stretched out on the sofa.

The room darkened rapidly in the deepening twilight of the late autumn evening. Taavi pulled down the blackout shades and turned on the light. It was good the city still had electricity. Their own men had kept the Germans from blowing up the power station. Passing a

69

mirror, Taavi examined his face. His beard had begun to grow faster of late. He had noticed it wandering through the woods, where shaving had been a difficult chore. Eedi of Piibu had usually scratched his face with a dull knife, so that Taavi's eyes had watered in sympathy.

"Would I trouble you very much if . . . I washed a little?" Taavi asked, entering the kitchen.

"Silly." Marta laughed. "Do as if you were at home. The bathroom is over there."

The table was set in the dining room. Only candles were burning.

"Surprised?" Marta laughed, pouring a golden brown liquid into the glasses.

"Cognac?"

"And genuine, too; quite an expensive brand! American cigarettes, French cognac and coffee. I don't know where the coffee came from, but it is genuine too. Only the beans stood on the shelf a little too long. Your health, Taavi!"

"Your health," the man replied, still hesitant and forcing himself to be amiable. He emptied the glass and put it on the table.

"Can't complain; the taste is excellent. No, don't pour me any more; that is enough," he said brusquely, when Marta wanted to refill his glass.

Marta only laughed, and paid no attention.

"If I say it's enough, that should suffice," Taavi said sharply.

The woman shrugged her shoulders and placed the bottle on the table. "Whatever you say," she murmured, giving Taavi a quizzical look. "Maybe later."

Taavi recalled suddenly the foreign officers who had sat there before him—also in candlelight, no doubt. The woman was very attractive, with her firm mouth, white neck, half-closed eyes and full breasts. But the whole scene was strange and revolting to him. It seemed so strikingly out of place in this embattled city, where shooting reechoed from ruins in the darkness of night, and where the howling wind was heavy with the rumbling of military vehicles. Riks was somewhere now, probably lying on his face with a black wound in his temple. Or more likely he had slashed his veins and bled to death in despair, for he probably did not have a gun.

Taavi emptied his second glass and said, "Thank you. Put me to sleep now somewhere. I'll have a hard day tomorrow."

"Whatever you say. It's still early, though."

"No, I'm serious."

"All right. Sit and smoke until I take the coffee cups to the kitchen and get you some bedclothes. Do you think you could sleep on this sofa?"

"Where else could you put me? I'll come and join you in the bedroom if this couch is not soft enough."

"Why don't you just do that," the woman said, resentment in her voice.

Taavi smoked his cigarette and walked back and forth in the room. Marta was hurt and gave him an angry, challenging look when she passed him on her way to the bedroom. Through the half-open door

Taavi heard the rustling of her clothes.

When Marta returned with the bedclothes, she was wearing a negligee and slippers. She did not look in Taavi's direction, but busied herself with making a bed on the sofa. Her morning coat had been left open in front—deliberately, it seemed—exposing a thin, transparent nightgown.

"Here, baby," she said, smiling.

Her voice seemed too self-confident to Taavi.

"Button your coat," he said abruptly. "What was between us once has been dead for a long time. Nothing will happen again. I'm not a . . . ," he added disdainfully, but stopped suddenly and listened. "What does that mean?" he asked with surprise. Loud knocking could be heard from downstairs, and the doorbell rang.

"Russians," Marta said mockingly. "Who else can be out at this time of the night?"

"You have betrayed me," Taavi shouted.

"Don't yell," she answered calmly, arranging her housecoat and hair, as if getting ready to receive visitors. "Stop. Don't break your neck. We are on the second floor," she warned, when Taavi wanted to rush to the window.

"Where the devil can I go?!"

Marta grabbed the bedclothes from the sofa and took them away.

Returning to the living room she took the bottle of cognac and the glasses from the table and hid them in a cupboard. Only then she answered. "Nobody has touched you yet. What are you afraid of? This is probably a routine check of papers. Haven't you gone through that before? Maybe they came to arrest somebody in this house. Why should that upset you so?"

Taavi bit his lip. Somebody had gone to open the door. The sound of footsteps and Russian voices carried upstairs. Taavi noticed now that Marta herself was as frightened as he. Her hands automatically tightened the robe under her chin, and her eyes roamed quickly around the room.

"Come!" she whispered excitedly on the threshold of the bedroom. "Go over there!"

She pointed toward the wide bed.

"Under the bed?" Taavi was startled.

"Yes, hurry up! I'll do the talking. I have good papers from the county house. Where's my purse? You keep that," she said, tearing the rings and bracelet from her hand. "And be quiet!" She switched off the light, but left the door slightly open.

Taavi stood in the middle of the room holding the jewellery, and hesitated. He heard Marta turn on the electricity in the adjoining room and put out the candles. The voices of the Russians sounded from the first floor. Every once in a while somebody knocked on a door, but Taavi could not understand what was asked. He measured the space under the wide, low bed, and groped around in the room. A hell of a trap! He tried the huge closet, but it was full of clothes. But the window! If he could climb out and stand outside on the window sill . . . he could jump down from there, if necessary. He peered out from behind the curtains and the blackout shades. Yes, the window sill seemed wide enough to support him. It was not exactly comfortable though. He placed his feet firmly on the outside ledge, but the hands had nothing to hold on to. His fingers ran quickly and helplessly over the cold, uneven stones. Damn it! He could only balance himself by holding on to the window panelling inside the room with the window open. If the Russians entered the bedroom, it might happen that one of them would become interested in the open window. He tried to close the window, trusting himself to the strength of his legs. Now the window was almost closed, and his fingers could only touch the narrow panel which framed the window on the outside.

Trying to hold on to the stone wall of the house was a strenuous task. A painful cramp twisted his fingers, and the cold, rain-heavy wind made his whole body shiver.

Suddenly he remembered that his passport and papers were all in order. He even had two passports and a job certificate, and yet he had run, stupidly and without thinking. If he should be discovered now, there was no excuse for his strange behaviour. No, he did not know yet how to live in the new world. He was not a "bandit" any more in a Finnish uniform, or a fugitive running around in the woods in borrowed civilian clothes! Then another fear seized him: his limbs were getting so stiff that he might not be able to climb back into the house. And if he should call and ask Marta to help him, she might unwittingly break his hold on the wall and push him down.

The window lit up. What was that? Was it Marta? But then he heard Russian voices and heavy footsteps inside. The footsteps and the conversation in the bedroom lasted a few minutes. Then the light was turned off again. But it took a long, long time before Marta's hesitant voice called his name in the darkened bedroom.

Taavi tried to ease his right foot along on the narrow ledge and open the window with the toe of his shoe. The attempt was futile. The window was closed too tightly. He tried to knock at the window with his foot. That brought results. A startled cry came from inside and the blackout curtain was raised.

"Careful!" Taavi whispered. "Careful!"

But Marta immediately realized Taavi's predicament and quietly opened the other half of the window, bending out to support him.

Taavi grasped the open window with hurting fingers and heaved his stiffened body into the room. He was quivering from the cold wind.

"Good Lord! If you had fallen down!"

"What did they want?"

"They were looking for Nazis. And checked passports. They were quite polite, but very suspicious."

"And did they search the apartment?"

"Yes, superficially, but they looked under the bed first thing when they entered the bedroom." Marta gasped agitatedly. "I almost choked to death thinking you'd be lost. Oh, Taavi!" She flung her arms around the man's neck.

"Oh, don't," was Taavi's tired response. "They are still in the house. Who knows, I may have to climb back."

"They are searching the attic now."

Taavi got up and did a few quick exercises; he had to get his frozen limbs quickly back in condition, for the game was not yet over. "Give me a drink, quick!"

"Poor man, you're all frozen like a. . . ." Marta hurried to get the bottle of cognac. Returning, she took her heavy overcoat from the wardrobe. "Take off your wet coat and put this over your shoulders."

"I don't know." Taavi was listening for footsteps in the house. "It's no fun to jump out into the rain in shirt sleeves. Why don't they get moving!"

But the Russians were already coming down the stairs. After a little while they heard the front door slam.

Marta helped Taavi take off his coat, and then made him sit on the edge of the bed. "Drink now! Drink the whole bottle! It will warm you up. What shall I do with you if you wake up with a fever tomorrow morning?" she said, bending down to untie his shoelaces.

"Oh, let it be," Taavi muttered listlessly and stretched out on the bed. In one aching hand he held the bottle of cognac, in the other his empty glass. The perfume of the woman rose from the bedclothes. He straightened himself up abruptly and walked back into the living room.

VII

Ilme had abandoned her plan to try to join Taavi. He hadn't gone to Tallinn to wait for her, she decided. And furthermore, Taavi had told his mother definitely that he was going to the coast. These words of Taavi's settled it. Ilme stayed home. She stayed with sorrowful thoughts and an aching heart, and whatever she did, she felt that all her work was in vain, foreordained to be unsuccessful. At night she tossed sleeplessly on her bed far into the morning. In the mornings she often had a headache, and at breakfast time she was frequently so nauseated that she could not swallow a bite.

"What's wrong with you?" her mother asked. "I hope you aren't. . . ."

"Yes, I'm afraid I am." Ilme smiled faintly. "I'm afraid I'm pregnant."

"Did it happen when Taavi first came home from Finland?" Krööt inquired.

"Yes. That's why I gave up the idea of taking the trip to Tallinn. I was afraid it might be harmful."

"Do you want it so very much, then?"

"I don't know. But since it's that way, I don't want anything to happen."

But Krööt was not so easily reconciled to the situation. She tried to keep from showing it to her daughter, but inside she was not a little displeased. It was not good during such a terrible time. When Ilme had given birth to her firstborn, she had almost been a child herself. With

73

the husband away who knows where—that was not the right time to be thinking of an addition to the family.

Ilme must have divined her thoughts. They were in the back chamber together.

"Do you have something against it?"

"What should I have against it, except it will be hard for you. Child, don't be silly," she scolded gently, seeing tears in Ilme's large brown eyes. "If God gives you a child, He will feed him. The Hiie farm is big. We'll need more people here."

"Don't worry. I'm not going to do anything to myself. I know you are scared of the times, and worrying, and thinking that it would be better if it hadn't happened. But I'm not going to do anything. If I should lose Taavi, I'll at least have the children."

The mistress of Hiie had nothing more to say. Her daughter was an emotional person—just as she herself had been in her youth. And Krõõt knew that she herself would be the first to pamper and cuddle the baby when it arrived. The same had been the case with Lembit, whom she had completely spoiled, as Ignas said, so that it was a question whether he'd outgrow it and ever become a man.

In his own mind Lembit was man enough already to walk around scowling and uttering the most terrible curses which he had heard others use, even though he did not yet know their meanings. So they had given up the trip to Tallinn! Why was it that Mother and all the other grown-ups could change their minds so easily? It had been the same with their trip to Sweden. They were all ready to go, and suddenly it didn't come off. It would be good if Father were still in Estonia. But Father had left the country, the grownups had decided, discussing world affairs after supper.

Lembit was always so tired at night that he fell asleep right in the midst of the most exciting discussion. No wonder—he had so much to do in daytime. When his father was still in Finland, Mother had taught Lembit to read, so he could surprise him. And Father had really been surprised, Lembit remembered. He had praised him and lifted him on his knee. So tall already, he'd said, and reading so fluently! Well, his reading wasn't fluent yet. Sometimes he stumbled on a long and peculiar word, which he could not make out even by pronouncing it letter by letter. And he hoped to grow taller still, to help his father when fighting days came around again. What the "fighting days" were like, Lembit did not know exactly. But he knew one thing: if he and his father had been making plans together, they would have carried them through. Father did not admit that anything couldn't be done. He had that on the authority of Uncle Värdi, the one with the wounded leg, and Osvald had confirmed the same thing.

One evening Anton of Lepiku came to see his neighbours. Ignas was a little surprised, for Anton left home only on very important occasions, such as when all the farmers came together to help somebody with the

74

harvest, or at Christmas time when a neighbour invited him to taste his home-brewed beer. He was not footloose like the farmer of Võllamäe, who roamed around and checked everybody's holiday preparation long before the holidays, as well as making the rounds when the beer kegs asked to be emptied. He wasn't churlish, though, like Juhan of Matsu right across the road, who was feuding with most of the village all the time and did not speak a word beyond a mumbled hello.

Anton of Lepiku was the oldest of the Metsaoti farmers. He had been the young companion of the fathers of the present farmers, and thus formed a link between the two generations.

"How is everything around your place?" Krõõt asked. "Is Luise still in good health? She used to complain about a pain in her back."

"It's the weather," Anton answered and began to fill his big, crooked pipe. He sat on a chair in the corner of the front room, the toes of his big boots turned in and touching each other, with his pipe in his bearded mouth and his rough, gnarled workingman's hands on his knees.

"Are you getting your potatoes out of the ground?" Ignas inquired. "I notice you have cleaned up the stubble already."

"I'm glad my fields are small," the neighbour replied. "If we keep at it from cock's crow to midnight, we can just manage. It's really too much for two people."

"Have you heard anything from your son Mihkel?" Krõõt inquired. "All the mobilized Estonians are supposed to be back. The Estonian corps is said to be in the islands."

Anton made an unconscious gesture with his hands and sucked furiously at his pipe, as if it were going out.

"Ah, nothing much. What can you hear so suddenly?" he mumbled in response. "I heard they'd taken your horse."

"And the carriage and harness, too. They aren't joking now on the highways. They take what they can lay their hands on."

Anton was silent for a while, as if preparing himself for a longer speech. Ignas understood that his neighbour had something on his mind.

"Did you want to talk something over with me?"

"Yes, I have some business."

Ignas gave a sign to Krõõt and Ilme, and the women went to take care of their kitchen chores. But Anton did not yet broach the subject that was weighing on his mind. They talked for quite a while about the general situation, about the battles in the islands, the withdrawal of the Germans, and the shortage of nails and tools, before the farmer of Lepiku said, "My boy has come home."

"Mihkel?"

"The same. That's the only one I have."

"Are his limbs whole and health all right?"

"His limbs are all right, but his health is gone. He's in the army."

"Did they discharge him or is he on furlough?"

"He just ran away. That's why I came here. I don't know what to do," Anton said.

"So that is how it is. He walked in just like that?"

75

"He ran away and now he wants to go back. But he's afraid they'll shoot him."

"When did he come?"

"Last night. He'd met your Taavi in Tallinn and talked with him and. . . ."

"So Taavi is still in Tallinn?!"

"He'd been there, yes. So he talked with Taavi and then he came home, cost what it may. He can hardly stay upright. Coughing and spitting blood all the time."

"Is it T.B. or what?"

"Who knows? I'm afraid it is. He was a sickly child. I told my old woman that we were too old, and that the child wouldn't live long. When he was still at her breast, he used to scream until he was blue in the face. Later he sort of picked up, but now, I see, he's through."

"It can't have been easy there in Russia. It's good he made it back alive," Ignas said darkly. "So Mihkel is back. I was beginning to think that nobody would come back from there."

"If they come in such shape it would be better they didn't come at all," Mihkel's father said grimly. "And he wants to go to the islands. The fear is so deep. I don't know what will come of it. I'd rather not let him go and die somewhere else."

"Maybe he'll recover? Maybe he'd get well at home?"

"Maybe. He was wounded. Right in the chest. Maybe that's what makes him croak. It's healed up outside, but who can see what it's like inside? I thought if your Osvald—they always got along so well—if your Osvald would come and talk to him. He just laughs at what we old people say, and we don't really know what to say now, anyway. The order is new, and the laws are different. I wouldn't want to have him shot as a deserter, either. I'd feel as if I'd killed him myself."

"All right. I'll call Osvald and come along myself. Let's see what would be the wisest thing to do," Ignas said and straightened up his bulk. "I can't give you any advice. You'll have to make your own decision in a matter like that."

"But two heads are better than one," Anton said, satisfied.

For several hours they sat in the front room of Lepiku by the light of a small kerosene lamp. Restlessness drove Luise to find all kinds of chores to do which gave her a chance to come in and listen to the conversation, although she held that it was unsuitable for a woman to mix herself into the affairs of men, especially when such important and incomprehensible things were under discussion. Luise was an old-fashioned woman. What was ordained from above was law for her, whether it came from the Russians, the Estonian republic or the German occupation authorities. But recently the puzzling ways of the younger generation had driven her to question some of her basic beliefs. There was Taavi of Piskujõe, Ignas' son-in-law, and an old friend and companion of Mihkel. Did he ever ask what the ruling foreign powers ordered or forbade? No, the boy did what he held to be right in his own mind, and

76

he wasn't any worse off for that. He was strong and well and went where he liked and did what he thought best. He gave his home folks heartaches and tears, but his life still his own and his arm was strong. Mihkel had been like that before he'd gone off to Russia. But look at him now—even if you cried your eyes out, death wouldn't take its foot off the boy's chest. And he was leaving again. How could they demand that of him? Even the army of the Czar would have considered him unsuitable and handed him his walking papers. But now—no. As if they were hard up for men! There were so many of them in Russia that nobody could count them. Kalgina and the whole country were full of their camps. Mihkel had already shed the better part of his blood upon their orders. That should be enough. No, she wouldn't let Mihkel out of the farm any more, come what may!

The men were not so quick in making up their minds. Ignas of Hiie did not give any advice. He did not recommend either course. He only inquired about life in Russia and listened to the story of the mobilized Estonian men, whose journey had taken them from prison camp to prison camp in hunger and cold. Mihkel, the former radical, did not speak much, and had seemingly forgotten how to complain and criticize. It had been hard, but those who were still alive were now coming back home. Osvald's decision was short and clear.

"I can see they haven't made a Communist out of you, and that is enough for me. As you see, I fled into the woods in 1941 instead of obeying the summons, and I'm still all right. I have been in some tight spots myself in the meantime, but it hasn't done to my health what your life has done to yours. And therefore, if necessary, I'll take to my forest hideouts again. That's how I feel."

Mihkel laughed helplessly.

"And what will become of you?"

"At least I'll be buried in our own earth," Osvald answered. "Or do you believe things will stay the way they are now?"

"Everything has changed already. We are allied now with the English and the Americans."

"Yes, we are allied with them, but who says for how long," old Anton broke in. "I cannot believe for the life of me that this alliance will last for long."

"And then what?" Osvald asked Mihkel.

Mihkel shrugged his shoulders.

"That's none of our business."

"It will be very much our business, for they'll give Ivan a real going-over and then we'll be needing every man. Everything is changed, because they have to boost up the tired Ivans with a new kind of propaganda which is able to move their minds. The game has gone too far for them to retreat. Communism has to play its losing game to the end."

"But if it should win?"

"You don't believe that yourself, so why speak about it? You should remember a little of what you used to think and believe in spite of their crude propaganda lessons. Try to recall. The world is still too big for one power to conquer it and keep it under its domination. But why should I be preaching to you! You remember very well what our republic was like before this mess. All the western countries are like that. Now put them side by side with that hell you're coming from, with its forced labour camps, millions of nameless graves, and masses of grey people vegetating through their hopeless everyday existence, and then choose."

After Osvald's impassioned speech there was a prolonged silence in the room. Even Luise, who had eavesdropped from behind the half-closed door was impressed. This hired man should have studied for the ministry. He would have wakened every last sleeper in the church.

Mihkel shivered. This unaccustomed talk stunned and confused him. Osvald's words came to him like old acquaintances from the time when he had worked in the cold of the Russian winter in wordless defiance and unbent pride, trying to meet the killing norms which were the only way to earn a minimum subsistence. But eventually the quest of that quart of grey, stinking water and the slice of black bread had become all-important and had usurped his whole being. Hunger, cold and the guard with the rifle—these three had kept them in check and driven them like herded animals. Osvald's words were only an echo from the past which had no weight among the living; no real purpose. And Osvald seemed like a young boy to him, whose development had been arrested for some reason, and who was still indulging in childish pranks, even though his body and beard were those of a grown man.

"What are you planning to do?" Osvald asked finally.

"Let him think for himself," Ignas said. "In such an important decision you must not try to influence him with your impetuousness."

But he wanted to be influenced. He was not capable of making a decision. If Osvald would come back tomorrow and the day after and speak like that, what had been taken from him might be restored. And then, if the time was ripe and he hadn't been shot as a deserter in the meanwhile, they could ask him again: What are you planning to do? And he might answer.

When he was lying on his bed close to the tiled stove, his future seemed completely unimportant to him. All these years he had had no future. Home had been a distant, forbidden, and yet persistently recurring dream. But now his past had come back, and his thoughts were already getting hold enough to break a small path into the future, although the road ahead was strange and shrouded with the shades of fear.

The crickets sang in the cracks of the stove, and the room was cosy and warm. His father was snoring in the back room as always, and a soft breeze caressed the eaves of the house. He was a small boy again, far from the dangers and fears of the world. He was sleepy and tired with that eternal fatigue which the shrapnel had thrust into his breast. Let the world go under—he was sleeping in his own bed.

When Ilme heard that Taavi had been in Tallinn, she was so disturbed she could not sleep a wink and was on her feet before dawn. A feverish urgency inside her made her forget everything else. She regretted bitterly that she had abandoned her plan to hurry to Tallinn at once after they had returned from their futile journey. If she should be too late now, she would not be able to forgive herself all her life.

She had felt nauseated again getting up, and she had not eaten enough for a bird, but she did not let anybody talk her out of her intention.

"We'll go as fast as we can. The way to the station isn't so long; only a few hours' walk."

"Three hours at least," Ignas said, looking at his daughter's pale countenance. "I could harness the horse. . . ."

"No," Ilme said firmly.

"Harness the horse," Krõõt urged. "There are enough hardships waiting for her on the train and in Tallinn."

"Now don't start going on like that," Ilme said sharply. "I'm not a baby any more."

"I'll go with you, then," Osvald announced. "I'll come with you at least halfway to the station. You can't go through the woods alone, with Russians camping all over the place."

The good-byes were long. Lembit was already at the gate, eager to go, when Ilme and Krõõt were still embracing as if parting for ever. All the Hiie people were out in the yard. Even Aadu, the old deaf-mute, was standing at the far end of the stable, and crippled Värdi was watching nearby, holding on to his crutch. He gave Lembit a brief wave of his hand and turned away, keeping his eyes on the grass which was white with hoarfrost.

Hilda's behaviour had disturbed Ilme most. She could understand Mother's crying, but Hilda had opened her mouth to speak and had burst into hysterical sobs instead, running into the house as if trying to escape from something. Hilda was a little peculiar. She was always afraid, and she dreamed bad, portentous dreams in which she believed blindly.

Their journey progressed peacefully. The autumn morning was crisp, clear and sunny. The grass on the side of the road glittered from hoarfrost, and the trees were dropping their last colourful leaves in the windless silence. When they passed the army camp and the county house of Kalgina, they saw the Russians at their customary activities, and the supply trucks coming and going.

At the crossroads in front of a store there was a Russian truck. Several men and women with their trunks and parcels were sitting in the open back. The engine was running, and the soldiers themselves were just coming out of the store.

"Want a ride? Come on," somebody shouted from the truck.

"Where are you going?" Osvald asked.

"Straight to Tallinn. If that's where you are going, you can save your feet. These are nice fellows. They'll stop the truck when you want to get off."

"Sorry I can't accompany you farther," Osvald said to Ilme. "This is a good opportunity and there is nothing to fear. There are a lot of passengers and half of them are women."

"Yes, but on an open truck it might be cold. I'm thinking of Lembit; he might catch cold. . . ." Ilme hesitated.

"Well, ride only to the station, then," Osvald advised. "It is still early. There should be a couple of trains during the day."

"All right. That is probably the best thing to do. So long, Osvald, and many thanks. We'll meet again, I'm sure."

The man laughed. "Why shouldn't we meet? But if you should catch up with Taavi, well . . . do what he thinks best."

Ilme looked at him with her large brown eyes and began to climb on the truck. Osvald lifted Lembit after her.

"Be a man, Lembit, my boy," he said, and stroked the boy's flushed cheek.

When they reached that station, Ilme regretted that they had not continued their journey on the truck. A long freight train was standing at the station, ready to move on to Tallinn, but nobody knew when it would be able to start. The railroad was reportedly blown up. Sabotage. The station officials did not say anything; just shrugged their shoulders nervously and hurried off to their duties. No, they did not have any information. It would be of no use to buy a ticket. It would probably not be possible to get through to Tallinn.

A number of Russian military men were at the station. They were sullen and tight-lipped, seeing traitors and criminals in everyone around them.

"Serves those asses right," an elderly woman said, full of gall, crouching on her baggage in the waiting room. "Serves them right. At least they'll see that they are not exactly welcome," she said loudly and fearlessly, her face drawn and tense with fatigue.

A man sitting close to her gave a quick glance toward the rest of the people in the waiting room and asked, "How did it actually happen?"

"Who knows, except those who did it, and they won't speak. But a whole munitions train blew up, so that only splinters of wood and iron are left scattered around. And the embankment is of course also torn up and flattened as if levelled with a bulldozer."

"Wonder how many Russians hit the dust?"

"I don't think there were many of them on the train."

"That's a pity," somebody whispered, and twisted restlessly on the bench. "But it's no use sitting here now. We'll have to thumb a ride on the highway."

"Maybe the Russians were just careless," somebody suggested.

"Careless or not, lots of heads will roll for this."

"Who said they were careless?" the woman said again energetically. "It would be disgraceful if our men didn't stir themselves a little. Why, right here in the prisoner-of-war camp, where they have rounded up some Germans now . . ."—she lowered her voice and addressed those close to her—"right here our boys have had some fun."

"What fun?"

"They have let out the Germans and have taken to the woods to-gether."

"Why bother about the Germans. . . ?"

"They'd been together on the Eastern front for years. That counts for something. And why should one harbour a grudge against a fellow soldier? Both are in the same mess now, anyway."

"And what happened to them then?"

"They installed Russian guards and made the rest of the Estonian guards line up along with the prisoners. Then they shot every tenth man in the line."

One of the men interrupted nervously. "What are you talking about? Why are you spreading rumours? You think that shows how brave you are? Think a little, good people, have you lost your minds? Right in the middle of the station!"

He left the room in a frightened hurry.

"Stalin's sun has made his head soft," somebody scoffed.

Ilme could not bear to stay any longer. She took Lembit by the hand and hurried out of the waiting room. On the way out she met some Russians, together with the man who had warned the woman. Were they going to arrest her? Life seemed much more frantic here than in the peaceful forests of Metsaoti. Ilme's knees were weak and she was again nauseated. They turned back toward the highway.

The soldiers of the patrol, who had only given them curious looks when they had climbed down from the truck, were now stern and de-manded papers. One of them scrutinized the piece of paper Ilme had received from the county house and asked something that the woman could not understand. The other soldier walked around them in circles, and a lustful smile appeared on his face, as he measured with open impudence her legs and hips.

Ilme snatched her identification papers from between the fingers of the soldier and turned angrily away. Nothing happened. They could continue their journey unmolested—the soldiers only laughed.

"How far is it to Tallinn?" Lembit asked, when they were back on the highway.

"Quite far." His mother smiled. "Are you getting tired?"

"Not yet," the boy answered bravely, although he had trouble keeping his feet straight and he often dropped a few steps behind.

"Let's see, maybe somebody will give us a ride."

Most of the cars, however, were coming from Tallinn, and the few that were going in the desired direction were full of Russians. Ilme did not dare accept a ride on those.

"Why don't we ask for a ride? I'll hold my own hand out for the next one," Lembit offered.

"Don't do that! I'll see first if there are too many Russians, then. . . ."

"You aren't afraid of them, are you?" Lembit sounded surprised. "Why, Mother, I am here with you!"

Ilme laughed. She was already getting some support and help from her young man.

81

The next truck stopped of its own accord and the soldiers offered them a lift. Lembit agreed immediately, and Ilme did not hesitate long, either, when she saw an Estonian farmer on the truck among the soldiers, smoking his short pipe. The driver stepped out and asked them to sit up front with him, sending his former companion to join the others in the back. So they were on their way.

The driver was a small Jew with quick eyes and jerky gestures, who addressed Ilme in German instead of Russian as soon as the truck rolled off. He was talkative, but his rapid tongue limited itself to meaningless phrases which seemed to reflect the propaganda to which every Soviet citizen was constantly exposed. He was furious at the Germans, though, and mentioning them he flared up like dry brush fire. Ilme could understand his anger, since she knew about the injustices and sufferings inflicted on the Jews by the Germans.

"I don't love these others particularly, either," he pointed his thumb over his shoulder toward his Russian comrades, who were sitting in the back of the truck. "They hate Jews. I have heard that your people did not hate us, and it has made me like them." He whistled a Russian hit tune and gave the woman at his side a critical, appreciative look.

"You and your brother going to Tallinn?" he asked Ilme.

She smiled. Strangers often thought that Lembit was her younger brother.

The closer they got to Tallinn, the more excited Ilme became. She had had luck up to now, but would it hold? Would fate be so kind to her that she and Taavi would get together after all these wanderings in the dark?

When she got out, her legs were weak, and she had to call on all her will power to force herself to walk. When the truck had rumbled off, she leaned against the wall and closed her eyes for a moment. She was deathly pale.

"Mother, Mother, what's the matter with you?" Lembit cried, grabbing her hand.

She tried to smile in response. "Nothing, darling, there's nothing the matter with me. Let's go on now. The ride tired me out."

Lembit answered seriously, "The Russian smell made me sick to my stomach too."

They turned from the Paldiski Boulevard up toward Kaarel Avenue.

"Do you still remember Tallinn?" Ilme asked her son.

"A little. Is it very far to our home?"

"This isn't our home any more. Some other people are living there now. Our home is at Hiie."

"Yes, Pontus is there and Grandfather," Lembit reflected. "But I think that our real home is where Father is. Right?"

Ilme sighed. In that case their home was somewhere on the wind.

And so it turned out.

"Holy heavens," Liisa exclaimed, opening the door, and gazing at them as if they were ghosts. "You, Ilme!"

"Hello, Liisa! We've come from the country. We've just arrived in Tallinn."

"Yes, but . . . do come in. You, Ilme! Good Lord! And little Lembit has grown so much! Taavi said you'd—you'd gone across the sea."

So Taavi was still in town.

"We didn't make it. We had to return from the coast and now we're here."

"Take off your overcoats. Sit down and—your own old home! So you didn't get out? That's bad news."

Lembit had already checked all the rooms.

"Aunt Liisa, isn't Father here?"

Liisa's hands dropped, and the excited flow of her talk stopped. She gave Ilme a fleeting glance and then looked in the corner.

"I'm afraid he has left already," she said quietly.

Ilme sat down. She might have expected that. And it was her own fault. Why had she stayed at Hiie as if in a daze? Why hadn't she followed her heart immediately and come to Tallinn right away?

"When did he go?"

"Today, I think. We saw him last night. He spent a few nights here, but then he was afraid of some informer and slept somewhere else. A woman came to look for him all the time. She didn't say who she was, but it seemed to me it had to do with his trip. Or maybe it didn't, for I heard Taavi tell her in the hall, "I'll go to the coast tomorrow for sure." That would be today. The woman took him along last night and—that is all I know. She came by here this morning and took a letter to him. One of Taavi's friends had just brought it. He asked for Taavi very insistently and when I couldn't tell him anything he left a letter. He said I shouldn't let anybody else have it, but when this woman saw his name on the envelope, she grabbed it almost by force, and tore the envelope open right here. She didn't show me what it was—some slip of brown paper—but she got so excited she ran out of the room. I was sorry later. Who knows what kind of a paper it was? Arno was quite angry when he heard about it."

"What did she look like?"

"She was dark and slim. Much taller than I. Very well dressed, but kind of uppity."

Ilme could not recall anybody among Taavi's acquaintances who would have fitted the description.

"What are we going to do now?" Lembit asked, waking Ilme from her stupor. "Shall we go to the coast, too?"

"Silly boy," Ilme answered sadly. "Now we have to start waiting for Father again, until he comes back home."

"But I don't like that," Lembit said stubbornly. "If he'll be away as long as he was in Finland, what's the use of having a father, then?"

Big tears were rolling down his cheeks, although he was making a manful effort to hold them back.

"He may stay away much longer this time," Ilme said, and her voice broke with grief.

Taavi Raudoja had had a bad day. He buried another hope of getting out: Inga had still not returned from the coast. Had they gone directly to Finland once they got the boat out on the open sea, or had they been arrested on the coast? The sea held many secrets.

Leonard had gone to Vääna. He was going around with a new crazy plan: to cross the gulf in canoes. He had done it when he had gone to Finland for the first time, and he tried to convince the others of the practicability of his plan. Yes, in summer he'd do it, Taavi agreed, but now that idea should remain their last resort. The sea was vicious in the autumn, and he was not such an expert in canoeing that he would venture it before death was actually at the doorstep. And Eedi of Piibu, born and bred in the country, did not have the least notion about these things. For him the sea was a strange, disgusting body of salt water, which he did not trust more than was absolutely necessary.

Taavi returned to Marta's apartment in a bad mood. He did not really want to see her, but he figured soberly that after the recent search by the Russians it was for a while the safest place he knew. And there was no lack of food at Marta's place, while his other acquaintances seemed to be getting short of supplies. Marta's cupboards were full of things which her former admirers had brought to her. He might hide there without much worry. Of course not for long, for who could guarantee that the Russians would not start looking there for Germans and other Nazis?

Marta was not in when Taavi arrived. He opened the door with the key she had given him, and suddenly felt as if he were following in the footsteps of some German officer.

Taavi sat down on the sofa and began to sift and ponder his plans for the future. He had a stupid, empty feeling, for he had not been able to realize any of his plans. That wouldn't do. Anger at himself flared up inside him, fury at his own incompetence. He went to the buffet and poured himself a large glass of cognac. It was good he had drunk that much yesterday after getting chilled—otherwise he would be down now with a fever, too sick to worry about his future. They were living on the other side of the end, as Richard Kullerkann had said. Poor joker! He had had rotten luck. To fall into the clutches of the NKVD so soon could only be called blind misfortune. Taavi had learned of Richard's end from his companions who were waiting for Inga's return. He had been found in the shrubbery near Schnell's pond. He had hanged himself. A Russian had been found lying in a bush nearby with a knife in his back. Taavi did not believe there was any connection between Richard and the murdered Russian. Riks would not have had the nerve for such a deed. But who knows?

Marta returned, excited but happy. She seemed to have forgotten the events of the night before and the insulted pout she had affected in the morning. She was sure of herself, ran up to Taavi and flung her arms around his neck.

"Oh, Taavi, dear! Do you know, we're about to leave the country!"

Taavi freed himself with a brusque gesture. This woman was completely out of her mind.

"I have a sure chance to go," Marta exulted. "Wait, let's celebrate it with a drink, and then get ready." She poured two glasses of cognac and threw her overcoat on a chair. "Cheers, Taavi! We'll go together! The two of us, you and I! Yes, the thing is serious. Good-bye forever, Kalgina county house and all this life here. We'll start something new and bigger now."

"Speak up; don't gush like that," Taavi ordered, disgusted.

"Why so gloomy? Look, the paper is here that will tell you all," Marta said, and handed Taavi an envelope containing a piece of brown wrapping paper.

"Where did you get that?"

"I went to your former apartment."

"Had the envelope been opened?"

"Don't worry; I did it. Nobody else knows anything."

"Why did you open it?"

"But there are no secrets between us, and I thought that. . . ." The woman tried to extricate herself from her embarrassment. "I wondered what this suspicious thing could mean."

Taavi gave up and concentrated on the crooked lines on the paper, drawn with a heavy hand. They represented the road from the highway to the coast past a farm in the woods marked "Siim of Kruusiaugu." "Jüri" was written at the bottom of the paper, which could only mean Jüri Paarkukk. But the map had not been drawn by Jüri himself.

Without saying a word, Taavi hurried to put on his overcoat.

"Going somewhere?" Marta asked.

"Yes. I'll go and ask the boys what this map means."

"Are you coming back for the night?" Marta asked, frightened.

"If I should not be back in a couple of hours, I'll have left for the coast. Otherwise I'll be back here for the night."

"But how. . . . If you go, what will happen to me? I could be useful to you on the way. I can speak Russian. And you wouldn't leave me behind, would you?"

"Why should you be so wild about going? This is no time for pleasure trips," Taavi replied coldly.

"Don't talk like that, Taavi! I won't stay behind. Taavi, dearest, I want to go with you, to take care of you, to. . . ."

"All right. I've already told you what I'll do."

"If you won't come home, I'll go to the coast myself."

Taavi was taken aback.

"Do you know the way?"

"I know the map by heart." Marta laughed.

They were playing chess as usual in the cooperative, and no excitement could be observed. There were more men assembled than at other times, and Vello Kasar was back from the coast. Jüri gave Taavi a searching look.

"You have made up your mind to go, haven't you?" Jaan Meos asked.

"Where? What are you talking about?"

"Did you get my note?" Jüri inquired.

"Yes, thank you, I did. What are the details? But another time don't leave things like that around so carelessly."

"How could we contact you then, running from one woman to the next? We didn't know where to look for you," Vello answered. "Today is Tuesday. We must all be there by Friday night. I've just come from the coast, and everything should be in order as far as I know."

"And is everybody going?"

"I don't even dream about it," Lieutenant Pihu answered carelessly. "This won't be the last boat, even if you should make it. Life is just getting exciting here."

"Yes, there are a few corpses lying around already," Taavi said sarcastically. "Are the others going?"

"Most of us," Jaan said. "Some have a few personal matters to take care of. They'll go later. We'll try to keep the line open. Some of our boys have already gone from that place. I'll stay behind myself, and Ugur is staying, too. He's still trying to find the Admiral."

"I wouldn't advise anybody to wait who has a chance," Taavi stated emphatically. "Who knows who will be the next Riks? How many places are there?" He turned to Vello.

"I have no idea. Right now they're counting on a little sailboat, but they are planning to get a new, big motorboat."

"This all sounds a little foggy, too," Pihu said ironically. But that did not bother Taavi in the least. In an enterprise like this you could not expect printed schedules with reserved seats and exact times of departure and arrival. Success depended on luck, the mood of the sea and the men themselves. This opening seemed to be more promising than any of the previous ones.

Details of the journey to the coast were discussed now, and the precautions they would have to take to elude the Russians. Some of the men decided to leave immediately. These were the ones who had not tied themselves to any job, and who had been completely unable to adjust to the new situation. They had tried again and again to get out, but all their attempts had misfired. Each time a new chance came up or reached their ears, their blood caught fire and life acquired new meaning. Others were simply curious to stay and see how the situation would turn out. Several were unable to leave right away because of their families. Some seemed to be remaining out of defiance, come what may. They were nervous and irritable and cracked obscene jokes, or sat in complete apathy. The fate of Richard had shaken some of them awake, but had stunned others into an even deeper daze.

Taavi, Jüri Paarkukk and Vello Kasar formed a threesome, but most of them planned to go in pairs.

When they were in the street, Taavi made a suggestion. "We should insure ourselves a little on our own. Wouldn't it be a good idea to get a travelling order, saying that we are being sent to Kuusalu to nationalize some fish cannery? In Russian, of course. We'll have to get it from the Food Administration, and we should get a document from friend

Tõnn, that we are taking the boat from such-and-such-a-place to such-and-such-a-place by order of the harbour master's office in Tallinn. We can't do that today. It must be done tomorrow morning, and at noon we'll go."

Toward evening Taavi stood before Marta's locked door. A stupid thing —he'd given back his key, and the curfew outside would start soon. Evidently Marta had gone off on her own. What a woman! Taavi had gone about his business in town, completely forgetting his promise to Marta. He would barely have time to go to their former apartment, where Liisa and Arno lived, and he'd have to hurry if he wanted to make it before the curfew. The autumn twilight was already deepening, and a cold, acrid-smelling mist was stealthily rising from the ruins—a combination of the odours of plaster, ashes and probably also decaying human bodies.

When he knocked at the door at Liisa's place and the door opened, he almost had a stroke. He couldn't believe his senses when Ilme embraced him with a cry of joy.

"Father, Father!" Lembit shouted jubilantly and tried to climb up his side, clutching his coat.

"Taavi, beloved," Ilme whispered, tears running down her cheeks, arms wound around his neck.

"You, Ilme?"

He was so stunned he did not even realize what was happening when he was pulled into the room and seated on the sofa. Somebody stroked his neck and kissed his cheeks, somebody climbed on his shoulder and ruffled his hair.

"Thank God we finally caught up with you!"

VIII

The unexpected reunion with his wife and son had filled Taavi's heart with great happiness, but on sober second thoughts it made every step doubly difficult. He had to be even more cautious and careful than he normally would have been. He had to fight for his whole family now. But their chance meeting was still an unexpected gift from fate. Everything could so easily have gone differently.

Taavi felt such tenderness toward his wife that he wanted to kneel in front of her. How much the poor child had suffered!

"Arrange everything as you think best," Ilme said. "Lembit and I will follow you. I'll try to rest a little now."

But there was not much time for resting, as they had to leave that very afternoon. Vello Kasar, who could speak Russian, came with them, but Jüri Paarkukk joined another group. There would have been too many of them.

When they reached the city limits, they walked apart, Taavi and Vello a little ahead, Ilme with her son behind. They had to avoid patrols because Ilme and Lembit had no travelling orders like the men. From the Lasnamäe hill they had a panoramic view of Tallinn. Below them was the valley called Kadrioru, and farther down were the churches and towers of the ancient city. To the right, the sea glittered and beckoned through a filmy haze. Ilme could not tear herself away from the view. Although she hadn't been born in Tallinn, she considered it her hometown, and the backlands of Metsaoti were only a refuge for her where one could rest and hide from the cruel world. Tallinn was alive and dynamic—ancient towers surrounded by bright modern buildings, lawns and hills reflecting their flowery ornaments in the blue water, the slender spires of the churches piercing the serene sky.

To Taavi, Tallinn was closer still, for he had spent most of his life here. But his eyes revealed no emotion, only sober calculation. It was not the first time he had left Tallinn as a fugitive. He had fought for his hometown, had liberated it and lost it again. He was used to leaving and coming back—to liberate or defend—and he knew that the hometown would be there waiting for him. It would be waiting, full of ruin and destruction, but patient and firm. Flags might change on the citadel, towers might crumble from bombings and fires, but Tallinn would still be standing on its limestone rocks, waiting patiently.

They had intended to make a big circle around the airfield, but had to give up that plan. There were so many Russian camps and supply depots around the field that they had to take the more dangerous direct road along the top of the hill.

"We must try to avoid the patrols; that's the main thing," Vello said. "When I came to Tallinn, they halted all cars right where the road descends from the hill to the town. We are already in their rear."

When they reached the eastbound highway, they did not notice anything suspicious.

"See," Vello exclaimed, "we got by. They're down the hill."

"Let's move on quickly. I'm still a bit leery. They're crawling all over the place," Taavi said, and pointed toward the tents and wooden barracks that could be seen everywhere. Even some side streets and backyards were full of camouflaged army vehicles.

After marching for a quarter of an hour they stopped, dumbfounded. A tree had been felled across the highway, and soldiers were standing guard next to it. Checkpoint!

"Look, those s.o.b.'s are everywhere," Taavi hissed. It was true; they were surrounded by Russians. There was no way to avoid the check.

Handing his papers to the sentry, Taavi began to worry about Ilme and their son. There they were already, right behind them.

Vello carried on a conversation with the soldiers in broad Russian, passed cigarettes around and cracked jokes. He knew how to handle them. One of the Russians became friendly and he laughed back, accepting the cigarettes. Those Estonians were generous. The soldier put one cigarette in his mouth and another behind his ear, and when Vello urged him to take a third, he was kindness personified. But the face of the other soldier became grim when he checked Ilme's documents.

"Could I help?" Vello approached quickly with his cigarette box.

"Where is this woman going?" the soldier asked and pointed toward the stamp on the paper, which was the only thing he understood.

Vello took the paper, made an officious face, and gazed at it for a considerable time. "Don't worry, I'll handle the son of a gun," he said to Ilme, inflecting his voice as if he had asked a question. When Ilme nodded, he explained to the Russian: "This comrade is going home with her little son. Her travelling orders? Her mother had suddenly become very sick. She had had no time to stand in line for papers. Just imagine, if your mother were lying on her deathbed, you'd forget too. You cannot think of anything else but your mother, who is about to die."

The soldier looked at him askance from under wrinkled eyebrows, and the corners of his mouth twitched. He returned the paper to Ilme with a tired gesture, and motioned to them to move on. Vello handed him the box with the rest of the cigarettes.

"Greet your folks at home, when you happen that way," he said to the Russian.

The soldier gave him a look that reminded one of a wounded animal and turned his back without a word. He looked down the side of the road, his back bent under the weight of his machine gun, his young face grey and worn.

The other soldier was helpful and lively. He pointed toward a truck standing on the other side of the barrier and told them to climb on it— they'd get to their destination faster and with less exertion. The travellers did not wait to be told twice, especially since the engine of the truck was already humming, and several people like themselves were huddling on top of the tarpaulin which covered the load.

They had been lucky again. They did not ask where the truck was going or how far. It was going in the direction they wanted to go. That made their journey shorter, and nothing else was very important to them at this moment. And Taavi was reunited with his wife and son. He took Lembit on his lap, so that the boy would be protected from the driving wind, and Ilme leaned against him. Vello pulled some of the tarpaulin over their backs. Darkness came quickly, for the sky had become overcast with clouds, and a cold rain was drizzling down.

Their luck held out. When at night the truck stopped in front of the inn at Koogi in pouring rain, a girl invited them all to her house. It would be dangerous to move around at night, she said, and it was raining heavily, too. She could offer them shelter and perhaps a cup of tea. Although there was not enough space for everyone to lie down, at least they might doze in the corner of a warm room.

A middle-aged couple joined them. The others were close enough to home to try to make it that night.

The kind hostess served them whatever food she had, and made Ilme and Lembit sleep in her own bed. She did not listen to polite arguments. They were her guests, and she was only sorry she had not known of their coming beforehand, so she could have been better prepared. They sat together in the warm kitchen, and their tongues seemed to thaw as the chilly stiffness left their bodies, especially when the woman who had come with them from the truck opened a quart of home-distilled vodka.

"I'm an old bootlegger," she said in explanation.

"Your health," her moustached companion laughed. "And I am an old revenuer, your mortal enemy. You better not ask anybody any more who he is or was, or you'll be in for a surprise, as you see. And I'm sure the two men here"—he gestured toward Taavi and Vello—"are carrying all kinds of secrets under their hats, in spite of their youth. Now what should they be doing here on the coast? You can't fool me. I've been fooled too often in my life"—he turned toward the woman—"by the likes of you."

Their hostess laughed. "I can tell you something that will surprise you. Officers of the NKVD are sleeping right on the other side of the wall. They requisitioned half of our house."

Luck was with them again the following morning. They did not have to walk more than half an hour, when another Russian truck picked them up. At noon they reached the supposed location of the fictitious fish cannery which they were officially to nationalize. This was the beginning of the road that had been marked with a red pencil on the piece of wrapping paper.

Ilme was depressed by the relics of recent battles on both sides of the highway: wrecked vehicles, pieces of torn clothing, boxes of ammunition lying around in disorderly confusion. Here and there a farmer's cart, a German military vehicle, or a monstrous Russian tank was perched on top of a stone wall, burned out, but menacing even in its destruction. Fresh graves without crosses were to be seen on the hillside. Here and there the Russians had ploughed their tanks into refugee columns, killing mercilessly whoever happened to fall under the chains of the tanks.

They had dinner in a farm nearby. The womenfolk were curious. So they were going to visit relatives? And although the travellers tried to make their story plausible, the expressions on the faces of the women showed that they surmised the real reason, even if they let the strangers talk. They did not charge anything for the food.

"That isn't worth talking about—potatoes and milk, a few mouthfuls of bread—we grind our own flour now, had to make a handmill," the old mistress of the farm said. "Put your money back in your pocket, children. You are on a journey, and you don't know what kind of people you might meet on your way. Here we are, don't know what to do—the Russians took my son into the army. Yes, just a week ago he went—took a change of underwear and a soup spoon and went. That's why I am wondering—you are young men, too, and there are not many young men left in this part of the country. Be careful; that's all I can say, and may heaven protect you!"

On the road leading to the coast through fields and forests they encountered very few people, and only a couple of Russians who were sitting on a farmer's wagon drawn by a small horse.

They stopped in the wood behind the house of Siim of Kruusiaugu.

"Why don't you go for a change and ask where we are supposed to go?" Vello said to Taavi. "I haven't seen him myself, but I've had enough of the coast people in the two days I roamed around here. I don't know what language they speak here, but you won't get very far speaking Estonian. They just let you talk and keep their mouths shut. If you're fortunate, they'll answer and say, 'I don't know.' They don't know a thing about anything; never saw or heard about a boat. They make such ignorant faces—as if they didn't know what a boat was."

"All right, I'll go and see what kind of a story I'll get from this middle-man between the forest and the sea. I'll be back in ten minutes."

"You'll do well to be back in an hour." Vello laughed and lay down calmly on the mossy ground.

Taavi walked down the narrow footpath leading toward a small house which was painted bright yellow. The house, a barn and stables were surrounded by patches of corn, vegetables and an orchard, and obviously formed the homestead of a forest ranger. A reddish-brown hunting dog greeted him noisily in the yard. A dried-out old man stood on the threshold, dressed in worn green pants, high boots and a leather jacket.

"Good afternoon," Taavi said.

The old man muttered something in response, called back the dog and gave the stranger a suspicious look from his hawk's eyes.

"Are you Siim of Kruusiaugu?"

"Some people call me that."

He inclined his head toward the house and entered ahead of Taavi. Inside he pointed with one hand to a chair and with the other signalled to his wife to leave the room.

"Then I'm in the right place," Taavi said, pleased. "I'll explain my trouble to you in a few words. I'm a volunteer, returned from Finland, and I came about getting back across the sea. Some friends of mine have recently gone back from here."

The man acted as if he had not heard a word.

"How about it?" Taavi demanded.

"About what? I don't understand."

"You can trust me completely. Look here, here's the map which led me to you. You must know the man who drew the map. It was Joonap Lahe himself, the owner of the boat. Please be so kind as to tell me how to get to him."

"To whom? What was his name again?" the old man asked, as if hearing something totally incomprehensible.

"Don't you know Joonap Lahe?"

"Never heard of him."

"Is the coast far from here?"

"A couple of kilometres."

"And you mean to say that you don't know anything about getting across?"

"Yes, during the German rule they did go, and the birds didn't sing about it in the woods. But now nobody can go any more." The man gave a short laugh. "I haven't been to Rannaküla myself for a long time, not even close to it."

And so it went on for at least an hour. The old man professed complete ignorance. Taavi spoke calmly, got agitated, walked back and forth in the little room, cursing. The old man only shrugged his shoulders.

"How many are there of you?" he finally asked.

"Right now no more than myself, my wife, son and a friend. But a few more are coming."

"How many?"

"I'm not sure. Perhaps four, five or six. Hard to say."

The old man took his beaked cap from the corner of the table, replaced it on his stiff grey hair and walked around the room, twisting his moustache and meditating.

"Now what shall I do with you?" he said, spreading his arms. "Do you think I have it easy? People are pouring down my neck like rain in the spring, directly from the bushes and with all kinds of drawn maps. Where the hell shall I put you? No, I'm harder up than the poor Estonian republic. Both of us are directly in the way of this mass migration. Do you have any food along? No? Of course, the little bit you have isn't worth talking about. That will be used up today and tomorrow."

"Isn't there any hope that we could leave sooner?"

"Sooner? If you have made the trip before, you should know how these things are. And you know it's much worse now. There has been a real ruckus down in Rannaküla. Who? Who else but the Russians. Some have got killed, and other things have happened."

"How far away does Joonap himself live?"

"About ten kilometres from here, or a little more. All right, let's go. I'll wait over there. You go and pick up the others from the woods."

On their way through fir groves and aspen thickets, alternating with meadows, Siim of Kruusiaugu spoke, "Don't get edgy if you have to wait a day or two. You'll have to wait; that's certain. The boat will leave today or tomorrow, depending on the weather, but there's no more room on it. It's a small sailboat, and the sea is rough. Joonap was in hiding here for a couple of days. They were closing in on him. That's what life is like. My old woman will bring you something to eat. We don't have much ourselves, so you'll have to tighten your belts. If we could get the other boat going. . . ."

"Is there more than one boat?" Taavi asked.

"I know of one more. It's a good craft, engine in good shape and everything, but the owner wants gold. It's his only possession, and he has a family to feed."

"We should look into that." Vello became interested.

"Yes, we should look into that," the old man agreed. "If you could get hold of some gold coins, you might have your passage right there."

They stopped near a hay storage barn behind a fir grove.

"I'm going back now. If a few more are on the way, then my old woman may get in trouble with them. She won't open her mouth, even if they threaten to knock her dead. You know the coast people. That wouldn't matter, except that she'd scare them away and they would go off on their own, looking for the sea, and get lost."

Eedi of Piibu was sitting at the entrance to the barn reading a book in the faint light of the evening sun. Before Taavi had time to open his mouth, however, Marta Laane rushed out from the barn with open arms and a jubilant shout.

"Taavi! Taavi, dear!" Then she stopped, bewildered, and her arms dropped. Her narrow eyes widened, seeing Ilme and Lembit, and the colour shifted rapidly on her cheeks.

"Why so startled? Aren't you acquainted?" Taavi asked.

"How? Mrs. Raudoja? But you were supposed to—to have left the country," she stuttered helplessly.

"We all came to leave the country." Vello laughed merrily.

"We didn't make it—we were too late," Ilme replied to Marta's question. She was not surprised at meeting her former schoolmate, as Taavi had already mentioned the possibility. But with her feminine instinct she sensed that the other woman would have been happier if she hadn't been there.

"So that's it," Marta said brusquely and turned around.

This greeting and conversation were quickly put aside, for the next head to rise to the high opening of the barn behind Eedi's back was that of Leonard. He was spitting out hayseeds, and a torrent of noisy, cheerful words spilled from his mouth.

"How did you get here? Didn't you go to Vääna?" Taavi finally managed a question.

"I thought I mentioned to you that I am one of the original members of the 'Erna' group," the boy answered haughtily. Jumping down from the high opening, he fell on his hands and knees. When he was excited his feet always gave way. He got up again and chuckled good-naturedly. "If my nose couldn't smell such things as are being hatched here, then it's good for nothing. There wasn't a single, solitary chance in Vääna, for Vääna is chock full of Russians polluting the air. So we decided to move on to this place. Eedi here, he turned white and pale, and said his stomach wouldn't stand the swaying of the boat, but he finally decided to come along."

"Do-don't sta-start over a-ga-gain," Eedi warned and stuck his nose deeper in the book.

Lembit had climbed up to the opening and jumped down into the hay. But his joy turned quickly into amazement. The stack of hay started moving, uttering heavy curses and rose up with the boy. Sleepy faces appeared from under the pile. Most of them belonged to former comrades of Taavi. There were shouts of greeting and demands for news.

"It's so damned cold at night," one of the fellows said. "If you fall asleep, you are stiff all over next morning. And there's nothing else to do in the daytime except sleep. It would be a different thing if we could play cards, but nobody has any money. What's the use of playing like that? Climb on the hay and make yourselves at home! If we get closer together, it'll be warmer."

Ilme was quite helpless. The presence of so many men in the same tight space embarrassed her. Taavi laughed when he saw her hesitant look.

"You'll get used to our way of life," he said. "A hay barn is a nice place, but you cannot use one very often. I don't see why people haven't built them right in the thickets instead of on meadows. What are you reading, Eedi?"

"I'm stu-stu-dying Sw-wedish."

"Do you hope to get a better job in the King's country?" Vello teased.

"Don't worry," Leonard said. "If Eedi becomes a locksmith, I'll be a safecracker; if he starts cleaning toilets, I'll foul up the world."

Toward evening the forest ranger brought some new people. There were two this time—Jüri Paarkukk with his strained, near-sighted eyes, and Ruudi Ugur, one of the organizers of the Admiral's commandos. The forest ranger had a heavy woollen blanket, which he handed to Ilme.

"That's for the boy," he said. "My old woman sent it." Then he turned toward the men. "The boat is leaving tonight. The weather is just right—clouds are coming up, with some wind. In a couple of days you'll have to go to the shore at night, for Joonap can't tell the exact time when he'll get back. He is hoping to get a new boat from Finland; they promised him one. We'll get into a tight spot with food if the waiting should last much longer. I'll bring you some potatoes tomorrow—you can make a little fire in daytime and bake them—and some salted fish. But there isn't anything much to be had here. The coast people haven't had a chance to catch any fish for a long time; the seas are closed. You should give some thought to that other boat; you're a big enough group here now," he said, turning to go back home.

Ilme found some food wrapped in the blanket: a bottle of warm ersatz coffee and some slices of bread with smoked fish in between. The forest ranger's kindly wife had sent that for Lembit. The boy ate hungrily and invited his mother and father to share his meal. They had to taste some of it, in order not to spoil his appetite.

"Yes, that other boat." Ruudi Ugur sounded interested. "I'm going back to Tallinn in the morning. If gold is all that's needed to get it, we should be able to arrange that. There must be some gold around somewhere."

"Why should we have to arrange anything, if one boat is already plying the route?" Vello replied. "Or isn't the way I organized it good enough for you?"

"Sure it's good enough, but if there's a boat available, we should put it into operation. The land behind us is full of people in trouble," Taavi said.

"I know enough about boats to chart a course to Finland," Leonard added. "If the engine doesn't conk out, you just keep going straight until you hit the rocks. It's a cinch to go in that direction, so long as you don't happen to land at the Porkkala base and give the Russians a scare. But coming back—that's a different story. You can't just turn the front end this way and blast ahead until you hit shore."

"That's true," Jüri Paarkukk admitted.

"It sure enough is," Leonard said emphatically. "You have to know each stone on the shore, and also where Ivan is waiting for you."

"We'll fix the other boat up in any case," Ruudi decided. "Perhaps I'll be able to prevail on the Admiral."

"What is the Admiral planning to do? You're close to him; you should know," Taavi said. "He surely didn't return from Canada just to give himself up to the Russians!"

Ruudi Ugur sighed in the darkness. "It's not easy with the old man. He's still believing in a third possibility. I can't really understand him. Sometimes I think that he's only too well aware of the situation, but I cannot comprehend his stubborn desire to remain in Estonia. 'The spirit of the War of Independence won't allow retreat,' he said once. And: 'Every step we take on the road of retreat and compromise, we will later have to pay for with blood.' But he is reported to have said much bolder things. He wants to continue organized resistance on such a scale that the noise will be heard outside."

The deep autumn night had descended over meadows and forests. Only a few cigarettes glowed in the dark barn. The smokers were holding them carefully over a hat or a coat. Every man had had some experience of this kind of life, acquired since the summer of 1941 when war had first rolled over the country. They seemed to possess a certain amount of natural talent for it—perhaps inherited from times long past.

Ilme approached her husband. "Lembit wants you, Taavi. He's in the corner over there where the hay is dry. One of your friends gave up his place for us. The roof has leaked and some places are quite wet."

She paused, then went on in an agitated whisper. "Do you know where Marta is? She acted so strange when she saw me. She seems to be still after you like she used to. . . ."

"Oh, come now," Taavi soothed her. "I'm not the only man in the world. Isn't she around?"

"No. Did anything happen between you two?" Ilme asked very quietly.

"Are you crazy?"

Right now it seemed to Taavi himself that this was a completely outrageous assumption, but still . . . yes, if he thought about it seriously, he had to admit to himself that it had been a near thing.

But where was Marta?

The storm had blown itself out a long time ago, and for a week now they had been down on the shore every night, waiting for the boat. But the boat never returned.

They had spent the last couple of nights in another barn closer to the shore, where a considerable number of Taavi's former comrades were hiding out—soldiers and officers, some of them wounded, a few already incoherent with fever, and everybody famished and stiff from cold. They had even encountered a Russian patrol one night. They had come close to a clash, for the men were armed, several even in uniform.

From a local girl who brought them a little food, Taavi heard about numerous Russians in the vicinity and other bad news that made him restless. Both his common sense and his instinct told him that this was not a safe place to wait for a chance to get across. And especially when there were so many of them together.

Early at dawn one morning, when the weary-looking girl announced that it would be no use waiting any longer, Taavi actually became calmer. Leading his group back to the forest ranger's barn, he felt as if they were leaving danger behind them.

But what now? Many were ready to return to Tallinn. Ilme kept her desperate eyes on Taavi. Lembit had a hacking cough. Taavi had tried to keep him covered with his own coat on the shore, but the thin over-coat had evidently not been enough. And Ilme had tearfully revealed her big secret to him: she was expecting another child. All that made the situation extremely difficult. Marta, who had reappeared, was gloomy and uncommunicative. This was her first trip, and she had probably expected it to be like a pleasure cruise. It wasn't Taavi's fault —she had rushed to the coast all on her own.

Leonard had exchanged his pullover for a bottle of home-distilled vodka in one of the farms. He'd gone to look for food, but returned with the bottle. Everybody got a few scorching mouthfuls.

"This will keep your spirits up," Leonard promised.

The small barn of the forest ranger was empty and abandoned, the trampled hay was moist and musty. Ruudi Ugur, who had gone back to Tallinn several days ago, had not returned.

What now?

"A damn lousy place." Leonard cursed. "One can die of hunger here!" He was still capable of mouthing his juicy curses. Eedi of Piibu got out his Swedish textbook, as if a few mispronounced words could carry him away from this wretchedness.

None of them really complained. The majority just gazed ahead, and pressed an occasional "damn" through their teeth.

"I'll go and see what the forest ranger has to say," Taavi decided. He was slightly older than the others, and his firm manner had made him the leader of the group. "There's that other boat they've been talking about. If there's no other way, we'll take it by force and set out with a fair wind. This waiting on the shore has been simply wasted time."

The old man was quite frightened when he saw Taavi. His sun-burned, narrow, wrinkled face remained immobile, but his moustache trembled when he fumbled for his pipe.

"Let me have a pipeful too," Taavi asked quickly.

"There you are. All out of tobacco?"

"We're all out of it. The boys are smoking hayseed already. They must have gone to the bottom with that boat."

"I'm afraid they have," the old man mumbled. "The weather was sort of thick that night. Are you in our barn again?"

"Where else could we go?"

"Yes, where else?"

"We should find out about that other boat now. The coast is full of people. That would help to clear the air a little."

"That boat is small. And the owner wants gold. I'll try to talk to him. We'd get the barn clear. My old woman is scared. There have been roundups in the villages all around. Life can't be very cheerful for you, either. How much gold or other stuff do you have?"

"Not a trace. What kind of a devil is he?" Taavi exploded. "He wants gold! The price of blood is always gold! Tell him, if he won't give the boat willingly, I'll go and knock him off!"

"No, you won't get it by pressure and force," the forest ranger mumbled. "He's a peculiar man. You can't bargain with him at all. And he won't show you where the boat is, either, before the gold is in a safe place. And if you got in a fight, the law would be on his side."

"The law, the law," Taavi mocked. "The barrel of a gun is the law. There's no other law in this country. I'm not going to leave my wife and child here in the clutches of the Russians like that and get hanged myself! Everybody is fighting for his life, and he who fights hardest will come out on top. Where does this man live?"

"The village is full of Russians, but I'll try to call him over here," the old man promised. "You won't get anywhere, though, trying to threaten him. He's a man from the coast, hard like a log that's been soaked in the sea. And he doesn't have it easy, either. He has a wife and family too, and the boat is his only possession. It's worth half of his life. How can you expect him to give it away for nothing? And he himself isn't going. He's expecting his eldest son back from Russia. That's whom he is saving the boat for. But he'd give it away for gold. He could exchange the gold for something else again."

"Does he think he'll be able to take the gold along to Siberia?" Taavi sneered. "Just how much does he want for that boat?"

"A hundred rubles in gold or an equal amount in valuables."

"I'll go and kill him tonight," Taavi exploded.

His anger had not yet subsided when he returned to the barn. He threw down the sack of raw potatoes and salted fish which the forest ranger's wife had given him, and climbed inside.

"D-did you bri-bri-bring some to-tobacco?" Eedi asked.

"Use your Swedish primer to wrap cigarettes with. You'll at least get a good smoke out of it, for nothing will come of that trip to the promised land, anyway. Here!" He threw the pouch, filled with home-grown tobacco, to his comrade. "The price of the boat is a hundred gold rubles. And there's no guarantee that it won't rise tomorrow, when our plight becomes worse."

"Is that all you got?" Leonard asked.

"There are some potatoes outside. Somebody make a fire. But watch out that you don't eat any until everything has been divided. Let's see how many valuables we've got together."

What they had didn't amount to much—a few rings and a couple of cheap wrist watches. Marta had left her rings and gold bracelet in Tallinn. A smart traveller!

"Why didn't you bring them along?" Taavi was amazed.

The woman shrugged her shoulders without interest.

"Go and get them, if you want to," she muttered. "What a fool! Listen," she said with increasing interest, casting a strange glance in Ilme's direction, "maybe you *should* go. I have more there than the price of the boat. I'll give you the key and tell you where to find them. It wouldn't be hard at all."

Most of the men had gone out to the fire. The baking of potatoes had a greater hold on their minds right then than the discussion about the boat, especially since their intellects, dulled by the hunger and cold, were unable to contribute any solution to their problem. Hot potatoes, burned almost black on the coals! Even Lembit was eagerly helpful, picking up dry twigs and branches for the fire. He had already made friends with everybody, and spoke a few words of Finnish.

Taavi sank into thought. Marta's idea wasn't as stupid as it had first seemed, and without gold they would never get away. What could have happened to Ruudi Ugur? They'd at least hear some news from Tallinn, if he'd return. But little could have changed in Tallinn during the ten days they had been away—a few more nightly roundups, a few more men slugged and robbed and a few more women raped among the ruins.

"I'll go," Taavi announced.

"Taavi!" Ilme looked at him with pain in her big eyes. They had got together after such terrible adventures, and now they would be separated again. It seemed to her that these long, hard days here on the coast had not lasted longer than a moment. Everything—the journey to the coast, the cold in the barns, and the waiting on the shore every night when they had to lie motionless on the frozen ground, huddled together so that the only warmth she had felt came from the bodies of her husband and her little son—everything had happened so quickly. It seemed to her that she had so many important things to tell Taavi, and that she should do it without delay, or they would never be said. But she did not say anything. She was accustomed to the fact that her husband would decide such problems without asking for her advice and opinion, using his own best judgement. She had been used to this since she was seventeen, and during these last years she had of necessity become accustomed to the fact that Taavi often left her side, plunging into unknown dangers.

"If I leave this afternoon," Taavi said, "I'll be there by mid-morning tomorrow. I'll have to travel on foot through the night. If I come back tomorrow at noon I'll be able to hitchhike. In any case I should be back by noon the day after tomorrow, allowing for unforeseen complications. Maybe even tomorrow night."

"You could spend the night in my apartment," Marta suggested.

"No thank you. I don't want to dangle from your window again. No, I'll come right back. We've lost enough time now. I've never seen a greater waste of time in all my life. Why didn't you bring your jewellery along? Did you expect to charter a plane in Stockholm and come back for your property?"

"I was far too excited to think," she said lamely, but without apparent shame.

IX

Before starting on his journey, Taavi had consulted the forest ranger about out-of-the-way shortcuts he could take to get to Tallinn at night. He did not trust the highways because of frequent patrols and the night curfew. And now he was on his way. Since the weather was windy, and a sharp, cold drizzle was falling, he had exchanged his thin coat for Jüri Paarkukk's heavy raincoat. Together with someone's wide-beaked cap it made him look a little like a German officer, but it was good to hear the rain splattering on his shoulders and to pour off water from the top of his cap. His back turned moist, to be sure, but that came from perspiration. In his own coat he would have been already thoroughly soaked.

His army training stood him in good stead. The journey progressed well. Where the road forked, he had to recall the directions of the forest ranger. Sometimes he just had to take a chance and follow his instinct.

It might have been around ten o'clock, when on a rutty country road in the wood he suddenly heard a voice.

"*Ruki vverh!*"

All at once two figures seemed to rise from the ground. Taavi felt the barrels of two submachine guns pressed against his ribs.

"What the devil do you want?" he protested.

"*Ruki vverh!*" The command was repeated, and the gun made a jerky movement on his ribs.

Taavi raised his hands slowly, even though they twitched with the desire to hit at the only light spot, which had to be his captor's face.

Instead of asking for papers, the men ordered him along. Taavi walked between the two armed men, holding his hands up at shoulder level. A fierce desire to flee burned in him—to shake off his guards and leap into the darkness. What a useless waste of time!

After a moment it was too late. One of the men exchanged passwords with a voice coming from the dark, and they arrived in front of a house. The sharp gables of the building jutted into the grey-black night sky. Damn it, wasn't it the sea that heard nearby? If that was so, he must have picked the wrong road at some crossing. Even the wind, a salty, open breeze, smelled of the sea.

Inside the blockhouse, in a small unpainted room, by the light of a kerosene lamp, Taavi was required to produce his identity papers. From the report which his captors gave to the young Red Army officer who sat in front of him, he had gathered that they took him for a German parachutist. Of course—the coat and the cap! They had not searched him, but their behaviour was more than careful and suspicious. The gun barrel in his back did not move an inch, and the other stolid-faced Russian in front of him was glowering at him, his finger on the trigger of the submachine gun.

Don't be stupid, Taavi told himself. The mistake will be cleared up right away.

He put his hand in his pocket to get his papers, and suddenly turned serious. A cold shiver ran down his spine. He fumbled through the other pockets of his borrowed overcoat. What a prince of fools he was! What an *idiot*! He had left his papers in the pocket of his own overcoat! The Soviet passport, the job certificate, the temporary identity card and the travelling orders! The only thing he found in his coat pocket was a card with his own real name—a small piece of paper with Estonian text, to which the officer paid only scant attention.

What a damnable situation! Taavi was furious at himself. All he could do was to grimace bitterly, when the soldiers now searched him thoroughly.

The only thing found on his body besides his wallet, wrist watch, pipe, and the keys he had received from Marta, was a piece of wrinkled paper on which he had drawn a rough map according to the directions he had received from the forest ranger. The officer scrutinized it from every side, and his face became even grimmer. Then he jumped up and thrust the paper under Taavi's nose, letting go with a volley of Russian curses. That would be enough to put a damned Nazi to the wall! The keys and the wallet were given back to him, and after a futile attempt to explain and protest he was pushed into a small storage room. The door was slammed shut, the bolt creaked, and Taavi Raudoja was a prisoner.

He fumbled around in the dark narrow room. Wide shelves rose on both sides, filled with empty glass jars and a few pots and pans. He stumbled over a box containing bottles with blueberry preserves. He sat down on the edge of the box, took off his wet cap and tore his hair. Hell, wasn't there somebody in the house, some Russian-speaking Estonian, who would have explained his situation? Who would have affirmed at least that he was a genuine Estonian, and not a German paratrooper? He stood up and began pounding on the door with his fist. He heard the voices of the Russians in the adjoining room and pounded louder. Somebody yelled at him to go to sleep. But Taavi was beside himself. He had to get out, get quickly to Tallinn and back, his pocket heavy with gold. His anger rose with every blow of his fist, and he beat harder and harder.

The door clanged open. Before Taavi could take a step, a short, heavy-set man with a broad, shiny face aimed a blow against his nose. Taavi was so flabbergasted by this unexpected treatment that he staggered backwards against the shelves. The door closed again to the accompaniment of raucous laughter. Taavi's eyes watered. He sat down on the box and fingered his aching nose. It was swelling already, and his face was sticky and wet with blood.

The situation had taken another unexpected turn. It was more serious than he had reckoned at first. He was sorry he had not tried to escape the moment he was arrested. In the rain and darkness he might have got away. Maybe yes; maybe no. It would have been stupid to run blindly into a barbed-wire fence and hang there like a ready target in the flashes of light from the shooting. Damn it all, everything had gone wrong today.

He sprang up and began to pound on the door with renewed vigour. This time he beat with the toes of his shoes, pausing only for short intervals to listen to noises and movements in the house. A good quarter of an hour had passed and the toes of both his feet were sore, before the door was opened. He was prepared for the next blow, clutching a bottle of blueberry preserves by its neck. But he was ordered out of the room instead. He placed the bottle on the shelf; there were too many Russians at the door to give rein to any wild impulses.

"Where are your companions?" the boy-faced officer asked. Taavi shrugged his shoulders. Wasn't there anybody around who could help him explain the situation? It seemed as if he'd have to spend the whole night under this roof.

"Take off your coat!" he was ordered.

Taavi shed his wet overcoat with slow movements. Somebody took his cap. The officer examined the quality of the coat and compared its size with his own measurements. Taavi's watch was already adorning his wrist.

"Give my watch back," Taavi shouted angrily. "My watch," he said, pointing to the wrist of the officer and taking a few steps in his direction.

His behaviour seemed to baffle the Russians. Then the young officer made a gesture toward the storage room and the hands of the soldiers grabbed Taavi.

Taavi was quicker and landed the first blow, putting all his might into it. The blow sat well. He saw his opponent fall on his back like a tree hit by lightning. But that was all he saw. The next moment he sank to the floor like a sack of flour, felled from behind by the blow of an automatic revolver.

When Taavi began to regain consciousness, he seemed to hear the earsplitting rumbling of a steam roller lumbering over the cobblestone pavement of some rundown street. Then it seemed to him that he was inside the drum of a threshing machine, whirling around like a handful of chaff. Finally he was sure that somebody was throwing crackling icicles in his face, while a dentist was simultaneously extracting all the teeth from his jaws. Choking and sputtering, he tried to open his eyes, only to be blinded again by another bucketful of icy water.

When he opened his eyes, a stifled groan escaped his lips. He became aware of his wretched condition. He had been beaten to a pulp while he was unconscious. He managed to bring his hand to his head. It was bloody—and cold from the water thrown in his face. There was no doubt that his face had been marked by the boots of the Russians. Although he still received a few disdainful kicks in the shins, he staggered to his knees. His bloody eyes had noticed a rifle with a bayonet leaning against the wall. Although his common sense told him he would never make it, an inexplicable force made him jump for the weapon.

The beating started again. The heavy boots trampled on Taavi's face, and this time he was aware of their crushing. Finally a chance blow behind his ear mercifully blotted out his consciousness.

He was cross-examined all through the night. From the questions, Taavi understood that the NKVD border guard unit which had arrested him took him for a very dangerous person. They tried to force him to divulge his identity. It seemed that they had not yet quite decided whether Taavi was a German parachutist, a Finnish spy from across the sea, or a simple bandit. In the morning he was left lying on the cold floor of the storage room, stiff and cramped, because the lack of space prevented him from stretching out. At noon he received a bowl of cold potato soup. He ate hungrily but repressed his desire to ask for some bread. After the meal two guards took him outside to a filthy latrine, and allowed him to wash his bloody, swollen face in a basin outside the door. Taavi looked around for a chance to escape, but there seemed to be none.

The building was a new blockhouse, resembling a settler's home with its barns and young orchard. Farther down across the road one could see the roofs of other buildings—probably a fishing village—and beyond it the sea. In the few short moments Taavi spent in the yard he did not notice any local people. This must have been one of the many dwellings left deserted in the great turmoil. Near the woodpile behind the shed were the head, feet and bloody entrails of a killed cow, and next to that was a machine-gun position, manned by a bleary-eyed Russian.

The fresh air and the cold water refreshed Taavi and revived his will power. He had already thought through every possible plan for escape, and found each one of them hopeless. He was seriously worried about his own fate and that of his wife and son whom he had left on the coast. What would they do without him? And if he should be detained for a long time, if he should be taken to a prison or even deported to Siberia, how long would Ilme and Lembit keep on waiting on the shore, frozen, starving and exhausted? And his wife in that condition! When Ruudi Ugur returned to the coast and they discovered another chance to get across—they were sure to find one, with so many energetic men together —would Ilme leave without him? That was hardly likely. He knew his wife and knew that under the present circumstances she would remain blindly behind, waiting for his promised return. No, he simply had to regain his freedom.

Driven by anger and pain, he began to hammer away at the door again. Those devils—to keep beating a man when he was already lying down. In his rage, Taavi began to smash the glass jars and bottles against the door. He'd force his way through the wall, if they wouldn't open.

But this time they let him rave until he exhausted himself. The door was opened only when he was sitting on the boards of the shattered box, surrounded by broken glass and debris. He was taken to another cross-examination. The broad-faced man cuffed him again a couple of times, hitting him in the face and on the back of his head. The cross-examination lasted until midnight. An older, grim-faced NKVD officer had joined the boyish-looking lieutenant. They demanded again that he tell about his fellow-parachutists.

At two o'clock in the morning they pronounced his death sentence.

Taavi did not grasp the full meaning of the statement at first. He saw that the older officer got ready to leave. He was pushed back into the storage room, worn out and tired. He heard the car leave. The noise of the engine was soon swallowed up by the distant roar of the sea.

Taavi boasted to himself that he would sleep, condemned or not. But he was mistaken—he could not sleep a wink. He sat on the cold floor, with a dull pain and numbness in his limbs. He had no idea of the passing of time. Only occasionally did the cold shivers and the pain of his wounds bring him back to his desperate situation. He could not believe that he would die, but nevertheless he experienced deep anguish. He was filled with grief when he thought of his wife and son. He pressed a piece of glass in his hand, not feeling its sharp edges cut into his palm.

Taavi had to fight also against fear of death. He had never experienced it as strongly as now. It was repulsive and weakening. It sneaked in like a detestable crawling animal from the floor, up to his fiercely beating heart and painfully throbbing temples. This will finally get me, Taavi realized. And then what shall I do, facing their rifles? I need anger—strong, irrational fury, so violent that I won't feel anything. Then I can step on my fear as on a worm.

Taavi began to move his stiffened limbs. He clenched his teeth, and cold sweat appeared on his forehead. He had to drive out the cold and the fear. He *had* to. At least he wouldn't die on his knees like a lamb. He'd attack them, so it would be easier. Move now—hands, feet, neck. He had to feel that he was alive. Every cell in his body had to yearn to be alive. What a foolish thought—he was alive—so far anyway.

The door banged open. Two soldiers with rifles and the young officer with a revolver were standing at the door.

The autumn morning was raw and grey. Darkness had not altogether disappeared from under the grey sky. Taavi's fingers became feverishly moist and his thoughts drifted aimlessly, finding nothing to hold on to. Crossing the yard Taavi kept pace with the men, fearing that if he moved a step ahead, the executioners would shoot him from behind. They turned around the corner of the shed, where the remnants of the killed animal were stinking in a bloody heap. So they'd take him to the woods.

But no, they stopped behind the shed. The officer said something and jeered, slapping Taavi's shoulder. Taavi saw his watch on the wrist of the Russian. Then they began to move backwards away from him, step by step. So here it would happen, in the same place where they had killed and dismembered the dumb animal.

Taavi Raudoja was later never able to comprehend how all that now happened had come about. He did not know what prompted him to raise his hand and point toward the house with a scream of surprise. His gesture and voice must have been so persuasive that all three turned their faces for a moment in the direction suggested by him. The next instant Taavi had dashed around the corner of the shed. He did not see or hear much. He acted like a well-oiled automaton, without a single thought he could remember afterwards. He saw in front of him the Russian machine gunner, saw his bewildered face when he leaped right over him, overturning the light machine gun and scattering sand in the face of his enemy with his shoe. When the first shots rang out behind him, he was throwing himself from under the barbed-wire fence into a wide ditch. He ran for about fifty metres along the wet bottom of the ditch and then leaped into the sheltering thickets. He had no time to listen to the Russian clamour which had arisen behind him, but he heard shots and bullets hitting the tree trunks. They wouldn't catch him, those devils! He ran and ran. When he heard the rattle of the machine gun, he gave a sigh of relief. They had not yet followed him into the woods.

A few hours later Taavi washed his bloody, perspiring face in a ditch. He must have looked frightening, he thought. There was a deep wound in his cheek, one of his earlobes was torn and swollen, his nose was swollen and aching, and he could barely open his mouth. One of his teeth had been knocked out, and another was dangerously loose. Taavi took off his coat and tried to clean it. He might have saved himself the trouble. He got the dust out, but where the blood and the dust had congealed into brown blotches even washing did not help. And a sleeve was almost torn off. His trousers were torn, too, baring one of his bruised, stained knees. He was amazed that his limbs had carried him this far, and wondered where he had got the strength to make good his quick escape. Right now he was close to collapse, half-starved and exhausted, spitting bitter saliva from his swollen mouth.

He had to hurry to Tallinn. He had lost two days and nights. But how could he get to Tallinn—without papers and in such a condition?

Seeing no trace of Russians in a small village, he made a quick decision and turned into a farm. In the yard he met the old farmer, who gazed at him, motionless and rigid. So here was one who'd got away from the damned Russians! He took the stranger quickly into the back chamber, did not ask many questions, ordered his daughter to fix a meal and began to treat Taavi's face with alcohol.

Taavi took a look at himself in the mirror. His face had changed beyond recognition. His wounds were black, and the swelling made them more frightening. He must not show himself to Ilme in daytime— in her present condition she might be frightened sick.

The old man treated Taavi like a prodigal son. He was a small, close-mouthed individual, but a righteous indignation at the Russians gleamed in his eyes, and he did not rest until he had put Taavi to sleep in his own bed after the meal. If only for half an hour, he said. His wife and daughter covered Taavi up solicitously, as if he were liable to freeze right next to the heated stove.

"I'll keep my eyes open," the man said. "We haven't seen them in our village much. They have only passed through a couple of times. If one should come, we'll put you in the cellar beneath the kitchen. That is a good place. There's a trap door in the floor with the dining table on top of it. Nobody will find you."

Taavi's half-hour nap turned into a long sleep. He did not even dream. When he awoke, he wanted to jump out of the bed in a hurry, knowing he must be late, but he fell back on the pillow with a groan, his limbs aching and stiff.

"We'll have to rub them," the old man said. "How do you feel? You've slept a nice long stretch. Now you should try to stuff down some food."

"What time is it?" Taavi groaned and touched his aching jaw.

"Eight o'clock."

Taavi did not understand. Eight o'clock? It should have been dark already. But the sun was shining brightly outside, and the light that fell on the curtain was warm as in spring. What, was it morning?! He tried to get up again. Had the old man meant that he had slept like a log the whole day and night? He must have been in bad shape. He had not even been aware that he had been undressed.

"I went out last night to see what was going on," the farmer said. "Nobody has seen the Russians. I brought you the old Soviet passport of my nephew. That may help you some. The boy himself has been in the grave since last spring. He had T.B., and nobody will be using it anyway."

That was good news to Taavi. He might get into the city with that passport. But he remembered also Vello Kasar's story, that it was easy to get into the city, but hard to get out. If only his face did not attract attention. He could get stuck in Tallinn as in a trap. But he had to take the chance.

He reached Marta's apartment door a little before dusk and curfew. With a broad-brimmed hat pressed low on his brow and a high-collared overcoat he had managed to slip into Tallinn through some residential suburbs without running into any patrols. He had met some suspicious Russians, but nobody had been interested in his identity. But the journey had lasted a little longer that he had expected. And he'd have to spend at least one day in Tallinn to get new papers. He would be lucky to get going again by the following evening. Cold and hunger in that barn would rob the poor wretches of their last hope. But it might have been worse.

He unlocked the apartment door and locked it quickly behind him. The room was dark. He pulled the blackout shades down and turned on the light. He'd have to spend the night here. He could not get anywhere else before the curfew. But now the jewellery, the gold he had risked his life for. It was supposed to be in a locked box in the left drawer of the nightstand in the bedroom. He hurried there in feverish haste. He was acting like a burglar, he chuckled to himself. Pull down the shade, take out the key and—what the devil, where was the leather box? He scattered Marta's night apparel on the floor, but the box she had described was not there. Perhaps Marta had erred about the drawer? Yes, of course, in the right-hand drawer he found several boxes and some bottles of expensive perfume. It had to be this bright yellow box. But the box was open. He had no need for the key. Taavi sat down on the carpet, holding the open box in his hand. Perspiration broke out on his face. The box was empty.

What did that mean? This was the right box, with an engraved dedication from Marta's deported husband. He looked feverishly into the other boxes, spilling powder on the floor and breaking a bottle of eau de Cologne in his impatience. He searched every drawer thoroughly, and his movements became faster and more disturbed as his agitation increased. He broke open the drawers to which he had no keys with a strong knife he had taken from the kitchen. He did not find a single valuable thing, and the glass beads that stuck in his fingers he threw angrily into a corner.

Taavi searched the whole room now with systematic thoroughness. How could Marta send him on such a fool's errand? The jewellery had to be somewhere; at least the rings and bracelet she had worn only a few days before. That would amount to almost half of the asking price of the boat. But he found nothing anywhere—not in the drawers, wardrobe, trunks, or pockets of her clothes. He looked under the mattress, behind mirrors and pictures on the wall. He lifted up the candlesticks and looked inside. He checked the upholstery, searched among Marta's shoes and even her lingerie and stockings. There was nothing.

Taavi drank a glass of cognac, smoked and tried to think calmly. But it was no use.

After midnight he threw himself hopelessly on the bed. What would happen tomorrow? He must get the gold, cost what it may. They must get that boat! He'd go to Arno and Liisa. Maybe they'd let him have their rings. And there was Selma, too. The girl wouldn't let him down in his present predicament; even though she did not have much herself, her aunt was wealthy. He would take it by force from someone, if he could get it no other way. He could not leave Ilme and Lembit like that.

Somebody shook Taavi awake in the morning. He had great trouble getting his swollen eyes open.

"Good Lord, what's the matter with you, Taavi?" It was a woman's voice, full of fright. Marta was standing at his bedside, still wearing her overcoat. Taavi straightened himself painfully and looked at her stupidly.

"How did you get here?" he asked sharply. He saw that her face was worn and thin.

"I just came. I remembered I'd taken most of my jewellery to the country. What has happened to you?"

"You damned fool," Taavi cried. "And now you came to tell me that?"

Marta retreated a few steps. She seemed unsure of herself and strange.

"I came to tell you that they are gone," she stammered.

"What?" Taavi shouted. "Who is gone? Speak clearly!"

"They all—Ilme and the boy and. . . ."

Taavi gazed at her with aching eyes.

Ilme had left the country.

"Speak!"

"Don't scream like that," Marta warned. "The boat returned the night after you left. Some of your comrades had taken a chance of going to the shore, and they got away immediately. There were not many people on the shore that night. The boat was large; they left half empty."

Taavi had sunk back on the bed.

"Speak, speak," he urged Marta.

"All the others left two nights later—last night."

"Ilme too?"

"Ilme and your son too."

"Don't lie to me!" Taavi shouted. He could not imagine Ilme leaving without him.

"I was there myself."

"And why didn't you go?"

Marta squeezed her fingers.

"I couldn't. I was thinking of you and—I just couldn't leave you like that, without knowing whether. . . ."

Taavi stared glumly at her out of his swollen eyes. Ilme could leave —although he could still hardly believe it—and *she* could not.

"When will the boat be back?"

"This boat won't come back any more," Marta said and swallowed. She was tired and seemed ready to break into tears. Her frightened eyes wandered from Taavi's wounds to her own scattered lingerie on the carpet in front of the nightstand.

"Why won't it return?" Taavi demanded.

The woman squirmed.

"They got the people all across and—there are too many Russians there on the shore, that's why."

Taavi bit his lips. So Ilme had escaped. Thank God! This was the only good news. It was a bitter irony of fate that he himself had left the coast. But what about the other boat?

"And the man told the forest ranger he wasn't going to sell."

So that was it. The road was closed again. The gate had been lifted for a moment, and now it fell shut again. Still it was good that a score of people had got away. Only Taavi Raudoja was on the same spot where he had started on his arrival in Tallinn.

"Where is your jewellery?" he asked sternly.

"I told you."

107

"Sure you told me. How can a person be so absent-minded that she does not remember where she has put her gold? No, I mean the bracelet and the rings that you wore recently."

"Didn't you find them?" Marta sounded surprised. "They are in the cupboard."

"There's nothing in the cupboard."

"On the top shelf. Didn't you look there?"

The woman went to the cupboard, followed by Taavi. Yes, Taavi had to admit, the jewellery was in fact there. He stared in disbelief. He lifted up the heavy gold bracelet. His eyes must have been half shut from the swelling last night, else he could not have missed it. But he was almost ready to swear that the rings and the bracelet had not been there then.

Taavi sat all day in Marta's apartment, stupefied and numb. He had slept deeply all through the night, but he felt that he had less energy than the evening before, when he had gone to bed, exhausted from his experiences and the desperate search for the jewellery. His limbs were heavy and sore from beating, and he had lost his zest for life. His head buzzed strangely, and the scab which the congealed blood had formed on his facial wounds felt like a mask that he wanted to tear off. But he realized that this mask had grown to be a part of him, that its roots were in his blood, reaching all the way to his heart.

So Ilme and Lembit were gone. They were now on the rock soil of Finland. They would not be able to stay there long—strong pressures were being put on the Finnish people, and dark clouds shrouded their horizon. But from Finland the way was open to the free world. They would soon go on to Sweden. Taavi was hardly able to picture to himself any more the happy workaday world of the old, free country, unscathed by wars for so long. And there Ilme would bear their second child.

Although Taavi should have been happy that his wife and son had managed to escape, he could not feel any joy. Even the knowledge that they were now far from mortal danger did not give him peace of mind. That was strange—he would not have believed he could be so selfish. And now his own hands were free. He had to worry about his own fate, and that had never troubled him much.

Marta treated and nursed his wounds. He accepted it. It was essential that his wounds heal quickly, at least those in the face. He had to move rapidly, had to get out to look for other chances to get across. This much he realized, regardless of his present lack of energy and determination. He had to start from the very beginning. When he touched his scarred forehead, he realized what was wrong. He had fever. The cold he had been exposed to and the hardships he had experienced had finally caught up with him. Nothing mattered any more; nothing made any difference. He swallowed the tablets Marta gave him and forced himself to drink several cups of steaming hot tea. Then he let Marta cover him with blankets, and lay there, shivering. He did not think about anything, did not care, and a deep, dreamless sleep enveloped his fever-racked body.

When he awoke, it had to be morning, for he heard the noises of early traffic from the streets. He remembered, as if through a mist, how Marta had changed the sheets on his bed at night when they had been soaking wet from perspiration, how she had made him swallow new tablets, drink hot tea, and perspire some more. And Taavi felt now that the heavy uncertainty and indecision which had plagued him yesterday was gone. His limbs were still sore and the wounds on his face itched from the sweat, but the roots of this pain did not now seem to reach all the way into his inner being.

Taavi jumped from the bed and began to dress. The day was ahead of him, his strength had returned, and the main thing—Ilme and the boy were safe in Finland!

Taavi had several errands planned for the day. First he had to provide himself with new identity papers, at least with a new work certificate, for otherwise he might get into serious trouble at the next check of documents. His experience had made him quite touchy in this respect, and furthermore, his face attracted much more attention now than ever before. The job at the railway station, together with his solid documents, had crossed the Finnish Bay with Jüri Paarkukk. It would not do to visit so soon the friendly girl in the Department of Personnel of the State Railways with a new name and different looks. He remembered that several of his comrades had got jobs in the shipyards—the officers of yesterday had turned overnight into trained mechanics, carpenters or bricklayers. Unfortunately he had no connections with these men. He decided to visit Liisa and Arno before Arno would leave for work.

"But why don't you take a job in your own field?" Arno wondered, having heard all that had happened in the meantime.

Liisa could not see why he didn't either.

"This would be the easiest for you, and not so hard to adjust to," she said. "And Arno is so hard up for help." She was still shocked from Taavi's account. Her round face was covered with red and white patches, her eyes wet with tears, and she had placed her trembling hand on the young man's arm in a motherly gesture.

"I've thought about that myself," Taavi hesitated. "But I wouldn't be much help to you, Arno. I'd leave as soon as I found a chance, and I'd bring you unnecessary trouble."

"I was considering that myself," Arno answered deliberately. "I'd wish, of course, that you would stay for a longer time—on account of the work. I'm the manager of the construction bureau, and I am responsible for the results. But it's clear that you cannot stay very long. Listen, I have to go now. Don't worry, we'll find a job for you, no matter for how long, even if it is in name only. I'll bring you the papers tonight."

109

Taavi mumbled something between hesitation and agreement. Sure, he would not stay long, but he needed the papers immediately. And he handed his friend the Soviet passport he had recently acquired, which had belonged to the young man who had died of tuberculosis.

When Arno left, Liisa started again from the very beginning. She wanted to know all the details. But Taavi was careful with his words. They had to keep in mind that the land was under Soviet rule. It would be better for Liisa herself not to know too much. Curiosity was dangerous at this time, and knowledge was downright deadly.

From Liisa he went downtown to the "cooperative," hiding his face under his broad-brimmed hat. There was not much pedestrian traffic in the streets at this hour—the workers had gone to their jobs, and the soldiers marched in formation.

The door in the archway was opened by the aunt of Jaan Meos, an energetic lady who had been the initiator and the soul of the whole enterprise.

"Is it you, Mr. Raudoja?" Her voice expressed amazement, and fear contorted her face. "I heard you had left the city. Good heavens, what has happened to you?"

"Nothing in particular," Taavi laughed. "The Russians stomped on my face."

The stout, energetic woman pulled him quickly inside.

"Tell me about it. Did many of our boys get arrested?" She was gasping from excitement.

"As far as I know, nobody but me," Taavi answered.

"Really?" The woman sounded relieved. "We here were already afraid that. . . . Please come in. Jaan is in the clubroom."

The woman disappeared in the office and Taavi entered their usual meeting room. Only two men were there today.

"You damned son of a gun," Jaan Meos shouted happily. He rushed to welcome Taavi, but stopped short in the middle of the room; his laughing young face turned serious.

"What are you gazing at with your mouth open, like a calf that sees a new pasture gate?" Taavi laughed and took off his hat, revealing his black eye sockets, torn ear-lobe, and swollen nose.

Jaan Meos stepped quite close and walked around him. Ruudi Ugur came closer too.

"You look as if you'd been through a threshing machine," was his opinion.

"Speak up!" Jaan demanded.

Taavi sat down on a chair and gave a quick account of his experiences. His eyes wandered around the room. It had changed noticeably during his absence. Red draperies covered the walls, adorned with pictures of Stalin and the marshals. Even the table was sporting a new red tablecloth, on which were displayed current numbers of the Communist daily paper and some propaganda tracts dug up from God knows where.

"So they got away!" Jaan rejoiced like a child. "They got away before the roundup! They are safe!" he shouted, pulling off the red tablecloth

110

with its load of Communist newspapers and trampling on it with his feet like a petulant boy. But when he raised his hand to pull down the wall decorations, Ruudi Ugur stopped him.

"What should we leave them up for?" Jaan asked indignantly. "We did all kinds of crazy things in the first fright. But if the men got away, why should we keep those damn faces up any longer? Down with them!"

"Let them be. We are still here," Ruudi said. "Do you know what kind of hell is loose on the coast right now?" He turned to Taavi. "I just arrived from there."

"I heard there had been a roundup."

"And how! You can't take a step without stumbling over a Russian. Whole farms have been emptied. I could exchange only a couple of words with the forest ranger's wife. She begged me to leave right away. The whole peninsula is teeming with Russians like hell with devils. And the woman was half crazy with fear; she didn't know what she was saying, only cried and begged me to go away. I understood that the forest ranger himself had been taken away. Nobody will get out from that shore any more, that's for sure. I'm glad that at least several of our men escaped: Jüri, Vaptas, Vello and whoever else was in that bunch."

"And what's new over here? Any new openings within earshot?"

"We'll have to start out again and be more quiet about it," Ruudi Ugur said. "This time the noise got far too loud—no wonder the Russians got wind of it. Men and women traipsing to the shore like to a county fair, and all barns full of Finland candidates. No, nothing is moving right now. There will probably be a sort of a lull for some time."

X

The people of Hiie were almost finished with their autumn chores. The grain was harvested, and the last potatoes had been brought home from the field.

Ignas had organized the work as well as was possible under the circumstances, but hardly anyone had had any leisure time to stretch his back. Värdi, Taavi's former companion, could already move without a crutch, and he had been delighted to assume the duties that went with drying the corn in preparation for the threshing. He had been quite helpless the first day or two in front of the huge stove, and, his eyes red and watering from the smoke, he had promised to burn down the whole shed in which the corn was drying. But Aadu, the old deaf-mute, knew every trick of the old stove, and had volunteered his help. Now they were both blissfully happy, sitting in front of the stove, enjoying the crackling fire, the sweet smell of the drying grain, and the delicacies they baked for themselves on the hot coals.

Every year Aadu Mustkivi looked forward to threshing time. As soon as the harvest began he cleaned the stove and scrubbed the floor of the drying shed every day. This year everything had been late. When the first flails hit the corn at Matsu, Aadu knew it immediately, even though

111

his ears did not hear a thing. Since that moment Aadu had kept at Ignas' heels like a dog, pointing toward Matsu and uttering his guttural sounds. He had already stacked the stove full of dry wood, carefully and expertly. Even the birch bark was there to start the fire. When Ignas gave the signal, the old man ran to the threshing floor as if he were late for something important. In the evening he moved all his possessions from the hayloft to the area back of the huge stove. And his earthenware bowl remained untouched in the kitchen for days—Aadu baked on the hot coals his own potatoes, turnips and salted fish. When Krōōt made bread in the house, Aadu stood at her side until her big bowl had been emptied of dough. It was his custom to wait there, until Krōōt would scrape the sides and bottom of the bowl and make a special little loaf for him. This time the mistress of Hiie made his round loaf bigger than usual and put some salt pork and sauerkraut in the middle—there were two of them on the drying job this year. Aadu would not let her bake his loaf together with the others, but grabbed it and ran to the drying shed, chuckling with pleasure. There they baked it, Värdi and he together, and it tasted good.

Saturday night, when the men were in the bathhouse and old Aadu puttering on his threshing floor, a visitor came to Hiie—August of Roosi. He was quite sober that day, although his eyes were still red from his latest binge. Hilda raised her eyes from her knitting, and a shadow of fear ran over her childlike face. She was scared of this dried-up runt of a man, who drove around with the Russians in his worn overcoat and fur cap, and whom nobody else took very seriously. But there was hardly anyone of whom Hilda was not afraid—fear was in her blood.

Krōōt did not even dream of being afraid of August. "He's a toothless dog. However loud he barks, he won't bite." She recalled Ignas' words when she observed the decaying teeth of the visitor and listened to his hissing talk. August was a kind-hearted man, who followed his nose wherever he smelled liquor. Only recently he had been hanging around the back door of the Germans who had stayed at Kalgina. Nobody had been any worse for that. What should they be afraid of now?

"Aren't your menfolk home?" August asked, pushing back the jaded winter cap which he wore all year round.

"They're in the bathhouse," Krōōt answered. "Sit down; you haven't rested your legs."

"I'm too busy." The old man sounded important. "Just heard some music playing at Harukurgu. I really should go and have a look."

"The Russians, or what?"

"Yes, who else? Who else makes music here these days? Everybody else makes a face that looks as if he'd stretched it on a shoetree. Now that won't do for long. Look here,"—he waved in Hilda's direction—"here's a young girl, sweet as a strawberry, knitting her eyes into a woollen stocking. Why doesn't she go among people and dance the worries out of her heart?"

He settled down in front of the stove with his pipe and tobacco pouch.

"Yes, I'm a busy man now," he continued. "I wouldn't have walked such a long distance for nothing. As far as I know, Ignas doesn't have a drop of beer anyway. So the menfolk are in the bathhouse? Listen, I'll go and join them, and beat the hangover out of my bones."

"Wait, wait!" Krõõt cried, in panic. Värdi was in the bathhouse. Even in their own village nobody had yet found out about him, and now all of a sudden there was the district messenger! "They should be through right away. Wait a little! Hilda, you go and tell them."

"Oh, I'll go myself," August answered and got up. "What kind of secrets could you have in that bathhouse? If you're just smoking a sheep or two in the chimney, who cares. I tell you: hide as much of your stuff now as you can! I hear a few things there in the county house. Soon it might be too late."

Krõõt was in a predicament.

"Wait now, August. I'll find something for you. I saw a little vodka somewhere in the bottom of a bottle. It's the vodka they gave out on ration cards during the German time—sort of weak, but if nobody drinks it, it will be wasted altogether."

"What do you know!" August said merrily. "And I've had a real dry day today. Bring Mäe's teardrops here, Krõõt! And I tell you: if you need to have your pigs cut next time, I'll do it for free. Sure thing! And I tell you, I always keep Ignas' welfare in mind. I remember the good days when the farmer of Hiie was district elder. A district cannot hope to have a more sensible man at its head. I had to toe the line, I confess it right here to the vodka bottle as if I were at the altar, but there was order in the house and the vodka tasted right, too. The whole life tasted right, for right men were in right places. Your health, Krõõt, and yours too, little slip of a girl! Watch out; the son of the house may marry you yet. And I tell you this: don't let the Russians get close to you. They'll tear you up like. . . . Cheers! I've seen enough of that already. Oh, yes, and I tell you. I'm drinking now, drinking like mad. I can't help it, but the whole thing doesn't have the same taste it used to have."

He passed his hand over his wrinkled face, which was already turning pink under the long grey stubble of his beard, and held the bottle so he could look through it at the glowing embers of the fire.

Hilda hurried to the bathhouse to warn the men. The farmer should come fast, for the vodka would soon be finished and August might again get the yen for a hot steam bath.

"You know, Krõõt, that my life has gone to the dogs," August said.

"Well, nobody can exactly boast right now."

"That's right, nobody has anything to boast about, that's for sure. I for one boast a little sometimes when I have a full bottle of vodka, but—I mean, my life went to the dogs a long time ago. Long before everybody else's did. My old woman used to keep me in line, slapped me from both sides. That kept me straight. But when the old woman died, and my daughter turned out no good. . . ."

"She's a clever girl, made a good marriage. She's doing all right even now."

"She's been gone for two weeks. Holde, the chairman of the executive

113

committee, keeps pressing me in the county house. Where is she? As if I knew. I'm the last person she tells about her plans."

"Where *did* she go?"

"Who knows? She must have run to Tallinn after some man. I tell you, Krōōt, and don't get me wrong. She's my own daughter, but she has no luck with men. Cheers! Let her run around, I don't care. But never mind all this rot."

"Yes, you are talking too much," Krōōt agreed.

"But I tell you this," August repeated, turning the bottle upside down to catch the last drop, "whatever should be going on in your bathhouse or on the Hiie farm or in the whole village of Metsaoti, August Roosi won't see or hear a thing. I'm a damn swine and a drunkard, but I'm an Estonian too. I told that to Ignas himself when he was district elder and when he fired me from my messenger's job. What else could he have done with a no-good sot like me? While the fair was on I didn't show up for weeks, and when I had a message to carry I got glued to the first beer barrel. The village elders had to run around themselves. I don't bear a grudge against Ignas. I tell you this: my kind of a bum is only good enough for the Germans and Russians, and in that case might even be useful to some better men."

Nobody could figure out whether August really intended to be useful on this occasion, or not. He was bringing the draft order to Tōmm of Hiie two days after the draft committee had met.

"I got it from the county house this morning," he insisted to Ignas. But the date was a week old.

"When did you take the orders to the others?"

"To Harukurgu I went last week. Their orders are all so mixed up, even I feel like crying when I look at them."

"Where should I send the boy now?" Ignas asked, annoyed. "He isn't home anyway. I don't know when I can catch him." He did not know whether to worry or to be glad that the order had come too late. Tōmm himself had gone to the threshing floor with Osvald and Värdi. Rumours about the mobilization had been afoot in the village for some time. They had heard about the draft board, and jokes had been made about the men who sat on it. But this turn of events made Ignas serious.

"Never mind about that. Just sign it and put the date down. I'll explain in the county house," August said lightly. "Those years won't be the first to be called up. Let Tōmm think it over. I'll tell them also that I didn't get to see Tōmm himself at all. That he'd gone to help an army transport or something like that and hadn't been home for some time. Or should I say that he's gone to live in Tallinn?"

Ignas stroked his high forehead. The light grey hair above his ears stood out slightly, drying in the warmth of the kitchen. He sat at the head of the table, and his broad, hairy chest glowed from beneath his white linen shirt.

"Well," he said, "it's your business to make it clear to them that you brought the order too late. Then we won't be to blame if there is any trouble."

114

"Jaak of Võllamäe said the same thing," August answered.

"Whom do they want there; the hired man or what?"

"No, nobody knows anything about the hired man. He's gone; he's in King Gustav's land for good." The messenger chuckled, blinking his small eyes. "They want Reku, the farmer's son himself."

"But he's an idiot." Ignas was surprised. "Even the Germans didn't want him."

"I guess the board wants to look at his teeth."

Ignas Tammela signed his own name on the draft order in place of his son's, marking clearly the date when the order had been received, and underlining the date twice so that there would be no misunderstanding.

"All right," August said, putting the signed paper in his pocket and leaving the summons with Tõmm Tammela's name on the edge of the table. "I had another thing on my mind. I wanted to ask your advice, or what you think about something. Your eyes are a little sharper than mine and your head is clearer."

"Go ahead, if you are in any trouble," Ignas urged him.

"I tell you: the trouble is great. What do you think; how long will this thing here last?"

"Not forever."

"I say that myself: not forever. That's as clear as the gospel," August agreed. "But it will probably last till spring. Or maybe longer still?"

"We don't know. But I am sure that when all is said and done, our own people will finally be ploughing our own land. The Russians aren't as strong as they seem. It's just that the others got knocked off their feet in the West, and are teetering. But the time will come when Ivan will be told a blunt word. Or slapped on his fingers for he can't understand when you speak like a human being. He can only understand a big stick."

"The reason why I'm asking is that they want to make me a people's representative here in Metsaoti—an agitator or something. I'm telling you about it so in case a new rule should come, they won't hang me on the spot; so you'll stand by me, if necessary."

"So, that's it," Ignas said. Well, this drunkard and pig-cutter was a fitting man for them. And he was fitting for his own people, too, better than somebody brought in from God knows where, or even a Russian who could not speak the language. "So that's it," he repeated. "I'll put in a word for you, if it should be necessary and if you yourself haven't done anything dirty. I think you should go ahead and accept the offer."

"I tell you, I have to look around for these part-time jobs," August confessed, "or else they'll cut me a piece from your field and tell me to start working it. Now what should I do with a piece of land in my old age? They just want me to make forced deliveries to the government."

They stretched out in front of the big threshing-floor stove, the three of them, feeling in their bones the pleasant fatigue that follows a hot steam bath. Aadu Mustkivi huddled a little farther back in the shadows, waiting for his turn. It had become a fixed custom that the men would take the first fury of the steam, followed by the women, and that old Aadu, the master bath-heater, would be the last. The men usually took the longest time, especially when they jumped into the river. And they did that almost every time, until the cold covered the river with ice. The women did not take long, Aadu knew that already. They could not stand much heat, and Ilme and Hilda had run into the river only on hot summer nights.

Tõmm stretched his strong young body. He was once again satisfied with his life. Yet he had not quite got over his bitterness against his father, who in his view had bungled their attempt to leave the country. Sometimes he blamed him for his long deliberations and slow decisions, sometimes his sister Ilme, who could not make up her mind whether to leave her husband behind in Estonia. Tõmm had never had much liking for Taavi anyway, because Taavi had always been set up for him as an example. Wasn't he, Tõmm, a man in his own right? In height and build he surpassed Taavi, and there was plenty of strength already in his arm. But no—everybody had to treat him like a boy, like a youngster who hasn't seen or heard anything. It was hard to hear your own father say it, but it was harder still to read it in his eyes.

Other things bothered him too. It bothered him that Osvald was so sure of himself when he expertly prepared secret storage places for the grain and the meat on the slopes of the pasture, or when he discussed possible hiding places with Värdi, in case the situation became critical. They listened to Tõmm's words too—he was the son of the farmer—but his words did not count for much. He had no resistance experience from 1941, and he had only been on the Eastern front for a very short time. It was enough to test the patience of any man that the hired man should consult with a crippled vagrant about how to manage the business of Tõmm's father's farm!

"Your missionary work with Mihkel of Lepiku bore no fruit," he said to Osvald. "The man ran to Saaremaa as fast as his legs would take him."

"It's a pity," Osvald answered. "The fear has robbed him of his senses."

"I should have talked to him myself," Tõmm said firmly.

"Talking didn't help. He was just about to stay, but suddenly he seemed to wake up or something. And he went. Who knows what is best for him? If he can stay alive until spring, he'll probably come back home. He hadn't turned Communist, and that is what matters most. That shows that Estonian men cannot be changed so easily. They can be broken, but they cannot be turned into tools for the new order."

"Isn't he a tool now? Fighting in the Red Army? What better kind of tool can you ask for? No, I would break all their necks. I can understand why they stayed in the army in Russia. That was their only chance to get back to Estonia. But that should be the end! But no, they just shout hurrah and go on!"

116

"Nobody is shouting hurrah. Even the Russians don't shout very loud, not to speak of our men. Fear is driving them. The kind of fear we cannot yet understand," Osvald answered, chewing on an ear of rye. "We are figuring now that we'll somehow wiggle through until spring, when the snow will be gone and the air free to breathe. But we don't figure that after spring, the next autumn will not be very far off."

"All will be settled by that time," Tõmm was convinced.

"But if it isn't, we'll have to wait for the following spring."

"And the next and the next and the next—better go directly to hell," Värdi growled angrily and gritted his teeth, as if he were chewing bitter gall, and his eyes flashed behind his glasses. He toyed with his sinewy, thin hands and turned his face toward the dark threshing floor. He remembered suddenly how on the first night of their return to Estonia he had strutted on a small table, drunk among his drunk companions, shot a bullet into the ceiling, thrown his big knife into the tabletop, danced an Indian war dance and chanted a Finnish doggerel. "Confounded Russian, soon you'll be dead! Confounded Russian, soon you'll be dead!" The foolish drunken braggart he'd been, and the others around him had been just as silly. How many of them were still alive?

"This is getting boring," Tõmm growled, leaning on dry rye shocks and stretching his feet comfortably toward the fire.

Osvald laughed and scratched his shaggy head.

"As long as it is boring, your little life will be nice and safe. When it gets more exciting, they'll be trying to get you. Don't forget that. It's just fine with me that they give us a little time to catch our breath and get things in order. That won't last for long. Don't get your hopes up."

The farmer came through the passageway from the house to the threshing floor, touched the shocks of rye to test their dryness, and handed his son a paper without saying a word.

"What's that?" Tõmm looked carefully. "A draft summons!"

Osvald burst out laughing.

"So life was getting too boring!"

"It came too late," Ignas said. "The last scheduled meeting of the draft board was day before yesterday."

"So it's mighty doubtful whether you'll manage to get into the Red Army and take part in the great patriotic war," the hired man teased.

"Do you think I'll show up? No, man! That's what you got by putting our names down on their list," he said angrily to his father.

"I said you weren't home," Ignas replied. "I said you'd left for Tallinn several days ago. Let them look for you. The order was brought too late. They can't blame you for not appearing before the draft board. This will give us time to think about it and figure out what is best."

"There's nothing to think and figure," Tõmm answered with spirit. "Your son is an outlaw now, who'll be shot when caught or sent to Siberia." He said that proudly, as if he had been waiting for it all along. It made him more of a man. It made him more important now than anybody else. At last he was somebody in his own right!

The village of Metsaoti, the district of Harukurgu, and even Kalgina had something to talk and gossip about, and even to laugh at in this mirthless time: Reku, the idiot son of the farmer of Võllamäe, had been conscripted into the Red Army. Reku's real name was Ebehart Kõhva, but, since he liked to bark and howl like a dog, he was called Reku, which was a dog's name. He was the only son of Jaak of Võllamäe, who had been a tricky horse trader at county fairs. Reku resembled his mother, who was small and freckled. From his father Reku had inherited only his large ears, his booming bass voice, and the ability to spit in two directions at once from beneath his teeth. But neither father nor mother could tell where the boy had left his wits. Sometimes they thought the trouble had been caused by an accident he had had at the age of ten, while playing with a gun he had made himself. The scar in the hair above his ear yielded to the touch. Besides the scar, no other mutilation was found, but the boy remained mentally retarded. He still played blindman's buff with little children now that he was twenty years old, and herded the animals in his father's pasture.

The dream of Reku's life was to become a general. Unfortunately he had had no luck with draft boards up until now. He had been called up several times by the Germans, but had been rejected every time. Maybe he did not have the right concept of war and army life. When men had been mobilized into the Estonian Legion by the Germans, he had been asked why he was so bent upon getting into the army that tears came to his eyes when it seemed that he wouldn't be accepted outright. He had given them a look as if they were all fools. My goodness, he wanted to kill somebody too and be made a general. "Whom do you want to kill so badly?" he'd been asked. "The Germans!" This had angered the Germans some, but finally they'd sent him away, laughing.

Now Reku wanted to join the Estonian Corps to kill Russians. He had learned from his previous disappointments that it was not good to tell right away whom he wished to kill. He'd see when the time came. His gun was ready, hidden in the woodpile. He had made it himself out of an old hunting rifle.

But it seemed that Reku just didn't have any luck. The order to appear before the board had been delivered too late, and his father and mother did not seem to take his anger at this seriously at all. When the boy refused to eat or drink that night, his father said, "Why don't you go to the county house tomorrow and ask about it yourself? If they want you, they'll accept you any time."

"Shall I take my gun along?" the boy asked eagerly.

"Stupid! Don't play around with the gun," Jaak said sternly.

Reku returned from the county house with a happy smile. The board would meet again to induct him into the Red Army.

"Don't talk nonsense," Jaak said, giving no credence to the boy's story. "The board may meet again, since quite a few orders were delivered too late, and when they met for the first time less than half the men showed up. But they won't do it just for you. They'll reject you anyway."

Jaak of Võllamäe did not have to worry. He knew beforehand that his son would be back home.

But a miracle was about to happen. The board, consisting of doctors and high officers, met again to accept just one young recruit—Reku. Ebehart, the fool of Võllamäe, was declared eminently suitable for the Red Army.

Nobody showed any interest at first in the son of the farmer of Hiie. Not even August of Roosi appeared to find out what was holding back the young draftee. August was now the representative and propagandist of the village of Metsaoti. He tried to keep up good relations with everybody: drank and caroused with Russian soldiers, and asked the farmers of Metsaoti how to act when new orders and directives arrived, so that he would not be hanged—now or in the future. Occasionally he wore a bright red necktie around his grimy collar, but usually he wore his shirt open at the neck. The tie, he declared, had been invented to torture people, and especially to make the roots of their beards sore.

Greater precautionary measures were taken at Hiie. Tõmm, Osvald and Värdi slept in the attic of the bathhouse, which lay some distance away from the farm, close to the woods and thickets. During the day-time they did their work, but kept away from open fields. They divided the night into three watches. In addition to this, Hilda slept in the storage barn, and her sleep was light like that of a bird. Ignas himself in the chamber listened to the sounds of night, getting up each time Pontus gave a sharp bark. Life on the farm had changed. Nobody knew how long the danger might last, and what trials and tribulations lay ahead during the impending winter.

The underground storage places in the pasture had been covered up. The following days were spent in fixing up the hideouts they had used in the summer of 1941. They went south at first as far as Ilmaotsa, and farther still, where the bottomless marshes of Verisoo stretched out toward the west. The bog of Verisoo had islands in it. A stranger would never have found the pathways leading to them, even in the dead of winter. The men of the whole district had used these islands as their hideouts.

Good news came from Kalgina and the county house. The numbers of the Russians decreased daily, as long columns of Russian troops moved toward Kurland, where the situation was reported to be critical. The Germans and Latvians were offering bitter resistance there. Certainly Estonian soldiers were there too. And the manpower of the Russians did not appear to be inexhaustible—the camps were not filled with new troops when the old ones left, and the filthy campsites remained rotting in the autumn rain, littered with old rags and empty tin boxes. The old farmers shook their heads in confusion when they read the words "Made in U.S.A." on shiny cans.

Although there was plenty of work to do, both Ignas and Krõõt found time to feel the emptiness that had settled over the farm. It was difficult to get used to the sudden absence of their daughter and grandson—all the more so because there was no news about their fate. At her chores Krööt would suddenly recall something, but when she tried to remember what it was, it would turn out to be something quite insignificant that she had forgotten to tell her daughter, something that now seemed extremely important. Even Ignas took time off from his busy schedule to drop by the front chamber now and then to keep the toys of his grandson in perfect order, as if the wooden horses and metal wagons required his special attention. It seemed as if old Ignas was reverting to his own childhood.

"I wonder whether they made it or where they are now," Krööt often said.

"Nobody has heard anything," Ignas would say and wrinkle his forehead. "I am quite sure that they are all three together, and that Taavi is looking around and doing all that can be done. Whatever you say about our son-in-law—and everybody has his faults—he is truly the son of old Andres in that he won't give up. If only he weren't quite so rash. When he has an idea, he goes ahead with it. But a young man gets many ideas, and he won't take the time to weigh every one of them."

"I know. There's so much to worry about now. Ignas, what about Tõmm? I can't get to sleep any more because of him," Krööt complained.

Ignas looked out of the window. His strong, straight nose and sharply formed chin were still full of energy. His large head sat firmly on his broad shoulders, and his forehead radiated almost visibly the primeval peace of forests and fields. Only his dark blue eyes had become tired and faded like the autumn sky, and his sunburned scalp showed through his silvery hair.

"What about Tõmm?" Ignas repeated. "I've given it a lot of thought myself. He isn't a child any more, whom we can coach at every single step. Even if he were, what could we tell him? Every day has its own truths, and a wise man finds them by himself. I suppose their own plan is the best one—to look around until spring. Maybe something will be settled by then. And the woods are close by."

"So you think that they are doing the right thing?"

"Yes, according to my own conscience and belief. There is no doubt or question about that in my mind. But what we hold to be right is a crime in the eyes of the Russians, and deserves the death penalty many times over. But we are Estonians. We cannot help but act in the way that our consciences prompt us."

The days were getting shorter and shorter. The night finally lifted its shadows by noon, only to begin soon a slow crawl back into the open from the woods. The rain in daytime and the hoarfrost at night had robbed the trees of their last ragged leaves, and the groves and woods were naked and bare. One of the most hopeless autumns that the old people could remember had arrived.

The people of Hiie and of the whole village of Metsaoti were busy

120

threshing. Tõmm and Osvald did most of the work, for Värdi was not built strongly enough to handle a flail, and his leg did not give him enough support yet, either. Ignas himself did the ploughing, being the only man who was not afraid of daylight. It was Värdi's job to take the rye shocks down from the drying racks, spread them out in orderly rows, and later to sweep away the straw. The grain, mixed with chaff, was then gathered by all three of them into sacks, barrels, bins or simply heaps in the corners of the threshing floor, to wait for winnowing weather. In the morning dusk Ignas himself lent a hand, and then the four-part harmony of the flails from the big old threshing floor of Hiie was audible all over the village.

Keeping watch at the farm had been entrusted to Hilda, while the men were at work. Of course, Ignas kept his eyes open in the field, and Krõõt never crossed the courtyard without casting a glance at the road to Haru-kurgu, when her chores took her from the kitchen to the stables. Without being aware of it, the deaf-mute Aadu and the dog Pontus enthusiastic-ally took part in the watch. They had both acquired the habit of stand-ing for hours under the chestnut trees at the gate and looking down the road in eager expectation. This had started the morning after Ilme had left with her little son. Everybody understood that Pontus would be looking for his young master, but that Aadu missed them so much came as a surprise to the farm folks.

Hilda was entrusted with the real watch, however, and there was nobody more conscientious about it. She could not sleep at night, waking up when the least twig moved near the farm. Three times she had sought out the old couple in the back chamber at night, shuddering from cold and fear. She had heard muffled steps and Russian talk. She insisted that it was real, but the others were inclined to believe that her imagination made her hear things. Ignas had come out, looked around in the dark courtyard, but had not found anything suspicious. Krõõt wanted the girl to quit sleeping in the storage house—the place was un-heated, she might get sick, and she was too scared anyway to sleep out alone. But Hilda argued back with tears in her eyes. She wanted to stay at her post. She took a big knife in a leather scabbard to bed with her and stayed. Whether she slept any better with the knife, nobody knew, but not even Krõõt's experienced eyes could detect any trace of fatigue on her face in daytime. She was pale and wistful anyway, but her young blue eyes were sharp and wide awake.

Hilda got along well with the three outlaws, and they accepted her almost as a companion, as one who shared their fate. The girl seemed to find it easiest to talk to Osvald. Sometimes she even talked to him about her lovely childhood home. She seemed to be just a little afraid of Värdi, and he never approached her with unsolicited conversation. They might have lived in the same room for months without exchang-ing a word. But their fates had something in common; that was clear to both of them, and it created a silent bond between them. Hilda had the hardest time with Tõmm. Everybody realized that the girl had a great, warm regard for the young man. When she served the food, the best morsels happened to land on the plate of the boy, the cream from the milk pitcher found its way into his cup, and warm water was waiting for him every morning. Tõmm teased the girl at first, but when her childish attachment became obvious to everyone, he did not care for it any more. He became sharp and thorny toward Hilda—such a scrawny, thin, slip of a girl. He, Tõmm, was not a shepherd boy, who could be won over by offerings of food. He would look for girls who had something better to offer!

"Don't poke your nose where you have no business," he said once, roughly, startling the girl to tears. "Take a look at yourself—you cry-baby!"

Hilda scanned herself secretly in a mirror. She did not think she looked so bad. And she was quite sure she was not a child any more. It was not her fault that tears came to her so quickly, and that she did not have a cheerful laugh or merry words to respond to Tõmm's teasing, when he happened to be in a gay mood. But Hilda was the last one to whom Tõmm showed a gay face. This did not diminish the attention she lavished on him—on the contrary; her care often turned into slavish service.

No wonder, then, that Hilda's watchful eyes spotted a strange man enter their pasture from the woods one afternoon. Seeing him, she almost turned on her heels and ran to the threshing floor. But there was something familiar about the approaching figure and so she remained where she was.

"Good evening, young lady," the stranger said. He raised his peaked cap politely. "Don't you recognize me any more?"

Hilda recognized him all right. The newcomer was Mart of Liiskaku, the man who had come out of the woods with Taavi some time ago.

"Do you know anything about Mr. Raudoja?" the girl asked excitedly.

"No. We separated soon after we left here. He went to Tallinn. Haven't you had any news from him?"

"No, only—I thought you might know something. No, we haven't had a word. His wife and son went after him to Tallinn."

"So, so," Mart nodded, letting his hesitant glance glide over the yard. "Are any of the men still here or are they all gone? Värdi with his crippled leg should still be somewhere."

"Yes, he is."

Hilda wavered for a moment. Should she trust Mart? She did not know him personally and had not heard about his political views. But that he had come out of the woods with Taavi dispelled her suspicions. She took the visitor to the threshing floor.

"Look there, by God," Osvald shouted merrily, reaching over the rye to shake the guest's hand. On the first and only night he had met Mart, the man had given him the impression of being a fighter who does his work and keeps his mouth shut. And that was enough for Osvald.

Värdi was equally glad to see the visitor. He wrinkled his nose, moving his glasses, and said just one word in Finnish: *"Perkele!"*

122

Tõmm did not know Mart, but soon heard his story and learned that he was hiding to escape from being drafted into the Red Army.

"I came to see how things stood over here."

"You see, we're all at work; no time to think about anything else," Osvald answered, stroking his calloused hand over the smooth shiny handle of the flail.

"Same at our place."

Tõmm took the guest inside. They stretched out in front of the fire, lit their pipes, and their conversation drifted to questions of common concern. Old Aadu went to sweep up the straw and separate it from the grain. The work day was over for the moment.

"I came to establish contact," Mart said. "There are several men besides me under our roof. Nothing to complain about right now; nobody has bothered us. For the Russians everybody is equally suspect, but it seems they haven't got their feet in these backlands well enough yet to start rounding up people. In Tallinn they are reported to be showing their teeth already—making arrests and throwing people into jails."

"So those pigs are burrowing already?" Osvald hissed.

"They are still weakly organized and staffed. And they have no clear picture how people feel and think. That's why they raise a big shout, saying that all is different now. They think they have enough time to put on their act," Mart said.

"We have a very good man in our group," he went on. "He's a captain, a genuine dyed-in-the-wool captain of the Estonian army."

"Then we can muster a regiment," Osvald said, rejoicing.

"He wants to keep quiet. The longer we can keep quiet, the shorter will be the time of the clash. He sent me to find out about the old hiding places. We should store up some food there. It will be easier now than with snow. Also, if there's a roundup here, please send us a warning. We'll do the same for you. I'm going over to Ilmaotsa from here. Men are supposed to be in hiding there too. And back around Kaku, a major is reported to have a whole battalion intact. He's let off the men on an indefinite furlough, but if necessary they'll get together in a matter of hours. It's a well-armed, regular unit that can strike hard."

"I like that!" Tõmm shouted.

They discussed at some length the condition of the hiding places and the indispensable supplies. They agreed also to keep in touch and to warn each other of roundups.

"And besides, there are suspicious characters wandering around the woods. Many of them are deserters from the Red Army, but some men from Vlassov's group have been seen," Mart said in his drawling, monotonous voice.

"What should we do with them?" Osvald asked.

"Shoot them—what else?" Tõmm said abruptly.

"We are partly in the same boat. . . ."

"They rob people on the highways and break into storage rooms," Mart continued. "In some places they have done all kinds of mischief and are a real plague. How can a farmer tell the difference, if they are dressed in Russian uniforms, come in and take what they please? And you don't dare raise your voice. We have to watch out for them, too, especially now when troops are leaving the district every day."

The same problem presented itself to the farmers of Metsaoti. Storage barns had been broken into one night at Harukurgu, and at Torisuu two hogs had been slaughtered and stolen the following night. This news made the sleep of the farmers uneasy. A week later Metsaoti got fresh news about the activities of the band. At Pudiküla a farmer had been shot at when he went to investigate suspicious noises in his barn. The bullets had missed him, but the dog who had chased the fleeing figures had been shot dead. A new, immediate danger had arisen in addition to the daily worries and cares.

Ignas of Hiie sent Hilda to carry word to the farmers of Metsaoti. They were invited to come Sunday night to confer at his farm. They all promised to attend except Juhan of Matsu, his next door neighbour, who said he did not have time. Ignas had counted on that. Matsu could not stand any new enterprise being initiated from Hiie, and opposed it blindly without any apparent reason. Juhan could never forget that the district had elected Ignas Tammela, when they both had been candidates for the post of district elder. Wasn't he a better man than the farmer of Hiie? He had more money in the bank, his horses outran those of Hiie any time on the road, and his own chest was so round with pride that it took effort to spit over it. Now neither of them had a red cent in the bank, and their style of living was badly cramped, but that did not make Juhan bend his head in deference, especially not in deference to his neighbour. They had not exchanged a word since last spring, and they passed one other as if he didn't exist. Yes, Ignas of Hiie had expected that Matsu would not come.

But an hour later the twin daughters of Juhan went from farm to farm, inviting all the farmers to come Sunday night and try the beer their father had brewed to celebrate the completion of their threshing.

Ignas clenched his jaws in anger. It was clear the village would be split in two factions. Linda of Piskujõe, who ran her own farm, had been invited to both places, but was sure to come to Hiie. So was Anton of Lepiku. But Jaak of Võllamäe and Paavel of Kadapiku were sure to turn in at Matsu. After a long struggle with himself Ignas decided to give in this time. All kinds of problems could be discussed over a mug of beer, and if Juhan was offering his hand in friendship, he'd take it. This was no time for bickering. They had to stick together. His wife agreed.

Ignas and Anton of Lepiku went together to Matsu. The other three farmers of Metsaoti were already seated at the table, with a big metal beer jug in front of them. The dark room was grey with smoke. The wide-bellied glass table lamp had been lifted on top of a dresser. Half of the glass shade was blackened from the irregular flame. Juhan himself was sitting at the head of the table, stocky and flushed, stroking his short brown beard with his palm. He had closed his eyes with deliberate disinterest when the new guests had entered, indicating by this that the newcomers were nothing special. With the silver that shone in his black eyebrows and hair, his big bluish nose, red cheeks and brown beard, he presented a variegated picture, as if the Maker had not quite made up his mind what paint to use in creating this man.

"You, settler of Kadapiku,"—he opened his eyes and addressed a square, short man sitting next to him—"you tell the man who lives on the other side of my gate that he should sit at the other end of the table, facing me. And you, farmer of Lepiku, you come here to my right hand, where you belong."

He closed his eyes again, waiting for his guests to sit down.

Paavel of Kadapiku, whom Juhan called "settler" because his farm was small, repeated the words of the Matsu farmer to Ignas. Everybody knew that when the neighbours were feuding, they did not hear each other's voice. The situation was still amusing to Paavel, and he did not mind acting as a sounding board for the two. He was the youngest of the farmers, although he carried the burden of almost forty years on his back. But compared to the hard countenances of the others, his pale, soft face seemed quite boyish under his light, pomaded hair.

Ignas sat down with an ironical grin.

"Jaak of Võllamäe, will you tell the man who lives behind my woodpile that I thank him and am ready to try his brew."

They drank each other's beer; otherwise the insult would have been too serious. Juhan himself pushed the beer pitcher toward the neighbour.

"The brew is good, as it always is at Matsu," Jaak of Võllamäe said, in his roaring bass voice, and wiped his sleeve. "I have respect for that kind of brew, hard and strong. It leaves a scab where a drop falls. Haven't you, you devil in Juhan's skin, soaked onions in it again? That will put my stomach over my heart!"

"That shouldn't make any difference to you. You've got used to all kinds of slush, going from fair to fair," Juhan replied. "Don't ask what I have put in. If your stomach can't hold it, don't drink. My beer was not made to water the ditches."

"Don't brag now, Matsu! You can soak the devil himself, horns and hooves and all, in your beer barrel. That won't do a thing to my kidneys," Jaak boasted. His wrinkled, tanned, sunken face was covered with long, black stubble. His eyes jumped like agile fleas from the beer jug to the mouths of the men. He drank slowly, with long draughts, enjoying the brew, placed the jug on the corner of the table, told a funny story, and drank again before he let the jug continue its circle.

Today their talk did not reach the boisterous heights it had done before the war. They had come together then to celebrate the end of the harvest season. Conversation was steady at the two ends of the table, between Juhan of Matsu and Paavel of Kadapiku, on the one hand, and Ignas of Hiie and Anton of Lepiku on the other. Jaak of Võllamäe followed the beer jug from one end of the table to the other. When they

125

were sitting like that, they always had to leave one side of the table free for him, so that he could move around and accompany his talk with broad movements of his arms. Jaak became a different person at a beer table. From a somewhat stooped, close-mouthed farmer, who always kept his hands in his pockets, he changed into a talkative, freely gesticulating back-slapper. He boasted about his horse trading and his experiences at fairs, revealed the tricks of gypsies, and sometimes reminisced about the times when he and Ignas had fought side by side in the War of Independence.

"I heard, Võllamäe, that your boy has gone to war," Juhan of Matsu said, with a certain amount of mockery in his voice.

"Yes, to war. Maybe a loud bang will knock his wits back into his head," Jaak said brusquely. He did not like that kind of talk. He had been taunted enough because of his retarded son.

Juhan laughed and closed his eyes, as if this question was not worth wasting words over. This irritated Jaak more than anything else.

"You with your daughters, you have it easy. You send them to bed with the chickens and have peace in the house. What do you know about the war or anything? You haven't been there yourself, and have nobody to send," Jaak growled angrily.

"Don't squeak, man from Võllamäe," Juhan answered proudly. "Yes, I send my womenfolk to roost with the chickens, but in the morning they walk behind the plough, if necessary. I don't have anybody to send to war, but it's gospel clear that even the war can't make a ploughman out of a swineherd."

"Listen, Ignas of Hiie, the rooster of Matsu is beginning to crow again among his flock of hens." Jaak turned to the other end of the table before the pitcher had completed its round. "The old rooster has no spurs left but he can crow louder than anybody else!"

Juhan leaned back in his chair, spreading out proudly his round belly in his grey knitted pullover. He closed his eyes again and said, turning to Paavel of Kadapiku: "You tell that horse peddler to go climb a tree!" He could not think of anything brighter to say at the moment.

"Ah, calm down now," old Anton mumbled, disgusted. "Hiie and I came here to take counsel but—what's the use?—you men should be old and sensible enough. . . ."

He seemed worried and melancholy, his moustache drooped and his grey head was bent down.

"We can take counsel all right. Nobody has anything against that," Juhan said. He respected Anton's grey hair and old age. "But first I want to say to that horse trader of Võllamäe what is on my mind. Tell him, settler of Kadapiku, that he should pass the word on to his neighbour, that cotter of Roosi—that August. Let this witless man appear before my countenance! Hang it—I'll drench that bundle of rags with beer and ask who put him in charge of the village of Metsaoti. And now ask the man behind my fence what he thinks about it. The power in the land may be in the hands of ragamuffins, but the village of Metsaoti will not tolerate every self-appointed rapscallion at its head! This is gospel clear, and something has to be done about it."

"You, Paavel, go ahead and ask the man who lives behind my wood-pile if he himself wants to become the "propagandist" and "representative" of our village, as they now call August of Roosi," Ignas asked in turn.

"Tell him to jump in the lake," Juhan answered.

"Tell him that Matsu should know that power is now in the hands of this kind of people. August will at least leave some seed grain in the bins of Matsu, whereas somebody else might make a clean sweep. August won't cut his farm and courtyard into separate small plots, as somebody else might do."

"Tell him that Hiie is going out of his mind, like everybody else! Isn't there a shred of justice left in this world?" Juhan puffed angrily, and drops of sweat appeared on his brow. "What do you think, Lepiku? Your son is in Russia or is already marching toward Berlin. You should have a clear notion. Haven't the English really stretched out a measuring stick and told them: Stop; thus far and no more! Let them do at Kalgina what they please; I don't care, but let them not give the big end of the stick here at Metsaoti into the hands of a punk like August of Roosi. Hang it—drink, men. Paavel, tell Hiie and Võllamäe to drink too."

"You speak about the real problem," Anton of Lepiku suggested to Ignas quietly. "Why should we otherwise waste our time here?"

Ignas knew beforehand that Juhan of Matsu would object, but nevertheless he straightened himself and said, "Men, we are all now here together and that has not happened often in recent times. Tell that, Paavel, to the man of Matsu, too. We should make some kind of decision here about what to do to make our lives more secure. There are all kinds of men now in the woods, some decent, others little better than highwaymen, who break into barns and storage rooms. Everybody knows what has happened at Harukurgu and Pudiküla."

"You, settler of Kadapiku, tell the man from the other side of my gate that I and my family have no time to start watching the woods," Juhan said, with his eyes shut. "For me, every man who roams around the woods is a vagabond and a loafer. Those people who keep their eyes on the thickets have somebody there themselves."

Ignas disregarded his neighbour's taunts and went on. "And tell the man behind my woodpile, Paavel, that several forest villages have instituted regular watches. At least there's a dog on every farm, and they have set up bells and wooden gongs. I think we should do the same."

"Yes, we should," Paavel of Kadapiku agreed. "My heart is heavy right now. My wife is home alone with her bunch of children."

"The noise would scare the thieves away. And if there should be a roundup or something—one never knows what might happen—it would be good if somebody would blow a horn in warning," Anton figured. "Võllamäe could let us know. He's the first one in line."

"I wouldn't mind," Jaak agreed. "I'd blow the horn from my hill down toward Hiie like Joshua did at Jericho."

"I won't have any part in such childish antics," Juhan of Matsu announced. "You, settler of Kadapiku, tell the man from behind my gate that those who didn't run to Pärnu, tails high up in the air, those men won't start playing the fool with a gong. Hang it all! Drink your beer and speak something that makes more sense. Juhan of Matsu is no shepherd boy."

"You, Paavel, tell Matsu that we won't keep watch over his sleep, either!" Ignas was annoyed. "If the man does not have enough sense, then let him go hang for all I care. If he thinks that he is in the middle of the village, that his storage rooms are protected—let him think that. But roundups don't start from the woods. They come from the direction of Võllamäe, and Matsu is next in line. Or does he think that he'll be left in peace forever? He doesn't have a son, and nobody wants his daughters. We don't know and can't tell, but at least we should keep our eyes open."

But Juhan of Matsu had closed his eyelids completely. Leaning back in the chair, with his hands in his pockets and his brown beard toward the ceiling, he was soon snoring regularly and peacefully.

"We'll have trouble with Matsu," Anton of Lepiku said on the way home. He followed Ignas to the Hiie courtyard, from which Ignas concluded that something was eating at the heart of his neighbour. Even his step was heavy on the grassy path, which was covered with hoarfrost.

"You can't expect him to behave reasonably," Ignas agreed. "He won't listen to reason. Whatever comes to his head, he sticks to, even if the world should come to an end."

"He has it easy, with no worries. Nobody will come to recruit his daughters into the Red Army and he hasn't done anything that would cast a shadow on him now. Even if they should take half of his fields, he'd get by."

"Who knows from where that shadow may fall nowadays?" Ignas said. "You don't even know it yourself, until. . . ."

"That's so right," Anton stammered.

"Come inside; let's talk."

"No, I won't any more today. It's Mihkel again. . . ."

"What about the boy?"

"He ran back home," Anton answered heavily.

"He's home now?"

"Yes, where else could I have put him?"

"How's his health?"

"It isn't any worse," the worried father answered. "If they leave him in peace and don't shoot him, he may last until early spring. But don't. . . . Let's leave it between us two."

"Whom should I. . . ." Ignas muttered. "So Mihkel came back, without getting to the front."

XI

Marta of Roosi had returned to Kalgina. Her absence had not been noticed much in Metsaoti—she hardly ever came down to the village. August himself came much more often, for all kinds of orders came now from the county house, demanding grain and horses for transport, and workmen for getting logs and firewood out of the forests, long before the winter had made the roads passable for sleds. Each farm was assigned a high quota of produce to deliver to the state, and taxes had to be paid. But even August could not tell how they might get hold of any Russian money to pay the taxes, for when the army camps were liquidated even that meagre flow of rubles ceased which had come from soldiers, who had foraged around for vodka and food and occasionally paid for what they took.

Linda of Piskujõe heard from August of Roosi that Marta had met Taavi in Tallinn. This news flashed like a restless flame through the head of Taavi's mother. Her thoughts had been constantly with her son but now she found a place to focus them. After August had left, she moved around as in a dream, carrying on her usual activities by sheer force of habit. In her mind she was already talking to her son.

The same afternoon Linda wrapped herself in a big shawl and hurried over the fields of Võllamäe toward Roosi. She wanted to talk to Marta. Was it really true that her son had not even sent greetings to his own mother? Marta had been back from Tallinn for quite a while but the news had taken so long to get to Piskujõe!

Marta was home alone. She had just arrived from the county house and her face was strangely drawn and tired. Seeing Linda, she did not even show her usual forced smile. A petulant, malicious expression hovered around her mouth. Although a cheerful fire was crackling in the hearth, the room felt cold and humid, as if it had been unheated for a long time, and the house was filled with a musty smell.

"Go on eating, child. Don't let me disturb you," Linda said.

"I've already finished. I'm just drinking coffee," Marta answered, absent-mindedly lifting dishes from the table.

"You know, of course, that I came because of Taavi," Linda began.

"What about him?" Marta turned round abruptly.

Linda arranged the shawl on her shoulders. She had never seen Marta act like this. August had said she'd got into trouble in the county house for having been away so long without leave. The present order did not treat gently those who were within its grasp.

"Go ahead and drink your coffee," she urged Marta, when she saw that the young woman began to brush the glass shade of the table lamp in the darkening room. "Don't bother about the light; kerosene is hard to get anyway. I'll just sit down for a moment in front of the fire and be off again. Don't let my coming stop you in what you were doing. You've worked all day. I just wanted to ask you about . . . Taavi and . . . the little boy. What has become of them?"

"Your son is a damn fool," Marta said brusquely and angrily.

129

"That I wouldn't know, but everybody is sometimes. . . ."

"He's been a fool all along!"

"Who knows? You may think what you like. Is he still in Tallinn?"

"Yes, he's in Tallinn and it seems he's planning to stay there. He refused to go across the sea when I was trying to find a chance to go."

"Perhaps because of his wife and son?" Linda hesitated. "Did he have news of them?"

"Of course he did," Marta said harshly. "By that time they were already in Finland."

"So they were already in Finland?" Taavi's mother repeated. Now she could not understand anything any more. She surmised that something had taken place between Marta and her son, but couldn't guess what it was.

"What about Ilme and Lembit? How come they got to Finland and Taavi remained behind?"

Marta explained briefly and impatiently. She brushed the sooty lampshade with the same agitated restlessness, until the glass cracked and broke.

"Come out into the light! You can't see there in the dark!"

But Marta did not want to come out into the light of the fire.

"The Russians had beaten him. I found him in my bed. No, the wounds were not too severe but they had kicked him in the face with their heels. And that tears you up. . . ."

Linda sat on a stool in front of the hearth, hunched and small. A low moan escaped her. So her son had been through hard days, terribly hard, but at least he was alive and he wasn't sick or seriously wounded. If heaven would protect him, then. . . . His mother could not believe that he would not try to follow his wife and son. What did Marta say—that he had given up a chance to go? No, Linda of Piskujõe could not believe that. Something had to be at the bottom of it that she could not understand, and that Marta could not know either, if she talked that way. Taavi would follow his family through fire and water, if there were a chance. His mother had no doubts about that. Ilme was in that condition, too. Taavi would surely know about it by now. And Taavi wasn't the kind of man who would send his wife out into the wide, strange world, without care or help. He could be reckless and harsh at times but under that hard shell was a soul, soft like that of a child. No, something was there she could not understand but it must have some connection with Marta's embittered impatience.

"He slept in my bed. I nursed him like a child."

Marta should not have spoken like that; especially not in that kind of a voice. It seemed as if Marta had forgotten the presence of the old woman, had forgotten that Taavi was a married man and the father of a family. Hearing the caress in Marta's voice it suddenly became clear to Linda why Marta was so grim and nervous.

The light from the hearth fell on Marta's silk-stockinged knees and on her absent-mindedly fidgeting fingers, which tugged at the seam of her

130

skirt. Linda looked at those white fingernails that stretched out from the darkness and suddenly she was afraid of something inexplicable and terrible. She felt as if she ought to flee through the dark autumn night—run and shout warnings.

"Keep your seat. What's the big hurry?" Marta said.

"No, what else should I wait for? I have heard everything," Taavi's mother mumbled. "You don't know where I could find him, if I should go to Tallinn?"

"Whom? Oh yes, Taavi, naturally," Marta seemed to wake up and her voice suddenly became grim. "I don't know. I tried to find him myself before I left town. Nobody knows. Nobody has seen him."

"Good heavens!" Linda jumped up. "You didn't say that before!"

"I told you I didn't know anything about him!" Marta almost screamed. "I don't know anything about him and I don't want to—whether he's in prison or at the bottom of the sea!"

"So that. . . ," Linda stammered, terrified. They faced each other in the glow of the fire and the old woman saw that Marta's head and shoulders were trembling.

"So that—whatever has happened to him, I don't know anything and I'm not interested, either," Marta said in a low voice and turned away into the darkness.

The anguish made the nights of Taavi's mother completely sleepless and her visits to the place where her husband had died became more frequent and longer. In the other farms the situation was not much better. Where the farmers had lost their sons in the war, or where they knew or hoped that their sons were still among the living, the prayers of worried mothers became longer and more frequent and the fathers walked around restlessly, trying to find a way out of the roadless wilderness of their thoughts. They threw themselves into work but stopped often as if awakening from a nightmare, with sweat on their brows and soreness in their gnarled hands, asking themselves the always unanswered question—why?

When the troops left the camps, the people breathed more easily. But new units rolled in on muddy transport trucks. When they in turn departed, leaving the land filthy and stinking under the pine groves and around the highways, news came that an airfield was being built near Suurküla village in Kalgina. Great numbers of military planes flew directly over Harukurgu, flashing their five-pointed red stars, and disturbed even the peace of the impenetrable forests of Metsaoti with their menacing rumble. Half of the population of Suurküla was driven from their inherited land God knows where, and the topsoil was levelled or carted away completely, baring the naked, flat limestone rocks. Farm buildings were moved to the edge of the pine forest, where they became temporary headquarters for the army and shelter for German prisoners-of-war and ragged forced labourers. New walls rose quickly close by,

131

built of brick and wood. They were immediately painted a protective khaki colour, surrounded by a maze of barbed-wire fences, and were patrolled incessantly.

So the people could not breathe more easily after all. Orders and directives came from Kalgina to Metsaoti and farmers had to harness their horses and travel scores of kilometres to haul building materials or even prisoners who were about to collapse from starvation. A young officer of the Red Army had enthusiastically explained to Ignas of Hiie their great fortification plans. In a few years the whole coastline, together with the islands, would form a single modern fortress, reaching far back inland.

It amazed Ignas to see the formerly arrogant and proud German soldiers humbly carrying stones or pushing wheelbarrows, feet wrapped in rags. He saw them in barbed-wire enclosures they had built themselves; he saw them being beaten with a greater brutality than they themselves had displayed when they had pistol-whipped collapsing Russians. Only their faces were not as flat and uniformly stolid as those of the unfortunates of yesterday, although hunger and despair were already stamping them with their standardizing mark, which bore a likeness to a death mask.

Back from the forced work, Ignas reported to the men what he had seen and heard. The men sat on sheaves of rye in front of the big threshing-floor stove and listened. Mihkel of Lepiku was among them. He had come on several nights to watch them work, dressed in civilian clothes, the collar of his heavy pullover up to his chin. He did not have much to say. He seemed to be still fighting a rearguard battle with himself after the decisive step he had just taken. Sometimes he looked as if he would put on his Red Army uniform right away and go back the way he came. He did not dare take a step outside in daytime, and nobody in Metsaoti except his parents and the people of Hiie knew about his being home. He had forbidden any mention of it, his face stiff with fear, as if he really expected somebody to carry the word from house to house: come and take a look; the two-headed monster of Lepiku is back from Russia and on display! No, it was clear to everybody without having to be told—the less people knew about it, the better for all concerned. The farmer of Matsu and his family were a churlish bunch, and Sessi of Kadapiku was a gossip. As for Võllamäe, their Reku had just been conscripted into the Red Army and nobody could tell what kind of thoughts that might give to his father and mother, especially since Jaak often hustled to Harukurgu to taste the beer of the neighbouring village. And Roosi—that was the real nest of trouble where anything might be hatched at any moment.

They were eating apples. Aadu had just picked them from the apple trees which had survived the cold of the previous severe winters. These were apples that had been growing too high or were so small that it did not pay to harvest them. Every fall the farmer of Hiie left a certain amount of apples on the trees for the deaf-mute. They remained out on the trees until the first night frosts came. Then the old man shook them down. Part of them he took up to the hayloft, where they sometimes rotted unnoticed; part of them he ate right away; and some he gave to everybody as a special after-supper treat, radiating happiness like a child.

Since Mihkel was always gloomy and afraid that others distrusted him, the men had decided among themselves that they would not keep anything secret from their new companion. This attitude might easily have fatal consequences, said Tõmm, but Ignas and Osvald thought there was no other way. Mihkel had to be treated carefully, as if he had a nervous ailment in addition to his other troubles. But he himself laughed disdainfully, as if the others were stupid children. They shouldn't bother about him. He knew well that when the trees burst into leaf in the spring his numbered days would be over, if he wasn't caught in a round-up before that deadline. Why should they feed him warm milk and honey, or why tell him about their hiding places in Raisanõmme, Päraluha, or the bogs of Verisoo? He wouldn't need them. He knew well enough that he had come home to die and everybody else knew it too. Why oil and polish his rifle? He wanted to forget the army, the dugouts, and the senseless plodding from battle to battle. He had carried his uniform and his rifle into the woods—let them rot there and rust; he wouldn't have anything to do with them. He had no desire to comprehend the senseless bantering of the companions of his youth, for he himself was already older than his aged father.

"We can't expect the load to get any lighter," Osvald said, when Ignas had reported the feverish building activities that were going on in Suurküla on the airfield, and farther away where great army barracks were springing up.

"It's all so far away," Tõmm consoled him.

"An hour or two by car," Osvald mumbled. "And if they have forces there to spare, they'll start combing the thickets."

"I didn't see many soldiers there," Ignas continued. "Hardly enough to guard the building sites and patrol the roads. And we can still talk here among ourselves without fear. But I'm sure they'll soon plant their spies among our own people."

"How do you know they don't have them already?" his son asked.

"I don't think there could be very many. Yes, it's possible that somebody could point his finger at somebody else from envy or jealousy, but the past has taught its lessons. Who knows what kind of a government we'll have tomorrow?—and then the spies and traitors will find themselves dangerously close to the gallows."

During the conversation it seemed to Mihkel that half-concealed glances were directed at him. It cut deep into his heart and made him shiver as if he had a fever. They must think him the most likely candidate for a spy. Good Lord. He, Mihkel Tümatõnu, whom they had treated as a sharer of their fate, to whom they had shown their secret hiding places and whom they had included in their survival plans for the winter—he was still a marked man in their eyes! Sure, there was his past. More than three years in the power of the Communists. They thought that something must have rubbed off on him. It was a pity these men hadn't been there themselves; they would have experienced some of the tribulations he had been through.

The men were very late getting home that night. No wonder—they had started out a little before dusk and it was quite a distance to Päraluha. Then Värdi's leg had begun to hurt and they could not move fast. It was only the weather, the hunchback insisted, and refused to let his companions lighten his load. They were taking supplies to their hiding places. It was high time already, for Christmas was getting close, and winter would start soon according to the calendar, although there was no trace of snow yet on the ground. The days were sombre and rainy, the ground froze only very seldom, and no morning had yet been cold enough to make the earth really ring underfoot.

On the way back Tõmm wanted to get his rifle from its hiding place. He had a new German rifle and he was afraid that the rain might damage it.

"We have plenty of weapons closer to home," Osvald argued. "I'm tired of turning around; my feet are wet and soaked clear through. All I want is to get my stomach full of food and stretch out in the attic of the bathhouse."

But Tõmm insisted.

"I cannot let my good gun go to waste. And it won't take long."

"All right, let's train ourselves for this kind of dog's life. No telling how soon we'll need the experience," Osvald mumbled. "I'll take my gun too and give it some fresh grease at home. We'll have to wrap them in tarpaulin and keep them in reserve in case the real fun starts."

Värdi also took his automatic. They turned back by way of a narrow forest path covered with puddles, crossed the pastures of Metsaoti and took the direct road to the village by way of Võllamäe.

The village was quiet. The wind drove the rustling rain. Pontus of Hiie, the only village dog awake, was growling somewhere at the far end of the pasture. The others must have crawled into warm woodsheds or sought shelter in the houses.

"The people of Matsu are turning over in their beds." Tõmm laughed.

"They're not that lazy. They'll soon be getting ready for the morning," Osvald answered. "Listen, old Juhan is away on a transport trip! There's no better time to pay a visit to the girls! Why didn't I think of it before? You did us a good turn taking us back into the woods, Tõmm. Now is the time!"

"All right, let's go and see what kind of welcome Lonni and Ella will give us. I'll take Lonni; she is bigger-boned. Värdi will get the old woman, if she should come across us." The hired man of Hiie grinned.

"Shut up," Värdi said sharply. "You should be grown men. Why don't you act your age?"

"A boy wouldn't dare think of such an excursion," Osvald answered. "It's only a joke. The girls won't mind. I've been thinking about it for some time, but old Juhan, bless him, is liable to knock your kidneys loose with his big stick."

They stopped on the road behind the storage barn of Matsu. The rain rustled on the straw roof, and the wind moved the barren branches of the thick lilac bushes. Osvald and Tõmm climbed over a small gate in front of the storage barn, where the wet pathway was covered with slippery moss.

"Keep a good watch," the hired man muttered to Värdi, who stayed on the road, not knowing what to do. Osvald knocked quietly against the wall of the storage barn.

Värdi was about to turn down toward the Hiie yard, when he suddenly stopped. A suspicious noise came from somewhere and reached his ears. He stood and listened intently. Damn that Osvald with his knocking—and now they were both giggling behind the house. Just like children! Then Värdi heard the noise again. It was a muffled groan or scream which sounded weak and seemed to be coming from a distance.

He hurried to join the others. "Will you shut up?" he hissed.

"Don't rush like that," Osvald whispered. "The little birds must be in the house behind their mother's back."

Värdi poked his fist angrily into Osvald's ribs. Tõmm had heard something suspicious, too and moved toward the house. When they got closer they all heard the noise coming from the living quarters. It was a woman's groan. When they passed the stairs they saw the door half open. Tõmm wanted to rush in through the front door, but Värdi held him back, grabbing his sleeve. They tiptoed to the window and pressed their ears against the glass. The next moment their hands moved to their guns as if on command. Through the glass they heard clearly Russian words and laughter, in addition to the high-pitched groaning they had heard before.

They did not say a word. Grabbing their rifles, they hurried toward the door. Tõmm's bayonet cracked, when he slipped it on the rifle. That fool, Osvald thought. He might run his own companions through with that weapon.

They had no time to take in the scene which faced them in the room. Later they could not understand how everything had taken place so quickly—like a well-rehearsed manoeuvre. Tõmm in his youth and inexperience was least aware of what was happening. Before his eyes could make out anything in the dim light of the kerosene lamp, he heard Värdi at his side let go with a burst from his automatic, and then he saw Osvald throw himself at a trouserless man, whose eyes were bulging with fright. And then a Russian was right next to him, tugging at a Browning on his hip. His glance was frightened and helpless, but Tõmm realized all of a sudden that this man would kill him the next moment. The young man pulled the trigger of his gun. He did not know what force pushed him forward at the same instant. His bayonet pierced his opponent. The feet of the Russian slipped against the wall, and he fell groaning in Tõmm's direction.

"Damn it, don't fall all over me," Tõmm hissed, staring at the face which was stiffening into a mask quite close to his own.

135

Fearing that this face would fall directly at him, the young man stepped back and jerked out his rifle. The soldier crashed to the floor, face downwards, arms spread out. Tõmm saw how the twitching fingers of one hand convulsively clutched a corner of the carpet, and then were suddenly still and motionless. Then he saw that dark blood was oozing from the man's sleeve.

When Tõmm could take his eyes off the clenched fingers, everything was over. He shook himself. His back was wet with perspiration and he was panting, as if he had been running for several miles. He thanked God that there had been only four Russians and that they were all lying on the floor. Anybody could now have knocked him down with the back of his hand.

Osvald's opponent was lying on his back, one leg over a chair, the way he had fallen. The hired man had by now run outside; he was probably worried that there might be more Russians around. The third Russian was hunched in the foot end of the bed, in dirty underwear, his black hair dishevelled, with a big splotch of blood on his back. Lonni of Matsu was staring at him from the other end of the bed. Her wide-open eyes had an insane look, her nightdress had been torn to shreds. Värdi was still clobbering the fourth Russian on the floor, cursing horribly. Tõmm stood and gaped at his hunchbacked companion with greater amazement than he had felt staring at the man he had just killed. Värdi's automatic was lying on the floor, and the man himself was kneeling on the chest of the helplessly struggling enemy and holding him by the throat with his hands. He pounded the head of his opponent against the floor and hissed his curses. His voice was sometimes shrill and triumphant, sometimes a low, angry growl, and only a few words were intelligible now and then.

"You damned pig! You damned toad, you devil, you damned swine! Pray now to Stalin!" Värdi screamed savagely. "Ah-ah, stare now! Stare now in the face of your killer! Stare, you damned filthy son of a bitch!"

Although his enemy did not move any more, the hunchback kept beating his victim's head against the floor. He was too hoarse to speak; he only hissed.

Tõmm had never imagined anything like this, much less witnessed anything remotely like it. His little bespectacled comrade must really have been containing within himself a terrible, painful fury.

"All clear," Osvald finally said, and touched his shoulder.

"Ah," Tõmm answered. "Listen, Pontus is raising hell!"

"Yes; now he's barking. Wonder where he was before," Osvald answered. "Well done, my boy," he then said appreciatively, nudging with his foot the soldier who was lying by the door. "Neat and thorough work! Wonder where these devils came from?"

"They're vagrants from the woods," Tõmm answered with a calm voice that sounded strange to himself. "See, the insignia have been torn off their epaulets."

When had he noticed that? Just now? No, probably when his opponent was about to fall on him. Then he had noticed that the man's eyes were grey and somewhat bloodshot, that the black stubble of his beard was quite long, and that the skin on the distorted face was of rough texture. So he had killed this man, so quickly and without planning? Strange how simply it had all happened. Only his back was wet, and he had a hollow feeling under his heart.

"Quit it now. How long are you going to beat him? He's stiff already," Osvald said to Värdi, hurrying to untie the bound, half-naked girls.

"He's still squirming," Värdi mumbled, but released his motionless enemy.

Tõmm untied Ella, who was lying on the floor in the doorway leading to the back chamber. A towel had been stuffed in her mouth, and her hands were tied behind her back with a torn sheet. The poor girl had struggled to exhaustion. Her chestnut-coloured hair was in disarray, her face was covered with sweat, and her half-naked, plump body was scratched and smeared in several places. She was staring at Tõmm as if he were an apparition, unable to utter a word and unmindful of her nakedness.

"Don't be afraid, Ella! How are you feeling?" the young man muttered bashfully.

Fright and shame shadowed the face of the girl.

"He didn't, he couldn't. . . ." The words came quickly, stumbling over each other, and crawling on her hands and feet, she vanished into the darkness of the back chamber, where she burst into hysterical sobs.

Lonni, the taller of the twin sisters, was still lying motionless on the messed-up bed. She was not crying, but was shivering all over as if in high fever, and pressed her face against a pillow. Osvald covered her carefully with a blanket and gave Tõmm a worried look, shrugging his shoulders.

Then they all heard the high-pitched guttural groan and muffled banging. It came from the threshing floor. That had to be Meeta, the mistress of Matsu herself. But before anybody could go to the threshing floor, the frightened face of Ignas of Hiie appeared in the doorway. He was fully dressed, wearing his high boots and carrying a heavy stick. Only his head was uncovered. His glance glided quickly over the room and stopped on his son.

"What's going on here?" he demanded sternly.

"You can see for yourself, Father," his son answered. "Everything has happened already. Nothing is going on any more."

"Juhan isn't back yet?" he asked.

"No," Osvald answered. "We just happened by."

"How? Are you all right, all of you?"

"Nothing wrong with us," Osvald said.

He then hurried to the threshing floor. The mistress of Matsu was lying near the door, a straw gag in her mouth, tied up with a thick rope. Osvald lit a match. The farmer's wife had almost managed to get her legs free from the rope. Osvald pulled the straw from her mouth. She spat and spluttered.

"Osvald of Hiie!" She recognized him by the light of the match. "How is it?" she asked quickly. "The girls? How are they?"

"They're all right."

"Those swine!" the heavy, strongly built woman panted. "Pounced on the girls. . . . They were still sleeping. And I, idiot, I thought it was Juhan. I opened the door and—those scoundrels! I heard the shots. Did they run away?"

"They won't run anywhere any more," Osvald answered.

"Are they inside the house?" The woman sounded startled.

"Well, yes, we couldn't take them out that fast. It was just lucky we happened by."

"Sure it was lucky. Oh, the stone floor was cold," she said and shivered. Her voice was hoarse and broken. "Those scoundrels! Pounced on the children!"

Her limbs were still stiff and her movements awkward. When she got into the room, she stopped for a moment. Her eyes dilated with fear, but she did not say anything. She was a strong, sturdy woman, with a broad, frank face; short, but squarely built, so that the width of her hips and breast easily filled a narrow gateway.

She rushed to the side of her daughter who was lying on the bed.

"Hey," she said, grabbing Lonni by the shoulder, shaking her vigorously, and then pulling the blanket from the girl. "Get up now," she shouted in agitation.

The farmer of Hiie turned to go.

"Where are you going, Father?" Tõmm asked.

"We can't just leave things like this," Ignas said calmly. "Listen, the dog is barking like crazy. Who knows who might be coming from the direction of Võllamäe? I'll send Hilda out to carry the word around. I'll go and tell your mother, too, that you are all here and that you're all right. We have to do something about this mess here, or else. . . ."

He went out, clutching his stick. Tõmm realized for the first time that this might be only the beginning of the story. Great troubles might arise from the events of this night, executions and revenge, so that the whole village might be erased from the earth. His companions did not seem to be much concerned yet about such a risk. Värdi was crouching on a chair, gloomy as usual, and Osvald was picking up the weapons and ammunition of the Russians.

The mistress of Matsu was shaking her daughter and shouting at her. "Lonni! Lonni! Listen, are you deaf or what? That's what I was afraid of. Come quickly. Wash yourself. Scrub hard. Holy heavens, my own child. Come, maybe you'll get rid of that filth. Those pigs!"

She pulled the girl out of the bed and took her to the threshing floor. Ella, who had already recovered enough to get dressed in the back chamber, followed them, clutching a small table lamp that shook in her trembling hands.

"Let's get started," Osvald said. "We'll get done before old Juhan comes back. God knows—he may give us a blow of his club for fouling up his living room."

Ignas and his men returned home long after midnight. The greater part of the work was done. The front room of Matsu had been washed and

138

the blood scrubbed off. The four corpses had been lined up behind the house on the edge of the field, where the rain washed their stiffening faces. Ignas went inside to talk things over with Krõõt, and the men went across the yard to the threshing floor, accompanied by Mihkel of Lepiku, whose lean face had appeared in the doorway of Matsu just when they were busy cleaning up.

Mihkel was frightened and wordless—he was the one who knew the Soviet régime best, and who could already visualize the consequences of the fateful night. His reaction made it even plainer to himself who he now was, and how strongly his fate was linked with that of his companions.

Krõõt went to the threshing floor and looked at her strong young son, as if she saw him for the first time. It seemed to her that she heard his voice for the first time, too—a strange, somewhat rough, strong masculine voice. The boy was really a man, then; the same youngster who not long ago had eagerly run to catch tadpoles in the ditches between the fields, full of enthusiasm and lively as a spindle. This same youngster had killed a soldier, killed a man a couple of hours ago. And now, there he was sitting, as if nothing had happened, his young, tanned, tired face reflecting no emotion. Krõõt turned back to the house. Her son had suddenly grown big and strange to her. And tears came to Krõõt's eyes.

Returning to the front room she found Anton of Lepiku sitting at the table opposite Ignas. The moustache of the old man drooped, and neither spoke a word.

"The rain is getting lighter," Krõõt remarked.

"The wind is scattering the clouds," Ignas replied.

"What about Hilda? She'll freeze out there," said Krõõt. "She did take her overcoat, but she ran out in such a hurry."

"We'll have to leave her at her post until we get the corpses into the woods," Ignas answered. "I'll go and harness the horse."

"How are you going to do it in the dark like that?"

"This funeral cannot wait for daylight. In the morning they must be under the sod and everything forgotten," the farmer said.

When Ignas opened the door, somebody was turning his horse into the courtyard of Hiie, accompanied by the barking of Pontus. The carriage stopped at the door, and Ignas heard the visitor throw the reins loosely over the back of the horse. They met in the doorway. Ignas recognized the visitor from his heavy gait and his puffing.

"You, Juhan?"

"Yes, me."

They stepped inside. Juhan of Matsu fell on a chair without waiting for an invitation, stretched his heavy boots out wearily and folded his hands on his chest. His shaggy beard trembled.

"Tell me, man from behind my gate," he addressed Ignas directly, "what have you done in my house while I was away?"

"I haven't done anything," Ignas answered. "I only cleaned up the mess behind my woodpile."

Juhan found it hard to keep his hands still on his chest, and all his affected calmness made a very poor show today.

139

"Hang it," he mumbled. "I turned my horse into my yard, and wondered what the devil was wrong. The animal snorted and balked and wouldn't enter his own yard. He wouldn't go, although his own warm stable was waiting for him. He backed up, until he almost broke down the Hiie gate. And then, what was inside? All those wailing women! And the walls full of bullet holes. That damned old woman of mine. I gave her a good whack in the face. Strong like a bull, and she let the Russians get at the girls!" His voice trembled in agitation, and not once did his eyelids sink over his eyes in his habitual attitude of impassive indifference. "What do you think of that, man from behind my gate?"

"What do I think?" answered Ignas, "Or what would my opinion amount to. I gave my advice. You didn't listen."

"Yes," Anton of Lepiku said in his low voice. "If we had listened to Ignas' advice and put up the alarm bells, this wouldn't have happened. Or if you'd had at least a dog in the house."

"Split that tree stump!" Juhan growled, but his voice was weak. "Now it's my own fault that the world is full of rascals! I'll go straight to the county house and break their windows. Let *them* come and clear away the carcasses.

Juhan got up. "Listen, man from behind my gate, tell your boys—I don't know how many you have there in the woods—tell them to throw the carcasses on the carriage. My horse is in harness. We'll get the yard cleaned up. And tell them they are real men. I won't go and shake the hand of every greenhorn. Let's do it here between ourselves."

He offered his hand to his neighbour. Now Ignas was Ignas again, and Juhan was Juhan. The "man behind the gate" and the one "behind the woodpile" were out of commission until the next feud.

They finished the burial in the first raw light of dawn. They were all muddy, dirty and wet, for it was no easy matter to dig a grave in the dark, although the soil was soft and marshy. Tõmm and Värdi had stayed home, the former to keep watch in place of Hilda, who was too cold to stand out any longer, and the latter to lie down in the bathhouse. He had exerted his leg too much in the fight. Mihkel of Lepiku, however, kept up with the others.

Juhan of Matsu himself selected the place. He picked the same spot near the bog where they had buried the ashes of a cow that had died of animal plague.

"If somebody should come to dig them up, he'll die of plague," he said gloomily. "Be careful yourselves that you won't catch your death from the dirt!"

Ignas was against the choice of the burial place but he did not want to start a new controversy immediately, especially as his neighbour seemed to derive a kind of grim satisfaction from this selection. It was not the business of Ignas to speak up for those vagrants.

Juhan countered his measured objections with: "Hang it all. That's the right place for the rascals to rot in. Take, men, and drink!" He passed a bottle of homemade vodka around. "You, too, son of Anton of Lepiku. I'd like to see you in daylight. The boy must have eaten a good sort of grain in his early days, or else he wouldn't be here now. I'd almost offer him my daughter."

"Damn it," he spat out, "you, Osvald, you don't want our Lonni any more? How could you now. . . . Those confounded lice! But this is for sure—and I say it on the graveside—if there should be any offspring from this, I'll kill the bastard with my own hands and bury him in this pesthole. Let them do with me what they please or roast me in hell fire. But we can't go on living like this. You, neighbour, you know it too—that we can't go on living like this. If there's no law in the world any more, then the axe must take its place. If they take your land away, if the horse you have raised yourself balks at entering your own courtyard, and the walls of your house are shot full of bullets, then the time has come when you gradually go out of your mind. Now speak up, men, do you understand what's happening? I feel that we'll be burying somebody in this pesthole every other morning. Split that tree stump! What kind of life is this? When you go to bed at night, you put a hatchet crosswise under your pillow, and when you get your eyes open in the morning, you start guzzling vodka, pour it in, or else you can't keep yourself on the road. Take, drink, men; this is a funeral of sorts!"

"It should be all right now," Osvald panted from the hole. "The water is rising above my ankles. And the mud is slipping back from the spade."

"We didn't dig such graves in Russia," Mihkel said. "We scratched the snow off the ground, gave it a few licks with the mattock, and piled the snow up again, adding a stone now and then. In spring we reburied them about a foot deep. Sometimes wild animals had carried them off. We didn't find a shred. Clothes were stripped off when the corpses were still warm."

The men filled up the grave in the sombre light of dawn.

"That's it. If it rains some more, it will wash out the tracks of the carriage," Ignas said. "But the skies seem to be lifting. It'll probably stop raining."

"We should dump a pile of faggots or dry branches on the grave," Osvald suggested. "I don't think anybody feels like going and cutting sod to cover it, and it will be visible here in the swamp otherwise."

They brought a load of faggots from the pasture of Matsu.

"If they don't come looking for them right away and it sinks a little, you won't be able to tell the place at all," Ignas said.

At home Juhan set up an alarm system. He hung up a wooden sounding board and rigged up a big bell under the eaves of the house. He bored a hole through the window frame and attached a string to the bell, so that in case of need one could sound the alarm directly from bed. When no roundups and arrests occurred during the next few days, he drove to Harukurgu and bartered some of his grain for a savage young mixed-blood dog, who gave promise of growing into a real killer in a few months.

"They were just vagrants," Ignas of Hiie decided a few days later. "So we didn't hurt old Stalin with that at all. They were just renegades who had deserted his cause."

XII

Taavi Raudoja's attempts to get across the Finnish Bay remained fruitless. It appeared that his companions had lost their first feverish enthusiasm. The failures were discouraging, the sea was growing more and more unfriendly, and the weather was unfavourable for crossing in a small boat. Nobody dared go to the coast on blind chance, for those who did go hardly ever returned. Taavi began to avoid the group who met in the cooperative on King Street. The meetings and discussions there were senseless in his opinion, reckless, and even childish. They were still eagerly organizing some kind of centre, a partisan outfit, and tried to keep in touch with all former comrades they could find. Hadn't the suicide of Riks and the disappearance of Voss sobered them a little and caused them to be more circumspect? Winter was approaching, and the more quietly one could hibernate, the better.

Although Taavi reassured himself and tried to wait patiently, the enforced inactivity was very hard on his restless spirit. Sometimes he felt such a painful yearning for his wife and son that he had to climb the hill to the old fortress of Toompea and send at least a glance out across the grey sea. Sometimes even that was not enough and he walked around in the harbour. When he returned to the city with the salty smell of the sea in his nostrils, his heart was a little calmer. He had to wait, he told himself. He had to wait and be patient!

After Marta's departure he had seriously begun to settle down for a while. He accepted the job his schoolmate offered him in the wood processing factory, although he considered it a little imprudent. According to his papers he was now Karl Heidak, a man with a perfectly clean slate, who had never belonged to any organization, let alone an army hostile to the Soviets. He completed long questionnaires, received the necessary documents, and then went to work. After a couple of days he was appointed Arno's assistant and deputy chief of the construction bureau.

"You're carving out a real Soviet career for yourself." Arno laughed. It was easy for him to laugh; he was not in Taavi's skin. But when the former schoolmate offered to let him stay at his own apartment, Taavi was upset.

"Are you soft in the head or what? Just remember, it used to be my own apartment! Don't gather too many live coals on your head. The fact that we know each other and work together may already be too great a sin for you, perhaps even a fatal one."

"I thought it might do temporarily. We have to give a room away in any case; we have much more space than the allotted nine square metres per person."

"Thank you anyway. Liisa is a kind soul. She'd take good care of me. But just consider what would happen if. . . ."

Taavi got himself a room quite close to the factory. It was a small room which a family he knew and trusted had to rent out because of the decree about space allotment.

"I'll try to be as small as I can," Taavi promised them. "I won't have any visitors and I won't butt into the living of others if I can help it."

He did not give his address to any of his acquaintances.

The only person whom he trusted with this information was Selma.

"If I should suddenly disappear, you will know where to look for me and perhaps take the news to my mother. Later, of course, when you don't hope to find me any more, Mother or the old man of Hiie should know what has become of me."

"I'll keep my eye on you," Selma promised, laughing.

Her laughter was brief but an undertone of faith and joy of living vibrated in it still, in spite of the fate that had struck her own family. She had overcome many difficulties to go to the country and visit her mother and sister. The trains could not be boarded without travelling permits any more and these were hard to get. Selma had said she had to go to her father's funeral. The officials had refused at first. Why should she, young woman that she was, go to the old man's funeral? He'd get buried without her presence. But she had kept on insisting until she had got the travelling permit.

Selma visited prison camps, too, looking for her brother. She was brave and fearless, in spite of her secret horror of the NKVD. There were three prison camps near Tallinn: one in Kopli, one at Maardu near the phosphate factory, and one at Nõmme just under the Mustamäe hill. But nobody knew anything about Selma's brother. The prisoners had not yet been sorted and screened and even the authorities were somewhat astonished at her inquiry. This girl must be out of her mind if she had the courage to look for a prisoner.

Taavi was not even aware of how it happened, but gradually Selma became his closest companion; the only one whose presence did not disturb him. If he had known how he filled the days of the lonely young woman, he would certainly have curbed his visits to her. But he took their friendship quite for granted. Selma left her aunt and rented a small room elsewhere. She often cooked dinner for him, after which they would sit up talking until it was too late for Taavi to go home. Then he would sleep on the narrow couch, two steps from Selma's bed.

Taavi Raudoja also appeared before the Red Army draft board. It turned out to be quite a simple procedure and he got his deferment papers easily.

The board, headed by a major from the political department, an Estonian from Russia, came directly to the factory. In the club room, in front of a huge table covered with a red cloth, Taavi gave a solemn account of his life and his past to the dignitaries who sat behind the table. The question that seemed to trouble them most was why he hadn't gone to Russia with the retreating Russian army in 1941.

"I was deferred from military service as an irreplaceable worker, and later there was no time to flee. The Germans came in too quickly. I considered it my sacred duty to remain at the post entrusted to me by the Soviet Government and people. I could not believe that the Germans. . . ."

"Do you have your deferment paper?"

"I'm sorry, I don't. When Tallinn was bombed, my house burned down with all my papers. Bombed by the Germans," he added with feigned anger, looking naïvely in the major's eye. The major should have known that the Germans had never bombed Tallinn, but evidently he did not know anything. Now he was interested in how Taavi had managed to live unmolested during the German occupation. How did he escape conscription? He emphasized the word "conscription." It was peculiar about the Estonians here. Only a short while ago they had fought the Russians on the Eastern front in large units, earning a reputation that spread far and wide and caused terror in the hearts of the brave Soviet soldiers. And now no trace could be found of the men who had been at the front.

The major sighed and concluded his political investigation. There were just no first-rate men left in this country to be drafted into the Red Army. And the better and healthier ones had to be deferred because they could not be replaced in their important positions.

Taavi left the room with a light heart. He could now settle down peacefully behind his drafting board and reconstruct war-ravaged Soviet Estonia, until the NKVD should decide to open his file and enter an order for his arrest in the dossier that had been started for him. The military authorities would not touch him any more. As far as they were concerned he could meet the patrols without fear and move around freely until the evening curfew. He called his deferment his "grace period."

Christmas came, greyer than any Christmas he had ever known. Even the weather was bleak—without snow or light. It was the Christmas of a forgotten people. The workers got one day off. Taavi felt it might have been better if the free day had not been granted, if the celebration of Christmas had been strictly forbidden.

Selma had invited him to spend Christmas Eve with her. She had bought a small Christmas tree and managed to get a few candles. Taavi was not quite sure whether he should go or not. He did not want to demonstrate how lonely and forlorn he was.

When Taavi saw the festive glow on the faces of the family in whose apartment he roomed, and when their little son began to decorate an evergreen branch with coloured paper streamers, he found it impossible to stay.

Once in the street he did not know where to go. He stood with his hands in his pockets and smoked his pipe. The weather was cold and damp. He could feel the moisture creep up his legs like wet ice. He began to walk fast and aimlessly toward the centre of the city. Christmas Eve. Holy Night. A starless, cloud-heavy sky over the dark, unlit city. The wind clanked the torn metal roofing in the ruins, as usual, and shots could still be heard in the darkness. This shooting had become a riddle which Taavi was curious to solve. When he walked in the daytime among the sooty, crumbled, stinking basements, charred timber and piles of sooty bricks, he never noticed anything suspicious. Some people said the shots came from bandits, others shrugged their shoulders, and still others were convinced that the Russians were executing German prisoners-of-war or even anti-Communist Estonian schoolboys.

Taavi was unaware that he had entered a street full of people, going somewhere in silent eagerness or in quiet conversation. Without thinking about anything, he joined them. Reaching the open door of a church, he realized that this was where he had wanted to come all along. He had never seen the church so full of people. There were young and old, men and women, and even tiny children.

Taavi felt his eyes become moist. He could not follow the simple, heartfelt words of the old minister. He was sitting in the back pew of the church with his eyes glued to the warm light of the few Christmas candles on the altar, which glimmered like a thousand sparkling stars through his tear-moistened eyelashes. He felt as if he were melting together with this light and with all his companions around him. His whole being was a sincere prayer and a communion with this two-thousand-year-old miracle, which repeated itself within him this Christmas night. Even if this service should cost the old minister his life, it would be given at a very high price. It was hardly possible that any of the congregation who filled the huge church could ever forget the experience that had been granted them this evening.

"Silent night, holy night. . . ."

Taavi felt as if he were soaring under the vaulted ceiling in the dim, mysterious light, rising higher and higher. The hymn billowed. Even the harshest faces were tender, even the gloomiest eyes soft and shining. Behold, we are trodden to the ground but a miracle is giving us strength.

Slowly leaving the sanctuary, Taavi noticed some suspicious activity near the church door. Figures moved excitedly, a car engine began to hum, and a black car disappeared around the street corner.

What had happened?

Some of the people began to hurry home, almost running. Others stood silently as if turned to stone.

"They nabbed them right in front of me. If I'd been a step ahead, the wife and children would have had nobody to expect home tonight."

"Even on Christmas Eve they keep arresting people! It's a wonder they didn't surround the church and take everybody."

"The minister will probably be the next one to go. They didn't quite dare drag him down from the pulpit."

"So church services are allowed now," somebody spat out in bitter irony, forgetting that he was standing at the church door.

That was all that was said. Those who had witnessed the incident hurried off, and those who left the church later knew nothing of the black car which had taken away two worshippers. Was it really true? Taavi wondered in his mind. The car might just have been passing by. What was so peculiar about that? Or maybe somebody was in church and the car was waiting for him. Silly; nobody owned a car any more for

145

pleasure driving. The rumble of a car had already become an alarm signal, for in the Soviet state only prisoners were transported by cars.

This was not to remain the only experience that disturbed Taavi's Christmas spirit. When he began to hurry home he heard somebody shouting in the ruins. He stopped.

"Hey, are you an Estonian?" asked a shaky, piteous voice.

"Yes, I am," Taavi answered, stepping toward the figure. "Who are you?"

A naked man appeared before him, a torn shirt on his shoulders, arms pressed tightly against his shivering chest.

"What . . . what has happened to you?" Taavi stammered.

The man was so stiff from the cold and seemed to be so close to collapse that he could hardly speak.

"The Russians. . . ," he whispered hoarsely. "They stripped me of everything!"

There was no time to ask any more questions. Taavi tore off his own overcoat, the scarf from around his neck, and the hat from his head. It was difficult to get the man's stiff arms into the sleeves.

"I live not far from here," he croaked. "On Vahtra Street. I was coming through the ruins but couldn't go on through the undamaged part of town, so I had to call out."

"How are your legs? Can they carry you all right?"

"Oh, yes. I don't even feel them much."

Taavi put his arm around the man, supporting him and at the same time trying to massage his ice-cold limbs. The man walked in a half-crouching position, groaning. His teeth were chattering.

"Oh, my feet hurt," he complained.

They were cut and bleeding, since he had walked through the ruins in the dark across broken glass and sharp stones, over charred boards where rusty nails were lying upwards. Without delay, Taavi pulled off his shoes and socks and put them on his companion's feet.

"Do you have anything hot at home?"

"Nothing, not even a drop of vodka," the stranger answered.

"I was thinking of hot tea. And what about the rooms?"

"The room is cold as a wolf's lair. I live alone."

Taavi took him to Selma's place.

The woman opened the door and stood there in amazement.

"Make some tea and give me a bucket of cold water. I'll try to rub this fellow a little before it's too late," Taavi ordered. "Don't be shy, my girl. Worse things than this happen every day."

He ordered the young man to lie down on the couch and began to rub his naked limbs vigorously with a cloth steeped in cold water. The man assisted him as well as he could. His legs were muddy up to his knees and the soles of his feet badly cut.

Selma brought hot tea. She made the stranger drink one cup after another. She found a remnant of vodka in the bottom of a bottle and made him drink that, too. Then she helped rub his legs, washed his feet, and bandaged his cuts.

"You're fixing me up like new," the man said. His name was Evald

146

and he lived in one of the two houses which had remained standing on nearby Vahtra Street. His limbs began to turn red and his face glowed. He was about Taavi's age, around thirty. From the way he spoke Taavi concluded that he was a former fellow soldier.

"Do you still feel cold?" Taavi asked, wrapping him in a heavy grey blanket.

"Hard to tell. The body is now hot and cold at the same time—mixed-up like."

He gazed at the small Christmas tree on the table and the unlit candles. Taavi guessed that Selma had expected him and had not wanted to light the candles alone. And now there were two visitors instead of one.

"How did it all happen?" he asked.

"How did it happen?" Evald mumbled, forcibly turning his glance from the Christmas tree, as if he had been awakened from a dream. "They acted as if they were patrolling the street and pulled me in among the ruins. Then they pressed a gun against my ribs and told me to strip. I argued that the cold would make me curl up like a pretzel. But when I raised my voice, one of them took a few steps backwards and was about to shoot. I hoped they'd be satisfied with the overcoat and the jacket but they even tore off my underpants. The shirt was torn to pieces in the scuffle, or else I'd have been naked as Adam. They left me the torn rags. I thought I'd call for help but I felt embarrassed. What kind of man is he, anyway, who lets two Russian bums strip him and then yells like a stuck pig? I clenched my teeth and began to crawl homewards over the ruins."

"Poor thing," Selma said, putting food on the table.

"Oh, that would have been nothing, but the weather happened to be so cold and damp and the wind blows clear through. A man can't hold out for long. My mouth fell open and my teeth began to chatter. Couldn't feel my legs any more."

"Don't bother about me." He tried to restrain Selma, who was setting him a plate. "I can't eat a bite. I'm so full of tea now that I need hoops around my stomach. I think I'll try to go home now. I'll run quickly around the corner."

"Naked? No," Taavi said. "Do you have a key? How are you going to get into the house?"

"Why, of course, I forgot that altogether," Evald muttered. "I didn't keep the keys hanging around my neck. They went the same way as everything else."

"I think we'll have to stay and bother Selma tonight. Tomorrow morning you may take my clothes and go home. When you have found something to wear, you can bring them back."

"The room is small. How can we? What will the lady say?"

"Don't worry; it will be better than among the ruins." Selma smiled. "If you're sleepy, you can lie down on the couch. I have plenty of blankets. I'll cover you up well. Just watch out you don't have a fever by tomorrow morning."

"That shouldn't get a man down—fever. But this cold really took all my strength. My feet prick and crackle like Christmas sausages in the oven." He yawned. The disorderly strands of his dark hair hung over his flushed forehead. "I'm scared to think what it would have meant if they had pulled this trick in real winter weather. No time to look around then—just kneel down in the snowdrift and commit your soul to the Lord. Ah-h!" A cold shiver ran through him and he shuddered. "But the couch is narrow. We can't quite sleep on it together, two grown men. . . ." He hesitated.

"I'll stretch out on the floor," Taavi answered. "You remember yourself when beds weren't always to be had for the asking. We dozed where we happened to come to a stop. You can't wish for a better bed than a piece of sod under your head and the corner of your trench coat over your face."

A satisfied smile stole over Evald's face. He was among his own kind and now he didn't care if the world came to an end. He fell asleep, the familiar smell of the Christmas tree in his nostrils, his head heavy and his body twitching from sudden spasms.

"He fell asleep as if knocked out," Taavi said, watching the man's relaxed but feverishly red face. Evald was lying on his back, snoring.

"It's a pity we don't have any medicine to give him—aspirin or something." Selma was quite worried. "He may catch pneumonia."

"He seems to be strongly built. And he's been hardened by army life."

They both fell silent. Selma offered food but Taavi had no appetite. He picked at a few dishes but was obviously absent-minded.

"I was thinking of the folks back home," Selma said. "A sad Christmas we're having this year."

"It's good that we have only one day off and will get back to work soon. This can't be called Christmas. Something is gnawing inside. Well, go ahead and light the candles. What are you waiting for?"

"I was waiting for you." Selma smiled. "I was saving them for you. Of course, I'll light them now. Wonder which of us will be needing candles next year."

"Ah, don't speak nonsense!"

Taavi took the blankets and lay down on the rug, fully dressed as he was. Lying in her bed, Selma listened to the breathing of the two men and could not sleep. Evald snored and groaned, tossing on his couch. The bitter-sweet Christmas smell of burned-out candles and scorched fir twigs hovered in the room. Outside, the wind whistled through the streets, rattling metal scraps in the ruins. Then a cold rain, mixed with sleet, began to rustle against the windowpanes.

Sleep did not come so easily to Taavi, either. Hazy dream images appeared before his closed eyes, but a refreshing sleep eluded him.

"Listen, are you sick?" Selma asked.

"Mh? I can't sleep," Taavi said and turned on the other side, so that the floor boards squeaked. Open-eyed, he gazed into the dark corner. Christmas night. Suddenly he saw his mother. She was sitting at the table, dressed in her Sunday best. She had her glasses on and she was reading the Bible. Candles were burning on the tree. Taavi saw clearly each object in the tiny room, as if he were actually standing on the threshold. Long striped runners covered the floor, and on the dresser between candlesticks of cut glass was his father's picture. Mother had placed lighted candles beside it.

Taavi opened his eyes and closed them again. Evald must have fever; he panted and tossed. Selma got up from the bed and arranged his covers. She checked to see if Taavi had a blanket and brought her coat to spread over him in addition to the blanket. There was a great deal of motherliness in her, too. She'll make a good wife for someone, if. . . . Ah, of course she will!

Taavi jumped up. Evald was snoring and moaning in turn, and the wind howled outside. Selma was awake, too. Her bed squeaked and her breathing stopped when she listened.

"What's the matter, Taavi?"

"I can't sleep any more," the man answered and took his head in his hands. He could not sleep that Christmas night.

After Evald had recovered, Taavi found himself a frequent visitor at his apartment. Often they both visited with Selma. Taavi was pleased to notice that Evald and Selma seemed to be getting along exceptionally well. It seemed to be developing into something more than friendship.

Taavi paid a visit also to Jaan Meos, to get news about the cooperative on King Street. Jaan seemed to be angry with him.

"You got lost like a needle in a haystack," he said.

"Have you got an opening, then? What else should I expect to find here?"

"We don't have a thing," Jaan answered impatiently. "The sea won't freeze over and how else. . . . Lieutenant Pihu has disappeared," he said. "One alarm follows on the heels of the other. He isn't home and he hasn't shown up for work. His wife doesn't know anything either."

"Where could he be, then? Maybe staying with some other woman; that could be expected of him."

"His wife was afraid of the same thing, but I don't believe it. Perhaps it's the NKVD. But his house hasn't been searched. It makes you damned nervous. And there's no trace of Ruudi Ugur. He went to look for the Admiral and that was before Christmas."

Taavi had a sudden hunch that it might be best to leave this place as quickly as possible. When some of the men had been arrested, then. . . . He didn't give his new address to his comrade.

"You don't trust me any more?!" Jaan muttered.

Taavi was sorry for him. He seemed manly and energetic enough, but he was still a boy, actually only an adolescent, and the shadows of implied future events were lurking around him. It was hard for Taavi to distance himself like that, knowing that he would remain more and more alone.

"When spring comes, then. . . ," Taavi said.

"Yes, if it comes," the other one mumbled and began to curse in a deep, masculine voice.

Their new cooperative met in Evald's apartment on Vahtra Street.

Only three of them belonged to it—Taavi, Evald and Selma. They made plans for future escape attempts. Just a couple of months and they might make a try, after the spring storms but before the returning sun made the nights too short.

Their meeting place was in harmony with Taavi's mood—among grey, battered and charred ruins, the unrelenting ugliness of which even the thick, white carpet of snow could not hide completely. In the streets between ruins and sometimes across demolished houses people had trodden pathways and shortcuts toward inhabited districts of the city. But the remnants of walls and caved-in roofs stood here, abandoned, just as the impact of exploding bombs and the greedy tongues of fire had left them a year ago. The snow fell into cellar-holes and the wind howled through glassless windows. Small boys and tattered old women dug up pieces of timber, half-burned logs, and broken furniture from under the snow, piled them on sleds and pulled them home for firewood. Markets often sprang up in the ruins, where wood scraps were bought and sold, and where the boys fought real battles for a piece of furniture or a better chunk of wood. Everybody was hard up and the younger generation had to learn to fight for its existence at a very early age.

Taavi began to enjoy looking from the window over the field of ruins. Always he felt melancholy, but never desperate. So what, he said to himself, even if we are down now, yet we have seen the time when these houses were standing and people were living in them, and we'll also see the time when the homes will rise again, smelling of fresh mortar, and when people will live again, turning their faces toward the sun.

One day Evald told him: "What would you say if Selma and I should get together in the spring?"

"You mean get married?"

"Well, I wasn't thinking of a wedding, but we'd just put our loaves of bread into the same cupboard. I'm just asking you—you're an old Finland fighter—what do you think the chances are of getting across? Will something open up in the spring or not? So I could make my plans accordingly, for a wife is not taken just for a short while. And my job at the shipyards—it's only temporary. One fine day they'll snatch me from behind my wife's back."

"That's for sure," Taavi answered. "They'll snatch all the men who are left, one way or another. Right now they're still keeping their claws in their paws, for we are desperately needed on the front, in the factories and everywhere else. But even now men are being mown down like grass, and if you read the *Voice of the People* you can hear the rumbling threats. The Estonian patriotic songs are not blared through the loud-speakers as often as before. Something has to come of our escape in the spring, if we are men and if we have any luck at all. I'll go across the bay, even if I have to swim. I don't know what kind of a spoiled brat my boy will become if he grows up without a father's discipline. I must get there in time."

"Then I'll marry Selma, even if the floods should come," Evald decided.

157

"Well, you could wait a little but—that's your own business. Life has to go on, brother; that's my opinion. A burned tree won't grow again, but the seed that falls before the disaster bears the proudest fruit."

"You are pronouncing the preacher's blessing ahead of time," Evald grinned.

Taavi did not doubt that this fellow whom he had picked up from the ruins on Christmas night would make a suitable husband for Selma. Yes, if they could only be permitted to live in peace. All depended on the length of the "period of grace."

But the sky arched up high and blue again, and the ice crackled in the streets in the mornings. Half of March and all of April—that made a month and a half.

XIII

Tõmm of Hiie glided through the snowy forest. He had always enjoyed skiing, especially on the high Koolu hills, where one could easily break one's neck running into the grave mounds which dated from the Great Northern War two hundred years ago. Covered with great pines, the steep and sandy hills rose from the prostrate forests within the triangle formed by Võllamäe, the estate of Kalgina, and the village of Haru-kurgu. This was where the real forests and moors began; the safe hinterlands of Metsaoti.

"Sticks right to my heels," the young man mumbled cheerfully, glancing back.

The Sunday morning sun glittered on the snow and the girl with her broad, brightly coloured scarf followed him from hilltop to hilltop, as lightly as a butterfly. She did not stay far behind the boy, although he had at first disdainfully told her to stay at home, and not to bother him with her helplessness. She'd surely cry before the day was over. But now —Tõmm almost got annoyed with her. A city girl, thin like a—bah! Where could she have learned to ski so well?

Tõmm felt a strange desire to hurt Hilda. The more the taciturn girl seemed to care for him, the stronger had grown his desire to hurt her. Sometimes he could not stand the sight of her; he was so disturbed by her soft mouth and tender, wistful eyes. Often he said things to the girl that hurt even himself. He could not understand why he did it.

"What a wonderful run," the girl shouted jubilantly.

"Real good snow," Tõmm muttered sullenly. Where did the girl get that laugh? Suddenly she was not their Cinderella-Hilda any more. The young man looked at her, as if seeing her for the first time. Her breasts were small and high, and her hips slender. Her hands, in big leather mittens, handled the poles with confidence, her strides were powerful, and she held her head proudly, letting her curls fly in the wind. Up and down the hills she went. The snow glittered in the sun, the squirrels jumped on red pine branches until the skiers were covered with silvery

151

hoarfrost, and birds rose from the white-capped firs, clapping their wings.

Competing with each other, they chose steeper slopes and more and more perilous curves amongst the tree trunks and bushes. Tõmm could not reconcile himself to the fact that the girl would not remain behind, even though she was using his old, discarded skis. He wanted her to fall, to break a ski, if necessary. The darned butterfly! There was nothing he could do to mock her. She only laughed back, as if she were living the first day of her life. And Tõmm was already getting tired from trying too hard.

He decided to make her fall and began to watch for a suitable chance. If he could slip his ski pole over the tip of her ski, or entangle his poles in hers, passing her on a curve, she would surely crash into the snowdrifts. But Hilda was only amused to see the boy chasing her. Laughing merrily, she crisscrossed between the trees, scattering snow into Tõmm's eyes.

On one of the sharp curves of the Koolu hills it happened. They collided and fell into a deep snowdrift, faces down, skis crashing. The tip of his pole hit Tõmm in the chest, but he was too excited to notice it. Their skis and ski poles got entangled and they grabbed hold of each other, falling almost against the rough trunk of a red pine. The girl shrieked in surprise, but her snow-covered face was still laughing. She was lying on her back and Tõmm had fallen on top of her. Suddenly the boy realized that the chase had had a much deeper meaning and he kissed the snowy, half-parted lips of the girl. Hilda held him strongly and pressed her lips against his. But she did not return the kiss.

Then suddenly her arms fell weakly to her sides and she turned her face into the snow.

"Hilda!" Tõmm whispered.

The girl was lying motionless and sobbing.

"I don't know how!" she shouted fiercely.

"Haven't you ever kissed before?"

She shook her head, pressing her face deeper into the snow.

Tõmm stood up and looked in confusion at his broken ski.

Women meant nothing but trouble. He got angry again. Was that necessary? Now he'd have to wade through the deep snow with a broken ski like a lame duck—good new skis, the best he had ever had! He hurled the broken piece against the trunk of the pine.

Hilda lay as she had fallen, her face in the snow, the hands in the big mittens helplessly at her sides. Only her shoulders rose and fell to the rhythm of her quick breathing.

Tõmm glanced at her and said, "Let's go! Are you planning to stay here or what? It's your fault, stupid. Look at my ski. If the Russians should come now, I'd be caught!"

The laughter had left Hilda's face. It was wet with tears and melted snow. She rose slowly and did not look at Tõmm. The young man followed her with his eyes, and he lost his urge to scold. These women— of course, she had to cry. He stood up to his knees in the snow and put a handful of snow in his mouth. Although he felt a little sorry for the girl, he did not stop her when she took his broken skis and put them on her own boots. Oh well, the boy thought, she has plenty of time to wade through the snowdrifts with the blunted ski. Without a word he mounted on the good skis, and they started toward home.

But Tõmm could not quite leave the girl behind with her broken ski. He led the way, as if he did not care, but often he stood and watched the yellow winter sun that had passed the midday mark, until Hilda became visible again between the trees.

Nobody came to look for the four Russians who had been killed in the Matsu farmhouse. They were evidently deserters whom nobody knew about or was interested in. There were not many army units in the neighbourhood camps during the last few months and when a carpet of snow covered the hidden graves in the marsh of Katkuaugu, those concerned breathed more easily. The village did not know much about what had gone on at Matsu that grim autumn night. Only the face of old Juhan had become more and more sullen and he did not stick out his chest any more like he used to. In February, when the Hiie people celebrated Independence Day with the traditional home-brewed beer, Ignas asked his neighbour about the consequences of the fateful night.

"Hang it," Juhan growled in response. "The girl is vomiting her heart out."

Then new, exciting rumours began to circulate in the village of Metsaoti: Reku, the fool of Võllamäe, had run away from the army. This was right after Christmas, at the time of the first snow. Nobody knew where he was, but the militia and a group of soldiers had come looking for him at home. Jaak of Võllamäe professed to know nothing about his son. Even when talking to Ignas of Hiie he made a show of ignorance—the dim-witted boy must have taken the wrong direction coming home.

Some other events occurred during the peaceful winter to keep the village of Metsaoti in a state of alarm. One of them was the roundup in the village of Harukurgu, caused by the fact that a dead Soviet soldier was found there on the road. Several people had heard the shot that night, but nobody paid much attention, since an army transport was encamped near the county house. But the following morning the soldiers were in the village. After the snowstorm during the night they had found one of their companions in a snowdrift with a charge of buckshot in his chest. Furiously, they teamed up with the militia looking for weapons. No firearms were found in the farms and the soldiers had shown no interest in identity papers. The outcome was lucky for the village, for in one farm the soldiers discovered a still with a quantity of freshly made vodka. There they celebrated the funeral of their slain comrade, and the transports moved on. The soldiers shook their fists menacingly at the woods but they did not choose to risk their lives in the snowy thickets.

Such upheavals had the good effect of keeping the young men who were hiding out on the farms from becoming too careless. They had to keep up a constant watch, even though the big, but lightly manned Russian army camps were situated some distance away, and the chairman of the executive committee, Jaan Holde, was a good-natured man. In some villages people already praised him as a better man than was possible for an official of the Soviet régime.

Tõmm, Osvald and Värdi had often found strange ski tracks in the woods. That gave them some food for thought. Could they belong to the men of Tenise, who were under the leadership of the captain from the peacetime Estonian army, or was somebody coming over from Harukurgu to rove through the backlands of Metsaoti? They had met no one.

One day in the late winter, when the alternating sun and frost had already made a hard, icy crust on the snow that crackled under the skis, they discovered an astounding fact. Their meat storage place in the slope of the back pasture had been dug up. Not much had been taken and the lid had been replaced on the barrel, which they had dug deep into the earth. There were many ski tracks beside the hole but on closer scrutiny they all turned out to be made by one pair.

"Who could this be, in the devil's name?" Osvald wondered.

"Who could have known where to look for it under the snow? And come exactly to the spot?" Tõmm could not understand it either.

Värdi looked sullenly toward the woods, examined the ski tracks, and looked again toward the woods. This was a suspicious matter. One could not trust the clean, snowy forests any more. It must be somebody from the woods—there was no doubt about that. With the cold and the hunger, he had found a good feeding place. But with what kind of instrument had he discovered that a barrel of meat was buried here in the ground under the snow? Even the marks they had cut into the trees were not clear enough for that.

They followed the ski tracks all day. With purposeless circles and roundabout loops they led into the depth of the forests. Exhausted, the men returned home at dusk.

Old Ignas did not want to believe their story in the beginning. Krõõt feared that it was the Russians again.

"It might have been Mihkel of Lepiku," Tõmm conjectured.

"He shouldn't be driven by hunger," his father countered. "He goes to the woods once in a while to try out his lungs. But he isn't much of a skier yet. He would not be strong enough to dig so deep. The ground is still frozen, although it has softened up a little now under the snow."

Mihkel did not know anything about the matter but he was quite intrigued. He took a great interest in the survival problems of his companions. He decided to join the others the following day in their hunt for the thief. Exciting things might happen again, just as they did last autumn in the Matsu living room.

But nothing came of it. Soft snow fell in the night and in the morning all the old ski tracks were covered up.

One day when Osvald was on his regular patrol trip through the woods, a hoarse voice yelled at him from the bushes: "Don't move, or I'll shoot your head full of holes like a sieve!"

Osvald stopped, dumbfounded. He did not even reach for his rifle that was hanging on his back.

"Who are you, idiot?" he shouted.

"I'll show you who is an idiot," was the growling answer, and now the hired man saw the tips of brown skis reaching out from behind a tree, and the muzzle of a rifle pointed at him.

"Don't play with the gun, fool!" Osvald shouted.

"Call me 'fool' again," the voice screamed furiously. "Call me 'fool' again, and you'll get the lead in your face like the Russian!"

"You can see that I'm no Russian. Stop playing around like that," Osvald remonstrated. "Be a man and come out from behind the tree!"

"If you won't grab me, I'll come out."

"Why should I grab you?"

"Swear like the holy father of Kustas of Tōnise that you won't!"

"Of course I won't. What are you babbling about?"

Reku, the feeble-minded son of Jaak of Vōllamäe, skied out from the bushes, dressed in a white sheepskin coat, carrying a two-barrelled hunting rifle.

"You, Reku!" Osvald was surprised. "So you shot the Russian at Harukurgu?"

The boy's face broke slowly into a wide grin.

"Reku has shot several," he answered simply. "See, you have a big tobacco pouch. It would have paid to shoot you."

A cold chill ran down Osvald's spine.

"I'll give it to you. You don't have to shoot for that. You must not shoot our own men."

"That's what Father said," the boy admitted. "But if they grab you?"

"Our own men won't. They won't grab our people. Speak up, how did you get here?"

"Father told Reku, don't speak! But Reku can speak to our own men, can't he? Reku ran away from Rakvere."

"Didn't you like army life?"

The boy looked at him with his small grey eyes.

"That is no army," he said with infinite disdain. "They gave me a wooden gun. And then, those devils; they wanted to make a fool out of me!" he spat out.

"Weren't they stupid," Osvald laughed.

"Don't laugh!" the boy threatened. "They wanted to make a fool out of Reku. They grabbed him and brought doctors to look him over. I stuck my tongue out at the rascals and when they got too bossy I shit in my pants. Don't laugh. And then I ran away. I'm no fool."

"You did the right thing." Osvald praised him.

"And now Reku is the general of the outlaws," the boy boasted.

"And that's a much better job. How many men do you have?"

"Oh, very many. They aren't here right now. But when they get

155

here, we'll go and give the Russians hell. Even old Andres of Piskujõe is in my band."

"How come? Andres is dead."

"Fool; he isn't dead. We had a long talk yesterday. He said, 'Watch out, Reku. Don't go near the villages. Later, when the Russians come into the woods in big gangs, then we'll beat them.' Old Andres is the greatest fighting man in my group. You'll never make such a fighter," Reku said to Osvald.

They were skiing side by side. The bluish dusk of the early spring twilight began to gather in the thickets. Osvald began to have strange misgivings about the son of Jaak of Võllamäe.

"Listen, wasn't it you who dug up our meat barrel in the back pasture?" he asked suddenly.

"Yes, it was," the boy answered simply. "I had a watery taste in my mouth. I wanted something salty."

"How did you know? How did you find out?" Osvald marvelled.

The boy laughed.

"Reku has the nose of a dog. I found the graves of the Russians too."

"What graves?"

"Those at Katkuaugu. Reku hasn't dug them up yet. They're buried too deep. There are three or four of them in a heap. Let them rot. Who cares? Andres told me not to touch them, and said I'd die of the plague if I did."

Osvald, the hired man of Hiie, was a courageous man, but this kind of talk scared him. He looked at the dull, blunt face of the boy and felt it might have been better if he'd never met him. This fool could do God knows what mischief here in the peaceful forests. He was capable of digging up the bodies from Katkuaugu, dragging them off, and lining them up in front of the county house at night.

They separated on the high bank of the river.

"Be careful, Reku," Osvald warned him. "And watch out that you don't touch our own men. They are all on your side. I think you had better not shoot any Russians right now either."

"I'll shoot them wherever I can," Reku said firmly. "Let me just see one, and I'll send a charge of lead into his face. And I'm not alone, you know."

"But if they send a whole battalion to catch you. . . ."

"I'll send two battalions against them. Reku won't ever run out of men. If Andres gives us directions, we'll beat them so that not a single one will get back home. Good-bye, Osvald. Stay well and go to hell," the boy said in his hoarse voice and turned back toward the woods.

Osvald looked after him with a queer feeling. Reku stopped on the slope and began to gesticulate with his arms and ski poles, silhouetted against the pale yellow evening sky. His movements were jerky and vehement, as if he were giving orders to men who had assembled around him. Then he slung his rifle on his back and vanished between the trees in a flash. Only the high-pitched barking of a dog sounded from the bushes now, as if the animal had found a fresh spoor.

156

Osvald pushed off and skied quickly down the steep bank of the river. The weather vane on the fir tree behind the Hiie farmhouse was pointing due north. At least everything was peaceful in the village of Metsaoti, and he could cross the pastures without too much caution. What a crazy turn of events: the safe, free forests had become dangerous and had fallen under the whims of a feeble-minded boy.

Ignas of Hiie faced the first thaws of spring with an apprehensive heart. This time it was not the usual pleasant restlessness, when the ears were attuned to the song of the first lark and the eyes followed the melting of the snow on the slopes in eagerness to start the labours of spring. The restlessness of this late winter was of an altogether different kind. Ignas was on transport duty for days without end. He left before cockcrow in the morning, when the roads were hard and icy, and returned at night through the melted snow, sometimes when it was quite dark, so that he could not keep the runners of the sled from screeching over bare stones. And all through the day he had no time to catch his breath. All the time he was conscious of working under compulsion, of being driven and ordered about by strangers. He could not imagine what would become of him if he'd be forced into a kolkhoz. And he knew things were moving in this direction, regardless of what anybody said. In the village of Harukurgu, where the village representative was a dyed-in-the-wool Communist, strong pressure was already being exerted on the farmers.

"I have to go to the county house and talk it over with Holde," Ignas decided.

Although the chairman of the executive committee felt respect for Ignas, even bordering on awe, it was not easy for the former district elder to talk with the representative of the new régime. Ignas tried to avoid him, mostly for the sake of his son, who was in hiding. Nobody had come to inquire about Tõmm yet, but the old man felt that the chairman of the executive committee suspected him and would have liked to teach him a lesson about living under the new régime. This was Ignas' opinion of Jaan Holde, whom the people of the county believed to be a good-natured and just man.

And he probably was. He did not like envious hints and secret denunciations. Although he was strict in demanding that the farmers of the county fulfil the obligations imposed upon them, he showed no interest in anybody's private life. If somebody went to him with complaints, he listened patiently. He even tried to ease real hardships, and often asked the men whether they were able to meet the heavy taxes, transport obligations and delivery quotas. He talked to the men about collectivization and advised them to think it over and to discuss it with neighbours.

The farmers, especially Ignas, could not complain about the representative of the village of Metsaoti, August of Roosi. When the old man ran into trouble, he always came to ask Ignas for advice. How should he act so as not to be hanged now or in the future? After the departure of the Russians from Kalgina his sources of vodka had dried up, and he went diligently from farm to farm, where he expected to find beer, or where he knew that the farmer was distilling vodka.

"You'll drink yourself blind," Krõõt of Hiie warned him.

"Why blind?" August objected. "I don't pour it into my eyes. And I tell you, if I don't oil my thinking apparatus, I'll soon be both blind and crazy. I have to look a long way ahead now, like a statesman should. I don't have such a clear head as Ignas. Without the help of vodka I don't see a thing."

Ignas went several times to the county house to speak about the telephone. Ever since he had been district elder there had been a telephone at Hiie, and since the line was still there, the administration wanted to make Hiie the telephone centre for the village. Ignas was against it—he was no functionary of any kind. Why should he be responsible for the telephone? He could foresee all kinds of complications. Since the line was still out of order, Ignas took the bold step of dismantling the telephone without permission and taking it to the county house. From the expression on Holde's face he could tell that the official did not like it.

"Why didn't you apply for the job of village representative?" Holde inquired after giving the farmer of Hiie a long, silent scrutiny. "Or does that position seem too small for you in our Soviet society?"

"I don't apply for any jobs," the old man answered gravely. "I didn't offer myself for district elder either. It was the will of the people who elected me. Our people are not a herd of cattle who don't know what they want."

"I realize that," Jaan Holde said, tapping with a pencil against the five-pointed red star on his chest. They were sitting in the small office at the county house, which was quite familiar to Ignas from former times. "I realize that," the new occupant of the room repeated. "Our people are far ahead of the other republics in their development. Only our development has been led astray. And this makes it all the more difficult now."

"That depends," Ignas muttered. "Before, we did not have any prescriptions about how a person had to think. The law and order that reigned did not choke anybody. If I didn't want a man to be in the government, I gave my vote to somebody else, and in my house or on my property I did what I pleased. Nobody interfered. I am an old man, and I have seen many people during my lifetime. I can tell at first meeting what kind of a man I have in front of me. And if I should ever have to say a word in your defence, my mouth wouldn't stay shut."

The chairman of the executive committee seemed pleased. He liked the firm words of the old man. "The people don't want to understand that I am one of them, too," he confessed. "But I am. Here everybody looks at me as if I were a nobody—a vagrant who has come from Russia. All right, I don't pay much attention to that. I have a lot of work to do and I believe the people will gradually change their attitude. The war is approaching its victorious end," he said proudly. "All of us will have to exert ourselves now many times over."

Old Ignas did not share his enthusiasm. Yes, he wouldn't mind exerting himself, for he had never been idle in his life and would not really know how to loaf, but he could not rejoice at the victories of the Red Army in Germany, not even at the signs that predicted the end of the war. Well, peace conferences were supposed to follow then, and the case of Estonia would be brought up too. That was the only thing that gave any hope.

Peace conferences. New frontiers drawn on the map. That fired Ignas' blood. Let them redistribute lands here in the district of Kalgina any way they pleased. The real boundaries would be drawn later, and the old boundary stones were still deeply in the ground and would yet be taken into account. Taking the telephone to the county house gave Ignas an amazing amount of new strength and will to live. It was as if he had clearly dissociated himself from the present régime.

One evening a little after sunset, when the twilight on the smoky plains still had the bluish transparence of early spring, Mihkel of Lepiku was arrested. Later it seemed to everybody as if the invisible hand of fate had paralysed their senses, robbed them of their power of decision, and kept them in a daze until that moment when the snow crackled under the feet of foreign soldiers in the Lepiku farmyard. The people of Lepiku rose from the dinner table, unswallowed food still in their mouths. Then they heard clearly the angry barking of Pontus of Hiie. Now their own old dog was growling in the direction of the door, the hair on his neck bristling like thorns. Then the door shook under strong blows.

"Flee!" the mother whispered to the son.

But the helpless voice of the old woman provoked no response at all in Mihkel. He swallowed painfully the food he had in his mouth and sat down at the table, fumbling for the soup spoon, as if he intended calmly to continue his supper. His mind and his limbs were paralysed and pain was racking his wounded lung. Strangely, the pain spread in long, hot streams into his shoulder, arm and wrist. The spoon did not stay in his hand and fell on the floor.

He touched his aching arm with his other hand. The fingers and palms were wet, as if soaked in water.

"Open the door," he said to his father, who was calming the dog. Mihkel's voice had an angry ring, as if the old man were somehow to blame.

Mihkel did not put up any resistance nor fight back. He did not even make a move to run, when the room filled up with Russians. Knowing this to be the end, he only longed for it all to be over with as quickly as possible. When the soldiers seized him from one side and his desperate mother from the other, he felt sharply that he had been torn long ago by the two forces that claimed him. When he saw his father surrounded by the Russians, clenching his fists, and when he met the grey, penetrating eyes of the old man, the son smiled apologetically. Didn't his father

159

secretly expect him to fight back? Mihkel's confused feeling of shame increased as fear stiffened him. That might be good, too, for in a way it strengthened him to face what was in store for him. And that was not easy. It was much harder than grabbing a gun at the decisive moment. It was many times more difficult than falling, weapon in hand.

"Mother, Mother," the son mumbled trying to comfort her, but his voice sounded in his own ears like sobbing. Then he was silent. He felt like a caged, fluttering bird.

The old woman was brutally torn away from her son. She shrieked and raised her hands in agony, but shining bayonets separated her from him. They were not permitted to say good-bye.

"The trees will soon be in leaf!" flashed through the mind of the prisoner.

XIV

Men building up their hopes on this earth cannot predict the whims of the one who rolls the many-coloured pebbles of fate. The grace period of Taavi Raudoja came to an abrupt end also.

Taavi had employed every possible means of precaution at his work. He knew that many people were watching out for him, considering it their self-evident duty.

Taavi was familiar with the procedure of arrest in the factory. When someone was called by telephone to the department of personnel, plain-clothes men and uniformed soldiers were waiting for him there, and he never returned. There were too many "nationalist-fascist" suspects among the people of Estonia, and the NKVD with their newly formed contingents had no time for secrecy, no time to stage a mysterious "disappearance" of their victims, as had been their custom before.

Taavi had become well-acquainted with the factory and had prepared an escape route for the time when the innocent invitation should come from the department of personnel. But it never came.

One night toward the end of March somebody rang the bell of the front door. It was half-past eleven, but nobody suspected anything sinister for the ring was short and modest, as if a tenant who had forgotten his key did not want to disturb the sleep of the others. As nobody from the first floor went to open the door, Taavi's landlord went downstairs. Taavi came to the corridor, sensing something suspicious in the air. He was wearing the slippers his landlady had made out of cloth for him last Christmas.

From the top of the stairs he saw three men enter. Two of them wore the uniform of NKVD officers. One looked like a tramp with his long, shapeless leather jacket and his spineless slouch. The men stood for a moment, looking awkwardly around, as if they were surprised at being admitted so readily. They held their hands in their pockets, clutching their revolvers. It was a check of passports, the captain of the NKVD announced. The other uniformed man had the rank of lieutenant.

Later Taavi could not curse himself enough. He stood in the corridor as if dazed, although he had long before thought out a plan of action for a case just like this. Why didn't he dash back into the room, lock the door, and then jump out the window? He knew exactly how far he should jump in order to land in a deep snowdrift without injuring himself. What was he waiting for? Everything was clear. Later he thought the reason why he did not move was that he had no shoes on.

The men were not interested in the ground floor. They came directly upstairs, still holding their hands in their pockets, looking around with frightened, suspicious eyes. Taavi handed his passport to the captain. He demanded also Taavi's deferment papers.

"What is your rank?" he asked in Russian.

"Private," Taavi answered, also in Russian.

The captain laughed briefly, like one who laughs at a bad joke in good company, and the other two pressed close to Taavi.

"You are an officer," the captain said.

Although a cold wave ran over Taavi's back, he forced a laugh in return.

"And your name is Taavi Raudoja," the captain announced.

Now the situation became all too clear to Taavi. He was the sole object of their late visit.

They entered his room. The captain waved him to a chair and sat down opposite him, taking his Browning out of his pocket. He wants to have it handy, Taavi thought, in case I should pull a trick. When the frightened face of his landlady appeared in the doorway, the captain hid the gun from her. The landlady withdrew without saying a word when she saw two strangers—the lieutenant and the man in civilian clothes— searching the room. It seemed to Taavi that the men were looking for weapons. Fools; he wouldn't keep any arms under the bed. The lieutenant picked up the few photographs Taavi had in the room, a notebook and a few other insignificant papers. There was nothing suspicious lying about—Taavi knew only too well how dangerous even unimportant trifles could become. The plain-clothes man pocketed unashamedly the old silver fountain pen Taavi had received from Selma as a Christmas present.

"Come along," the captain ordered, getting up.

We'll see about that, Taavi thought, putting on his shoes and his thin overcoat. His landlord and landlady were pale and speechless from fear. Only their little son, awakened from his sleep, ran to Taavi. He grabbed the man's hand and looked at him with large, pleading eyes.

"Uncle, you won't stay away long, will you?" he cried, frightened.

Taavi's own son Lembit appeared before his mind's eye. No, damn it, he wouldn't let the Russians take him—back to the wall from where he had already once escaped. Thoughts flashed through his head in feverish haste—clear and sober thoughts.

They descended the stairs, Taavi first; the three men who had arrested him at his heels. The door of an apartment was opened on the first floor and closed quickly again. A rapid move going out and he'd slam the

161

front door in their faces. In a moment or two he'd be around the corner, gone. The hall was dimly lit and it was quite dark outside. Not knowing why, Taavi abandoned the plan.

When they reached the street he thanked God he had not attempted to escape. The captain gave a short whistle and men emerged from behind the corner of the house and from the lilac bush beside the door. They were carrying submachine guns crosswise on their chests, and Taavi counted six of them. Three and six—that made nine. They must really have considered him a topflight bandit. Nine to one; these were high stakes, and this time they had not been interested in anybody else in the house.

Taavi was ordered to walk down the street toward the railroad terminal. They'll put me directly on a train and send me to the great fatherland, he thought with bitter irony. They marched off, Taavi a little ahead of the others, and some of the men marched parallel to him on the other side of the street. Although he had been searched in his room, he was not permitted to put his hands in his pockets. That's all right, Taavi thought; if he started running it would be easier to take the first jump that way.

They marched slowly. The recent spring-like weather had thawed the snow, and the ensuing freeze had covered the streets with ice. A few inches of fresh snow had fallen in the evening, covering the streets which had not been strewn with sand, so that every step required much effort. It seemed as if fate itself were against Taavi—the glazed streets robbed him of a firm foothold, and he was sure that the Russians noticed this and gloated over it with obvious satisfaction. The night was dark, and the streets empty and gloomy, but some stars showed in the early spring sky, glittering from between sparse, rent clouds. What a stupid time to let oneself be dragged to prison. Soon the meadows would be green, and warm winds would sweep along the shores.

Taavi recalled clearly his sudden arrest on the pitch-black road that autumn night. He had made a mistake there in not dashing into the woods right away. No, cost what it may, this time he wasn't going to let himself be treated that way. Without looking back he tried to figure out how the men were holding their guns. Could he surprise them and gain a few steps that way, or would the shots ring out at his first leap? Perhaps their number made them careless. He decided to flee on the corner of Tornimäe Street, which was narrow and crooked. If he could jump around the corner, he'd be gone. Just calm down and get your foot muscles taut like springs, he told himself.

Reaching the street corner, he slowed down as much as he dared and tried to find a firmer footing on the sidewalk. If he stumbled here, a few bullets would whizz through the night and his adventures would be at an end. At the same moment that Taavi's sole found a handful of sand on the pavement, he noticed a big pile of snow on the street corner, shovelled there by a janitor, whose diligence seemed peculiarly out of place in this time and age. The plan did not materialize. Taavi was almost ready to swear out loud. He realized that by running around the

162

pile of snow he'd be riddled with bullets long before he could reach the protective corner of the house. A little later a heavy army truck passed them. Was the driver afraid of the marching figures in the street, or was it an accident that the bright headlights came on for a moment? The shadow of the NKVD captain who was walking right behind Taavi fell on the wall and Taavi saw clearly that he was carrying his gun in his hand. He was grateful to the unknown janitor, whose snow pile had saved him from certain death.

The captain and the lieutenant, who was also walking behind him, tried to carry on a conversation with him in Russian. They seemed to think that Taavi understood the language sufficiently, for he had used a few words he knew. Or was this a device to keep him from making escape plans? Passing the cooperative of Jaan Meos, Taavi began to wonder who else was arrested that night besides himself.

They marched directly toward the railway terminal. They passed the old city hall with its spire blunted by bombs, and walked down Nunna Street, past the Imperial restaurant. On the corner of Kloostri Street they crossed over and entered a big, grey, stark house on the corner. Taavi cast a quick glance at the black, majestic silhouette of the citadel and the intricate lacework of the leafless trees near the adjacent pond. That's where Riks hanged himself, thought Taavi.

The interrogation began in a plain room on the second floor. Taavi's curiosity was slightly aroused. The situation did not seem as desperate as he had expected. He had not noticed a single armed guard in the dimly lit corridors and halls of the house, and all the soldiers who had escorted him remained downstairs. Instead of the lieutenant who had been along when he was arrested, another one entered the room, a one-armed invalid.

The captain waved to Taavi to sit down. There were only two chairs in the room, one on each side of the desk, so that one of the three would have to remain standing. Taavi got the strange feeling that the captain had arrested him because of boredom. He had gone out on his own to get some work to do. He had strong features and small, sparkling black eyes. The impression he made was not really terrifying, although his mouth was brutal and his teeth yellow. He took a big topographical map of Estonia from the corner cupboard and cut it into letter-size pieces with a pocket knife. Then he sat down on the other chair, facing Taavi, and placed his Browning ostentatiously on the corner of the table. This last move evoked an ironical smile from Taavi. All according to the book, he thought.

The interrogation began according to the pattern already familiar to Taavi: name, father's name, time and place of birth, and so on. The face of the captain remained grave and formal. Taavi discovered that the one-armed man, who remained standing, was an Estonian from Russia who served as interpreter. Taavi decided to hide as much as he could. He must only keep track of what he was saying, so that he would

163

not contradict himself when interrogated again. Everything went smoothly with the year 1941 and the German occupation.

"Why did you go to Finland?"

Taavi made an astonished face. He'd never been to Finland.

"The damned swine; listen to him lying," the one-armed man hissed, grey in the face, as if racked by severe internal pains.

"Why did you change your name after you escaped from the border guard unit?" the captain asked.

Taavi felt cornered at the beginning of the interrogation.

"I haven't escaped from anywhere. There must be a mistake," he said firmly. His self-confident, brazen denial made the men furious. The captain was the first to jump up and slap his face. Taavi's face was still sensitive from the beating he had received on the coast, and he was not certain he could remain composed for long under such treatment.

"Tell us your name!" the captain demanded.

"Karl Heidak. I have already told you. You saw my passport and my deferment papers."

A new blow fell on his ears.

"Who do you think I am?" Taavi shouted, angrily. "What right do you have to drag me here like this?"

Taavi saw that both men became slightly nonplussed. This emboldened him and he made an even more indignant face.

"But you were in Finland, weren't you?" the captain insisted.

"I have never been in Finland," Taavi said, emphasizing each word.

"Say it again that you've never been in Finland, you damned skunk," the one-armed man screamed behind his back and began to beat him hysterically on the nape of the neck. The initiative of the other seemed to encourage the captain. He grabbed the Browning from the table and pressed its muzzle against Taavi's ribs. He threatened to shoot immediately, if Taavi did not admit who he was. Although Taavi's face hurt and his head buzzed from the blows, he forced himself to be calm. The comical eagerness of his attackers would have been ridiculous, if the situation had not been so serious and the blows so painful. He knew that the threat of shooting was as far as they would go in this room, and furthermore he noticed that the captain had not released the safety catch on his pistol.

"Tell us who you are. Then you'll be released. If it turns out to be a mistake, you'll be released immediately and can go home."

"Of course it's a mistake!"

Without saying a word, the captain went to the cupboard, took out a photograph and showed it triumphantly to Taavi.

"Do you know this man?"

Taavi swallowed and shook his head. His throat had become dry.

"I can't recall having met him."

Of course he knew Mats Luukas; he knew him very well. They had been in the same platoon when they both attended military school in Finland. So Mats was in their clutches. When he had been arrested last autumn, Jaan Meos and his cooperative had considered it an accident.

164

"This man knows you very well," the captain said.

"If he's happened to see me on the street. . . ." Taavi shrugged his shoulders.

"You were together in Finland."

"I told you I haven't been in Finland."

Thus it went for a long time. The captain advanced questions and accusations, and Taavi denied everything. This drove the men to desperation, as if their own lives depended on the confession of their prisoner.

"Don't forget, you scoundrel, where you are!" the Estonian from Russia threatened venomously.

Taavi acted as if he hadn't heard him.

"It's useless trying to deny anything. We'll find it out anyways," the man said importantly. "We have graduated from schools for that purpose in Russia." He exchanged a few quick words with the captain and added, "You are in the special department of the NKVD for the investigation of war crimes, and nobody has yet left this house alive!"

Taavi did not show any reaction to these words. He looked toward the window. Bright daylight shone from between the blackout curtains.

"You are a Nazi!" the captain screamed.

Taavi burst out laughing at this accusation, so that the captain realized his mistake.

"Just keep laughing, you rascal," the one-armed man growled behind his back. But the blow Taavi expected did not come.

"You are a counter-revolutionary, a betrayer of the fatherland, and it would be a sin to waste a bullet on you," the captain said. He had not got any further than the first page of the interrogation protocol, and a whole pile of sheets cut from the map was still waiting—sheets on which he had planned to record the recitation of the sins of Karl Heidak or Taavi Raudoja. Taavi became tired. He expected to be beaten again and he didn't care. But he was not beaten any more.

A tall man with a rough-hewn face entered quietly, wearing the uniform and insignia of a colonel. Taavi deduced from his casual, superior manner and the apprehensive faces of the others that he was the head of the department; perhaps of the whole establishment. This assumption was confirmed by his impatient look at his wrist watch and his commanding voice, which sounded displeased that they were not yet ready.

They conversed for a long time in Russian. Taavi could not make out more than that he was the object of their discussion. The sallow, sombre face of the colonel and his ominous scowl portended no good. The interrogation was nevertheless over. The captain put the papers in the cupboard. Taavi Raudoja was taken to the first floor. The lobby was filled with bright daylight. It would have been mid-morning.

Taavi was not given much time to look around on the first floor for he was pushed down the steep stairs into the basement. Only the one-armed man followed him, brandishing his revolver.

A weak bulb was burning in the basement. Taavi was met by a

Kirghiz, whose sleeves were turned up, displaying a pair of strong hands in which he held a knife almost eighteen inches long. There was no use denying it; this scared Taavi. The dark, gloomy cellar with black, moist stone walls and the tiny bulb covered with a metal net created the impression of a medieval torture chamber. The NKVD agent with the long knife, with strands of matted black hair falling on his forehead from under his greasy cap, and with long rubber boots on his feet also looked sinister.

But no, Taavi was only searched again with new thoroughness. The man who was going through his pockets put the knife under his arm, so that the blade often touched Taavi. Then the searcher rolled himself a cigarette and began to smoke, at the same time cutting off the buttons from Taavi's clothes. He seemed to take a special pleasure in gliding his shiny blade past the face of his victim and blowing smoke casually into his eyes. When this was done he took Taavi's suspenders and threw them into a corner, undid his shoelaces and took them off, and bundled together his overcoat, cap, scarf and gloves.

"Say now what your name is," the one-armed man screamed. "Say it right away, or you'll never get out of this cellar! You'll only fly out as an angel." He repeated the last sentence several times, obviously pleased with his witticism.

Taavi did not answer. The unexpected arrest, the terror and the exertion had made him tired and had dulled his brain. His mind did not work well, and it was difficult to breathe in the stinking basement. They were not going to shoot him now. He was too interesting and unknown a specimen for them, and they had not yet got from him what they wanted. The removal of the buttons from his clothes indicated that they meant to keep him in prison.

"Come, you filthy toad," the one-armed man growled and pressed his gun against Taavi's back. He was pushed quickly along a dark corridor, where he noticed the stolid faces of armed guards.

The next room was damp, but he sensed here the smell of dirty clothes and sweat and felt the warmth generated by sleeping bodies. He made out a number of hazy figures; some of them crouching on a long bench, and others on the floor. Then he was roughly pushed into a narrow cell and the heavy door was locked and bolted behind him.

So that was it. Entering, Taavi had bumped his head into the ceiling. He leaned against the door, holding up his pants. He stood motionless, with the toes of his shoes touching the opposite wall, and his head drooping on his chest, until a chill shook him. He groped along the ice-cold walls and ceiling of the room. It was too small to stand up in, and too narrow to sit down. Cold, humid air gushed into the cell from holes in the ceiling. A fear arose in Taavi that he had been placed in a refrigerator to be frozen to death. Groping again at the stone walls around him he located two oblong openings in the ceiling where cold air kept blowing in. No light came from the openings and Taavi could not determine whether the air was blown in by ventilators or whether it was the natural flow of outside air.

His mind was feverishly at work trying to find a way to close the openings. There was not enough room for him to take off the few clothes he had left. Then he recalled the woollen socks he was wearing. He bent over, but could not reach his feet with his hands. The unlaced shoes came off easily, but he would never have believed that taking off one's socks could have meant such an exertion. It did one good thing: at least it warmed him up a little. With great effort he stuffed the socks into the air ducts above his neck. That did not help much, and soon his feet began to freeze in addition to his back. Chills ran up his legs, stiffening the muscles that were tense from long standing.

Then he heard voices outside and muffled steps. Taavi hoped somebody was coming to open the door. He heard imcomprehensible Russian words, and then muffled thuds. They seemed to follow at regular intervals, accompanied by desperate screams. When the walking stopped and the voices were silent; only the muffled thuds continued, resembling the sound one hears when tough meat is beaten to make it tender. Finally that stopped too.

Taavi tried to sleep standing up, his knees pressed against the wall, his neck against the icy ceiling. He doubted whether he would be able to fall asleep like that, although he had always tried to gain strength from sleep even in the most hopeless situations. He relaxed his limbs as far as it was possible in their cramped condition, and tried not to think.

He could not tell whether he had actually slept or whether he had only been in a dazed half-sleep from exhaustion. He became aware of his body again when he found himself shivering all over. He breathed quickly and moved his shoulders back and forth. His mind was wide awake and the apathy was gone. He felt anger again and a desire to fight. He had to do something. Suddenly he realized that he had to get out of this hole, and quickly, or else very soon he wouldn't be able to move even his little finger. He began to pound against the door with his fist. His arm was stiff and weak. With every blow he felt prickly thorns penetrate from his palms up into his wrists. That was a queer feeling and offered a certain amount of novelty. He remembered the door of the storage room he had pounded when he had been imprisoned in the house on the coast, and the Russian who had hit him in the face when the door was opened.

What time was it? He felt as if he had spent an eternity between these walls. He could not recall any more what he had told the captain who had interrogated him. He could not even remember the faces of his interrogators. The one-armed Estonian from Russia and the lieutenant of the border guard who had sat at the table in that house on the coast seemed to melt into one. Many things began to get mixed up in his head. The back of his neck, pressing against the ceiling, felt like a stone, growing bigger and bigger until it reached the back of his eyes, which were hurting from the darkness. And there was no room for thoughts in his head any more. Taavi felt that his thoughts were being pressed down into his throat. The saliva that collected in his mouth tasted of gall. He was hungry.

He pounded harder with his fist but nobody came to open the door. He became scared that he had been forgotten, and summoning all his remaining strength he pounded on the door again and again. Then he heard screams, this time quite close, and soft, muffled thuds. All of a sudden he realized that there were more people like him suffering in these dank holes in the wall, and his arm sank down, discouraged. Why exert himself? He was in the clutches of the NKVD. Even a mouse could not get through this wall.

Then he heard the rumbling of a car somewhere. The sound seemed to come from the ducts in the ceiling. Was he in a dungeon beneath the street?

By now Taavi had lost all ability to tell time. He could not even make a guess. He became dazed again from strain, cold and hunger, and had no desire to move even his fingertips. He began to look forward to the moment when the rigour of death would rise up higher from his legs. Nothing mattered any more.

When the door was opened, he slumped backwards on the floor. But he felt no pain from the fall. Only his legs felt rigid like breaking icicles. He could not tell whether he had been hit in the face again or whether it was merely the bright electric light that cut into his pupils like a sharp knife. He could only look around for a few moments in the lighted cell. To the right of him, on the bench, he saw the legs of sleeping men. They were sleeping on the floor, too, their bearded faces pressed against the wet stones. Then the guards grabbed him from either side and pulled him out from the cell into the corridor.

He was taken upstairs again into the familiar room, where the sallow-faced captain was waiting for him. The Browning was ready on the corner of the table. The sheaf of paper cut from the map was in front of the captain. He was holding his pen in his hand and looked at Taavi with his restless, sharp eyes.

"Comrade Raudoja," somebody exclaimed behind Taavi's back.

Taavi turned around, realizing at the same moment his mistake.

The captain laughed triumphantly and told him to sit down, with a satisfied expression. The man who had called Taavi was an elderly, bald Estonian, dressed in black. He served as interpreter this time. He was a fatherly-looking man, who had the appearance of a clergyman.

"So you are Taavi Raudoja?" He repeated quietly the captain's question.

Taavi rubbed his stiffened limbs.

"My name is Heidak," he said.

"But it was Raudoja just now?"

"I heard the voice of an Estonian. That's why I turned around."

"Don't make the comrade captain angry," the black-suited interpreter advised him. He then translated the words of the interrogator: "Is your mother alive?"

"None of my relatives is alive," Taavi muttered.

The captain laughed again triumphantly. He took the revolver from the table, went to the cupboard, and took from it a folder with broken corners and greasy blue covers. He waved it across the table in front of Taavi's face.

"This is your dossier," the interpreter said.

Taavi only shrugged his shoulders. Although he was tired to death and the stubborn chills had not yet left his body, he resolved to go on denying everything. He saw no immediate hope in it for the future but he was more afraid that the death sentence which had been passed on the coast would be carried out, than that he would be returned to the icy torture box. It was clear to him that he could be shot at any time in the cellar where the man with the shiny long knife was holding sway, without ever getting a chance to escape. If he refused to speak, they might torture him, but at least he wouldn't have to face immediate death. Or would he? Who could tell? "Your death will not be heroic. They won't give you a chance for heroics," Richard Kullerkann had said. "Your death will be made uglier than you can imagine." The death of Riks had not been glorious or heroic—suspended from a bush with a piece of rope, feet dangling in the water of the pond. But in a bush nearby there had been a dead Russian lying on his face, with a Finnish dagger in his back. It was well done, in spite of everything. But Taavi felt so squeamish from hunger that he was nauseated at the thought.

The interrogators had much more self-confidence this time. Or did it only seem so to Taavi because of his own wretched condition? Last time he had faced them with haughty defiance, considering even the blows he received only the overcompensated self-assertion of individuals who suffered under great inferiority complexes. Today the captain seemed actually to have grown taller. He was still waving the blue folder, with his eyes on Taavi with the expression of a beast of prey who is sizing up his victim.

"We have gone to a lot of trouble for your sake," he said. "Too much trouble for a White counter-revolutionary and traitor. Do you know how much your arrest has cost us? Of course you don't. It has cost a thousand rubles. A thousand rubles for your miserable presence." He laughed out loud. "The Germans have left some well-trained men behind; former S.D. men. Ha-ha-ha. Now the poor wretches don't know whom to haul into our hands. Even one's own brother isn't too much for them. What do you think? Is a thousand rubles too little for you or too much? Ha-ha-ha. I'll say—too much. But then it turns out the counter-revolutionary has already been sentenced to death once as a German spy. Too little; a thousand rubles is too little, I say. It's less than too little, for the man didn't get a penny, only a black eye. Ha-ha-ha."

So he had, in fact, been betrayed. Somebody had pointed with his finger—look, that man is suspicious. He's done such and such: avoided forced conscription by the Russians, hidden out in the woods, fought in the German army. But of course, there was the fear, the instinctive desire to hang on to one's wretched life. A new way to extend the days of your existence—by betraying others. Denounce, run around, search, spy on others; or else the trap will spring shut on your own head.

"What is your name?" he heard the ministerial voice of the interpreter. "It will only simplify your situation if you confess; if you tell everything nicely just as it has been."

"I have nothing to tell," Taavi answered. "Do you want me to start telling fairy tales?"

"A man who knows you very well has given us your real name and all the data. There's no use denying, when. . . ."

"If that man knows me, he should know also that my name has been Karl Heidak ever since I was born. Is the NKVD stupid enough to be misled by a liar?"

This answer infuriated the captain. He threw the folder angrily on the table and grabbed the Browning, scowling at Taavi. His eyes were bloodshot, his face flushed, and he was spluttering Russian curses through his teeth.

"We'll have to drag a woman here from the country. The name of that woman is Linda Raudoja. If you want to spare this old woman from getting acquainted with a certain room you already know, admit that your name is Taavi Raudoja!"

Taavi's head sank on his chest. He was in greater trouble than he had imagined. He did not doubt that the NKVD would bring his mother here if he should keep up his denial. The NKVD needed information, needed a confession, cost what it may. The torture and death of an old woman did not matter in the least. No, for heaven's sake, they must not touch his mother. But would Taavi's confession save her? Wouldn't they arrest her anyway? But she was really too old. What could the NKVD gain by arresting her? She knew nothing about the things of which her son was accused. She could only be valuable as an object of torture, as a means designed to open the closed mouth of her son. But would his mother ask him to speak? Hardly. She was an old woman who had already lost much. Her mouth would remain closed even under torture. And Taavi decided to persist in his silence. Beads of perspiration rose to his forehead but he bit his teeth firmly together.

"My name is Karl Heidak," he said indifferently.

The captain bent quickly over the table and punched his face several times with his fist. Taavi tried to dodge the blows, but his head sank weakly over the back of the chair, leaving his face exposed.

"Tell this scum that we'll bring his mother here immediately if he doesn't admit that his name is Taavi Raudoja," the captain screamed angrily to the interpreter.

Taavi staggered to his feet. He felt that it was the power of a tremendous fury that lifted him up and gave him strength. Blood trickled from his nostrils over his unshaven chin.

"My name is Taavi Raudoja," he said, holding up his buttonless trousers with his hands. "And remember this, captain: you can kill me, but you cannot escape your own fate. And your fate will be worse than mine."

The captain was as triumphantly happy as a boy. He spoke rapidly with the interpreter, unable to conceal his glee. Then his squeaking pen ran greedily over the paper. Is he recording another death sentence, Taavi wondered.

"Sit down, sit down," the captain made a generous gesture toward the chair. "Would you like to eat something? You might be a little hungry?"

"Could I get a cigarette?"

Both men fumbled through their pockets, but in vain. The captain waved to the interpreter, and the latter went out, returning after a few minutes with a big piece of newspaper, on which there was some coarse, greyish-brown, home-grown Russian tobacco. Taavi rolled himself a crude cigarette and began to smoke with cautious, short puffs, knowing that hungry smoking might make him sick. He noticed that his fingers were thinner, that his hands were dirty and trembling. The captain smoked a cigarette he had rolled from the leftover tobacco. It was very thin, burned quickly, and filled the room with the bitter smell of smouldering paper. Taavi asked also for some water. The black-coated man brought him some cold water in a metal tankard.

"Why did you change your name?" the captain asked.

Taavi had a good reason.

"As I had been sentenced to death on the coast, I had no other choice. I was arrested that time for no reason at all."

"What were you doing on the coast?"

"There was no food to be had in Tallinn after the liberation. I went to get some supplies from a farm I knew," Taavi lied.

"You wanted to flee to Finland again," the captain shouted.

Taavi shrugged his shoulders.

"Why should I have tried to flee to Finland?"

"Because you are a traitor. Why did you return from there in the first place?"

"I haven't been to Finland at all," Taavi answered stubbornly.

The captain jumped up again. Taavi was afraid he would punch his face once more, but the colonel with the long, rough-hewn face entered at that moment and the captain began to report the results of the interrogation to his superior. It was morning again outside.

Downstairs in the corridor Taavi received some food—a bowl of lukewarm, watery soup and a slice of dark bread. The man with the long knife sent him into a washroom to clean his bloody face. Then the heavy door of the tiny cell swung open and closed again, and Taavi Raudoja began to wait hopelessly, convinced that he would freeze to death.

XV

Taavi confessed the following night to having been in Finland. He smiled weakly while doing it. What the NKVD wanted, it had to get.

If somebody had predicted that Taavi would confess his "guilt" so

171

quickly, he would not have believed it. He did not quite believe it even when the pen of the captain was squeaking on the paper, recording his service in the White army of Finland. But that did not matter, Taavi thought. He did not want to go back into the ice-cold cell for a third time.

Then the captain asked the next question, which showed Taavi that he had already gone too far in his confession.

"Tell us the names of your comrades who were together with you in Finland."

"I won't tell that," Taavi answered firmly to the one-armed lieutenant who was again acting as interpreter. "I won't tell that," he repeated, as if seeking strength in his own words.

The captain only smiled confidently.

"So you won't tell that, eh?"

"You didn't want to tell your name either, you son of a bitch," the Estonian hissed angrily behind Taavi's back, as if Taavi's words made him choke.

Taavi did not answer.

"I'll give you my word that we'll do everything to ease your punishment, if you stop denying everything," the captain promised.

"I don't remember anybody right now," Taavi answered.

"Loss of memory," the one-armed man laughed. "We've seen that before. Do you know that even those who have really lost their memory get it back before they leave this place."

Taavi did not deign to look at the one-armed man, considering it beneath his dignity. He hated him, for they were of the same blood. He only turned his head slightly and mumbled with the greatest disdain of which he was capable: "You shouldn't be talking to me like that. You can't even remember who your parents were."

Before Taavi could finish, the renegade fell on him with insane fury. Taavi felt with satisfaction that he had caused his enemy greater pain than he himself was experiencing from the blows. Saliva spluttered from the lips of the enraged man, and he attempted to sink the dirty nails of his only hand into Taavi's eyes.

"What the devil," Taavi shouted and jumped up. Forgetting where he was, he nearly disregarded the need to hold up his buttonless trousers with his hands. He nearly sprang at his enemy's throat. But he heard the click of the captain's pistol, and paused. The captain was standing and aiming at Taavi. Angry curses sounded from behind Taavi's back.

"We'll have to freeze you for a long time yet," the captain said. The triumphant grin reappeared on his face when Taavi slumped back on the chair. "Stand up," he ordered.

"Stand up, you dog," the one-armed man cried.

Taavi stood up and swayed. He was really quite weak.

"Tell us the names of your companions," the captain demanded.

Taavi did not answer. He refused to speak even when the lieutenant pressed his revolver against Taavi's shoulder blade until he touched the bone. Taavi knew that the man would not dare to shoot him without orders from his superior.

The captain went to the cupboard and brought from it a woman's stocking. He waved it in front of Taavi, sneering.

"Do you recognize it?" he said, looking searchingly at his victim.

"A woman's stocking," Taavi replied with indifference.

"Yes," the captain jeered. "This is your wife's stocking!"

Taavi winced. No, that was impossible.

"Do you recognize it? The man doesn't even know his wife's stockings. What kind of a husband are you? A good stocking, see; torn just a little. Do you recognize it?"

"No."

The captain went back to the cupboard. This time he produced a brassiere, and threw it on the table. It was pale pink and soiled.

"Do you know that? The husband doesn't recognize his wife's brassiere. Ha-ha-ha."

"That doesn't belong to my wife," Taavi said firmly.

"Do you know where your wife and son are now?" the captain asked.

Taavi hesitated. Marta had seen the boat take off. Holy heavens, had they been captured at sea? Taavi looked at the stocking and the brassiere. No, he was not so familiar with his wife's underwear that he could have recognized these items as belonging to Ilme. Could this be a trap?

"I believe they are in the country," Taavi muttered.

"Ha-ha-ha," the captain laughed. "The man doesn't recognize his wife's stocking and underwear and doesn't know where his family is. Why did they attempt to go to Finland?" he asked.

Taavi staggered toward the chair but the lieutenant pulled it away from under him.

"I don't know. . . . They didn't want to go anywhere."

"They certainly wanted to, but they didn't get off the beach," the captain chuckled.

"This is a lie," Taavi shouted. All of a sudden he was convinced that they were trying to trap him. If Marta saw them in the boat, setting out from the shore, then the last sentence of the captain and his whole story were pure invention. Through Arno or some other acquaintance of Taavi's the NKVD might have learned about the whereabouts of Ilme and Lembit, but his wife and son were outside their grasp. Why didn't they show him Lembit's cap or overcoat or gloves? He would have remembered those more clearly than his wife's underwear. Or was a brassiere such a marvel for the Russians that every man should remember it in their opinion? Those fools!

"If you want your wife and son to be set free, tell us the names of your companions. Now are you going to talk?" the captain asked.

"No," Taavi mumbled. Regardless of what happened, he would not betray his comrades. He hadn't sunk that low yet.

His sullen, indifferent silence irked the captain. When the horse-faced colonel came to make his morning round of inspection, the reporting voice of the interrogator was perplexed. The tall colonel, decked with medals, gave Taavi a scrutinizing frown and issued new instructions, which Taavi did not understand.

"Think of your wife and little son," the colonel warned in his booming voice. "And the third one who'll be born soon."

It was a long time after these words had been said before Taavi grasped their significance.

To his surprise Taavi was not hauled into the familiar icebox this morning, but was left in the anteroom of the torture chambers, which was lit by a bare bulb in the ceiling. The cell was about twelve feet long and ten feet wide. A sleeping bench of rough boards occupied one end of the room. The stench had bothered him when he was descending into the cellar. Now it almost suffocated him. The room was so full of sleeping or crouching men that Taavi had trouble finding a place to stand. He leaned against the wall, holding up his pants with one hand. Near him next to the door was a hot iron stove, and by its side a stinking metal container about the size of a washbasin. In the opposite wall he saw two heavy, narrow doors, which he knew led to the icy cells. As if in response to his wandering thoughts somebody's hand began to pound on one of the doors. The blows were weak and hopeless.

"A new man?" somebody asked.

Taavi looked at the floor. Several pairs of eyes watched him from thin, shadowed faces. The heads of the men were shaved but they were all more or less bearded and looked dirty and unkempt. They gathered closer to Taavi and even the men lying on the boards gave him curious looks. He estimated that about sixteen or seventeen men were crammed together in this room. He could not count them exactly, for they were lying around in heaps. Right at his feet a middle-aged man was snoring, his face under the edge of the stinking basin. He looked like a labourer and there was a fresh bloody wound over his pugnaciously jutting chin. An old man with a long white beard crawled toward Taavi from the other side and touched the leg of his pants. A boyish-looking man was sitting cross-legged in front of him, tilting his head expectantly on one side.

"Sit down!" the old man said. "It's easier that way."

Taavi sank to his knees and then into a sitting position on the floor.

"What kind of men are you?" he asked. But the others only looked at him without saying anything.

The white-bearded man straightened his neck.

"Betrayers of the fatherland!" he said darkly. "Where do you come from?"

"I hardly know myself. . . . From Tallinn."

"Why?" somebody asked in an annoyed voice, as if Taavi had been caught lying. He noticed that the eyes of the men reflected as much curiosity and desire to ask questions as they revealed suspicion which

174

forced them to be silent. They had gathered into a tight circle around him, but they gave him sullen, scowling looks.

"Because of the Finnish affair," Taavi answered.

An understanding nod came from the shaven heads of the men. Their faces brightened.

Then they began to ask questions.

"Say, what's new outside? What date is it?"

"Have you heard anything about the Atlantic Declaration?"

"Are there any Englishmen still in Tallinn?"

"Do you have any news from Sweden?"

"What about the war?"

Taavi was not strong enough to speak much. And he did not know much, although the answers seemed vitally important to the men. Oh yes, they had their own answers ready for each question, answers which they believed in and which gave them confidence and support.

"Did you hear our former prime minister's speech on the Swedish radio?" the old man asked.

Taavi had never heard about this speech. Nobody had mentioned it outside, although people risked their lives, secretly listening to hidden radio receivers. No, Taavi hadn't heard it. The old man looked sadly in front of him. So the newcomer didn't even know that. In fact, they knew much more about world affairs here in the dark prison than the young man who had come from the very midst of life. The faces of the men sank dejectedly.

"Have you really not listened to the speeches of our ministers from abroad?" the white-bearded old man repeated. "Well, if you haven't got near a radio, that's possible. We don't know much either of what's going on in the world. We've been in five or six months or more. We don't soften up; that's why. But if you soften up, you disappear," he whispered.

Taavi was already too "soft" in his own opinion and too indignant to follow the questions and remarks of the men. The words he had brought with him from the interrogation room tormented him: "Think of the third one who'll be born soon." Ilme was supposed to bear the child in May. And he would remain here now for months to "soften up," as the shaven-headed men had said. This was one of the torture methods of the NKVD: to "forget" the prisoner for a while, until one day he is willing to confess to all the real or imagined crimes which the NKVD desires. Ah, if he could only sleep. Drop to the floor as if dead and sink into forgetfulness in the heavy, oppressive air.

The guards entered with great rumble and noise. Reveille. It must have been about six o'clock in the morning. Taavi Raudoja's first grey prison day began. Quickly and silently the men fell into a close single file and moved out of the cell, holding up their pants with one hand. The labourer with the bruised chin, who was too exhausted and sleepy to get up, was kicked awake by the guards' boots.

"Hurry up! Hurry up! No talking!" a guard shouted incessantly, although nobody said a word.

The row of men marched along the gloomy corridor toward a dirty, wet-floored washroom.

"Be quick now!" the old man whispered to Taavi. "This is as much as you get out of the cell all day and night. There, you can take care of your needs in that corner." Taavi noticed that his adviser was a stocky, broad-shouldered old farmer, whose one knee seemed to be stiff. His hands were big and strong.

Washing went quickly. There was no soap; they could only rub their faces with cold water.

Taavi felt his wounds in his cheeks and nostrils. They were painful. His face was covered with sharp, long stubble. Still, the cold water refreshed him. He stayed under the faucet until the guard pushed his automatic into Taavi's ribs. Even the time for washing one's face was limited.

"Hurry up. Hurry up! No talking!" the guard shouted.

After the morning cleanup, when the prisoners had been driven back into their cell, Taavi was taken to the man who had cut off his buttons. This time he cut off Taavi's hair. The procedure was careless and rough. The hair-cutting machine was old and out of order and Taavi had to grit his teeth several times with pain. When he touched his bare scalp, his fingers were bloody. But he did not pay much attention to that any more. Too often had his fingers become blood-stained touching his own face. He was a prisoner whose blood could be shed at any time, in any manner.

Breakfast was dished out after that in the cell. Taavi, too, received his portion—a thin slice of dark rye bread, a piece of smelly codfish and two cold boiled potatoes. He saw that the men put the greater part of the food carefully into their pockets. Why didn't they eat it?

"You'll have to get by on that until tomorrow morning," the greybeard said.

Taavi looked at his handful of food, smelled the stinking fish and shook his head. His head was heavy and he kept his eyes open with great effort. Greedily and mechanically he ate the fish and the bread, but when he wanted to peel the potatoes with his fingers the old man said: "Don't waste them. Later you'll be looking for the peelings on the floor, and some other man will have eaten them up. Put the peelings in your pocket if you can't get them down now. They'll be good to nibble on later."

Then one of the guards brought in a bucketful of water and a drinking mug, placing them next to the stinking metal container. One of the prisoners had emptied it during their morning trip to the washroom but evidently he had not had enough time to wash it. Knocking sounded again from behind the door of one of the freezing cells, mingled with Russian screams. It was the weak and desperate voice of a man on the verge of collapse.

176

"A Ukrainian, one of Vlassov's men," said a prisoner who was crouching next to Taavi. "They torment him, but he's tormenting us!"

"What if we opened the door?" Taavi asked. It was hard to listen to the choking, gasping voice.

"It's locked," the man answered. "And you'd better not touch it. The other cell is empty right now. Or have you already got the taste out of your bones?"

"He'll probably die today," the old man mumbled. "He's been in several days now, and they won't take him out before nightfall. He's a real tough character," he said with respect.

The men gathered again around Taavi.

"Speak up now," they demanded. "Tell us what's going on outside!"

"I'm not well enough to talk much now," Taavi muttered.

"Come on; give him time," the old man took Taavi's part. "You see, his head is shaven too. He won't get out from here very soon."

"I thought maybe I could get some sleep," Taavi said, turning toward the bench.

"Oh no!" the old man exclaimed. "They'd kick you into the icebox right away. Try to lean against the wall behind the stove. We'll keep you covered in case a guard should stick his nose in through the door. Oh no, you can't get away with sleeping in daytime. Try to doze a bit right here. Lean your head on my shoulder, I won't mind." He whispered the last words, suspiciously eyeing the haggard faces of his cellmates. One among them was an informer.

Taavi Raudoja was not yet familiar with the deadening daily routine of the prison. He was too tired to be wholly aware of his environment and before long his eyelids became heavy and his head sank on the old man's shoulder.

In a few days Taavi Raudoja became acquainted with prison life and with most of his cellmates; at least with their faces, for it was much more difficult to see inside everybody and nobody spoke about his past. It was as if they were embarrassed to talk about it, as if the days they had lived through had been too insignificant. Only the expressions and the eyes of a few younger men bore witness to their inner troubles.

"Hope is our last mouthful of bread," the grey-bearded old man insisted unswervingly. He did not tell Taavi much about his life, but a friendship had developed between them ever since the first few hours. The name of the old man was Tõnis. He came from somewhere on the coast. When Taavi asked for more, he answered: "My life isn't the most important thing. Why keep talking about it? I am an old man. My life is over."

All that Taavi could make out from his talk was that the old man was the sole survivor of his family and that his son had fought in the German army all through the war. He had been killed quite near his home village. The old man's conversation was mostly patriotic and idealistic

177

like that of a schoolboy. Taavi was quite astonished at the faith and hope the man displayed in their hopeless situation. Not a day passed when they did not discuss the Yalta conference and make plans for the enforcement of the Atlantic Declaration. Everything was just a matter of time. If only the days would pass a little faster. They were sure that when the war was over they would be released. But many of them had lost count of the days and were not quite sure of the date. Violent arguments arose about that, which helped pass the monotony of the days.

It was hardest at first for Taavi to get along without tobacco. Then he began to suffer from hunger. The old man sometimes slipped him a mouthful from his own meagre portion.

"I have no appetite today. It'll be left over anyway," he said.

Taavi accepted, although he knew Tõnis was lying. He accepted because he was too hungry to refuse.

One morning they were all thoroughly searched again. Their clothes and the whole cell were examined. The guards looked under the sleeping bench, behind the small iron stove which was heated with sooty, soaked pieces of timber from the ruins, and even under the stinking metal container. The search was supervised by an Estonian from Russia who looked like a genuine political commissar. Taavi heard that his name was Kuusk. Nothing was found. To the men who had lost count of the days he made a triumphant remark.

"The war is coming to an end. Our army is on the outskirts of Berlin. Soon we'll hang Hitler and then the smaller Nazi fry—like you!"

This was news from the outside to the men, and interrupted even their habitual lice-hunt in the shirts which had become black and stiff with filth. One could discuss it and argue about it, and some began to reconsider the deadlines they had set up.

Taavi was greatly bothered by lice. The first night he could not quite tell why his body was itching. His tired and tortured brain did not even register the presence of the vermin. But the following nights he could not fall asleep so easily.

"Your shirt is clean. That's why you are in such a fix. A louse won't even get through our underwear any more. It's as tough from dirt as a calf's hide tanned into shoe leather. Hasn't seen soap and water for half a year. The louse is no fool," Tõnis said.

"We must taste like corpses already," one of the middle-aged men remarked, whom the others called "dairyman" because of his big, flabby stomach. His real name was Johannes and he was a bookkeeper by profession. He and a young man, Hendrik, looked more exhausted and worn than the rest. Their shiny eyes were sunk deep into dark sockets. The deepest facial wound belonged to Valter, the thirty-year-old labourer who had arrived only recently. A man about forty named Otto was said to have severe wounds on his back from being beaten with a leather whip. He never spoke a word, and he was suspected of being a spy.

Battling the lice Taavi understood why the young man had scratched his neck and his whole body until they were covered with blood. Taavi had to do the same. The feet of several men were swollen and their toes bright red and inflamed. Somebody was coughing, and he spat on the floor where his companions slept at night. Taavi had no socks and his feet froze at night, although he took off his shoes and pulled the legs of his trousers down. He was thankful that he had picked up no worse disease from the icebox than a head cold, although this was annoying enough under present conditions. Tõnis offered him his own torn socks. Although Taavi sometimes accepted a bite of food from the old man, he refused his socks. Then Tõnis asked the guard for an extra pair, but the guard kept forgetting.

Taavi marvelled that the men had been able to hold out for several months under such conditions. Only once he saw Johannes, his face livid, lean his forehead against the cold wall and beat his fists against the stones. Then the man turned around and began to gaze at the ceiling with an apologetic face, as if he begged to be pardoned for this weakness, and asked strength from heaven.

Strength—they all needed much strength. Days passed. No more men were brought into their cell. Of course this was not the only cell in the prison. The freezing boxes were in frequent use. Toward dawn a victim would be pushed into such a cell, and the following night be hauled away again—probably to be interrogated. Some did not utter a sound behind the locked doors. Some raved and kicked for half a day, until the blows became tired and feeble. Some cried and prayed. Their voices were harder for the men to endure than the deadening hunger.

One morning Tõnis said: "Listen, men. It's the Ukrainian again!"

"Yes, the Ukrainian," the child-faced man whispered. He had always looked at Taavi with awe, and probably had had older brothers in Finland. "I saw the Ukrainian when he was brought in," he said, frightened. "His mouth had been beaten to a bloody pulp. He didn't seem to have any teeth left."

"But listen to him; how he tears loose," somebody muttered with respect. "He's tougher to kill than a cat. Wonder if he's gone out of his mind or what?"

"He won't confess; that's all."

"What could he have to confess?" Tõnis sighed. "Got taken prisoner by the Germans, and there he was clobbered half to death. Then they put the uniform of Vlassov's army on him, and now the Russians are squeezing out his soul. The life of a native citizen in the Soviet paradise isn't much to brag about either."

"Why don't they shake off the shackles of communism, then? Why don't they rise up?" Hendrik shouted, suddenly jumping wrathfully to his feet. "They are used to revolutions. All their celebrations are bloody. Why has he come here to tear my soul out with his yelling?" He ran furiously to the door behind which his fellow-sufferer was writhing and began to beat on the door in turn. "Shut up!" he screamed.

The pounding stopped.

"Don't you start it again, you creature. You are driving me insane," Hendrik shouted in desperation.

179

Only in the afternoon did the men hear his croaking voice again. The prisoner pounded on the door a couple of times, resembling the last slow ticks of a rundown clock. Nobody paid much attention to that. At midnight, when the guards came to take him to the interrogation room, he crashed backwards on the floor, stiff in his crouching position like a piece of wood. The spirit of the tough Ukrainian had departed hours ago.

Lying on the floor near the stove, Hendrik began to sob like a child, his shoulders twitching.

Although the men had lost track of the date, it must have been around the beginning of May when exciting news from the outside began to penetrate the cell. Kuusk, who looked like a political commissar, and other guards brought it. Even the girls who handed out food in the mornings seemed ecstatic at the long-awaited joyful news—the end of the war was at hand. The end of the Second World War; more victorious and glorious for the Soviets than anybody would have dared dream only a short while ago. Kuusk considered it his duty to stop by every day and report the victories of the Red Army.

"The cannon are roaring their salute! From two hundred and forty mouths!" he shouted, his face wildly happy. "The Red Army is in Berlin! Don't you hear the jubilation from our great capital Moscow?"

The faces of the prisoners remained grey with indifference. They did not hear or see anything. Only pain flashed through the hardened hearts. When Kuusk rushed out of the cell, they discussed the news.

But the roaring salutes and raucous jubilation of Moscow began to resound louder and louder in the underground torture cells. Kuusk had to return again and again, for he had nowhere else to express his joy. Berlin had fallen. The German forces had capitulated in Italy and in Austria. The Russians and the British had met at Wismar and had drunk vodka to celebrate eternal brotherhood. Hurrah. And then Kuusk arrived with the final news: Germany had capitulated unconditionally. The protocol had been signed in Berlin on the eighth of May. The Second World War had ended in Europe.

Kuusk raced back and forth in front of the narrow cell door. His hands were spread out and he spouted hissing screams of joy in Russian and Estonian. He spoke in a continuous stream and his voice was almost gone from drinking and shouting for joy.

"Comrades, shout for the health of great Stalin!" he cried, hands raised over his head. "Hitler is down! For whose sake are you here? For Hitler's sake. He's down now, down in the dust, broken, smashed. Our great fatherland is free of danger for ever. Estonia is free for ever."

"Will we be freed now?" somebody asked with a motionless face.

"You'll all get free," Kuusk croaked, red in the face as if he were suffocating. "Comrades, shout hurrah to our great leader, father, and teacher! Long live great Stalin! Long live Josif Vissarionovitch Stalin!"

He dropped both arms abruptly, but no sound followed. This enraged him, so that his eyes almost popped out of his head and he frothed at the mouth. The blunt, bearded faces of the men around him remained impassive. Was mockery lurking in their sunken eyes? "You damned scum!" Kuusk screamed. "We have to get you quickly under the earth, out of everybody's way. There will be more to come. Half of Europe will go through these cells before we are through. Get the filth out of the way."

He rushed out, slamming the door with a crash. Even through the door the men heard his spitting, cursing and wild hurrahs.

Moscow had won.

"Now we're that far," Tõnis remarked, sat down on the floor and stroked his white beard

The others, too, sat down. The rapid succession of news items from outside had made them dizzy and tired. So there was finally peace in Europe.

"Red peace!" the grey-bearded old man mumbled. "My daughter said those words before she died. Red peace. This is the most terrible thing that could have come. So the British—no, I can't believe that! I wish they had killed me before I heard this."

No one said anything.

It's spring outside, thought Taavi; full, blossoming spring. Spring had come too late for him. He was a hopeless prisoner now, whose companions predicted he would get twenty-five years of forced labour, if nothing worse. Taavi knew what that meant. A Soviet forced labourer, even if he was in the best of health to start with, did not last more than a few years. And it was much worse than a quick death, for hope died, leaving only an animal instinct, a brute desire to live. This made a man lower than an animal, until death came and redeemed the soul from the decaying body. But he knew that if he had to choose, he would reach for forced labour instead of death by shooting, for he wanted to live. He hoped. His face and neck were heavy with bruises but he believed in a miracle. Because of the instinctive urge to survive he did not feel ashamed to accept the meagre mouthfuls of food from the old man, when he offered them to Taavi. Taavi accepted them and swallowed them greedily, wondering only how the old man was able to give them up. He had made up his mind long ago that he would not accept any more, but still his hand took the potato and his mouth swallowed it hastily, although his throat was tight with suppressed tears and his eyes were rigidly glued to the shaking, thin, sinewy hand of the old man.

"I don't eat as much as I used to," Tõnis said. "Well, it's easier that way, and the vermin won't attack you either, if there's nothing to be had. This is just a trifle. Take it!"

And Taavi took it.

Taavi kept thinking of the spring outside. And there was still freedom to be found in the forests. There were many men who were alive and fighting. They were outlaws, but they were free to move and escape.

They were free to fight and die fighting. Taavi began to realize what a blessing it was to be able to breathe fresh air, if only a few draughts. And the sea was free now; cruel and savage, or glittering calmly in blue and silver sparkles.

"The sea is free now," he said to the old man.

Tõnis winced and his hands became restless.

"Yes," he said and did not speak any more.

A few hours later, when Taavi had had time to torment himself with many thoughts, the old man said, "Yes, the sea is free, but I belong to this land, and the land isn't free. But hope is our bread. This land will become free."

It was good to listen to the words of the old man. He was the unfailing source of faith and strength for the whole cell. He called the men his sons and he was a strong father, inspiring hope and confidence in their tortured hearts.

The war is over but, believe me, it won't stay this way. Some of them will be saved too. But those who won't be saved should remember that life will go on in those who are left and in those few who escaped over the restless waves during the great storm. Though many innocent prisoners will die, their right to justice will remain, even if the Western allies bring shame upon themselves by drinking vodka and pledging eternal friendship with the greatest murderers of mankind. Let them keep in mind that every pact they make with the Communists becomes their own epitaph.

It was past midsummer when they again began to drag men to nightly interrogations. All at once their forgotten, tormented lives became full of sinister excitement. The interrogators seemed to be suddenly in a hurry to liquidate the cell. They used new brutalities instead of the freezing boxes.

"The prisons of Tallinn are in socialist competition with each other," Tõnis remarked. Since the news about peace in the spring he had become sickly and feeble.

"It seems that way," the labourer called Valter stated. He had just returned from the nightly strain. "It seems to me that they don't even share their information about the prisoners. It's all the same NKVD, but they seem to be jealous of each other."

Taavi remembered again the woman's stocking and brassiere he had been shown before he had been "forgotten." He remembered even more sharply the warning about the third child who was to be born soon. When his heartaches and suspicions about the unknown fate of his wife and child—or children—became too intolerable, he insisted to himself, speaking out loud: "They are in Sweden. They are in the free world. Marta saw with her own eyes how the boat took off. The Russian lied when he said that they had never set foot outside the country."

Taavi was longing for his turn to come. If only he could find out something for certain. If only something would happen. But he was not called up.

Men began to disappear from their cell. The first who did not return from a nightly call was Otto, the one whom they had considered a spy. Valter, the sturdy labourer, came back, but did not walk on his own feet any more. His face had stiffened into a painful grimace. The men watched him as he tried to reach the sleeping bench, holding on to the wall, but he sank to the floor with a hoarse groan. He did not complain. Only the muffled sounds of pain and swearing issued from his lips, although he tried to keep them tightly together. His cellmates watched him silently, too stunned to offer help, as they saw him crawling on the floor on his hands and knees. When he reached the low bench, he took off his shoes and exposed his feet. They had been burned bright red with boiling water, were skinless in places, and swollen all over.

The men shook their heads. This meant that none of them would be spared, otherwise the butchers would have hidden their brutalities. Now the beatings and tortures of their comrades were deliberately used to torture them all, just as the freezing cells had been used in winter. And yet once a week their beards were trimmed—simply cut shorter with shears. And once a week comrade Kuusk came to discuss politics with them—to reeducate them by preaching "the gospel of Stalin," as the men said. For what purpose, then? Although they had already suffered here for long, nameless months, there were still many things they did not understand.

Those who were not taken to be interrogated at night were disturbed by muffled shots. The sound was not far away, and there was no doubt that it came from pistol shots. The youngster with the pale face winced each time and moaned quietly. Hendrik, the tall man who looked like the shadow of death, gritted his teeth and covered his ears with the collar of his coat, as if he were cold. Taavi could not believe that they were killing people right there. In his opinion it was easier to drag living prisoners into a clump of trees than corpses. Or was something afoot again in the political sphere, that they had to rush to destroy the prisoners? No; that was a futile hope. After the Russians had left in the war summer of 1941, there was not a single one among the prisons the NKVD had occupied where executions had not taken place. It was part of the NKVD tradition to leave the blood of their victims on the walls of the rooms they had used. And they buried them under the floors.

It was hardest for Taavi to watch the sufferings of the boy. The executioners had not yet literally laid their bloody hands on him. Up to now his torments had been mental. He came from a simple, good family, and it always touched Taavi when he folded his hands in prayer at night, frankly and without embarrassment. He prayed for his parents, his brothers and sisters, and prayed for strength for himself. He was very weak and he cried more and more often. He tried to hide it and be strong but he could not help it. He was still a child. And what was his

183

guilt? Was he really a criminal, dangerous to the great Soviet state because the last forced mobilization of the Germans had dragged him from his home into some kind of auxiliary labour company? He had never got to the front and could hardly handle a gun.

Old Tõnis tried to console him and slipped a piece of boiled potato into his hand during his comforting talk. But the youngster paid no attention to the mouthful of food. His long white fingers fidgeted with the potato, and words exploded from his mouth, sounding incongruous and unnatural, considering his weak, childish looks.

"Why don't they kill me right away? What are they waiting for?"

Then he placed his head on the breast of the old man, and dry, tortured sobbing shook his whole body. The old man stroked his shaven head.

Hendrik, tall and thin as a skeleton, looked at him and gritted his teeth.

"Quit whining," he shouted angrily, bending over as if he had painful cramps in his stomach. His dark eyes rolled over the low, damp ceiling, and he gnashed his teeth again, without looking at anyone. Then his glance caught the small electric bulb in the ceiling and he laughed hoarsely. "They are wasting electricity on us!"

Several men had already disappeared from the cell. The disappearance of quite a few was not noticed right away, for there were no beds to remain vacant. The number of those who had to sleep on the floor because of lack of space became smaller and smaller and at night all could now find room on the sleeping boards. But their sleep was restless. The men listened, wincing, for the shots; or lay awake, expecting their names to be called.

Taavi began to get worried about the old man. It seemed as if Tõnis wanted to starve himself to death. He hardly ate anything at all, although the food they received was barely sufficient to remain alive. When Taavi did not accept the food the old man offered him, he put it in his pocket or handed it to someone else. His body seemed to dry up. All that was left of him was a bundle of stocky bones and tuft of white beard. His chest rattled and he hunched smaller and smaller. At night he was racked with pain. His straight leg gave him a lot of trouble. The morning trip to the washroom became slow and painful for him. But his spirit refused to break. When the guards kicked him because of his crippled slowness, he cursed them in Russian with such strength that they began to show him respect. And within the cell he remained a source of defiance and firmness to everyone. Many a man would have felt more self-pity had it not been for Tõnis.

"If they destroy me, they haven't yet destroyed the whole people. They are really all wrong to think that way. There are more people outside right now than were left after the Great Northern War, and they won't be able to uproot everybody here either."

And he exhorted the men: "Remember my words. They won't cost me anything any more, even if somebody does report them—somebody whom fear of death has turned into a spy. Whoever of you should be sent to Siberia, try to save your souls. And if you can, flee, dash into the woods. If you don't succeed, the end will be short and clear. But if you do, you'll manage to live somehow, no matter where. Nobody will find out. And when they begin to crack down on Russia, then turn back to your ravaged country. Yes, you must try to escape. You must not stand there like a calf seeing the gate closed. If you do that, they'll bring the stick down on your bare skull. I am old and won't amount to anything any more, but you have to keep your eyes open. Even between these walls you must keep your thoughts moving, making plans. And if no crack opens up anywhere, then remember that the people won't come to an end if you should be put to death."

Six new men were brought into the cell. Half a dozen of their number must then have received their patrimony or been sent to Siberia. Without exception the newcomers had been arrested much later, although they, too, had suffered for quite a long time under the same roof. They were wordless and numb. Silently they looked around the cell for acquaintances. Taavi did not find any Finland fighters among them. There was no hurry to ask questions. Their fate was the same; there was nothing to ask about, and the newcomers were no better informed about the outside world than they themselves. They all knew that summer was in its full glory over Tallinn. What was happening at peace conferences and what kinds of boundaries were being drawn on the maps, nobody had any idea.

"The Russians must be getting ready to pull out again," one of the newcomers said. "They are clearing up the prisons and cleaning up the rest."

"But we are through," another of the newcomers said. "We were brought here, and this is the death cell."

"Where did you get that, damn it?" Hendrik shouted, ready to attack the speaker.

"This is what we know about this cell. And it smells that way."

The following night three of them were taken away and did not return any more.

A night later the name of Taavi Raudoja was called.

XVI

"Haven't we met before?" The familiar captain laughed mockingly at Taavi from behind his table and measured him with a critical look. He's checking how much meat is left on my bones, Taavi thought bitterly. Walking up the stairs he had realized with horror how weak he was physically. Now they began to test the remaining strength of his spirit.

The sullen one-armed man served again as interpreter. Seeing Taavi,

185

his mouth seemed to water like that of a hungry beast of prey in front of its victim.

Taavi did not know whether he should go on hiding his past or begin recounting the names of his companions. In the months he had spent in the cellar he had invented scores of non-existent names which he planned to use if necessary. But walking up the stairs he had suddenly become giddy. He had breathed fresh air. The clean air of a summer night. In his mind he saw all at once the dark blue summer sky, shady trees, rustling fields, inviting streets. All these deliriously seductive smells. And how many of them had penetrated into those corridors, even into this interrogation room. Taavi's limbs began to tremble with excitement.

Even while he was standing in front of the captain his heart pounded savagely and his eyes bored into the blackout curtains, behind which, he knew, was the sky. If he could only take one look at the summer night sky. He did not hear what he was asked and the interpreter had to kick him repeatedly before he awoke.

"Are you going to tell us the names of your companions now?" the captain asked.

"Yes!" Taavi answered quickly.

"You have had plenty of time to make up your mind," the interpreter sneered.

The captain eagerly seized his pen but all of a sudden Taavi was unable to remember any of the names he had invented down in the cell.

"Speak up, you swine," the one-armed lieutenant screamed. "We won't play with you long. If you won't talk, we'll make sausage out of you."

He began to dictate names, summoning his total will-power to invent new ones. It was difficult to devise even the most everyday names. His head was simply empty and sounds seemed mysterious units which refused to be combined into a name. When he got hold of an animal's name he had to fight against making all the following ones into names of wild or domestic animals. When he recalled the name of a tree, by and by he had names with which to populate a whole forest, and the Estonian interpreter might begin to doubt their veracity.

Addresses were important for the captain, too. But Taavi was in an even greater pinch here than with the names, for during the few following nights this would have exposed his total deception. And what if the NKVD should return empty-handed each time, without finding anyone of that name at a given address? He would be beaten into a bloody pulp, there was no doubt about that.

"I don't know where they might be living now," Taavi said. "I have been here so long. I didn't have much contact with them before, either."

The captain and the interpreter counselled with each other. Taavi's story seemed credible. But names alone were not enough. If Taavi would only recall some addresses. If only just one.

Taavi got an idea.

"If you would give me a couple of days to move around freely in

186

Tallinn, I could find out for you where they live." Perspiration came to his armpits when he said that.

But the others burst into disdainful laughter. The proposition was too transparent. The captain even passed his hand over the pistol which was lying on the corner of the table, as if that would help dispel such thoughts from the head of the prisoner.

Taavi saw that, but he could no longer stop his thoughts. They came from the fresh air, as if dictated to him, although he did not yet know where they would lead.

"If you want more names, then," he said, "I have a paper with the names of all those who graduated from the military school in Finland. It is Mannerheim's order of the day, and they are all listed on it."

Something unexpected happened.

Hearing the name of Marshal Mannerheim, the captain jumped up as if stung by a viper and the interpreter fiercely clasped Taavi's shoulder with his one hand. The captain rolled his eyes, his lips moved, but he could not say a word at first.

"Why didn't you say that right away?" the interpreter hissed, as if about to choke.

"I didn't remember," Taavi apologized.

"Where is the paper? We'll go and find it at once."

"Strangers won't find it," Taavi said calmly.

"Confess. Where is it hidden?" the lieutenant said hoarsely. The captain was still staring at him with feverish eyes.

"It's somewhere . . . where I worked. Very difficult to describe."

The captain made Taavi swear that he was telling the truth. They both seemed to overestimate the importance of it all, probably because of Mannerheim's name. Taavi was secretly surprised that the NKVD had not already got hold of that order of the day in which Mannerheim promoted the Estonian volunteers who had graduated from military school to officers of the Finnish Army. Many of his comrades must have been taken prisoner; several the previous autumn. Yes, if the prisons were in socialist competition with each other, perhaps this particular institution did not yet have a copy.

Greater weight and significance were attached to Taavi's casual words than he could have foreseen. The warden of the prison, the horse-faced colonel, was summoned in a hurry. He was no less startled by the news. He scrutinized Taavi from head to foot, endeavouring to get the right picture of this haggard, shaven-headed man, who was holding up his trousers with one hand. Was the comrade really telling the truth?

The interrogation was stopped and Taavi was taken back to his cell. He did not quite understand yet what had happened. But when he heard that the captain and the colonel continued their agitated discussion, Taavi began to hope that something might yet happen.

He looked around the small cell and now his heart began to pound from the strain he had gone through. Suddenly he felt a terrible lack of air. How had he managed to go on living here for monotonous days and months—for half a year? How could these men sleep here side by side on the boards of the sleeping bench and on the filthy floor? Hopelessly they vegetated here, plagued by vermin, hunger, lack of air, filth and fear. Their companions returned from interrogations, beaten into cripples, their bodies covered with bruises and wounds. Often they never returned.

Tõnis stirred on the boards. Taavi approached him carefully, stepping over the sleepers on the floor.

"You got back whole, and so quickly?" Tõnis marvelled. Taavi squeezed himself to his side.

"Who knows? Something is up," he muttered. Then he told the old man in a whisper about his sudden inspiration and the effect it had produced. The old man touched Taavi's wrist with his feeble hand.

"So, so," he repeated excitedly, and rose to a sitting position. "The Lord Himself gave you that idea!"

"Wonder if they will be stupid enough to take me outside?" Taavi doubted it.

"You'll see, you'll see. But if they do? When you are outside, then— act like a man. If they took me out, I wouldn't hesitate," the old man said firmly. "You have grown weak. Keep that in mind. But if you should get away, then tell everybody. Shout it to the world. Tell them that even the stones cry here."

He fell back on the boards, exhausted.

For a while they lay there, motionless and silent. Their companions groaned and twitched in their restless sleep. Muffled thuds sounded from somewhere afar.

The old man fumbled in his coat pocket.

"Take them," he said, handing Taavi two small potatoes. "Eat them right away. Maybe they'll give you a little strength. Eat. These potatoes grew in our own soil!"

When the morning trip to the washroom and the handing out of food went according to the old routine, Taavi Raudoja's hopes began to wane. They must have found out that he had been lying, and the following night would be much worse.

Halfway through the morning the door of the cell was opened and his name was called. He got up with feigned calm and went out. The captain was waiting for him in the corridor. So it was really true? Taavi feared that his face would betray his excitement and he tried to look as nonchalant as possible, shuffling his unlaced shoes slowly over the wet floor.

He was taken to the oily-looking, grinning Kirghiz who had cut off his buttons the first night and who usually cut their hair and trimmed their beards. Taavi was handed a razor and a pair of suspenders, and the captain in person accompanied him to the washroom where he was to shave. The razor was dull, and shaving without soap, with cold water, was a painful procedure. But the captain checked with fatherly care that Taavi's chin was clean.

Then they returned to the Kirghiz, who in the meantime had sought out Taavi's thin overcoat and hat. When he handed a pair of shoelaces to the prisoner, it was discovered that he had no socks.

"Where are the socks?" the captain asked.

Taavi, who had stuffed his socks into the air vents of the freezing box, pointed at the official, who spread his hands and argued back. But when the captain began to swear, the frightened fellow produced a pair of socks from somewhere.

Taavi dressed slowly and calmly. All this was part of the game and every suspicious, hurried move or expression of joy would have betrayed everything. The captain who followed him all the time must have had experience in judging the behaviour of men, considering his record as an interrogator.

But the most strenuous acting was still ahead of him. He was taken upstairs to the familiar room and questioned with renewed thoroughness. To hold his own under the crossfire of questions required greater and more sustained effort than the flight from the executioners the previous autumn. A middle-aged woman, wearing a beret, acted as interpreter this time. She was a Communist who had returned from Russia. Two sharp-eyed critics were there, judging the quality of Taavi's acting. The game was made even more difficult by the blue summer sky seen through the open window and the city which breathed its life straight into Taavi's thin face. Daylight half blinded him and made him dizzy.

"Aren't you lying?" the captain asked again.

"When we get there, you'll find out immediately whether I'm lying or telling the truth!"

He looked the captain straight in the eye and saw that the Russian believed him. This gave Taavi a great deal of support and confidence.

And then they actually went outside. The miracle Taavi had hoped for actually happened, the miracle he hardly dared to believe in even now. He put on his hat, which was too big now for his shaven head, and pressed his hands into the coat pockets that now felt strange to him. But the shoes fitted well and the suspenders held up his trousers.

He was not permitted to look back when they descended the stairs. Thus he could not find out the number of soldiers who escorted him. The one-armed lieutenant walked right next to him, and the captain came along too. There were probably about ten; as many as had been there when he was arrested. The heavy black door of the house swung open, and Taavi Raudoja stepped into the street.

He could not tell whether it was the sight of the well-known pavement that startled him so, but he would have fallen on the doorstep if the captain had not grabbed his arm and supported him. This showed Taavi that he was weak and should not overestimate his strength. Perhaps it also lessened the watchfulness of his escort. A man on the point of collapse would not escape very far if he tried. But taking his first step outside, Taavi resolved he would not be taken through the door of that house alive.

Taavi looked at the city and the people on the streets, as if he saw them all for the first time in his life. Now he knew the value of each free step. The people he met did not seem to hear the singing of their steps, but Taavi heard it. Although horror flashed in their eyes and they hurried past him and his guards like animals scenting the proximity of death, Taavi was still able to hear the song of freedom in their walk. It was a powerful call. All the streets were full of it, every corner, the whole town, the sunny summer world.

He remembered from that March night when he had been arrested that the captain did not seem to know Tallinn very well. This led Taavi to conceive his first escape scheme when they reached the marketplace. There were not many people in the market, but nevertheless Taavi dived into the midst of the crowd. He did not succeed; without saying a word, the captain and the lieutenant seized his arms. Taavi felt how empty his sleeves were and how thin his arms and shoulders. They moved slowly, for Taavi was too weak to take quicker steps. Here among the people he noticed the shocking impression his face made on those who saw it. Women stopped and stared at him as if they had seen a ghost.

No other chance of escape opened up for Taavi. They reached the end of the boulevard and turned into Masina Street, where the office building of the cellulose factory was located. Taavi had no choice. He had to stand by his initial plan, although at the moment he had misgivings about his chances of success. But at least it speeded up and simplified the execution of his death sentence.

Taavi's former office, where he had said the paper was hidden, was on the second floor. It was lunchtime and the building was empty. In a corridor he noticed an acquaintance whose name he no longer recalled. He was a middle-aged man and he let his cigarette fall in amazement at seeing Taavi.

Taavi stepped into his former office and stopped in the middle of the room. Somebody else must have been working at his desk, for it was placed differently from the way he remembered having left it. But he was not given much time to catch his breath and rehearse his new part.

"Where is the paper?" the captain asked.

Taavi took a letter opener from the table, tested the point, picked up a pencil, and again took the letter opener. The captain's eyes followed him with curiosity and excitement; those of the lieutenant looked gloomy and askance, and the soldiers just stood around. Without looking back, Taavi went to the window and pointed up with his hand.

"Where?" the captain came nearer.

Taavi looked up again, holding the letter opener, and then climbed up on the window sill after opening the window. Standing in the open window, he began to bore in the plaster. He felt his fingers become moist with tension. He also realized that the only thing that made it possible for him to balance on the ledge was the letter opener.

There had been a huge pile of sawdust in the yard below the window. Sawdust mixed with oil was used to clean the floors in the factory.

Glancing down, Taavi saw the sloping edge of the pile of sawdust. At the same time he tried to guess whether the revolvers of his guards were directed at him or just held without any specific aim. He could not look back; the matter had gone too far already and his glance would have betrayed everything.

Then Taavi Raudoja threw himself out of the window. He was still in mid-air, hardly gone from the opening, when the first shots rang out. He did not know how he managed to land from the second floor without injuring himself. He felt as if he had been running already in the air. Only his hat fell off from the shock, and sawdust filled his gasping mouth.

Taavi found himself in a courtyard surrounded by blocks of houses on three sides. Instead of running directly out of the yard, he rushed along the sides of the house toward the corner. There was a door that led into the factory. He knew the factory thoroughly and knew how to proceed there. But the door was locked. He pressed himself desperately against the wall. How dare the door be locked just today, when it had always been open before. The unexpected obstacle jolted him so strongly that all went black in front of his eyes for a moment.

Pressed against the closed door, Taavi looked back. He was afraid the Russians might jump out of the window after him. Even bending down from the window they could have reached far enough to get a shot at him. But suddenly everything had become silent. Had they begun to run downstairs? That must be it.

Not deliberating for a moment, he ran back the way he had come, under the window, and then, summoning all the remaining strength of his strained muscles, he dashed out of the courtyard. It was simpler from here on. He tried to breathe regularly, so he would not collapse. Great exertions were still ahead of him and the past moments had already used up much of his limited store of strength. From here on his escape proceeded by the shortest route. He ran through the powerhouse and the boiler room into the lumber yard and there climbed over the wall. Then across the Tallinn-Narva railroad, and he was in the wood by Lake Ülemiste. In a few minutes he had gained almost six hundred metres.

He fell on the ground and pressed his face into the moss. He was out of breath but he was free. He was free; he did not care for how long.

When the workers returned from the lunchroom, they could not understand what had happened in the factory during their absence. Only a few of them had happened to see a shaven-headed man, gasping for breath, running through the boiler room. Their tongues remained silent when they recognized their former colleague. Nevertheless, the story of Taavi's escape spread through the factory like wildfire.

The Russians completely lost their heads when their prisoner escaped. They ran back to the street the way they had come, and jumped back and forth on the pavement, screaming. The one-armed lieutenant fired a few shots into an upper window, as if he saw there the haunting face of Taavi Raudoja. Some of the soldiers followed his example. The captain collected his wits only very slowly. He drew up a cordon of soldiers around the factory, ordered that the prisoner be shot on sight, and telephoned for additional forces. A truckful of NKVD men arrived with a bloodhound. Dragging the dog by its leash, the captain rushed under the window from which Taavi had jumped and let the dog smell the ground. The dog seemed to sniff greedily the smell of the "bandit's" tracks but when the captain hopefully released the animal from the chain, it dashed to the nearest garbage can and began to hunt energetically among the rubbish. The sight of the captain running after the dog in the yard, revolver in one hand and chain in the other, was so comical that it provoked laughter among the bolder ones who were looking out of the office windows.

Intensive, week-long interrogations began now in the cellulose factory. Surveillance was kept up night and day, and one search followed another. The men from the boiler room who had seen Taavi run through walked around with a sudden feeling of importance and swore before the interrogator's table that they had not seen anybody. The prisoner must be in the factory. The one-armed interpreter promised to stuff all the workers into the boilers if the escapee did not give himself up at once. But to no avail. The captain walked with a hunched back and his face became narrower and darker every day.

These were sad days in the history of the new prison on Nunna Street; some of the most humiliating that the NKVD had ever experienced. Nobody knew for sure whether the reecho of the event reached down into the cellars. It might at least have given old Tõnis some strength for his last hours.

Taavi Raudoja rose from the soft moss. His heart was still beating savagely and he could hardly believe that he was free. But the air did not intoxicate him any more as it had when he was taking his first steps between the guards. He had kneeled on the moss not from a feeling of gratitude or overwhelming emotion but from weakness.

When he struggled to his feet, he did not hear the soft rustling of the pines. He strained his ears to catch the sounds of his pursuers. When he did not hear anything except the audible beating of his heart, he quickly walked along the railway track toward the station, and from there back into town along Veerenni Street. He had to act quickly—change his clothes completely, and get himself some kind of hat to shield his shaven head.

His acquaintances who lived on Veerenni Street were not at home. Taavi stood in the hallway of the small house and hesitated whether to knock on the first door and ask for a cap. He did not know how much Tallinn had changed during the past few months and how many of his acquaintances were still left. He could not get far without a hat. And the militia station was right here, too. He had to knock on a door.

An elderly woman opened it. Taavi found that he had done the right thing, for the questioning look on the woman's face turned into a terrified stare when she saw him. She could not say a word when Taavi explained that he had escaped from the Russians and would like to ask for a hat. The woman ran quickly into the back room, as if she, too, were running away, and with trembling hands brought him a blue beret. When Taavi thanked her and promised to bring it back some time later, the woman merely said, "May God keep you, son!"

Going out, Taavi at first wanted to hurry to Arno and Liisa on Pärnu Avenue but gave up the idea. Arno had been his friend and co-worker. His apartment would be the first they would search. But Selma lived not far from here. He must go somewhere, for his face attracted too much attention in the street and his pursuers would recognize him by his clothing. There was no time to look up acquaintances who lived farther away. But would Selma be home? Hardly, for this was working time. Had he not made a great mistake in returning to Tallinn? Of course, but it was too late now to go back to Ülemiste—right into the hands of the Russians. But who knew how well the approaches to and from Tallinn were guarded? With his feeble strength he would not have escaped anyway, setting out aimlessly like that.

To his great surprise he found Selma at home. She met him at the door, wearing her summer coat. He was lucky again; she had been just about to leave.

Taavi feared that Selma would faint with emotion and astonishment. She was unable to say anything except Taavi's name. She pulled him quickly into the room and locked the door. Then she touched Taavi's hand carefully, as if she feared it might crumble. Her lips moved, but no words came, and her wide-open eyes were suddenly filled with tears.

"I'm alive," Taavi said. His husky voice was merrier than his face. "I got away from them!" The words came with difficulty, as if they were hewing a way for themselves through a wall.

"Taavi! My God! Taavi!" Selma exclaimed and seized his shoulders with both hands. She pressed her face to Taavi's chest and her trembling hands groped down Taavi's arms until they reached his hands.

"Don't come so close. I'm full of lice," Taavi warned.

The woman threw back her head and laughed hysterically, eyes brimming with tears. It seemed to Taavi that she was like a child who did not know what to do with the joy that filled each limb, until it finally threw itself on the floor, laughing and kicking. Taavi sank on a chair. Selma was still in Estonia. She hadn't escaped to Finland this spring. What had happened here, outside, in the meantime? Life seemed to be going on slowly, day by day. And now the war was over. He wanted to make small, simple, everyday talk. But he did not know what to ask. And Selma only looked at him. She had not reached the stage of speaking yet.

"I cannot stay here for long," Taavi said.

The woman winced.

"No, you must not stay here!" she said, terrified. "How did you dare come here at all?" she asked with a strange tension in her voice, which was somehow related to her recent hysterical laughter. "How did you dare come, Taavi? I'm in their hands, too!"

Taavi jumped up.

"For the past month. They've kept interrogating me and threatening. I haven't told anybody. Evald doesn't know anything either. He doesn't understand me. I can't marry him like this. What would come of it? I cannot bring death upon him, for he is living with false documents. Oh, Taavi! Don't be surprised, we are all being hunted here like animals."

Taavi sat down again.

"Do you have a cigarette?" he asked.

Selma brought a box of cigarettes from the table and lit one for herself, too. So she had taken up smoking. Taavi inhaled only briefly. He did not dare to smoke much, for he felt nauseated.

"Nothing came of getting across in the spring," Selma said. "Maybe it was just as well, for they say that the Finnish police are extraditing all refugees to the Russians."

Taavi wanted to spring to his feet again.

"That cannot be!" he cried in disbelief. "The Finns wouldn't do that. I can't believe that of the Finnish people."

"Nobody will ask the people for permission, if the powers demand it."

"This is mere rumour. This is a rumour the Russians themselves have started, to keep people from fleeing," Taavi said with conviction.

"What shall we do?" Selma asked, worried. "My God, how they have worn you down. Tell me, did they torture you, too? Do they torture very badly? It is difficult to recognize your face. No, don't tell me anything. It's better if I don't know."

"I need a change of clothes," Taavi muttered.

"Oh yes, of course," Selma said mechanically. "And for the night? Where will you go for the night? Wait, I have Evald's key. I'll go and get you some of his clothes. Do you need underwear too? Of course, what a silly question. Go ahead and eat in the meantime. Take anything you want. You know your way around here. I'll think of a way to put you up for the night. I'll lock the door from the outside in case anybody should come. They've been here a couple of times to search the place when I was away."

She took a small suitcase from the foot of the bed and hurried out. That's how things are, Taavi thought. Bad indeed. He was still looking at everything from a distance. He could not take an active part in life yet, as if his freedom were still a dream. Take and eat what you can find. Selma would not have said that before. She would have forgotten everything else to prepare some food to sustain his starved body.

When Selma returned, Taavi was still sitting in the same position, with his overcoat on and the blue beret on his head.

"Quickly now, put these things on," she said, opening the suitcase. "I didn't get an overcoat, but it is so warm now."

Taavi was happiest about a big peaked sports cap which would hide his shaven head. It was a wonder that Evald still had so many clothes

—he who had been stripped down to his shirt in the ruins that Christmas night. Then Selma took off her overcoat and began to prepare him a meal. It did not take Taavi long to change his clothes, for his own dirty, stinking rags were without buttons.

"Let's burn these," he said to Selma, "or else your room will be full of lice."

Selma burned Taavi's prison clothes in the stove. With big scissors she cut the coat and pants into pieces. The soiled underwear fitted into the hearth without cutting.

Selma had recovered her composure. She was more talkative and matter-of-fact. No matter what happened later, she had to take care of Taavi, so he could sleep the night in a safe place and get quickly out of town into the protective embrace of the forests. Not a minute should be wasted, for the same night a general check of papers might begin in the city and a big manhunt commence for the escaped prisoner. The war was over and the Russians had unlimited manpower at their disposal.

Taavi let Selma take care of everything. She arranged things well. At nightfall they departed together and went to one of Selma's friends. This woman had rented out a room to an old maid with Communist sympathies, who, in addition, was a notorious gossip. But luckily the lodger was not at home and the two women hit upon such a clever scheme that even Taavi was astounded. The spinster had left her key at home and this became the basis of their gamble. The woman told the people in the next apartment that she was going out of town and would not be back for the night.

"What will happen to the lodger?" Taavi asked.

"She has plenty of friends with whom she can spend the night."

The women left. Taavi sat down in the comfortably furnished living room and something very like a smile appeared on his face. The women were smart. He was safe here for the night, even from a random check of passports. He might even sleep in the old maid's bed.

The idea appealed to him so much that he went straight to the spinster's room. There were no Communist pictures or literature to be seen and the bed was made. He undressed and climbed under the covers, and fatigue and sleep engulfed him almost before his head touched the pillow.

When Taavi awakened, startled by daylight, he could not understand for a long time where he was. Then he got up hastily, fearing that it might already be noon. It was five o'clock in the morning. He took a quick bath and now for the first time he became fully aware that he was really free. He felt it in every step, in every movement. But fear pervaded his heart at the same time. He had never experienced such fear before. Not even on the coast the previous autumn when he had escaped from the firing squad. He suddenly found that fear, too, must be cultivated slowly in a human being—at least the kind of fear that can be sensed with the whole body, that lurks in the brain like a compressed spring, dictating every thought and giving to every move a strange direction, which conscious effort cannot always control.

Taavi stroked his chin. It was rough and bony. He could not find any shaving utensils in the apartment. The powder box on the dressing table gave him a new idea. He began to make up his face. He did it slowly and thoroughly, like an actor who was to step on the stage in a new role.

He painted his eyebrows dark, put rouge on his lips and tried to give himself a somewhat tanned complexion. The dark eye sockets were hardest to cope with. He was not at all pleased with the results of his work. Anybody taking a close look at him would have burst out laughing. And his shaven head, covered with white scars, scabs and bloody scratches, spoiled everything. The cap improved the general impression a little, however.

He wolfed down some cold food he found in the kitchen cupboard, made up the bed, and covered up his traces as well as he could.

At half past six in the morning he knocked at Evald's door. His friend had just got up.

"You darned son of a gun!" he shouted happily, seeing Taavi, but covered his mouth immediately with his hand and pulled the visitor inside. He locked the door and went on with great joy in a startled whisper: "Selma told me. You and your tricks! You make a working man lose his sleep. Even the cellars of the NKVD won't keep you in. But you've squeezed yourself thin, brother. Speak now; what are you waiting for? I have nothing to tell. Listen, let me look at your face. I wouldn't have recognized you, except for the cap."

Evald began to dress and Taavi briefly recounted his story. Taavi's face-lifting efforts made him laugh. He thought it a priceless idea. They decided that Taavi must leave Tallinn at nightfall, taking the suburban train from an outlying station, and moving in the direction of Saku.

"My uncle has a farm there," Evald said. "I'll tell you exactly how to reach there. I won't go to work today. We must plan this very neatly, so you won't get tripped up anywhere."

"Are you still a locksmith?"

"I'm still a locksmith in the Harbour Works. By now I've just about learned the job and there are a couple of half-Russians under me. Oh, I'll wriggle through somehow," Evald said carelessly. "Let's cook some soup now. Selma has taught me how, and, believe me, it will turn out first class, if we don't let it burn."

Taavi had to summon all his will power to bridle his appetite. His hunger could not be appeased and he knew he might become sick from overeating. He recalled cases of men who had been drafted, shipped to Russia, and taken prisoner by the Germans. Upon arriving back home, many had died from eating too much too soon.

"I could eat a horse," Taavi said, looking at the food with gleaming eyes, "but. . . ."

"No, you must not," Evald asserted. "That would be an inglorious

end, if you should eat yourself to death. It's lucky we don't have anything very filling here. From time to time I have brought some food
from my uncle—in secret, of course—and the old man has been to town
a couple of times, too. It's tough with food now in Tallinn. Only party
members can grow fat. The others have to hold body and soul together
by pulling in their belts. Food is rationed out according to political
reliability."

Taavi did not listen to his friend's talk; his mind was concentrating
on the food. He tried to chew each mouthful slowly, but some invisible
power pulled it down his throat the moment it arrived in his mouth.
He could not raise hand to mouth as quickly as his throat could swallow.
When his companion took the plate away from him, Taavi looked at
Evald as if he were his enemy.

"Don't hit me," Evald warned.

"My appetite is just beginning to grow."

"You can have some a little later. The pot is full of soup."

"Oh, how the men in the cell would eat," Taavi said.

Suddenly he saw their sunken cheeks and lustreless eyes. The wrinkled
face of old Tōnis was as white as his beard. No, his face seemed dark, as
if the bones under the skin were covered with soot. And it was only
yesterday morning that he took two cold potatoes from the bony fingers
of the old man.

"Come, look," Evald said suddenly with excitement and pulled Taavi
to the window.

Taavi looked down into the street. The sun was shining on the pavement. Ruins stretched out on the other side of the street, growing luxuriant dark green nettles and purple blooms on their ash-covered shoulders.
A haggard man was loitering on the sidewalk. Another man strolled
casually across Tuha Boulevard and turned into a side street. Taavi
looked after him absent-mindedly. It was a little strange to see people
taking their slow Sunday stroll among the ruins on a weekday.

"Well?" Evald said.

"Spies," Taavi mumbled.

They had a good view from the second floor window. In a short space
of time they saw several men following each other's slow meandering
down the streets. There was no doubt: they seemed interested in the
house from which Taavi and Evald were observing them. Taavi felt a
defiant fury raging inside. Damn it, surrounded again. Trapped again.
A cordon drawn around the whole block. Hot and cold flashes alter-
nated through his limbs. Evald's face had become grim.

"Have you any kind of weapon?"

"Are you crazy? How could I keep it here? It's hidden in the ruins.
They are walking over it."

"If I could get hold of it, I'd break through."

"They would shoot you. You are in no shape to run from them."

That was true and Taavi knew it.

"This way they'll take you, too."

"What the hell," Evald said, looking hard at Taavi. "Do you think

I'm not good enough for them or what? Sure they'll take me also, if they come to get you."

For several hours they followed the movements of the spies among the ruins. It was very difficult to understand what they were aiming at. Why didn't they begin the roundup? They could not be so sure about their catch that they would spend the whole day ruining their victim's nerves. Then Taavi realized what it was all about. It was foolish of him not to have hit upon it earlier. His former apartment, where Arno and Liisa were living now, was located in the same block, with an entrance from Pärnu Avenue. Since the plank fence which had separated the lots had been destroyed in the bombings, people used shortcuts through the ruins from Pärnu Avenue, passing by Taavi's former residence. The NKVD must have assumed that the escaped prisoner would try to sneak through the ruins to get to Arno and Liisa to change his clothes, and therefore spies were assigned to watch the back of the whole block.

"I'll go and find out," Evald said resolutely.

He put on his light hat and left. He passed the spies without seeming to arouse much interest. Taavi remained at the window.

Evald returned after an hour or so. His face was gloomy but his eyes were laughing.

"What a manhunt they have staged in Tallinn. I went almost downtown on back streets and came back by way of Pärnu Avenue. The thing is clear. I saw more than ten of them, hanging around smoking, some with hands in their pockets and, I guess, fingers on the trigger. A big black car with curtained windows is waiting across the street from the Luther Company. NKVD men are marching on the sidewalks, burp guns on their bellies. They all have such self-confident faces that they'll have you in the next minute."

"We'll see about that," Taavi pressed through his teeth.

"Shall we wait until dark, or will you try to break through now?" Evald asked.

"I think it is safer right now. When it gets dark, they'll come too close. It's hard to decide what would be best. This is getting on my nerves."

"It doesn't matter, except for Selma," Evald sounded worried. "She is free in the afternoons now. She works at night. She might come right here from work."

"She gave me her key, in case. . . ."

"Listen," Evald said suddenly, stepping close to Taavi. "Let's try to get it done before she comes. In case we should get caught, you know. . . ."

Taavi understood. Evald did not want to expose Selma to danger. Poor fellow, he did not know that Selma had been involved for a long time already and that she had been bearing silently the burden of nightly interrogations.

"I think I'll go right away," Taavi said.

"Let's change clothes, then, and you take my documents."

"Yes. Wait, I wanted to tell you something first. Let's keep it between ourselves, but it is better for you to know. You and Selma should try to get away. Go to some other town. Why didn't you go to Finland in the spring?" he asked with increasing agitation.

"Why?" Evald repeated. "It was not so easy as that. I don't know of anybody who did. I have heard, however, that refugees are extradited to Russia. That would be the end. And to another town—that is easy to say. No, a Soviet labourer does not go where he wants. He has to stay where he is, and wait for his fate."

So that was it. The Estonian people were divided into two categories: one formed by the outlawed refugees in the woods, the other by slave workers chained to their working places.

"You must do something for Selma before it is too late," Taavi said, putting on his friend's faded light grey summer suit.

Evald winced.

"Do you know something more?" he asked urgently. "I have noticed some things. . . ."

"I don't know more than—you know what. She told me yesterday."

Evald's limbs were suddenly full of lead. He did not say a word, and he felt no interest in the spies sauntering down the street. What was the use? Nothing mattered any more.

But Taavi Raudoja concentrated all his attention on the impending dangerous enterprise. The spies in the street were unknown to him. He had not seen them in prison. He assumed that this was mutual. They had certainly been given a description of Taavi and of his clothing. Now he had changed his clothes. Only—his face. The hat was of a light colour and did not accentuate his thin, pale face too much—but still. . . . He took another look at himself in the mirror. He was suddenly pleased with the rouge that was still lending a healthy pink glow to his cheeks, and with the sharply drawn black eyebrows, which gave him an unfamiliar appearance.

"I'll send the passport back with Selma," he said. There was not much more to say. He saw that Evald opened his mouth at hearing Selma's name but he did not utter a word. Yes, there was no other choice.

Reaching the street, Taavi slammed the gate with deliberate carelessness. His heart pounded until he could hardly breathe. It was more difficult than he had imagined. Stupid thing—he could not control himself any more. Noticing two spies on the corner across the street, he felt an irresistible urge in his legs to start running. Crazy! Where could he run? Perspiration rose to Taavi's forehead. All of a sudden he was not afraid of the NKVD any more but of the strange compulsion in his legs that forced him to run. Fighting this morbid desire, he passed the men with slow steps. Turning his back to them, he felt still worse. If he did not run now, bullets would pierce his back and he would be thrown prostrate on the sunbaked sidewalk. You fool; walk calmly. Wipe your brow and take one step at a time. Only when he reached the house where Selma lived did it suddenly dawn on him that he had escaped for the time being. It had been so simple. Incredibly simple. He had walked past the spies, and nothing had happened. He was covered with sweat, however, and his heart was pounding against his ribs until it hurt.

Selma had just come home.

"You are walking around as if it were Hallowe'en." She laughed. "A new suit again, and your face—good heavens, Taavi!"

"Take the documents back to Evald. He may get into trouble otherwise."

When Selma had left, Taavi looked around for food. He laughed at himself, stuffing the contents of the kitchen cupboard into his mouth. What had become of him? Barely had he wiped the sweat of terror from his forehead, when his teeth were tearing into food like those of a wild animal.

About three-quarters of an hour later Selma returned with Evald.

"They stopped us," Evald said. "We barely made it. We were walking slowly and holding hands, but they seemed to be jealous, damn them. And they took our names down."

Selma was grim and silent.

"Don't swear," she said to Evald. "Taavi is out, and that is what matters most right now."

"Oh, why should I swear," Evald mumbled. "Nerves, that's all. My nerves are all through. He couldn't even write, just printed the names with big block letters, the son of a bitch. Damned half-Russian! Now we are as good as married, and the NKVD will pronounce the blessing."

"Evald," Selma cried.

The young man began to murmur an apology. His nerves were really in bad shape and Taavi was sorry he had hinted at Selma's secret.

"The people are coming from work. I think this would be the best time to get on the train," Taavi said. He must hurry. Tomorrow, perhaps in a couple of hours, the thread of his life might be twisted into new knots by the careless fingers of fate, if it did not snap altogether.

Taavi changed his clothes again with Evald, who went to the suburban station of Lilleküla to see if the coast were clear. No Russians were in sight and no more suspicious characters were hanging around than usual. The electric trains going toward Pääsküla were crowded with people going home from work.

Selma embraced Taavi when they said good-bye. She did not say anything. She did not cry either; only squeezed his shoulders. Then she quickly wrapped a small sandwich and stuffed it into Taavi's pocket, along with most of her rubles.

Evald and Taavi went to the station together. Evald bought the ticket, and they waited behind a fence until the train rolled in.

"Thank you," said Taavi and shook Evald's hand.

Evald did not answer. When Taavi jumped on the moving train, Evald looked after his friend with a feeling of deep satisfaction. He wished him success. His own heart was aching. He wanted to fly from the approaching thunderclouds, like a bird into the protection of the thickets. But he could not. Even this road was closed to him.

The following evening all trains were stopped at the Lilleküla station. A more thorough check of passports took place than anyone had ever seen before.

Taavi Raudoja recalled clearly his flight from the enforced mobilization of the Russians in 1941. He was walking along the same familiar path now. At that time they had gone in broad clear daylight, his friend and he. It seemed to him now as if they had not been able to realize then the immensity of the lurking dangers. They had simply walked, walked across the moors, met with some adventures in Saku, and had arrived at Kiisa without plans or worries. There the real outlaw life had begun. They had been young, bold and fearless, and they had been very lucky.

This time he turned to the right in the direction of the village of Asmu. Taavi knew the village from the first summer of the war.

He stopped in a pine grove on the roadside. The whole district of Pääsküla was full of Russian soldiers. They were billeted in private houses and housed in camps. Taavi could hear clearly the spluttering of a car engine and the broad cursing of soldiers above the din of the motor. The place was full of danger but it was the only road Taavi could take. By dawn he had to be far from here. He walked carefully in the forest at the side of the road, listening intently from time to time so that he would not run into a sentry in the dark. His past experiences had made him all the more alert and he knew that in his present physical condition he would be unequal to carrying through a sudden feat of bravery. The fact that he did not possess any kind of weapon, not even a pocket knife, made him feel quite helpless.

When he approached the village, he was annoyed by the barking of dogs. The animals were watchful, and discovered him from afar. Their yelping carried sharply through the night. As the dogs had been quiet up to now, Taavi concluded that there were no Russians moving around the village. Encouraged by this, he stepped on the road and went straight toward the houses among the dark trees.

He was not at all prepared for what happened next. A powerful electric light on a tall pole flashed on in the courtyard of the first farm, throwing light over all the buildings. Taavi stopped. That was strange. There were no Russians here. Only the dog ran to meet him with an angry growl. He tried to calm the fierce animal but then somebody began to strike a booming iron gong. The banging sounded across the fields and into the forest behind Taavi's back.

He stood for a long time, until the situation became clear to him. The villagers had mistaken him for a thief and this was their alarm. But it also confirmed his assumption that there were no Russians ahead of him, or else the warning gong would not have been sounded just now. He heard voices. Somebody slammed a door. The barking of the dogs accompanied him down the village street. In the next farm somebody blew a horn and then lights came on in the whole village. Taavi began to look forward with joyful anticipation to the moment when he would be caught.

When he turned into the yard of the farm to which he had been directed by Evald, a gruff man's voice barked out in Russian: *"Kto tam?"*

Taavi lingered behind the fence in the dark shadow of a tree, ready to hide behind the buildings in case he had to deal with Russians. He shouted back in Estonian.

"Christian people?" The man called and came to the gate, a big stick in hand, ready to strike. It was Evald's uncle himself. When he heard who the stranger was, he shook Taavi's hand in greeting and threw his cudgel to the side of the house. "I heard Pärtli pounding the rail, and then Rein blew the horn in his courtyard. I thought that the thieves were coming again from Pääsküla. There's hardly a night here that some door is not forced open and a pig or sheep spirited away."

"Are things so bad?"

"Worse than bad. Last winter they wouldn't give us a chance to breathe. You didn't happen to see anybody suspicious walking around? All right, I'll give the signal that all is clear again."

The farmer blew some short notes on his horn, someone answered in the village with the same signal, a few slow strikes were given to the wooden gong, and the iron rail sounded a calm note in place of its former excited boom. Even the dogs calmed down.

"You've got it well arranged," Taavi said.

"Necessity has taught us. It does help some. The big noise shames them a little, if it isn't good for anything else. And they are afraid of light and of bold eyes. But sometimes even that doesn't help," he said, waving toward the darkness. "You can still smell the burnt ruins of my neighbour's house. They burned it down. About a month ago three Russians came to the door at night and asked the farmer to let them in. The farmer speaks good Russian. He swore at them through the door and told them to make themselves scarce. They wouldn't budge, and kept pounding at the door. They wanted to enter and smoke a cigarette inside. Who's crazy? If you let the beasts in for a smoke they pounce on the women first thing. Finally the Russians left. A little later there was just one rifle shot, and the house caught fire and burned to the ground. They had fired an incendiary bullet into the straw roof. Since then we have lived here in a state of emergency, so if a stranger moves about— well, you saw for yourself."

Taking a closer look at Taavi in the lighted room, the farmer lost his talkativeness. He and his wife both stared at him, listening to his story, and shaking their heads in silence, as if afraid to express their thoughts. The mistress of the farm, her eyes wet with tears, stroked Taavi's bony wrist.

"But I got away," Taavi said happily.

"You got away," the farmer repeated, and his grim face, marked with sorrow, brightened up as if he had found his prodigal son. "You got away and they won't catch you again."

"They won't?" Taavi muttered. "They won't!" he repeated victoriously. He felt a strong urge to run out again, to run across the meadows, fields and roads, to move every limb in his body, to throw stones into the bushes and jump across ditches. He was really free. Away from the room, out from between walls. Free! The whole world was open in front of him. Everything belonged to him: night and day, sky and forests, the songs of the birds and the rustling of corn in the fields.

Evald's uncle and aunt kept staring at him in consternation. Yet they probably understood him, when he walked around the room, gazing at the chairs, the pictures on the wall, the curtains on the windows, and when he touched the tablecloth, as if wondering what kind of a thing it was—that white, fringed piece of cloth. And he laughed out loud without apparent reason. When the farmer's wife invited him to the hastily prepared table, he folded his hands unconsciously as if in prayer. He did not say anything. He only looked at the dark everyday bread, almost with a lump in his throat, took an unpeeled boiled potato in his hand and looked at it thoughtfully, as if it had something to tell them.

"The white-haired old man fed his life to me with potatoes like that," he muttered. "His life and his strong faith. If he should hear of my escape, it would give him great joy. It would be the last great present that life could give him."

Then he began to eat, quickly and greedily.

Taavi stayed at the farm for a couple of days to recuperate. The farmer invited him to stay longer but he wanted to get farther away into the forests. It was too dangerous to stay here, so close to Pääsküla and the Russians. Then he began to recall the places he had known during the first summer of the war—trustworthy forest farms and homes of his comrades. But he could not place much hope in these, for the intervening years had thinned out the number of his former comrades. The farmer recommended some people he knew who lived farther inland and who he knew could be trusted. Nobody would deny his help to a man in the woods at the present time, if he wasn't a Communist. There were almost none of that ilk among the farm people. Suddenly Taavi remembered the home of Eduard Tähn. Eedi of Piibu had talked about it often. What a good hiding place it would be among the moors and forests.

Taavi decided to make his next stop at the farm of Eedi of Piibu. He would bring his parents the good news that their son had succeeded in getting across to the free world. Taavi would stay at the farm for a few days. Great moors were within reach there. Mahtra was not far away and Kohila and Järvakandi were familiar and quite near. He could count on meeting forest wolves like himself out there.

The trek to Eedi's farm gave him deep pleasure. From somewhere, Evald's uncle had procured an old revolver with some cartridges, and Taavi felt quite safe on the forest trails. He felt like a real man again, after his recent privations. He ate in the farms, got to know some fellow outlaws, absorbed news from all sides, and laughed boldly at the worries of the farmers. The wind and sun burned his pale face and he let the sun redden even his hairless scalp. For hours he lay in the sun in little clearings in the woods, listening to the twittering of the birds, his loaded revolver at his side. He felt no sorrow, no worry, no anger. He had plenty of time. Sometimes he asked himself why he should hurry to get to Eedi's farm. He might just as well join a group of men hiding in the woods and live no matter where. But he did not do it. It was almost as if he dreaded that the troubles of the locals would disturb his free carelessness. On the other hand, one must have some kind of a purpose. He had two right now: Piibu Eedi's farm with the moors of Mahtra behind it, and the flight across the Gulf of Finland in the autumn. The latter was his most important goal. He did not doubt that he would find a small seaworthy boat somewhere on the coast. This time he'd go alone, be extremely careful, and he'd row across. He was convinced that he would succeed. Now he was confident about everything. And as for the rumours that Finland would extradite the refugees—stupid; there was no need to give himself up to the authorities. He had enough friends there upon whom he could depend. A man who had come out of the death cell of the NKVD would not find it difficult to get across the Finnish-Swedish border. If nothing should happen in Estonia in the meantime, then he would go sometime in September. The gulf would still be calm as in summer but the nights would be long and dark. His unexpected arrival would be a birthday present for his wife.

He was sunburned and his muscles were charged with their former energy when he opened the gate of Eedi's homestead one afternoon. All of a sudden his heart began to beat excitedly. Will there be any Russians on the farm, he wondered. Certainly not, for he never ran into a house any more without first watching it for some time from the woods. He fixed the outline of the farm in his memory, marked possible escape routes for unexpected emergencies, took note of protective ditches, underground storage mounds, and woodpiles. And when he entered a farm, he always placed his cap on the light, stubborn hair that grew so reluctantly. The shaven head of a prisoner or a deserter might startle the people.

The home of Eduard Tähn was small and shabby. Luxuriant climbing plants covered the walls from which the paint was peeling. Nasturtiums and irises blossomed next to the gate and suggested to Taavi that the farmer's daughter must live at home. The courtyards, gardens and pathways of the farms indicated to him from experience the kind of people who lived there. He was seldom wrong and, when he was, something had occurred which had upset the normal habits of the people.

Eedi's mother was lifting a milk pail from the well. Her face resembled Eedi's, but in contrast to her son she was short and bent. Her eyes stopped searchingly on Taavi. He had become used to meeting this kind of glance this summer: a little suspicious, but warm and understanding.

"Good day. I came at the right moment—the mistress of the farm lifts the milk pail from the well, almost as if the thirsty wanderer had requested it."

"It's warm, so you'll surely be thirsty," the woman answered. "And your stomach can't be very full either."

"It certainly feels empty just now." Taavi laughed. He liked the woman—a little worried, but helpful and kind.

"So you've been on the road for some time?"

"In a way—yes. A couple of weeks."

"Getting away from something bad?" she inquired pointedly, hinting by her tone that she considered Taavi an honest man.

"You must be Eedi's mother?"

"I don't know." The woman smiled. "Let's go inside."

Taavi took the heavy milk pail.

"I'm in no hurry," he said. "Don't stop because of me."

But the woman went inside and began to set the table. The farmer soon entered, too. He greeted Taavi with a handshake when he heard that he was one of Eedi's acquaintances, but he didn't know anything about his son. He didn't have one, he said. Taavi smiled to himself. They didn't quite trust him yet. The farmer's daughter was quite upset when she saw his shaven head.

"Prisoner," Taavi said.

"Yes, they've got you branded," the farmer remarked and stuffed his pipe, shoving his tobacco pouch and a piece of white paper toward the visitor. Taavi showed him the scars on his chin and nose, as if hoping to win his sympathy.

"Of course, you don't know anything about your son now," he said quietly, but triumphantly. "He was lucky. He got across last autumn!"

Instead of the joy Taavi expected to see on the faces of the people of the farm, he noticed a peculiar shadow passing over their eyes. The farmer gave him an intense, searching look and then blew smoke toward the ceiling. The daughter made a quick, panicky move, and the mistress of the farm gazed at Taavi, her mouth open from amazement. Taavi could not understand their behaviour. The farmer's wife turned her back on him and the girl rushed out of the room. Had he come to the wrong farm?

"This is the Piibu farm, isn't it?" he asked.

"Yes, it is," the farmer drawled. He took the tobacco pouch from Taavi and put it in his pocket as if he were afraid it might get lost.

"You have a son Eduard, don't you? Of course; he has his mother's features and his father's stature. I can't be mistaken. Don't worry about him. He is in a safe place. I thought I would be bringing you glad news, but—what the heck, haven't I? I don't understand anything now."

The farmer stood up and gave him a stern look.

"Eat all you want," he said. "Nobody has left this house hungry who has come with an empty stomach. But after you've eaten, see that you get going as fast as you can. It will be better for your health."

Taavi jumped up.

"Are you a Communist?"

"I am who I am," the old man answered quietly. "That is not the business of any vagrant who comes with the story that. . . ."

He turned his back to Taavi and walked out of the room.

Taavi was perplexed. He had come with the best of intentions and with good news, or so he thought. And now this unexpected reception?

If that's how it is, then—thanks, but he would not eat a bite here. Or was the farmer planning to call the Russians while he was eating?

He stepped up to the mistress of the farm.

"Tell me, you aren't Communists, are you?" he asked insistently. He would not let them play a dirty trick on him.

"Holy heavens!" the farmer's wife said and took a step back. Fear and repulsion sounded in her voice. She looked for a long time into Taavi's eyes, as if trying to see through him. "I must say the stranger has an honest face," she said. "Please eat now."

Taavi spread out his hands.

"Tell me, you are Eduard's mother, aren't you? Or else I will have to run back into the woods, for how could I know that the farmer didn't go to bring somebody to catch me."

"Sit down. My son's name *is* Eduard," she said softly, keeping her eyes on Taavi.

"Call the farmer back! There must be some kind of mistake, for. . . ."

His mouth remained open in amazement, for the door was opened at the same moment, and two men in addition to the farmer were standing on the threshold.

"What the devil," the shorter of the men shouted in Finnish and ran toward Taavi, overturning a chair.

And the other one said to the farmer: "Wh-what di-did you sa-say ab-about trai-aitors—this-is Ta-Taavi Ra-audoja! The-the last rem-maining of-officer from our gr-group!"

Taavi's surprised eyes had not deceived him: the two newcomers were Eduard Tähn and Leonard Kibuviir, who had crossed the gulf last autumn. What a trick fate had played on him. They were both in Estonia, hiding in the forests just like himself!

"So he's all right?" The old farmer was still doubtful.

"Of co-ourse he is-s all ri-right," his son answered.

"For Heaven's sake," Leonard shouted happily. "Tell us quickly how you got here."

"I?" Taavi repeated confusedly. "How? What about me? I am here. But. . . ," he got up with mounting agitation. "But you tell me how it is that *you* are here?" His hands made a gesture toward Leonard, as if he wanted to grab him by his chest. "What happened there on the coast?"

"That is a long story," Leonard answered. "It can't be told in a few words. You sit down and get some food under your belt. I tell you. You'd better not ask at all. Lightning struck in all directions. It's a wonder we are not all singing with the angels."

"That means—what? You were in the boat going across?"

"Some went directly to St. Peter."

"Speak up," Taavi demanded. "Quit that fooling. You know my wife and son were there. Don't squirm and wriggle like that."

"This is a crazy story to tell—sure thing. It's just as if I had to swallow an inch-thick rope," Leonard said. And now Taavi realized that the words did not come easily to his companion. His expansive boasting and joyful energy were suddenly gone. Leonard Kibuviir touched his chin and his shiny bald head helplessly. His thick lips seemed somehow slack and his eyes gave Eedi a furtive look. Eedi was looking on the floor, like a schoolboy who had been sent to the corner. It was obvious that they had bad news.

They stood like that for a moment or two. The farmer and his wife looked at each other in turn. There was still much that was not clear to them.

Leonard's words were simple. He did not understand himself why he had to make such an effort to say such simple words.

"They were taken prisoner."

"You're lying," Taavi shouted, although he knew instinctively that his friend was telling the truth. "How could they be taken prisoner, if Marta saw the boat leave with them?" he asked with a desperate voice.

"The boat didn't even get clear of the stones on the coast."

"And everybody was taken prisoner?"

"Yes, and s-some were ki-killed on the s-s-spot," Eedi added.

Taavi felt delirious. He could not keep his feet quiet but stumbled helplessly from Eedi to Leonard and back, in desperate confusion.

"What kind of special types are you two, then, that the Russians sent you to bring me the news? Everybody else was caught in the net, except you! Well now, my two friends. . . ."

"You won't let us talk," Leonard complained.

"What else is there to be said, if they're in prison," Taavi said hopelessly. "Go ahead and talk, then. What are you waiting for?"

"Well, it so happened that the boat arrived from Finland the same night as the people began to leave the coast. Only a very few got across: Jüri Paarkukk from our gang, and a few others who went to the shore just in case. Damned bad luck—we were snoozing in the barn and a big strong boat sailed off with a handful of men. The following night they were supposed to come back. The shore was black with people—men, women and infants, some who had been waiting their turn for weeks, frozen, hungry and wretched. It was a sad sight. Your wife and son were with us, of course. Your wife said that she would stay behind and wait for you. She was not going to leave without you. We tried to persuade her, telling her that you would come after her, and that it would be simpler for you to make plans for yourself. She stuck by her words, although she came along to the shore. Well, it must have been quite a while after midnight. We were shivering on the slope under some trees and bushes, when it happened that Eedi and I both had to go to the wood. Actually, it was just I, but Eedi came along, sort of for company's sake. There we were squatting on the ground, when all of a sudden I saw a Russian lurking a couple of steps from us. I took a better look. There were two of them tiptoeing past us, burp guns ready. I whispered to Eedi to keep his teeth pressed tightly together, so they wouldn't chatter. Sweat began to run down my face. I couldn't move a finger. What a miserable feeling. Then we heard the soft humming of the boat's engine. It was already quite close to the shore. A thousand thoughts jumped to my mind all at the same time but there was nothing

I could do. Yes, I could have shouted out an alarm but who knows how many could have escaped, and the killing might have been much worse in the confusion. And it all went so quickly. The shots were already falling. The boat had reached the shore. They had opened fire from every direction. Only those who were flat on the ground stayed alive. But the women, they screamed and jumped up and. . . . But most of them were probably taken alive. As for Eedi and me, we stretched our legs as straight as we could—and ran. Somebody must have betrayed us to the Reds. The whole place was surrounded and right at the moment when the boat touched the shore, the blitz came from all around."

Taavi sat down. He could picture to himself in minute detail everything that had happened on the coast. The strength had gone from his limbs, although he appeared extremely calm and detached.

Silence reigned in the room for some time. Then Eedi's father said slowly: "And I thought that if nobody except Leonard and Eedi got away, how could the stranger bring me any news. I thought right away that this man must be the traitor. But see. . . ." He stepped to Taavi and touched his shoulder. "Forgive me, that. . . ."

Taavi paid no attention. The food remained on the table, untouched. The others did not touch it either. The expression on Taavi's face was such that everybody walked on tiptoe around him.

Leonard Kibuviir said to Taavi, who barely listened to him: "Don't think that we haven't had our black days here, too. The winter passed quietly. We just kept ourselves out of sight here at Piibu, and no trouble came up. Sure, they were looking for men who were hiding out from mobilization but most of them had never registered and so nobody was wise enough to look for them. They knew well enough that men were hiding out in back rooms and threshing floors of the farms, but it seems that they simply ignored it. In their own interests, of course. They did not put up a friendly front to win over the people, but they simply did not have the necessary forces. The great Russian bear was quite low on the eve of the great victory and the end of the war. He was practically down on all fours, believe me, brother. You were in Tallinn working on reconstruction and did not see these times. And the NKVD got the city under its thumb in the autumn. But here in the country the NKVD's fingers were still quite short. Eedi and I and a few others have roamed around in several districts and we know. But now you have to keep your eyes open or else your hind quarters will be cold before you know it. Are you listening?"

Taavi was lying on the grass, fingering a blade absent-mindedly, and looking at a white cloud that seemed caught in the crown of the aspen which quivered in the windless air. When he grunted something like an affirmation, Leonard went on.

"Damn it, when the end of the war came with all that terrible hurrah-shouting, our lives also took on a different colour. They began their roundups right away. Wherever an army unit happened to encamp, they hustled back and forth on the forest roads and searched outlying farms. But they still kept their noses respectfully out of the forests. In Tartu province they are said to have used old members of the Estonian Corps but with no great results. They couldn't make brother shoot brother.

"We had our first baptism in June. News began to trickle in that Russian troops were concentrating at Järvakandi. We were just snooping around at Särge and keeping our eyes peeled, as the Finns say. The troops were concentrating all right, but very slowly. Probably so that they wouldn't attract attention and reveal their plans prematurely. But there was no doubt that a big roundup was in the offing. As our intelligence reported that NKVD units had not yet arrived, and as the troops stayed at Järvakandi, we assumed we would have a week or two. These damned skunks disperse their units before a roundup like the teeth of a comb, and then all set off at the same time like a swarm of bees. We figured that by that time we could withdraw back behind Vahastu, toward Anna and Kuimetsa. We could have remained out of the reach of their encircling moves that way, and our right wing could have remained open, for the left was protected by the swamp between Vahastu and the Lelle-Türi railroad. We considered it improbable that they would try to come all the way around Käru and Türi. And if such a thing had happened, we would have retreated through Järva-Madise and Ambla, all the way to Virumaa. Then let them try to catch us. Türi and Paide were teeming with them, but no movements were reported from there. The men around Käru had behaved nicely and politely. We assumed the roundup would cover the counties of Järvakandi, Lelle, Rapla and Keava, and that's how it actually turned out. You see, we aren't as stupid as you may think. Eh, are you listening or not?"

"I'm not deaf," Taavi answered. He began to get more interested in the story than he had at first expected. Leonard could talk sensibly, if he chose. And Taavi did not yet know how men of his kind actually lived in the woods. He had been leading this kind of life himself for only a couple of weeks but he had somehow been quite far from reality. Now he found himself face to face with the facts. The roundup that had taken place in June might be repeated every day. "Go on," he told his companion.

"Well, there isn't much more to tell. I got my thrashing so unexpectedly and stupidly. The others got by easily. They just sat in the bushes and held back their chuckles. One night—it was raining cats and dogs and the weather was cold as in March—I went to a farm I knew to get some tobacco and stuff. Before I got to the farm the weather cleared up, and I had to huddle for hours in the pasture before midnight came and I could slip into the house. I heard at the farm that two Russians had been there the same day, had asked for food, and had ambled on again. What the devil, I thought, just like reconnaissance. But the brother of the farmer had served in the Czar's army, spoke good Russian, and he insisted that they were just deserters, dressed in fags and poorly armed. It began to rain heavily again outside. The farm people suggested that I stay for the night and at least get my clothes dry. And I, damned fool that I was, piled up my bones in a heap in the back room and lay down on top of them. Let the floods come now, I thought. I slept like dumpling dough. The lightning struck right in the middle of my snooze. At half-past five in the morning they shook me awake—the Russians were in the yard! In my daze I got only my sweater on, when I heard the skunks already in the kitchen. In a flash I was through the window, in my underpants as I was, and in a few jumps I was flat on my stomach under the hedge."

Leonard caught his breath for a moment. Recalling the experience, he had become excited again and his eyes and hands moved together with his words.

Eedi of Piibu chewed indifferently on a blade of grass and studied a textbook that promised to teach ten foreign languages for everyday use. The book had become sadly worn from being carried in his pocket, but instead of the Swedish Eedi had studied on the coast, he had already progressed to English.

Leonard continued, rising to his knees in excitement. "Of course, everything happened in less than a minute. I had no idea of the situation. The first thought I had when I jumped out of the window was to get down on the ground as fast as possible, for I thought they would shoot right away. But lying under the hedge I realized that the house was not yet completely surrounded and that I had not been noticed. I realized also that I was holding my revolver in my hand. How I had managed to grab the weapon so quickly and automatically, I don't know. But it must have got into my blood during these years, become a kind of reflex. My heart began to beat more calmly right away and my head cleared up. Believe me, I have always liked hedges—they are just made for summer love-making—but that hedge I liked especially. It was so dense that after a while the Russians walked right past me, though they were only about a step away. I was afraid that the white underpants would really make a good target. When the Ivans were a little farther away, I scraped some dirt and rubbish over me—quite a wet and uncomfortable blanket, believe me. I began to shiver so hard under it that I almost had to hold my teeth together with my hands, or else they would have jumped out of my mouth. The farm and all the barns were thoroughly searched. It took them a couple of hours of hard work. The only suspicious thing they found in the house was a pair of German army horse bridles. They had a tough time explaining to the Russians that the bridles were war spoils. They were not hiding any Nazi horses in their stables. Then the Russians produced an old German army rifle and bellowed, 'A-ha! It was found in your hay barn. Where are the bandits?' Later it turned out that the Russians, who had roved around the village the day before, had really been spies who were investigating ways to approach farmhouses without being seen. Meanwhile, I, poor soul, lay buried under wet earth and leaves under the hedge, half-naked. Believe me, brother, the cold almost made me burst. When the Russians were gone the farm people came to get me. I was frozen stiff like a stick.

They poured homemade vodka and other stronger stuff into me and tried to save my soul. I thought that I would get at least pneumonia but not a thing happened.

"The whole roundup began earlier than we had thought. But their spoils turned out to be quite small. They tracked down one man in Keava, who just happened to be home. The fellow did not notice the Russians until the house was completely surrounded. He made a straight decision and began to snipe at them through the window. The Russians soon had the house in flames with tracer bullets, and shot the man and his mother when they tried to flee from the burning building."

"And how many did you shoot?" Taavi inquired.

"We? I told you what happened to me."

"I mean the others," Taavi said, looking at Eedi with angry expectancy.

"We d-didn't do a-any-thing," Eedi muttered, closing his book.

"What do you carry these rifles around for then? To scare the children and the dogs in the village, or what? The old spirit is gone from the men—too afraid to turn the guns at the Russians. They might shoot back! The man who began to shoot at them through the window was the only honest one left. At least he got under the sod with honour!"

"So that's where we should go."

"Go to the devil," Taavi said, stood up, and walked slowly away.

Taavi had the feeling now of being completely exposed and defenceless against the fury of his anger and pain. After the recent free, sunny vagabond days, he was a prisoner again. The dirty brassiere and torn stocking he had been shown in the prison had actually belonged to his wife. Whether she was alive or whether the tatters had been taken from her dead body, he did not know. And why didn't they show him Lembit's clothes? Or had the boy fallen on the coast from the bullets of the executioners? Taavi felt that the peaceful forest-refugee life they were enjoying at the moment in the neighbouring hay barns would drive him out of his mind. There was only one thing he could do in his impotent anger. He wrote a letter in pure Estonian, addressing it to the NKVD on Nunna Street. He mailed the letter personally from a county house twelve kilometres away, thereby risking his life. In the letter he declared, swearing solemnly in the name of Comrade Stalin, that his escape had been successful only because he had bribed the captain who had interrogated him. The captain and the one-armed interpreter had helped him escape and had received a thousand rubles apiece for their assistance. This was all he could do for the moment to satisfy his craving for revenge.

The sun was descending toward the dark green forests, and Taavi Raudoja was sitting alone under a tree at the edge of the meadow. The fragrant midsummer night descended on the fields, blue and soft, milky with mist, full of tenderness and love. The gold from the northwest spread over the sky. Shades of red and deep purple blended with it in the south; yellow and pale green in the north. Stars came to life above his head, one by one; small like silvery dust. A little night insect buzzed through the air and crashed into the leaves of the birch tree. There it buzzed again, aiming directly toward the banks of fog which rose from the river. The windless air carried scents: the suggestion of resin melting in the sunshine from the fir grove, where the woodpecker still sent forth its eager calls; the fragrance of withering wild flowers that had fallen before the scythe along the banks of the river, where the grasshoppers began their endless chirping; the smell of potato fields and the bitter hint of turnips from the vegetable garden. So many homey, familiar smells. But Taavi did not feel, hear or see anything. His thoughts and feelings were wandering on much more distant paths, bottomless paths that did not lead out of the gloom of night toward the morning dawn.

He had Eedi and Leonard tell him everything over again in detail but before they could finish, he had shouted to them to stop. He could not stand any more.

Marta had seen Ilme and Lembit sail off. Something must be out of order there, too. Yet he remembered the words of Eedi's father: "And I thought that, if nobody except Eedi and Leonard got away, then. . . ." Of course, the old man had every right to suspect him. But Taavi had a greater right to suspect Marta. She must know what had happened. Why had she sent him back to Tallinn from the coast? Just *what* had happened on the coast?

Taavi rose and walked back and forth on the freshly mown grass that was drying on the edge of the meadow. Absent-mindedly he heard the rustling of the hay under his feet, but he did not notice the honey-sweet smell. The coolness of the evening penetrated through his open shirt into his hot breast.

Taavi's faith and hope had been shattered. The faith the grey-bearded old man had fed him in the cellar—wasn't that faith any stronger than this? Was the family really the only content of a man's life? For some women, that was so. But there was the old man, who had lost everything, and had said that nothing could be taken from him any more. He was above earthly losses; above death itself.

Hadn't Taavi Raudoja known, when he returned to his homeland as a soldier, that he had thrown his gauntlet to fate, that he had added his life to that of his people? To share the fate of the people in victory and in defeat, in life and in death—that had been the resolve of their regiment. If his wife and son were called away before him—it must be so. If he was allotted a longer span, there must be some purpose, some reason.

He looked at his hands. They were strong, tanned by the sun, capable of holding a weapon. What else should he hold in these hands? There was freedom in Europe but that was not for him. It was the names of his blood brothers that called him. He was forced to continue in his role as soldier. And he would do so, for only blood could wash off his sufferings.

Eedi followed him, whistling softly. His whistle resembled a bird's call—that was their signal. Oh, yes, they were preparing to leave the farm, to stay for some time deeper in the woods, where comrades were waiting for them. It was a fortunate accident that he had found Eedi and Leonard at home. A fortunate accident indeed. It was the mocking sneer of fate.

Eedi was carrying a rucksack on his back and his gun on his shoulder. He walked slowly, bending forward under the weight of the load of food destined for their comrades hiding in the woods.

"Eh?" he asked. "We th-thought it w-was ab-bout t-time we were mo-moving."

Without saying a word, Taavi turned around and walked at his side toward the farmhouse. Leonard was busy with his rucksack in the farmyard, alternately cursing and cracking jokes. The farmer was filling the third rucksack, which was meant for Taavi.

News had reached them of the arrival of large army units at Rapla. Apparently another roundup was in the offing. When reports of similar concentrations had come from Kohila and Kose, Taavi and his companions gathered around a torn map, trying to figure out the possible directions the anticipated move would take. But they did not care much —least of all, Taavi.

"Come what may," Leonard said, "it cannot be much worse. Now we'll shoot our irons nice and hot!"

"Now we'll sh-shoot th-them n-nice and h-hot," Eedi repeated with conviction.

They took their rucksacks and, leaving Eedi's home behind them, they disappeared into the wide embrace of the forests.

PART TWO

I

Ignas of Hiie had dragged a huge whetstone to the meadow on the banks of the river. On dew-wet mornings he and Hilda went out to mow the hay, while the mistress of the farm and Linda of Piskujõe took care of the animals and chores around the house. Ignas felt a little uneasy, leaving the house for the whole long summer day like that. Except for the deaf-mute Aadu, not a man remained at home, and Russians often strayed into the village from Kalgina. But Krõõt was not afraid in daytime. She was still a strong woman, although her health bothered her these days. It had been quite bad in the changing weather of spring, when pain had gnawed at her every limb. The heat of summer attacked her legs with new vigour. They swelled, and she had a hard time getting them to limber up in the mornings. But she did not complain. The day was full of work from dawn to dusk.

The fugitives had been living in the woods ever since Mihkel of Lepiku had been arrested. They had settled down to a strange pattern of life. Since new troops had arrived at Kalgina, the men did not dare to work in the fields in daylight, when roaming soldiers might have noticed them. But they worked during the light summer nights, walking through the fields in elf-like fashion. They had even planted potatoes in the dark, not to mention harrowing and rolling. Värdi, the hunchback, who was inexperienced in farm work, acted as a lookout. He had a bicycle hidden in the bushes and he carried a flare gun. The men slept during the day, chopped faggots, mended fences, or went to faraway thickets to keep their hideouts in good condition.

Everybody in the village knew by now that there were men hiding in the woods. The people of Matsu and Kadapiku suspected also the presence of Reku, the fool of Võllamäe. But not even the men themselves knew how many others had taken refuge in the forests. On a forest trail one might nowadays meet a man from a village several counties away, with a revolver in his pocket or a gun defiantly over his shoulder. Nobody knew much about Reku. He went his own way, although he had joined the people of Metsaoti several times when they were eating or on other unexpected occasions. Sometimes he was quite normal and did not talk about his army of ghosts. At other times he seemed quite mixed up, so that even his father Jaak had to remark bitterly: "What the devil, nobody comes to my fields at night. The boy burrows in the bogs. An idiot is no use to anybody."

Ignas had much help from the men in the woods. He and Hilda carried food to the meadows. The scythes were usually waiting, honed to a sharp lustre, lined up on the sturdy branch of an alder on the river bank. Osvald, the hired man, was sometimes already at work. At other times he would arrive later, alone, his forehead covered with sweat from great hurry. Ignas did not inquire about his comings and goings. They had given up the farmer-hired-man relationship long ago. But the others did not keep quiet, especially when it was difficult to rouse Osvald from his midday nap.

"What the devil is wrong with you?" Tõmm said to Osvald one evening when they were returning to their camp. "That Marta seems to have gone to your head."

The former hired man of Hiie only laughed. Even his laughter was different now. He was full of good spirits, and bold to the point of recklessness.

"You seem to be in love," Tõmm scoffed.

"In love," Osvald mimicked him. "What should I love her for? I'm not your age any more. But sometimes it's simply necessary, you see. And there are all kinds of advantages too. Now we know exactly what they are planning in the committee and how the Russians are moving around."

"I don't care for that slit-eyed one, and this I know, that she has never got along with the same man for long. She is supposed to have played old Laane into the hands of the NKVD. That's what people whispered when it happened. I wouldn't be surprised if the Ivans will carry you one morning out of the storage barn of Roosi toward the district administration house, singing as they go."

"Fool, I'm not blind," Osvald said, annoyed. "Why do you have to stick your nose into it? What business is it of yours? Are you jealous, or what?"

"Jealous, jealous," Tõmm mocked. "You're as blind as a chicken with a sack over its head. You don't see or hear anything any more."

"What kind of an animal is this woman?" Värdi inquired.

Osvald was hurt.

"Animal," he muttered and did not open his mouth any more. Little Värdi shook his round head and strained his cheek muscles, chewing with an empty mouth. He was a big and powerful man, this Osvald. It would be a pity if he were ruined by a crazy woman.

Hilda and Värdi took turns keeping watch during the mowing, although Osvald assured them that it was not necessary at the time—according to his intelligence reports. But neither Hilda nor Värdi were much help with a scythe. Both managed to strike the scythe into clods even on the smoothest meadow. Värdi kept trying, straining his facial muscles, naked to the navel, his hunched back bent around the scythe handle, but nobody expected him to become a real mower, and he himself had no faith in it either. During mealtimes he stuck his feet in the river and looked morosely at the lukewarm ripples. It was lucky that mowing by hand lasted for only a week on the back meadows of Hiie. Then Ignas began to sweep along with the machine.

When the hay was being turned over, Värdi and Tõmm took shifts as lookouts. Tõmm did not consider swinging a rake a man's job, and Värdi was awkward even at this chore, breaking one rake peg after another. Old Aadu and Linda of Piskujõe came to help stack up the hay, and this year the hayricks grew faster than in several preceding years.

"We work like Stakhanovites." Osvald laughed.

Ignas was pleased with their fast progress. "I think you might help the

Lepiku folk now for a couple of days," he said. "Cut down as much as you can. I'll go later and help them rake it up."

"All right, farmer," Osvald answered. "This year we're ahead of everybody at Metsaoti. Even in Matsu's meadows they're still whetting their scythes."

"Well," Ignas said, "one of them has to be counted out, and Meeta herself has to stick around the house. Lonni's day is near; she can't be left alone. I told Krõõt at home to look in there once in a while. They might need help. The girl's feet are all swollen and she looks wan in the face. It's not easy during the hot summer months."

"No, it isn't, farmer," Osvald said thoughtfully. He felt somehow sorry for Lonni of Matsu. These damned Russians. It was an awful thing they did before they died.

Life went on at Metsaoti. The farmers discussed the general situation, when they happened to get together on the edge of the fields or during their forced transportation duties, but most of the troubles were kept behind closed mouths, unless strong home-brewed beer or vodka from Harukurgu unlocked them. And very, very seldom did this happen.

Ignas did not have anything special to do in the courtyard, The darkness brought the fir groves closer and closer, leaving the glowing western sky without support. His heart ached. He even felt it in his limbs, as if he had been chilled or stood in the draught with a perspiring back. Linda of Piskujõe, who came to help with the chores, complained about heartache too. Ignas would not have paid any attention to the woman's talk, but now he was in the same kind of trouble. His heartache was more physical than mental.

Old Aadu Mustkivi came from the house, shuffling his feet. It must be late then, for the old man had emptied his earthenware bowl and was going to the hayloft to sleep. He walked across the courtyard with hurried, impatient steps, with Pontus at his heels, whining softly. They both stopped near the fence. Aadu pulled a handful of fresh blades of grass from the ground and chewed them noisily. So it would rain. Ignas was relieved. That was why he had felt so heavy and oppressed. Aadu's grass-eating was a sign that never failed. The dog was more likely to make a mistake than the deaf-mute.

Pontus, too, bit off a few blades of grass, softly whining. Then Ignas heard that Aadu responded to the whining of the dog. It was something Ignas could not understand. Yes, Aadu began to whine just exactly when the dog had finished. This was repeated several times, as if Aadu were communicating with the animal. Then they both went to the dark gate together. Pontus sat down in the middle of the road, and Aadu leaned on his heavy clublike stick. They looked down the road that led to Võllamäe, as if they were sure that somebody was to be expected from that direction. Whining from time to time, they shared with each other their feeling.

Ignas shook his head, unable to understand it, and turned toward the house. The times made everybody crazy, one by one.

"You're late," Krõõt remarked. "What kept you? The food is already cold."

Ignas sat down at the table, unwashed as he was. He felt tired, and had no appetite.

"Linda of Piskujõe was here."

Krõõt looked at her husband, as if she had said something extraordinary.

"Mm," Ignas answered, and let his glance wander slowly around the spacious farm kitchen. Everything seemed far too strange: Aadu's empty bowl on the corner of the table, the glowing embers under the stove, the blackout shades on the windows. Why those? The war was over; no airplanes roared above any more. But they were so used to the blackout now. It protected them and seemed to shelter their thoughts from the world behind the windows. As if they were afraid of the dark, or of the evil that had forced its way from the high roads into the forests. Ignas felt suddenly that there should have been more people in the room, more people around him. His heart froze, and the house, his home, seemed empty. Hilda had moved her bedclothes out into the storage barn again. She watched over the farm like a faithful watchdog, although the men came only rarely to sleep in the attic of the bathhouse in the meadow.

"Is Hilda asleep already?" he asked.

"She ran away again with wet eyes," Krõõt answered. Ignas noticed now that the eyes of his wife, too, were filled with a strange frightened restlessness, and that the movement of her hands were needlessly fidgety.

Ignas put the spoon back on the table and leaned against the back of the chair. The question in his eyes was enough for Krõõt.

"Linda said," Krõõt began, holding tightly to the corner of the table, "that she had met the youngest daughter of Toomas of Kuuse at the store. Selma had sent word from Tallinn, that Taavi. . . ."

"What about him?"

"He's been arrested. He was taken away in March."

That was bad news. Ignas would rather not have heard it after a hard day's work.

"So that's it," he mumbled. "And Ilme and the boy got across the bay."

"Yes, the poor things. She has two children already," Krõõt lamented, with tears in her dark eyes. "Linda has taken it very hard, though she didn't cry. She just talked about Andres and wondered why she should continue to live now that the son and father are together. Why should she wander around alone any longer. I am afraid she'll end by her own hand, go into the river or. . . ."

"Don't," Ignas forbade her, feeling a chill run down his spine.

"She was so strange, so calm, as if she were already on the way." Krõõt sobbed.

"So Taavi has been arrested," Ignas muttered. "I wouldn't have believed that of him. I thought he'd be like old Andres. That when he saw there was no other escape, he'd tear into the Russians with his teeth, if there were no other way, and that would have been the end. Don't weep now, Krõõt. We have to get over it. This loss won't be the last."

"That's why. . . ." The woman turned her tearful face toward the wall. "That's why—because this won't be the last!"

Ignas noticed, as it were for the first time, that his life's partner had somehow shrunk, that she stooped and that her thick hair was more grey than black. Unnoticed by him, the recent years had broken her.

"Is it your legs again?" he asked, when he saw that she walked stiffly, dragging her feet.

"A little," Krõõt answered wearily. "It will probably rain. I'd like to know how Ilme is among a strange people."

"Well, they are out from under the terror and that's the most important thing. That should give us strength; the knowledge that the children can grow up in freedom."

Ignas stood up and walked out again, although he knew that his wife was suffering and needed his presence. He was sorry for Krõõt. He was sorry for the whole world and perhaps most of all for Linda of Piskujõe.

Ignas stopped at the corner of the house under the apple trees, looking across the fields toward Võllamäe. Was he, too, expecting somebody from that direction? Foolishness. Only Russians could be expected from over there, and they were still wary enough not to venture close to the woods at night. Only in the daytime would they drive their trucks to the gate, and if the gate were open they would even drive into the yard to ask for vodka. Ignas never gave them anything, but pointed imperiously toward the gate. Anger made him reckless.

He heard Pontus still whining at the gate, and saw the dark figure of the deaf-mute huddled over his stick. The snorting of a horse sounded from the field across the road and the quiet creaking of a harrow's springs in the soft earth. Osvald, that carefree soul, had come so far into the open to complete his harrowing! The old man felt that he should go and send Osvald back into the forest. Why should he be so far out in the open at night and in the middle of an open field? If something should happen. . . .

Suddenly something did happen! A muffled revolver shot sounded from the Koolu hills, and a yellow flare soared in a semicircle across the sky. So the Russians were on the move! Pontus and the young vicious Saulus of Matsu began to bark furiously. The dog of Võllamäe howled with excitement, and the high-pitched yapping of the hound of Kadapiku sounded from the pastures. The peace of the night was suddenly broken.

Puffing hoarsely, old Aadu ran down the path from the courtyard gate, his heavy overcoat flapping and his stick clanging against a stone now and then. Making his guttural noises, he climbed quickly into the hayloft. Ignas heard him close the trap door behind him with a bang, and fumble at the hook with his awkward fingers. Then Ignas heard the heavy thud of horses' hooves, which went from behind Matsu over the

221

lands of Kadapiku toward the forests. Osvald was quick. Only the harrow remained in the middle of the field, waiting for the morning. At the same time Värdi was pedalling his bicycle on the road across the Koolu hills toward Verisoo, across the small wooden bridge, and nobody would be able to reach out far enough to catch him there.

Ignas strained his eyes and ears, took off his cap, and stepped into the field, but he saw or heard nothing except the agitated barking of the dogs. Gradually they calmed down, only mimicking each other now and then. A manoeuvre, Ignas decided. Yes, it was probably only a manoeuvre, but the situation was serious enough, and no one knew what the morning would bring or what might happen even before the morning.

Krööt and Hilda were both waiting for him when he returned to the courtyard. Hilda was already in her nightdress, bare-legged, but she had her overcoat over her shoulders and her clothes tucked prudently under her arm.

"What is it?" Krööt asked, frightened.

"Doesn't seem to amount to much. Everything is quiet. It's nothing right now."

"If Hilda heard a shot, how could it be nothing?"

"It's nothing right now," Ignas repeated abruptly, as if he were annoyed. "We'll see what comes later. Try to get some sleep, Hilda. A young person like you needs a good night's sleep."

"Sleep, a good night's sleep," the girl repeated, as if she did not understand what Ignas meant. She repeated the words even when she turned around and went back to the storage barn.

The sky with its glittering stars arched calmly over the world. It had no secrets to keep, unlike the black earth beneath.

A new morning came, and nothing happened. Fragrant days went by, full of light and sound. There was no spot in the sky above the earth from where the song of larks did not trickle down like blue sparkling dust, mixed with sunlight. It fell everywhere, it covered everything, and after a winter that had been tortured with the irons of death there were still some people left whose hearts reached for the blue gold of the sky to adorn themselves with it, as if the world were still the same, and as if the blossoming of life were still the only meaning of summer. One of these was Hilda. In spite of the evil times, she began to live together with the summer. The mistress of the farm noticed it first, and rejoiced in it, for she was already at an age when she needed shining eyes near her, sparkling with joy, even if it was only for a brief moment.

But life did not come to Hilda suddenly like the breaking up of ice, and certainly not like the blossoming of trees. Her laughter and joy flashed forth even more quickly—like a handful of sun rays from a cloudy sky. They passed over her face like lightning, and shone in her eyes. Then the weight of sorrow clouded her cheeks again, and tears crowded into her eyes. This could be seen from the outside, but inside a slower and firmer change seemed to be taking place. The soft hues of flowers in the garden, which she watched for hours, seemed to be forcing the bloody glow of fires from her soul, and their fragrance dulled the acrid smell of collapsing houses in her memory.

"She's getting well," Krōōt remarked to her husband.

"Seems that way," Ignas answered thoughtfully. "She has to, or she will not be strong enough to meet new blows."

Taavi's arrest was a great shock to Hilda. She barely knew the man, but she knew Ilme, and she loved Taavi's mother, Linda of Piskujōe, into whose little house she ran now every day. Linda called Hilda her daughter and they walked together under the firs of Piskujōe, in the place where crosses were cut into the tree trunks and where Hilda would not have dared to go a short while ago, even if driven by fear of death. Now she began to cherish the quiet place where Taavi's father lay.

But the chief reason that Hilda began to blossom was a living human being, who himself had no idea of what was happening. Tōmm, the farmer's son, could not know anything about it, for, instead of her former slavish adulation, Hilda had not shown him even a kind face since the winter. All of a sudden the girl had thrown her head up, and the boy was not worthy of a look from her eyes. Even more, when Tōmm had tried to keep up his former teasing, she had said bitingly, "You think you're somebody, don't you?"

Tōmm's mouth fell open, and he felt like a nobody. The girl had skied home miserably and humbly from the woods with his broken ski. But look at her now! The boy looked at her supple body and the mocking arch of her mouth, and suddenly felt like a young wet sparrow. He was embarrassed and confused. Trying to be superior, he had suddenly played out his superiority. Hilda did not even fill his plate at the table any more, or, if she did, mockery played in the corners of her mouth. Sometimes it drove the boy into a frenzy. He rushed at the girl ready to hit her or tear out her hair, but his hands fell down, although the girl crouched in fear. Even the boy's mouth had remained shut for some reason that he did not know.

Suddenly they lived like a dog and cat, and, odd as it seemed, this gave Hilda new life. Or perhaps it was that kiss on the Koolu hills, when they were lying in the snowdrift on the bones of men who had been buried there hundreds of years ago. Hilda did not know, and Tōmm felt that it would be foolish to mention it again. At the same time he felt that he was in love with the girl. He began to look at her and realize that he had never seen a girl in all his life quite like the one he saw now that his eyes were open. Love made him feel helpless and stupid.

II

The man who took Holde's place as the new power in the white house with the large green blinds was named Michael Turban, and he was a man cut from a completely different cloth. He did not have the stature of his predecessor, and the first impression he left was that of a wretched and helpless person. He wore high boots and a simple soldier's coat with a five-pointed red enamel star on its breast pocket, but on festive occasions he could cover half of his narrow chest with decorations and medals. He was an Estonian from Russia, a war invalid, a former officer, taciturn, glum and suspicious, and the few words he uttered sounded like raucous barking.

The atmosphere in the big office of the district administration house remained stifling and restless after the change of the men in power. Marta spent the first days observing her new superior. The man seemed even more sickly and pale than the departed chairman. When Holde had sometimes had long fits of coughing he had hurried into his private office. The newcomer was plagued by a constant short dry cough, and his sunken face with a deep scar on one cheek was grey and almost colourless from pain. He put pomade on his smooth hair and black moustache, and he resembled Hitler a little. He scrutinized everyone with suspicion and disdain, and when Marta happened to meet his glance, he turned his scarless cheek toward the woman. There was a sickly strained smile on his lips as if he were about to spit. Usually he tried to hide his hands: standing, he would pull down his sleeves, and when he sat he held at least one of his hands under the table. They were almost without fingers, deformed like clubs. He was a man who had been marked by the war, a wretched cripple, so much so that nobody really understood the reason for the recent change of chairmen.

Another new official was Peetal Rause, the militiaman, who soon became the terror of the district. Even Marta was scared when she saw this giant for the first time. The man's face was covered with pockmarks, and his eyes were naked like those of a fish, without a single hair where the eyelashes and brows should have been. His mouth was big and thick-lipped, full of strong yellow teeth, and the nostrils seemed placed directly into the face. At first glance he appeared as witless and dull as an ape, and the impression was strengthened by his long hanging arms. He was not stupid at all in reality and seemed to know his business, boldly driving his motorcycle even into the forests. When he went without his motorcycle his journeys boded no good, as he always brought somebody back with him. Woe to the victim who tried to resist—Rause beat him unconscious. In a few weeks his fame spread beyond the limits of the district. Little was known of his past, except that he had done some time in jail during the independence of the republic for raping a young farm girl.

Peetal Rause was the only man on the horizon of whom Marta was afraid. She tried to suppress this fear by every means possible, reasoning that, after all, the man was nothing but a rough tool in the hands of the ruling authorities—an unimportant axe. This did not help much, for she was afraid of him as one might be afraid of a beast, in spite of the fact that she knew he would never dare to touch her even though he gave her lewd looks. Marta was happy when she received a permit from the NKVD to carry a revolver—ostensibly to defend herself against the bandits in the woods. She was also a candidate for membership in the Communist Party now.

It was one of the last days of haymaking. The weather threatened rain, and the Hiie people expected Linda of Piskujõe and old Aadu to come to the meadow after midmorning, to help them stack the dry hay. But only Aadu appeared just before noon, out of breath from running. All were busy finishing the work and none would have paid much attention to Linda's absence—women could find unexpected chores in their homes which demanded immediate attention—if the deaf-mute had not been so obviously agitated. He ran straight to the farmer and began to gesticulate excitedly to the accompaniment of high-pitched guttural sounds. It was clear that he was trying to communicate something.

"Wonder what's on his mind?" Ignas said, when Aadu followed on his heels like a dog. "Would you, Hilda, run and look? Your legs are fast. Just take a quick look at the yard. And don't run yourself out of breath."

"Yes, yes," the girl said, eager to go, throwing a hurried glance in the direction of the young man, who was carrying big loads of hay to the stack, clad only in shorts, his bare back browned from the sun and his perspiring face shining like copper. If somebody were in danger, of course Hilda would run, and already she was hurrying through the willow bushes and between the young birches toward the pastures of Metsaoti.

Hilda's departure seemed to calm the old man a little. At least he left the farmer's side and sat down on a clod of earth. There he mumbled to himself for a long time and fidgeted with his hands. From time to time he put a blade of grass into his bearded mouth, looking at the perspiring workers, and then at the woods, behind which was the village of Metsaoti. When he finally joined the others in their work, he stopped raking every now and then and talked in excited, broken tones.

The workers were eating their midday meal, when Hilda returned. The girl was breathing heavily from her run, and her glowing face was more excited now than when she had left.

"There are Russians at Hiie! A black closed car is standing in the courtyard and two men in NKVD uniforms are keeping watch at its side. I watched for a long time from the pasture, but that was all I could see. The village is quiet. Not a soul is moving around."

"The devil," Osvald growled. "Listen, farmer, the rain will get us. See, the clouds are coming up fast!"

"Two men in uniform," Ignas muttered.

"Yes, with submachine guns in their hands."

"We'd get some good weapons," Tõmm said, throwing the bite he was about to eat back on the outspread paper. "What do you think?" He turned to Osvald.

"What? Are you crazy?" he answered. "A black closed car, an evil-smelling affair and the NKVD."

Instead of hurrying back to work, Ignas began to stuff his pipe, casting an indifferent glance at the approaching thunderclouds. He did not notice that his gnarled fingers shook a little. So the car was in the farmyard. They might take the women away. And if they frightened them enough, being women, God knows what they might confess. It was probably for Tõmm's sake. They might have expected it any time. And the boy himself—all he could think about was the prospect of getting good weapons!

"I told Värdi," Hilda said.

A cool breeze ran through the tops of the birches. Then came the first warm drops of rain. They were big and heavy, and became more and more frequent and cool. The men packed the food together, pulled their shirts on in a hurry, and ran toward the hay barn. Aadu brought up the rear, arms swinging like a pendulum, holding his rake in one hand and his stick in the other. Ignas alone stayed in the rain. He looked at the raindrops that fell on the dry, rustling hay, quickly turning it dark and beating it close to the earth, and he had an empty bad feeling in his breast.

In the afternoon, when the rain had thinned out into a drizzle and when the men had tormented themselves enough with futile suppositions, Linda of Piskujõe herself arrived at the barn, accompanied by Osvald who had been keeping watch on the road. She was wrapped in a big shawl, and her feet were soaking wet.

"The air is clear again," Osvald announced happily, before Linda had a chance to open her mouth.

The face of Taavi's mother was tired and tortured. She sat down on the hay, stooped, small and old.

"I came to tell you that I don't know what all this means."

"Whom did they want to take away? Were they looking for me?" Tõmm inquired.

"No. They were looking for Taavi."

"For Taavi?" the men repeated. And Ignas said, "How could they be looking for Taavi, when Taavi is in prison?"

"That's what I don't understand," Linda answered. "They came to my place and searched all the buildings. They asked when I had last seen my son, as if they didn't believe me when I said it was last autumn. They asked to see photographs and took all of them. Then they began to threaten me. They said they'd take me along if I didn't confess where the boy was. I answered that I didn't care what they did with me. I didn't care where I died. A man in a black coat, looking a little like a minister, put my words into Russian. He seemed to be a good man, quiet and serious. I told this Estonian that my son was in prison and that they ought to know his whereabouts better than I. Then they all became angry, and asked me how I knew that my son was in prison and who told me? I answered that Marta of Roosi had been to Tallinn, and that I had heard from her. Who was Marta of Roosi? I answered that she was working in the district administration house as a secretary or something. What kind of relationship did she have with my son that she should know so much? I said that they didn't have any relationship.

They just went to school together when they were children. Then I suddenly remembered that it wasn't Marta at all who had told me that, but the younger sister of Selma of Kuuse. I wanted to straighten this out, but they began to bother me with all kinds of other questions, and that was that."

"Didn't they really ask about me?" Tõmm inquired, full of excitement.

"No. Only for Taavi. They yelled at Krõõt and asked where the men were, but she answered calmly that she didn't have any more men than her own husband, and that he and the hired girl were in the hayfields. Krõõt treated them so proudly, that I almost expected her to open the door and tell them to get out. They did not do much at Hiie though—only looked at photographs—but at Piskujõe they really went to town."

The shoulders of Linda of Piskujõe shook under the great shawl when she recalled her experience. She stopped for a while, fighting back the tears.

"They acted so strangely. Some of the men kept aiming their rifles at the woods, as if they expected goodness knows what from there. They threatened me, but in the pasture they looked at every tree and bush, and spoke only in whispers."

The men began to laugh. This was pleasant to hear. The Russians must have got their fingers burned in the woods or else they would not have been afraid. NKVD—the word alone made one shiver with terror—but see, they were scared of the bushes. So they themselves, the men in the woods, were strong enough to make even the NKVD men tremble in their boots!

"I cannot understand," Ignas said thoughtfully, sitting in the hay, "why they are on Taavi's tracks now, if they arrested him in the spring. Listen, Linda, don't you think that your son has played some kind of trick on them?" he said, his voice full of joyous excitement. "Seems that way. I wouldn't be surprised if he walked up one day, saying, 'Hallo, old man of Hiie.' That's what I think." Ignas began to stuff his pipe.

"May God grant it!" Taavi's mother whispered. "A thought like that flashed through my own mind too, but I didn't dare to say it. How could anybody get out of prison?"

She passed the back of her hand over her wrinkled cheeks.

The younger men did not believe in this possibility, although they did not voice their doubts in the worried mother's hearing. For even the wildest hope gave some comfort and it was cruel to dash it.

Little Värdi even said seriously and convincingly: "Why not? Men have escaped from the prison trains into the woods of Virumaa, and Taavi would have done it right away if he'd only had half a chance."

Only Osvald went to the village with the Hiie people that night—for reconnaissance, as he said. Tõmm and Värdi decided to spend the night in the dry hay of the barn, for the hideouts on the moors were wet from rain. Mart of Liiskaku, who was helping the old couple of Lepiku, returned to the camp alone to bring word. The old captain, the leader of their group, had to be kept informed of the whereabouts of the men.

The weather vane on the Hiie flagpole pointed toward Matsu. That meant that there was no direct danger. Linda and Hilda went to the farm, while the men stayed in the pasture to wait for developments. Aadu had not caught up with them yet. After a while the girl hurried back together with Pontus. The dog jumped and whined happily.

"The mistress is not at home. The doors are open but she isn't in the stables, nor in the storage barn." Hilda stopped and looked over her shoulder.

Ignas, too, gave a look in the yard. The cows were stamping from one foot to the other, waiting to be milked, and the chickens were drifting toward the toolshed. The yellow rays of the setting sun glistened on the wet fields. They glowed with many colours on the surface of the water, and dripped in a reddish glow from the leaves of the trees.

"Where could she be?" The farmer was perplexed.

"If the Russians. . . ," Hilda began apprehensively.

"Don't talk nonsense," Ignas said, annoyed, and stepped quickly into the yard. Only one set of car tracks showed on the grass. The Russians had not returned, as he had feared for a moment. Even the tracks that were there had almost been washed out by the rain. Krõõt was nowhere to be found. The potatoes that were being boiled for the hogs in the barn kitchen were already cooked to a pulp, and the food stewing on the kitchen stove was hardly warm for the fire had gone out. They all stood around not knowing what to do.

Old Aadu caught up with them. He had turned up his trousers almost to his knees, and he was carrying his soft leather shoes by their laces. The wet grass had washed his feet clean and white. He too waited for some time in the pasture and looked around carefully before stepping into the farmyard. He inspected the car tracks and beat the earth with his heavy stick, as if he were killing a snake. After paying a visit to the kitchen, checking the porridge pot, and expectantly placing his bowl on the corner of the table, he hurried to the gate. There he leaned against the post and turned his face toward Võllamäe.

"Look," Hilda said, excitedly. "Aadu is expecting something."

"He's crazy," Ignas muttered. "He's always waiting for something."

To everyone's surprise the mistress of the farm came from the direction of Matsu. Her face glowed and she was in a cheerful mood.

"Now it's all over," she said with relief.

"What?" Ignas asked. He did not comprehend. "You run off for no reason at all, like a young girl. The cows are in pain. They have to be milked. And we don't know what to think," he scolded.

"Ella ran over and called me," Krõõt said. "A thing like that just can't wait."

"So that was it," Ignas mumbled. "Which is it, a boy or a girl?"

"A nice big girl, strong and healthy," Krõõt answered. She had somehow grown younger herself. "The mother is doing fine, too, except that she is afraid."

"Afraid of what?"

"Of her father of course, of Juhan. Right after the birth the girl was

228

so scared. She made us hand the baby to her. Now they are both asleep, side by side. Meeta herself is quite happy. She put on a frown when I called her grandmother, but smiled and said, 'It's my daughter's child, and that's all I care about!' "

"So it's a girl," Linda of Piskujõe repeated. She smiled too. "Then we cannot expect another war for a long time. Only girls are born this year —at Harukurgu and Kalgina and even Tenise; only girls. Wonder which Ilme has, a boy or a girl?"

When the peace of the evening began to descend upon the farm and Osvald had gone his own way, Juhan of Matsu came to Hiie. Ignas took his neighbour to the back chamber, for he knew that Juhan had something weighing on his mind. Here, away from the women, they could talk undisturbed.

"You keep sentries at the gate," Juhan remarked. "Several of them— the dog and the old man. Both take a good look at you. The old man has a stick in hand, and seems to watch out or he'll let you have it, if he doesn't like your face. I heard that the Russians paid you a visit today."

"That's right."

"That damned breed of red plague. I wish there was some weed that would smoke them out!"

"They understand the smell of powder."

"That's the only thing they do understand. What were they looking for now?"

"I don't know. They were chasing my son-in-law. I'd heard that he'd been sitting for some time in a cold place."

"A rascal is your son-in-law." Juhan guffawed. "Don't believe everything you hear. If they're looking for him, he isn't sitting anywhere any more. He must have given the Ivans a good kick between the eyes. Do you think he'd let a stupid Ivan cut off his balls? Ha-ha-ha, the footloose son of old Andres isn't that big a fool. Even if the dog herd of Võllamäe takes to the woods, then—but I'd better shut up."

"So you think that. . . ."

"Hairy hawk! Do you think they would be looking for ghosts?" Juhan was in an unusually expansive mood, chest stuck out and beard pointing upwards. Was that because of the granddaughter just born? Ignas wondered. When, however, his neighbour produced a bottle of vodka from his pocket, he had to say it aloud: "I suppose one may congratulate you now, upon having become a grandfather, or what?" Ignas ventured.

"Split that tree stump! I had nothing to do with it. Had it been a boy, believe me, I would have broken its neck, but why should I bother about a girl. I took a mouthful of vodka at home and thought that it is good it turned out to be a girl. She'll be all right to have around, when she grows old enough to run after the herds. And my own conscience will remain clean, too. Here, take a shot. Yes, if it had been a boy I would have buried him under the woodpile. How could I have watched him grow up—my own grandchild, yes, but a Russian, damn it! There's no

229

need though to get worked up about a girl. My heart feels lighter already."

Looking at his massive neighbour, Ignas realized that everything had not gone as easily as the lightly said words seemed to indicate. But the final decision had evidently calmed Juhan to the extent that it brought him to Hiie in a cheerful mood, vodka bottle in hand.

"All right then, your health, and good wishes that the girl will grow into something useful!" Ignas said, raising the bottle.

"What can a split-tail be useful for?" Juhan retorted. "A woman. That's a weak vessel."

"Well, may she become a useful vessel," the former district elder corrected himself. That was a minor detail, and certainly not worth wasting words over. They had many more important knots to untangle here with the help of the small bottle, for all of life now was one big bundle of knots, whichever way you looked at it. Every day turned up bigger problems that stubbornly refused to be solved.

Osvald was walking alone through the wood. The summer night was full of fresh, ripe fragrance after the rain. Mists rose in the warm evening and muffled all the sounds that had rung out far in the clear, dust-free air at sunset. Osvald recalled again how it had all begun, the whole affair with Marta of Roosi.

It had been a night in the late spring. He had just completed a long reconnaissance trip to Kalgina, collecting information about the Red Army units that were camping under the pines—their number, character and possible plans. On his way back through the early morning dusk he had almost run into Marta of Roosi. Osvald realized immediately that she was coming from the district administration house, where a noisy party had been in progress all through the night. To his surprise he saw that the woman hurried into deep thickets, away from the fields of Harukurgu. She must be completely drunk, Osvald decided. Following on her tracks he began to wish that she would lose her way completely. His wish was fulfilled, and he felt happy like a boy. It seemed to him as if it was he who directed the woman into the dense forest with the invisible power of his desires.

Roaming around the forests in the springtime, Osvald had had enough leisure time to mull over in his mind the time when he had come to the Hiie farm as a young farmhand and had fallen desperately in love with Marta of Roosi. Marta, however, was then running after Taavi of Piskujōe, and was almost reckless enough to have run after him to the altar, regardless of the other woman. How would she have noticed Osvald, a hired boy with angular limbs. And later, when the girl was about to make a profitable match by marrying a rich old man, Osvald had spit out in anger. He had of course been right, for every passing year made it clearer that August of Roosi's daughter would not make a wife for any man. Even his anger at Marta faded, and he began to think of her with contempt when she was at a distance. But when he happened to meet her again face to face, the old strange feeling returned. He was awkward and angry at himself. She was only a tramp that had been at the beck and call of every German, and yet he could not help running after her with hot feet.

Still, following her like that seemed only a pleasant diversion for Osvald. It did not happen every day that women got lost in the thickets. Marta seemed too deep in thought to find her way, or else she would have turned right immediately. No, she seemed to be drifting more and more to the left on the moss-grown path. The fool, she would end up at Ilmaotsa by night.

On the edge of the back field Osvald could not constrain himself any longer. He could not wait for Marta to get up from the tree stump where she had sat down. He went around her and walked up to her, seemingly coming from the opposite direction.

"Osvald!" Marta exclaimed, getting up and taking a few steps in his direction, as if she had been expecting him.

"Well, what do you know. Good morning." The man feigned surprise. "You sure have taken a long early morning walk. Lost? Ha-ha-ha. What about me? I was going to Metsaoti. I've just come from home."

Marta's face seemed tired and pale. The long hike had failed to bring any glow to her cheeks, but she seemed almost happy to have met Osvald.

"Don't tell me fairy tales. Do you think that I don't know where you have come from? Both you and Tõmm of Hiie are living on the moor."

"Tõmm is in the army," Osvald lied, "and I am not staying here for long either. I have a job in Tallinn. I'm just taking a vacation."

Marta laughed. The laughter sounded forced, but it indicated that she did not believe Osvald's words.

"Tell me what you please, but don't take me for a fool. After all, we are from the same village. I'm not trying to find out where you live. I am only sorry you don't trust me. I gave the passports to Taavi last autumn, and helped Ilme and the boy across the bay. But let's not go into all that. Say, is it going to rain?"

"Yes, it seems that way," Osvald agreed. He was sorry for a moment that he had let himself in for that game. The devil only knew where it might lead. The woman was just coming from a drinking party with the Russians, and plenty of wild stories were being told about her already.

Thunder broke over the moors, crashing into the slender trunks of the pines, soughing in the branches above their heads. Half of the sky was covered with black clouds.

So suddenly! They both marvelled.

Osvald pulled Marta into the woods. They had to hurry, or else they would soon be soaking wet.

"We won't make it to the village any more," Osvald panted. "We'll have to wait out this rain somewhere else."

"I don't care," Marta answered. "We can sit under a tree somewhere."

"It's dangerous under a tree in a thunderstorm."

"And if we should get wet, so what," Marta said defiantly.

They had barely reached the meadows, when the heavy downpour caught up with them. A whitish grey twilight surrounded them all of a sudden, into which the lightning mingled with yellow fire.

"Didn't make it," Osvald said.

"So what."

"So what," Osvald mimicked her, running. "Come quicker. Run. It's easy for you to say 'So what.' You go and dry your clothes at home and that's all. But I have to crouch like a soaked rag in the wet thickets. The hay barn of Kadapiku is right here."

Sitting on the remnants of last year's hay in the barn, Osvald remained glum, as if the unexpected storm had been Marta's fault. This seemed to offer secret satisfaction to the woman.

However, Osvald was angry with himself. What should it matter to him whether this woman was drenched by the rain or got lost on the moors? He was acting like a boy again, following childish whims.

For a long time they sat apart, listening to the thunder. The glow of the lightning reached every corner of the barn. Marta had lain down on the hay.

"Osvald."

"What is it?"

"I am cold."

Sitting away from Marta, Osvald had only been able to see her wet feet with the tattered stockings that had been torn in the woods. Now he raised his eyes. The woman nudged closer to him, lying on her back, her breasts rising high from the opened coat.

"Osvald, I am cold," she said again, and reached for the man.

The thunderstorm rolled over the meadows and forests, but they heard nothing.

The night was warm and stuffy, as if it were hatching a new rain. Raindrops were still dripping from the crowns of the trees to the moss-covered roof of the Roosi storage barn. They dropped into the puddle in front of the barn, and some fell even directly on Osvald's neck.

Osvald knocked against the wall of the storage barn, giving the signal they had agreed upon, and listened intensely. Could it be that Marta was not at home? But no, now he heard the quiet squeaking of the bed, and soft footsteps approaching the door.

"Is it you, Osvald?"

The voice of the woman sounded tired.

"Who else?" The man did not quite understand, and was surprised to find Marta fully dressed.

"You haven't gone to bed yet?"

"No, I was waiting for you."

That was strange too. Osvald shook his head. Her voice did not sound as if she wanted him. He slipped through the door and Marta bolted it.

"What's wrong with you?"

"With me? Nothing." The woman laughed mirthlessly. "I was just sitting and thinking. This business is getting on my nerves."

"What business?"

"The Russians and—everything. Don't light the candle. Let's sit like this in the dark. I don't know, I may have to move to the district administration house soon."

"Why over there? To live there or what?"

"Well, there's an order like that, and there is plenty of room. Wait. Don't right now. I don't feel like it. Forgive me, I am peculiar today, I know. Let's talk a little. We have never had any time to talk. Say, Osvald, do you think that I am a very bad person because of all you know and have heard of me?"

"No, silly. Why should I?" Osvald observed. He felt a cold draught rise up from under the floor of the barn. His arm went around the waist of the woman and she leaned against him, sitting on the bed, as usual. Yet suddenly everything was different.

"The NKVD were at Hiie today, weren't they?" Marta asked.

"Yes, they did drive up to the farm."

"Well, Taavi has escaped clean away—from prison."

"You don't say!" Osvald rejoiced.

"Yes, I can see you are glad. I was glad too in the beginning, but then I began to think no good would come of it—no good at all. I have a feeling that now we are in for it."

"In for what? They won't catch him any more, now that he's gone."

"They may not catch him any more, but that's even worse. You don't know what kind of big trap the NKVD is. I am afraid that many things will come back to life now. Even the dead may come back to life," she whispered with a lustreless voice, as if she were talking to herself.

Osvald felt her back tremble under his hand.

"Listen, what's the matter with you? You seem to be completely beside yourself."

"It's the times; it's my nerves. Don't pay any attention to me, Osvald. I should have married you a long time ago, and we could have had big children by now. Children. See what foolish thoughts I have. I never wanted children, and now, suddenly. . . . Why don't you say something. What name would you have wanted to give to our son?"

"Our son?" Osvald mumbled. No, that would have been impossible. He could not picture it any more.

"Of course it's silly," Marta repeated weakly, as if she could read the man's thoughts. "It's always too late when we learn how to be good and wise. I have never known how to be either. I would like to go away from Kalgina now, to Tallinn or somewhere. This accursed new order won't let me, though. It keeps everyone on a halter like an animal that is being led to slaughter. Would you like a drink, Osvald? I have some vodka today. Listen, why don't you take off your shoes? I can't get over this worry without drinking."

Marta had never received Osvald like that before. She had always been in a hurry, she had always been burning and thirsty like the earth after a long drought. He tried to find the bottle in the dark.

"Light the candle," Marta whispered. "Or don't you want any more? Is it already too boring for you?"

"Don't talk nonsense," Osvald muttered, fumbling in his pocket for matches. His hand touched the revolver. Everything was very strange today.

"This may be our last night," Marta said, looking into the candlelight, her face pale and tired. "Have you ever had the feeling that somebody will suddenly appear on the other side of the wall and knock? Knock in a completely different manner, not like you at all. Russians maybe? Or God knows who. And then what? I have a revolver, but will that be of any help? Oh, hell, I'm out of my mind. Let's drink! Your health, Osvald."

Osvald drank, but the vodka did not taste right. This drinking was somehow forced, false and superfluous. Osvald's heart froze. He thought about Taavi. Ilme's husband was quite a man, if he had managed to struggle out of the irons that held him.

"Let's drink to Taavi's health. He needs it right now," he said.

The glass in the woman's hand moved suddenly, as if it were about to fall.

For a long time Marta looked into the dark corner of the barn and then gave Osvald an anguished look, as if she had awakened from a nightmare. She emptied her glass in one draught and threw herself on the bed, face toward the carpet that was already a little warmer from the vodka. The moods of a woman. . . . After a little while Marta touched his back. Her face glowed and her eyelids were heavy.

Their last night, Marta had said. Strange, how a person can be so right sometimes. She did not move to the district administration house, as she had said. She found it unnecessary, for a group of NKVD soldiers was billeted at Roosi. They were young men, armed to the teeth, who dug foxholes around the little farm. They set up a heavy machine gun right in front of the house, covering the forests and the fields of Metsaoti, as if an attack by a considerable force might be expected from that direction.

When a similar group was stationed at Piskujõe, it became clear to Marta, Osvald, and the people of Hiie that these soldiers were expecting Taavi Raudoja from the forest. Perhaps they even intended to go looking for him in the thickets.

Even living in the old bathhouse of Piskujõe, Linda awakened early in the mornings. At her age she did not need much sleep any more. By the time the sun of the harvest month reached high enough to throw a handful of gold over the slender fir trees, she had already been up and dressed for some time, had milked the cow and driven the couple of sheep to the meadow. The soldiers who lived in the farmhouse now slept almost until noon. Only the sentries who kept their eyes on the forests were vigilant. When Linda went under the firs where the crosses were carved into the tree trunks and folded her hands in prayer, there were always two gloomy men standing nearby. This was the longest walk she was permitted to take. For weeks she had been in a strange kind of confinement. Nobody had forced her to leave the little farmhouse of Piskujõe. The Russians had merely moved in like the real owners, made beds for themselves on the floor of the front room and placed their rifles in a corner. Linda had slept the first few nights in the back chamber, while the strangers made themselves at home in her household, taking from the pantry and drawers what they pleased, noisily rummaging around all through the night. Then the woman had not been able to stand it any more. For half a day she had carried her bedclothes, some dresses and a few more personal items into the little bathhouse, leaving the rest at the disposal of the intruders.

Linda did not ask herself what the coming days had in store for her. She knew that her life had been lived, that it had been over ever since Andres had died. She had been born at Piskujõe, the small cotter's homestead built on the land of the big farm of Hiie, had grown up here and spent here the years of her youth. Her widowed mother had raised her, working hard at odd jobs in the village. Everybody had thought that she would be the future mistress of Hiie. However she did not become the mistress of any farm, for fate decreed otherwise and sent along Andres, a hired man, sailor and jack-of-all-trades, who, because of his restless spirit, was often disdainfully called an adventurer. A woman's heart is a strange thing indeed, for Linda had preferred him to anybody else. In the little house of Piskujõe their son Taavi had been born, and then they had gone out into the wide world. For years they had lived in a small coastal village, and had then moved to Tallinn. Andres had gone to sea again, had tried many a business, and had made good for a while. But more often unexpected obstacles had been thrown into his path, for he was reckless and regarded life as a gamble. After the death of Taavi's sister he had taken a special interest in the upbringing of their son. "Study," he had told Taavi, "or else you'll become a wild wolf like me, who cannot even offer a roof to his wife and children. You have better opportunities than I had in my youth." So Taavi had studied. He had become a construction engineer, but he too was now unable to provide a shelter for his family. He was an outlaw, a wilder wolf and outlaw than Andres had ever been.

Linda had returned to her birthplace when the great upheavals began. They were by then related to the Hiie people, and the Russians had begun to harass Andres on the job. Then Ignas of Hiie had let it slip that they might find shelter at Piskujõe. His big farm would be carved up anyway by the new masters. Andres could have a part of it. Thus Andres Raudoja had become a farmer on the land of his former rival. Of course, Ignas and Linda were now well along in years, their lives were behind them, and the blood of both of them flowed in their grandchild.

The day before, August of Roosi had brought Linda a summons to appear at the district administration house. She set out in mid-morning, accompanied by an armed soldier. On the way she met farmers who were returning from the dairy with empty milk cans on their wagons. They looked at her with amazement. Some who knew her better even opened their mouths. But nobody said anything beyond a greeting. A soldier was with her, and the bad news spread rapidly through the district and frightened people into silence. Only Ignas of Hiie, who happened to be taking the milk to the dairy instead of Hilda, stopped his horse.

"Where are you going with that Ivan?" he asked. When he heard she was going to the committee he became thoughtful. "What should they want of you?" he muttered.

"Just drive on. It's better you don't talk to me," Linda said bitterly.

"Yes, you are right," Ignas answered. His own son was in the woods, and he was quite sure now that he himself was marked by the new authorities. It only depended on fate, when his hour would strike. The decision might be made already. Ignas had no contact with the men in the woods now. He had even forbidden his own son to come near the village. They were all afraid of the reprisals that would follow if a Russian were killed, for they remembered what had happened last winter when Reku had killed a Russian in Harukurgu. Nobody had met him in the woods recently, so they had not been able to warn him, and the atmosphere was explosive. NKVD units had arrived from Tallinn, and their eyes were watching the backwoods in Kalgina county. The slightest rustle in the thickets might set large forces in motion.

Ignas followed the woman with his eyes for another little while. The years and the worries had made her thin and frail. Then he shook the reins, and the wagon began to move, empty milk cans rattling. Day by day the scope of their lives became narrower.

The chairman of the executive committee gazed sternly at the old woman, as if he were in a quandary and did not know how to begin.

"Why didn't you apply for land, when land was offered?" he asked finally.

"What could I have done with land, old woman that I am?" Linda answered with a question. The reception room of the committee had become filthy and sordid. The unswept wooden floor was covered with sand and cigarette stubs.

"Why didn't your son stay here and cultivate the land for you? Why did he go into the woods as a bandit?" the invalid asked angrily, as if the words hurt him.

"I don't know anything about my son."

"You're lying. You yourself brought him up that way. But that's nothing for me to worry about. What I am interested in is why you haven't registered your cow and sheep. Why haven't you listed them with the committee?"

"One old cow—and nobody has asked for it."

"Yes, I know, my predecessor was a damned weakling and a counter-revolutionary. It is hard to straighten out the mess that he left behind. Everything is out of order here. The whole district is disorganized." He seized his forehead with the stumps of his fingers, as if his predecessor's incompetence gave him a headache. "You have no land, but you keep a cow," he growled. "You pay no taxes, you fulfil no obligations toward the district, but you keep a cow. You'll come tomorrow and you'll bring your cow here, for keeping a cow like that is a scandal. It is robbery of the state and the people. Do you understand that?"

No, Linda did not understand that.

"And secondly, the land you are living on has been assigned to the state land reserve. It is the property of the people. How dare you live on land that belongs to the people and grow your cabbages there?"

"I am one of the people too."

"You are nothing—the mother of a bandit! I hear that you have moved into the bathhouse. That is sensible of you, for the farmhouse doesn't belong to you anyway. I warn you though, if your son doesn't come out of the woods you will have to take your bathhouse on your back and move it off the people's land."

"Where to? Where is there any land that doesn't belong to the people?"

"Shut up, citizen. You are nothing but a disgrace to the whole district. You may go now, and make sure that you come tomorrow with the cow."

"Yes, but. . . . How shall I live then, or what shall I eat?" Linda hesitated. Everything became blurred before her eyes.

"That's something for you to worry about," the chairman sneered. "Why don't you gather pine cones in the forest?"

Linda looked around the office. She cast a glance in the direction of Marta of Roosi. She was a real Red now, the people said. Linda could not tell anything from her face. She was busy and did not look in Linda's direction.

Linda backed out of the door, followed by the Russian. She saw acquaintances in the waiting room, but they were looking at the floor and acting as if they did not know her.

III

Ilme did not believe that she could possibly survive giving birth this time. It was possible that she received better care because of her condition than other prisoners, but she was still too weak, and she feared for the child that moved restlessly under her heart.

She did not know much about the people who had been caught with her in the autumn. They had received their sentences long ago and had been sent to Siberia. Ilme had been kept in a solitary cell for months. She thought that she had not yet been sent to Siberia because of her pregnancy. It was strange that they had not yet sent Lembit, her son, away either. They saw each other only very rarely, but the feeling that her son was still within the same walls gave Ilme much strength. The boy had become thin and sickly, but he did not cry, although fear darkened his childish eyes and their look cut deeply into his mother's heart. She endeavoured to put on a cheerful expression when she saw her son, and tried her best to comfort the child.

"Why doesn't Father come?" Lembit asked every time. He believed firmly that his father would come soon and set them free. The men in his cell befriended him and tried to comfort him as much as possible. The confidence of the boy was probably an even greater source of comfort to the grownups, but a boy seven years old is not blind and without sense, unable to observe and relate to each other the happenings around him. The disappearance of men who had become his friends depressed him deeply, and the wounds and stripes of his grownup companions on their return from interrogations hurt him as if he had received them himself. The men tried to hide the ugly truth from him, but he discovered it on his own.

Lembit was used as a spy in the big cell, but he learned to deny what he had heard, and instead of the promised candy he received beatings. He was told propaganda stories, he was promised his freedom, and often became so mixed up in his mind that he spoke freely about things he should have kept secret and kept silent about things that had no significance.

Even before she gave birth, Ilme was afraid that she would not be allowed to keep her child. She was a prisoner, and forced labour awaited her. The new order could not reform her any more, and thus she knew she was slated for liquidation. But the child would be planted into the seedbed of Communism, fatherless, motherless, a being without a homeland or nationality, who would grow somewhere in a children's home into a faithful slave of world revolution.

Ilme could not recall many details of the birth later on. It had come prematurely as a result of beating, and then the pains had made everything else remote and unimportant. Whatever came within her field of vision bounced back from it without penetrating any deeper. The male nurse, dressed in the uniform of a prison guard, treated her with the roughness of a butcher, but Ilme trusted him. There was nobody else from whom she could have expected any help.

The woman's silent pleading did not remain unnoticed by the middle-aged medical technician, but there was not much he could do. All he wanted was that everything should go as quickly as possible and according to rules. He did not believe the child would live, and that was none of his business anyway. As long as the woman did not scream too much —he could not stand screaming women. Fortunately, she uttered only a few short cries. He could not be blamed for that. He had no experience in maternity cases, and no help could be expected from the Russian girls.

When Ilme was told that she had given birth to a girl, and heard the sickly crying of the child, she fell into a short, deep, blissful sleep. She forgot her fate and the place where she was lying. The exertion had been almost too great for her exhausted organism. What with the narrow confinement, mental suffering and the bleakness of the prison walls it was a great miracle that everything had turned out as it did, and the child was said to be well.

Ilme and her child were somewhere in an upstairs room, for the bright, unaccustomed daylight hurt her eyes even when she was asleep. Her sleep was profound, and for the first time for a long while it was refreshing and without nightmares. Only rarely she winced, opened her eyes and grabbed mechanically the edge of the grey blanket. She raised her head, a restless look in her frightened eyes, but as soon as she saw the ragged bundle in the white wooden box, her head fell back and she fell asleep again. She was still in pain, but the pain had somehow risen above her. It had the shape of a star, and it stood at the head of her rusty iron bedstead, almost within reach on the right-hand side. When she woke up next, she noticed that the rays of the sun focused there, shining at an angle through the barred window.

And then the sun began to disturb her. As a little schoolgirl she had drawn pictures of the sun. She had drawn a circle with her pencil and added bundles of rays around it. "Is that the sun?" the teacher had asked. "No, it isn't," she had replied. "The sun is yellow." She coloured her sun bright yellow, but she was not satisfied with it. "The sun is golden," she exclaimed. She painted the sun golden. "Is that what the sun is like?" the teacher had asked again. "No, the sun is white, white, shining white!" But she could not find a colour for it. "See," the teacher had said. "The sun is a masterpiece of nature, and no artist can imitate it." She had not wanted to accept this. She had observed the shimmering light of the sun on the water, on the dew in the morning, in the whiteness of blossoming trees. She had let the sun and the wind play on her skin until it was golden brown and glowing, and until even the curls of her dark hair had turned into dark gold. "I did not know that every last ray of the sun can find room in your eyes," Taavi had told her. "The sun goes to sleep in your eyes at night," he had continued. "How could that be," Ilme had wondered. "My eyes are brown. The sun could sink into your eyes much more easily. Your eyes are blue." Taavi would not be contradicted. "No, your eyes are the real home of the sun. They were made that way. My eyes are too icy. The sun would die in them." The sun had been everywhere then. There had been so much sun in their lives that they had had no place to store it, and finally they had realized that the biggest sun in their lives was their son Lembit. Now even the sun had been thrown into prison, had been chained to the bottom of the earth and left to die of cold.

She awakened with a start, feeling as if she had stepped on a sharp-edged piece of glass with her bare feet. When she was awake, she felt again that the pain had risen higher. It was a blunt pain, and she did not pay attention to it. The cell was almost dark, and the male nurse was standing at her bedside. Ilme asked for something to drink. The man shook his head and left, locking the door behind him. It did not matter, Ilme thought. At least she had her daughter. She was too weak to hear the breathing of the baby, but raising her head she could still make out the white wooden box on the floor in the twilight.

Ilme could not fall asleep any more. Thoughts kept coming and going, and the burden of her troubles oppressed her. Her weakness and the blood that rang in her ears built a wall within walls around her and separated her even further from her anguished life.

With open eyes, she saw everything in the darkness. Everything that had happened to her during the recent months, beginning with the arrest on the shore that autumn night. The blasts from the automatic pistols of the Russians had sounded just when the first people, glowing with the hope of escape, had begun to climb from the stones into the large boat. She saw the fires dancing between the bushes, heard the high-pitched scream of a woman, the frightened wail of a child and the dark curse of a man that turned into a husky groan. She had pulled Lembit down to her side and pressed her face against the moist, cold moss and the sharp pine cones. It was hot all of a sudden, a storm roared over the shore, and she felt as if they were being trampled under the feet of a thousand wild, stampeding cattle. She could not think of escape any more. She could not think of anything. On the long march, when some of the wounded had collapsed and a man who had happened to stumble in the morning dusk had been killed by a blast from a machine gun, she had been barely able to walk. She had hoped to wake up from this evil dream. She remembered that Marta had not been among them then. Ilme had not seen her on the shore, either. Had she been hit by the first bullets?

Ilme saw the interrogations, which in her case had not started until a little before Christmas, and had gradually become more and more brutal. When she had told all she knew, they had demanded more and more. They had beaten Lembit in her presence to make her confess. A thin, scraggly-haired woman who seemed to bear a grudge against her had been her chief interrogator. The woman seemed less interested in the questions and answers than in the torture she could inflict on Ilme during the interrogations.

"You are a victim of the Soviet order yourself," Ilme had once told her, exhausted.

Later she had been sorry for her words, for the woman had run her fingernails into her face, crazed with rage. Ilme had been too weak to defend herself.

Ilme was convinced that the woman would finally kill her, or that she would kill Lembit before her own eyes, but then the woman had developed a fiendish interest in the still unborn child. She had made the guard, who had laughed out loud like a horse, tear the clothes from Ilme's body and had said that she would cut out the foetus with her own hands. Shivering from terror and cold Ilme had tried to retain consciousness, but she had nevertheless collapsed. She felt that she was about to lose her sanity. The expressionless eyes of the inquisitor stared at her day and night during her semi-consciousness. She had not really slept for months, and she had not been quite awake either. She asked herself sometimes in a loud voice, "Am I still a living human being?" Her voice echoed back from invisible cells, although her own cell had been silent like a grave already for a long time, the air in it congealed and dense like grey ice, in which the tiny electric bulb burned with a reddish glow.

During the most recent interrogation the woman had beaten her mercilessly, until she had suffered a hemorrhage and the male nurse had been summoned. Ilme had been barely conscious all the time, convinced that this was the end, until the labour pains had begun. She had been stronger and braver than she had ever expected herself to be, and she had given birth to a healthy daughter! Miracles still happened in this world.

Ilme slept much during the following days. She spent most of her time somewhere in the anteroom of unconsciousness, in downey, soft peace that was nevertheless pierced by the sharp, steely pangs of fear and anguish. She was content each time when the male nurse brought her lukewarm unsweetened tea in a big tin cup and handed her the baby for nursing. She had begun to trust the silent, morose man. The woman needed that knowledge that there was at least one human being near her who did not hate her, but was helpful.

She inquired about Lembit. Oh, her son was doing quite well. She asked whether the boy could see his little sister sometime. The male nurse thought he could; he might be able to do it quite soon.

"Thank you for everything," the woman whispered and leaned back on the straw mattress. It was hard and lumpy, but still so much better than the bare moist boards of the cot in her former cell.

The male nurse gave her a startled look. He could not understand why she had thanked him. He left the cell in a confused hurry.

From day to day Ilme felt her hunger increase. It was because of the baby, she decided. She had milk in her breasts, and she was afraid she might lose it if she did not get more to eat. The food was better up here, but when she was through with her lukewarm maize soup and her slice of rye bread she began to feel ravenous.

Food became suddenly the dominant thought in her mind, and she dreamed about meals in the big front room of Hiie, about the bounty stored in the larder of the farm, or simply about great brown loaves of bread, which she devoured with her eyes, knowing that even in her dream that they would vanish if she only lifted her hand toward them. She asked the Russian girl for food, the one who brought her the soup and who changed the wet rags of the child once a day. The girl only laughed stupidly. She spoke to the male nurse about food. He promised to do what was in his power, but evidently his power did not reach very far, at least not far enough to satisfy Ilme's hunger.

Ilme did however appreciate one of his gifts: an old comb and a piece of black, polished wood with which she could comb the vermin from her hair. Ilme longed to wash herself. She yearned for the bathhouse of

Hiie and the fragrant bundle of birch twigs, but the girl brought her only a basin of water and a stinking rag for a towel.

Her thick hair became thinner with each stroke of the comb. Her curls had hung out straight long ago, and she remained quite indifferent when she discovered several thick grey hairs among those she had combed out over the piece of wood. She knew that the woman who had interrogated her had plenty of reason to rejoice at the change in her looks. She remembered well how she had surveyed her. "You look pretty like hell," she had remarked. "Never mind, soon you'll look like me, or maybe a little worse." Maybe. The outside of a person could be changed. Even his soul could be destroyed, but it was a different question whether the outward ugliness could be planted into his heart right away. Ilme began to arrange her hair again, not because she cared what she looked like, but because she was accustomed to keeping her hair neat.

As soon as Ilme was able to think again she began to worry about the name she should give to her little daughter. She had mentioned it to Taavi once on the shore, but the man had had no time for such problems. Down in the cellar Ilme had not believed any longer that she would be able to bear the child, so she had not bothered about a name, but now suddenly she began to like the name Hilja. So when the nurse asked her for the name of her daughter one day, she said Hilja. The man wrote the name down on a piece of paper, and that was the total christening ceremony.

Ilme had revived together with the child. She began to rejoice in the small privileges she now enjoyed. She no longer mouldered in the cave-like cell that had been hers before. Not much daylight fell into the room through the small, barred slit in the wall, but it was nevertheless something to be thankful for. The fresh air seemed to penetrate through her skin, and late in the afternoon even a few sunrays fell onto the wall near the corner of the window. One day when the gold of the sun glittered again on the wall, she arose and stepped on the floor with her bare feet. She could not remember later how she had managed to reach the window, for everything had become black before her eyes when she had raised her head. It must have taken her some time to reach the window, for the sun had been gone for a long while when she stretched her hands, thin and fragile like a bird's, toward it and grasped the bars with her fingers. A new fainting spell made her face sink against the rough wall, but she did not let go of the bars. She hung there, too weak to raise her eyes to the window level to look out, until the male nurse entered and carried her back to the bed. There she lay motionless like dead, but her hands were still stretched out toward the light.

A few days passed before she trusted herself to attempt to reach the window again. She was secretly afraid of what she might see. She might see nothing—a few grey rooftops or the courtyard of the prison, where prisoners were sometimes walked around like animals in the stockyards. She was afraid that she might fall, hurt herself and leave the little girl hungry for her milk. But the window enticed her, the light intoxicated her, she was obsessed by it day and night. So she went again, leaning against the wall, falling to her knees once, but rising again with difficulty. Her ears sang, and darkness fell over her occasionally like a heavy blanket, but she did not lose from her eyes the light that drew her toward the window. This time she raised her haggard face up to the iron bars. She remained there a long time, and the picture she saw made her moan. She knew she would remember it until the end of her days, like a child remembers a vision which has entered its soul without requiring conscious action of the brain.

There was not much to be seen: only the shining sea, silvery in the evening sun. It was the same sea by which they had been arrested in the autumn when only a few steps had separated them from freedom.

She knew that she had to drag herself back to her bed, but she was unable to tear her eyes away from the sea. The sun did not reach her face. She stretched her arm out between the bars, and the sunlight fell on her hand. She laughed with excitement, feeling something marvellous flow from her fingers into her body. She laughed and cried simultaneously, until she sank to the floor, barely conscious. She looked at her hand and then pressed her fists tightly against her breast, as if she feared that the big bird of light she had just caught might escape from her heart.

Hilja was a sickly child. When Ilme looked at her crooked, almost transparent limbs or her bluish face, such pain and anguish overcame her that she could not even cry. The child herself could not cry either, although she whimpered all the time. The woman feared for the child's milk, and the fear further lessened the amount she was able to offer the baby.

One day the male nurse announced that they would have to go back to Ilme's previous cell. The face of the man was sad when he announced it, although he was accustomed to brutality and roughness.

"Back there, in the dark?" Ilme repeated, as if she could not believe it. Her glance turned toward the barred window, behind which glittered the sea. Back there? That meant being buried alive again, not seeing the light of day, not feeling the warmth of the sun. Nightly interrogations, beatings—oh Lord!

"But the child?"

"Will go along."

She did not ask any more questions. The protest she felt as a mother, the resistance that rose in her against taking the baby into such terrible conditions, swelled up and almost blinded her, but she knew only too well that any opposition would be useless. It would only harm herself and the child. She had to be as calm as she could possibly be, whatever might happen to her.

She was taken back to the windowless, small, airless cell, which according to her calculations had to be located below ground level. A guard supported her on the stairs, and another carried the child before her, as if knowing that the mother would follow the child. The cell was not the same one in which Ilme had spent long months, but it did not differ from the previous one in any essential detail. There was a sleeping bench made of rough boards, and a tiny electric bulb in a wire net in the ceiling. There was no stove or radiator in the narrow room. The air was dank and smelled like a grave.

One of the guards placed the child in its box on the floor, and then they both went out, locking the door behind them. For a moment Ilme saw an eye peering through the peephole in the door, and then the steps sounded farther and farther away, echoing from the stone floor of the corridor. Ilme sank on the bare bench. She breathed hard for a long time, gasping for the stinking air, and everything was black before her eyes from the recent exertion.

A chill shook her. After the birth of the child she had become more sensitive to cold. The sleeping bench consisted of bare boards, which her unfortunate predecessors had already rubbed shiny. She noticed a few brown bloodstains near her hand, and a little farther she discovered a few letters that had been scratched into the wood. Try as she might, she could not make out a single word.

She looked again at the bare boards of the cot, shivering from the dampness and the cold, although it was midsummer outside. She had only a wide nightshirt that had been given her when her own clothes had become too tight, and around her shoulders was the coat she had worn to the shore. She looked at her thin, naked legs and the torn socks on her feet. They were a man's old woollen socks.

She rose and began to pound the door of the cell with her fist. They had to give her at least a blanket to sleep with. She did not care what kind of a blanket. She pounded with all her might, but the sound, muffled and weak, was lost in the walls of the cellar. She heard no response from the neighbouring cells, no footsteps seemed to come nearer. She stood and hesitated. No, she had to take care of herself for the child's sake, and she beat the door again. After a little while she heard the footsteps of the guards, but they passed by her door, paying no attention to her intensified pounding. A lock creaked a little farther down, and somebody's brutal voice shouted orders in Russian. She heard the scream of a woman. Then the steps passed by her cell again, accompanied by the trembling sobs of the woman and somebody's laughter that ended with cursing and spitting. Ilme's hands fell down. It was night—the busiest time in the prisons of the NKVD.

She returned to the sleeping bench, which she was allowed to use only during night-time, as she well knew. She sank upon it, sitting at first, then crouching helplessly, prostrate before her fate, shaking from chills. Her mouth uttered prayers, mechanically almost, for the pain that stiffened her neck like an iron bar robbed the words of any meaning. Her legs grew cold and lost their feeling, as if they were being gradually cut off from her living body.

Every morning Ilme believed that she would not live to see the next breakfast—a few cold potatoes and a mugful of lukewarm water. But she did—for weeks, and marvellously enough the milk did not disappear from her breasts, although she was barely able to raise herself to her feet. She knew only too well that it could not last for long. Often she heard footsteps passing her cell door. Prisoners went by in droves, escorted by guards. The prison was crammed full of unfortunates. It was strange that she had the cell all to herself. Usually a cell like that, although built for only one occupant, contained about ten women. She had been in one like it during the first months of her imprisonment.

The child whimpered constantly from unsatisfied hunger. She had never been washed, and the rags the Russian girl had given her had been torn from dirty men's shirts. She was constantly wet, and her reddened skin broke out in a rash. Oh Lord, why did they torment the little one so? After a few days Ilme had changed her mind. It would indeed be better if they would take the child away from her. She was unable to bear it any longer. But she had to—there was no other way.

She had inquired about Lembit. In desperation, she had begged the guards to let her see her son. Had he been taken to Siberia already? Why didn't they send her after her son? She could not get any information about him.

Day and night got mixed in her mind. A day seemed to last a week. Sometimes she talked to herself. She moved arduously from one wall of the cell to the other and asked herself, What are you looking for? Then she shouted out an answer: I'm looking for food. She really was looking for food. She dreamed about bread again. It had to be hidden somewhere in her cell.

Watching the child's face that was stamped with the shadow of death, she conceived the idea of killing it. Her mouth prayed, but the sudden idea did not disappear even when she called the Lord's name aloud. This convinced her that she was about to lose her reason. Thoughts raced wildly through her head, contradictory, raving, exhausting thoughts, just as if her head had been a metal box full of jumping little stone-hard peas. The child had to die sooner or later. Why shouldn't she end its sufferings right away? After this thought she remained on her knees on the floor, as if lightning had hit her in the face. She knew that she could not turn the face of the baby down into the rags and let her lie and suffocate. She began to be afraid of herself.

She did not believe her ears when her name was called one night. With her coat over her bare shirt and ragged socks on her feet, she climbed the stairs to the interrogation room, filled with strange forebodings. What now? Was it the beginning of her journey to Siberia? Somehow these questions did not preoccupy her very much. The sufferings had numbed her beyond caring.

To her surprise she found several people waiting for her. In addition to the familiar woman interrogator, there were men in the uniform of NKVD officers, and some in civilian clothes. The woman who sat behind the table looked at Ilme with a sour, sickly smile, as if she felt embarrassed because of Ilme's wretched appearance. Ilme was offered a chair. This was an unusual courtesy that she had rarely experienced before. The woman spoke with the men in Russian for a long time, and it seemed to Ilme that they were somehow divided into two groups. She gathered from the glances and the gestures of the speakers that they were talking about her.

A swarthy NKVD officer was brusque and demanding in talk, gesturing toward the others with a sheet of paper in his hand. A one-armed man supported him, gritting his teeth audibly now and then. They both seemed more than a little insane to Ilme, especially since the others, too, seemed to treat them with a certain amount of disdain and suspicion.

Then the dark-faced man handed Ilme the sheet of paper. It was a photostatic copy of a letter.

"Look here, do you recognize the handwriting?" the woman asked her.

Ilme could not read, for the letters and the words began to dance before her eyes. She looked, and when she raised her eyes, not a word came from her mouth.

"Well?" the one-armed man hissed, leaping toward her.

"Taavi," Ilme stuttered. "Where is my husband?" she asked, rising calmly to her feet, although her legs swayed under her.

"There's nothing wrong with your husband. Only he is driving some other men here crazy," the woman muttered with contempt. It was directed this time at the one-armed Estonian who was staring at Ilme, and at his companion, who was decked out with numerous ribbons and decorations. After that Ilme was ignored again. The excited Russian conversation went on.

The men left the room in a heated argument. The dark-faced officer had a miserable stoop. Ilme recognized among them some of the higher officers of the prison whom she had gotten to know during her earlier interrogations, and concluded that something must have happened or was about to happen. She looked at the woman behind the desk. What was the meaning of her strange words and the photostat with the familiar handwriting?

The woman, who had laughed at first, grew serious, took a revolver from a desk drawer and tossed it roughly back again. Then she began to look Ilme over—her feet, her clothes and her hands that were covered with sores. Ilme knew from experience that such silent scrutiny boded no good. And sure enough, each time the woman's glance met her eyes, her face seemed to have become more and more cruel. She built up anger in herself, looking at Ilme thus, as if there was anger to be extracted from Ilme. The interrogator became livelier and livelier.

"They want to take you away from here," she muttered. "They want to let the bird fly away from under my care, and I already had my plans all laid out for you. Your husband is no fool. No man will ever be trapped with you as bait, even if they were to pour sugar all over you to make you sweeter!"

"Please, what do you know about my husband?"

Ilme had been worried all along that Taavi might have returned from Tallinn to the coast, where the NKVD was waiting.

"Those idiots, they have let your husband escape," the woman shouted. "Those pigs, monkeys, asses! They can't keep what they've got.

Now they're in trouble, and I say they'll be hanged, both of them. Those two idiots are sorry now that they were ever born."

"So my husband was. . . ."

"Don't ask so much!" the woman screamed. "Your husband will be caught again anyway, if he hasn't been caught already. Don't you worry about that. You know, your help won't be needed for it. Come here." She took the revolver from the drawer and stood up. "Come here, right under my eyes. Look at me," she screamed. "Give me your hand. So. You are all covered with scabs. What are you shivering for?"

"Where is my son?" Ilme asked quietly.

"Your son! Just listen to her. She has a son and a husband—and who knows what else. A husband, houses and landed estates. And she thinks she is pretty, what the devil, and she comes to throw a litter in the prison. The devil. . . ."

In a fit of fury, she seized Ilme's hand, pressing it tightly against the table, and before Ilme knew what was happening, the shattering blows of the iron handle of the pistol fell on her hand, her fingers and fingernails. She could hear the heavy breathing of the woman, until she collapsed with a moan.

Before regaining full consciousness she had felt that she was being carried somewhere. When she came to, she was lying on the cot in her cell, her hand covered with a bloody bandage. To her surprise she found a ragged blanket at her side. The male nurse was standing in her cell. When their eyes met, the man turned quickly and left. Ilme saw the guards lock the door. Then she cast a quick glance toward the box of the baby. It was empty. They had taken little Hilja away!

Lembit was eagerly busy changing the cold compresses on his mother's feverish brow. He had had the foresight to fill a cup with cold drinking water from the pail. The rags that he now dipped into the big bucket soiled and discoloured the water. He kept changing the wet rags on his mother's forehead, for the male nurse had told him that otherwise his mother might die.

Only a year ago, Lembit had run through the farmyard and the meadows of Hiie, yelling like an Indian, Pontus yelping at his heels. The same Lembit knew very well now what death meant. It was an ugly and terrifying state that resulted from beating and shooting. A person did not move or speak any more after that. Sometimes he could open his eyes, though, and look at you as if he planned to attack you. That had been the case recently with the young fellow Paul, who had known Lembit's father in Finland. Lembit had become a great friend of Paul because of that, but Paul had been tormented and beaten to death. Nobody believed that he was that far gone—all the men had said that— but he was, and Paul had died right at Lembit's side. That had been awful, and the boy had not gotten over it yet.

Lembit was afraid that his mother might die now just like that, and then what would happen to him? What would he tell Father, when Father came to set them free?

Lembit knew that his mother was very sick. The nurse had said that, and Lembit could see it for himself. Mother's hand was wrapped with bloody bandages and it must have hurt her very much, for she did not say anything that the son might have understood. She pressed the bandaged hand against her face and moaned. Sometimes she said something, and when Lembit tried to answer her their conversation became quite mixed up. Sometimes she looked at Lembit, intensely, but with a strange expression on her face. Then she suddenly closed her eyes and her forehead was drawn into painful wrinkles.

Lembit had not seen his mother for a long time. He had heard from the male nurse that he had a little sister. He had not met his little sister yet, but her bed was right here on the floor. The name of the sister was Hilja. A strange woman was feeding her now. This strange woman had had a child too, but the child had become so big already that it had been taken away from her. It was a strange, mixed-up story, and Lembit did not quite know what to make of it.

When the male nurse came to see his mother, Lembit asked: "They aren't going to give my sister to this strange woman?"

The nurse checked Ilme's pulse and listened to her breathing.

"No, of course they won't. She is only feeding her, for your mother does not have enough milk. The fever makes the milk disappear."

"Disappear? Where?"

"Don't ask too much, young fellow."

Lembit did not ask any more, although everything remained as muddled as before. But he liked the male nurse. He wasn't a Russian. That was the main thing, although some Estonians were said to be even worse. Those who had tied him up after they had caught him praying on his knees had been bad enough. From that time Lembit had dared to pray only secretly. He had seen his grandmother pray on her knees under the fir trees, where his grandfather had been shot, and therefore he had tried it. A man will try anything in a tight spot, as one of his friends in the cell had said.

When the nurse was gone, Lembit took his coat off and shoved it under his mother's head. A piece of soiled cloth was too hard in his opinion, and he was not cold. The coat was too tight for him anyway. All his clothes had become too small for him, and when the buttons had been cut off the clothing of the other men, his buttons fell off on their own.

The boy had placed the food that had been brought for his mother on the edge of the sleeping bench. He looked at it, his mouth full of water, fighting with himself. No, he would not take it, although hunger was already tearing at his heart, as the grandmother of Hiie used to say. He would only taste a little of it—take the peel off a potato and suck the tail of a salted fish. When his teeth were about to sink into the fish, drawn by an irresistible urge, his mother groaned, and this brought him back to his senses. He pressed his head against his mother's breast and began to cry. He had forgotten the new laceless boots he had received in the meantime and had wanted to show his mother, forgotten the deadlines the men had set for their ultimate release, forgotten the news he had wanted to tell, and the questions that burdened his heart. The son crawled up on the bench to his sick mother, his heart full of pain, tenderness, and a great longing to find there shelter and protection.

Ilme did not know what awakened her. She tried to rise, but felt as weak as she had been after her labour. The Russian girl placed the child in the box and left without saying a word. The guards locked the door. Confused, Ilme looked at her son who was asleep at her side, his thin face pressed against the bare boards of the cot, his little limbs clinging to his mother, his hands blue and cold like ice.

For a moment she could not understand anything. She looked at the baby in her box, wrapped in rags, as if she feared that somebody might tear it away from her again by force. She looked at her bandaged hand, felt the pain throbbing in it, and gradually she remembered what had happened. Yes, that madwoman had smashed her hand with the revolver, and then suddenly there had been the sleeping box of little Hilja, and it had been empty. Then she had fought her fever. That had left her so weak that she was hardly able to move. Her daughter must be hungry.

With a sudden fear she tried her breasts. She still had some milk! Poor Lembit, poor little boy, exhausted from suffering. Ilme noticed the boy's coat under her head, and tears came to her eyes. She took the wrinkled and spotted coat and covered the boy with it.

Ilme looked at the stone walls of the cell. She was not quite back to normal yet. Right now she had wanted to feed the baby, had forgotten it again, and when she remembered it she realized that she was too weak to lift the child. How long had she been unconscious? Was the child still alive? What had they done in the meantime with her child?

Then again she forgot the questions which had flashed through her mind and looked at the sleeping boy with surprise, touching the overcoat of her son to make sure that what she saw was real. Then a sudden light burst through her brain: Taavi had escaped. Taavi must have been imprisoned, then, or else he could not have escaped.

Lembit woke up suddenly with the leap of a startled wild animal. His boots touched the floor with a loud bang, his coat fell to the floor, and he looked at his mother without recognizing her.

"Lembit," his mother whispered.

The boy approached her, trembling from the cold.

"My son, my dear son," Ilme said, embracing him with her whole arm. "How are you doing?"

"Oh, I'm doing quite well," Lembit said manfully. "You have been very sick. I was changing the wet packing on your face and I don't know how I fell asleep. You know, I dreamed about Father."

"Father is free again," Ilme said. "They had taken him prisoner in the meantime, but he escaped."

"That I believe," the boy said happily. "I have told the men that if my father had been here, we'd have been out long ago, in Finland or Sweden or. . . ."

"Have you looked at little Hilja? You haven't seen your little sister yet, have you?"

"She was taken to a strange woman, the nurse said. Why, here she is!" The boy stood up and approached the box. He bent slowly down, but when he straightened up again, the joy was gone from his face. "She is such a. . . ."

"She's still very tiny."

"Very tiny and ugly," the boy whispered. "Mother, she doesn't even look like a baby."

They were both silent. Ilme could not answer anything to the disappointed remark of her son. It was as if these words had made her dumb. Footsteps sounded from the corridor, names were called and doors creaked and slammed.

"They are taking somebody away again," Lembit whispered, clinging to his mother. "I was scared all the time that they would take me away and leave you here."

"They won't do that."

"They will!" Lembit answered violently. "They can shoot you and they can do anything."

"Lembit, don't. They may be taking them somewhere else, to set them free."

"They won't let anybody out from here," the boy said and swallowed. "They won't let even Hilja out. Only Father got out, only Father! Nobody but Father can get us out from here."

IV

Taevasaar had been the scene of intense activity all through the summer, but now, when the first yellow leaves appeared on the trees, the work became especially urgent, almost feverishly so, since the enemy had pushed closer. It had settled down at Piskujõe and Roosi. This cut off any significant help from Metsaoti. Although others, except for the Hiie people, did not know what was going on on the moor, they nevertheless offered their assistance. Even Juhan of Matsu, that clumsy insensitive man, had donated a whole barrel full of salted meat, and had said to Ignas: "Let your boys take this—for cleaning up my front room one night. And if they are hard up for something, tell me, and I'll look around. Split that tree stump. The boys in the woods need something to keep body and soul together, and who else should be more important. You can also tell your hired man, that rascal, when he happens to come this way or when you happen to meet him, that our Lonni is all right again and pretty good to look at. The boy should make it his business to see her sometime, otherwise she'll get all mixed up in her mind—one

250

gospel song after another in her mouth. That won't do. Holy Scripture should not be used every day. It is too strong for the weak wits of a woman. Well, if your moor-moles need something, just tell me, and I'll take a wagonload back there myself on a windy night, when the creaking of the wheels won't carry too far. And tell them to keep closer to the village during these dark nights, so that they will be handy to call together with the gong if necessary."

Fear has got under the skin of the man behind my woodpile, Ignas thought bitterly. The same fear drove Paavel of Kadapiku, the full-bodied, soft-faced smith of Metsaoti, to consult with Ignas. He had belonged to the home guard during the German occupation, and this was now a very valid reason for trembling.

"I'll be the first one to be taken from Metsaoti, I bet," Paavel smiled sadly. "But we have decided, my wife and I, that as soon as anything suspicious comes up, I'll jump into the woods. That isn't as simple as it sounds, with that bunch of kids of mine, but I know it already well enough. They make you sign that you have requested, damn it, to be resettled in Siberia."

These rumours had reached Ignas' ear already some time ago, and since Paavel had formerly taken his threshing machine from village to village, he was now slated to become director of the tractor station at Kalgina.

"They want to put me on the sieve, that's all," Paavel said. "But when they begin to shake the sieve, I'll be big enough to stay on it. When the grain falls through and is swept up, then I—well, I'll fall through the sieve any time." Then he offered his help to the men in the woods. He'd squeeze as much as he could from between his own needs and the quotas he had to deliver.

"Do you happen to have some nails in your smithy, some big ones, or some two-by-fours somewhere hidden away?"

"So, they are building something?"

"Well, not exactly, but something like it." Ignas hesitated. Help was surely needed, but they could not take everybody into their confidence. Paavel had the strong fists of a smith, but his chin was a little too soft and round. His jowls began to shake too easily with fright, and might let slip all the secrets. His wife Sessi was of much tougher grain, dried out and dark, as if she had been soaked in poison. A person whose skin is tanned like that will not open his mouth and cry to save his life. However they had six children, and that was no laughing matter. But Paavel carted his wagonload back to the moor and unloaded it where Ignas had suggested. When he walked over a few days later to check up, there was no trace left of the building materials he had brought. This made Paavel happy and sad at the same time.

Ignas approached Anton of Lepiku himself and asked for his help, for Anton left his farm on few occasions now. Sometimes he sat on the bank of the river at dusk, full of thoughts, until Luise came and touched his shoulder. Then they gave each other an understanding look, exchanged a few words about the weather and walked quietly back to their darkened farmhouse. Even so, Anton too delivered his share from the farmhouse into the woods.

The men of Tenise, though, topped all that. The road from Tenise led through forests, and their comings and goings were undisturbed. Old Captain Jonnkoppel had been organizing cooperative work there all through the summer. His popularity swept the whole district, and everybody would have been glad to help him, but he used only those who had relatives in his company or who had reserved a place in the "green army." In the opinion of the men of Metsaoti the captain was too hesitant and lacked initiative. He thought of nothing but passive resistance. He would not allow any of his men to carry out retaliatory raids, and forbade them to give any sign of their existence. He did not even approve that the men of Metsaoti helped with the haymaking.

"But who will feed us then?" Osvald asked, annoyed.

"We don't have many hiding places, and there is not enough space to manoeuvre in," the captain answered. "You can hear it yourself. The woods resound with the roundups. The thickets are made so hot that even the wild animals have to jump out."

"If we give the Reds a few kicks in the pants, they'll be more polite," Värdi figured. "What do you expect of those swine? If we had resisted the Russians when they first occupied the country, we wouldn't have the shame and suffering that we have now. The leaders we trusted and praised sold off the state and the people, and gave their honour and their lives in the bargain. It seems to me that the higher an Estonian rises, the more rotten he becomes. Cotters, farmhands and schoolboys— these were the ones who fought for our freedom. High diplomats and generals sent it to the devil. Are we really such a degenerate and stupid race that when a crofter or a farmhand rises a little higher, he is struck with blindness and gets rotten to the core?" And Värdi kept spitting and gnashing his teeth, as if even the simple captain were rotten like that.

When haymaking time was over, the work at Taevasaar became more intensive every night. Spades cut through the ground, saws whined, axes and mattocks crashed into earth and wood. In the mornings everything looked dead again: the heaps of earth and sand were covered with branches, logs and boards spread with heather, and the men asleep under khaki-coloured tents. Russian reconnaissance planes circled over the moors and forests. Even the smallest suspicious clue could ruin everything. One day a plane fired a few rounds at a neighbouring moor island. The bullets mowed down the tops of some heather plants and fell into the moor.

Their first job in the spring had been making a road through the moor. This shortened the trip to Taevasaar. Except for the men of Metsaoti, only a few boys from Tenise knew the secret path through the bog. A dugout they had built during the first summer of war was waiting for them there, half caved in and full of bats and hissing snakes. They christened it the Snake Pit, and the men of Metsaoti built their bunker here. They had found a bed in the Snake Pit, made of old hay. It must have been a man with an intrepid heart, who had shared his bed here with the reptiles.

"Who else could it have been than the fool of Võllamäe," Tõmm said with contempt.

The thought of sleeping here made the men's hair stand on end.

"You must not drink any milk, or else they'll crawl down your throat when you're asleep," Mart of Liiskaku warned. He had been on the eastern front with Osvald and had voluntarily joined the men of Metsaoti when the group had been divided in two.

The nightly work at Taevasaar proceeded only very slowly, and that made the captain glum and nervous. His worries might have been caused also by the fires they often saw on the horizon at night—flashes of fire, followed by the bright glow of burning houses, and the rumbling of firearms in the distance, as if the front were getting closer. These were battles between terror squads, regular units of the Russian army, and groups of partisans. Why should they keep sticking their noses out? Why didn't they dig in and wait until they could really beat the Ivans' shirts into their pants? The question was whether they would be left alone on the moors. That worried the captain and made him nervous. And for how long? How long would it last?

When the floors and walls of the bunkers were finished, they lived in the new dugouts in daytime, sheltered and camouflaged by the branches they had brought from the woods. Excess sand was carried away and covered with sod and peat on the edge of the moor. Every night the perspiring men travelled the swaying pathway across the bog, carrying ammunition, food, building materials and arms. The captain plotted strategy, Osvald and Mart laid mines in the moor, and heavy machine guns were placed into fortified positions. They felt childish joy at every new achievement, be it ever so little. When the men of Tenise, led by Mart of Liiskaku, dragged an anti-tank gun to the island, even Värdi laughed and stroked the barrel of the gun.

"What's the use of this," he finally said disdainfully. "No tank will get close to us anyway. Scare them a little—that's all it's good for. If we only had a mine-thrower," he dreamed.

Messengers went around, information was brought in from faraway villages, and one night the men of Torisuu hauled in two German mine-throwers. One was a small portable model, but the other was heavy, and the men had a strenuous time lugging it for several miles across the bog.

"Soon we'll have such an arsenal here that if the Ivans drop an egg in the middle of it, we'll all fly straight to heaven!" Osvald rejoiced. "Tackling a regiment, nothing less, would give second thoughts." He jumped up and down, happy like a child. "What the hell, brothers, how well we are going to live here. You'll see how fat we'll get." He wiped his forehead with his hand, dirty from the brown peat soil, and kept hopping. Life had become much more secure, and their self-confidence had risen high. It did not matter that the weather turned more and more autumnal, that not a single ray of brighter promise shone from the darkness of the future, and that the frosts of winter would freeze the moors solid so that a lighter tank could cross it at will.

The dugout of the men of Metsaoti—the Snake Pit—was roofed over before the Froghole of those of Tenise, for the men of Tenise had to be away often. The villages in their district were clear of Russians, and they could still arrange a thing or two over there. And the supplies had to be transported to the woods before the frosts came, because later the wheels of the wagons would make noises that would carry far in the wintry forests and moors.

The Snake Pit had been built according to Värdi's directions, but with Osvald as foreman. The little hunchback could talk well enough about the bunkers they had lived in on the Finnish front, but neither simple sawing of logs nor spadework progressed at all in his hands.

"Like a real thing!" Värdi said approvingly one morning after the last rafters had been put in their places and camouflaged. They stepped down into the oblong cavity. Tõmm of Hiie lit the small kerosene lamp his father had contributed, and then they began to measure and study the building. The logs of the walls were partly new and full of resin, partly old and dry. Fringes of peat moss hung from between the beams like yellow, green and red streamers.

"Next night we'll cover the roof with dirt," Osvald promised. "But see, we could live here already. There's a decent storage room and everything."

"We'll put our rifles here. Here we'll set up a little stove. We'll have double bunk beds," Mart of Liiskaku said.

"Yes, in case we happen to pick up more men," Osvald spoke up. "We have to take this into account. If some come looking for shelter in winter, we can't drive the poor devils away, and then it will be too late to build a hut. We'll find a place for them somehow, and the more men we have the warmer it will be in the cold. Now we can start doing indoor work and sleep at night like Christian people. Only—I have such a crooked feeling in my bones. Hasn't that always been our sad experience, that hardly have you planted your hind end on some clod, when you find such an ants' nest in it which burns your rear black inside out."

The rifles were the first items to be carried into the new bunker. Then Osvald brought a big bottle of home-made vodka from his private stores.

"This is to celebrate the roofing of the new house," he said happily.

The captain and his group came to look over the bunker, as if they had smelled the vodka. Captain Jonnkoppel was a short, stocky man, with a rather prominent stomach, and he had a round black beard that made him look comical and bellicose at the same time. He had sported the beard since the first summer of war, wearing it sometimes short, sometimes long, but refusing to shave it before times turned bright. He wore air force trousers with leather patches on their knees, high boots that his orderly kept scrupulously clean and shiny, and a leather jacket. His beard was oiled and perfumed. This latter fact had startled the men at first, but soon they got used to this idiosyncrasy, for the captain had the polished manners of a peacetime staff officer. Perhaps these particulars were designed to remind him here on the moor that he was a civilized man in spite of everything. He thanked them for the proffered drink and sat down on a sawed-off beam.

The room was filled with bearded, dirty men. The last to enter was Peeter of Valba, a shrivelled old man of sixty, shy and taciturn. He had been hiding in the woods since spring with a cow and a horse. He entered with unsteady steps and remained standing in the doorway, looking embarrassed. Nobody would have guessed that this grey-haired old man, whose face was burned the colour of red clay by the sun and the wind, was a veteran of the War of Liberation and the best companion of the young ones. Even the manner in which he had left his farm had been unusual, and not everyone would have had the guts to do it that way. Yes, fate had hit Peeter Valba hard. The war in the East had taken his only son, and the stray bullets of some drunken Russians had felled his wife in her own farmyard. That had been early in the spring, when the war had long since passed over the land and had almost come to an end in Europe.

Peeter did not give his wife a big funeral. The resources were too meagre to send his life's companion off in a fitting and dignified manner, and the man's pride would not let him insult the departed one with chicken feed. He thought: "My wife has devoted all her life to God, the farm and me, and if I cannot send her on her last journey with a decent brew of beer, if I cannot kill a fatted hog and call together all relatives and friends, then I won't do anything. I can't insult my wife with soggy, mouldy bread and a drop of burnt home-made vodka." And thus only a few neighbours from the village came to carry her to the grave, and that had been all.

So they were drinking to celebrate the completion of the new building? All right; Peeter would drink its health too. He drank and rubbed his nose. Well, they had things to discuss and talk about here, but Peeter—he had completely different things on his mind.

Peeter had spent a long time in the graveyard. They had lowered the coffin into the grave with the help of the old cemetery guard, his wife and son. Then Peeter himself had read the Holy Scripture in his loud, clear voice, and they had sung a hymn. Together with the cemetery guard they had filled in the grave, and when Peeter had had no vodka to offer, the guard had left in a huff. Peeter regretted most that he had no flowers. He had sat at the side of the fresh grave until evening, and suddenly an insoluble question had begun to plague him. Who would be buried in their large family plot? The place for their son would remain empty, for he had been buried by his friends somewhere in the frozen earth of the East. And the death of the son had interrupted the succession of their lives so completely that the old man could not even fill his family's cemetery lot any more.

The vodka mug reached him again. The talk of the men became more and more lively, and their hands moved quickly as they passed the cup around.

There was not much to think about any more. Returning from the cemetery he had found his farm looted. A gang of Russians had stopped by, and broken open doors and locks. It was as if the Reds had thus celebrated the funeral of his wife, their own victim. This shocked the old man so deeply that he set the stock loose, nailed the doors and windows of the house with planks and wrote on the door: "Whoever comes to live in this house will be shot." Then he loaded his wagon with a sack of food, some clothes, a few dishes, a milk pail, water bucket and feeding bag, tied a cow to the wagon and drove away from his farm into the woods. Now he was here, and nobody had yet settled on his farm. The corn that had been sown in the spring ripened and dropped to the ground, the hay in his meadows dried and rotted. His movable belongings had been carried off from the buildings, but the executive committee could not find anybody who would agree to settle on the farm.

"Listen, Peeter, why don't you sit down for a while," somebody said, and tugged at the leg of his pants.

"Well, I don't know. I should go and look after the animals," he said. The cow and the horse were real trouble now. He could not possibly take them to Taevasaar with him. That would have been the limit. The men had already enough to bother with. He had cut hay for the animals from the edge of the moor and from the dried places in the bog. He had heaped it into several nice haystacks, but shelter for the winter was really the main trouble. Right now a roof made of branches sheltered the cow at night and during rainstorms, but that was not enough during the winter frosts. She was due to calve soon, and he would probably have to kill both the cow and the calf later in the autumn. That was what the men advised, too. No, it would be impossible to keep the cow through winter. He'd try somehow to keep the horse.

"Where are you going now, Peeter?" the men asked, when he turned, about to leave. "It's bright daylight outside. Don't go out to the moor."

"It's still early and foggy," he answered modestly. "I've got to go. The cow is about to. . . . I've got to look after her. I'll be back at night when the work gets started."

"All right," the captain mumbled, "but watch out that the Russians don't see you. We can't let you risk the lives of twenty men because of one cow."

Peeter of Valba shrank from him fearfully. He was scared of such words. Or rather of the words that were supposed to follow now, but that remained unsaid. They probably thought that he should understand them himself. Well, but the animals, living animals, how could he leave them? His wife had raised the cow, and only a few years ago his son had ridden the horse. The animals were a link between the old man and his dead. How could he explain that to the men? They would not laugh, if they knew, but an old man cannot go around talking about such things.

"That old Valba is a drag on us," the captain growled, when Peeter had gone. "Another one was that vagrant from Metsaoti last spring, that fool of Võllamäe. He's probably been eaten up by lice in the meantime, and a good thing it is."

"Death won't take him so easily," Osvald answered. "There's nothing particularly odd about it that he doesn't show himself. He sits quietly in some bush and watches us. If he sees something he doesn't like, he aims his gun at it."

"That devil!" Jonnkoppel swore.

"Perhaps he is afraid of you?" Tõmm suggested.

"What? Of me?" The captain seemed to like the suggestion.

"What's new on the radio?" Osvald asked the men of Tenise. "We could bring it here from the tent now. There's more room here."

"The battery is getting low. All we get with it is Sweden, but that doesn't help any. Nobody knows a word of Swedish," the owner of the radio complained. "And the Estonians over there, their mouths are all full of the King's sweet custard; they don't utter a squeak. The Swedes are handing over Baltic refugees to the Russians. I did understand that much from the Finnish broadcasts."

"Bring the radio here right away. Värdi here, he speaks Finnish like a native, and his English is smooth like butter. So the Swedes are handing over our people." Osvald growled, and his big angular body stiffened with bitter spite.

"Most of them are Latvians."

"Moses was a Latvian too, as they themselves say. That doesn't matter. A Latvian or an Estonian, it doesn't make any difference. That's almost the same, and in our present predicament it's exactly the same. A Latvian is a man, although he has some tricks up his sleeve, but ever since the Winter War I haven't counted the Swedes among men. All they can do is suck sugar water. When a Russian lets out a guttural growl, they have more in their pants than anywhere else." Osvald heaped abuse on the Swedes.

"Don't swear like that," Mart reproved him. "Just think how many refugees they have accepted."

"Yes. What's the use cursing them," Tõmm added. "If you're in trouble yourself, why do you have to sink your teeth into someone else's heel."

"The trouble is that there's no place to sink your fangs except your own heel," the hired man of Hiie answered.

"God knows what has gone to your head," Tõmm mocked. "The Russians have moved in at Roosi. The militiaman is said to be visiting Marta."

Osvald looked at Tõmm, angry and embarrassed, and his talk was suddenly cut in two. He only wished that he and Marta could be left alone. To a certain degree, this was an affair of the heart, and the others had no right to dig into it. The adventure had remained strange to Osvald himself. He was not clear about it in his own mind, and he regretted its sudden end just as much as he disliked the bad taste it had left in his mouth. The hired man of Hiie felt no desire at all to swear

257

at anybody any more. Yes, the militiaman was reported to be paying frequent visits to Roosi. Peetal Rause, that big, horse-faced man on his motorcycle, who raped minors and broke the bones of prisoners. The daughter of August of Roosi really had strange desires.

"The English spout such nonsense too that it's better not to listen. Damn them. They are all faithful allies of the Russians."

"This would be the perfect time to defeat the Russians," the captain said.

"The perfect time," Värdi muttered. "Who would be the one to beat them. They are all lying together in a heap on the back of smashed Germany, and the Americans are kicking around the Japs. Victory. Victory. Only the Russians are the victors. Only the Ivans! The damned black devils."

"Pass the vodka cup."

"The devil take it all." Värdi gnashed his teeth. "Why do you tempt us with that drop? The bottle is empty. The vodka is gone, too. The Russians, these beasts; they have even drained the land of vodka." The few times the cup had made the rounds had made Värdi drunk enough. His customary gloomy calm was suddenly gone. He jumped up, his eyes flashing behind his glasses and his fists wildly gesticulating. "I say men, and I tell you too, captain, that we'll show these bastards yet. That is all I wanted to say. Clear and simple. Damn it. The knife is already so deep in the back of Finland, that they have to yield up our brothers who have fled there. Now they already have their fingers in Sweden. Then this moor here is the safest place after all. Here the relationships are clearly defined, and your soul won't be a pawn in the hands of other nations. Who has the right to give up refugees? Who are the leaders of the Swedish people? If a people elects leaders like that, then the people are rotten and cannot claim any right to live. The people punish themselves with their leaders. If the leaders lead the people into death, then the stupid mass of people have brought it upon themselves."

"Stop now, stop," Tõmm shouted. "Did your people ask for the destruction that came over us?"

"Of course they did," Värdi answered with unswaying firmness. "The people accepted the cup of shame and humiliation through their tired and gullible leaders, although the men behind the guns were ready to accept something else."

"Defeat! Utter destruction!"

"And what have we now?" Värdi cried with flashing eyes.

"We are a sober people," Captain Jonnkoppel remarked. "We were alone; only a handful of us."

"Soon there won't be even a handful. All those praises of fatherland and liberty—bah! All during the independence they pumped patriotism into the people, so everyone would be ready to defend his plot of land. If a people has leaders who keep mouthing such words until they finally spit in the faces of those who listen to them and believe in them. . . ."

"Don't, damn it," Tõmm said and rose menacingly.

". . . then the people themselves are full of boils too and need to be cleansed."

"I believe Värdi is right in several respects," Osvald said.

But Tõmm warned: "Don't start messing up history with your own fuzzy minds and personal disappointments, or else you'll be playing into the hands of the Soviets. And whoever says a bad word about our leaders, I'll punch his nose in myself. I would like to see a people healthier than our own."

"Look at the Finns," Värdi said. "Can you cast a stain or shadow on them?"

"The Germans—a healthy, vigorous people," Osvald retorted.

"Don't spout nonsense, you damned nitwit!"

"Watch your words a little," Osvald warned.

"I tell you," Tõmm shouted, "go and drown yourselves in the bog, both of you. That should leave the people a little bit cleaner!"

Captain Jonnkoppel tried to calm down the unruly men.

"As far as our leaders are concerned, we have no right to criticize their actions at the present moment."

"They gave everything to Estonia—their best knowledge, their best years, and finally they sacrificed their lives," Tõmm added.

"Their lives! The life of one is no dearer than that of another. If a simple farmer gives his life, is it too much for the elected and ordained leaders of the people to give their lives? They gave their lives and left the whole population in a whirlwind. Damn it, don't you understand that one always has to give his life for liberty? The mistake and the tragedy was that these lives were considered too expensive. They began to bargain and haggle for them. As if the seven hundred years of serfdom had not been a long enough lesson, as if the taste of it was too tempting. One should not bargain for freedom. One should value the homeland higher than one's blood."

"That is only wisdom after the fact."

"The captain now—I don't care how you take it, but I say that even some military men belong among those who would hurry to unbutton their pants, if only their souls would flicker a little longer on the wick."

The captain opened his mouth abruptly, but Värdi gave him no time to say anything. The hunchback was in the middle of the room like a little devil, fists pressed to his hips, arms akimbo like the wings of a plucked bird. Although the whole room was full of talk—the few draughts of vodka had relaxed the customary rigidity—he did not allow anybody else to argue.

"Confounded Russian, soon you'll be dead," he sang in Finnish and hopped up and down like one who had lost his mind.

In the afternoon of the same day—it was Sunday, but the men in the forest had not realized it yet in the morning—most of the people of Metsaoti were sitting in the front room of Matsu. Home-made vodka

259

was not lacking here, either, although the talk never became very boisterous. Juhan had brewed a small keg of beer. All his life he had never seen such a small brew of beer, but the times were bad and tight, and seemed to get ever greyer, the closer autumn came. Today Juhan's face was flushed with pride for the first time in years, for a baptism was about to take place in the front room of Matsu. A baptism, as had been the custom in the good old days and as the Saviour himself had ordained.

Ignas of Hiie performed the ceremony. The farmer of Hiie did not assume this task lightly, but since there was nobody else he finally consented when Juhan kept insisting. Their preacher, although of pure Estonian blood, had left before the great storm began and gone to Germany with the Baltic Germans. The most recent wave a year ago had taken even the organist, who had served the congregation in the meantime. Russian soldiers lived now in the rectory, and the fields that belonged to the church had been assigned to two families who had come from Russia. They could not speak a word of Estonian and knew even less about what to do with the fields. The doors of the church remained closed, as if the Creator himself had shut his ears and turned his back on the people. In such circumstances Ignas of Hiie had to baptize the little daughter of Lonni of Matsu. He did it upon the request of the grandparents and the mother of the child, and in the name of Jesus Christ.

As district elder, Ignas had often addressed the people on festive occasions, and in his short talk today he mostly tried to console the young mother in an indirect way.

"This people will not perish or be thrown into the wind like chaff, if it brings its children to the Lord," he finally said. "And I would like to say this to the mother of the little girl, that she should plant this young flower into the soil of the homeland. The young plant has been entrusted to her care in such a strange way that only the Lord himself can understand it. This must be the will of the Lord. For, if he has decided to shake our lives so deeply to their very foundations, then we with our human understanding cannot say anything else but, 'Jehovah, your will be done.' "

From then on Ignas' own words got mixed up and he had to call upon the Scripture for help. Even reading the old, familiar lines he did not take in what he was reading, and he felt that perhaps he too was violating something. He felt as if he had cast everything that was so dirty at the feet of the Lord, so that God should lift up what was too heavy and repulsive for a weak human being. Was God really there only to tidy up his children, wipe the drops of filth from their angry faces and gently fold their fingers in prayer when they were crooked from grabbing after sin? And Ignas Tammela, an old farmer, who had directed the affairs of a whole county, was demanding that of his Creator.

He finished reading the Bible, so deeply in thought that the people looked wonderingly at him. Didn't he know what to do next? His glance had stopped on the child in her mother's arms, on the little girl dressed in a long, white robe made of the confirmation dress of her mother. Her eyes were open, calm and undisturbed, and were directed at her young mother. Suddenly Ignas could not see anything but the snow-white dress of the little Kai, her soft downey hair, her innocent face, and the hands of her mother pressing her to her heart. Ignas felt a bitter lump in his throat from his recent doubts and dark emotions. Looking at the child like that, he felt a great clarity come to him, pure like a morning in the early spring, with hoarfrost and sunshine. This child that had been born from violence was nevertheless clean and pure to enter into the presence of the Lord. Whatever shadows might later fall into the life that had just begun must not rise up from the past.

The other people of Metsaoti however could not have shared the clarity of vision that Ignas had achieved from his brief encounter with himself. After the ceremony the women left, excusing their hurry with the urgency of household chores. Even Krõõt of Hiie left, and Ignas could not understand that. Krõõt had been the first whose hands had touched little Kai in this world. Then Ignas realized that their departure was caused by fear. They had reached a time when people were afraid of all kinds of gatherings that were not official meetings held in the district administration house or the school. True, even those were feared in a way, as if the people had to hide a guilt in their hearts, that would unmistakably rise to their faces in the sight of red flags. A man had the urge to crawl under the bark of a tree like a little worm, but the Red authorities stripped everyone naked to his soul. Men began to keep their mouths shut even in the circle of their families, as if they carried contagious diseases. They began to avoid the company of their fellow human beings, as if they were ashamed of their nakedness. And there was something else yet connected with the farm of Matsu. Who could tell whether that which had just taken place here would not soon be considered a crime to which each one of them had been an accessory? Who could say that the recent past would not be dug up one day, that the happenings would not be traced down, happenings which some of them knew, and which plagued the others through intimations, suspicions and rumours that had arisen from God knows where? Those who suspected felt as if something loathsome had happened here. Those who knew looked with open eyes toward the black grave in the bog, and they were in a frightened hurry. Hilda of Hiie had even refused to come along.

The men remained—not so much for the sake of the beer jug or the vodka bottle, but from the need to look into each other's eyes. Some neighbours were still able to look at you as honest men. Others lowered their eyes and began to study their boots. Even Paavel of Kadapiku returned from the courtyard, where he had gone together with his wife. He could sit for a while, he guessed, if his wife went home to keep a watch on the children. He did not know what made them so mischievous. The middle two had come with the mother to the baptism, for the two older ones mistreated them all the time. The two youngest were safe, for the older ones were more merciful toward them, and even buttoned their pants and wiped their wet noses.

Jaak of Võllamäe did not mind at all sending his wife home. He did not like to have his wife close to him outside of their own home, and when she remained crouching somewhere for a little while during a fair or a big party, the man shouted at her: "Woman, see that you go home. The fool will begin to play with matches, and the fire will soon rise to the rafters."

This time the woman was a problem. She had come with Jaak only because she was afraid to stay home all by herself. Across the road at Roosi the Russians swarmed in and out, and one might come by any time to ask for eggs, meat or vodka. What should she do alone at home? She could not understand a word of what they were saying, and although they had always come to the farm in pairs and had behaved decently, one could expect anything from them. The darkness would fall soon. She was afraid of being alone, when the machine guns of the Russians were so near and when she had not seen her own son for such a long time. But she began to walk home quite briskly, when Jaak told her: "Go on home, woman! Look, the other wives are all gone. You go ahead. We'll talk a little. I'll join you in a little while."

Jaak had no intention of leaving soon, and he was not as much interested in the talk as he was in the drink. To taste the strong vodka and to swallow some beer to relieve the burn, yes; that was the best kind of rest in this life that was heavy with quotas and taxes. At home he felt guilty because of the work that he could not get done, for the woman at his side was beginning to grow old. It was impossible to get hired help, and old age had begun to burrow in his own arm like a worm in a tree. In addition, the trips from one fair to another that had been his favourite type of relaxation had ceased automatically.

"They drive your life into a new rut!" he said aloud. "They turn you into a slave on your own land. Can't even think about business any more."

"Go hang! You're an old man. How long were you planning to go from fair to fair? They'll turn you into a farmer yet," Juhan of Matsu retorted. He was sitting at the head of the table again, his chest, stomach and legs all stretched forward.

Lonni had gone to the back room with the child. Her great day was about over, for she did not see any connection between the food and the drink and the recent holy sacrament. She had been pleased that the whole village had come to the baptism of her child, but the talk of the men, enlivened by the beer, began to disturb her. They had come for her sake, not to hurt her sensitive heart, had come as if they had been under an obligation, or else the women would not have hurried home leaving the men with their drink. Lonni became quite bitter about it, and she had to recall the beautiful, weighty and admonishing words of Ignas, gather them together like the broken shards of an old, heavy crystal vase.

Meeta herself, the sturdy mistress of Matsu, was displeased with the departure of their women guests, although she kept carrying food to the table together with Ella.

262

"So that's it," she said with her strong masculine voice, when the women were gone. She placed her fists brusquely on her hips. "So that's it," she repeated, as if she were facing a great fight, but she only emptied a big glass of vodka and said a few harsh words to Ella. The times were like that.

"The times, the new times," Paavel began.

"Cut it out," Juhan said in a ringing voice. "Shut up." This topic was by now threadbare. These times were not new any more. Their nightmare had already lasted an eternity. "Drink yourself and pass the beer jug," he ordered. Yes, they still dared to look into each other's eyes, but they did not want to discuss their everyday life under the Soviets. A few ironical remarks, ordinary small talk about small troubles—that was all. They did not even discuss rumours. Did they distrust each other? Perhaps yes. They knew too much about each other's lives, things that one had to be silent about now, and they knew that there were men in the woods, with whom everybody was connected in some way or other. And to hold a meeting—why should they do that? Their lives rolled on just as fate threw the dice, and meetings were held all over the country anyway, with ranting full of accusations.

"Just like a big Russian dogs' wedding," was all Juhan would say about politics.

Of course, when vodka heated them up, they were more liable to say something. They valued the drink, for it made a weak man strong. Right now it almost turned them again into the former farmers of Metsaoti. The fist of Juhan began to fall on the table more and more often, and Jaak began to follow the beer jug on the free side of the table with his former agility.

But before their innermost thoughts could rise to their lips, they heard the noise of an approaching motorcycle, which stopped at the gate of Matsu.

"Split that tree stump," Juhan said gloomily. An undertone of fright sounded in his voice, and his fist remained hanging in the air. "Old woman, light the lamp. One can't even see the nose one wants to punch in this darkness." He commanded to give himself courage.

Fright was clearly to be seen on all faces by lamplight. August of Roosi and Peetal Rause, the militiaman, walked in through the door. Their movements indicated that they were both drunk.

"That's what I say. Matsu, don't get offended," August began. His nose was wet from the driving wind and his winter cap was pushed far back on his head. "I heard that you had smoked up some beer. Well, what do you know, the nose of the old pig-cutter of Roosi cannot go wrong. It will lead you even to an old dried-out still, not to mention freshly brewed drink! All of Metsaoti here together! Greetings! Rause, the devil, drove so fast that my old eyes got caught in the stone fences. Now I've a hard time making you out. Well, if all of Metsaoti is together, why did you leave old August out? Isn't he a man or what?"

Juhan's mouth formed a very bad word.

"Sit down, if you're here already. Don't trample around," he forced

263

himself to say and tried to close his eyes, pretending superiority he did not feel.

"Let's sit down, comrade Rause. Let's sit down," August said to his big companion, who kept his hands in the pockets of his sack-like raincoat as if embarrassed. He wore his uniform cap and a broad leather belt with a big holster for the Browning. He was a husky man, with suspicious, browless eyes full of naked brutality. His glance stopped on the small table in the corner with its white cloth cover, on which the half-burned candles and the Bible still betrayed the recently performed ceremony. When August of Roosi carelessly threw his winter cap on the table like a member of the household, the militiaman did not even unbutton his raincoat. They sat down next to Jaak of Võllamäe, and Rause fingered the handcuffs in his pocket.

Anton of Lepiku fidgeted at the end of the table and rose to leave. He said good night in a calm voice and excused himself on account of the late hour.

Peetal Rause measured the back of the old farmer, and when Anton had left he spit out two words: "He's afraid!"

"Why should he be afraid of you?" August did not agree. He did not want the men to leave. They were all fellow villagers of his, and he had not had much chance to sit with them recently. And August loved company.

"He's afraid," Rause repeated, enjoying his pronouncement. He emptied the vodka glass of Jaak of Võllamäe. Jaak was scared too. He only moved his hand helplessly, when the militiaman filched his glass. He was slumped over the table, as if he had had the air squeezed out of his lungs by the big man next to him. When Anton had departed, he jumped quickly to Anton's seat.

Everybody could see that Paavel of Kadapiku was also having a hard time sitting right across the table from the militiaman. He tried to eat quickly and mechanically, without raising his eyes from the plate, but that was not simple when he felt the eyes of the militiaman constantly upon him. His jaws became stiffer and stiffer and his throat contracted like a dried-out goose's neck. He backed out of the room at last, trying to leave the impression that he was sick from the jellied meat and the vodka or that he had to go on some other urgent business, but everybody could tell from his face that the smith of Kadapiku was hurrying home.

Juhan beckoned to his wife, and the mistress of Matsu brought the militiaman a clean set of dishes. August reached for the plate that Anton of Lepiku had used. He did not want to bother his hosts, just so Juhan would fill his vodka glass. Rause measured the mistress of the farm from her face down to her thick legs, and then began to ogle Ella, who turned red under his stare. She had heard much about the violence to which the militiaman had subjected young girls, and her embarrassment made her stumble.

August was the main talker, for the mouths of the others had stayed shut since the arrival of the uninvited guests. Ignas looked directly into the eyes of the militiaman from across the table. He had never seen that terror of the district at such close range. He suddenly decided that the man must be quite a weakling inside, so that brute force and his revolver were the only support he had. The times were favourable to him, and he threw his weight around. That was all. A cruel and help-less victim of life from the bottom layer of society, who had now risen to the top. He did not seem to feel comfortable here at all. Evidently he had not drunk enough yet to lose completely his little bit of sense.

But August said: "Look here, Matsu, don't hold it against us that we walked in like this without being invited. We're old friends. Comrade Rause here is a regular fellow. He does squeeze the kulaks and the damned fascists now and then, but you have to allow for that. Sure, that's what I say and that's what I always have said. The men of Metsaoti are pure-blooded men. They don't have to drag their tails between their feet before the Soviet régime, as long as August of Roosi is their repre-sentative and assistant militiaman. The title of August rises and rises, for he knows that hanging was not good for a man's throat in the olden times, and it isn't good now, and won't be good in the future. Hallelujah and cheers! And that's what I say. I'll always come to ask your advice, honoured farmer of Hiie, comrade Tammela, when my own attic is full of empty draughts. All the comrades and commissars could ask advice from you, for your grey head is not full of chaff, but holds the sense and wisdom of several men. Cheers! Marta tells me at home, my only child, you know, she says that I have the sense of a calf, and I say, sure enough. What do you think of these things, Matsu?"

"What on earth is that August spouting about?" Juhan asked Ignas quietly.

"Ha-ha-ha. August is spouting like a fountain in the Garden of Gethsemane. He doesn't know a thing. He is neither the Saviour, nor Judas, nor Peter, nor any one of the soldiers—simply a fountain." He laughed into the suspicious face of his bulky companion. "You, Rause-boy, don't understand that. I myself don't either. That's what I say: it's Holy Scripture; that's what it is."

The militiaman began to laugh too, suddenly and raucously, as if he had just caught on to the ingenious joke. August chuckled on a high pitch, while Peetal laughed in a deep voice like a horse. Their laughter infected Jaak of Võllamäe, and all three of them laughed together. It was strange and repulsive to the others.

Juhan endeavoured to close his eyes, but did not succeed. The baby whimpered in the back room. The child's voice affected Juhan strangely. He remembered a gloomy night a year ago, when he had returned from transport duties and had found this same room full of crying and blood, and corpses lined up behind the house. He had carried a burning hatred in his heart against the child in his daughter's womb. He had sneaked close after it had been born, holding his breath, his hands ready to strangle it, and with it the humiliation that had trampled him to the ground. His body had broken out in perspiration at the thought, sweat had even dropped from his beard, when he had heard the news that it was a daughter, for he had pictured to himself a boy, a Russian. He, then, in his great weakness, had sat alone on the threshing floor and collected himself like a cup that had been broken into a thousand pieces. And only a few hours ago the words of the Scripture had convinced him that the will of the Lord must be done. Now his strong chin with the grey-red beard suddenly began to tremble. What did these bums find to laugh about here in the front room of Matsu? What on earth did they know about the life of a man?

"Listen, you manure-spade of Võllamäe," he shouted to Jaak, who was winding himself with laughter at the other end of the table. Then he turned to Ignas and shouted, "Hiie, you tell the man of Võllamäe to go hang himself. Hiie, tell that damned old goat of Roosi: 'Hang yourself, by the devil!' " He rose, full of anger. "Hiie," he again addressed Ignas, as if in desperation, "tell them to go hang themselves, both of them. Or I'll walk out of this house backwards. I'll walk to the woods, because—hang me if I don't!"

The word "woods" swept the laughter from the face of the militiaman. He began to glare in front of him, and his browless face became tense. The laughter of the two others subsided gradually. Juhan remained standing, as if waiting for something, his thumbs stuck into his waistcoat.

Peetal Rause raised his black, wide-open nostrils, emptied his glass, swallowed a few mouthfuls of jellied meat, and said to August: "Let's go."

"What's the matter with you?" His companion was shocked. "Where can you expect a better welcome? Here you have vodka, fun and laughter, kind hosts and pretty girls. That's what I say: there's no better place in the whole wretched world. Pour yourself a drink and. . . ."

"Let's go!" Rause pressed his uniform cap firmly on his head and jangled the handcuffs in his pocket.

"Well, if we must go, then we must," August muttered sadly, spreading his hands. He threw a glance at Juhan, as if asking for help, but Juhan was standing at the end of the table like a statue, his eyes closed.

"What are you afraid of?" August turned to Rause.

August almost paid a high price for these words. The militiaman made an angry motion toward the old man, but did not hit him. He only glowered at Ignas with his bull's eyes, but there was such rock-like firmness on Ignas' face and a barely perceptible smile around his mouth, that the big man went to the door like a boy.

"Let's go, damn it," he growled.

August said good night and followed him.

Jaak of Võllamäe looked for a moment at his empty vodka glass, and he rose too.

"Maybe they'll let me sit in the rumble seat. I'll get home faster in the dark. Good night, Matsu people."

Juhan did not open his eyes yet, although the room became quite empty. It was only when he heard, from the courtyard, raucous laughter, the roar of the motor, the barking of the dogs, and a few shots from the pistol of the militiaman that he raised his eyelids with a start.

266

Walking down the slope toward his own farmyard, Ignas Tammela had a very bad taste in his mouth and a queasy feeling in his stomach. Neither August of Roosi nor Jaak of Võllamäe was worthy of the name of a man. But the worst thing was that the fool Ebehard carried everything to his father that happened in the backlands of Metsaoti.

V

Ilme's son was again taken away from her. A couple of times each day little Hilja was taken to a strange woman to be fed. Sometimes she was kept for a long time. Ilme was desperate and pounded the door with her fists. Nobody ever came to open the door, and she staggered back to the bunk.

Her hair kept falling out when she combed it, and she found more and more grey strands in it. Her feet in the rags that had been socks were ice-cold and swollen. The sores that had been caused by filth began to suppurate. She tried a few times to wash herself in the bucket of drinking water, but this made it worse. Instead of healing, her injured hand developed an abscess, although the orderly smeared her fingers with a black smelly salve that reminded her of cart grease. She shivered in a continuous fever, and sometimes she realized that only her concern for the baby kept her from collapsing altogether.

One day when she was leaning on the door and waiting for Hilja to be brought back, a strange woman, holding Ilme's child, was pushed into her cell. The woman was strongly built and seemed to be about thirty-five years old. She wore winter clothes of the kind that are worn in the country, and her step was vigorous. She did not say a word, gave Ilme an indifferent glance, laid the child on the bed and started rearranging the rags in which it was wrapped.

Ilme rushed toward the child.

"Is it wet?" she asked.

The strange woman gave her a sullen look, but did not answer.

But when Ilme wanted to bend over the sleeping child, something unexpected happened. The woman barred her with her arms. She gave Ilme a long, searching look, studied her face, hands and clothes, and then her fleeting but intense glance took in the whole cell. Suddenly she seized the child with her large peasant woman's hands, as if some unseen danger were threatening the baby.

Ilme watched her, and a strange foreboding rose to her throat.

"Wouldn't you like to put her here? This is her bed," Ilme said and pointed toward the box on the floor.

The woman clutched the baby to her breast, and her suspicious glance fell on the box, where Ilme had made Hilja a bed of rags. She touched the box with her foot.

"Put the child here? The child is not a dog," she said, a vicious note in her voice. Her whole being expressed anxious tension and a readiness to fight.

"Yes, isn't that terrible?" Ilme answered. "Here they treat the child worse than a dog. When she was born, I thought we both would die. But life is stronger than I could have believed." Ilme felt strange, talking to the other woman. The joy at her presence brought a sudden flood of words, but she seemed to have forgotten how to talk. And the strange woman behaved very peculiarly. Ilme's words brought to her rigid and tormented face the expression of an animal that had been trapped and was now baring its fangs.

When Ilme wanted to take the baby, she refused to give it up, although the child made little hungry noises.

"Hilja wants to eat," Ilme said.

"Hilja?" the woman muttered, and strained lines appeared between her eyes. "Her name is Leili." She sat down on the cot and began to feed the baby at her breast. A bloody stripe ran over her full breast. "Her name is Leili," she repeated.

Ilme staggered closer.

"Hilja! She is my child!"

The woman winced, but pressed her hands tighter around the sucking child.

"Please, give her to me at once!"

"My baby—to you?" The woman measured her with disdain. "I know you want to take her from me. I know. Don't come any closer. Now you are under my eyes. Now I see. The milk is gone from my breast with the trouble and worry. Now I know why!"

She rocked the child tenderly. The baby began to cry when the breast slipped from her mouth.

"I tell you, don't come any closer," the woman cautioned. "The child is feeding. Don't disturb it. Where did you get this child from? You stole it from me. You devil."

"You are really out of your mind."

"I—out of my mind? You are all crazy, except me. Look here, Leili looks exactly like me. Even my husband said so. Just like two apples from the same tree. Those hangmen. First they took my husband; now they want the child too. What sins could she have committed? Little sweet one. Leili, my darling. Feed now, little birdie. Don't be afraid. The strange woman won't get you. Mother is watching."

Ilme sat down next to her, holding her throbbing head in her hands.

"Give her to me," she screamed, seizing the child. She succeeded in getting hold of Hilja, but the woman plunged toward her. Ilme pushed the child into the corner and protected her with her body from the attacker. The woman grabbed her by the shoulder and hair and struck her head with her fists.

Ilme wrested herself free and turned round. She hit back, although she knew that she was no match for the strong peasant woman. Her body was hot and trembling with anger.

The strange woman panted hoarsely. A dull madness shone in her eyes. The child's crying drove her to another desperate attack. Ilme held tightly to the edge of the cot and kicked with her legs, for her abscessed hand was torn from its bandages and hung limply at her side.

She feared that the woman would push her backwards over the baby and suffocate it. She began screaming for help.

When the woman had kicked and beaten her into a crouching heap under the bunk, an unseen power suddenly pulled the assailant away from her. The child was crying, and the cell was full of the sound of heavy boots, the thud of blows and the screams of the woman. Ilme struggled painfully to her feet, grasping her baby. She bent her whole body over her daughter, as if she were in mortal danger. She feared that her mind would give way. My Lord, how long are they going to beat her? Why don't they take her away?

The jailers left, leaving the woman on the floor, bloody and groaning. She tried to rise, whining like an animal, and then turned over, her face toward the muddy stones. She sobbed long and hysterically. Her throat rattled when she breathed. When the child stopped crying, Ilme hurried to her. Sympathy, compassion and despair banished her own pain. She touched the woman's bloody head and limbs.

"Does it hurt very much?" she asked.

The woman only groaned, remaining motionless, her face toward the floor. Ilme took a tattered cloth, wetted it in the bucket and washed the wound at the back of the woman's head, where she had been beaten with a revolver. When she tried to turn her over to one side, the woman held herself obstinately in her previous position.

"The floor is cold. Come on, I'll help you to bed!"

The woman did not move, but she began to cry instead of groaning. She wept, her whole body trembling, as if she had been freed from unseen chains.

"My God, my God," she said in a humble, suppliant tone.

"Come on; you'll get cold!"

"Take care of the child," the woman begged. "Traitor!" she then hissed, her voice a blend of hate, despair and pain.

Ilme staggered to the bunk and sank weakly to the child's side. She passed her hand over her aching face. It was scratched and bleeding. She hurt all over—her torn scalp, shoulders, chest and feet. Pus ran from her hand. It was yellow between her fingers. Her long, dirty fingernails pressed into her palms in a painful cramp. Which one of them was insane?

She gazed stonily at the little face of the child, asleep in its rage, at its swollen and reddish eyes, whitish mouth, and the hair that was grey with dandruff above an abnormally angular forehead. Good heavens, this was her own child, whom she had pulled back from the hands of death.

Later on they got along fairly well. The name of the woman was Elli Saluste. She never spoke about herself. Sometimes she simply did not speak at all for days.

Ilme was not able to convince her that the child was hers; Ilme's.

269

When she began talking about it, Elli snatched the metal drinking cup and was ready to hit her with it. She did not keep Ilme from feeding the baby. They had a silent agreement about feeding times, but the changing of her wraps and everything else remained the province of the stranger. She simply kept Ilme at a distance, holding the metal cup as her only weapon ready at hand, as if Ilme were threatening her life.

They feared and watched each other, and Elli would not sleep on the bunk, although there might have been room for both of them. No, she shivered on the floor next to the baby's box. Her limbs, black and blue from beating, were so stiff in the mornings that she could hardly move.

Ilme gathered gradually from Elli that she had been arrested the previous winter together with her husband and month-old daughter. Sometimes she talked to herself about her household and her stock. But more often she talked about them to little Hilja, who was Leili to her.

"Don't teach the child a wrong name," she said to Ilme. "She is growing. She is beginning to understand."

Ilme did not answer.

She had to cry each time she saw Elli rocking the baby in her arms and singing lullabies with her sick, hoarse voice. Mostly they were mournful folk songs, or just humming, with an undertone of mute suffering. The face of the woman became tender and soft. She spent all day making a fuss over the baby, holding it in her hands while sitting or standing. Sometimes she let it sleep all night in her lap, while she sat in the corner on the floor. When she tore up her shirt to make dry wrappings for the baby, Ilme burst out crying, as if the child had really been taken from her by the greater love of the other woman.

"Look, she is laughing. Good Lord, she's really smiling already. Oh, you sweet thing. The apple of my eye, my tiny sugar-dumpling. There she smiles and smiles." Elli was jubilant about the baby.

Observing all this, Ilme feared to lose her balance from jealousy. She felt like flying for the other woman and tearing the child away from her by force. Perhaps it was the heavy tin cup that held her back. More likely it was pity.

Their life wore on in the feebly illuminated cell, unreal and ghost-like. They scratched each other's bodies where they were itching from the filth. They swallowed their miserable mouthfuls of food, as if afraid of each other's hungry hands, and watched with hate the caresses which each bestowed on the baby.

Ilme was astonished to find so much malice in her heart, when suffering should have made her pure like living water under God's eyes.

It was strange, really. Through many dark months she had yearned and cried in her solitude for another human being. And now, when a human being, a woman and fellow-sufferer, shared her cell and her days, her heart foamed over with hate and contempt. Could this person be she, who had once been tender and noble, and a stranger to the ugly realities of life? She wished that Elli might be taken away, even

270

executed, for that was everybody's ultimate fate anyway. Ilme wanted to be alone. She wanted to free her mind of the presence of that woman. She wanted to yield to her desperation and thus escape from the iron cage of madness. Oh Lord, don't let the mind die before the body.

Their new nightly interrogations began at the same time. The tow-haired female interrogator demanded from Ilme new information about Taavi. Ilme answered the questions as if she were reciting something she had learned in a book, sometimes forgetting simple things out of her own life. This infuriated the interrogator, who used black rubber gloves now to beat her. When Ilme remained insensitive under the blows and collapsed too quickly, they began to direct a blinding beam of light into her eyes. But that made Ilme lose her consciousness even faster. She was already too weak to suit her interrogators.

It was demanded of her that she confess to Taavi Raudoja's guilt as a murderer of working people, a traitor to the Soviet state, a collaborator of Hitler and a fascist butcher. To her own surprise, Ilme answered: no. She dared say it because she knew that she would lose her consciousness each time a new brutality was inflicted upon her. Fainting had become her escape. Sometimes she fainted when she was merely threatened. Usually she was then taken back to her cell, and when she awoke there the pain was not so terrible any more. And a peculiar change took place in the cell. Elli began to care for her now as if she were her child, too. Sometimes she even covered her with her overcoat. She was not always able to do it, and there were many mornings when they groaned side by side on the muddy stone floor, with the helpless crying of the baby in their ears.

Then a whole week passed, during which she was not taken from the cell. Two thick blankets were brought her, and the male nurse cleaned and bandaged her wounds.

"How are you feeling?" he asked.

Ilme did not know what to answer to such a question. How could the man ask anything like that.

The most startling change, compared with the recent past, was the fact that Ilme was suddenly given almost a double ration of food: warm watery soup twice a day and big slices of black bread with it. She tried to share the food with Elli, who was starving, but she was not permitted to do that. When she did not pay any attention to the orders, the guard stood in the cell while she ate. Elli began to hate her more because of it, although Ilme gave up every bit of her morning rations as well as one of the blankets.

Elli was taken away almost every night, and then a morning came when she was not brought back any more. Ilme waited the whole day. The child was restless and kept crying, as if she understood she had lost her second mother. Steps passed the door. Ilme was brought her food, and the male nurse came to see her, but Elli was not pushed into the cell. Ilme waited for the night and then for the next morning, measuring

271

time by the steps and movements in the corridor. A couple of times she thought she recognized Elli's voice in the distant scream of a woman, but she was not sure. All at once her wretched life seemed still more wretched and empty. And the child kept crying, hungry because Ilme did not have enough milk to satisfy her.

"Where is Elli? Please tell me where she is? Why doesn't she come back?" she asked the male nurse.

He shrugged his shoulders.

"The baby is starving."

The man suggested that Elli might have been released.

"Released!" Ilme laughed hysterically. This reminded her of Lembit. What had happened to the boy? Why hadn't her son been brought to her?

The male nurse left. His face was tense and unsympathetic.

At dinnertime Ilme fed the crying baby some soup. Hilja sucked the food greedily, caught it in her throat, and cried even more. Only later, when Ilme had also breast-fed her, she calmed down and fell asleep.

Ilme was still waiting for Elli's return.

One morning she did not believe her ears, when the male nurse said: "Get ready now. You have to take a bath. The director of the prison wants to see you."

"A bath?"

For almost a year she had suffered here from vermin and from indescribable filth, and now—a bath! She had dreamed about bread and the bathhouse. Now she received almost enough to eat, and she was told to get ready to take a bath. What had happened? Had she really heard right? The director of the prison wanted to see her. No, she could not understand anything any more.

Ilme had not known that there was a bathhouse in the prison. She did not know much about the inner workings of the big house. Thick walls surrounded each prisoner, and after a short while not even thoughts penetrated them any longer. The bathhouse was barely warm, but the water was quite hot, and Ilme shuddered for a moment at the thought of touching it. The touch of water on her skin was peculiarly exciting, so that she felt a mixture of tears and laughter rise to her throat. She felt an irresistible urge to throw herself into the water, for ever. Water—it purified everything.

She was not able to wash herself much. Two Russian girls did it— without soap.

After the bath she was handed a clean shirt in place of her soiled one. She was given underwear, a dress, stockings and shoes. Everything had been worn before, but the clothes were clean and neat and fitted her. Oh yes, she was supposed to be taken to the director of the prison. The male nurse came and tied a clean bandage around her hand and treated her leg wounds. Only the shoes bothered her. Although they were big enough, they hurt Ilme's feet, somehow tying down her body which was glowing from the bath and feeling light and airy.

"You're looking pretty good," the male nurse said. "Why don't you dry your hair here? It's too cold and humid downstairs. The girls will wash the baby, too."

"Yes, yes," Ilme agreed eagerly. Of course, the child needed a bath much more than she. It cried and whimpered bitterly all the time when it was wet. It was so tiny, helpless and always sickly.

"Does my son have a chance to wash himself?"

"Oh, over there they wash their faces every morning and take baths too."

Ilme was not taken back to the dark cell any more, but the guards took her upstairs into the daylight.

"Don't look back. Don't look around," one of the guards, who was an Estonian, warned her.

Dizzy from the light, she found herself pushed into a small room furnished with a couch, a table and a chair. Through the barred window she could see the roofs of houses. When the door was locked behind her, she ran to the window, as if the light were pulling her with irresistible power. She stretched out her arms and moaned. Houses, and people lived there, free people! Free people under the open sky—what a thought. She looked at the clouds, and suddenly she felt something like fear of the winds and the clouds that were hanging heavy in the sky.

It was a strange feeling. She noticed trees among the grey roofs, and she was startled to see that they were almost bare. Only a few yellow leaves fluttered in the wind.

A year had gone by.

A spring had blossomed and sung without her. She had missed the golden gifts of a summer—the sun, the water and air. Meadows, fields and forests had been for her a forbidden fairyland. Coloured leaves were dangling in the treetops, faded reminders of a summer that had bloomed and ripened—a song without a melody, a refrain one has heard in a dream and cannot recollect any more in the morning.

Little Hilja was carried in and placed on the couch. When the guards had left without saying a word to Ilme, she turned toward the baby. She looked at the little girl, who was wrapped in clean diapers, and marvelled. The child was soundly asleep.

Ilme sat down next to the child, unable to understand what was happening to her. These simple matters, like taking a bath and dressing as a human being, were tremendous, unheard-of events in her life, and left her more shattered than the nightly brutal interrogations. For a long time she could not take her eyes from the child. The breathing of the baby was heavy and difficult. Her face was colourless and strange in the daylight. This five-month-old child had barely seen daylight during her whole existence.

A fat girl in a white apron brought Ilme's dinner. It was served on a wooden tray which covered the whole table. Ilme stared at the warm, steaming food, and although her mouth ran full of saliva, she did not dare touch it. It could not be meant for her. It had to be a mistake. All through the past year she had only received a couple of frozen potatoes every morning and a piece of stinking codfish or a few raw salted fish.

No, it was impossible that she would now be served steaming soup and roast meat with pan-fried potatoes! The smells made her wild. Was this a new kind of torture?

Her eyes ran around the room and stopped for a long time on the door. The door was locked. She could not hear a single step. She was bending forward toward the food already, when she got up, her hands poised in the air. She admonished herself to eat slowly, but her hands could not take the food to her mouth as quickly as she could swallow. She could not see or hear anything. She swallowed and swallowed, taking an occasional deep breath. She ate soup, meat and bread all at the same time, grabbing the bigger pieces first, as if she were apprehensive that they might disappear.

"Watch out!" She heard the voice of the male nurse behind her. Ilme had not heard him enter. "What have they brought you?" the man asked, throwing a glance over the tray. Before Ilme could answer anything, he lifted the meat from her plate. "This is too strong for you."

Ilme looked at him as if he were her greatest enemy.

"I would not deny it to you, but I have seen both: people who have died of hunger, and some who have died from sudden eating." He removed the roast from the tray. Although Ilme understood that he was right, she submitted to it only as a new violence.

"What—what does all this mean?" she asked the male nurse.

"Orders," he shrugged his shoulders. "You'll probably be released."

Ilme shook her head. Something buzzed there strangely.

"Released?" Wasn't it she herself who had laughed out loud at that word—a short, husky, mirthless laugh? "Released?" she repeated over and over again, as if that were the only word she knew.

"I don't know. People are always released after they have served their sentences. Soviet justice is fair."

Ilme had not noticed how the man had entered. Now she did not notice when he left. She gazed through the barred window at the grey sky, and her lips formed this one word, sometimes aloud, sometimes whispering, sometimes without any sound. She did not believe it. She could not picture it. All of a sudden she did not know, understand or feel anything.

The prisons of the NKVD are dead in daytime. The prisoners are not allowed to sleep then. Often they may not even sit. All the business of the prisons begins at night. From midnight to early morning the cells, corridors and rooms behind sound-proofed doors are filled with brisk activity. Dossiers are taken from shelves, and Brownings from their holsters. The dictator of the Soviet state works in the Kremlin at the same time. Why shouldn't his henchmen follow in the footsteps of their leader and teacher? And there was no doubt that their victims were more helpless at night, that courage failed them more easily then. The vast country of the Soviets is managed at night, for its real ruler is fear.

Ilme Raudoja was taken to the director of the prison at night. She had never been in that large room before. The first thing she noticed when the guards opened the door were huge portraits of Stalin and

Beria on the wall, surrounded with red and gold draperies. Above and below the portraits were a series of Russian slogans that Ilme could not understand. A table was located in the centre of the room, covered with telephones and open dossiers. A tired-looking, middle-aged man in the uniform of an NKVD officer was sitting behind the table. He raised his face slowly, uttered a polite greeting, and pointed toward a chair. His face was startlingly benevolent, stern, but frank, reminding one most of all of a high state official; certainly not of a professional member of the NKVD. The tow-haired female interrogator was standing at the far end of the table, hands folded behind her back, in a posture of respectful expectation.

"How is your family?" the man behind the table asked, and the female interrogator translated his words.

"Do you mean the children?" Ilme queried. "I haven't seen my son for a long time. Maybe a month or two. I cannot recall."

"Why haven't you seen him?"

Ilme looked at the Russian with surprise.

"He hasn't been brought to me. He will be eight years old soon."

The director of the prison said something in Russian to the interpreter. It seemed to Ilme that he was displeased with her. Fear flashed in the eyes of the interpreter. This was in its own way interesting to see, and it gave Ilme courage.

"You have a little daughter," the man addressed the prisoner. "How is she growing?"

"She is undernourished, and has bed sores, for I haven't had any diapers. . . ."

"Why haven't you asked for them?"

Ilme looked at him again in astonishment.

"I haven't had a chance to wash her. Today she was washed for the first time since she was born."

Hearing this, the man began to swear angrily. Ilme could not understand the man's ignorance. Or was this only pretence, a pose, deliberate make-believe? Yes, that was possible. That was more than probable. For a moment Ilme felt the urge to show the director the wounds and stripes she had received from beating, but she decided against it. This would be nonsensical, even silly, for her face could not but testify eloquently enough to her sufferings, and she was not so naïve as to do this in order to accuse the female interrogator. It would merely increase the hatred she already felt toward her. No, Ilme sat on the chair, slumped together, and waited.

The man studied for a long time the paper in front of him.

"Do you smoke?" he asked Ilme.

Ilme shook her head.

"You'll be released tomorrow, if . . . ," the man said slowly, and paused, waiting for the words to be translated.

Ilme rose slowly, holding on to the chair. She was not overwhelmed by what she had heard. Released—only that word remained in her ears, a strange incomprehensible word.

". . . if you comply with the following conditions. Now listen carefully. Do you want to be free?"

Ilme could not answer. Only tears came to her eyes. Do you want to be free? The words sounded from somewhere far away, booming as if they had been said in a vast empty church. Do you want to be free? Do you want to be with me? I am Taavi, your own husband. Come, Ilme, come. My God in heaven, of course she wanted to be free! Of course!

But she could not say anything. She could only cry.

"Listen carefully," the man repeated. "You'll be free tomorrow. You'll go into town, walk on the streets, you'll go to the country—anywhere. You'll go and find your husband Taavi Raudoja and you'll send him here."

"Him? Here? What for?" Ilme's lips moved.

"We want to see him. Don't get scared. Nothing will happen to him. This is a mere formality. He'll come here to get your children."

"Can't I take the children with me tomorrow?"

"No, they'll stay here as hostages until your husband comes."

"Then I won't go," Ilme said in a tired voice. "I won't leave my children. This is a cruel trick," she shouted. You'll never release my children, and you want to get my husband too. My daughter will die, if she stays here. I'm still feeding her from my breast. I won't go without my children."

The man listened to the interpreter and busied himself with the papers on the table.

"That's a pity," he said. "Think about your children."

Ilme sat, hiding her face in her hands.

"Could I see my son? I can't decide it alone. I don't have the strength. I cannot leave my daughter here. That is impossible. She is too small. Why don't you try to understand? Please, do understand!"

The man talked again in Russian for a long time with the female interrogator. Ilme noticed a sneer on the woman's face that arose from the sharp, bitter corners of the mouth, but did not reach her chilly eyes.

"All right, you may take your daughter along. But that is all. Don't ask any more questions," the man said firmly. "And if you plan to deceive us, if your husband doesn't give himself up, then your son remains here. Don't forget that. Then you'll force us to use stronger measures, and we will always get you—anywhere."

"So you'll kill my son?" Ilme whispered.

The man shrugged his shoulders.

"No, we won't do that. I told you that we can catch you whenever we please. The country is too small. You won't be able to hide from us. We'll find you together with your husband. As you see, we are simply being generous. We are giving you a chance to start a new life. Remember, you must not say a word to anybody about what you have seen and heard here."

"I know that. Only could I see my son before I decide? I don't know, I still cannot. . . ." She tried to think, but she could not. She saw the sea, saw the blue sky arching over golden fields, saw the dark forests of

276

Verisoo. Everything was quiet, holding its breath, silent like a picture, or like something seen through a barred window in a thick wall. "Could I see my son before I. . . ."

"No," the man said. He had been discussing something with the female interrogator in the meantime.

"Maybe he isn't here any more?" Ilme cried in desperation.

"He is here and he will remain here, until your husband gives himself up."

"I won't go if I can't see him."

The man rose. Ilme noticed for the first time that he was excited. Impatiently he lit a cigarette, throwing the match into the corner.

"You bargain too much," he warned. "The door to freedom is open, and you don't want to use it. Sign this. It's your pledge to silence!"

"I am not signing anything until I have seen my son. I won't go until then. You can do what you want with me."

"Don't be a fool."

Ilme did not answer. She did not have the strength to talk any more.

"All right." The man smiled. "I'll have your son brought up. You may talk to him. Just sign here. This will validate our agreement, and in the morning you may take your daughter and go wherever you please."

Ilme signed her name in many places. Writing was difficult and required much exertion. The letters came out strange and angular. The man read some paragraphs aloud to her—warnings and threats that Ilme did not understand. She felt as if she were signing the death warrant for herself and her whole family. "Then you'll be released" rang through her head. You'll be released.

"You are free now. I congratulate you. If you send your husband here, your son will be set free too."

The guards took her back into the room where she had waited for her interview.

"Don't look back. Don't look around. Hurry up. Faster, citizen."

Ilme sat with Hilja, waiting for Lembit. She was excited, for she had not seen her son for a long time. She was supposed to be free now. Free? What did that mean? Was there a single free person in the Soviet Union?

When her son was pushed into the room, Ilme arose, but she was too weak to run and embrace him. An inarticulate scream rose from her heart, and she only gazed.

"Mother, there's nothing wrong with me," Lembit said and swallowed, pressing himself against her.

"Dear child! My dear little son," his mother whispered. "How thin you are. What have they done to you? What have they done to your arm?"

"That's only the bone. It's beginning to heal up now. The male nurse said it would grow together very soon, as if nothing had happened."

Ilme held him tenderly in her embrace, as if she feared that all his limbs might break like the arm that was wrapped in dirty rags, set with rough splinters, and hung limply in a ragged sling.

The muddy overcoat slipped from the boy's shoulders. Ilme had the feeling that only the dirty, torn shirt held the bones of her son together —the skin on the small, sharp bones was too full of sores, scabs and wounds.

"Lembit, Lembit," Ilme whispered. "My dear little son!"

"Don't cry, Mother," the son said. How serious he was, how like a man.

Ilme did not cry. She had no tears. She only looked into the ashen face of her son, at his sunken mouth, shaven head and big dark eyes.

"How did it happen? How did you break that arm?"

"That was an accident," the boy said in a matter-of-fact way. "We were driven into another cell. There were very many of us. The guards kept shouting and hurrying us up. I stumbled on the stairs, and then the Russian hit me."

"How did he hit you?"

"Well, with the butt of his rifle," the boy answered simply. "The bone broke—split and broke, the male nurse said. That really hurt."

"And how is it now? Is it still. . . ?"

"It still hurts."

She could see it in the face of the boy. He was bearing it like a man.

"Mother, may I look at Hilja?"

"Of course, of course," Ilme mumbled.

"She has grown, you know! She almost looks like a baby now," Lembit exclaimed.

"When we get free, we'll run around together, the two of us. No, the three of us—Pontus too! I'll let Hilja ride on Pontus' back. Won't we, Mother?"

"Come here, Lembit. Sit down. I have to tell you something."

Ilme felt embarrassed, and she found it difficult to speak. The tormented eyes of her son looked at her.

"Yes, Mother. Tell me."

"They are sending me tomorrow to find Father."

"Are you leaving, Mother?" The boy sounded frightened.

"They want Father to come and get you."

The son was silent. His lips throbbed, as if he were about to cry, but that was all. He thought hard.

"Don't leave me here, Mother! I know that Father will come to get us, but he doesn't know where to look for us. The men have told me that there are many prisons in Tallinn now, and Father cannot find us. It might be better, if you did go. I don't want to be alone, but Father is sure to come. Father won't leave me here. Go, Mother, and speak to Father. I'll wait. . . ."

"So you think Father will. . . ."

"Yes, Mother. Father will understand."

When the guards came to take Lembit away, the son kept repeating: "Mother, I'll be waiting. So long, Mother. Oh Mother, Mother."

Then the crying child was dragged out of the room. He went, stumbling, holding his overcoat under his whole arm. Ilme stood up and wanted to run after him, but the door between them had been locked. Ilme beat on the door with her fists and then fell on her knees.

VI

When the car stopped with a jerk, Ilme felt that she would wake up now from a dream. She sat and waited, holding the baby on her lap, but the expected awakening did not come. The car door was pushed open and a man dressed in civilian clothes signalled to her. Ilme began gingerly to move herself. The footsteps of passers-by sounded strange —familiar and yet almost forgotten. She climbed out of the car and stared around.

"So long," the driver said, and the car rolled away.

Ilme stumbled a few steps after the car, as if she were afraid to be left alone. Then she stopped, one foot on the sidewalk, the other on the street. She had trouble breathing and was so weak in every limb that she feared she might collapse on the very spot where she was standing. Half-dazed, she walked up the slope and sat down on a bench.

It was too much all at once, and her senses refused to absorb everything so suddenly. She began by looking at the ground at her feet. She saw each individual grain of sand, small and large, brown, yellow, black and white; blades of grass, some dry, others broken, some bright green and straight; fallen leaves, round, oblong and wide, with serrated edges, covered with brown, red, purple and black spots; zigzagging light and dark green lines and patterns; a piece of coloured paper, a rusty nail, and a bright white pebble on the black earth, where night crawlers had dug small holes. That would be enough for one day, without raising her head to the drooping flowers, the bushes and the tree trunks or, God forbid, even higher, where the sun shone sparkling at the windows, upon the white stone pavement of the streets, and the people walking there; where the wind played with the branches and where white clouds were soaring high above the smoke, above the chimneys, and even above the church steeples which seemed to penetrate straight into the sky.

She was free, but she was not intoxicated by her freedom. Rather she was frightened, dazed and cowed, afraid to take a single step, like a child who has had a bad fall on its first attempt to walk.

It seemed to her at times as if she had been here only the day before— everything was so familiar. At the same time she felt as if it had been ten or twenty years ago, even several lifetimes ago—as if she had been set back by force, to lead some former bungled existence all over again. Nonsense, she had no more life. Even her freedom was violence. Listen to the birds. Sparrows, still brown—the colour of summer.

"So long," the driver had said to her.

"We may meet again," the female interrogator had said.

"So long, Mother. Oh Mother, Mother." The lips of her son had said these words.

When the sun passed behind a cloud, Ilme noticed that the air outside was chilly, although it was light and seemed to lift her somehow by her shoulders. The air in those cellars pressed one down, as if what one inhaled was part of the ceiling and the walls. A chill shook her whole body.

Don't look back. Run, droned in her ears. Where might Taavi be? Where was she supposed to start looking for her husband? The hourglass had been turned over. The sand dribbled slowly and calmly through the opening.

Her coat half-open, the baby clutched to her breast, Ilme began to run. Down the hill, to the street, looking into the face of every passer-by, glancing at everybody's back. Wasn't that the well-known blond hair, the quiet grey eyes of her husband?

Although it was late afternoon, traffic was not heavy. Ilme heard much Russian spoken, practically on every step she took. She was afraid that she was being followed, but she did not dare look behind her. She hurried as if driven by an invisible whip. Soon it felt as if she had been walking for miles and everything turned black before her eyes more and more often. She was forced to lean against the wall of a house with empty store windows decorated with red flags and portraits. She began to deliberate where she should go. She noticed the startled and inquisitive looks that people gave her.

She was afraid that she would sink down to the ground on her knees, that people would gather round her and ask questions. She sneaked into a dark back yard and fed the baby, straining her eyes and ears, her body ready to jump as if she were about to steal something. She leaned against the wall, and a weariness filled her tortured limbs like lead. There was so little milk in her breasts that the child did not stop crying for hunger. When the crying became loud, Ilme lifted her from her knees and hastened back to the street. The child calmed down although it was wet.

Ilme figured that her strength might suffice to let her reach their former apartment where Liisa and Arno now lived. Why hadn't she gone there straight away? Liisa would have been curious and talkative, but she could simply have said that she could not explain anything at the moment. At least not until she had been told where Taavi was.

She rang the doorbell, sat down on the steps with the baby, and waited. A sloppily dressed strange woman opened the door.

Ilme tried to get up but did not have the strength. She mentioned Liisa's name. The woman looked at her for some time. Her face was quite expressionless, and only her eyes widened when Ilme repeated her question. Then the woman mumbled something in Russian and withdrew from the doorway.

Ilme bent over the baby, but was too weak to lift it up and to run away. She was kneeling at the door when Liisa came. Was that the same Liisa, Arno's pink-cheeked, good-humoured wife. The woman's face was pale, her cheeks hollow, and her eyes framed by deep black circles, while her mouth was squeezed into a thin, bloodless straight line.

"What do you want?" she asked Ilme with a gruff voice, but her eyes were full of frozen terror. She did not move her hands. One of them was on her stomach, the other on the doorknob ready to close the door.

"Liisa?" Ilme muttered. Her lips moved but no more words came.

"What do you want?" the woman asked impatiently.

"Don't you really recognize me, Liisa?" Ilme mumbled, leaning on the wall and rising slowly from her knees.

Liisa looked directly into her face. Her hand touched her throat. She swallowed to catch her breath, and her eyes flew open, as if ready to drop from their parched, inflamed sockets.

"God, it cannot be!" she said and took a step back, sweeping her hand across her eyes. "Ilme? Say no." She looked at Ilme again, touched her sleeve and stuck her fingers between her teeth.

"Yes, it's me."

"No," Liisa shouted, "But you went to. . . ." She covered her mouth abruptly with her hand and covered her eyes again. "Have you seen Taavi?!"

"No, I haven't. Please let me come in," Ilme mumbled. "Take the baby. I've got no strength now." Not waiting for an answer and not seeing anything she stumbled across the threshold into the hall. She sat on a chair next to the mirror until she began to make out the pattern of the wallpaper across the room. Then she noticed an overcoat hanging on a peg. It was the overcoat of an NKVD officer. She rose and turned around, ready to flee, take the baby and run. She felt nothing but a panicky fear. Liisa had taken the child. It was crying in the bedroom.

But Ilme could not move from the spot. She was unable to move hand or foot; not even her little finger. She was standing in front of a mirror. She had stood in front of the same mirror many times before. How often had she thrown a last glance into this mirror before going to a concert with Taavi, or to a theatre or party. Was the mirror now telling lies?

"Is that me?" she asked Liisa who came to her side.

"I don't know."

The crying of the baby called her and Ilme stumbled into the bedroom.

"Do you have a few dry rags?"

Liisa brought her some clean pieces of cloth. She did not say anything, but questions were carved into her face.

"Where have you come from?" she finally demanded. "From the prison?"

Ilme winced. "I am free now, and Lembit will be released too."

"So they even release some people now?" Liisa mumbled. "So they set some people free." Her body twitched. "I'll bring you something to eat. I was just warming up the soup from yesterday."

When Ilme had taken off her overcoat and was feeding the baby, she heard Russian voices in the next room. She winced, ready to jump up, a questioning look at Liisa.

"It's a Russian couple, I'm subletting a room to them. The husband is an officer of the NKVD—a nice man, a little brutal maybe, and drinks a lot. The woman is worse than our lowest country bumpkins—a complete imbecile."

"U-uh," Ilme muttered. "Put the soup here. Thanks. I'll give a little to the child. It isn't too salty, is it? Her name is Hilja."

Liisa sat down on the bed, holding her plate of soup, and began to eat too.

"Tell me, do you know anything about Taavi?" Ilme begged. "Tell me," she demanded excitedly, when she saw that the questions made Liisa nervous. The child was satisfied and quiet, but Ilme was too impatient to eat anything herself. "Tell me, where is Taavi?"

"I don't know where he is," Liisa sighed. "And I would rather not know." Ilme's stare made her uneasy, frightened and helpless. "Don't look at me. Don't ask. Perhaps he is in the woods. Yes, of course. Where else could he be? I don't know."

"In the woods, you think? Hasn't Arno seen him? When will Arno come home?"

Her questions made Liisa sink weakly to the bed. She closed her eyes.

"I don't know. Arno does not know. Arno was taken away," she whispered.

"Arrested?"

"Yes. Right after Taavi escaped. It was a long time ago. It all came because of him. It's all his fault."

Taavi was in the woods then, somewhere in the forests, hiding from his hunters. How could Ilme go looking for him with her little baby? But she had to, for Lembit was waiting. She had to.

"Please, may I have a little more soup?" she said.

"I'm sorry, I don't have any more," Liisa answered. "I'll bring you a piece of bread and some tea."

When Ilme had eaten the bread and drunk the tea, Liisa asked: "Where are you going?"

"I don't know." Ilme was tired, and the air in the room made her dizzy and almost paralysed her, after she had spent such a long time in the fresh air to which she was not accustomed. The room had become quite dark. Liisa switched on the light.

"I wouldn't ask, except it's getting late already, and you should find a place where you can spend the night."

This was like a blow in Ilme's face. She understood that Liisa might shrink from her because of fear of vermin, because of her looks, and because she had been in prison, but she could not have believed that her former friend would not give her and her baby shelter for one night. Liisa's voice had a barb in it. There was no use mentioning it any more, and Ilme could not force herself to plead with her. She would have begged mercy from a complete stranger, yes—but not here in this room, where she was sitting on furniture she and Taavi had bought together, which they had turned over to their friends along with the apartment for nothing more than a thank-you. When Liisa wanted to send her back to the street, she would go right away. She could not comprehend how one year could have changed Liisa so completely.

Later Ilme did not know how it all happened. She remembered that she had looked at Liisa for a long time, as if trying to find in her face her former friend. An urge to run away had arisen in her. A fear had overcome her that all of life and all people had changed during the past year as much as she had herself. She grabbed the baby.

"So long," Liisa said indifferently and closed the door behind her. So long! Why did people use this phrase? Liisa did not want to see her again. This was evident from her voice, her look and her annoyed gestures.

The night was windy. Drops of rain fell on her bare forehead. She bent forward and began to walk against the wind. Ruins were on one side of the street; whole houses on the other side. The windows on the first floor were mostly dark, but some windows of the upper floors were lighted.

She heard steps behind her. She ran faster. She had to get somewhere, before the late evening turned into a pitch-dark night.

Russians materialized from somewhere in front of her—Russian soldiers who asked for her papers. Before Ilme had even had time to think about the paper she had been given at the prison, they grabbed her by her overcoat and dragged her along. The startled woman saw that they were heading toward the ruins. There were five men. Were they going to shoot her? For God's sake, not that, for she had to find Taavi. She tried to explain to the soldiers, but they only laughed. When she tried to turn around, she was held more tightly. They talked among themselves and laughed, brutally and hungrily. They stopped under a roof, in a room that had only two walls. Water trickled somewhere in the dark. Metal squeaked somewhere in the wind.

"What do you want of me?" Ilme screamed, when their hands grabbed her and tried to take the sleeping child from her arms. "What do you want, you madmen?" she shouted.

The soldiers had thrown their rifles on the floor, and suddenly the situation became clear to Ilme, although she could not believe it. She had heard of their violence. Even in prison she had been threatened with it, but that it would be like this—no, no! The stories of ten, even twenty, men attacking one woman were not as terrible as reality.

Somebody offered her vodka, but when another stretched out his hand for her breast, she began to scream. This became the signal for the fight, turning the men into maddened animals wild at the sight of their prey. Ilme was pushed to the floor, and the crying baby was torn from her hands, but Ilme was fighting for her child above everything else, and suddenly she had incredible strength. She did not care about anything. If she had been able to pick up a stone in her twitching hands, she would have hit them with it in their faces, putting all her strength into the blow.

A rag was stuffed into her mouth, and her arms were pressed against the floor, but she did not give up. She heard her child cry in the hands of the Russians. Her clothes had been partly torn from her, and her brain warned her to be careful, or else she might hit her head too hard on the floor. Then she might lose consciousness and remain helpless in their power.

She did not know how she had escaped from their clutches. She remembered one had lighted a match. Did they see her face, and had her face startled them for a moment? Ilme felt only that the hands were not holding her down, and the next instant she was rolling along the length of the crumbled wall. She did not feel any pain from her fall. She did not feel the stinking mud and the sharp stones. She ran a few steps, pulling the wet rag from her mouth. She ran and fell, crawled and stumbled. The rain fell on her face and her shoulders. She gasped for breath, her heart thumped against her ribs from the exertion. The blood roared in her ears, drowning out all other sounds. Away, farther away! In her imagination she felt the hands of the Russians about to grab her again.

Her feet got caught in rusted metal and she crashed on the slippery stones, as she had done several times already. When she had freed herself from the bottom of an old iron bedstead, she took a few more steps and sank then to her knees, leaning against a heap of half-burned beams.

She could not measure the length of time she had crouched there that way. When she began to hear the rustling of rain again, the first thought that came to her mind made her move quickly. Where was the child? Where was Hilja? What had they done to the baby?

Giving no account to herself of what she was doing, she began to retrace her steps. She did not ask any more what would be her own fate. That did not matter. If only the child. . . .

Lord, Lord, be merciful. Did they take the baby along? Had she sacrificed the child, saving herself?

The soldiers were nowhere to be found. It was as if they had never existed. A nightmare—if Ilme could not still feel their hands.

It was a wonder she did find her way back. The room with two whole walls was empty. The dry corner, where she expected to find her child, smelled of bitter dust. A light bundle she saw was not Hilja. Her fingers found a picture frame with torn canvas, sticking out from a heap of plaster and torn wallpaper.

Ilme called for the Russians. She did not care what they did to her, if they would only give back the baby. But she heard neither the raucous voices of the soldiers nor the weak crying of Hilja. A door squeaked somewhere. The wind. A piece of metal roofing rattled. The rain fell quietly upon the grass that had grown through the ashes on the ground.

Then she found the child. Hilja was lying in the rain, had kicked the wraps off, and her fragile limbs were ice-cold and stiff. With a muffled scream, Ilme fell over her daughter. She clutched the child to her heart and crawled back under the roof.

Ilme tore off some of her underwear and wrapped the child in it. Hilja was too weak to cry. Life seemed to be barely clinging to her exhausted and sickly body. Ilme rubbed her carefully. It seemed that the child's limbs became less stiff, but the warmth did not return to them any more.

Old Aadu Mustkivi was strangely restless that day. His heavy stick kept thumping the ground between the buildings, in the vegetable garden, in the apple orchard. It even made the rounds in the meadow. The only place where he would stop to take a rest was at the gate of the Hiie courtyard. This was the goal of the restless walks of the old man.

Even there he would not stay long. Bending over his stick he would stand for a minute or two, looking intensely toward Võllamäe, and then he would come back down to the courtyard, half running, his overcoat open and his shoes sloshing through the mud. On his way back, the dog loped at his heels, and when he turned back to the gate, Pontus jumped ahead of him.

The restlessness of the deaf-mute was no news to the others. Fits like this one, incomprehensible even to himself, had often chased him around the farmyard like that. Rain or shine, he was at his self-appointed post as watchman.

It was a rainy Saturday, and the farm people, as many as were home, busied themselves with inside work. In the morning Ignas had taken the potato wagon to the field and Hilda and Krõõt had stooped over the furrows until noon. Then the farmer had hauled the wet potatoes home and said: "Ah, why don't you quit for the day. There's plenty of mending and cleaning to be done in the house. Right now we still do our work according to the hints the heavens give us. Even the orders of the authorities cannot clear the sky."

So they did not go out to soak themselves and their clothes in the afternoon, although everyone knew that the orders of the authorities were even more powerful now than those of nature. Ignas repaired and cleaned farm machinery in the barn. The two women patched potato bags in the chamber of the old house, and Aadu was dispatched to the bathhouse to start the fire. There was more than enough to do, more than they could have done even if they had not slept a wink at night, for after the haymaking in the summer, no helping hands had reached from the woods to the farm.

Communication with the men in the woods was almost broken off, for Russian soldiers were still stationed at Roosi and Piskujõe. They did not exactly terrorize the people, but the coming of the autumn made them gloomy; especially those at Piskujõe. Perhaps the threatening sound of the wind in the great forests had a bad effect on them when the long dark night commenced. They swaggered as usual during daytime in the village, but the night and the forests were stronger than their bravado, even when they were holding on with both hands to their machine guns.

When Ignas saw that Aadu had even left his job at the bathhouse to run to the gate, he shook his grey head. The old man was going mad.

Soon you would not be able to trust him with the fire in the bathhouse and on the threshing floor. Wonder what it was there at the gate? Hastening toward it, the old man made excited, expectant noises. Returning he sounded disappointed and complaining, as if someone had mistreated him.

Aadu's restlessness infected Ignas strangely today. He came to the barn door each time and watched the old man as he hustled through the rain, almost running, stopped for a moment at the gate, leaning on his stick, and then turned back, the sides of his open coat flapping in the wind. Ignas thought he could predict the time of his next trip, but when he stepped to the barn door, Aadu was already returning from the gate. So it was repeated over and over again, until the farmer could not put his hands to his work any more. Excited for some unknown reason, he went down to the bathhouse in the pasture. Crazy, he muttered to the old man who ran past him. Aadu stopped for a moment and spread his hands, as if to say that he could not help it at all.

The rain rustled on the fallen leaves. A few red leaves still fluttered on the maple, but the ash trees were already black and bare. The water in the river was high; one could hear it roar. The dam at the Kalgina sawmill was open, which hastened the up-stream current. They were probably again cutting two-by-fours for the Russians. All sawmills, even far inland, worked now at full blast, for the Russians needed a large quantity of building materials to fortify the coastline and the islands. White tree stumps, discarded branches, and wide open stretches gaped in the forests like open wounds.

Ignas left the bathhouse and returned uneasily to the threshing floor. The women were working in silence, and they seemed more stooped than usual, as if they were freezing in the warm chamber. Ignas inspected the potato sacks. They were almost in tatters. They might take this autumn's delivery quota to the vodka distillery and the railroad station—the orders were there already—but that would be their last trip. Grain sacks were all accounted for, and new ones simply were not to be had. The cooperative store was empty. It was a lucky day when they had some inferior matches and grey salt, but there was no thread, no needles, and nothing else. Oh, yes, they did have some coarse yellow cornmeal, but Ignas did not know whether the store had kept it since 1941 or received a new delivery.

"I thought we should let the cattle in," he began. "Leave those sacks now. The chamber is getting dark."

"You're right. I told Hilda the same thing," Krōōt answered. "We were just saying winter is on us again."

"You can't keep it back," Ignas muttered.

"Winter is coming again, and nothing has happened," Krōōt complained. "A whole year already!"

"How long will it last like that?"

"Not for ever."

"That is what you always say," the woman complained. "But how long can we go on living like this?"

This was as far as they got for the time being. Krōōt stood up. She had nothing more to say.

The conversation in the chamber of the old house did not bring Ignas any peace. His heart was torn so painfully that he wanted to rise up and fight, although his common sense told him to stay quietly on his knees. Ignas Tammela realized more clearly than ever before that he was a reluctant but helpless slave of the new régime.

He hoped that the warm bath and the heat of the bathhouse would dispel the heaviness that had gathered on his soul, but he was mistaken. It afforded no relief. Worries seemed a little more remote, but even his cleansed body was affected with the same restless sickness. Had Aadu's running back and forth between the courtyard and the gate infected him? When he returned from the bathhouse, his feet wanted to take him on past the threshold. Was he crazy? He had nobody to expect. His son who was hiding on the moor islands of Verisoo would not drive up at the gate in a four-horse coach.

When the women were still in the bathhouse, the deaf-mute came to Ignas, who could not make out anything from Aadu's excited mumblings and gesticulations. The door behind the old man remained open, and Ignas' glance rose to the black square that led out from the hallway. Aadu pointed to the courtyard with his hands, asking Ignas to accompany him, and was angry when the farmer failed to understand his insistent noises.

The night was pitch dark. Rain fell as before, rustling lazily. Ignas wanted to turn back into the front room, but the old man would not let him. He held Ignas' shirt sleeve in his wet hand, whining like a dog. This simile reminded Ignas of Pontus. Was the dog still keeping watch at the gate? Ignas took his overcoat from a peg in the hallway and went out with Aadu. The mysterious bond of understanding between the dog and the old man intrigued him.

Pontus was not at the gate. The gate was open, as if somebody were really going to drive through it with a horse. When Ignas closed it, Aadu was annoyed again and dragged it quickly wide open. He pointed with his stick toward the dark road. Suddenly Ignas felt a strange fear that was different from the everyday terror of the Russians. He called for the dog. Pontus did not appear.

Aadu was probably waiting for the dog. This was what caused his excitement and made him so stubborn in keeping the gate open, the farmer consoled himself. He was an old man, childish and crazy. He was afraid of solitude when the dog was not there to keep him company. The dog may have run off to the village.

Returning to the house, Ignas filled his pipe with tobacco and began to smoke. Was his own mind getting fuzzy? When the women came from the bathhouse and asked for the deaf-mute, Ignas had a guilty feeling.

"What's wrong with that Aadu recently?" Krōōt wondered. "He used to be waiting in the front room of the bathhouse, but now he seems to have forgotten what the house is for. We'll have to clean him up our-

287

selves soon. I laid out fresh towels and a new bunch of birch twigs for him."

"Oh, he'll go," Ignas mumbled. "The sauna will be warm until morning. Let him eat supper first. Then he can go from the bathhouse straight to the hayloft."

"What's the matter with you? You look so gloomy." Krōōt cast a searching glance at her husband.

"Me? Oh, nothing," the farmer of Hiie answered. "I was just looking at the boy's horse and—nothing. Set the table. Hilda is in the kitchen already."

Krōōt's glance stopped on her grandson's big wooden horse in the corner. When she had suggested taking the toys to the attic, Ignas had grumbled. The boy will take them there himself when he comes. Well, it was no use discussing that now. Words were too rough to touch such things.

Aadu came to the table, soaking wet. He took only his old cap off, grabbed his bowl with the greediness of a hungry man, and ate quickly on a corner of the table. In a few minutes he had emptied his bowl. He did not hand it back to the mistress of the farm to have it refilled, but licked his spoon clean, wiped with his wet sleeve over his face, and rose again. Standing up, he folded his hands in prayer, pressed his cap deep down on his white hair, grabbed his stick and left.

"Say, Ignas, what's the matter with him today?" Krōōt was quite startled.

"He's probably rushing to get to the bathhouse," Ignas suggested, although he did not believe it.

"Yes, but why has he soaked himself in the rain all day? See, all that water on the floor, as if someone had poured it from a pitcher."

Melancholy rested upon them that Saturday supper. They were all tired from a week of heavy work. Tomorrow was Sunday by name, or rest-day as it was called now, but they had not observed Sunday for a long time. Their work was mostly limited to the farmyard and the house for that day, but nobody could afford to take any time off for a Sunday rest.

"Would you, Ignas, read the Bible after supper," Krōōt finally suggested. "Hilda and I will listen."

Hilda raised her face from her plate, where she had been picking at her food without appetite, and said: "That won't help any."

Her voice sounded strained, defiant and pleading. The two old people did not know what to reply to that. Without knowing it, a person could say something these days that shocked others into silence.

The farmer of Hiie nevertheless took the Bible. He felt that he had a deep yearning for the ancient and living words, although even keeping the Bible in one's house was a deadly sin now in a country where worship was supposed to be free.

He had not read a single word when he heard the howling and barking of the dog in the distance. He began to listen to it, his hands on the open book. It was the voice of their Pontus. The women looked at him with questioning eyes.

The deaf-mute rushed into the room. He had not gone to the bath-house after all. He left the door open behind him and hid in the farthest corner of the room.

Ignas rose together with Hilda and Krōōt, and the eyes of all three were turned toward the black opening of the door. Aadu in his corner looked as if he, too, could hear the barking of the dog, which now turned from the open gate into the courtyard.

Then a strange woman entered the doorway, hesitating in the glow of the lamp. She was carrying a nondescript bundle, and water ran from her face and her clothes. Pontus whined in the hallway behind her.

The woman stood for a long time on the threshold, before she said with a broken voice: "Don't you know me? Pontus recognizes me. I am Ilme. Forgive me, that . . . I came . . . home."

Ignas looked suddenly on his hand on the open Bible. The large letters of the Holy Writ had jumped out from the page and trembled on the back of his gnarled hand.

VII

Tōmm stuffed new firewood into the small iron stove. It was safe to keep the fire going today, for it was raining steadily outside. The wind pressed against the chimney opening now and then and forced bitter smoke down through the stove, irritating the eyes of the men who were lying on the upper bunk beds, but it was warmer on the upper bunks and you did not have to worry about the water that was rising from the autumn rains. It could easily happen that it would rise up to the lower beds, for they could hear it sloshing under the floor boards when they walked.

A small kerosene lamp was standing on a little table in the middle of the bunker. Hilda was sitting in the circle of light, and her fingers were busily knitting a sock of grey home-grown wool. The men on the bunks were asleep or half-dazed. Only Värdi was puffing in the centre of the room, pulling plugs through the barrel of a rifle. He had returned from sentry duty; his feet were wet and his spirits low. Hilda glanced now and then at the men and arranged the covers of the patient on the bed behind her back.

Ilme was sleeping peacefully today. The crisis had passed, and she had survived the heavy bout of pneumonia that had broken her down right after she had arrived home.

Hilda thought back over the time since Ilme's return. It seemed like a wild nightmare. She was just beginning to comprehend the dreadful facts that were, little by little, coming to light.

Tōmm climbed past Värdi into the corner behind the table. His sun-tanned face was haggard, and his long dishevelled hair made him look older. The quick look of Hilda's doe-like eyes took in his arm in a heavy grey pullover, his strong shoulder, and flashed for a moment to his chin that was covered with a sparse, short black beard.

"You should sleep a little," the girl whispered. "You are next to go out."

She did not expect an answer. Quickly moving her knitting needles, she felt that the young man was looking at her grimly, but kindly, for Ilme's return had somehow made them very close. Without saying a word, they had begun to understand each other.

Hilda knew that Tõmm could not sleep for worrying about his mother, for both the mother and the daughter were bedridden now. How could old Ignas get along over there all alone? He had, however, ordered Hilda here to watch over his daughter. The women of Matsu came over to help, and the deaf-mute Aadu cleaned the stables. Everything was too terrible to recall, even now, after many grey days and sleepless nights.

At first they had simply stood there. Then it had been Hilda herself who had closed the door behind Ilme. When she had turned around, Ignas and Krõõt were gently leading Ilme to the couch next to the tiled stove.

The mother took the bundle from her and placed it on the table. Carefully she freed the face of the little girl from the covers, and the corners of her mouth sank suddenly, but she did not cry. Bending quickly over the child, she touched it with trembling hands. The child was stiff and dead.

If Aadu and the dog had not whined quietly and sadly, the room would have been silent like a grave. The air was like ice, that would not allow for any movement. Then the people began to move, as if they were afraid to freeze. They all looked at the little corpse on the table and then at Ilme, who was sitting motionlessly, looking at the floor.

"Where are you coming from?" Ignas asked. His strained voice sounded strange, almost threatening.

"From the prison," Ilme's lips moved. "From the woods, from the city, from the highway—from everywhere. I've come . . . from everywhere."

Her mother stumbled toward her and touched her wet hair. This hit Ilme like a blow. She clutched Krõõt's skirt with cramped fingers and hid her eyes in it, sobbing wildly. Her shoulders, her mud-covered clothes, her whole body shook and trembled.

"Where is Lembit? Where is the boy?" Ignas asked, as if that were suddenly a question of life and death to him and as if even his own daughter were only a stranger.

Then Ilme spoke, incoherently, but with a calm voice: "Taavi has to give himself up. Then Lembit will be released. I am free, too. I can go to Finland now." She gave everybody a burning look and stood up. "Has Taavi gone to get Lembit? You think that I am mad. No, I am not. Hello, Hilda. Oh yes, we have met already. It's good you closed the door. They'll be after me soon."

"Child, child don't!" Her mother tried to restrain her.

"Save me, hide me, until Taavi comes with Lembit. Father, Mother, save me, until Taavi comes."

She hid her face behind her bandaged hands and slumped onto the couch, crying, her head bent unnaturally backwards. Her tormented face, framed by wet, sticky hair, was suddenly flushed.

That night was not easy for Hilda to recall. She looked around the small bunker, her glance restless like a dancing butterfly in a beam of light. Why was Tõmm sitting there outside the lighted circle? Värdi was holding the gun barrel against the light and looking into the hole. The nightmarish vigil went on. The man who was groaning in his sleep on the upper bunk did not know anything about it. Why did he groan? Hilda moved her fingers. Quickly, mechanically the sock grew. Her eyes were turned elsewhere.

There was a peculiar connection in Hilda's mind between that night and the destructive bombing of Tallinn. She remembered tiny details of both nights, the rigid faces of people frozen into silent horror, their uncontrollable movements silhouetted against the flames, and at the same time she had felt as if she did not see or hear anything.

Aadu had left the room—after all, it was his turn at the bathhouse—and they carried Ilme to her bed in the back room. Hilda noticed that neither the mistress of the farm nor she herself was crying. Their looks turned from Ilme's closed eyes to Ignas' taut face.

"Take those rags off her," Ignas said. "Help her, Hilda!"

"Take me away," Ilme shouted. "They are coming. They are coming right away." She closed her eyes again, shaking from fever, muttering incomprehensible words.

They did not exchange a word as they stripped the wet rags from Ilme's body. The festering wounds and stripes that appeared on her skin shocked them into silence.

"Let's leave her alone now. Give her something warm to drink," Ignas said and stepped into the front room with measured steps. Hilda followed him with the lamp. Ignas closed the Bible. His lips moved, when he looked at the corpse of the child. Then he walked up to the window, put his hand to his forehead, as if he saw something through the curtains, the blackout shades, and the night behind them. He was bent and stooped, and his left arm hung lifelessly beside him.

Then Hilda had run through the forests in the night for more than an hour. Forests, meadows, forests again. She held her hands protectively in front of her face, but the wet branches scratched it nevertheless and tore her hair. When she reached the moors, she realized that she had missed her bearings in the dark. Sheer instinct finally guided her to the beginning of the pathway between the bog holes. She felt the beams under her feet in the sloshing water and hissing peat moss. She walked with outstretched arms, for she had no stick to balance with, and searched for the landmarks with her hands, soaking wet, muddy to her waist. When she reached solid ground, she heard the call of the sentry. Fortunately it was Osvald with his big raincoat wrapped around his shoulders and head.

Then they had hurried back through the hissing bog, she and several of the men. She could hardly keep up with Osvald, who was carrying ropes. Tõmm breathed heavily down her neck. They did not have to wait long on the edge of the bog. Soon they heard the quiet creaking of wagon wheels in the wood and the neighing of the horse. Everything went by silent agreement, in a wordless hurry. The men made something like a litter from a couple of young trees and used the ropes to secure Ilme, who was wrapped in blankets and tarpaulin. She was raving in delirium and shouted for light.

"Stay with her," Ignas had told Hilda.

"Yes, yes. But if the Russians. . . . If they come to look for me, and I am not there? And how is the mistress going to get the chores done without me?"

Nobody could give any thought to that at the moment. Too much had happened already.

Ignas took the horse by the bit and turned the wagon around under the pine trees. He had to hurry. The grey dawn was already turning to light in the east. If only the wind and rain would last, so that the rattle of the wagon would not reach the ears of the Russians in the village.

Hilda saw clearly in her mind the following morning at Hiie—the two old people with the corpse of the child they had to hide. Krõõt had washed the baby, Hilda had heard, but she also knew that the next morning the mistress of Hiie had not arisen from her bed, although she had tried with all her might. She had no fever, she did not complain of any pain anywhere, she spoke very little, but when she put her legs on the floor she could not get out of the bed.

Ignas Tammela, owner of a big farm all his life, who had always had many hired hands to whom to assign the chores around the farm, had to pick up the milk pails and go to the barn himself in the morning. Hilda milked the cows in the afternoon. She had found the farmer on the threshing floor, planing some new boards.

"I'll just smooth them a little on the inside. They'll look nicer that way," he said quietly. "The grave is ready, on the river bank under the birch tree."

"Won't you take her to the churchyard?" Hilda asked with dismay.

Ignas did not answer right away. He looked on the clay floor and touched his grey, bushy eyebrows.

"She was not baptized. Hilja was the name they'd given her. A beautiful name. The earth is a churchyard everywhere now. The ground is just as blessed here as over there."

Next evening Hilda could not keep Tõmm from coming home with her. The son wanted to see his mother, whom the shock had felled. His eyes flashed angrily when the girl tried to persuade him to stay with his delirious sister. They walked together for more than ten kilometres through bogs, moors, and pitch-dark, wet forests. The weather was warm as in summer after rain, windless and foggy, predicting a continuous drizzle. The sounds fell where they had arisen, too weak to echo very far.

Krõõt was asleep in the back room. Her cheeks were hollow and her lips were forming silent words. She had probably just fallen asleep, since she did not wake up during their tiptoed visit. A circle of light fell on the table from a little lamp. The bed of the farmer was empty and untouched.

They walked through every room with their wet, splashing feet. Ignas should have heard them, but he was not in the house. Neither was he to be found in the courtyard at the storage barn, the stables or the threshing floor. Tõmm hushed the merry yelping of Pontus and ordered him back to the gate.

Then Hilda guessed where the farmer might be. They hurried through the meadow to the riverbank. Over the rushing sound of the waters, made powerful by the recent rains, they heard the sound of a spade passing through sand. Ignas was filling in the grave of his grandchild. They did not exchange a word. Tõmm bared his head, following Ignas' example, standing in front of the little grave where his niece was resting. They stood for a moment like that, and then turned back to the house as if by silent agreement.

"She who came last into our family was the first to go," Ignas said. "I said my prayers all alone, and wondered who would go next. Why did you both come home again?" He stopped suddenly. "This is no joking matter," he said brusquely to his son. "Do you think I sent my dying daughter away from home just for fun? You know well enough what happened to Mihkel of Lepiku. He was sick unto death, and they dragged him practically from his deathbed."

"How is it with Mother? Is she better?" Tõmm asked.

"I don't know." The old man hesitated. "She wanted to say something last night, but could not speak. I don't know what it is."

"She was asleep when we went to her room."

"That is good. She hasn't slept much; the shock is still in her blood. How is Ilme?"

"She has high fever. She gasps and talks in her delirium. Värdi thinks it is pneumonia."

"Well, she'll probably go too," the father said heavily. "I shouldn't have taken her to the moor. There's nobody to help her. No doctor among the men."

"Värdi studied medicine before he took his law degree."

They were standing near the bathhouse and speaking with muffled voices. Some wet leaves fell from the branches. There were still a few left, fluttering in the wind. The night was sticky like glue, penetrating everywhere, clinging to their faces and hands.

"Hilda should stay home," Tõmm said. "You can't manage everything all alone. The stock, the cows to be milked, the harvest. . . ."

"The grain will rot and spoil, but I can't help it. The deliveries, yes, I'll haul them to the railroad station, straw and all," Ignas said bitterly. "Only, if it should turn cold all of a sudden, the potatoes will stay in the ground. We'll see what will come of it. The mistress of Matsu comes over to milk the cows. She seems to guess something, but won't ask any questions. Well, go now and look after Ilme."

He sent them back from the courtyard, although Tõmm wanted to see his mother once more. He wanted to talk to her, but Ignas said: "No, Tõmm, later. I'll take care of her. She cannot speak right now. You'll only make her excited."

"Oh Father, do understand."

"No, we don't understand what is happening to us. We don't know what it means. When they sent Ilme to look for Taavi, they baited a trap with her. They could not get him any other way, for the weather is ideal right now for crossing the sea. They must be on Ilme's trail. They could surround the house any minute."

"Now? At night?"

"Don't forget the soldiers right here at Piskujõe and Roosi—behind this pine grove here and there across the fields. In daytime they could pick you off with their guns here in your own courtyard."

Returning to the camp of the men, together with Tõmm, Hilda had stumbled at every step, weak from sobbing.

"Don't howl like that, silly," the boy had said impatiently. "You are nothing but a crybaby."

Hilda could not control her tears. They had accumulated in her for quite some time. She walked a long way behind Tõmm, her hands over her eyes.

"Quit that whining," Tõmm ordered her. He had stopped and was waiting for her. "Stop it now, that's a good girl, or you'll get hysterics. Listen, the birds are twittering. It will be morning soon. We have to hurry. We can't cross the moors in daylight. If an airplane should spot us—you know. They seem to be smelling something. They circle up there all the time. Oh you little fool. I was hoping and looking that you would soon make a pretty good wife, but if you go on like that. . . ."

"What would you do with a wife?"

"What does anybody do with a wife, don't you know? I'd take her to the moor with me. She could at least knit some socks for me and. . . . There wouldn't be much else to do with her," he said sadly.

"How far will it go like that?"

"What? Taking a wife. . . ."

"Stupid! I wouldn't marry you anyway. I mean everything. How did Ilme get arrested? And now all that. . . ."

"I don't know. I don't know anything about Taavi, either. Ilme screams and talks about shooting in her fever."

They walked silently side by side.

"I have a feeling that. . . ," the girl said, but stopped abruptly.

"A feeling of what?"

"I can't say it; it is so terrible. How should I say it?"

"Well, what is it?"

Hilda thought it was so dark that the boy could not see her face, but her voice became strange even to herself, and a peculiar weakness came over her when she said: "It seems to me that—you can gather it from what she says—that they attacked her on the way. They wanted to

—like with Lonni of Matsu—but she ran away, and then it seems to me they killed her baby."

"Filthy swine," Tõmm hissed, after a long silence.

When they walked between the bog holes, he took the girl's fingers in his palm. Her hand was hot and trembling, but it held tightly to his hand.

Now these same fingers were rapidly manipulating knitting needles in the yellow light of the small kerosene lamp, knitting socks for Tõmm and for everyone else in turn, as quickly as she could get around to them. Thank God, the crisis of Ilme's sickness was over. Maybe her lungs which were so desperately gasping for breath would soon breathe peacefully once more.

When Osvald was carrying Ilme across the moor, feeling for the beams with his feet in the black water of the bog, he had not said anything. He had been silent on the following days too. He remembered vividly the day when Ilme had gone to Tallinn with her son—to look for Taavi. Osvald had carried Lembit on his back up to the cooperative store. A whole long year and some days had passed since then. There was no use denying it, Osvald held Ilme in great respect, almost as much as his own mother. Osvald would not have wished to meet her again under such circumstances—never like that—not in the bogs of Verisoo.

Hearing the name of the daughter of Hiie from the mouth of Hilda, who had run herself breathless hurrying to the moor, his body had become hot and his head dizzy. He could not really realize what was going on. But when they were carrying their burden over the swaying footpath, the questions began to burn within him. Marta had said that they had crossed over to Finland. How come Ilme was here? Marta had seen with her own eyes the boat leaving. How come Ilme had been in prison? He was unable to believe that the groaning creature they were carrying was really Ilme. But when he had looked into the face of the sick woman, his strong hands had become weak, and a pain had gone through his shoulders. When he became conscious of himself again later that night, he found himself standing behind the bunker on the edge of the open bog, looking into the dawn that was rising behind the rain.

Impatiently he pushed the hood of his raincoat back and took off his cap, letting the rain fall freely onto his tousled hair. He stood in the rain like one who prays, but he did not know for what to pray. He felt he wanted to wash himself, to jump into the river, head first, diving deep into the bottom. He wanted to rise from the wet darkness, to take an occasional breath on the surface, where the warm rain left ripples on the smooth water. He felt dirty and soiled, like someone who had wallowed in mud and suddenly comes out into the daylight. He pulled up a scraggly moor pine and shook it until only the bare white roots remained dangling from the trunk. He looked at the little tree and felt sorry for it. Only a very few of them grew on these islands in the moors.

It was not the fault of the tree that the wind had carried the seed into such bottomless ground. Bare-headed, his wet coat open to the wind, he tried to plant the tree back, but failing in that he threw it away. The branches rustled, and the tree fell at his feet, white roots pointing toward the sky. He turned grimly back to the bunker.

Osvald sat for hours on the edge of his new bed. This bed had been empty until now, waiting for a man or two who might happen to join them. It stood in the wettest corner, where water seeped in between the logs and gathered under the bedboards. Now it belonged to Osvald. Mart of Liiskaku slept in the upper bunk. Osvald had given his own bed, the widest one, close to the small iron stove, to Ilme. He was glad to be able to do this, only regretting that he had not made the bed wider still. But then, the whole building should have been made wider.

Hilda caught a nap now and then on Tõmm's bunk, when Tõmm practically ordered her to bed, otherwise she would not have had any sleep at all. They were all eager to take care of the patient, but unfortunately there was nothing much they were able to do. It was hard to listen to her sudden husky screams, her pleading voice calling for Taavi, Lembit or little Hilja. Hilda had hung a blanket in front of her bed, so that the light would not disturb her, but Ilme often tore it down, with hands stretched out toward the light, as if she expected help from there.

Most of the time when Osvald did not have sentry duty and could not listen to the delirium of the patient without doing something drastic, he spent his energy building bigger storage rooms. Tõmm and Värdi took care of arms and ammunition. Värdi cleaned and oiled the light machine gun several times a day. He picked it up at night, too, counted the cartridges and predicted the death of several hundred Russians. Although the men of Tenise had provided them with plenty of hand grenades, Värdi wanted to make some more out of explosives, taken from land-mines. He wanted to use the hollow metal spokes of wagon wheels for that, as they had done during the first summer of war, in 1941.

They had planted land-mines on the stretches where they expected the enemy to make an attempt to approach the island, where the bog was solid enough to carry a careful man. Osvald planned to surround the entire moor island of Taevasaar with a strong, fortified trench to which zigzagging ditches would lead directly from the bunker. This was a huge task, and winter was liable to catch up with them before they could get very much done.

The captain in the staff bunker, the Froghole or Mudbath as the men had christened their neighbouring bunker, was against such great undertakings. He felt they had to avoid battles for the sake of the surrounding villages. Osvald had a rather low opinion of the air-force officer. He was no coward, but Osvald was particularly annoyed that the captain disapproved of their bringing Ilme to the moor. Why had he not been consulted?

One grey day after rain, when Osvald slouched in the sentry's box they had fashioned out of pine branches, and thought his gloomy thoughts, his eye noticed something moving on the moor. Somebody was on the slope of the next island, where the fallen yellow birch leaves shone like a patch of bright light. The Russians! The thought flashed through his head, and he grabbed his binoculars. No, it was only one grey figure that seemed to contemplate how to get to Taevasaar. He was wearing a wide-brimmed hat that almost covered his face, and had a rifle slung across his back. He seemed heavy from a load of sacks and parcels. It appeared he was a man of the woods, carrying his rain-soaked household with him.

Surely he wasn't planning to cross over where the open bog holes were? He would be lost at the bottom of the bog before they could even try to rescue him from here. Even if the surface would carry him a few more metres, the mud would be too deep below for them to drag out the body. If he would keep a little more to the left, where he could find a foothold under the black water, then—there were the land-mines, their thin wires level with the surface of the water! The crazy man began to move along, advancing slowly between the bog holes. Osvald's binoculars fell down and a hot flash went through his body.

When he lifted his binoculars again, he recognized Reku of Võllamäe. Reku, the deserter, who had been out of sight for several months, and who, according to rumour, had been considered caught and shot. He was alive, and came now to seek his death here on the moor.

But no, Reku swung far to the right, as if he wanted to draw a circle around Taevasaar. He walked between the bog holes, feeling with his stick in front of him. Then he jumped from one clod to another, crouched on bushes of heather and held on to low willow branches with his hands. Osvald followed his progress along the banks of the moor island. He was still convinced that the boy would begin to sink at any minute. Sometimes he saw quite clearly that Reku was up to his loins in water.

When Reku reached the next stretch of fairly solid ground. Osvald shouted a warning: there were land-mines ahead of him. The boy did not hear him, but he had stopped of his own accord, bending tensely forward, as if he could see the lurking danger. He probed the moor with his stick and waved his hands, as if he were talking to someone. He took off his hat for a moment and wiped his face with its inner side. Then he turned around and began to move toward the left.

When Osvald had reached his former post, after a complete circle, Reku was directly in front of him, walking quite fearlessly, skipping along merrily on the dry, high moor. Evidently it was possible for a determined person to reach Taevasaar. The pathway they had built between the bog holes was not the only way!

Osvald looked at Reku as if he were a ghost. The boy was carrying a heavy load on his back, topped off with his gun and his high boots. The tops of his rubber boots were covered with dried-out mud, indicating that he had crossed moors before. Even his grinning face wore dry mud splotches as well as the fresh ones he had just acquired. The strangest thing was a hairy skin on the boy's shoulders. It could have only belonged to a dog.

"Hello, man," he said to Osvald, like to an old friend. "Reku is out of tobacco again."

Osvald handed the boy his tobacco pouch, still looking at him as though he were a vision. Reku sat down on a clod and began to roll a cigarette.

"Don't you want anything to eat?" Osvald asked.

"Not this time. You have plenty of eaters here yourself, and we aren't short of food."

"How many of you are there?"

"Ha, ha," the boy laughed. "Many. Some have been put out of commission for the time being, but there are still many of us. Give Reku some fire too." He sat down again and began to inhale greedily. Smoking seemed to intoxicate him. His eyes began to roll wildly and excitedly.

"Don't smoke so fast," Osvald warned him. "Where are you coming from? We haven't heard anything about you for some time."

"We were over there," the boy pointed with his hand across the moor, "in several places, at Ilmaotsa and even farther away. There was some fighting."

"I heard there had been some big roundups. The roar of it carried to us here."

"We put plenty of them to sleep," Reku said proudly. "All summer we sent them on a dirt diet. When the men over there would not listen to Reku any more and called him a fool, then Reku took his men away from there. Reku is no fool. Andres himself said: 'Let's go away, or else that will be the end.' Those who stayed are gone now, but Reku's men are all right."

Osvald always had a peculiar feeling when talking to Reku. In his opinion the boy was out of his mind. Nobody doubted that, not even the parents of the boy. Nevertheless, Reku was a peculiar idiot, one whose insight and talk raised goosepimples on a man's back.

"There will be a lot of killing here soon," the boy predicted gleefully.

"Where did you get that?"

"Why, it's clear. Everybody thinks that, and why else would Reku have come here? Even Andres had to hurry to get here before his son."

"Before whom? Taavi?"

"That's what they say. But Andres won't let Reku start. We have to wait. Andres stays at Piskujõe keeping watch. No, he says, you mustn't fight toward winter. But after summer the winter comes again, and then another and another, and how will we ever get it done? Andres says: 'Wait, save your cartridges, a great day of reckoning is at hand.' Reku has plenty of ammunition. Reku never misses a shot. Each time he shoots, a Russian stays in the ditch—stiff. Reku shoots straight into the face. When half the head is shot away, then he'll remember. Osvald, give me some more tobacco!"

"There you are, take it. Take it all. Then you won't have to walk over the moor so often."

The fool's homecoming was likely to prove a nuisance. He could cause a good deal of trouble with his impetuosity. At a single shot from his hunting rifle the Russians might swarm toward Verisoo like provoked wasps. If the winter turned cold, they might approach straight across the moors on their skis.

"Say, Reku, how do you know that Taavi of Piskujōe is still in Estonia?"

"Where else should he be? His wife and children are still here. Where could he go?"

"You have a lot of respect for Taavi's wife, don't you?"

"Reku does," the boy admitted, blushing and simpering, looking at the ground.

"She is very sick now."

"Reku knows."

"How do you know that?"

"Reku has a dog's nose."

Osvald looked silently at the skin of a black dog on Reku's shoulder and then across the wide moor. The nose and the senses of a dog—this explained the boy's safe passage between the bog holes. He heard in his ears Ilme's delirious raving and her cries for Taavi, and he said: "Do you think you could find Taavi, if you went to look for him?"

"Reku will find the grave, if. . . ."

He stopped, because Osvald's eyes bulged from sudden fear.

"Stop that nonsense!" Osvald shouted. "See that you get going, you damned fool!"

Reku stood up and looked askance at him for some time. Then his eyes turned grey and ominous and finally he slowly took his gun from his back, retreating step by step.

"What do you want now?" Osvald growled.

"Reku will shoot you like a sick pup," the boy said darkly. "Then you won't call Reku a fool any more."

"You do all kinds of foolish things. Leave your gun alone. We are allies. We are men of one and the same gang!"

"All right—for the sake of the tobacco," the boy muttered. "Andres would have come between us anyway. Reku will go and bring Taavi of Piskujōe here."

He turned around and went back the way he had come.

When Ilme began to see and hear again, she had to figure out many baffling things, but the colourful rug which hung in front of her bed separated her from actual life. It reminded her of sleigh rides in winters when she had still been a child. She heard the ringing of sleigh bells in her ears, saw hoar-frosted forests and snow glittering in the pale sunlight, and smelled the sweat of the spirited horses. They were riding to church, out to pay a visit, or perhaps father was taking her to the railroad station. She was wrapped in furs, and on top of everything was this same rug, made of wool, that had been dyed with treebark, herbs and moss.

She breathed heavily and huskily, croaked and gasped for air, her weak limbs covered with perspiration. She began to recognize faces—Hilda, Tõmm and Osvald—but she did not have sufficient strength to ask them for anything. When she did speak she herself did not understand from where the strange words came, for she was still dwelling on the other side of reality.

It was her own hand that began to fit together the torn shreds of her thoughts into the pattern of her life—her own bandaged hand. She looked at it now every day, with curiosity and interest, as if the hand belonged to a stranger.

"How long are we staying here?" she asked Hilda.

"Until you get well."

"I am well already," the patient said. Then she remembered something. "May Lembit come to see me tomorrow? Might he come the day after tomorrow?"

"He may come soon."

"Why are you so sad, Hilda? You are up so late at night."

"I am not sad, and it is daytime now."

"When Lembit comes, I think he'll bring some flowers with him. On Mother's Day he brought me flowers. He had picked them himself."

The next day she asked: "Is Taavi still at the front? They were supposed to end the war right away. Say Hilda, what are they doing there, all that noise in the middle of the night?"

"The men are bailing out water from under the floor."

"Water from under the floor? Hilda, tell me, where am I? Tell me, what place is this?"

"In the moor of Verisoo, on the moor island, on Taevasaar. This is a very safe place now."

That was something else Ilme could not understand. Surely they were in some kind of building. She asked for something to eat and fell asleep after eating. She said she would sleep until morning, and then everything would be clear.

She awoke at night when Tõmm had just returned from his watch.

"Where is Hilda?" Ilme asked her brother.

"She went home last evening. They needed her help. I'll turn out the light. It might disturb you."

"Oh, please don't," Ilme pleaded. "I just had a terrible dream. Please let the light burn, Tõmm!"

"This is a place for dreams all right. Even I begin to see them. I must be getting old, for I cannot sleep. Formerly such things didn't bother me."

"The Russians attacked me," Ilme said, trembling.

"Uh-uh," her brother mumbled, looking thoughtfully at Ilme's hair. The grey threads shone in the light of the lamp. "Well, God damn them, they are that kind. They always try to attack," he said and began to fix his rifle.

"What are you doing?" Ilme asked in a frightened voice.

"Nothing much. I'm just oiling it. It's so cold outside that it turns moist when it's brought inside."

"But that is a rifle."

"So what? What of it?" Tõmm laughed bitterly. "A good weapon, a faithful companion, tested in trouble. When you get a little better, I'll tell you all about it."

Ilme's glance stopped again at her bandaged hand. She had placed the wounded hand over the other and in the lamplight looked at the bandages.

"Tõmm, have I lost my memory?"

"Why? What makes you think that?" The boy was startled. "Losing one's memory—that would be a blessing to everyone," he muttered to himself.

Ilme must have heard him, for she winced. Suddenly she was in a hurry to get somewhere. Her questioning spirit was like a man running with desperate speed through corridors and disarranged rooms in an empty house, opening doors and slamming them behind him.

"Ilme," Tõmm shouted, hearing her breathing become a low groan. He pulled the curtain from the bed and bent over her. "Ilme, what happened? Silly, why did you tear your bandages off? Hilda had only just dressed your hand. Wait, I'll look for some new bandages. These are covered with pus. The pine resin will draw the inflammation out."

Ilme did not answer. She could not talk. Even breathing was painful and difficult. She did not even notice Tõmm bandaging her hand, not even the painful similarity of her surroundings with her recent prison cell. And Tõmm's solicitous voice—how was she supposed to hear that?

She was fleeing with the child, running out of the city, to the country, into the woods, before the betraying light of the rising sun fell upon her. She hurried, bent over with pain, blowing her own breath on the cheeks of the child. She feared the patrols she met and did not stop when she was hailed. Let them shoot, let them kill her, it did not matter any more. Nothing mattered any more. Nothing. Only the last spark of life in the baby in her arms—only that. Her tiny Hilja, the little un-baptized starving baby, only she mattered any more.

A strange farm woman had picked her up from the road and had taken her into the house. Ilme was afraid and refused to let the baby be taken from her. She was scared of everyone now. They might take her child from her. They all wanted to take Hilja from her. They were all Communists, sent out to catch her. Even in honest eyes she saw lurking a wild desire for her baby. The farm people became speechless, looking at her misery. The baby in Ilme's arms was dead.

Why was she punished like that? What sins had she committed? Looking at the stiffened face of her daughter, she would have cursed herself and God with the ugliest words she knew, if she had had the strength to do it. But all she could do was to push back the hands that were offering help, as if they had been hissing snakes which were raising their heads toward her, and to run out of the house, clutching the child. She screamed when people wanted to stop her. They were all her enemies. When the farmer's wife ran after her and put a piece of bread in her pocket, even that seemed to her like violence.

301

The same slice of bread, which she had forgotten to throw away because she was concentrating on the baby, probably saved her life later on. She had eaten it somewhere but could not remember where or how.

So she had reached the home where she had been born, shouting aloud for Taavi and frightening the people she happened to meet.

VIII

Three men sat down to eat in the forest. They were on the moor, near the caved-in roof of a peat-drying barn. The sinking sun had succeeded in drying out one side of the slanting roof. The old cracked shingles had burst open and were sticking out in every direction. The men had found dry branches, crumbled moss, and heather under the roof—the bedstead of a former occupant.

"We'll stay here for the night," Taavi Raudoja had said, and that was that.

They were all glum from the continuous rains, and their wet clothes made them uncomfortable. The autumn made them sick.

"G-god-d-damn cr-crooks!" Eedi of Piibu cursed, without apparent reason, and looked across the moor where the straight-lined ditches from where peat had been cut were brim-full of pitch-black water. He munched a slice of bread, looked across the moor and said again: "G-g-goddamn cr-crooks!" as if to confirm his heavy thoughts. There were the peat ditches, covered with bright green moss, neat and sharp-edged, which could not yet carry a rabbit on their surface. The old peat ditches could not carry the weight of a man either, although the moss on them was much thicker. They stretched out far behind them, lighter in colour than the rest of the moor. The roads that led to the centre of the moor were crooked and dangerous. Attack and escape were equally hazardous here. Eedi spit onto the ground and stretched out on one side, picking at the moss.

"Ha-ha, the little fellow has tears in his eyes!" Leonard remarked. "Well, if his hind end is wet for days, it makes his stomach run and his eyes drip. You two brothers are no good for anything any more. I get the feeling, ambling around in your company, that I am swimming in a sea of manure. My nose is barely above the surface and if a wind should come up, the waves of stench would meet above my head. Then it would all be over. Leonard Kibuviir is drowned, and neither of you will throw me a rope. Swear a little, throw up some of the filth. There is plenty of it in the world; yours won't make it any worse. But no, they press their jaws together and don't give their souls any relief."

"Quit that," Taavi said, bored. "You're an old man already, but you talk like an idiot."

"Old age makes an idiot out of me. I feel that I am turning gayer and younger every day. All that others can see is that I am turning into an old fool. Now what is the trouble with us at this moment? We've just stuffed a mouthful of bread into our stomachs, and there's the bed waiting for us. Tomorrow is another day, if the damned Ivan doesn't spit lead into our gills. Well, my clothes are wet, and that turns the screws on my rheumatism, so that by morning my last strands of hair will be loose from the pain. And there aren't any women here. One would certainly come in handy to keep body and soul warm. Don't scowl at me like that. That is just what is missing from our lives, and it's a crime."

"You are crazy about women, aren't you?" Taavi said. Let him talk, he thought. But when he had a talking fit when all three of them were gloomy, their situation seemed least tolerable.

Right across the moor Taavi could see the black thickets, from which the night was approaching, step by step. He had plenty of problems, more important than listening to the blabbering of his companions.

"I have figured," Leonard now said, thoughtfully, "that I should go out of the woods for a while."

"Are you crazy?" Taavi asked sharply.

"Id-idiot," Eedi added.

"No, I have considered it from every possible angle. I won't be the first one; plenty of others have given themselves up in response to Russian urging. They say they are sorry, make a tearful face. They say that they were forced into the German army, scared to death, but at heart that they have always been staunch Soviet patriots."

"Don't spout such foolishness," Taavi said angrily. "If you go, you're lost. You know that better than anyone. You must be going out of your mind out here in the woods."

"Sure enough, I'll get lost sooner or later—back into the woods." Leonard chuckled. "I have figured it out to the last detail. That's all you read in the newspapers and hear on the radio: 'Come out of the woods. Be nice boys.' We have heard for a year that they'll give you farms and good jobs, that nobody will pull a single hair from your head. They'll let you live for a little while, to lure a few others out, and then you're gone, lost, so that even a dog won't bark after you."

"What are you talking about then?"

"Yes, brother. But what if I should lose myself again before getting lost, and should creep out into the open somewhere else, with a new name and a new repentant face? It's a dangerous game, but winter is getting near. I could get through the winter that way, keep alive until next spring. The snow and frost, damn them, they strangle the last breath out of you. And women! Just imagine, I'd get a passport and I'd be able to move around freely for a while. I'd get a chance to live. Warm rooms, a little food regularly under my nose, maybe even sheets on my bed, and—women!"

"Many men have been destroyed by women."

"How else would a man perish? A man is always destroyed because of women. This way or that way. Even a damned domestic tyrant, who keeps his wife under such pressure that the poor scared woman runs around like a burning spindle, even that kind of a bull is finally destroyed by his enslaved wife. There is nothing that can be done about it, and it's a fool who doesn't realize it, but I am seriously considering returning to the Soviet paradise."

Their conversation ended here, as they began to make a bed under the old roof. There was nothing to be afraid of here at night. They could sleep safely, if only the cold would let them catch a wink. The cold began to bother them more and more every night. It was better in hay barns, but the danger was greatest there, and one man had to keep watch outside every minute, regardless of the weather. That was a strict order Taavi had given.

Why were they wandering? Taavi often asked himself. It was time to settle down somewhere for the winter. In a place where they could get food, where there were not many Russians, where there was a degree of understanding between the people and the local Communists, and where no terror squads had been organized against the so-called "bandits." Restlessness, however, drove Taavi from place to place, and his two companions followed him. The situation had become unfavourable at Eedi's home because of roundups in the summer and because of the continuous presence of the NKVD. They had agreed to go into the forests of Pärnumaa for the winter, where Taavi knew that some of his former comrades were hiding, but for some reason he did not seem to be in a hurry.

"Damn it all!" Taavi said, when they had gathered some heather and wind-dry moss to spread on their bed. He could not get rid of a great anger and gloom in his heart, try as he might.

"Spit it out," Leonard chuckled. "Blow it out, or you won't even catch a wink."

"I won't get any sleep anyway."

"It's hard for me, too," Leonard said. "Eedi snores so loud that it echoes back from the woods and straight into my ear. Like a tractor, my word of honour. Even if I were to stuff my ears with moss, the vibration would shake it out."

Taavi did not answer. He pulled off his boots—old German army boots he had got from one of the villages—arranged the wet and dirty rags around his feet and slipped into a potato sack. The sack served as a sheet under him and a blanket over him, and it reached exactly to his navel. The coat he had taken off covered his chest and head. Leonard and Eedi slipped into another bigger sack. They were warmer together, and they had two coats to cover the two of them. Even their usual bickering warmed them a little, especially when they began to pull the coats off each other. Leonard had the warmest place, for he usually slept between Taavi and Eedi. He would not exchange places with the latter, although they sometimes got into serious fights over it. Leonard claimed that his bald head was especially sensitive to cold.

"I h-ha-have a f-feeling th-that-the-de-devil is st-still after us," Eedi muttered.

"And for several days straight. What kind of a joke is it?" Even Leonard was perturbed.

They had begun to imagine that someone was on their trail. Not the Russians, but someone who they could not picture very well. When they were keeping watch outside at night, they returned to the others pale and frightened. Once Taavi had found Leonard peering into the darkness with insanity in his eyes, his fingers on the trigger. "He's there, I saw him, the terrible beast! Without shape, like. . . . Wait, I'll shoot the devil." Taavi had a hard job calming his companion down. There was nothing except what their own nerves conjured up. The nights were long, dark and heavy.

"That is called a persecution complex," Taavi said. "It is the fear within you which is already taking the shape of some ugly beast. You've got weak nerves."

"What the hell," Leonard cursed. "You know, Eduard, we are getting soft in the head, that's all. I have heard a dog howl every night now. I slap myself in the face and against my ears. May the wolves eat me, but the dog keeps howling. Nothing will stop it."

"I-I-have heard him-him t-too."

"Go to sleep, damned idiots," Taavi said angrily. "I haven't heard you two talk like men for ages. If you aren't spouting foolishness about women, you are fighting among yourselves and slipping each other ants in the pants. Now this crazy story about a hellish dog. A dog keeps howling! It's the wind."

"Last night he sniffed at a bush, sniffed right behind my back," Leonard said violently. "I could swear by my immortal soul that it's true. It was a weird feeling, so weird that—ugh! The devil."

"D-d-don't get all w-worked up ab-about it," Eedi answered. "I hav-ve he-heard him sev-veral t-times."

"Stupid. We are getting crazy, my dear bedfellow. You heard Taavi. He won't believe us. We believe that someone is on our trail, but Taavi says that. . . ."

He growled for some time quietly into his beard.

Taavi was sick and tired of hearing the story about the big dog who was sniffing on their trail. He marvelled to himself how quickly men could lose their nerve, although they were tempered in battles and dangers. They had both begun to fear the forests and the night, their protectors and friends. They were not afraid of Russians, but they were too scared to keep watch at night. Going out to relieve each other, they shouted the password from a long way off, and their guns flew to their shoulders even when only the breeze passed through the dry grass, or a piece of white bark fluttered on a birch tree. They were happiest when they could slip into their potato sack, as if that protected them from all haunting dangers.

A big dog, jaws dripping with saliva, a dog of the night, a beast with ice-cold eyes, a man-shaped hell-hound of a dog, Taavi thought sarcastically, crawling closer to his companions. It was difficult to fall asleep when the cold kept drowsiness away. Eedi of Piibu was already snoring. His lips made jumping noises like a tired machine gun, stiff from cold oil. When Leonard poked him in the ribs he mumbled some incomprehensible curses and began to whistle between his snores. Taavi rolled still closer to Leonard, until he felt the pleasant warmth of his body behind him, and closed his eyes. The sack of food and ammunition under his head was too high, straining his neck muscles painfully, but it was better than a wet clod, stiff with hoarfrost.

It was much colder here on the moor than in a haystack or under the tall trees of the forest. Well, it didn't matter. Before dawn they would be up again and on the move. Should the weather turn out nice, they could rest for an hour tomorrow in the low noon-time sun, in a protected place somewhere. But the weather would hardly be warm. The wind rustled in the heather and sniffed in the collapsed roof of the peat barn. A big, shapeless wind-dog, spitting cold rain like saliva from his jaws.

Suddenly Taavi shuddered and listened intensely. He smiled tiredly at his own foolishness, and his head fell down again on the sack. The silly stories of his companions had begun to give him nightmares too. He pulled his coat over his head again.

Was he, too, going out of his mind? He pushed the coat brusquely from his eyes and strained his ears, open-mouthed. He could have sworn he heard the whining of a dog. Listen, now he heard it again. Now it came from the other end of the roof, where the bushes had grown through the broken rafters. Taavi sat up. This dog story—perhaps a homeless dog was really on their trail. A hungry animal, beaten half to death, who had lost his master and was afraid of cruel people and did not dare show himself. Perhaps he sniffed at the places where they had eaten, where a few crumbs of their tiny rations may have fallen into the moss. The times were hard in the land for animals as well as humans.

Taavi wanted to lay his head back on his knapsack. Everything had been his own imagination, he decided. Suddenly he was overcome by the strange feeling that someone was looking at him from the darkness. Someone was looking straight into his face, searchingly and penetratingly, with rigid, suspicious eyes. This was a shocking realization that made him helpless, almost paralysed him. Taavi wanted to laugh out to break the spell, but he could not. In his mind's eye he saw a dog that had climbed with all four muddy paws onto the leaking shingled roof and was looking down at him. The dog had a human face. Taavi's stiffened fingers moved slowly toward his revolver.

"Don't move your hand," a rough, angry voice said. "I'll shoot your face full of lead!"

Taavi shuddered.

"Who are you, you devil?!" he hissed.

"A dog. Reku is a dog. The dog was sent to tell you, Taavi of Piskujõe. Run quickly to Verisoo. Your wife is on Taevasaar and she is sick to death."

"Where? Who? Where? Who are you?" Taavi shouted, kicking helplessly in his potato sack, his revolver finally in his hand. He heard the bushes rustle, but when he took a dazed aim at the bushes, the dog howled quite a distance away.

Eedi's snoring had stopped.

"What are you making all that row about?" Leonard growled, annoyed.

"The dog." Taavi shouted and sprang out from under the roof. Rain drizzled on his face, and the wind rustled in the heather. The night was humid and cold. There was nothing to be seen, although he looked hard and strained his ears, listening. He ran around the barn, stumbling over old boards and crumbling pieces of peat. Once he thought he saw a dog jumping over a peat ditch, but this was only an illusion, caused by eyestrain, for at the next moment he saw black dogs here, there and everywhere, leaping into the darkness. It must have been a vision from his childhood, the way he had pictured it, when his father had told him the story of how his grandfather had fought with wolves when he had been a boy. When Leonard and Eedi joined him and were standing at his side, they all heard a howl across the moor.

"Well, well," Leonard croaked. "Well, don't you hear it now? Don't you hear it yourself? Which one of us is crazy?"

"It's a wolf," Taavi muttered, rubbing his forehead fiercely, as if he were trying to wake himself up.

"A hellish creature," Leonard muttered. "I'm going tomorrow to give myself up to the Communists at the nearest district administration house. This kind of a joke drives you mad and your stomach can't hold even blessed pure wheat when you see such spooks all around. If only I knew how to say the Lord's prayer backwards. . . ."

"For goodness sake, cut out your endless blabbering," Taavi said angrily. "You have driven every one of us crazy with your talk, so that even I begin to see and hear God knows what."

"So-s-so you st-still don't belie-lieve?" Eedi was amazed.

Taavi was still touching his forehead. He could just not understand how they could all three be losing their minds at once.

"Run quickly to Verisoo. Your wife is on Taevasaar sick to death!"

These words would not let Taavi sleep any more that night. He heard them again and again in his tortured half-sleep. When he jumped up, there was nothing. These words rang in his ears even in the morning, although the daylight almost convinced him that it had been only a bad dream.

That his imprisoned wife could be on Taevasaar seemed to him wildly impossible. What a pity a man's dreams were so devoid of logic.

But why not go into the forests of Verisoo anyway? Why not go to see his mother? He had wanted to do this for some time. During the summer he had thought about it several times, especially when he had rested on the moss somewhere, exhausted from battles. It seemed that there had been so much to do all through the late summer after they had left the farm of Eedi's parents, that his plans had not materialized into deeds. There had been great roundups in central Estonia, and they were forced farther and farther eastwards. Because of the anger that was smouldering in him he had almost enjoyed the situation. A whole division of the regular Soviet army had been deployed against them, plus special units of the NKVD, airplanes and tanks. It had been worth their while to be a part of that. A general of the Red Army had been in personal charge of the whole unsuccessful operation. These were not battles in the normal sense, for the partisans had avoided setting up any front. They did not have sufficient men to do it. But they were mobile and reckless like angry wasps, they stung the clumsy army units as they stumbled through the thickets. They were rarely seen, but their deeds spoke for themselves. Only a very few of them fell, and their crushed corpses had been hung on trees by the Russians. But the losses of the enemy had been ten times as high, although the Russians outnumbered them a hundred to one.

As the thickets became quiet, they realized that autumn was upon them. When Taavi had heard of the fate of his family he had given up his plans to cross the sea. He had nothing to look forward to in the new world, neither now nor in the future. Yes, the village of Metsaoti, the house of Piskujõe where he had been born, his waiting mother—these were still calling him. But what if his mother had been arrested after his escape from prison? Perhaps, perhaps Ilme's parents knew something about the fate of Ilme and Lembit! Marta! Marta had to know.

A few days later they walked across the Koolu hills down toward Piskujõe. They had spruced up a little in a forest ranger's farm, had shaved and clipped their hair. Even Taavi's shaven scalp was covered with light blond bristles. They walked in single file, a few paces apart, revolvers ready to shoot, Taavi first in line.

The sun was sinking toward the west, throwing its last red glow into the crowns of the pines. Taavi hurried along the tops of the ridges, from where one could see farther over the bushes and the almost bare underbrush in the hollows. Soon he would see his mother face to face. If only his companions would hurry a little. In only half an hour his mother would rummage through all her storage rooms and spread the table with the best her farm could offer. Leonard and Eedi, two men who would never grow up, kept lagging behind picking half-frozen whortle berries from the slope, angry with Taavi for his rushing. The distance between them became greater, but Taavi did not care. He would rather run than walk. One could not but hurry going to his own mother.

Then he heard a dog howl right in front of him. It was quite close, a brief warning howl, ending in an angry growl. Taavi's pace slowed a little.

"Well, do you hear it now?" Leonard said, a confused expression on his face.

"And in b-b-broad d-daylight to-too!" Eedi muttered.

"Stupid," Taavi answered. "There are plenty of homeless dogs around. Why should this be the same one?"

"It used to be behind us, but now he begins to growl right in front, and even before the sun has set." Leonard would not be interrupted. "This place feels like a graveyard."

"You are right in the midst of a graveyard. The people of several villages were buried in these sandhills during the great plague," Taavi said. "Let's go."

Before they could take another step they saw a strange figure coming. Even his approach was unusual. He jumped from behind one tree to another and peered at them, his rifle ready to shoot.

"What the hell! Who is that?" Leonard said. The newcomer must be a woodsman. That was obvious.

The stranger stopped at about ten paces from them and leaned against a pine. He was a boyish-looking man. His chin was covered with a light beard and his eyes were small and sharp. He carried heavy bags on his back, had high boots on his feet, and over his shoulder wore the skin of a dog.

"Hallo, men," he said.

"Hallo. Who are you?" Taavi asked in surprise.

The stranger laughed.

"I am Reku, the dog, but don't call me Reku the fool. If you do, Reku will shoot you down like a mangy puppy." The boy's voice had a warning in it. He looked at Taavi and his companions as if they were old acquaintances who did not interest him very much.

"Are you Ebehard of Võllamäe?" Taavi asked. Of course, he was the fool of Võllamäe. He used to call himself a dog.

"Reku is Reku. Reku is a general now. Don't laugh, Taavi of Piskujõe. You're almost a city slicker. Reku doesn't have much in common with such people. But Reku came because of Ilme of Hiie. Let's go," he said, and turned around.

"Speak," Taavi shouted and grabbed him by the shoulder. "How did you know that we were here?"

Reku tore himself away from Taavi, startling everyone with his fierce, dog-like growl. Leonard and Eedi stared at him as if they saw a ghost. Was this strange man the beast that had trailed them at night? The same creature that had sniffed at their tracks, looked from the woods with burning eyes, and leaped high over the peat ditches? Damn it, this thing took their wits away even before the sun could vanish completely behind the thickets.

"Stop playing like that," Reku growled. "Your father is Reku's adviser. Andres said: 'Watch out, or else Taavi will run to Piskujõe, and that will be the end of everybody. Piskujõe is full of Russians.' Let's go now. Ilme of Hiie is waiting on Taevasaar."

Taavi looked at Ebehard and his companions in turn.

"How did Ilme. . . ? How did she get to Taevasaar?"

"The men carried her. She came from prison, and now she's there. Don't ask so much. Let's go!"

They began to walk quickly behind Reku.

"What about the Russians? How did they get to Piskujõe? Tell me, what has happened to my mother? What is Lembit doing? My son Lembit?"

"Reku hasn't seen him. The Russians are at Piskujõe waiting for you."

A chill ran down Taavi's spine. The sun had set, and it was beginning to get dark under the trees. The evening star twinkled through the striped clouds. Reku trotted along. It was impossible to have a sensible talk with him. He did not stay in one place long enough, but jumped into the bushes and ran short circles around the tree trunks. Near his mother's farm Taavi halted. He heard the accordion playing of the Russians. The fool of Võllamäe had told the truth, although it was hard to believe. Russians at Piskujõe! An NKVD unit here in the midst of forests. It was strange to imagine.

They walked quickly and silently through the dark wood. Taavi knew the forests around his home, the meadows and the thickets. He knew about the islands in the bog of Verisoo, and he knew that after the autumn rains it was almost impossible to approach Taevasaar through the bog holes. It was getting darker all the time. The evening was like night, starless and without light. Men had lived on Taevasaar during the first summer of war. Even Osvald, the hired man of Hiie, had lived there. They had had a cabin made of a few short beams, covered with sod. Men from Tenise had stopped there, some even from much farther away, until life had become too dull and they had begun to move in the direction of the approaching front.

"Don't sink into the bog," Ebehard of Võllamäe warned them, picking up a long stick from the edge of the moor. "Reku knows several pathways, but this one here is the shortest, and it won't make you wet above your knees. The men have put logs into the moor."

They sloshed right through the bubbling and hissing water. Their hesitant feet found the logs. Damn it, everything was true after all! This was a tangible sign right here in the bog—the beams that supported their swaying feet.

Not even insignificant words were exchanged any more. The water gurgled in the dark, giving off a soft and bitter smell. Taavi swore through his teeth when the water came over the tops of his boots. Leonard in his short boots was wet to his knees. Soon the ground became more solid.

"There are land-mines in front of us," Reku said, turning toward the right. "They'll split you up like a butchered hog."

The men on Taevasaar had organized their defence well, Taavi found. He was suddenly pleased with it.

"Hey," a warning voice called from the bushes and said a word, to which one obviously was supposed to answer with the correct password.

"Don't shoot!" Reku shouted in return. "Our own men. If you shoot, you'll get a shot of lead right in your face. This is the dog of Võllamäe and Taavi of Piskujõe."

The little figure of a man rose from the bushes, touching them with the barrel of a submachine gun, as if to get the feel of the strangers.

"Well, I'll be dog-gone," he pressed out from between his teeth without moving his lips, and then gnashed his teeth together.

"You, Värdi!" Taavi grabbed him strongly by the shoulders.

"Taavi himself! The prison was not good enough for you, eh? And Leonard and Eedi of Piibu. The old gang!" Värdi rejoiced, shaking the hands of the others with his stiff hands.

"Say now, Värdi, is my wife really here?"

Värdi gnashed his teeth for some time, beating Taavi's ribs with his fists to express his delight. He was wearing a thick, heavy army overcoat that reached to the ground. Whether it was German or Russian, Taavi could not tell in the dark.

"Your wife is in the bunker. Let's go. I'll take you there."

"How's your leg?"

"Oh, the leg is all right. I got it back long ago."

Värdi was the same old Värdi. Taavi felt as if this meeting brightened up the darkness around them. So they had a bunker, and everything.

Climbing down the steep stairway into the bunker, Taavi suddenly imagined that he was again on the Finnish front in Karelia. Everything was so familiar: the damp and stale air that met them, the shining bottoms of metal food containers, a willow mat on the muddy floor, the yellow light of a small kerosene lamp that greeted them when the door was opened in response to their stumbling steps.

He stood in the doorway and felt that the circle had been completed. He could not realize yet how wide a circle it had been, but his instinct told him that fate itself had whirled them around wildly like rotating toys, until their motion subsided and they sank down on the ground. He saw men jumping from their bunks, shouting in astonishment, hurrying to shake his hands—Osvald, Tõmm, Mart. He saw Hilda behind the small table, whose knitting needles stopped with a jerk and whose hands rose suddenly to her breast. Taavi saw much in these first moments: the weapons of the men, their clothes, the little iron stove and the wet beams of the ceiling, but no detail penetrated far into him or took a clear shape in his mind, except for the woman who rose from one of the bottom beds. Quite suddenly the air was silent like a grave, motionless and heavy around him. It was strange. Taavi's limbs were lighter than air. His hand rose and remained hanging in the air, light like a feather and full of pain.

Hilda's eyes flashed to the woman, and she, too, got up, as if she wanted to run to the aid of the patient, who was straightening herself with the support of the sleeping bunks. But she remained in her place. They all remained in their places.

"Taavi!" This was a strange voice. The big black eyes looked at the man. Her head seemed to make a great effort to stand straight, but her shoulders sank weakly forward, and her fingers were white from the strain of holding on to the side of the upper bunk. They seemed like the cramped fingers of a drowned person around a piece of wood that had sunk with him.

Birth and death took place in Taavi at that moment. He saw the sufferings of a human being in front of him, an unwritten passion, holier than the Scripture. The man staggered toward his wife. He could only whisper her name. Her haggard limbs pressed against him, weakly, like a cut blade of grass.

Ilme did not cry. She could not speak. Her body trembled, her mouth twitched, and when she threw her head impetuously back, her eyes shone with tears, but only hysterical laughter came from her lips.

The men looked for something to do. They moved around awkwardly, as if the cold had stiffened their limbs. Värdi climbed out of the bunker —he recalled his duties all of a sudden, and this relieved him greatly. He was like a man who had lost his way in the woods and suddenly came upon the right path, although the warmth of the bunker had made his glasses misty and he stumbled over every clod. It was dark and you could not see anything either with glasses or without.

Osvald and Mart, too, went out.

"Put your hand over your cigarette," Mart warned the hired man of Hiie, who was smoking so violently that sparks flew around him. "If your fire shines as far as Kalgina the Russian fire brigade will come to put it out."

"We'll turn our hoses on them and spray them with lead," Osvald growled. He could not take pleasure in the return of the son-in-law of Hiie. Although he had wished it all the time, he had not believed it to be possible. A hope without belief is sometimes better than the fulfilment of that hope.

When Tõmm stroked Hilda's arm, the girl took it as a great kindness. At this moment Hilda would have liked to have held Tõmm with both her arms, to have held him tight. This touch on her wrist, perhaps accidental, but more likely an intentional caress, affected the girl like a great gift and released her tears. Tõmm himself began to question Leonard and Eedi about outside news. Where had the men come from, and how. Their conversation, although uneven and often incomprehensible even to themselves lessened the tension and seemed to restore the former friendly, yellow glow to the little kerosene lamp.

The many-coloured rug had fallen to the floor from Ilme's bed. Taavi made Ilme sit down. His face had become motionless and grim. Its tautness seemed to be a rigid, defensive iron mask, set up to protect the fragile glass that was inside from careless shattering.

Ilme's face was completely different—an unprotected open window that exposed the shattered interior.

"So you are back with me," Ilme said tiredly. "Why didn't you bring Lembit with you?" Reproach rang in her pained voice.

"Where is Lembit?" Taavi demanded.

"Don't you know?" Ilme shouted. "My Lord, you don't know. I have told you often enough and begged you to bring him back. He is waiting. Just think of that. He is a little child. He cannot wait patiently like an older person."

"So he is still in prison?" Taavi muttered. He looked again and again at his wife. He began with her hair, which was strongly mixed with grey, let his glance glide to her distorted face, to her eyes that seemed to burn in their deep sockets, to her formerly full-lipped mouth, which had become a narrow grey line, somehow pulled inside. He looked at the slumped shoulders of his wife and her caved-in chest, her bony knees and legs that were narrow and straight. He saw the ruin of a human being, crushed by suffering.

He took his wife's quivering fingers in his hands.

"They said: 'Send your husband to get your son, and then you'll all be released.' They said: 'If he won't come or if you plan to deceive us, then....'"

Ilme burst out crying.

So that was it! It was impossible to imagine a more satanic trap. He knew that the NKVD did not choose means to reach their ends, but he could not have pictured to himself such ingenious devilry.

Suddenly Taavi remembered something. He looked again at the haggard figure of his wife and asked:

"But what happened.... What about our second child?"

Ilme gave him a desperate look. Taavi feared that she would have another fit of crying.

"She is dead, thank God," the woman said, swallowing. "She died...."
Ilme wanted to talk but only her lips moved.

"At birth?"

"No, no! It was a girl—Hilja. They told me that Father buried her in the meadow, there on the river bank under the birch tree, where ... remember?"

Yes, Taavi remembered. They had decided to unite their lives there, for better or for worse, and they had both expected only happiness.

"Hilja died in the ruins!" Ilme said. She was looking down and bending more and more forward. When Taavi touched her trembling shoulders she winced, as if she wanted to rise and flee from the man. She looked at Taavi for a moment and then closed her eyes with a great effort.

Taavi put the coat back on her shoulders. It had slipped down to the floor. He tried to persuade her to lie back on the bed, but she would not listen to the man's suggestion.

"Taavi, go and save our son!"

Taavi stood and stared, baffled and helpless. The bunker was quite silent and empty. Of course, the men did not want to disturb them, and had gone out into the night. Only Hilda was crouching at the table. No, Tõmm was also sitting in a dark corner with Leonard and Eedi, and then Värdi returned and began quietly to dry his misty glasses. His near-sighted eyes squinted helplessly in the light of the tiny lamp.

"I'll have to think about it," Taavi murmered.

"You must not think. They'll kill your son," Ilme shouted huskily.

"But they'll kill me too...."

"Oh no!" Ilme sounded surprised. "They only want to see you."

"You don't understand," Taavi muttered darkly. "If I should go, then—no, that is impossible! I would have to betray everybody else, bring them here to the moor. Betray and betray until I have nobody to betray any more—and that would be my own end. They simply want to get hold of me. They want to avenge themselves, because I managed to escape from their clutches. Woman, we have nothing to save any more! Nothing!"

That night turned into the hardest struggle Taavi had ever had with himself. A struggle with his convictions, the life he had led, with himself and the world. He remained calm on the outside, his face rigid like stone, his manners clumsy and absent-minded. He could not understand the useless, probing questions of his companions. Why? Why did they keep looking at him?

Think of God. Think of our child, Ilme had wailed. Yes, Taavi did think. He thought of everything a human being can think of, but to no avail. Suddenly he did not believe in anything any more—in God, or justice, and least of all in himself.

He exchanged meaningless words with his companions, asked and answered questions mechanically, forgetting every word a moment later. So they had two bunkers on Taevasaar, machine guns and a solid supply of food for the winter? Hell, what did he care about that. A little more than a dozen men. What did that amount to? They might hold back a company, maybe two companies of Russians if attacked across the moor. What did that matter? They might even destroy a regiment, but that would be of no help to Taavi Raudoja, whose wife kept calling him in her dreams, when she had finally fallen asleep, weakened from the emotional shock. He was a brave soldier, for whom his tortured little son was waiting, his own child, a little man who hero-worshipped him. A brave soldier—what mockery!

They showed him a bed, seemingly happy that the bunker would now be full of men, of strong fighting men. The fools. A man who has been kicked by fate right in his face is no fighting man. Every man, even the strongest, has a limit beyond which he cannot endure. What stuff are you made of, my friends? He looked in their faces. He saw motionless shadows on their faces and pulled back. Hilda, the orphan who had suffered so much, why was she looking at him like that, her eyes burning with pain? Why did this girl bring her life here to share their fate? Gratitude toward the Hiie people did not oblige her to run between the moors and the farm.

"Be careful, there are land-mines in several places in the moor," Osvald said.

What? Oh yes, he was going out. Why did Osvald think it necessary to warn him? Did he look as if he were going to drown himself in the moor? No, foolishness, the men were stupid. Taavi Raudoja did not care about land-mines or bog holes. He had a Browning in his pocket. If the land-mines should tear off his legs, he would still have enough strength to give himself a decent end. This would be fate, and he could not do anything about it, but he was not planning to look for that kind of an escape. He was not planning anything.

The cold, sticky night clung to him as he stumbled through the darkness. He passed the other bunker, met the sentry and said simply and calmly: "I'm getting some fresh air. It is a little tight there in the bunker. I'm not used to that kind of life yet, so don't shoot at me while I lumber around here."

The sentry was from the other bunker, a stranger to Taavi, but he, too, warned him of the land-mines. Taavi sensed that they all knew everything and would be watching him tomorrow and on the following days, waiting to see what he would do.

IX

Ilme had it easier now, for she could place much of the burden on Taavi's shoulders. He would know how to take care of things. When Taavi was not nearby, she thought he had gone to get their son, and she waited in agitation for their return. Her first question to Taavi was always: "Where is Lembit?" Good Lord, has Taavi lost his mind, that he can waste precious hours like that? Every minute was important, every single minute.

Taavi could not stay for long inside the bunker walls, but it was no better outside, no better anywhere. He participated in the doings of his comrades. He even volunteered for sentry duty, but nothing gave any relief to his thoughts. The work he liked best was placing mines. It somehow calmed him down when he handled explosives.

Captain Jonnkoppel invited him in several times. The leader of the group seemed worried about the steps Taavi might take. The captain had a corner separated from the general room by a partition. He had a flowered blanket thrown over a sack filled with heather, maps and pictures on the wall; even a row of books on a small bookshelf. Everything was pleasant except for the floor, where the black moor water splashed with every step. Water was the biggest curse of the Froghole, for the builders, desiring to make their living quarters as roomy and comfortable as possible, had dug too deep. Now water was constantly up to their ankles, in the mornings sometimes even halfway up to their knees, and the men, tired of constant bailing, were looking for a pump in the villages. They threatened to break into the dairy if they could not find one elsewhere.

Captain Jonnkoppel treated Taavi with the respect due to a fellow officer, and his first words were accompanied by an embarrassed smile: "Actually, Mr. Raudoja, although I have not had any dealings with the Finnish fighters under field conditions, I have a great deal of respect for them. If you see something wrong somewhere, you have younger eyes and more recent training from the war academy, go ahead and correct the situation. All right?"

"Sir, I don't have a very clear picture yet of the life and situation here, and now—you understand—I am in a special position. . . ."

The captain interrupted him quickly, as if he were afraid to hear something unpleasant: "Of course, of course, I understand. We'll try to

315

find a way." He moved his strong stocky body on the bed. Taavi walked on the wet floor—two steps, turn, and again two steps. "Of course, of course," Jonnkoppel said and scratched his curly beard. "You are in a special position, but in any case I expect you to stay here and to submit to the discipline of the camp, that is, to my orders. You'll take over the command at the Snake Pit. All right?"

"No, sir."

"What? If I say that. . . ."

"No sir. There is no sense in playing war. I won't accept any responsibilities right now, for I don't know what will become of me. If I should stay here, then I would of course take orders from you, that is natural. But I may go after my son."

"Are you crazy?"

"Sir, this is my personal business. I have wasted many years of my life already, but the boy's life is still ahead of him."

"You'll betray everybody."

"The scars are still on my face from my earlier imprisonment. I did not betray anybody. I have thought of going, but they would only get my corpse."

The captain lit his pipe and handed the tobacco pouch to Taavi.

"Listen to me. I won't say more than a few words," he said heavily. "Of course, nobody could keep you here by force, although, frankly, I have considered that too, for not only the lives of the men here, but also the lives of their relatives in several villages are at stake. Yes, I have considered arresting you, if you should do anything foolish."

A contemptuous grin appeared on Taavi's face.

"You seem to want, sir, that we should fight our last battle here on Taevasaar between our own men? At least half of the men would be on my side. Take that into consideration. Thank you for warning me!"

But the older man continued undisturbed. "All right, you'll give yourself up to the NKVD and blow your brains out under their eyes. Fine, your sufferings are over, but do you think they will be satisfied? You are gullible if you believe that your son will be set free as easily as that. Listen, listen—and if you should give yourself up alive your son will be the means by which they will make you talk. You will tell everything you know, and you will lie, make up fantastic stories, if you don't have anything more to say."

"That won't happen," Taavi muttered, but then he remembered how simple beating and freezing had been enough to make him admit that he had been to Finland. The man was probably right.

Taavi had a similar talk with Osvald, when he went to take over his watch the next night. Osvald stayed with him under a low pine on the edge of the moor and unloaded his rifle, trying to appear busy.

"Wonder if it is going to snow soon? Look, the ice won't melt from the creeks even at noontime, and it seems to be clouding up," he said without expecting an answer from Taavi. "We should try to cut some more firewood for the winter. It will be easier to carry it in now than in winter with snow on the ground. Of course, we have to keep an eye on the weather when we make a fire, so the airplanes won't spot it or somebody see it with binoculars across the moor. You haven't told Ilme about what happened to Krõõt? It is better not. She might get upset. They are having a hard time at Hiie now. Paralysed—what can you do. Ignas is taking it hard too. It's a blessing that he picked Hilda up from the snowdrift then. Are you listening?"

"I have ears, don't you know?"

"Oh, well, come on," Osvald said with embarrassment and began to swear. He spit and cursed to himself, looking down, as if he had dropped something into the moss. "Why is it that all these blows have to hit you at the same time? One after the other, like lightning out of a clear sky. You don't hear much thunder, but there it has hit you and you lie on the ground."

"The thunder may come yet."

"I am sorry for Ilme and your son. Thinking about them often keeps me from sleeping at night. I have even pulled my boots on several times, but when I start to move I ask myself—where?" Osvald stopped talking and gave Taavi a penetrating look. "What do you think? Would they set Lembit free if you were to go?"

"You mean if I gave myself up to the NKVD? Yes, I believe they would set the boy free, if he isn't already in such a condition that Christian eyes dare not look at him. Yes, I believe they would release him, but deport him somewhere in Russia."

Osvald opened and closed his mouth several times, finding no words to express his feelings.

"Are you going?" he finally managed to ask.

"No," Taavi said quietly.

Osvald backed away from him, looking at him with wide open eyes.

"If I were in your shoes, I think I would go. Your own son! I would go—come what may. How can I say what I would do. I cannot compare my life with yours. I don't know; I cannot say. I don't know anything. Have you made a final decision?" Osvald asked angrily. The whites of his eyes flashed, and he tried to keep his eyes down, looking at the moss. "You wouldn't have far to go. They are waiting for you at your home. We would have to move then. I have a feeling that if we settled in too well when the time came to move we'd leave a nasty burned-out trail behind us. Listen, I'll come with you if you want me to. No, don't think that I have gone out of my mind, but I could say I caught you. I must be going crazy right this minute. Now where did I get this idea that I caught you? So they'd give me a lighter sentence. . . . Hell, have I really sunk that low already? At night, when I listen to Ilme's screams in her sleep, I used to think that I would go together with Taavi, that I would put my head on the block too. So what, I thought, we have settled our accounts with the Russians pretty well already. Let it be a glorious end. We'd march in and say: here we are! Then we'd shoot our burp guns empty and. . . . But look now, what kind of an idea should have come to my head!"

Osvald's talk became a confused murmur, and his wide shoulders stooped forward like those of an animal who is freezing in the rain.

"Go to the bunker and lie down," Taavi advised. "Get some rest. Sleep, if you can. Don't let your thoughts kill you. We are ordinary people, simple soldiers. We can fight against the enemy, suffer hunger and thirst, but we cannot fight against thoughts. They'll always get the better of us. That is why I am not surprised when some men who were good fighters yesterday go out of the woods today and give themselves up to the Communists, although they know what is actually in store for them behind all those fine promises. The men have no purpose, no orders. Nobody has prepared them for the situation we are in at the present time. They have been left alone with their thoughts. I know what this kind of struggle means."

"And you are not going?"

"Don't ask me. I don't know! Now I'm saying no, but in an hour I may be going." And looking absent-mindedly out over the open moor, he said: "If there were something to do, something that would engage the spirit a little. A battle would be a great relief now. It would shake us up. If we could at least take a bath, but we can't even wash ourselves."

"I have already caught a couple of lice in my shirt."

"What?"

"Yes, I think that—Ilme brought them from the prison in her clothes."

"My wife," Taavi muttered. He was silent then for a long time, as if he had forgotten everything. When he awoke, as from a stupor, he began to scan the moor and the woods beyond carefully with his binoculars, as if he realized only now that he was out on duty. "It's foggy and dark. The binoculars are not much help. If they should learn about our nest here they could sneak up on a dark and windy night such as this. At dawn they'd jump up and run across. We should have more land-mines, several circles around Taevasaar."

"So you are not going?"

"Leave that up to me," Taavi answered sharply. "If I should go, you would need the land-mines more than ever, for who can guarantee that I won't be the first one to lead the Russians to you!"

Ilme was staring at the ceiling of the bunker where sooty moss was hanging down from between the logs. The light flickered on the rough-hewn beams, some of which were grey from age, while others were still stained with the fresh juice of the bark. The fire in the stove cast a reddish light, to which the flame of the kerosene lamp added a dull yellowish glow reminiscent of the atmosphere of a threshing floor or the light of the rising moon. The shadows played on the walls, and Ilme followed them, sometimes for hours. At times they put her quietly to sleep, but then again the objects that happened to meet the eye acquired corners and outlines where the light was sharply cut and broken. The boards that formed the bottom of the upper bunk began to drop little sparks and red and blue circles. The bright pattern of the rug became black, and flat surfaces formed sharp angles, so brilliantly golden that they hurt her eyes. Then she had to close them quickly. Even inside the protective eyelids the wild whirling of the circles went on, until they

318

felt coarse like sand in her eyes. The bunk bed swayed, rose and fell with her head and feet. The sides of it bent and shook. The quiet voices of the men sounded from far away, as if through gushing water. Above them Ilme heard other voices, words that rang out ominously, as if everything were a void around them, like a huge ice-cold cathedral. The words reverberated against the walls and then receded into the darkness. There was a hollow, metallic, grave-like echo as the voices sounded in the silence: "Send your husband, send your husband. Then you'll be set free, then you'll be set free . . . free . . . free. . . ."

Then Lembit would be released.

Ilme sank and swayed. She raised her hand to her moist forehead, which seemed to be farther away than the walls, separated from everything. Even her hand was separated from her, insignificant, nameless, lifeless. Then Lembit would be set free . . . set free. . . . The words that resounded from afar were all that was left.

Sometimes Ilme managed to break herself loose from the spell of the words that hammered at her brain. She opened her eyes with an effort, raised her head a little, and said in a barely audible voice: "You want my husband. You want him."

She was perplexed by her own words, and at the next moment she was often struck numb: "Now you know what fate has in store for Lembit. Now you know."

"This is a trap. You want Taavi. You will never release anybody who is still alive."

"This is a formality, a pure formality. . . . You'll all be set free. . . . Your son may begin a new life, if only. . . ."

The light was still flickering on the beams of the ceiling. The nightmarish glitter continued, the words rang out in metallic space. Ilme's own thoughts whirled at a dizzy speed and left her gasping for breath.

Perhaps they really only wanted to see Taavi? Perhaps they would really let Taavi come back—together with Lembit? My God, there had to be some solution! She, Ilme, had served her sentence and had been set free. A whole year's imprisonment. Perhaps she was really guilty. Yes, she had tried to escape to Finland. That was it. According to Soviet law this was a crime. But why didn't they let Lembit out? He was only a child. That was because of Taavi. Taavi should go, and then Lembit would be set free . . . free. . . .

Her desperate glance hurried from face to face. Who would tell her the solution? Who would show her the way?

"Hilda!"

The girl looked up, placed her knitting on the table and bent toward her bed. Her face was haggard from lack of sleep, and the shadows from the lamp played on her cheeks.

"Hilda, tell me. . . ."

"Would you like something to drink? Peeter of Valba brought some milk this morning. He has a cow in the woods."

"No, thank you. Milk? No, I don't want any." The patient turned impatiently to one side. "Tell me, would they set Lembit free if Taavi should go?"

Hilda stepped back, fright in her eyes.

"Tell me, Hilda!"

The girl saw that Ilme's shoulders were trembling. Her own throat was dry, and she could only stammer: "Taavi . . . Taavi should not go. . . ."

"Would they set Lembit free?"

"Yes, perhaps—yes!" Hilda burst into tears.

The men were slumped forward and seemed to be preoccupied with things that were very close to the damp floor. Tõmm straightened the floor mat that was woven out of willow twigs, as if somebody's stumbling foot had just mussed it up.

"Tõmm!" Ilme turned to her brother.

"What? The damned mat, the men don't know what a decent piece of work is, all these thick sharp ends sticking out right in front of the bed. . . ."

"Would they let. . . ."

"How do I know? They want to get Taavi; that's all."

Ilme gasped and coughed, pressing her hands to her breast. Hilda tried to cover her with the blanket, but she pushed the girl away.

"Then—then I'll go myself. I can't leave Lembit like that."

Osvald had been growling angrily for some time in the corner. Now he straightened himself brusquely.

"You and your talk!" He scowled at Tõmm. "Boy! Of course they would set Lembit free." He puffed and gesticulated wildly with his hands, pivoting on one spot. "What do we know about it? We cannot know, but this is certain, that they would set the boy free."

When Taavi entered with Värdi, they all looked at him with guilty faces.

"Taavi," Ilme shouted. "Osvald said that they would set Lembit free, if. . . ."

The man threw the rifle into the corner.

"Go and take Leonard's place," he ordered the hired man of Hiie. "Osvald said. . . . What does he have to say? Idiot! What do you say?" he said, turning to face Osvald.

"I . . . what would I . . . I would shoot the gun empty and—period," Osvald mumbled.

"Then shoot it empty and don't stick your nose where it doesn't belong. Understand?"

"Damn it, I may do just that," Osvald growled and climbed upstairs.

Ilme turned her face toward the wall. Taavi did not want to go. Taavi did not want to save his son.

X

Days passed without relief. Taavi was often away from Taevasaar. He only wanted to be alone to take leave of the one he would never see alive any more.

320

Taavi remembered Lembit well—the birth of his son, his own pride, Ilme's happiness, and the satisfaction of the grandparents. He remembered how his son had gradually begun to take notice of life around him, how he had stretched out his hands for this or that object, how he had smiled for the first time, how he had begun to sit up, stand, and take his first stumbling steps, how the first words had come as a surprise to himself, how his joyous laughter had become louder and louder, how the floor began to resound from his running, and how his light curls had gathered sunlight for everybody: a little bearcub, everybody's darling, the healthy and lively child of young parents. There were thousands of images in his memory, thousands of ties that bound him to his son, that he could see and feel now with a strange clarity, feel as part of his own life, the part that meant most and was most valuable.

They had beaten Lembit in the prison with their rifle butts, when the boy had stumbled on the stairs. They had beaten his child, his own little son. Rage and despair filled Taavi, bringing tears to his eyes when he thought of it.

Roaming restlessly through the forest, Taavi met Peeter of Valba. The first thing he saw was the horse of the old man. The mare was tethered on the slope, and, noticing Taavi, she began to point with her head toward him. Taavi stood and looked at the animal for some time. When the horse approached him slowly, moving her head up and down all the time, he heard the voice of the old man behind him: "Miira is saying hello. She thinks you are a friend."

Taavi turned around. The old man was standing quite close to him, holding a piece of rope in his hand, and smiling. In spite of the cold weather he was only in his waistcoat. The sleeves of his shirt were rolled up and his old, peaked cap was pushed far back.

"The animals are good company," he chuckled. "I spent the night here, had to keep an eye on the cow. I slept at Miira's side. She is smart, and funny, too. She won't lie down until I have stretched out under the bush. Then she comes and lies down at my side. Funny how the animals long for human company. When I went to see the cow under the shelter, she was up just like that and wanted to come with me. And then in the morning there was a little black and white bull-calf. Come and take a look."

"A calf is a calf. What's so special to look at?" Taavi answered indifferently, but walked nevertheless with the old man toward the dense thicket of young fir trees.

"They sleep together at night, the cow and the horse. They are used to that. But when I come from the moor, then they run to meet me like children, and they're happy. Well, here is my family."

A farm wagon, covered with tarpaulin, was standing among the young firs under a couple of ancient, sturdy pines. A small shelter, made of branches, was nearby. A fire was burning in front of it. A metal kettle was hanging from a raw alder branch that was placed on two forked sticks stuck into the ground. Peeter took Taavi straight to the shelter.

The cow was ruminating, and fresh hay was heaped in front of her. The calf was in an enclosure in the most protected corner.

"Look! It's going to be a fat bull," he chuckled, looking at the little animal that he had wrapped in his own coat.

"How are you planning to keep them until spring?"

Peeter's laughing mood disappeared, and his bearded face became serious. He backed slowly out of the shelter and looked at the roots of the fir trees.

"Well, the calf could be slaughtered pretty soon, but I don't have the heart to kill the cow. She just came into milk. That would really be a pity. Yes, it's too bad. My wife nursed that animal. She was a sickly heifer, that's why . . . that's why I took her along, because my wife had taken such pains with her," he said reverently. "The rest of the cattle stayed behind. I suppose they suffered plenty at night, before the neighbours noticed and had mercy on them. But I took along my wife's cow and my own workhorse."

Yes, Taavi knew the story of Peeter of Valba.

"What are you cooking here? Tar or resin or what?"

"This is medicine for your wife's hand," Peeter answered, poking the embers together. "What can you do here in the woods? I looked at it. It's still full of pus. It will get well all right, but the healing process needs to be speeded up. I went to the village at night, got some honey from my brother-in-law, and am now brewing it here. Resin from the fir, honey, ironweed roots, and few other herbs. You have to be careful cooking it, so it will be just hot enough and boil long enough. This will draw out the fever from a wound and heal it."

The old man looked at him with his grey eyes—kind and helpful, Taavi thought. He felt sympathy for him. Such old men had repeatedly proved to Taavi the vigour of their people, the understanding between young and old, their mutual interdependence and solidarity. They stayed so strangely unmoved on their last journey, as if they no longer fully grasped exactly what was happening to them. When life would not let them stay in the background, the old men joined the young even in reckless gestures—shared the trenches with their sons and grandsons, nailed the windows and doors of their homes with boards and posted a warning: "Whoever comes to take over will be shot."

Peeter milked the cow, and then cooked a milk and egg custard in the small iron kettle.

"This makes me swallow my tongue," Taavi praised. They ate straight from the kettle, taking turns with the only spoon that the old man had in his wagon. "I can't recall when I ate anything so good."

"You have to cook it just that long. If it gets too much, it will be tough and spoiled. My blessed wife, she really could cook. I don't know much about such things." Each time Peeter mentioned his wife he raised his glance and looked directly into Taavi's eyes, whilst his finger swept past his nose, diverting his gaze again into the fire, the mossy ground, or the tips of his boots. At length he said: "Your son . . . they say he's in prison?"

"In prison, since last autumn," Taavi murmured.

Peeter did not speak more about it. Taavi's situation was a little worse, he figured, than his own. It had been easier to nail down the doors and windows and drive off into the woods, with the cow tied to the wagon. Peeter had lost his son, lost his wife too. Nobody's advice would bring them back.

Yet each other's company was pleasant to them, for they both knew how to pass by painful wounds without hurting the other, and this was great wisdom.

Taavi remained in the forest for the whole day. He walked around, sat on the clods smoking, watched leafless trees, red pines, and the cold sky above them that was pale blue and comfortless. He seemed to have forgotten the moor of Verisoo and Taevasaar with its damp earth huts. He picked some cranberries from the ground, felt the pangs of hunger, and smoked again. He did not return to Taevasaar for the night, but climbed into a hay barn to sleep. He dug himself deep into the hay, slept a little, but lay awake most of the night because of the cold, which became very cutting just before dawn. The ground was frozen in the morning, and the pools were covered with ice. The ice was rather thick for one night's frost, Taavi thought, shivering. Sparse snowflakes began to fall about noon.

"They fall in circles. They won't stay on the ground for long," he muttered to himself, his hands in his pockets and his head on his chest. The snow, but even more so his increasing hunger awakened him from his stupor. He decided to visit his daughter's grave and to speak a few words with the farmer of Hiie. Days were quickly passing and he had to tell Ignas how things were. In any case he ought to get his skis from Hiie, and this would be the right time to go. He would reach Metsaoti before nightfall.

It was dark already when he stood on the river bank near the Hiie farm. He had come directly across the Lepiku fields, had climbed over fences, and was now looking into the black water which contrasted sharply with the snow-covered banks. The firs and alders on the opposite bank stretched their snowy branches like white arms toward him from the darkness. Snow was still falling quietly and peacefully. The sky was clouded, but when he turned his face upward he felt the snow on his cheeks like the touch of the sky.

Taavi found a little sturdy wooden cross under the familiar birch tree. He swept the snow away from one arm of the cross, but left it standing on the other—he liked the snow; it was like a decoration. Then he folded his hands for a moment and turned through the meadow toward the house.

Pontus ran to meet him by the bathhouse. The dog's barking turned into delighted yelping when he smelled Taavi. He recognizes me, the man thought. There was no doubt the dog knew him. This meeting gave Taavi as much pain as it brought joy to the animal. He ordered the dog to be quiet, but Pontus was too excited and let loose a short happy yelp.

Ignas, who had heard Pontus bark, was standing at the doorway, holding his hands in the pockets of his trousers and leaning motionless against the doorpost.

"You, Taavi!"

They shook hands and entered the hallway together.

"How is Krōōt?" Taavi inquired.

"Not too well," the farmer answered quietly. "Her right side is paralysed. But she is talking again, and we can make sense of it. I think it would be advisable not to see her. Everything is still too recent," Ignas said. He added in a whisper: "I'll take my coat and we'll go to the threshing floor. It's warm there. Or would you like something to eat?"

"Yes, I would. I haven't eaten a bite for two days."

"Well now," Ignas said with reproach in his voice, "why do you starve yourself like that? But go to the threshing floor anyway, and I'll bring something for you as quickly as I can."

Taavi found a black figure in front of the stove who jumped up when he saw him. It was old Aadu Mustkivi. He mumbled excitedly and stared at the visitor with wide open eyes. Taavi tried to make some encouraging gestures, pointing at his chest, but Aadu retreated behind the rye that was drying on the rafters and piled on the floor, and observed Taavi from there.

When Taavi had settled himself comfortably in front of the big open fireplace, Ignas came, a little basket of bread and meat under his arm, a pitcher of milk in his hand. Without saying a word Taavi began to devour the food. The farmer of Hiie pulled down a sheaf of rye, sat on it and filled his pipe.

"Hilda went over to Taevasaar last night. They were worried about you over there. The men were afraid you had given yourself up to the Russians. I don't know what you have decided, but I don't think it would help one bit." There was a long silence. Aadu's mumbling became louder.

"It might not help, but it might make my conscience clean," Taavi answered.

"I have thought about it too. But they will demand others. And you must not hold one any more precious than another if you want to be just!" Ignas said heavily. "It means that one must be sacrificed for perhaps a larger number."

Taavi could not answer anything. Even the food he was eating suddenly became irrelevant, so that he had difficulty in swallowing.

"You're threshing rye?" he asked.

"That's right, Aadu and I, and Hilda helps sometimes. The threshing machine won't get here from the tractor station before the spring, but nobody will extend the deadlines for deliveries and taxes."

"Are the taxes heavy?"

"What do you think?" Ignas turned his face toward the darkness. "The life of a farmer was better during serfdom than it is now. At least there was less terror. Life is getting worse here than it would be in prison, and for what? Just because we are like God created us, because we are human beings, not bums or vagrants. But it's no use talking; it only makes one feel worse."

"We'll see how long it will last this time."

"Only those who will live will see," Ignas agreed. "They are discharging some men from the Estonian corps now—invalids. You can hardly tell that they were ever men."

They were silent again. Speaking somehow seemed a little strange to them, for their incoherent, anguished thoughts were crowded out by fresh ones before they had materialized into words.

"Hilda didn't sleep again last night. She ran to Taevasaar to . . . or did you see her?"

"No, how could I have seen her?"

"Of course not. She really went for your sake, because your mother was here today."

Taavi moved as if to get up, but remained nevertheless on his seat.

"She is quite worn out and sick. No wonder—she's living in the unheated bathhouse. The committee took her cow, the Russians slaughtered her pig, she doesn't have a chicken left. She managed to harvest some of her potatoes."

"She came here? How . . . how could she get away?"

"She was out of bread, and then she had heard that you were nearby. She had heard all the rest too. I tried to comfort her as best I could, but she is not a child. She wanted to go to the woods and try to find you. She'd lived all these months without any news, with the soldiers after her at every step."

"How could she get here then?"

"The soldiers packed up their belongings this morning and left."

Now Taavi jumped up. Why hadn't Ignas said that right away? That meant the way to his mother was open!

Taavi's mother remained quite calm when she saw her son. She had been waiting for him, sitting near the fireplace in the sauna and feeding the fire with faggots. She pulled her son wordlessly inside and lighted the lamp, shaking it worriedly to make sure there was some kerosene left in it. Only her eyelids were wet with tears.

At first Taavi was unable to say anything. His eyes wandered over the tiny square room, taking in the big stove, the bench that served as his mother's bed, the little table, and a couple of chairs. Trunks and parcels were under the sleeping bench, and his mother's clothes were hanging on the walls. The floor was covered with fresh fir twigs, and their smell together with the crackling fire created an atmosphere that reminded one at once of Christmas and of funerals.

"This is how you live," Taavi sighed, shaking the snow from his clothes.

"This is how I live," his mother repeated. "It's difficult at times, but that is not because of the way I live. Thank God, I have a roof over my head." She took the lamp and looked for a long time at her son's face in its light, caressing with her fingertips his scars and his scraggly beard. Her mouth twitched painfully. "You are tired," she said. "But—now that I have seen you, you must go again. Here. . . ," she took a little parcel, wrapped in a kerchief. "I put some things together for you, some food, a woollen sweater, some underwear."

"You shouldn't have, Mother." Taavi remembered that his mother had gone to Hiie to ask for some bread, and now she gave it all to him. She gave the last bite from her own mouth. "Thank you! But we are really not hard up for food right now. We have plenty of everything. We live like human beings."

"But you look like skin and bones. Your mother still recognizes you, but somebody who is a little less familiar will think you a complete stranger. Let's go, I'll walk with you for a while. It's safer to talk in the woods, and you can get away if anything should happen."

"And leave you behind?"

Mother took his wrist.

"Don't take a single step because of me, son. My life is over, and I have Andres, your father. I am not alone, and it will make no difference whether I go to him a day earlier or later. Now I have seen you again—it was over a year, like always—I have received my share."

Linda wrapped herself in a big shawl and put out the lamp. Taavi noticed that his mother had aged markedly during the past year. Her face was covered with wrinkles, and her hair had much more grey in it. She was somehow fragile and ethereal—like tenderness personified.

She arranged the burning faggots away from the mouth of the stove, and then they went out. It was still snowing, slowly and peacefully. Taavi stopped and looked at the dark windows of the farmhouse of Piskujõe.

"I went in there today," his mother said. "It would have been better if I hadn't gone."

"Have they left it so filthy?"

"Yes, it is awful to look at. The rooms cry at you, as if they had been violated. I'm glad Andres didn't see it, and you too," she whispered.

"We'll clean them up and put everything in order again," Taavi promised. "Perhaps I may come and help you."

"No, Taavi, don't come here any more. Nobody must come here. One has to be afraid of me now, and everybody is afraid of me. Ignas, too, not to speak of others. The mother of an outlaw. Everybody has to keep away from me, as if I had the plague." Linda's voice was quiet and sad.

"So it's all because of me," Taavi whispered, and his voice turned into an angry hiss. "The mother of an outlaw."

"Let it be, son. It won't last for ever. Although my own eyes won't see the new day, I can see clearly with my mind's eye that everything that is now will become insignificant. Let evil triumph. It is only because it feels its end coming. That's the only reason."

They were walking in the snowy woods up toward the Koolu hills.

His mother was breathing heavily—not from the walk, Taavi knew, although even her step had become short and stumbling and her body stooped forward.

"This has been a hard day for me," Linda said. "It hasn't been as hard for a long long time. Every day has its own troubles, but when I went to Hiie today, everything opened up at the same time, and it was too much all of a sudden," she whispered.

"Poor Mother. It was really too much."

"Never mind, son. If it has gone that far, the solution must be somewhere near. It must be very close, although we cannot picture it yet. I went to her grave, too. Her name was Hilja. I looked at the grave—my granddaughter, I thought. She was born, and the light went out before anyone had the chance to hear her laughing voice. Why? What did God want to say with that? Maybe worse times are ahead, and it was God's mercy that He called her away. Don't worry, son, I'll take care of the grave if I live."

"I was there myself," Taavi murmured somberly.

"Yes, it is hard. It is very hard. I thought that you ought to go, but . . . they will want all the others."

"Yes, they want all my friends. I know already what they want."

"Yes, you were in their hands, you know. Lembit is your own son. How can God place such a heavy burden on a man? How can He forget that a man is only a weak human being?"

Taavi had a feeling in his legs that seemed to force him to his knees, force him prostrate on the ground in shame, humiliation, pain and despair.

"I am torn in two, Mother! There must be some meaning in this, too, some higher purpose," he tried to stammer, but it pierced his brain like a steel chisel. You are merely trying to justify your step.

"Yes, there must be some meaning. God sacrificed His son too. He demands the same from man." She spoke with great exertion. Taavi heard how hard it was for her to breathe. "How—is Ilme? This isn't going to do something to her? To leave one's child there . . . and she's in the woods too. They said she was very sick."

She was silent again. They were standing in the shade of the fir trees, whose dark shadows formed big black circles in the night that was white from the snow. Then Linda said: "I am not holding you back, son. You yourself know best. If you think that . . . it would be your duty . . . but you have no right to bring death to the others!"

Then they turned back toward Piskujõe. Linda would not let her son accompany her to the courtyard. They stopped to say good-bye.

"Be a support for Ilme," she begged. "I know how Andres supported me, and still does. A woman needs support, and Ilme—what she has had to bear is more than a human mind can carry. Taavi, stay with her. She has been a good wife to you."

"Yes, she has been very good."

"You'll get over all this some day. Go now, Taavi. God be with you, son."

Taavi followed her with his eyes, as she vanished into the snowy night, wrapped in her big shawl. When the darkness and the trees hid his mother from his view, he could still hear her careful, tired steps in the soft, clean snow. They made him weak and helpless.

XI

The snow melted. Even the frozen earth thawed up again. This pleased the men, although it meant a lot of work. Taavi worked from morning to night, often soaked from the rain and covered with mud up to his loins. The mines they had placed in the moor had to be taken out and carefully stored on the edge of the bog, to wait for snow. Taavi specialized in the handling of explosives, as if he had discovered a favourite game that absorbed him completely. He liked this activity, for it demanded his complete attention, so that he could not think his own thoughts. It was a kind of rest for him.

When Taavi left the bunker in the morning, Ilme looked after him with desperate eyes. If she happened to be asleep when Taavi returned, the man's glance stayed long on her face, which, even in her sleep, was distorted into a screaming mask. Ilme's dry cough had not become any worse, but she remained on her narrow, hard cot for days. She did not talk to anybody, shrieked and cried in her sleep, and Tõmm was the only one from whom she inquired news about her father and mother.

This situation made the men in the Snake Pit uneasy, and they tried to be outside as much as they could. Osvald had butchered the calf of Peeter of Valba in the forest, and its meat was salted in a barrel. Since it was to be expected that the cow, too, would have to be killed, they dug a new storage room—simply a hole in the ground, for they had no timber to line it with—and covered it with branches. Seeing these preparations, Peeter himself walked around with a defeated mien and brooded new plans for keeping the cow over the winter. Sometimes he was very melancholy and crushed, but he never forgot to bring Ilme some milk from each milking. This had become his duty, and he fulfilled it rigorously, until one day the captain forbade him to cross the open moor in daytime.

The men passed by Taavi with their faces choked up with questions that nobody dared ask. One night, when Taavi was still busy with the mines, Leonard came to him.

"Don't play with them like that," he warned. "It will take half your head and your back molars along with it, if it blows up."

"That's what it was made for."

Leonard was silent. When Taavi passed him and stood under the dwarf pines, his companion ambled after him. Taavi took his pipe from his pocket and began to stuff it with tobacco.

"I wonder whether you should. It's dark already!"

"It sure is," Taavi mumbled and stuck the pipe back in his pocket. "What did you want?" he asked brusquely.

"Nothing—that you could give me. I feel that life is getting damned dull here. I'm going away."

"Going away? You should know by now that one doesn't leave Taevasaar on his own. Whoever comes here is subject to the laws—one for all—and does not leave except with orders to be carried out."

"Just like prison!"

"It's a little better than that—like protective custody."

"I won't hold out until spring—without women like that. If we could only take a trip to the village now and then. I have been thinking—that I'll go out, as I told you before. If I am able to live like a human being for a little while, my mind will get limber again. Here in the moor you rot like a carcass."

"Uh," Taavi growled and returned to the bunker.

To everybody's astonishment, it was Eedi of Piibu who disappeared from Taevasaar a few days later. His traceless departure caused much concern, especially as not even Taavi would have expected him to undertake such a step. The nightly watchmen had not seen him go. Nobody had noticed his preparations, how he had packed his rucksack and left the bunker. He had faithfully performed his sentry duty and then vanished. The captain invited the men of the Snake Pit for a parley. He was grim and sombre.

"This is nothing but a dirty mess. This is a thoughtless playing with the lives of everybody. Now tell me what will come of it—a man of officer's rank, whose sick wife has found shelter with us, is lost for days. Now one of his companions is gone, has packed up his things and gone. Where? Would Lieutenant Raudoja be kind enough to enlighten us? He should know his companions."

Taavi seized the rough boards of the bunk bed with his hand, as if he needed support. Actually he did it in order to find contact with reality and not to lose his self-control under the direct accusation of his superior. He realized that the old officer was losing his composure because of fear, and because his authority was being flaunted. He saw the angry eyes of the captain directed at him, and the expectant faces of the men.

"Shut up, you lout," Värdi muttered, gnashing his teeth, crouched in the corner of the bunk bed.

"The problem of leadership has been the greatest misfortune of our people," Taavi said in a hard, sarcastic voice. "The general level of our people is too high, and that of our leaders too low. We have had more back-room politicians and cowards than you could shake a stick at during these last years. The men who could look the people in the eye and say that this is it, and this is what must be done, have been deported to the slave labour camps of Siberia, and new ones have not yet had time to grow up."

"You don't seem to have the slightest notion about military discipline! None of the men who have come from Finland seem to care about it. . . ."

Värdi hissed again, with a warning in his voice.

329

"Excuse me, sir," Taavi said calmly. "If you have a grudge against the Finland fighters, if you yourself did not succeed in getting across the gulf, don't hurl that at me. You personally know as well as anyone who was at the front how the Estonian soldier has had to search and find his way in his fight for the homeland. Don't forget that many of the Finland fighters were formerly on the eastern front, and there have never been misunderstandings among the fighting men themselves. We have also understood those who, even in spite of their officer's rank, have kept themselves aloof from the battle! If some man finds it hard to stay here, he leaves. Hangs himself from the branch of a fir tree or does something even worse. This group here consists of men who have joined it voluntarily. It is not a military platoon. Quite apart from our military lives, we all have our private lives—our families and homes outside Taevasaar. Every problem should be discussed, and your word will be listened to, but the decision of the majority should prevail. Of course, if we have to wage a battle, your orders will direct the operation."

"And at all other times we'll have a parliament?" the captain asked mockingly, red in the face. "Would you answer what kind of a man was your companion?"

"He was a real man, sir," Leonard answered impatiently from the corner. "When he started to hit the Russians, we could all have learned a lesson from him."

"Maybe he'll come back?" someone hesitated.

"Damn it, that won't do!" The captain got so angry that he jumped up. "That won't do, if everybody leaves without a moment's notice, as if he's got to go, nobody knows where or for how long. I must know where the man is going. If you don't understand that, then we'd better leave Taevasaar right away, for the Russians will get here sooner or later."

"That's for sure, they'll be here sooner or later," Taavi said.

The mouth of the captain twitched, but he did not say anything, only sat down.

Mart of Liiskaku, whose turn it was to keep watch, entered at the same moment, and announced excitedly to Taavi: "Ilme wants to go home! I caught her at the edge of the moor. It's lucky the mines had been taken out. I persuaded her to go back to the bunker. Come quickly, she may run into a bog hole!"

"That's what you get," the captain mumbled, but Taavi had no time to listen to what else he had to say. He ran out, with Mart after him.

Halfway down to the Snake Pit, Taavi saw his wife back again on the open moor, some distance away from Taevasaar. She did not know the pathway the men used, but had begun to run at random, aiming for the nearest wood, not knowing that a completely impassable stretch of bog holes was directly ahead. Taavi ran after her as fast as he could.

When Taavi came within calling distance Ilme paid no attention to his call, but seemed to try to plunge ahead with even greater speed. She looked across her shoulder once and staggered on, stumbling between the clods.

330

"Are you crazy?" Taavi panted, grabbing her by the sleeve. His grasp was so strong that the woman swayed and fell to her knees.

Then she struggled to get free from Taavi's hold, rose to her feet, in a blind hurry, panting in a wild effort: "Let me go! I am going after Lembit. I won't let them kill my child."

"Silly. There are bog holes ahead. Be sensible. You'll drown. You won't get anywhere'"

"You are lying! You want to cheat me again. Let me go, I won't ever come back. My mother is in bed, paralysed. I want to see her, before. . . . I want my child. I want Lembit."

Taavi pulled her roughly.

"Turn around, Ilme!" he shouted. "Right away, and we'll go back. Do you understand?" And then Taavi did something he had never done before. He hit his wife. It was more a rough push than a blow, but the woman sank between the clods of the moor, overcome by surprise as much as weakness. She looked at her husband for a moment with wide open eyes and then pressed her face against a bush of sharp-edged grass, screaming in a fit of hysteria.

"You hit me, Taavi. You hit me," she wailed. "I only wanted to save Lembit. I have never done anything against your will. Never, Taavi. They are killing him." Her voice broke into an unintelligible whisper.

"And you would have told them that I am here. You would have sent the NKVD to get me." Taavi's lips moved, and his voice sounded inhuman.

"God, be merciful! Lembit—your own son."

When Taavi attempted to lift her, she refused to get up, dug her fingers into the moss, and resisted him with all her might.

Taavi lifted her up and took her in his arms. Ilme had no strength to struggle any more. Suddenly she was weak and limp. Her eyes closed. Her arms hung lifelessly down.

It was fortunate that Tõmm had hurried after them. The young man did not ask any questions. He seemed to divine what had happened. Ilme was carried back to the prison island of Taevasaar.

When Osvald, who had hurried to the edge of the moor, saw how Taavi struck his wife, something welled up inside him so strongly that he was almost ready to shoot Taavi across the moor. However, he shook his rage off, startled at the dark flash that had taken him by surprise. Was a screw loose in his head, too, here in the moor, he asked himself. If it went on like that, soon there wouldn't be a single sober-minded man left among them. Every word of their companions offended them, they were unkind and edgy toward each other, gnashed their teeth like Värdi and were bent low under their burdens.

It was Taavi's mother who brought up a grave question. She sent word by Hilda to her son. Taavi should come immediately to Päraluha. She would be waiting near the hay barn there.

It was a stormy winter night just before Christmas. The snow fell in heavy circles, wet and sticky. The skis did not glide right and the night was too dark. Taavi was startled by his mother's sudden wish. A great sorrow must be troubling her. In daylight, Russian patrols circled the village of Metsaoti. Only the darkness and the snowstorm made it possible for his mother to contact him. The NKVD had even been to Hiie, asking for Ilme.

Taavi cursed when wet branches hit him in the face in the dark and dropped slushy snow between his neck and his collar. His mother was crouching near the corner of the barn, leeward from the storm, frozen and small.

"You came so quickly," Linda marvelled. "Hilda only went an hour or two ago. You shouldn't have strained yourself running so fast. I am not in such a great hurry. How is Ilme? Still waiting?"

"Still waiting. She looks at me as if I were a criminal."

"Because of Lembit?" Linda sighed heavily. Taavi took off his skis and leaned them against the hay barn. "Don't get angry with me for calling you, at night like this, but a question has bothered me for a long time, and God knows how everything will turn out. I'll begin to walk toward home, you can walk with me."

When they had walked in silence for quite some distance, she suddenly stopped and asked in a calm voice, hiding her inner disquiet.

"What was the story of the capture last autumn? Were they caught at sea?"

"No, on the shore."

"On the shore. Did Ilme say that?"

"I haven't got around to asking her. How could I dig into her with questions like that—and now!" He realized suddenly that he had asked almost nothing from his wife. Everything had been so shocking. He had not known what to ask. "I have two companions who got away from the shore, probably the only ones who escaped. Frontier guards and army units encircled them the very moment when the boat arrived. Many were shot right then and there. . . ."

"How was it that Marta was unaware of that, when she got away too? How could Marta say that she saw the boat leave? Tell me that!"

"I don't know. Maybe she left the shore earlier," Taavi muttered. His former suspicions flared up again.

"Ask Ilme. Marta said that she saw them sail away with her own eyes. How can she lie about something like that? She said it to me. Taavi, you haven't . . . there hasn't . . . been anything between you two?"

Taavi remembered how shamelessly Marta had tempted him: how she had come to him when he was lying in bed in Marta's apartment, sick with fever. Even the memory repelled him.

"No," he answered gloomily.

"Of course not. What was I thinking about!" His mother seemed angry with herself. "But I have such a feeling that there's blood on her hands. I have always felt uneasy about her, ever since Marta's husband was arrested, that she did it herself. Wanted to get rid of the old man.

And then the rumours. I cannot believe them, but it keeps nagging. Marta told me that she does not care about anything."

"So you think that Marta. . . ."

"May God forgive me my thoughts, but I am sure that she knows more than we do. She had something to do with it, and that something is no good," Linda said with conviction.

Yes, Taavi's own thoughts had wandered the same way. Suspicions had gnawed at his soul, but he had been unwilling to believe them. He could not believe so much evil of a woman, and he had suppressed his suspicions and doubts.

"How could I see her?" Taavi asked.

"Marta?"

"Yes. Otherwise we'll never have it straight. They say there are Russians at Roosi. I can't go there."

"Keep away, son! Keep away. Marta—she can bring nothing but trouble. She means destruction. I don't know anything else, but I know that."

Although they did not speak more about it, the question remained on Taavi's mind like a smouldering fire that had been fanned again to an open flame.

Yet it must have worried Taavi's mother even more, if it made the old woman come at midnight into the faraway forests to ask her son for clarification.

Taavi slept in the bunker a couple of hours toward morning, but his sleep was restless. He had not slept soundly for a long time.

Most of the men were still asleep, when he went to his wife and sat down on the edge of her bed. Ilme, who had also been awake for a long time, moved away from him.

"How did you sleep?"

The woman did not answer, making only a repelling movement. This question was superfluous.

"How long do I have to stay here?" Ilme asked in return, her tired voice barely audible. She kept her eyes glued to the wall. The air in the little room was warm and stuffy, because the iron stove had been heated.

"As long as the rest of us. Nobody knows. Tell me, what actually happened last autumn when you were arrested? When did you see Marta last?"

Ilme was silent for some time and then answered slowly: "In the hay barn. I don't remember. Perhaps I saw her on the shore, before she fell. She must have been shot or remained between the boulders, wounded, for I did not see her later among the prisoners."

"How did she come to be shot?" Taavi interrupted her. "Marta is right now at the district administration house of Kalgina, living at Roosi. How could she have fallen? She came back from the coast and told me that she had seen you sail off in the boat!" Taavi had raised his voice in agitation.

But Ilme was still more excited from what she had heard. She struggled to sit up.

"Is Marta at Roosi? How can she be at Roosi? I saw her fall myself. Didn't I see it?" she asked, as if Taavi should know.

"Marta of Roosi is at home and is working in the district administration house," Taavi repeated impatiently. "I told you she came to bring me word, a couple of days later, that you had left. I was in her apartment. I went to get the jewellery, you remember. She did not have anything. I could not find anything. When she came home herself, she showed me some jewellery in the closet, which she must have put there later to deceive me."

Taavi spoke hurriedly. The men had awakened and were listening to their conversation. Osvald, who had been thumbing in the language textbook Eedi of Piibu had left behind, bent low over the book.

Ilme was silent for a while, as if she could not understand anything any more, and then exploded with a scream: "It was Marta of Roosi! She called the Russians! She informed the frontier guard. Good Lord, it was Marta herself."

The men listened to her quietly, and more than one pair of eyes turned toward Osvald. The hired man of Hiie threw the book against the table and stood up, his eyes dazed and rolling. He remained standing, as if he did not know all of a sudden what to do with his big body. Taavi, too, had risen to his feet, leaving the bed of his wife so quickly that the coloured rug fell to the floor.

"Damn it," Tõmm swore, his voice still sleepy.

"We have to consider that seriously, men. We have to add up the facts and weigh them one by one," Taavi said coldly. He felt suddenly that the room was oppressively hot. It made his voice husky. He walked back and forth in the free space between the beds. Water sloshed under the floorboards.

"Was it Marta? Was it really Marta?" Osvald mumbled. He remembered the peculiar way Marta had acted when they met for the last time in the storage barn of Roosi, and his body became hotter and hotter. He remembered Marta's words from that last night: "I am afraid that many things may come to light now. Even the dead may come back to life. I would like to leave Kalgina now. I'd run if I could!" Osvald did not remember everything, but he remembered how Marta had acted because Taavi had escaped from prison.

"Marta wanted you for herself," Ilme stammered to her husband. "She has wanted you all her life, and that's why she sent you away from the coast and betrayed us."

The truth was too naked to be believed at once. The men jumped from their cots one by one, and began to pull on their boots. Värdi puffed and swore, spit out and looked for his glasses, swearing even louder.

"We should drag this woman here," Leonard said.

"Throw her into the bog hole, head first," Mart of Liiskaku answered.

"Later, of course," Leonard sneered. "But first. . . ."

"Keep your damned jaws shut," Värdi snarled at him. "Where did you put my glasses?" he growled at Mart of Liiskaku, his bedfellow, with uncontrolled anger.

Tõmm fumbled with the coffeepot at the stove. He threw a glance at Osvald and said: "You should open your mouth a little, too. You know Marta better than anybody. You really found the right one!"

Osvald slammed Eedi of Piibu's language textbook on the table again, and went to his cot. He searched for a long time in his rucksack, did not find anything, and remained sitting. He growled a few confused oaths, but when he noticed that the light did not shine directly into his face any more, he began to calm down. He wanted to be left alone. He had to smoke and think. And Marta had said that they could have had big children by now. Damn it to hell!

Taavi sat down behind the table and began to clean his revolver. His hands moved quietly, and he did not even raise his eyes any more.

"You think that. . . ," Mart of Liiskaku blurted.

"There's nothing to think. This must be cleared up!"

"You can't get close. The Russians are all around," Tõmm said.

"Be quiet, all of you," Taavi answered with a cold ring in his voice. "I don't care much about anything right now, and I have my revolver in my hand."

When the snow melted again, Taavi began his reconnaissance trips around the farmhouse of Roosi. He spent days there, not achieving anything. Only soldiers were moving in and around the farm. Watching in the forest between Roosi and the village of Harukurgu gave no results either. He did not see Marta on the forest road, neither in the morning dusk nor in the evening. Taavi just could not figure out which road the woman used to go to work.

One day when he was in the woods together with Leonard, they met the fool of Võllamäe. Reku told them Marta had been living in the district administration house for the last few weeks. "It's easier for her to fuck around there, that's why," Reku explained seriously.

Taavi was disappointed by the news. In the district administration house! Then she must really be afraid. "Ah let's go," he said impatiently, walking on.

Leonard's attention was turned to the demented lad.

"Why did you let her move into the district administration house? Now your bride is gone for good," he teased.

The boy backed away, his mouth open with surprise.

"Reku has no bride. Reku's bride is still in the top of a birch tree."

"Aren't you a man or what?"

"Of course Reku is a man. Reku is a general, and you, silly, don't know even that."

When Leonard moved on, Reku ran with him.

"Reku wants to talk about his bride," the boy announced shyly, and his little eyes were suddenly bright. His long hair was hanging in

335

dishevelled strands over his forehead, giving a wild expression to his face that was covered with a short, stubbly beard. He looked altogether savage, with black rings of dirt on his neck, the wet and stinking dog's skin over his shoulder, and dirty straw in his boots. He walked along, stooped under his burdens. Evidently he was on a long journey again: he had his rucksack with a sooty metal kettle on his shoulders, his rubber boots attached to his belt, and the hunting gun strapped to his back. "Reku wants to talk about his bride!" he repeated eagerly.

"What is there to talk about? Don't you know yourself?"

"Of course Reku knows! But Reku is not allowed to."

"That's what I said, that you aren't a man or anything."

The boy stopped abruptly.

"Just say once more that Reku isn't a man, and—damn it, you'll get some lead in your face right now!"

"Oh-oh!" Leonard was suddenly frightened. "Well, now, come on," he muttered, and the back of his neck became moist under his cap. "All right, we'll talk about women."

"Reku does not want to talk about women. Reku wants to talk about his bride, don't you understand? Let's talk about Marta of Roosi."

"Agreed," Leonard forced himself to say. "She's a ripe morsel."

"Marta is a tramp."

"So she isn't good enough for you?" Damn that Taavi, walking away and leaving him at the mercy of this crazy bastard! And the boy was clinging to him like a cocklebur, mouth watering and eyes sparkling.

"Why not," Ebehard of Võllamäe smiled, flushed red in the face, and lowered his glance bashfully. "She would be good enough, but. . . ," he turned his back slowly toward his companion.

"Well, why don't you go ahead?"

The boy looked at him for a long time full of suspicion. Then he shrieked suddenly at the top of his voice, threw both arms up over his head, gave a long and triumphant howl, and ran off into the woods.

Leonard had lost his breath, and his body was covered with goose pimples. When he set out to catch up with Taavi on his wobbly knees, every small clod made him fall flat on his face.

Taavi himself met Reku again a few days later. He was surprised, when he saw the familiar burdened figure right behind him in the wood near the district administration house.

"Why are you following me?" Taavi was annoyed. He was even a little frightened, for he had not heard anything—neither a step nor the breaking of a twig. His instinct told him to turn around, and he found himself face to face with the madman.

"Why should I follow you?" the boy said contemptuously. "What should Reku care about Taavi of Piskujõe? Even Andres says that Taavi is still wet behind the ears."

"Don't talk so loud! The Russians. . . ."

"Are you scared? There's nobody near whose soul is still in his body."

"How do you know?"

"Do you think Reku is a fool? Reku knows. Don't jump at me like that. The times have changed. Now Reku can slap the face of every city slicker!"

Taavi felt suddenly that there was something between him and the madman. The superior airs of the other disturbed him, and the boy's unshakeable self-confidence made him uneasy. The look from the little eyes of the boy was not at all friendly.

"What are you looking for? See that you get going!" Taavi said angrily.

The boy only laughed.

"Reku is looking for Marta."

"Marta?" Taavi was embarrassed. "Why are you looking for Marta?"

"Because she is good to look at."

"Good to look at?" Taavi still did not get it. The boy shifted his weight bashfully from foot to foot. "What do you want with her? Speak up!"

Now Reku retreated behind a bush, giggling idiotically.

"Reku wants!"

"Wait now, wait!" Taavi got excited. "Have you seen Marta?" He hurried after the boy, but Reku had vanished without a trace. A solitary dog barked somewhere in the distance.

Taavi himself watched for several days on the other side of the village of Harukurgu and took trips quite close to the district administration house of Kalgina. One morning he even crawled into the garden of the house and hid in a dense hedge of young firs, where he stayed for half a day. He shivered from the cold, but could not bring himself to leave his hideout. His eyes were glued to the whitewashed walls of the building, and this time he had luck. For a moment he saw Marta's slim figure between the buildings and heard her voice. The woman was laughing and talking merrily. Taavi's hand slipped to his gun, but this was a futile move. If he should kill Marta like that, the secret would never be revealed. Then he also saw a big, hulking man, dressed in a black raincoat and a militiaman's uniform cap. They both sat on a motorcycle behind the corner of the house and drove away. Taavi's tongue was prickly from cursing, and he could not find words that would have been juicy enough. He had no luck, or perhaps Marta had too much of it. He should be standing on some roadside now, ready to shoot the militiaman, ditch the motorcycle, and if the woman's neck remained unbroken, to stand face to face with the truth. His limbs stiff from the cold, Taavi climbed out of the hedge and walked directly across the open fields toward the woods. He did not even look back to check if he was observed from the district administration house or whether any soldier was taking an overdue interest in the passing figure.

Then he got the reckless idea to break into the district administration house. Investigate the place thoroughly first, and then step right in front of Marta. If he poked his gun in her ribs when she was asleep, she would surely keep quiet and say what she had to say. Taavi got so carried away with his idea that he suddenly felt very hot. He did not think of what he would do to Marta. He only wanted to know the truth.

But fate had different plans. It began to snow once more, wet and sticky snow that clung to skis and made it completely impossible to undertake such a long journey on foot. Taavi remained on Taevasaar and helped his companions to salt away the cow of Peeter of Valba in a barrel. After submitting to the strict orders of the captain, Peeter was as if struck with a grave illness.

Since the winter was now beginning in earnest, the captain issued several other orders, or rather repeated rules he had laid down earlier. All traffic between Taevasaar and the villages had to be stopped. They could go out only on skis, in a snowstorm. The bunkers could be heated and food could be cooked also only on stormy nights. Young fir trees were brought from the woods and stuck into the snow near the bunkers and the pathway that led to the sentries. A sentry was posted at each end of Taevasaar at night, in place of the former double watch in one spot. The captain also forbade Hilda to come to Taevasaar, except to bring word of impending danger. No action must be taken against the Russians, even if there should be some arrests or deportations in the villages. If somebody should happen to get into trouble with the soldiers, he should try to struggle loose and escape in a direction leading away from Verisoo. If somebody should be wounded and be in danger of being taken prisoner, he had to kill himself—blow himself up with a hand grenade or shoot a bullet through his head. The captain distributed poison among those of the men who thought that they might not have the nerve to finish themselves in a soldierly way. The majority laughed at his suggestion, although their hands were ready enough to accept what was offered.

Actually nobody was ready to believe that his final hour was near.

They had a one-sided radio connection with the outside world, but in spite of that many of them believed the rumours that reached them from the villagers. These were to the effect that the Russians would not be allowed to plant their roots into the country, that the Western allies wanted the Baltic countries to be free. They also heard that people were receiving letters from relatives in Sweden.

Thus the Christmas holidays came, without anybody paying much attention or counting the days. But when Christmas Eve arrived the men of the Snake Pit and the Froghole both brought a green tree into their dugouts. The kerosene lamp was hung on a nail on the wall. The Christmas tree was placed on the table on a stand carved by Osvald. The ice melted from the branches and fell like teardrops on the floor. The hut was filled with the clean, nostalgic fragrance of the fir sapling. When the tree had been brought in, the men set about cleaning their shabby living quarters and smartening themselves up as if by silent agreement. To the great surprise of everyone, a childlike smile flashed even over Ilme's tortured face. A little later she helped to sweep out the hut. She even asked if they could not make some candles out of tallow. They could not. Although the day was cloudy and gloomy, they did not want to light a fire in the stove before twilight.

Peeter Valba had left early in the morning. He had gone deep into the woods to prepare jellied meat, the traditional Christmas dish. He had saved the head and feet of the calf they had recently slaughtered, had wrapped them in a cloth soaked in brine to keep them fresh. In the evening the men were supposed to carry the meat cauldron home, so that there might be at least a little Christmas fare.

Large, light snowflakes began floating from the sky at dusk. The men went out to look at the falling snow. It was refreshing, soft and peaceful. It hurt them, but washed their hearts clean. Every one of them remembered some particular Christmas—driving to church to the accompaniment of sleigh bells, the chiming of church bells, the flicker of candles which shone from childhood all through a man's life. Some pictured their Christmases in the country, on the family farm; others in town apartments, richly or poorly furnished. All divisions crumbled on that evening. The men did not speak. Those stern, forgotten soldiers, left in an eternal night, they just watched the peaceful falling of the snow and kept their own counsel. Each of them felt as if he were just about to reenter the warmth of his home, of his own family, which he had missed for years.

Ilme uttered two words: "Christmas Eve!"

If one counted separately all the sounds in these words, the sounds would number less than there were feelings in this statement—entreating, yearning, unhappy, desperate feelings. She made a sudden move toward Taavi, as if she wanted to rush to him for shelter and protection, but instead she turned her unsure steps toward the entrance of the bunker.

Hilda came at dusk. Since Peeter of Valba and his men arrived simultaneously with their jellied meat, there were so many voices outside that many of the men could not resist going out.

Hilda had covered the long distance on skis. She was white all over from the falling snow. Even her bright cap was completely white, and the white tassel stuck out like a rabbit's ear. The men helped to carry her heavy knapsack inside. This fragile girl had strength. The sack felt heavy even in Tõmm's strong hands. The girl was always serious of late, but her voice sounded bright when she wished the men of the Snake Pit a merry Christmas. She shook the snow from her clothes and her curly hair and took off Krõõt's short sheepskin jacket, which she had worn over Ilme's old skiing suit. Her face glowed from the exertion of the long journey.

The men kept gazing at her, as if she were a being from another world, who somehow had been compelled to cross their paths. Her coming always brought excitement, but today, because of the significance of the season, it became a gala affair. After reporting the latest news of the village and the district—these came first in order of importance—she busied herself with her knapsack. She fussed with it under the Christmas tree, and the men gathered around her like expectant children. And behold, there was something there for everyone, in addition to the freshness of youth and the purity of the snowy winter evening that she carried with her. Hilda's own eyes began to sparkle while she distributed the presents: a pair of woollen socks for one, fly-patterned mittens for another, a soft, fringed muffler for the third. Tõmm was singled out for special attention: he received a grey sweater, with a pattern in the national colours—blue, black and white—in the front.

"Did you knit it yourself?" the youth asked, not knowing how to thank her. Such marked attention in front of everybody made the son and heir of Hiie feel awkward. He could not show his appreciation of the sweater by giving it a closer look, since his hands were sooty from the fire he was lighting in the stove. Nevertheless he suddenly felt anger rising within him at Leonard. He saw that Leonard seemed to be getting a little too close to the girl with his funny stories. Let that story-teller stop in time—nobody other than Tõmm would have anything to say in this particular matter! Hilda was his. He was startled—not at the thought, but at the feeling, which now seemed so natural. It seemed to him that he had felt this for a long time, and suddenly he felt hot and quickly started to work at the stove.

But then everyone was in a hurry, for Hilda's knapsack now yielded a quantity of half-burned candles, saved from previous Christmases—blue, red, yellow, white, even a whole candle or two. She seemed to have brought all the Christmas decorations of the Hiie house! This was a special treat, almost a miracle that none would have dared to expect. The men's faces shone like those of children, and many an unwashed rough hand came forward to touch the silver, the icicles, and the spark-ling little glass balls in their boxes. Even Ilme touched them with her hand, as if she did not believe her eyes.

"Hilda, you are an angel. A Christmas angel!" Osvald said, his face shining with joy.

Taavi suggested: "Let's call the men from the Froghole now. What a Christmas Eve they are having—cursing and bailing water out of their dugout."

"Let's put the candles on the tree first," Hilda said. "Let's surprise them."

Hilda had still more surprises in store. All kinds of food began to emerge from the knapsack—apples, cookies, roast ham and white bread.

"Don't make me blind!" Leonard shouted. "Oh Lord, what I must see before I die." And then the words got mixed up in Leonard's mouth, and he had to turn his face aside as if he were hiding tears. "Why are you bucks looking like that?" he demanded of his fellows. They had all become silent. Their faces, so accustomed to wearing the mask of gloom, were all at once tender and soft.

"Piskujõe mother brought the raisins," Hilda said. "God alone knows how she managed to save and hide them—for so many years."

Taavi did not know it either. So it had been his mother! He recalled

340

that when he was still a little fellow he had imagined that Mother had every good thing hidden away somewhere. Later he had been quite disappointed when he found out that there was much his mother had to do without. Now he realized again that his mother's secret treasure-chest contained everything one could desire.

"But the apples," he marvelled.

"Those are from the young trees near the fir grove, where the winter cold couldn't get at them," Hilda explained.

"Yes, I remember seeing a few stunted ones last summer," Tõmm added. He had now stepped behind Hilda's back.

"So Father saved them and sent them all here." Ilme's lips trembled.

"Yes, all of them," Hilda answered. "One, the biggest one, he saved for Mother and another one for me. He said I wouldn't eat here anyway. He was very worried, and kept counting them to make sure that every-body would get one. This roast was sent over from Lepiku. They killed a pig recently—to deliver their quotas. They brought the whole ham, but I couldn't carry all of it."

She placed the cookies on a clean towel on the table and offered them to the men, but they were slow to reach for them. This surprise was somehow too solemn. It was more to be looked at and admired than to be eaten. It was quite enough if one could look at it and pick up frag-ments of memories from a happy time long ago.

"I baked them myself. I don't really know how. It was the first time I tried. Hiie mother taught me, and I did as she told me. The gingerbread dough was ready weeks ago, but I couldn't get all the necessary things to put in it. These butter cookies I made as I remembered my own mother making them. They didn't turn out as good as Mother's, though."

"They're delicious. They melt in the mouth!" Värdi said. This was real recognition for Hilda, and somehow Tõmm felt glad too, really proud, as if the guests were praising his own farm, his stock, and his wife's hospitality. And why not? Who could say that it might not turn out that way one of these days? Why couldn't Hilda, the poor orphan whom his father had picked up from a snowdrift, become the mistress of the great Hiie farm some day?

From the bottom of the knapsack Hilda handed Ilme a small package. When Ilme opened it, she found a wedding ring and a sheet of paper with the following lines:

Dear daughter-in-law,

I heard that your wedding ring had been taken from you, and there-fore I am sending you mine. I pray to God that He may transfer to you herewith all the blessings that have accompanied Andres and me all through our lives. All that has happened has been the will of the Lord. May He save you for each other, you and Taavi. Listen to the good tidings on this blessed evening. It will bring light to the darkness now and evermore. May the Lord give the light and peace of Christ-mas to both your hearts.

For a long time Ilme read the lines on the wrinkled paper that had been wrapped around the ring. She felt the need to be alone, and withdrew into the dark corner of her bed. She held the ring tightly in her hand, until it became wet with perspiration. The fits of pain that had receded a little during the activities of the day overwhelmed her again, but she felt a great tenderness with the pain. Goodness had not yet vanished from this world. Good people could still be found.

But then Ilme hurried to Taavi and offered the ring to her husband.

"I can't," she stammered helplessly. "I cannot accept it. It is . . . good of your mother, but . . . Taavi, I can't. Sometime when you yourself feel that. . . . Then put it on my finger. I have no right to it any more. God wouldn't forgive me, if. . . ." She hurried back into the dark corner.

Taavi looked long at his mother's wedding ring in his hand. He watched the men rejoicing with a childlike joy, decorating the Christmas tree and fixing the candles on the twigs. Taavi lowered his face toward the floor, as if he could not stand the sight any longer. Why wasn't Ilme among the others? Why didn't her eyes light up? It was Christmas Eve, but their son Lembit was not there to enjoy the shining candlelight.

The men arrived from the other dugout. Soon their boisterous shouts of surprise gave way to a festive solemnity, which words are too clumsy and commonplace to express. The hosts made room for them, and they sat down side by side on the bunks and on the floor, or simply stood and looked. Hilda and Tõmm lit the candles, logs crackled in the small iron stove, and the men stood motionless, almost stiff, as if they were one body—the Estonian soldiers of yesterday, from the battlefields of the War of Independence, from the Russian front, the Estonian Legion, the frontier guards, the home guard, from amongst the Finland fighters. How different had been their fields of combat; how united had been their purpose.

Who started the song, nobody knew, but all at once they were all singing: "Silent night, holy night. . . ."

They sang calmly, not self-consciously, instinctively, and they neither noticed nor cared about the tears that rolled over many a rough cheek, falling on bearded chins or collars. Had they been conscious of it, not a few might have relieved their embarrassment with a profane expression, but they paid no attention to it, for their eyes were drinking in thirstily the little trembling flames of the candles—the great, bright light of Christmas.

Old Peeter Valba hurried back to Froghole and fetched his Bible. He had taken it along when he returned from burying his wife in the cemetery the previous spring. Between the leaves of the Bible he kept the pictures of his son and his wife, and his personal identity-card bearing the stamp of the Estonian Republic. Only those things deserved to be kept in the holy book. And when the song was over, Peeter read the Christmas story in a clear, monotonous voice. Neither he nor the men really understood what he was reading, but they all stood up and recalled how their fathers had read the Bible at home long ago, or how the minister had preached his Christmas sermon in the candlelit church.

Peeter Valba stood for a while, slouched and silent, as if the newly begun Christmas carol pained him. He kept his hands crossed over the Bible and threw furtive glances around him, until he stole out of the room unnoticed. Reading the Gospel he had suddenly remembered his dead wife and how she had always carried bread to the barns and stables on Christmas Eve, to let the animals share in their celebrations. Peeter himself had carried the lantern for her. How the cattle had licked the hand of their mistress in the warm stable. Peeter went without further hesitation to the Froghole, broke a large hunk of bread and started walking across the moor in the snowstorm. He remembered the horse Miira, who must be waiting for her Christmas bread.

Osvald did not feel well at all this Christmas Eve. He had not been feeling well for days. Marta's part in Ilme's tragedy worried him. On Christmas Eve, by candlelight, Osvald could not get rid of an impure, soiled feeling. Now he felt truly polluted, as if he had been an accomplice in treason. This interrupted the carol on his lips and bent his strong body forward, until his eyes did not see more than the muddy willow mat underfoot.

Nor could Taavi join in the Christmas cheer of the others. He could hardly sing with them. He held his mother's wedding ring in his hand and marvelled how Christmas Eve could penetrate into the depths of this bottomless swamp—so suddenly and unexpectedly. When he heard his wife singing, he raised his eyes in surprise. Ilme had approached the Christmas tree. The light of the candles shone in her eyes. Her hands clung rigidly to the edge of the table, and often her head fell weakly forward. Each time, however, when she raised it, she rejoined the carol. Her whole being reminded Taavi of the pitiful shivering of a reed that is being pulled from the waters, and the Christmas light was unable to kindle any joy in her sunken eyes. Taavi himself—hadn't he pushed her away, struck her, instead of comforting her? Hadn't he destroyed the former bonds between them instead of offering her support? Hadn't he done all that in his human weakness and pain, as if the unfortunate woman had been guilty of something? What shelter, what support or mercy had Taavi offered to his suffering wife? Not even human understanding. He felt miserable.

When Taavi went and stroked her hair, Ilme stopped singing. Suddenly she pressed herself close to her husband and embraced him.

"Forgive me," Taavi muttered. "I have been so weak, and left you alone. We still belong to each other." His words became confused. He realized that the words did not matter. They could not express anything anyway.

"It has all been God's will," Ilme's lips moved. "All—that."

Taavi placed his mother's wedding ring on his wife's finger.

The candles burned fast, although the short stubs were replaced by others as long as any were available. The room had become hot and stuffy, but the men hated to leave the tree. The warmth and the smell of scorched fir needles seemed to bestow upon them a strangely comforting bliss. The silence had become a pact among those sitting around the tree. Even memories of former Christmases were banned, for everyday words in everyday mouths were not good enough to describe them. Words were unworthy stumbling blocks on the road leading to the treasures which each one of them still hoarded in his soul.

XII

All signs showed that spring was near again. The sun was high in the sky, the winds were soft, and at noontime one noticed how the snowdrifts shrank. In the low bogs open water could be seen already and the higher spots, such as the bunker roofs on Taevasaar, were bare even on the north side.

The weather brought one of the most impossible periods to Taevasaar. Contact with the outside world, which had become irregular after the snowstorms had ceased, was now interrupted completely and had to remain so for several more weeks.

"We can die of hunger here," Osvald grunted.

They had not lived in abundance throughout the winter, for after Christmas they had received nothing from the farms—vast stretches of forest were being cut down in the woods and the hauling out of the timber lasted for months. The huge, empty stumpfields made the men's hearts ache—it was their house that was being torn down, their great green home.

"If they keep on slashing like this, we'll have a direct view to Kalgina in the spring."

The cutting did not turn out to be quite that extensive, but when the men heard that wood was being cut down all over the region, they realized that the Russians planned an equally merciless struggle against the woods of their homeland as they were waging against the free men.

Although the men were out of bread, they had enough meat to tide them over the lean days. The calf and cow of Peeter of Valba had provided plenty. Sometimes they made a dough of flour and water and tried to bake it on top of the iron stove at night, but there were never enough of the sticky unleavened cakes to go round and the flour was mostly used to cook porridge. There were many days when their food consisted of tough beef and half-frozen potatoes.

The spring thaw brought a special plague to the men of the Froghole. Every morning their house was flooded with moor water, which often reached to their knees. The men who slept on the lower bunks began to get seasick. Everything that was left on the floor in the evening was found floating in the morning, including the willow mats which served as floor coverings. The men waded to their buckets and dishpans, muttering curses while bailing water out of the bunker. Frustration made them provoke fights among themselves. Every day brought its quarrels, which often were not far from breaking into open fights.

The men of the Snake Pit were also busy bailing out water from

344

under the floor. Up to now their bunker had not been flooded, although the water sloshed under the mats every morning.

As soon as most of the snow had melted, Taavi Raudoja's journeys began again. Sometimes he stayed away from Taevasaar for the night, for it was difficult to cross the moor because of the spring floods. He slept in hay barns where there was still some hay left, or kept watch near the farmhouse of Roosi or the county house at Kalgina. Several times he had even sneaked past the Russian sentries to the Roosi farmyard. The game was dangerous and he enjoyed it. He waited for a good chance to break into the county house, a loaded Browning in one pocket and a hand grenade in the other. He knew by now where Marta slept. Her room was in the attic.

He enjoyed waking at dawn in a hay barn, limbs stiff from the cold, nostrils full of the morning coolness and the smell of fresh earth and moist hayseeds. Life became more exuberant each morning even in the farthest backwoods. At first only the robins sang, the woodpecker walked on a pine trunk, or beat the tree with his busy beak. But then all the singing birds took over the forests, and mysterious cooing sounded from the thickets. Taavi stretched and moved until his limbs were warm and, strange as it was, he began to feel new strength flowing into his sinews.

When he returned to Taevasaar, Ilme never asked him about Lembit any more—not with her lips, anyway, although her eyes still questioned him. Taavi had ordered the men to keep an eye on her. He did not trust his wife, for Ilme had refused to promise not to leave Taevasaar. She remained deaf to Taavi's persuasions and looked stubbornly and blindly away. Although Taavi tried to influence her, Ilme remained unchanged, withdrawn and aloof. Sometimes she broke down and cried on Taavi's breast, her whole body quivering. After that she was usually quite calm for a few days. She took an interest in life, cleaned the bunker and took care of the men's food, but soon she hit an unconquerable wall again and bent low under her hopeless burden. This tormented and exhausted Taavi, until it became one of the reasons that kept him away from Taevasaar. He roamed in the forests until he felt it was high time to return to his wife lest some misfortune should occur.

"Damn it to hell," Leonard swore. "This is worse than a prison. This is hell; cold and filthy hell. Tell me, Mart of Liiskaku, you are a proper and well-balanced person; tell me how long one is supposed to hold out like this?"

"What's wrong with you?"

"Wrong, wrong?" Leonard mocked. "Oh nothing. Nothing at all. Everything is wrong. Damn it to holy hell."

One day, as Taavi was just leaving on his trip, he met Osvald in the woods. The latter walked slowly and wearily home, carrying a sack of food on his back.

"No luck?" Taavi inquired.

"Luck!" Osvald muttered. "I have a hunch that Marta knows we are on the lookout. She must sense it somehow."

"What have you got there in the sack?"

"Hilda filled it. I guess it's mostly bread. Life at Hiie seems to have become pretty tight too. Ignas and Hilda cannot keep the whole farm going. They have threshed rye all winter. Even old Aadu flails away at it, but every grain they get out of the straw goes to the delivery centre. I saw last evening how Ignas ate. He dipped cold potatoes into herring brine. Used to be, even the Hiie shepherd boy had fried eggs for breakfast. Now, damn it, the former district elder has to eat pig food. I asked Ignas how he was getting along with the taxes and quotas and everything. The old man just shrugged his shoulders—no hope of getting everything paid on time." Osvald sat down on a rotten tree stump and held his face in both hands, pushing his grey cap back on his head. Taavi broke himself some bread and ate hungrily.

"They're getting along all right at Võllamäe," Osvald said thoughtfully. "Jaak barters stuff to the Russians and takes in plenty of rubles. The plain Ivans don't have much but when a man of higher rank happens to be in on the deal he pays quite well. Jaak and August of Roosi are partners now. Jaak provides the vodka, and August brings in the customers. He gets a few drinks for free, but the rubles go into Jaak's pocket. He's an old hand at this. He can smell money from far away. This makes him all right in the eyes of the Russians, too. The rubles have a little power after all, mainly because the farmers never see any money."

"What could one buy with rubles? Nothing."

"Who knows," Osvald said. "I have thought that we should leave this district before they begin the roundups. When the ground under the woods and edges of the moor dries up a little, they'll come after us. I have thought about the other side of Lake Peipsi. The country is familiar there from war days and nobody would think to look for us inside the Russian borders. If we take a sack of potatoes along, there's plenty of fallow land over there where we could dig a few furrows and the potatoes would grow."

"For how many years are you planning to settle down?"

"Until the sound of a new war reaches my ears. I have plagued my brain quite a bit recently and I think it would be best to prepare for the worst. If then it should turn out even a little better, we will have cause to rejoice. Let's say it will take another couple of years. . . ."

"Go to the devil!" Taavi got so angry that he pushed the sack of bread away and began to stare gloomily ahead. The western allies were demobilizing. The men were greeted with jubilation in their homes, their wives and children welcomed them, everyday life accepted them back. Peace. Peace. Where is peace? Why did those in the west close their eyes and bury their heads in the sand? Why didn't they take a look at that peace they had bought for themselves at the price of betraying half of Europe?

Two years. . . .

That summer it would be two years since they returned from Finland to the harbour of Paldiski. Two months later their regiment had been destroyed. Many had been killed in the last frantic battles. One or two fortunate ones had reached the shores of free countries, many were suffering within prison walls, had been murdered, or perhaps fate had granted them a short reprieve in forced labour camps. Only a few were defying their fate somewhere in the thickets, like himself.

They had been silent for a long time, looking at the pine cones that had burst open from the wind and the sun.

"Why do you chase that Marta so hard? What score have you to settle with her?" Taavi asked.

Osvald did not raise his eyes. After a little while, he answered: "I, why should I. . . . I simply want to—end our relationship if I should meet her. That's all. Last summer for several months I was just like a boy. Damn it. Now I want to have a final reckoning. I won't kill her. I don't care what you do. I'll give her my last token of affection, that she'll remember all her life." With a mean grin, Osvald took a big fir cone out of his pocket, dry and bristly and hard as wood.

Taavi looked at the fir cone, without comprehension.

"Shove it in backwards and give it a good kick with my fist. Then let her howl," Osvald said gloomily and spat on the moss.

It was Osvald who met Reku in the woods one spring day. They had not heard about him all winter and the men assumed that Jaak of Võllamäe was hiding his son somewhere around his farm. But the boy's thin, wind-tanned face did not confirm their assumption.

"Where's the general coming from?" Osvald asked.

The boy laughed. When he had emptied Osvald's tobacco pouch into his own, he announced: "Oh, from far away! From there, where earth and sky touch each other."

"That was a long trip all right. Why did you come back from there?"

"There were no women, that's why. Reku wants to see Marta."

Osvald stared at the idiot for a long time.

"Don't start mocking me," he mumbled in confusion. "What is Marta to you? What do you know about Marta?"

"Reku knows. Marta is good to look at."

"What do you look at her for?" Osvald asked excitedly. He had a peculiar feeling, standing there like that. Reku's little eyes penetrated him as if he were made of some transparent material. The boy was laughing at him, at the big, hulking man who roved in the woods like a shepherd boy. "Just leave Marta alone!" Osvald said.

"But I won't. Marta is good. That's why Reku came back. Marta called him."

"Did Marta? Did Marta come into the woods herself?"

"Stupid!" The boy looked at him contemptuously. "The hired man of Hiie is as dumb as the white wether of Matsu. At night, when the lights were almost out and the men were asleep, then Marta said: "Come, Reku boy, Marta is Reku's girl friend. Marta is good. Nobody is as good as she.""

347

"Are you speaking the truth?" Osvald shouted, grabbing the boy by his sleeve. "Where did you see Marta? Speak up."

Reku wrenched himself loose.

"Don't touch me with your paws. Reku will silence you like a sick dog. Reku saw Marta in the county house."

"You fool. Did you go to the county house to inform on us?"

Now Reku got angry too. He took a step backwards and growled.

"Are you asking for your death? Do you want to get lead in your face?" he snarled. "Just call Reku a fool. Just go ahead." And before Osvald could move even his fingertips, the madman had raised his gun, so that Osvald looked directly into the two barrels.

Only one clear thought flashed through Osvald's mind. He'd die like a hunted animal.

But something quite unexpected followed instead of the shot. Reku suddenly looked aside, as if listening to somebody's peremptory orders. The rifle sank down and Reku backed off, crouching from fear. His body trembled as if invisible hands were shaking him, and the gun almost fell from his hands. Osvald broke out in a sweat. Now he could see with his fear-dazed eyes that Reku's face, too, was covered with beads of perspiration.

"What is it?" Osvald stammered. He felt cold and hot air on his face, although the day was quiet and windless.

"Andres. . . ," Reku stuttered.

Osvald could not speak. He believed that he would wake up the next moment in the dank, stuffy bunker, his sides hurting from sleeping on the hard bedboards. He was still standing in the same place, as if turned to stone, when Reku ambled off among the trees, head sunk on his chest. When the boy had been gone for some time, Osvald began to move slowly and deliberately, as if he had to pick up his stiff limbs one by one.

Taavi had heard long ago that his former schoolmate, Tiit Kalmre, who used to spend his summers at Harukurgu, had returned from Russia and been discharged from the Estonian corps. He was said to work as a truck driver in Tallinn. Taavi remembered Tiit from their schooldays as a curly-haired social lion, a good companion, always merry and full of high spirits. Now he was supposed to have grown into a man, and gossips had it that he drove down from Tallinn to Matsu on Saturday nights to see Ella. He was said to have serious intentions, for a man who has been wounded in every imaginable place would not undertake such long trips merely for entertainment. During his last visit at Matsu Tiit had inquired about Taavi. When he did not receive a direct answer he had gone to Hiie and Piskujõe and much had become clear to him even without words. And Tiit had left an invitation for Taavi to meet him at Matsu next Saturday night.

Taavi took a reconnaissance trip around the village of Metsaoti during the day. He went to Piskujõe, shaved, asked his mother to cut his hair, and changed clothes. Instead of his customary high boots he put on his father's shoes, so it would be easier to run, if necessary. His mother had moved back into the house and with the arrival of spring the burden of her worries seemed to have lightened a little. She spent most of her time at Hiie now, helping Hilda and Ignas.

"It is good that you can feel like a human being on a Saturday night," Mother said.

The evening dusk was deepening into night when Taavi approached the buildings of Matsu by way of the sheltering hedge between the fields. The spring air was misty and cool, but full of the smells of the earth fermenting from the sun, the odour of decaying leaves, and the fragrance of fertile nature. Frogs croaked in the ditch, a crow cawed sleepily in the fir grove near Võllamäe, and the melodies of birds were full of the jubilation of spring. Stars began to twinkle in the sky and the pink stripes above the serrated edge of the woods turned a cold yellow. It seemed as if the sun, sinking into the shadow of the earth, had lit a green fire in place of the recent red one.

A truck was standing at the gate leading to the farmyard. Evidently the bridegroom had arrived. Taavi did not enter immediately, but walked several times around the house and listened to the sound of conversation behind the windows. The people of Matsu and their guest were eating supper.

Then they stood face to face, Taavi and Tiit. When they had shaken hands long enough and had measured each other from head to toe, they sat down without talking. Taavi was invited to sit down at the table, right across the table from Tiit.

"Miracles still happen in this world," Tiit said and there were tears as well as joy in his voice. Tiit had not changed as much as Mihkel of Lepiku, who had been arrested. His bold shock of hair had been cut off and the new bristles, about an inch long, were still too short to follow any fashion. His face was that of a man now, bony and thin, and the former sparkle in his eyes had given way to an opaque dullness. But he did not seem to be noticeably crippled.

The table was loaded with an abundance of heavy peasant food and the presence of the guest had conjured up some delicacies like fresh barley muffins and fried eggs. Juhan of Matsu was sitting at the head of the table in the seat of the master of the household, a litre-sized vodka bottle in front of him from which he had just filled the glasses on the table. One could read from the faces of the company that the visitor's proposal had been accepted.

They ate and drank and soon their voices rose as the liquor took its effect. The women kept themselves apart from the men's talk, as is proper in a well-bred household, but the mistress of the house raised her vodka glass with the aplomb of an innkeeper's daughter. She could drink an average man under the table without batting an eyelid, and could give quite a merry battle even to a strong-headed man.

Juhan, the thunder-proud farmer of Matsu, was quite delighted at Taavi's coming. He stuck his thumbs in his vest and said: "Split that tree stump. This is the kind of man I like. Damn him, he escapes from

349

prison, out of the seventh death cell, the devil take him, runs away and into the forest as clean as a whistle. The Russians run after him, run their gills into the twigs like smelt that are strung on a stick, can't even catch the smell of him. And then the vagabond son of Andres of Piskujõe walks through the doorway of Juhan of Matsu, sits down at the table and begins to break bread as if nothing at all had happened. A hairy hawk, damn him. This is the kind of man I like. How big is your regiment now there in the bush? Eh?"

At Juhan's frank talk Taavi cast a sidelong glance in the direction of his former schoolmate. Their eyes met and Tiit winked familiarly. The vodka had broken through the dull film on his eyes and they began to gleam with their former joy of living.

"Oh, not many. . . ," Taavi muttered. "I myself, and—that's all."

"The hairy hawk," Juhan growled. "Take a good drink. It will warm you up. You haven't got the chill of the moor out of your bones yet. But when you start hitting them, don't forget to mention it to me. I want to try how hard the Russian skulls are before I die."

Then Tiit's heart overflowed too with hatred of holy Russia.

The conversation circled for a long time around Communists and Fascists and how they should be handled. Taavi marvelled at the boldness of the men, as if they had not seen any trouble yet, as if the conversation was a wonderful new toy, a fire that was fascinating to look at if you forgot that it might burn. The men on Taevasaar did not talk like that.

The women did not like this kind of talk either. Lonni soon rose from the table and went into the back room to stay with her baby. She had not even placed a vodka glass for herself on the table. Ella began to chatter in short, simple-minded sentences in the midst of the conversation, receiving angry looks from her mother. Then Tiit made a suggestion that showed how the former boyish spirit still dwelled in his patched-up body. There was said to be a big dance at Täoaru. Why couldn't they drive out there?

"Sure, sure," he said, standing up and thrusting his hands deep into his pockets. "Let's climb on my truck and we'll be there before you can look around. If we can't find any other entertainment, at least we'll punch the noses of a couple of Reds. And the most important thing," he turned to Taavi. "I'll introduce you to the commander of the terror squad of the district of Kalgina. I know him well from the Estonian corps—he's a lieutenant. He was the political commissar in the corps. There are only two battalion commanders in the whole district and they don't know each other."

"Split that tree stump," Juhan said, and for the first time he looked at his future son-in-law as if he doubted whether he were quite normal. Tiit received a similar glance from Taavi. Only Ella was all eager to go to the dance. Why not? Why didn't their parents understand? But the mistress of the farm did not even want to hear about it. She had barely allowed her daughters out of her sight, and all her caution had not

350

helped. Now—to the dance. Almost fifteen miles away in the small town! They must be out of their minds.

Taavi suddenly remembered that even his presence here was extremely dangerous to all concerned and that it might bring death to half the village. It was high time for him to go. Another time, yes. He liked to talk with Tiit. It was a sort of relief. Then he suddenly had a startling idea. What if Marta should be at the dance too?

"Let's go," he said calmly.

"I'll introduce you to the commander of the terror squad," Tiit shouted. "This will turn out a real big joke. This we'll laugh at until our dying day."

"Just so your dying day doesn't come too soon, if you take me along," Taavi muttered grimly.

Both Ella and Tiit had to use a great deal of persuasion before the parents gave their consent. It was never given expressly. Juhan merely closed his eyes and went to look after his horse in the stable, while Meeta went to the back room, scolding her daughter on the way. Ella knew her parents and knew that this was as good as consent.

Standing in a dark corner of the garden, behind the clubhouse, Taavi realized for the first time how dangerous this adventure could turn out. He could not deny, however, that the danger had attracted him as much as his desire to meet Marta. Tiit and Ella had entered the dance hall. Through the half-open window sounded the singing of a choir.

When Tiit returned, Taavi had already reconnoitred the surroundings, had smoked two pipefuls of tobacco and was just stuffing his third. "Pardon me, for having kept you waiting so long," his friend apologized. "But I could not take you in there without precautions. Everything is in good shape. I alerted the men I know and they will organize their own friends. They are keeping their eyes on the door and every movement of the leader of the terror squad is being observed. A girl is taking care of the telephone."

"You didn't see Marta of Roosi?"

"No. I looked around and asked those who might know her. But I don't believe she's come so far. There are no Russians either; the only uniformed man is the terror squad leader. He's looking for a wife—that's why he's here so early." Tiit laughed. "Let's go in." He handed Taavi a new bill. "Buy yourself a ticket and act nonchalantly. We'll say that you are a factory worker from Tallinn and that you came with me to have a good time, in case somebody should get interested."

Taavi slipped his Browning from his hip pocket to the inside pocket of his coat and they entered the dance hall. The lights in the hall and in the dining room made Taavi blink his eyes. The program had just ended and the chairs were being pushed together to make room for dancing. A peculiar chill—perhaps brought along from the outside—ran down Taavi's spine in the warm, brightly-lit room. The dance hall was decorated with red cloth, and pictures of bearded Communist idols were hanging on the walls. Otherwise the atmosphere was the same as it had always been at a dance in a back-country town. Most noticeable was the great preponderance of women, who were standing around the walls in groups, with disappointed expressions on their faces. The orchestra consisted of an accordion, a piano, a violin that always stayed half a measure behind the other instruments, and a drum in the undisciplined hands of a young red-kerchiefed Communist. They played a waltz. One of the older men cut paraffin shavings from a candle and spread them on the floor. Couples began circling around him, looking serious as if they were performing hard work. The recent years had wrought havoc among the menfolk. The former band had been broken up and only very little was left of the old festive spirit.

Taavi was already sorry he had come along with Tiit and Ella. It was ridiculous and dangerous. He tried to dance with Ella but this seemed most foolish of all, especially as the girl was a bad dancer, her eagerness notwithstanding.

"Come, let's go to the restaurant and get some drinks into our bellies," Tiit said. "The ride cleared my head completely and if you should suddenly get sad in the midst of the party—then what are you going to do? There aren't even any Russian noses here to punch."

When they turned toward the restaurant they ran into the commander of the terror squad in his Red Army uniform. Before Taavi could stop Tiit, his friend had introduced him to the officer. Taavi's new acquaintance and closest enemy was a straight-backed man of approximately thirty-five, with strong, energetic features, even intelligent-looking. Thus he was a fitting opponent both in body and spirit.

When Taavi recalled this meeting afterwards it always seemed to have a dreamlike quality. Everything had been unreal—how they shook hands, how the man watched him with his dry eyes, how they ordered tea, sandwiches and vodka, and sat down at a table. It was good that Ella was too startled to speak. He was not worried about Tiit, for the fellow enjoyed the meeting of the two deadly enemies as much as he would have enjoyed a superb comedy.

"Where does comrade Raudoja come from? From Tallinn?" The lieutenant looked at him with the suspicious eyes of a genuine Communist.

"Yes, from Tallinn. Just came to have a good time. The travel conditions and work—can't get out like this every day," Taavi answered. One thought disturbed him suddenly and brought perspiration to his forehead: how did the lieutenant know his name? Had he noted it so faultlessly from Tiit's introduction, while he himself had not caught the name of the lieutenant at all? He was the head of the terror squad in his own county and Taavi was being hunted all over the district. No, Taavi had never made an equally magnificent blunder. He had only one lousy card to play—that the enemy had forgotten his name, that he just thought he had heard it somewhere. His scrutinizing, thoughtful looks seemed to indicate that.

"Where do you work in Tallinn?"

"Oh, at the Red Krull factory. My father was a mechanic there and so I almost inherited my job. My old man was a furious revolutionary in 1917—what else could you expect—worked all his life in the metal shops at Krull. Your health, comrade lieutenant!"

They raised their glasses. The dance had got into full swing in the ballroom and flushed couples entered the restaurant now and then. Taavi knew that he had to dispel the suspicions and doubts of the man next to him as quickly as possible. He could not permit the situation to develop so far that it would have led to open shooting. This could have brought much trouble to innocent people.

"We made it fast to Estonia this time," he said proudly. "It's a pity I could not take part in the mopping-up myself."

"It didn't go so quickly at all," the lieutenant growled. "Our own boys—these traitors fought back from every bush! These whelps should be killed, all of them! The régime is too soft. They are too mild and merciful, expecting them to readjust. And the woods are still. . . ." He interrupted himself abruptly but Taavi did not even move his little finger. Did he remember now? flitted through Taavi's mind. Well, there was still enough time to draw the revolver. And when Taavi passed Tiit his cigarette so Tiit could light his own, the lieutenant asked: "Why didn't you take part in the fighting in Estonia if. . . . Were you in the Corps or what?"

"They got me . . . under Velikiye Luki," Taavi pressed angrily through his teeth. "The doctors did what they could but I was beyond repair. Well, then I was sent to recuperate—working on a kolkhoz, and that's where I stayed. It's a shame to come back to your homeland like a vagrant when the comrades have finished the job."

"Where did you get hit, comrade?" the lieutenant asked, brightening up and striking a more intimate note.

"Right through the lung. Those cursed Fascists!"

"Oh, comrade, that was really bad luck. What unit were you in?"

"Wait, what was his name now—in comrade Mihkin's platoon."

"Do you know Paul Kaarna?"

"Wait a little—Kaarna, Paul Kaarna. . . . Was he sort of medium height?"

"No, he wasn't. Big as a horse, with his front teeth knocked out."

"Why, of course. Why shouldn't I know him—of course I do! Where is he now?"

Their conversation really got going. Taavi soon began to believe himself that he had actually taken part in the Russian expedition. Tiit helped along when he thought his friend was on dangerous ground, and Ella fought with laughter.

The one thing that disturbed Taavi was the lieutenant's caution in drinking. Although everybody kept urging him on, he was even more careful than Taavi. They watched each other and each considered the other's behaviour suspicious. The lieutenant seemed nervous and kept looking at his wrist watch.

The lightning struck suddenly through the doors and windows. Excited whispers passed through the people and a group of armed Russians entered the ballroom door. Everybody was ordered to stay in his place. This was a routine check of identification cards.

Taavi's hand slipped into his inside breast pocket but before his fingers could touch the handle of the revolver he received a hard kick on his shin. His eyes met for an instant the grim, commanding eyes of Tiit and his hand brought forth his pipe instead. He realized Tiit's gamble. He continued his conversation with the lieutenant, nonchalantly stuffing tobacco into the pipe. It was too late now to act anyway, for several of the Russians were already in the dining room, as well as in all the doorways. The windows were closed and it would have taken too long to jump through the glass panes. The dance had ceased, the orchestra was silent, and the people were hurrying to produce their identification cards. Fear spoke from the eyes of quite a few of them. Taavi's leg hurt from the kick he had received from Tiit.

Tiit played his game still further. When Ella began to look for her papers in her handbag, he said contemptuously: "Don't be silly. Now what could be suspicious about you?"

The girl gave him a confused look. Even the lieutenant gave him a sidelong glance, but that was the end of it. Tiit offered Taavi a cigarette before the latter managed to light his home-grown tobacco. This, too, was a sign of Tiit's sober presence of mind, for the pungent smell of country tobacco might have seemed strange coming from the pipe of a city worker.

The officer in charge of the check, a Russian NKVD man, came to their table, greeted the leader of the terror squad in a comradely way, emptied the vodka glass Tiit offered him, and talked about something that made him laugh. Tiit sat closer to him and so Taavi had no reason to enter the conversation. He knew where to join in the laughter of the others, without understanding much of the story.

The check of documents in the dance hall went on for some twenty minutes. But as soon as the Russians had left their table Taavi considered himself saved for this time—with the help of Tiit and the terror squad leader. On the next round he emptied his vodka glass with one gulp.

"It's beginning to taste right," he said. "When you get a little warm, then you really begin to enjoy it."

"It sure is beginning to taste right," the lieutenant agreed.

When the passport check was over, the Russians remained at the dance, and now the real party began. Even Taavi grabbed the nearest wallflower and vanished between the other couples. Suddenly he found it very amusing to bump into the Russians in the wild swing of the waltz. He laughed aloud in their faces and whirled and whirled as if the devil were driving him.

"Don't kill me," the girl shrieked. "You act like a savage who has just come out of the jungle," she shouted, pressing herself close to Taavi. She was quite decent looking, he discovered.

354

But this discovery, as well as the girl's words, made Taavi think, and he slowed down his momentum. What was he doing here? The warm body of the girl pressed directly against the revolver in his breast pocket and this had awakened a thought in his mind that dispelled the effects of the vodka and the joy at his recent escape. He was back in thought at Taevasaar in the darkness of the sod hut. He was sober all of a sudden, tired, and repulsive to himself. The dance that had begun with such a swing ended quite lamely. Taavi returned to the dining room and walked straight through a group of Russians who were standing at the door.

"Taavi!"

Taavi knew this deep woman's voice. It sounded excited, startled, even mixed with joy. And then their eyes met. No muscle moved in Taavi's face and his calm step did not falter. Marta was standing in front of him, the same proud woman with her fur coat and genuine pearls. She stared at Taavi, her mouth still open from calling his name, her hands raised to her breast, her long fingers spread apart and seemingly frozen. Raising his hand to his breast pocket, Taavi passed the woman, the towering militiaman, and the Russians who surrounded them. His fingers cramped around the handle of the revolver but his step remained as calm as before and he did not look to either side as he walked out through the door. Everything seemed unreal around him, the people looked like wax figures, the air buzzed in his ears. His body was as taut as a spring, ready to be released if somebody should call to him to halt. He would duck down and to the side, shoot his seven bullets right in the midst of them and then dash into the darkness—be it life or death. But nothing happened. Only Marta's startled cry still rang in his ears for a long time after the spring night had enveloped him.

Marta left the party when the dancing had just reached its climax. She had only recently arrived, had danced a little without much interest, had somewhat nervously drunk a few glasses of vodka and then returned to Kalgina in the car with the Russians. That was enough for her.

She rushed to her room, locked the door, pulled down the blackout shades, checked the hooks on the windows, and took the Browning out of her purse. When she had convinced herself that the revolver was loaded she put it back in the purse, took off her overcoat and sat down on the couch, placing her purse next to her. She was shaken. She felt she wanted something but did not think of lighting a cigarette. Finally she did it mechanically, not realizing what she was doing. But the same feeling continued.

The dead had come back to life after all. Those whose return she had feared more than death, and he whose return she had yearned and hoped for. She had felt for a long time that Taavi Raudoja was back, but when she began to surmise from the allusions made by the NKVD boss that something was being kept from her, she had moved immediately to the county house. Despair and fear had overcome her. When she

355

had asked comrade Kasinski, the NKVD boss, about the fate of Ilme Raudoja, the man had laughed sarcastically and mockingly: "Is my little birdie getting worried?"

He did not say any more but Marta concluded from his remarks and his nervousness that something had happened in connection with Ilme Raudoja. In Marta's opinion the woman should have been sent to Russia and forgotten long ago. It seemed strange to her that Ilme's name should still be on the lips of the NKVD men. The private questions Captain Kasinski asked about Ilme seemed equally peculiar.

"You are not planning to release her?" Marta had shouted in excitement.

"The NKVD will never let anybody out of its hands," the captain had laughed frankly but with a clear warning, and it seemed to Marta that the warning had been directed at herself. She, too, was in the hands of the NKVD.

She played with the men who held her life in their hands in the hope that she might steal some of their power. But although they considered themselves powerful, these men trembled with constant fear. They suspected and watched each other and also Marta. Only he had power who could uncover something about another that could endanger his life, but this kind of power was only relative and brief and everybody was afraid of invisible eyes. Even when they did not exist, everybody could conjure them up in his imagination, and Marta had begun to feel and create them too.

She hated the Russians. She hated the ruling régime. She hated comrade Turban, the chairman of the executive committee. She hated the chief of the NKVD, Captain Kasinski, that fat man with pig's eyes. She hated the ape-like militiaman. She hated them all, every one of them. She hated them from the bottom of her heart. She abhorred everything that had happened between her and these men. The only man she had been able to turn into her slave was the militiaman, the greatest idiot of them all.

She had often asked herself how it had happened that she had become so evil. Why? Could the love of one person justify what had happened? She must have been out of her mind. She was sure of that. She had had to do it to save her own life. Although she had wandered around the frontier guard post that night with wild thoughts in her head, she had not had any definite plans. When she had run into the Russians she had had no choice. If she had not done it, she would have been arrested and the people on the shore would have been caught anyway. She had saved her own life and everything else had been the whim of fate.

And today she had met Taavi Raudoja.

Taavi must know much he had not known at their last meeting. Marta could not guess how much. But the instinct that had driven her to leave Roosi had not erred. She had realized that from their brief meeting, from Taavi's single look and his tense walk when he had passed her.

Marta could not shout: "Arrest that man!" She felt powerless in front of Taavi Raudoja. She would probably be unable to move a finger, even if Taavi should stand right there and say that he had come to take revenge.

Ah! Marta threw herself on the couch and tore its cover with her fingernails. She closed her eyes and beat with her fists against her forehead. Then she turned around, quick as a flash, her mouth open to scream, eyes wild with fright. But nobody was behind her. She grabbed the Browning again from her purse and pressed it flat against her forehead. No, it was certain that she could not spend this night alone. Even if she should drink herself unconscious she would not be able to face this night. Should she call comrade Turban from downstairs? The man would come. He was always ready to come, in spite of his wife. No, not that. No. She must spend the night without sleeping, keeping the light burning and pressing her back against the wall.

Marta knew what such nights were like—she had had them before. The hours before dawn were darkest, for then fatigue tore her thoughts to shreds and their sharp steel shavings grated on her brain.

The roar of a motorcycle sounded outside. The vehicle stopped in the courtyard of the county house. Peetal Rause, the militiaman, clambered up the stairs with heavy steps and Marta suddenly felt much better. She threw the Browning into her handbag and went to open the door. When the giant figure of the man loomed up in front of her, she stepped back in terror. The militiaman had lost his hat, his face was pale and distorted with pain. He was holding his left wrist with his right hand and his fingers were bloody.

"Damn it!"

"What has happened to you?"

"The bandits," the man gasped and sat heavily on a chair. "Come, bandage my hand a little. The blood just keeps gushing out."

Marta had much trouble in getting off the militiaman's raincoat and jacket. He was groaning with pain, although the bullet had passed through his arm without damaging the bone.

"This isn't too bad," Marta said bandaging the arm.

"The damned swine. Who was the man who marched out of the dance hall?" he asked abruptly.

"Oh, an old acquaintance—from Tallinn," Marta muttered, straining to steady her hands that refused to obey her.

"They shot at me on top of the hill. It was lighter up there. They recognized me from my uniform cap. I pulled off the road, into the ditch, barely escaped hitting a tree. I threw myself down, heard one of the devils ask me whether I was alone. I was quietly trying to get the gun out of the holster when he asked me again whether I was much hurt. Then he shouted out of the woods with a savage voice: "Drive off, devil, before I kill you." I thought he would kill me anyway, and was just too scared to come close. That was all. I crouched there for half an hour and held the blood back but then I began to worry that I might bleed to death. I started the motorcycle and he laughed right there from behind a tree. So long! And he did not shoot. Just imagine, he did not shoot me." Peetal Rause marvelled with confused joy, as if he realized only now that he had escaped with his life. "He was a bandit and he did not shoot me. He asked if I was alone. I wonder whom he wanted to shoot?"

Probably me, Marta said to herself. She cast an appraising glance at Peetal Rause and decided that in spite of his great horse-like body and his gorilla-like cruelty he was a wretched weakling in the present circumstances.

"Scare up some vodka, Marta. He did not shoot me," the man repeated. "Give me a mouthful of vodka."

"Get going," was Marta's short answer. "Be gone, and quick."

There was something unfathomable in the woman's eyes that made the man retreat. He heard Marta lock the door behind him—two brusque turns with the key.

Marta sat down on the couch and pressed her back against the wall. The gun was on one side of her, within easy reach. A package of cigarettes and a box of matches were on the other side.

XIII

The roundup came earlier than anybody had expected, although they had talked about the possibility now and then. It was limited to the villages of Harukurgu and Metsaoti. The soldiers only searched the farmhouses and walked once across the Koolu hills. The terror squad did not venture farther into the woods. The militiaman with his wounded arm and the leader of the squad drove back and forth between the village of Metsaoti and the county house of Kalgina, adding weight to the operation with the rumble of the motorcycle. The young Communists piled up their guns in the woods, and August of Roosi told them dirty jokes. No results could be expected.

The outcome was favourable for the woodsmen. Soon afterwards the NKVD unit left Roosi without having participated in the roundup. What their task had been in the first place remained obscure. They had not made any excursions into the woods, except in the winter when they had worked together with the farm people cutting down timber. The behaviour of the Russians remained mysterious, and Taavi suspected that new moves were being planned, guided directly from Tallinn. The spring was peaceful, fragrantly blossoming everywhere. Was this only a pretended peace, a rearrangement of forces, a feigned manoeuvre? Taavi knew that the NKVD would never retreat like this without results. The grace period allotted to them in such an incomprehensible way was only a breathing spell on the threshold of bigger events.

But the majority of the men did not share his apprehensions. They interpreted the mysterious behaviour of the enemy as an exhausted retreat. Although they well remembered the huge roundups of the previous year in Central Estonia, that had lasted through the whole summer, they believed they would remain untouched throughout the season. They began to extend their reconnaissance trips to remoter villages, and when Captain Jonnkoppel added up the information he could not see any signs of danger in the immediate future: Russian units of any size were only to be found some fifteen miles away at their air bases and airstrips. Everywhere else their units were smaller than before, and they were used only as guards. The terror squads were weak in numbers, could only engage in intelligence, and pass the alarm to larger army units.

The men moved around more freely and visited their homes. The depression and melancholy of winter faded from their faces. Everyone tried to spend as much time away from Taevasaar as possible. Thus the men of Metsaoti began to work in the fields again at night. They worked not only in the fields of Hiie but all over the village. The acres of Lepiku needed help more urgently than any others, for Anton and Luise were elderly people and they had not got over the tragic fate of their son.

Hilda and Värdi took over the nightly watches again. Taavi, too, watched sometimes behind the lilac bushes of Roosi. Osvald, the hired man, was the one who worked the hardest in the fields of Hiie. He arrived with the first evening dusk and did not leave until the sun flashed up from the horizon. He offered to stay at Ignas' side in daytime, too, but the farmer would have none of that.

The passage of time had somewhat reconciled Ilme to the inexorable fact that she had lost her children. While her body recovered a new hope began to grow in her that Lembit had been taken to Russia and that he was being brought up there. Perhaps she might see her son after all sometime in the future?

Ilme lived wholly absorbed in her unfounded belief until one day some news from the village unsettled her again. The rumours concerned a complete stranger and did not involve Ilme in any way. A labourer who had been arrested last winter near the army bases had been released from prison and had returned to his home. The reason why the man had been arrested—a drunken brawl—made no impression on Ilme. Her senses absorbed only the words: Released from prison.

It meant that people were released from prison after all. Lembit could have been free ever since the autumn.

Since it had been decided that she should go home that night with Taavi to see her parents, nobody saw anything peculiar in her strange excitement, and Taavi did not have much time for her. Before they started, the woman talked only about going home, as a child talks about a long-expected visit. On the way she tired quickly, sat down several times and breathed heavily. Sometimes she coughed sharply. This cut into the heart of the man as if it were his fault.

"The way is so long," Ilme complained. "It has never been so long before."

"It isn't any longer now than usual, only you are weak and not used to walking."

"Yes, that must be it. How fragrant everything is. The spring is here and it came so suddenly. There is so much cooing and singing now on the moor. I have been sitting in the sun—even the lark sings now over the moor. When I heard it the first time, a long time ago, there was still snow on the ground. I thought it could not possibly be a lark. But it was, right above the moor. There are many of them now. The butterflies are out, too, and the wild bees hustle back and forth. Then I keep thinking—what right have you to hold me back and watch me, that I cannot get away to my child? If people are released from prisons now. . . ."

"Stop that, Ilme," Taavi said grimly.

"I—I think only. . . ."

"Why do you torment yourself and me?"

"What are our torments compared to his?"

"Let's go on."

"The summer will be here soon and—the men could go away. They could go to some other woods so that you would not even know where they are. If you would. . . ."

"Should I go and let them kill me in cold blood?"

Ilme began to cry.

"If I should go now. . . ," she sobbed. "Tell me, Taavi, tell me. What are we going to do? Nobody will tell me. Nobody. If I only knew whether he is dead already. Oh Lord. Taavi. He is your own child; think of that."

The man could not stand it any longer.

"If you won't quit that right away, I'll take you back to Taevasaar. If you want to kill me, then I'll shoot myself right here."

"Then kill me first!"

"We *must* live! We *must* fight," Taavi said. "Life was not given to us that we should end it by our own hand. You should understand that. Be quiet now. After all, I am a human being too. I cannot take it endlessly either."

"You are not human," the woman whispered. "Why don't you give me my child back? This is in your power and you know it. He is still alive. I feel that he is still alive. I feel it every day."

"Be quiet, Ilme. Please be quiet."

"His large eyes look at me: Mother, have you abandoned me too? I cannot wait for Father any longer. Mother, have you forgotten me too?" Ilme burst out crying again. "Does the child have to die?"

"Lembit is—dead already." Taavi could finally talk again. "He was one of the martyrs of our people—one of many thousands."

Ilme did not answer, although her lips moved as if she wanted to say something. They walked as if they were mute and blind.

When Taavi began to make out the heavy trees in the dark night, the stars and the faint glow of the sunset, when his feet stopped stumbling and began to find the pathway again, when his nostrils sensed the dew-heavy smell of the black alder blossoms, he realized they had reached Metsaoti.

"Black alders," he said quietly, pointing toward the trees that were white in the darkness of the night.

Ilme only swallowed.

Behind the courtyard of Lepiku they turned under the high trees of the river bank. Ilme stopped here for a brief moment. Fragile webs of mist were rising from the river and moving away with the stream. The air was still ringing with the song of the birds. The singing was quiet, peaceful, dreamlike, as if tiny little pearls were running down the branches that were soft from the darkness, breaking into shining shreds the moment they fell on the ground. It was a white spring night of the North, more fragrant than anywhere else. The birch leaves were still crinkled from the sweet sap, but the sun had already coaxed open the apple blossoms, and the white candles of the chestnuts would burst aflame in a few days. The summer was coming, proud and high amidst the green luxuriance, crowned with blue and gold in daytime, wrapped in white and pink veils at night.

Ilme and Taavi were standing on the river bank in the meadow of Hiie. The round high bank of the river rose in front of them from the dark waters and under the birch tree was a little grave with a white cross—the grave of their daughter Hilja.

Ilme fell on her knees in front of the cross and stroked with her hand over the earth into which someone had placed fresh flowers. She seemed calmer. She kneeled for a long time, her head sunk on her chest, and when at last she moved she stroked the mound again.

"Let's go now," Taavi reminded her.

But Ilme remained on her knees. Her glance passed now over her surroundings—the steep river bank, the deep pool of water in front of her, and the tall, old trees on the other side.

Taavi turned toward the meadow, hoping that Ilme would follow him. He could not stand there any longer. Why did people have to torture themselves?

He had only walked about twenty steps when he heard Ilme stepping into the river. She slid herself quietly into the water, as if trying not to bother anybody.

The man was back on the river bank with one leap. Dashing toward the water, he threw down his overcoat. Air bubbles rose from the dark waters. Taavi pulled off his high boots, which seemed to have grown to his feet. He pressed his teeth tightly together so that he felt pain in his cheeks. His eyes tried to pierce the water. It had been too simple. But he had no time to yield to any feeling. All his strength was concentrated in his hands that were tugging at the boots, and in his eyes that were waiting for the woman to rise to the surface. Then he dived into the black, cold depths. The clothes hampered his movements and brought him up again. He was surprised that he could not reach the bottom and even more surprised that his searching hands did not find his wife.

He rose to the surface, his chest tight with fear. The cold and the darkness under the water stunned him and he could not understand how Ilme could have sunk like a stone that way, with her clothes on; even her overcoat. She might have inhaled and filled her lungs with water and the current might have carried her downstream.

Taavi dived once more a little below the deep pool. This time his hands found the woman's shoulders, head, her hair, and the overcoat that was floating in the water above her. She was strangely crouching on the bottom of the river, almost in a sitting position. When Taavi tried to pull her up his hands touched a big, rough stone in the woman's lap. Ilme had grasped the stone with all her might and Taavi had to struggle to get her free.

Taavi did not see anything around him. He did not hear the whining of the big shepherd dog of Hiie nearby and did not see the black figure of an old man who was standing on the river bank, trembling with fear, mumbling incomprehensible words and gesticulating with his arms. Or rather, Taavi heard and saw them both but his senses refused to admit anything superfluous. Aadu was already running toward the house anyway.

Ilme had drawn water into her lungs. She was half unconscious. Instead of breathing she made uncontrolled movements and her body twitched with convulsions. Taavi held her around the waist, letting her head lie lower, and tried to get the water out of her lungs. Ilme's arms became limp and she did not start breathing.

Taavi worked furiously. He pulled the wet overcoat off and began applying artificial respiration, sweat and water running together from his forehead.

When the deaf-mute returned, the startled Ignas at his heels, Taavi told the farmer: "Rub her! Rub her!"

Ilme began to moan. Her breath came back, but it was painful and irregular.

"Did she jump in the water?" Ignas asked quietly.

"She stepped in. Walked—right to the bottom."

"Intentionally, of course?"

"Yes, there," Taavi pointed somewhere with his hand. "Let's carry her inside now, and quick."

"Yes, but—it will upset Krōōt again," Ignas said, startled. "If she gets upset again it will be the end of her. Wait, let's carry her to the bath-house. It is still warm. Then I'll go and say that there was an accident. Don't tell Krōōt that she did it herself. Just tell her that she slipped and fell in."

Taavi remembered the big stone in Ilme's hands. He must not tell even Ignas about that. No, that was so incredible even to himself that it drove chills over his wet back all the way to his stiffened knees.

Nobody in the villages knew what had actually happened to Marta of Roosi. The rumours that reached Metsaoti through Harukurgu were too strange to be given full credence. The only sure thing was that Marta did not work any more in the office of the country house. The people knew that she had been found one night in a wooded grove nearby, after her wild cries for help had alerted the neighbourhood, and had been taken to the hospital. There were plenty of people who rejoiced in her misfortune and mocking laughter could be heard all over the district.

Taavi asked Osvald whether he had anything to do with it, but the latter only spat out and did not answer.

Ilme of Hiie stayed in bed in her childhood home for a long time. Although Taavi did not want to expose everyone to the danger that her presence entailed, the calm patience of Ignas had come to an end.

"I don't care what happens. I cannot take it any more."

It was hard to hear this from the lips of a strong man. Ignas knew the responsibilities that lay upon him but his own counsel no longer sufficed. The events around him were beyond his control. Some solution there must be, but he knew it could only be either death or complete insanity. Yet the resinous woods sent up lavish fragrance, the sun sparkled over the fields, the golden globe flowers gave way to flaming phlox, and the exuberant Queen Anne's lace outgrew the stick fences. Bees hummed from flower to flower, filling their combs with abundant honey, and butterflies fluttered above the meadow. Ignas hauled milk to the dairy and met farmers from neighbouring villages who made small talk and predicted a good harvest. Both threshing machines of the tractor station hummed in the villages, threshing last year's oats and barley. Life might have gone on but Ignas was impatient, yearning for a solution with the petulance of a child, with the presentiment of one who believes in dreams.

The heat of the summer became oppressive.

Ilme's return to life had been painful this time. She could not remember any awakening in her life that had been so tortured. Life cut a return path for itself into her with iron chisels—by force, as it had been cast away in the first place. Ilme stretched her arms out toward her own birth. When she recovered from the pain she was left with a feeling that she had given birth to another child.

Ilme looked long at her mother. She could not despair any more, looking at the mistress of Hiie. Krööt came, supported by Ignas or Hilda, a crutch under her arm, and sat down on a chair near the head of her daughter's bed. Sometimes she came alone, getting up from the bed by supporting herself on the headboards and then putting the crutch under the arm of her paralysed side, leaning on the wall. This frightened her daughter but her mother was able to take care of herself.

Krööt had trouble talking. Her lips did not form words clearly and her thoughts had become fragmentary, but her mind was still busy with the farm chores and she gave Hilda detailed instructions. She was still the mistress of Hiie.

"You have suffered much without any guilt," she told Ilme. "You have had to suffer for my sake, for I did not want you to have another child. I thought that. . . . The times are hard and . . . and I sinned that way. You had to suffer, for the sins of the parents are visited on their children for three and four generations. What was it that I wanted to say. . . ? I have been thinking so much every day, but I do not know how to put it into words. Too much thinking is not good and will only make one's life narrower and narrower, until finally one cannot take a single step. Then one begins to blame God for this predicament. A human cannot understand the acts of God."

The next day Krõõt was restless.

"You must go away from under this roof," she told her daughter. "You must go back into the woods. I told Father, too, that if anything should happen, he should go. Just leave me behind. I cannot do anything to help anybody now. If the new day comes the farm will need him again. Perhaps even the district will need him again, for life must go on. I have done as much at Hiie as I could; planted the garden and worked in the fields and meadows. I was proud of our livestock. I don't think I have been the worst kind of wife to Ignas. My work is done now. It is not finished but all human work will remain unfinished."

"Father won't leave you."

"That's what he said himself. 'Don't worry Krõõt,' he said. 'Our lives have been lived. We belong together and even death could not separate us for long now.' That is what he said." The sick woman repeated her husband's words with tenderness. "I feel that it won't stay that way. Something lies ahead. The fields can lie fallow and the livestock can go astray—that does not matter if only the people can save their lives. Everything can be built up again if the lives are saved. Every life that we can keep until the new morning is like a handful of good seed corn."

Ilme admired her sick mother. Nobody could talk like that except someone who had made a final reckoning with her own life and continued living only for the sake of others, continued living in her children and in the future.

They were silent for a while. Krõõt swayed back and forth on her chair as if the soft, warm, fresh breeze that came from the open window, together with the sun and the fragrance, were cradling her. Robins whistled in the trees and a wagtail twittered right under the window. The cuckoo called from the meadow, clear and bold. Suddenly Ilme had ı great desire to lie on the soft grass among buttercups under the hot glow of the sun; to lie with closed eyes, all thoughts banned from her mind. She was suddenly happy because of that wish. Life began to well up in her again, giving her new strength.

Marta of Roosi soon returned to the county house. Everybody who gazed at her now to satisfy his curiosity could see the change in her face. She rarely raised her eyes directly to another's but when she did the look in her eyes made the other step back instinctively.

Open arrests and mysterious disappearances that began to happen again in the district were now connected with Marta of Roosi, justly or unjustly. After the return of August's daughter the Communists of the district seemed to become generally more active. The woodsmen were singled out for great attention. Posters were glued to the walls of the waiting room in the county house, on telephone poles, crossroad signs, and plank fences, exhorting the men to give up their resistance and to report to the nearest executive committee. Everybody should come voluntarily and without fear. Nobody would be hurt in the least. Everybody who had been led astray by the terror propaganda of the Fascists was needed now to build up the great fatherland. Everybody was necessary to consolidate the victory and to assure a better future. Everyone would receive land and good jobs.

At the same time propagandists began to move from village to village and from farm to farm, trying to persuade the relatives of the men of the futility of their resistance—begging, exhorting, making promises and threats. The young Communists were also employed in this task. Their real purpose showed only too clearly in their scrutinizing eyes that seemed to try to remember every detail of the layout of the farm and the political opinions of every inhabitant. The propagandists took an interest also in the environs of the farms, their stables, meadows and pastures.

Marta of Roosi pondered over several problems. Her behaviour was curt even toward the chairman of the executive committee; not to mention others. Strangely enough, the blunt-mannered comrade Turban seemed afraid of her.

On Sunday Marta basked in the hot sun, lying on the edge of the field right behind the county house. She lay there with a secret purpose, for she kept a loaded revolver hidden under the blanket on which she was enjoying the sun, and her hand rested on it. Here she had recently met Osvald of Hiie.

"Take this for destroying innocent lives!" she heard Osvald's husky voice in her ears. "I am not going to kill you. But next time. . . ."

So Ilme of Hiie had really been set free. The chief of the NKVD, whom Marta had sounded out about that, had confirmed it. Osvald's act dispelled her last doubt that Ilme was free and with Taavi. Marta had to fight for her own life now, destroy whoever was necessary, until she could get away from Kalgina. She had to get away, for destruction was stalking her. Crying was useless and it was too late for that.

She had ceased to care about anything. She turned the lives of her fellow workers in the county house into living hell, watching and checking them, enjoying their frightened eyes and startled wincing. She ran into the room of the chairman of the executive committee at night, dressed in her nightgown, and embraced the man in front of his wife. This gave her pleasure. The more she suffered herself, the more she wanted to make others suffer, for it gave her some relief.

She was lying naked today for she knew that she could be seen through the window by comrade Turban. He had binoculars and she could almost feel his stare moving up and down her body with brutal desire. His crippled hands turned moist while he was standing at the window and he paced back and forth in the room in a frenzy, hurling angry words at his elderly Russian wife. Marta enjoyed even the woman's tears, and turned her naked body in the hot sun.

Suddenly Marta felt somebody else's eyes on her breasts and hips.

She winced, for she thought it might be Taavi. But before Marta's hand could grasp the revolver, she heard a raucous, angry voice from the bush: "Don't move!"

A twig cracked. Marta's helpless fingers touched the blanket, under which was the loaded Browning.

"Don't move. I tell you," the voice hissed.

"Who are you?"

"I am Reku, the dog."

After a little while Marta began to laugh with relief. The fool of Võllamäe!

"Don't laugh," the boy hissed furiously.

"I'm not laughing at you."

"But you are. Reku knows. You have always laughed at Reku. Reku will kill all who laugh at him."

Marta swallowed.

"You are a good boy, Reku."

"No, I am not. All the good ones are in the ground."

"How did you know to come here?"

"Reku has a dog's nose. And you smell."

"What?"

"You are that kind of a woman. You smell good." The boy's face emerged from the bushes—a sunburned face with gleaming eyes. Marta also saw the double-barrelled shotgun that was aimed at her.

"What do you want?" She sat up, holding her arms over her breasts.

"Reku wants," the boy panted, coming closer, crouching like a cat that is stalking a bird.

Marta saw his ragged clothes, his body that had grown to full manhood, and the hand grenades at his belt. These gave her a new idea.

"Don't come, Reku."

"I will!"

"They can see us from the county house."

"I don't care," Reku answered recklessly.

"Wait. They'll shoot you."

"Let them shoot."

"You won't get anything like that. I tell you something. Have you seen Ilme of Hiie?"

"Why not? Of course I have seen her. But she does not amount to much now. She is grey and old, and both her children are dead."

"Where is she? Are she and Taavi together?"

"Yes, she is with Taavi of Piskujõe. But Reku won't say where they are. Only our own men know that."

"Then you won't get anything! I am one of our own people too."

"They are in a cave on Taevasaar. Sometimes they are also in other places."

Marta saw that the boy did not dare approach her after all. He had become very embarrassed and shy. His eyes gleamed as before but he did not dare look Marta in the eye. His hands had sunk down together with the rifle, as if the woman's naked body paralysed him. This delighted Marta. She did not hide her breasts any more but sat up, leaning on her arms, and stretched herself. The boy swallowed and gasped, breathing huskily.

"Reku. I'll come into the woods with you if you go to Taevasaar and throw a hand grenade into the cave. At night, when they are all in there."

The boy looked at her, open-mouthed, and then retreated.

"Don't tell anybody about it," Marta warned. "When you have thrown the hand grenade in, I'll come to the woods with you."

The boy was still unable to speak.

"Andres wouldn't let me," he mumbled finally.

"Why do you have to tell him? You must not tell anybody. Anybody at all."

"Andres knows without telling. He knows everything. The old man of Piskujõe, don't you know? Taavi's father."

"But he is dead."

"That doesn't matter. He is one of my men."

Now it was Marta's turn to stare at the boy in confusion. The fool was really standing there at the side of the bush as if he had risen from another world. The soldiers had been looking for him at Võllamäe, and he was not afraid to come to the county house. He was not afraid of anybody, free and fearless like a wild animal.

"Throw the hand grenade in, throw two or three in there together," Marta said. "But don't tell anybody. Remember that. Neither before nor after."

The boy turned his face away and began to shift his legs.

"Reku does not know."

"If you don't want to come with me. . . ." Marta smiled and moved herself.

The boy winced.

"Then you'll come to the woods with Reku?" he panted, half bent over, holding the rifle crosswise in his hands.

"Yes—then!"

Reku turned abruptly around and ran quickly into the bushes. The branches cracked and the corn on the field rustled, the young soft corn. Marta stared after the boy and conflicting emotions seized her. She looked at her slender legs and then all of a sudden she pressed her fingernails into her own thigh with angry violence, so that a few drops of blood appeared and a moment later high red welts rose up on her skin.

Marta turned her face down. Suddenly she did not care in the least what happened in the world.

August of Roosi, who had wanted to set his steps so his life would not be in danger under the new régime, and so that he would not be hanged or thrown into prison for a long time under any other power either, found that the game was getting too difficult for him. Even when he was drunk he found it hard to get things clear in his mind, but when he was sober he could barely stand it. Lying and denying began to be too much for him and in spite of himself he was pulled along into doing things that left such a foul taste in his mouth that even the strongest vodka would not wash it away. August of Roosi, that tireless carouser, began to get tired.

Why couldn't they leave him alone for a few days, sitting peacefully in his hut with a bottle of vodka and some salted herrings? Let the old man enjoy life, hum a song to himself and rest. Let him throw himself down on the camomile-mixed grass under the old poplars and take pleasure in the singing of the birds, the humming of the bees, and the cool shade. Let him walk from village to village on his own and turn into any farmyard he wanted where he knew that the farmer had some beer left in the bottom of the beer keg. Let him use his crooked knife to cut off a little something from a piglet that would only spoil the meat anyway and let him be the August of Roosi he was before, whom everybody knew and nobody took seriously.

But now he was taken seriously and he was forced to take himself seriously. This brought problems that robbed him of his peace of mind, so that even the good old vodka could not save him from the tight spot in which he found himself. Formerly he had walked, chest stuck out, a red handkerchief in his breast pocket, but now his feet became unsteady near the county house and his body stooped fearfully, as if he wanted to make himself invisible.

August had begun to hate spying on the farms, for he had openly promised Ignas of Hiie, his adviser, and the other farmers that he would not be interested in anything that happened in their back rooms. But the others were interested. August's generalized, wordy reports did not satisfy them, regardless of how the old man twisted his statements. He began to hear threats and warnings.

After his daughter returned from the hospital he feared his own child more than ever before. He realized that she would try to get her revenge, and what would be the result? A bloodbath in the midst of the dry summer?

One evening Marta invited her father to her room, a place the old man shunned. When he saw his daughter's grim face and her sharp, nervous gestures, he became helpless and sank into a chair, trying to make himself very small. He rolled his worn and faded winter cap in his hands and looked at the floor with a penitent face like a schoolboy who expects a scolding. He looked askance at his daughter's back when she closed the windows with a crash.

"Listen, old man," Marta said, turning around and placing her hands on her hips. "I hear that you are too negligent!"

August fidgeted on his chair and made his old cap rotate on his blunt thumb. He felt his armpits getting bristly. It was hot in the room.

"I think I'll have to disown you soon. Think who you are—assistant militiaman, member of the people's defence force, village representative. Something is expected of you, but you only laugh. Why do you laugh when they demand work from you? Haven't you learned yet that they cannot stand laughter if it isn't drunken neighing. A Soviet citizen does not laugh—only screams and neighs, or is quiet. Everything in between is suspicious."

Marta walked back and forth in the room, smoking a cigarette.

"They are all such fools—Turban, the militiaman, and everybody. Or are you laughing at me?" she asked bluntly and stopped.

"Why should I laugh at you?"

"There might be a reason," Marta said with a warning in her voice. "There might be more reason to laugh at me than at anybody. But it will cost them dearly. You know, old man, I'll have them in my hand soon and I'll squeeze them hard. Those idiots! That leader of the terror squad is the biggest fool of them all. Just imagine, he sat at the same table at the party with a bandit, almost drank brotherhood with him, and yet he should know even in his dreams what the name of Taavi Raudoja means. Later he jumped at me, furious that I was there when the bandit ran into the woods. He did not run at all, but marched out through the door as if on parade, past the militiaman and through the whole gang of Russians. Why should he try to hang his own stupidities on my shoulders? Crazy! I'll turn the screws on them yet. I have sent in already so much information about Turban that he will disappear soon, and the militiaman won't be able to hang on much longer either. That rapist. Don't worry, old man. All these big shots are in my hand. Look here, in this same hand!" Marta shook her fist in front of her father. Her cheeks were covered with red splotches.

August fidgeted again. He cast a worried glance toward the door. Marta's voice was too loud.

"What did you want of me?" he muttered.

"Be careful, old man," Marta said quietly. "Lie to them, pretend that you are more active. They are planning something—maybe a deportation. We have to make sure they won't succeed. Warn the people ahead of time so they can be on their guard. I shall try to get as much information against them as I can and present it directly to Tallinn. Then there will be a purge among themselves, for they all have information against each other that they will be using to save their own lives. But my information is better than theirs. Go now! Warn the men in the woods and everybody else."

The old man rose but stayed in the same place and rolled his hat, as if it were too warm for his fingers.

"What else do you want?" his daughter asked.

"If . . . if . . . I am afraid your game is not as simple as that. That's what I say."

"Why should you worry. I have already looked up a new job. I'll finish up and disappear. But I cannot leave everything half done here like this. I have no reason to leave right now and it would seem suspicious. They might put the screws on me. I don't want anything to happen to you but—you understand. A person has it much easier when he has no relatives. Look, I have talked myself quite calm now. Here.

Have a better cigarette. One more thing—perhaps it will give you some assurance. These officials here, in uniform and out, only seem to be powerful but you do not need to be afraid of them. They are all under the surveillance of the secret section—even the captain. Remember that. And I am one of those who control them. Don't bulge your eyes. If you should hint at that somewhere, you'll be a goner. Now go and do as I tell you."

August of Roosi left his daughter's room with stumbling steps, as if he had left much of the sight of his eyes there. The old man could not have any peace, try as he might. The only thing he realized was that what was asked of him would perhaps keep him from future imprisonment but would bring the possibility of being shot quite close.

A few days later when August of Roosi was whispering his warnings in the villages and Marta assumed that Reku's explosion might already have sounded on Taevasaar, she received a blow that stunned her senses for a long time. Panic was in her eyes and her hands tried to wipe from her face a moist, sticky cobweb that was not there. She stared blankly at the wall on which she had happened to lean. The wallpaper had split open, and a hidden microphone appeared in the crack. Every word she had spoken in this room had reached somebody's ear!

XIV

On these beautiful summer evenings, when the meadows seemed bathed in milky light, one could often hear the melancholy howl of a lonely dog in the dark forests. At times it sounded near the village of Metsaoti, sometimes even right behind the garden fence of Piskujōe under the great fir trees. In the soft light of the summer night, filled with the smell of fresh hay and the singing of the crickets, it sounded eerie and unnatural. It was the complaint of an abandoned animal seeking the tracks of his master, and it sounded especially hungry and desperate in the early hours of the morning. Those who happened to hear it felt a chill in their hearts and tossed and turned long before they fell asleep again.

Reku roamed and sniffed in the forests, his face haggard from sleeplessness, his small eyes gleaming feverishly between his eyebrows and cheekbones. He was looking for his companions, for he found himself suddenly abandoned and alone. This unheard of situation at first startled him. Then it began to torment him and now it drove him to desperation. He did not know how to arrange his affairs any more. He could not understand what had happened. He saw only the naked woman lying in the sun and this picture made him lie breathless on the tree roots, where he crouched until the cold made him quiver and tremble.

When he got up he called for his companions and shouted warlike orders to his army but his words reverberated in the night as on silent waters where the nightbird's skirting barely left a ripple. Sometimes the owl answered him, a crow cawed which he had frightened out of its sleep, or a bat fluttered silently over the river. Reku shook his wildly dishevelled hair and howled. He ran around big trees, sniffed at dark bushes, felt for tracks on grassy forest trails and turned to some glen in the woods where he raised his face toward the stars that were veiled in opaque blue light.

He had never gone through anything like it before.

He could no longer recall exactly how the men had joined him when he escaped from the Red Army but it seemed to him now as if they had helped him to crawl through the barbed wire fence, as if they had greeted him joyfully and led him to the forests near his home.

A young fellow had shouted one night in the barracks, his hands balled into fists: "We have nobody to help us but the ghosts of our ancestors. If all those would rise from their graves who have been killed and who have fallen on battlefields, then we would show them. I tell you, they will rise from their graves and ask us who we are, that we dare mock their struggle with our wretched slavery." The boy had checked himself, sat down on the cot and wrung his hands. "Nerves, damn it," he had muttered with a pale face. "But I am going to get out from behind these wires. I'll shout until the dead rise from their graves and help me fight. I'll fight until I go to join them."

These words that Reku had forgotten long ago had taken hold of his imagination. He had begun to see soldiers at night outside the barbed wire fence—old and young, with shattered limbs, with grievous, bloody wounds, but with bold, firm faces. He saw familiar faces among them— he did not remember their names any more—but there had been very many of them.

Then Reku had run away. He realized that he was being played for a fool, that he was being mocked, that they did not intend to give him a gun but wanted to make him into an idiot. He had joined the army to kill Russians and become a general with a long, shiny sword, rattling spurs, and golden stars all over his chest. Reku's flight had been the step of a person who is deeply disappointed and hurt, who has finally realized that he is on the wrong path.

Reku had led his great army through the rains of the autumn, the frosts of winter, through spring and summer. They were not always with him, but they came when he called. Sometimes they came in little groups; sometimes in an endless procession. When Reku was cold and lit a small fire in the thickets, he enjoyed watching their camp fires that filled the great forests. Then the boy lay on his back on the moss, listened to the steady footsteps of the war horses, the conversing voices of the soldiers, the rattle of their weapons, and the singing that rose from the fires. The boy knew that even when he could not see or hear them, they were near, waiting for his orders. At least Andres of Piskujõe was always near; he whose coat was bloody and chest pierced with bullets.

Reku had understood that only he was able to see them, but no other living person. The others were stupid. Although they said they were on the same side, they sometimes acted so that Reku's companions shook their heads. They did not act at the right time and place, and if

371

they did something it was wrong, as if they had been blindfolded. Reku, too, would have made mistakes, had it not been for Andres.

But now Reku was in trouble. He ran through heaths and birch forests, crossed the meadows that were covered with bright blossoms, got caught in the thickets and broke wildly through the underbush. Every night he made big circles in the forests of Verisoo and his aimless wanderings brought him sometimes to the camp of the men.

He found it easy to sneak past the sentries, for they stood far apart. The camp was small, for some of the men of the Snake Pit still slept on Taevasaar. The other bunker had become filled with water and had been temporarily abandoned. It was also difficult to feed such a large group. This was the reason why the men of Tenise had built shelters of branches near their homes. They had not started setting up supplies for the winter yet and it seemed to Reku that the men were somehow hesitating. Sometimes Reku inspected the places where they had eaten. When he did not find anything there he shot some animal in the woods when he had a lucky day. On a worse one he was satisfied with newly matched young birds. But Reku had tried everything that was edible in the woods, even frogs and grass snakes.

Then one stormy night, when Reku had howled long enough in the glare of the lightning and complained of his loneliness on the moor, he began to cross the bog toward Taevasaar. He hurried over the gurgling earth, growling, cheeks still streaked with tears. A witless child, freezing in his loneliness, who saw nothing but a naked woman lying in the glow of the hot sun. So he went, disregarding the logs that had been placed into the bog holes to provide a foothold, leaping from clod to clod in the darkness and rain over the open moor. Sometimes he crawled on all fours, searching for a way with his hands in the wet ground that swayed and gurgled under him. Then he threw himself again from bush to bush. The barrel of the gun hit him painfully in the nape of the neck, his feet sank over his knees into the mouth of the bog, but his hands grabbed the sod, pulling his body forward before the bottomless bog could begin to suck him down. Again he crawled and groped, guided by senses for which human beings have not yet found a name. He made wide circles until he reached the land-mines.

"Don't go there, Reku," he warned himself. "The mines will tear you to pieces. You dog, don't take the pathway either—there's a man keeping watch. Reku will shoot his eyes out but the others will hear the bang. Reku must go quietly so that nobody can hear or see him, and then throw in the whole bundle of grenades so everything gets smashed to pulp inside!"

Suddenly Reku felt as if he had found what he had been looking for, running around for long days, perspiring and tired, pain and thirst burning in his throat. What he had been crying and howling for through the white summer nights. Throw in the grenades and—pulp. Red blood flowing on the floor, shattered people groaning and gurgling like the bog that he has left behind. Strange—in that wild hallucination he saw clearly a naked woman. There were many of them, the whole

372

field was full of them, waiting for Reku. Throw in the grenades and—pulp.

The bunkers under the dwarf pines lay silent and lifeless in the brisk shower of rain. The thunderstorm had reached its height. Reku saw the bolts flashing with metallic crackle. The boy was forced several times to his knees against his will; once even pushed flat on the ground where he lay for a moment, shivering. Then he jumped up and rushed forward, gasping for breath. The grenades and—everything to pulp, bloody and stinky like the bog.

Reku busied himself with the grenades on the roof of the bunker. His hands shook from fever, his throat was hot, the rain flowed down his soaked body. He hid his face in the earth and the sharp branches each time the lightning flashed. He had tied the grenades together with a willow twig several days ago. All he had to do was to ignite them and throw them down the chimney.

At the very moment when Reku was about to complete his errand, the whole place lit up with blue light. Andres of Piskujõe stood in front of him, with a stern face and a paralysing accusation in his eyes: "What are you doing?"

Ilme had again become a little more reconciled to her fate. After Taavi had dragged her up from the bottom of the river, she had remained almost strangely calm. She followed her husband, obeying without argument his least word. What amazed Taavi most was her childlike, almost playful return to nature. She could sit for hours somewhere near a bush, gingerly touching the moss and stroking the blades of grass, or looking into the dewy eyes of wild flowers as if she saw there a new, hitherto undiscovered miracle. Most frequently she lay leaning against a resinous tree trunk and looking at the blue sky through the branches. Her face opened up somehow and became soft, the wind played with her hair, and the sunlight poured lifelike colour over her pale face. She coughed painfully, germs of death were in her chest, but she stretched out instinctively toward life and sunlight, her arms resting limply and her fingers opening and closing.

Taavi could not altogether understand her but he waited patiently. He looked at his wife as a gardener looks at a delicate plant. He knew how healthy and full of life Ilme had been before.

The men of the Snake Pit had decided unanimously to go to Taeva-saar for the night. A thunderstorm was brewing and it was no fun to stay under the trees in the rain since there was not enough room for everybody in their little tent. The captain had advised against building huts from tree branches—the roundups could reach their hiding place any day and their huts would be strong accusation material against the people of the neighbouring villages. Living in the forests from day to day they had to manage so that they left as few traces as possible. The group of Tenise with Captain Jonnkoppel at its head had become more mobile. The men of Metsaoti remained stationary mostly for Ilme's sake, but also because of the help they could give to the haymakers. They kept their heavier weapons and munition supplies on Taevasaar.

"I would rather not go to Taevasaar," Ilme said. "It is so stuffy there under the earth—just like living in a grave."

Nobody cared much for walking across the moor, although their limbs had become stiff with rheumatism from sleeping on bare ground, especially Värdi's. Tõmm refused abruptly to go along, and went into a hay barn.

"If it should rain you don't have to fear even the devil himself in the hay barn. I have my gun with me. I am sick and tired of rotting there on the moor."

"You should come along to take your turn at the watch," Osvald suggested.

"I'll watch in the hay barn. Watch, watch. . . ," the boy mocked him. "He must be completely soft in his head who comes to look for you there on the moor."

It remained that way. Osvald and Leonard gathered a load of dry branches for a fire, and when the dusk came they followed the path across the moor. Black thunderclouds rose on the horizon and the air was heavy.

The situation in the Snake Pit was really not very encouraging, although Osvald began to build a fire and the yellow light of the kerosene lamp made a weak effort to reach the four corners of the room. The light was just strong enough to reveal the stinking, wet mats on the floor and the green mould on the walls. Gray wet stripes ran across the ceiling. Sand and dirt had dropped in places on the sleeping cots. Sleepy frogs hobbled in the middle of the room.

Värdi shook the sack of moss on his bed, gritting his teeth as if he were chewing the moist, stuffy air to make room for himself to breathe. Even his narrow shoulders and humped back remained stiff and tense.

"Don't eat up all the frogs," Leonard sneered.

Värdi began to pant and jump in response, as if he had sat down on glowing coals. He whirled like a top and his eyes were almost bulging out from behind his glasses. He had pulled a big whitish snake from his bed, thrown it on the floor, and was trampling on the writhing reptile with both feet.

Ilme felt so repelled by it all that she wanted to run outside, especially since the cold stove sent out bitter blue smoke, blinding everybody in the room. She could not understand how they had lived here all last winter.

"Leave the stove alone," Taavi scolded Osvald. "Do you want to smoke out all of us and the whole zoo here?"

"It won't start, damn it," Osvald answered, crouching in front of the stove on all fours. "The air is so heavy outside, as if a cat had got stuck in the chimney. Wait until it starts to draw. We could at least make a cup of tea."

"With what? The water here in the bog is pure sewage."

The chimney began to draw after all. Ilme and Taavi tried to make up the damp beds, Värdi took the light machine gun apart, and Leonard cleaned his rifle, humming a song. The roar of the thunder made the earth reverberate. Osvald went out to check the chimney. When he returned, his clothes were wet and his hair clung to his forehead in dark strands. The heavy beat of the rain sounded on the roof. The thunder seemed to penetrate deeper and deeper into the moor.

"Brr. That rain is really something," Osvald purred. "It's good we have a hole to hide our heads in such weather."

Ilme was standing in the doorway, turning her face toward the bluish flashing lights. The raindrops broke into thin mist. The flashes of lightning reflected in them and formed a whitish wreath above her head. She stepped back a little each time when the bright sky seemed to bend down toward her, filling the doorway with eerie light, but she no longer feared the thunderstorm. Today it seemed to have a strange fascination for her. The water that blew in her face seemed to caress it. The thundering sky, torn by lightning, made her so small she almost did not exist, and that was good, for then she was unable to think about herself. Suddenly she felt the urge to walk alone across the moor, in the rain and the glow of the lightning, to stumble through the thunderstorm at night, barely conscious, frightened, helpless and small. When the morning came she would not remember anything but just find herself somewhere in a strange forest on the warm earth that steamed from the hot sun—washed clean and pure.

The fire was burning satisfactorily now in the stove but the bitter smoke and the mouldy smell had not faded from the room. The men were all sitting on the lower bunk beds, stooped and tired, their faces turned toward the hearth. Taavi had hung Ilme's blanket near the fire but the warmth was barely sufficient to dry it. Nobody seemed to care about sleep. Osvald had found a sack of peas in the storage room. They were soft from the humidity. Osvald rolled them between his fingers and then passed the sack to Leonard, who alone was lying on the bed behind Osvald's back.

"What are we waiting for?" Ilme asked with a strained voice when she had sat down and the men were still silent.

The looks that slowly reached her did not provide any answer. She thought she saw that all these sunburned, strong faces were only masks hiding inner exhaustion and desperation.

The eyes of little Värdi began to flash and his mouth chewed impatiently. Osvald bent down as if Ilme's words had urged him to force some more logs into the stove. The fire blazed up so that even the metal chimney pipe rattled.

At the same moment there was an explosion above their heads. Smoke, ashes and burning firebrands burst from the crashing metal stove all over the room and the chimney they had fitted together from pieces of pipe fell apart. Choking smoke mingled with the smell of explosives, sand rained from the ceiling and the weak light of the kerosene lamp flickered miserably like an expiring eye.

Ilme thought at first that they had been hit by lightning. She stood there, paralysed by fear, her eyes, hair and even her mouth full of ashes. Coals that had flown from the stove were smoking near her in somebody's old clothes. The stove itself had fallen over on one side, probably burning Osvald, who was spitting out and cursing, holding his big hands between his knees. Värdi was again kicking at everything and everybody near him, as if the whole room were filled with writhing snakes. This time he was stamping out burning firebrands.

"A bomb!" Taavi gasped.

Then they all stopped for a moment, notwithstanding the smoke and ashes that took away their breath and blinded their eyes. Above them on the roof, sounded somebody's wild scream. It broke down into moans and trailed off completely, only to begin again still more desperately.

Without wasting any words the men grabbed their rifles and rushed toward the door. Leonard, getting up in the dark, banged his head loudly against the upper bunk.

Taavi was the first to bend down over the wounded figure. He could not understand at all what had happened. Nobody could understand anything. The rain was falling, warm and heavy, although the thunder had rumbled across the moor toward Kalgina. In the light of the fading flashes a deep crater was visible in the roof, reaching down to the beams of the ceiling. The groaning remains of a human being had been thrown on to the lower earth cover of the doorway.

While Osvald and Värdi searched the neighbourhood for their supposed attackers, Taavi concerned himself with the wounded man. He was screaming and writhing in pain and his cramped limbs were bloody in their tattered and torn rags. Wherever Taavi touched him, his fingers found sticky warm blood or cold mud. Then he picked up the weapon that he felt lying under his knees. It was a double-barrelled shotgun. He touched again the boots and clothes of the wounded man and jumped up. He had recognized Reku of Võllamäe.

What could it mean?

Taavi called for his companions. It was ominously dark and raining hard. Leonard rushed out from the bunker, rifle in hand, and threw himself down among the earth clods with a thud. Taavi heard how he loaded his rifle with a loud click.

"Come here!" Taavi shouted to him. "You, Leonard! Come quickly, he is dying!"

But Leonard did not understand. Osvald and Värdi arrived first.

"Reku," Taavi said. "Give me a hand, let's carry him inside. He's badly wounded."

"How come?" Osvald muttered.

The wounded boy screamed as they dragged him inside. He was conscious, but terribly mangled. His movements were weak and convulsive. It seemed that he had only enough strength to moan and croak, breaking this monotony with an occasional piercing scream.

The air in the smoke-filled bunker was suffocating. The scattered firebrands were still burning on the floor.

"Hold me a light!" Taavi shouted. "Throw these firebrands out of the door! Quickly! And bandages, hand me some bandages! They are in the box up there."

Someone handed him the bandages. Someone panted, throwing fire-brands out of the door.

"Quicker. Faster. He is dying. I can't see anything but blood. Ilme, hold me the light. Come closer with that lamp. Osvald, is your shirt clean? Come, see if you can stop the bleeding somehow."

Taavi pulled off his coat, then his blouse and undershirt.

"Here," he threw it to Osvald, "tear it up. The other bandages are too small."

He kneeled on the floor, naked to his belt. He had no experience in bandaging wounds and at the moment it was impossible to estimate their extent. He tore shreds of bloody clothing from Reku's shattered body. The boy's hair and half his face were singed, his neck was black with blood. He kept his eyes closed but his mouth gasped for breath. His hands twitched on his stomach—one was whole but bloody. the other torn to pieces up to his shoulder.

Värdi bent down at Taavi's side. His hands seemed to be more used to wounds.

"Hold the light closer," Taavi ordered. Realizing that his wife could barely hold herself up even on her knees, he motioned to Osvald to take over the swaying lamp. Ilme withdrew and remained huddled on the floor, pressing her face against the edge of the sleeping cot.

"That won't help any," the hunchback panted. "It won't. . . ."

"How did it happen?" Taavi asked in return.

"He wanted to blow us up."

"No!"

Then Reku said it himself, as if he had understood their words: "Throw the grenades in . . . ah . . . nothing but pulp."

"Speak up," Taavi shouted, seizing the wounded man by his shoulders.

"Taavi." It was Ilme's voice. "Taavi."

"Marta . . . Marta. . . ," the wounded boy mumbled.

"Marta of Roosi? What about her? Speak up!"

Reku squirmed helplessly, his face distorted with pain.

"Marta . . . grenades . . . throw in . . . and . . . pulp. . . ."

Taavi was still shaking Reku.

"Speak up."

"Don't do it," Osvald said quietly.

Reku's words came quickly now, like jerky rounds from a machine gun: "Grenades . . . in, all of them . . . pulp. Ilme-of-Hiie-two-children-all-pulp, Ilme-herself-too. Don't jump like that, the dog will blast your face in. Andres don't come. Our own men. Andres! Andres . . . came . . . wouldn't let me. . . ."

Reku opened his eyes and gazed at Taavi, who had relinquished the hold of his bloody hands. The boy seemed to recognize Taavi and his lips moved but they did not form any words. Then Reku began to howl, plaintively and gravely. He did not move any more. His eyes were open and clear, but his mouth wailed, until blood gushed forth from his lips.

Then he was silent, pushing his chin higher and higher until his whole body gradually became limp.

The men covered the shattered limbs of the corpse with white bandages, even tried to clean his face, and then lifted him on to a bed.

Taavi carried the news to Võllamäe in the grey light of the dawn, describing what had happened as an accident. The old people were both already up, although Jaak's thinning hair was still standing straight up in the nape of his neck from lying on the pillow, the buttons of his shirt were still open, and his feet bare. The face of the old horsetrader became grey and hopeless, and the mistress of the farm, a small woman, busy and self-effacing, aged before her time under the tyranny of her husband, looked at the bringer of the news, her mouth twisted to one side and her freckled face rigid. It took a long while before her wrinkled cheeks began to tremble and tears ran from her eyes, faster and faster. Neither of the parents complained, although the grey morning would never usher in another bright day for them.

"Was his end . . . very bad?" Jaak asked. "Did he suffer long?"

"No, not long."

"What are you crying for?" the man said roughly to his wife. "Whatever he was, he was our son, but now we don't have even that much. Those thugs!" His hands made some quick unconscious movements and he began to search for his tobacco pouch. The woman retreated quietly to the back room.

When Taavi left, the farmer of Võllamäe accompanied him to the woods, barefooted and unwashed as he was, eyes rudely opened from their sleepiness. The mistress of the farm hurried with busy steps across the farmyard, milk pail in hand, her other hand raised to her eyes. The feet hurried and hurried but the body seemed to get there faster. Her body was bent forward as if the tears must fall directly into the blooming camomile of the yard without touching any of her clothes.

Taavi had felt much heartache these last days. It was good that there was something to do now—go somewhere and consult with his companions and the farmers of Metsaoti. But since all these trips and meetings arose from the happenings of that stormy night, he had found no real relief from tension.

He had heard about the fate of the four vagrant soldiers in the autumn two years ago and had seen their shrub-covered graves in Katkuaugu. He knew other graves—of strangers and of their own—which had come into being during these last years in the woods nearby and even on the moor. He knew that there were many more to come—outside the graveyards and the empty, deserted farms, haunted by howling, homeless dogs.

The funeral of Ebehard of Võllamäe took place three days later. When the soft, white summer night slumbered over the moors they placed the corpse on a homemade stretcher. Up to the bog holes four of them could carry it together. Then the corpse was entrusted to Osvald and Tõmm, who were the toughest. Taavi and Leonard walked behind.

The procession moved slowly. They could take only short steps and it took time and strength. It reminded Osvald of how they had carried Ilme to Taevasaar one rainy autumn night—again it had been he and Tõmm who had carried her.

"Don't stumble there in front. You'll drag all of us into a bog hole," Tõmm growled.

"My foot . . . slipped," Osvald retorted. Into a bog hole, his thoughts mocked him. They were already in a bog hole, all of them. It was impossible to sink much deeper. "It was stupid of me not to kill Marta when I had the chance," he mumbled to himself, barely audibly.

Jaak and Leena of Võllamäe were waiting for them at the edge of the moor. A new coffin made of white boards was on the wagon. The farmer was holding the horse by its mouth, as if the old, steady animal were quite jumpy and shy. He had even tied the reins around his arm. Leena ran to meet her son on the moor as soon as her eyes distinguished the approaching figures. She did not speak to the men, grasped the side of the stretcher and stomped through the moor grass and the huckleberry bushes toward the heath. When Osvald and Tõmm lowered the stretcher on dry ground, the mother kneeled down at the side of her son's corpse and tenderly stroked the white bandages.

Jaak was still standing on the same spot, but his feet took slow steps without getting anywhere.

"Shall we put him in the coffin?" Taavi asked quietly.

"Yes, what else?" Jaak mumbled. "Yes, into the coffin."

When he did not leave the horse Taavi and Leonard lifted the coffin from the wagon. It was a little peculiar to do it that way. Both parents seemed to be watching them from the side.

"Don't howl like that, old woman," Jaak said roughly, although suffering ran in his voice. "Put the clothes on the boy! You can see that I have to hold the horse. . . ."

"Yes, yes," the little woman now rushed eagerly to the wagon. She threw things around until she found her son's new suit. Jaak stood all the while with the horse, while the woman dressed the corpse with the help of the woodsmen. The unhappy mother wiped her tears courageously but her movements were nevertheless awkward and clumsy.

"He must have grown in the woods. Look, the suit won't fit," she complained. "Poor thing. Poor child. You had to suffer so much. . . ."

"Why didn't you take my church-going suit?" the father remonstrated with her. "I told you to take it—it would have been bigger and more comfortable. Whom are you saving it for?"

When Reku was dressed and lifted into the coffin Jaak came to look at his son. He kneeled for a moment near the coffin, wiped his hand over its smooth side and got up.

"Don't howl," he said quietly. "He has it better now." Returning to the horses he added sternly: "Lift the lid up and screw it on. And let's go! If you want to, Leena, you can climb on the wagon."

But the woman walked at the side with her short steps, hand cramped around the corner of the coffin. So they went along the winding road through the heath, Jaak leading the horse, Leena supporting the coffin, and Taavi following with his three companions.

They had dug the grave on a slope in the woodland pastures of Võllamäe. Jaak stopped the horse near the hay barn. Ignas of Hiie, little Värdi and old Peeter of Valba were waiting for them, Peeter with a big armful of flowers.

"Where are the others?" Jaak inquired.

"There are no more," Ignas replied.

"How come?" Jaak could not understand. "I invited the whole village. I told everybody to come to the funeral. I even sent word to the men in the woods." His voice sounded disappointed and hurt. "Why didn't they come? Look, I hauled food and drink out here to fill half the hay barn so it would be a decent funeral. I don't have a son to bury every day. Tell me, farmer of Hiie, why didn't they come?"

"The times are such—people are afraid. . . ."

"The times," Jaak muttered. "The times, of course it's the times!" He repeated his words several times, while the others stood around, waiting. "Well, lift the coffin down and put it in the grave. If the neighbours are afraid to come to bury one of their own number, then—the times. . . . What road are they themselves planning to take? Will they go to heaven in a fiery chariot or remain unburied? The people of Kadapiku are scared, of course. Worry about all these children makes them soft. Juhan of Matsu, you know that bull. He is so proud that he thinks himself too good to come to the funeral of a fool. But this fool was a human being too." He was silent for a while and then asked Ignas: "Say that my son was a human being too!"

"Yes, he was. He might have grown into a strong tree if this accident hadn't happened to him when he was a child."

"Then we'll bury him like a decent Christian."

Ignas of Hiie sent Reku off with a handsome speech. He spoke in a quiet, calm voice, sounding a little tired, surrounded by the dark night, facing the black open grave around which were standing the dark figures of the funeral party.

And then he said the Lord's Prayer. Peeter of Valba scattered his flowers over the coffin, everybody threw in his three handfuls of earth and then only the sound of the spades could be heard filling up the grave.

In the midst of this silent activity the mother of the deceased, little Leena of Võllamäe, suddenly began to sing: "A mighty fortress is our God. . . ."

She stood on the edge of the grave and wailed in her pained, clear voice. The men stopped swinging their spades and stood as if paralysed. They had all heard Reku's barking and howling in the dark forests and the singing of the unhappy woman reminded them of that. Then Jaak, too, the horsetrader, joined in the singing. Their voices blended well, although Jaak could not remember when he had last sung a hymn. The singing of the woman in the quiet forest suddenly moved him so deeply that he forgot the funeral meats and drinks that were waiting near the hay barn, forgot the hurt and disappointment caused by the guests who had ignored his invitation, and all the heavy sorrow that lay on his soul.

The men would have slipped quietly away into the thicket if they had not been holding spades that reminded them of the necessity of covering up the grave.

XV

Soon after the funeral of Ebehard of Võllamäe a fateful event took place one hot July day which proved decisive in the tragic developments in the district of Kalgina.

Since nobody had touched the food Jaak of Võllamäe had hauled to the forest for the funeral meal that night, he had left it near the hay barn for the men in the woods—freshly baked bread, butter, meat, and a quantity of home-brewed vodka. Taavi and his companions took part of the supplies with them that same night and a few days later they returned to get the rest.

At Leonard's instigation they sat down on the edge of the woods between the roots of great alders, spread out their delicacies and began to enjoy them. As could be expected, they poured some of the stinking home-made brew into a field bottle and let it go around from hand to hand. They did not speak much, devoting their main attention to the food, the drink and the refreshing shade. From time to time they stretched out their hands, picked blueberries from the bushes and stuffed them in their mouths. Late white blossoms shone from the bushes in front of them, the hot air quivered over the meadows, and the smell of the peppermint plants they had inadvertently crushed mixed with the heavy aroma of the ferns among which they were lying. A little bird twittered in the branches above their heads.

"If heaven would send us more funerals we could get jellied meat and white bread every day," Leonard laughed irreverently.

Everyone looked at him reproachfully and Värdi's eyes flashed angrily from behind his glasses.

"Oh Leonard, Leonard, when are you going to grow into a man?" Osvald retorted. This time there was serious displeasure in his voice; even some bitterness. Reku's death had affected him so deeply that when he sat in the wood alone with his thoughts he often found his big hands trembling.

"What can you expect from the swine," Värdi growled, holding the field bottle for a long time on his lips. His sharp Adam's apple moved quickly like a pump.

Tõmm of Hiie took the bottle from him. Almost as if the levity of Leonard's words drove them on, they all rushed to the vodka. Although they knew that it would be pure stupidity to get drunk on a hot day they did so as if from some secret compulsion, to dispel the memories of the funeral. Soon they stretched out recklessly in the blueberry bushes and

Leonard became really talkative. His black moustache had grown together with his untrimmed beard, under which his cheeks had turned boyishly pink. The general conversation grew louder and louder, but it remained bitter and gloomy. Even their laughter was mean and violent, staying in the back of their throats like the growl of an angry wolf.

"Let's get going," Taavi suggested. He did not like the idea of returning to the camp intoxicated. Captain Jonnkoppel and his men had stayed in the woods near Tenise and he had sent word of lively movements among Russian army units near the airstrip and the military bases. True, all that seemed to be taking place at some distance from their location in the forests of Ilmaotsa and the moor of Verisoo, but they had to be prepared for any eventuality, especially since they were beginning to set up supplies for the winter. "Let's go," Taavi repeated and got up.

"What the devil," Tõmm said suddenly, crouching behind an uprooted tree stump. Since the vodka had made him lose control of his voice his shout had been louder than necessary, startling the others into silence.

Looking across the meadow they saw several strange men in front of the Võllamäe hay barn. They were holding rifles in their hands and their new cartridge belts gleamed in the sun, leaving no doubt as to their identity. Two soldiers of the Red Army emerged from behind the barn.

A roundup!

With feline agility and smoothness the men hid the supplies of food and the vodka bottles in the branches of an uprooted fir tree. Värdi swallowed the last mouthful from the field bottle, mechanically readying his pistol in the meantime.

"That means new funerals," Osvald muttered.

"That's what they are asking for out there in the open," Leonard answered.

"Shall we mow them down?" Tõmm asked.

"Hold it, you idiot," was Taavi's agitated reply. "This handful cannot be all of them. We must watch out that they don't get behind us. Leonard, run to the camp and tell them that the men of the terror squad are out and that Russian soldiers are with them."

He then sent Tõmm to guard their rear. Värdi and Osvald remained in their position on the edge of the meadow. Since the bushes were in the way and hindered observation, Taavi climbed a fir tree. His head buzzed and his limbs had become light from the vodka. He felt an irresistible urge to hurt the enemy some way. Although he knew that his fighting instincts had been aroused by the drink, he could not suppress them completely with his reason.

There were about ten young boys standing near the hay barn, close together like a herd of hesitant sheep. A few soldiers of the Red Army were among the group. A little farther down, on the meadow of Lepiku, was a moving line of soldiers. They were evidently combing the forest

382

meadows of Päraluha. Taavi climbed down, disappointed. From the last branch he looked again, straining his eyes. The group near the hay barn had become excited, moving back and forth, gesticulating with their arms, pointing to the ground, and then moving into the bushes toward the slope where Taavi could see Reku's sandy grave.

"Hey," Taavi called his companions.

"They're leaving," Osvald said when he reached the fir tree.

"They are about to dig up Reku's body. They are digging in the grave with their bayonets."

"What can you expect from the swine?"

At the same moment they heard the call of a grouse from the wood. Before any of the three could have answered, Leonard raced out from the bushes and crashed again to the ground, stumbling over some twisted branches.

"Come quickly, men, damn it," he panted, flushed from the run. "The terror squad is attacking the Hiie people! Near their hay barn. They have already pressed Ignas against the wall."

"Let's go," Taavi interrupted him.

They ran across the meadow, leaping from bush to bush. Nobody was to be seen. The horse was ambling across the field and the load of hay was leaning against the side of the barn.

"Shh!" Taavi stopped.

Then they heard voices from the barn: coarse laughter, a man's voice and the muffled, desperate cries of a girl.

Disregarding all caution, the men rushed around the corner of the hay barn. Osvald, Tõmm, and Värdi saw vividly in their mind's eye an autumn night in the living room at Matsu—dead Russians piled over raped women.

"Hands up, you devils," they shouted with one voice.

The picture that appeared before their eyes was not much different. Hilda was tossing in the hay, legs bare, her cotton dress torn to shreds around her breast and hips in the unequal struggle. Two startled men rose from their knees, raising their hands—the gigantic militiaman Peetal Rause and August of Roosi, their clothes in wild disarray.

They might have been shot right away but before any of the men could have done it Tõmm jumped into the hay barn, hissing like a wild animal, and began to beat the men with his strong fists. He hit them in the face and on the back of their heads, as the blows happened to fall.

"Don't beat me, I haven't done anything," the old man moaned weepily.

"So you haven't done anything," the boy puffed. "So it wasn't you at all!" He gave the old man another blow in the face. But before August could begin to spit out the remnants of his front teeth, Tõmm seized him by his shoulders and threw him face down into the hay. "So you haven't done anything and I saw you holding the girl's arm tight, you damned beast! Where is my father? What did you do to the old man?" he shouted to the militiaman, raising his rifle butt for a savage blow. It enraged him that he could not crush the ape-like face of the militiaman with his fists.

"Wait!" Taavi grabbed his rifle. "We'll take care of that. See what's happened to Hilda."

Hilda had turned her face into the hay and was sobbing hysterically but without tears. She ignored Tõmm's shy touch. She did not answer any questions, and was barely able to breathe because of her convulsive weeping. Help had arrived at the last moment. Suddenly realizing this, she rose and sprang out of the hay barn, without looking anybody in the face.

"Hilda," Tõmm cried.

"Let her run and recover from the shock," Taavi replied.

"We didn't do anything to her," August of Roosi hurried to reassure the men. "Nothing at all, my word of honour. Rause is such a boar of a man. He's born like that—just grabs them and. . . ."

Peetal Rause moved himself stiffly, as if his big limbs were frozen. His black nostrils were open like those of a nervous animal, but otherwise his face remained immobile. The brutality that had grown into his features hung somehow loosely in his face, especially around his mouth, and naked fear looked out of his browless eyes.

"Where is the farmer?" Taavi asked. His stern quietness was more ominous than any rage.

"The boys—the boys took him along," August puffed, his mouth bloody. "They won't do anything to him—they'll let him go again."

Värdi was gnashing his teeth impatiently behind his back as if they had already wasted an intolerable amount of time.

Suddenly August became lively and talkative. He wiped sweat from his face and the words ran from his bloody mouth like a babbling brook: "Taavi of Piskujõe, be human. That's what I say. You see I'm an old man. They drag me to the forests by force, make me run along, old though I am. That's what I say—just like a clown. I tell the boys dirty jokes and carry my gun crosswise on my back. See, they ordered me to catch the Hiie horse. The animal is no fool. He won't let an old stupid ass like me catch it. Rause here grabbed the girl. Well, I came to tell him he shouldn't, crazy. . . ."

"Don't lie like that, you were holding the girl yourself," Tõmm cut in, ready to attack the old man again.

"Don't come again with your fists," August wailed. "I couldn't help it when the militiaman ordered me. His strength and power is greater. I can't let myself be killed! That's what I say. I told the girl too, that—it wouldn't hurt her, if. . . . Believe me, men, I have always been on your side. Always—my word of honour and amen." He climbed out of the hay barn, beaten and wretched.

"Keep your hands above your head," Osvald ordered him. "Shall we finish it right here?"

"Let's take them to the moor," Taavi answered. "The shots will call the others. Tõmm, take the militiaman's arms and uniform cap."

The militiaman was squatting at the entrance to the hay barn. Tõmm gave him first a powerful kick with his foot, so that the giant crashed to the ground, face first. His belt and his uniform trousers were open and bared his body. Värdi, who could finally get close to the enemy, leaped at him as if propelled by a spring, grabbed a stick from a faggot heap and began to cane the militiaman.

"Look at him, damn it, how he loses his pants," he panted, his stick falling with increasing energy on the naked haunches of the lying man. The militiaman squirmed on the ground but each time he tried to rise, Leonard put his foot on the nape of his neck and pressed him down.

"There," Värdi gasped and handed the stick to August. When August looked at him without understanding, the hunchback cried: "Damn it, don't you know what this is for?" He gnashed his teeth for a long time, his chin twisted to one side and his vein-covered forehead wet with perspiration.

August held the rod without knowing what to do with it. When they began to move toward the woods and pushed him indifferently with the butt of a rifle or the barrel of an automatic, the old man realized that he had to do something to save his life. He had tried to follow his golden principle in these tough days—do anything to avoid being shot, either now or in the future. However, it seemed that the prospects of being shot right away were increasing every second. Whose fault was that? Hadn't it been Peetal Rause, that swine, who had taken the girl? The old man had stayed to watch whether Peetal would knock her unconscious first, as he sometimes used to do. But no—if August would help to hold her he could have his share too. That swine! And he himself, head still warm from the vodka they had drunk before the roundup, put his hands to the girl as if she were a little pig that needed to be operated on.

Sometimes Rause stumbled over his pants and on one such occasion August swung the stick, hitting his naked posterior. When the first blow had been struck, the others followed naturally. August was a little surprised by his own actions, but it somehow loosened the rigidity inside him. The closer they got to the woods the more energetically August whipped his companion.

"What are you mumbling about," he said menacingly. "Such a raper of children. Jump on the girl like that. Wasn't my daughter enough for you and all these others? Swine, that's what I say."

"Hit him harder," the little hunchback panted and knocked his automatic into August's ribs with undiminished ferocity. "Are you too weak or what? Is fear of death turning your blood to water?"

The sweat-covered limbs of August of Roosi were in reality quite weak. The sun was burning down, right on top of his head. August ran desperately at the side of the militiaman and his cudgel whistled in the air, leaving red stripes on the legs of the prisoner. Rause moaned and swore, staggering on, hands pressed against the back of his head. August was desperate. Only a few more steps and they would be in the woods, which meant that their death sentences would be carried out. Then he stepped accidentally on the pants of the militiaman that were being dragged at his heels: the prisoner lost his balance and almost fell.

Now August repeated this almost every step, getting more and more worked up the closer they got to the woods. The trailing pants of the militiaman and his bare, whipped haunches—for the moment they made up August's whole world and the narrow confines of his life.

"Make the devil quit," the militiaman moaned.

"We can't take his last pleasure from him," Taavi answered. "You can settle your scores in hell."

"Taavi of Piskujõe, be merciful," August begged, almost weeping. "Be human. I say. . . ."

"Are you human?" Taavi shouted. "Is your daughter human? Who killed my children? Tell me. Do you know that it was your daughter who played more than fifty people into the hands of the NKVD, including my wife and son? Your own daughter, your flesh and blood. Tell me, who has destroyed the lives of all of us, destroyed our freedom? The Red tyrants, with the help of your daughter, and other weaklings like yourself. Who has shown mercy to me, or who is planning to be human toward me? What is mercy?"

When they reached the woods, August's strength was gone. He kept goading the militiaman with the sharp point of his stick but he himself began to stumble over the clods. His bloody mouth was stiff and dry. Osvald moved ahead of the group, Tõmm and Leonard disappeared to the sides. The prisoners were escorted by Taavi and Värdi. Their guns were ready to shoot and their faces were stern. Värdi kept gritting his teeth. They moved in a direction parallel to the route the recent round-up had taken. August knew that the terror squad and the Red Army soldiers had returned to Kalgina by now and that they had no help to expect from anywhere. An airplane rumbled somewhere in the distance, increasing the feeling of complete abandonment.

Near the meadows of Võllamäe the men assembled again. Loads of food were taken out from under a wind-felled fir tree. There was enough to load the militiaman, August, and the men themselves. Then the procession turned directly toward the heart of the forests of Ilmaotsa. The field bottle, which had been filled with vodka, began to move from hand to hand. The drink burned their anger loose and Peetal Rause received new kicks.

"How far are we going to walk them this way?" the hunchback growled impatiently.

The bottle was handed to August once. The old man filled his mouth greedily with the home-brewed alcohol, but most of it ran down his stubbly chin. For a moment he lost sight and hearing from the terrible pain the alcohol caused to his bloody gums.

Yet the vodka raised August's sunken hopes considerably. Lest they should diminish again, he began to torment the militiaman with new vigour. Since his hands were full of supplies, he kicked his companion with his feet.

"Damn it, everything is your fault," he cursed, shedding tears of desperation. "Haven't I told you often enough to leave young girls alone? Your balls should be cut off, that's what I say. I should do it with my own hands, so you would not spoil the race with your robber's blood!"

The men stopped. The militiaman had fallen down again under his load, growling angrily at August's blows.

"Tie him up," Taavi ordered August.

"I—him? What should I tie him with?"

"That's your business. But be quick."

August took off his holster belt. He hesitated, looking from face to face, and then began to tear out young pine trees in desperate haste. The tough, pliable roots of the pines were the only available material.

"Do you have your knife with you?" Taavi asked.

"The knife—yes, I have. . . ." The old man stammered, his face haggard and sweaty.

"There," Taavi threw him a first-aid bandage. "As you said yourself—cut them off!"

August stared at him without understanding. He took his curved knife from his pocket, looked at the knife and at the giant who was blowing angrily through his nose lying on his back on the clods, black nostrils stretched open, hands and feet tied with bundles of white roots.

"Do you understand?" the little hunchback pushed the old man with the barrel of his automatic. "What did you expect of the swine?"

Then August of Roosi, that drunkard and pig-cutter, took off his coat in an impatient hurry.

August of Roosi was an outlaw now for the second week. Outlawry was harder for him than for the young wolves in the wood, for he had been left completely alone. The woods did not accept him and the county house was waiting to send him on his last journey. The first night he had gone home, but he had not had enough sense to take anything along except for a few mouthfuls of bread. He had even had to borrow a rucksack from Ignas of Hiie, for Russians were again camping at Roosi. There were twice as many now as the first time—a regular army unit sent there from the military bases.

August was squatting in the Matsu pea field near the woods, his gun under his arm, eating his scanty supper, when the first group of Russians reached him, led by his former companions—men of the terror squad. The evening was so dark that he could not make out the number of the men in the woods. The group came either from Kalgina or directly from Roosi and was moving along the edge of the woods around the village toward Kadapiku. What startled August most was the fact that they dared approach the great forest so late at night. That meant they must have plenty of men and felt safe in their great numbers.

August had not been able to change his position before he heard the approach of another group—footsteps and the quiet clicking of rifles. He lay as quietly as a mouse and let the soldiers pass. The wind stroked the cornfields and ran on into the dark woods, shaking the leaves of the aspen tree on the edge of the field. Soiled by the grey ashes of night, the red and golden clouds of the evening sky had taken on the dark hue of blood.

August of Roosi got up from the pea field and hurried into the woods. A lightness was in his feet and limbs as if he were a very young boy. When he wiped his nose with the back of his hand he noticed that his whole face was wet. No, it was not dew this time, as in the mornings when he woke up somewhere under a haystack or strawpile, stiff with the cold. No, it was sweat. Although he knew that Peetal Rause could not be among the soldiers he was afraid that the militiaman would be after him. The giant's screams of fear and pain had made him deaf, and when the screams stopped their sound continued to ring in his ears. All his senses had been blunted.

He was holding a gun but he did not know what he would do with it even in case of need. He dropped the rifle in a bush and moved on from the shadow of one tree to the next. Why had he carried the rifle for so long? But at the same time he found that his hands were wretchedly empty and his mind so confused that he began to look again for the weapon he had thrown in the bush, as if it were his only support. He circled around the bush like a black, injured bug, his face wet with perspiration, until another thought gave him a clearer direction.

He had to warn the men in the woods. They must withdraw farther inland until everything here blew over. August did not consider them his enemies, although the men had contemptuously turned their backs on him. Let them despise him. It did not matter, for all his life he had never been able to walk with a straight back or sit at the upper tables. Now he was sure that it was safer for a man to burrow in his own dirt like a little insect. High flights were short and it was dangerous to rise far above the earth, for everybody's grave was in it sooner or later. It would be more comfortable to roll oneself in the dirt quietly and deliberately, sipping some good wine, than to fall from some height with a terrible crash.

Stooped and small, he hurried deeper into the forest. He did not doubt that he would reach the men before the soldiers did. It was unlikely that they would start combing the forests at night. They probably only went to the bases of their attack somewhere between the pastures and the forest meadows. Then he hesitated again and stopped. Fool, he did not even know where the men were camping. He had to go back to the village and find Ignas of Hiie. Only Ignas could help now.

August came upon the Russians near the farmyard of Kadapiku. He fell on his knees behind the stone fence and tried to crawl away from the soldiers on the bottom of a dry ditch. Although he realized after a while that he had not been noticed he hardly dared to breathe. If only his old cough would not begin to plague him. If only he could keep from breaking a twig under his hands and knees. He crawled along inch by inch until he began to hear whispered Russian conversation from the direction in which he was moving. Then he began to comprehend that he had come right into the midst of Russians who were encircling the Kadapiku farm.

At the same moment the door of the farmhouse squeaked on its hinges. August peered cautiously over the stones, fighting a feeling in his throat that he should call out for help. Nobody came through the door—only the dog was let out. As soon as the animal had taken a few steps away from the threshold it began to bark loudly, jumping straight up in the air as if hitting an invisible wall. Then it stopped just as abruptly, ate something on the grass of the courtyard and growled. It's eating poison, thought August.

True, the dog did not bark any more after having swallowed the piece of meat that had been thrown him from somewhere. He growled and whined, trying to run away from the soldiers who were forcing their way into the yard. But that did not save him. A thudding blow with a rifle butt sounded through the night.

Frozen to the stone wall, August had to witness the events that took place in the yard of Kadapiku. How often had he, together with drunken Russians, forced his raucous way into farmhouses near the road, had bragged and boasted and demanded vodka, especially during the first autumn. He could not see anything wrong in that. However, when the soldiers entered the farmhouse now under his eyes it seemed to him a completely different picture.

The farmer appeared at the door. Quietly but menacingly he was ordered to raise his hands. Paavel was wearing a white nightshirt and was barefooted. August heard his voice tremble with fear.

"Where are the bandits?" The question was asked in Estonian and was addressed also to Sessi who appeared behind her husband's back.

The woman had evidently risen from bed and had thrown an overcoat over her shoulders. When she began to remonstrate with the soldiers, she was brutally pushed down on the doorstep and ordered to shut up. Her loud voice would warn the outlaws. Then the six little children of Paavel and Sessi were herded together in the yard.

"Dress the children. You have to come along, all of you." August recognized the voice of the chief of the terror squad.

"But where?" Paavel complained. "We are no criminals. Everybody knows I am not a rich man or an enemy of the people. We have lived quietly from hand to mouth. . . ."

"And carried supplies to the woods!"

"God help me, we have nothing to give away. It's not often that the children get to eat their fill," Sessi answered. This haggard woman, worn out by successive childbirth, was calm and courageous and her voice remained quiet. "Where must we go?"

"You'll show us the way to the bandits. If you won't do it, the children will."

August began to move. Slowly, as if he were waking from a deep sleep, he became conscious of himself again. Across the yard and the vegetable garden he saw that the soldiers were swarming all over the farm—into the buildings, up into the hayloft, between the black currant bushes. From his uniform he recognized the NKVD chief as one of the men standing near the door. Suddenly, without realizing what he was doing, August of Roosi sprang out from the shallow ditch and began to run toward the woods. When he was already on the way he realized how stupidly he had acted.

"Stop, stop!"

Shots accompanied the shouts. Then everything was quiet, as if there were no living beings near, as if the soldiers were ashamed of the noise.

August of Roosi had fallen on his hands and knees in the thicket, had hit his head against a tree and had broken a heavy branch which had fallen across his backbone. When he attempted to get up the tree pressed him down, hurting so that he could not even crawl. After a moment a croaking sigh found its way through his throat. He had been wounded. As if he did not believe it, he touched the lower part of his body which was stiff with pain. No tree had fallen over him. Warm blood was oozing between his legs and the pain pulled his fingers into the rough earth. He had received a round from an automatic pistol in his thigh and hip.

Then black figures bent over him and instead of the kick with the rifle butt he had expected he was dragged to his feet. August of Roosi staggered out of the woods between his companions of yesterday.

In the morning Ignas had categorically declined Tõmm's offer to stay and help with the work: the meadow was too open, the roundup might start any time now. Tõmm stayed anyway. He had shoved hay into the barn, Hilda had received it and Ignas had hauled the hayricks to the barn. Hilda, too, had urged Tõmm to go back into the thickets but Tõmm found it easy to laugh at Hilda's warnings.

It seemed as if the whole Hiie household had moved from the farm buildings to the fields near the woods, to pastures and meadows. The cattle were kept in the woods at night under the care of Hilda and Ilme, the cows were milked under the trees, and with the help of Hilda, the deaf-mute, or Ignas and Linda of Piskujõe, the milk was carried to Hiie. Hilda did not dare go to the farm now and Krõõt would not let Ignas stay in the house at night. The farmer returned to the hayloft or to the bathhouse in the late evening without letting his wife know. Linda of Piskujõe helped in the fields, and the chores around the house had to be performed by the deaf-mute and the half-paralysed Krõõt. It was good the rye had been cut with the help of the woodsmen, who had come nightly to lend a hand with the work. The greater part of winter wheat had been harvested also. The men had begun to rebuild their winter quarters on Taevasaar, although the majority of them would have preferred to move their headquarters somewhere else.

Ilme, Hilda and Tõmm were waiting for Aadu on the back meadow. Every day he came with his little wagon to get the milk but today he came empty-handed. They could hear his excited mumbling from afar. Recently Aadu had often had cause to be startled, reaching the herd, for the men from the woods often came to get a drink of milk and some- times took some milk along. Aadu made friends with them—he had met some of them a year ago during haymaking—but nevertheless he was afraid of their rifles and their stern demeanor. Today the old man was quite frightened and the excited sounds he uttered seemed to ask for an answer as he took a folded sheet of paper from the flapping sleeve of his black coat and handed it to Hilda, stepping from one foot to the other.

She recognized Krõõt's handwriting in the few lines, written hurriedly with a pencil: "Hilda, there are Russians in the village. I dare not send the milk pails with Aadu. They might molest him when he returns. Let him stay in the woods with the cattle for a while. Milk the cows on the ground if their udders are too full."

"Russians again!" The girl trembled. "Let's drive the cattle farther into the woods."

Ilme agreed. She observed the shaking limbs of the deaf-mute, looked out through the trees, and suddenly felt a desire to be with Taavi—but not on Taevasaar, where the men were resting now to be ready for their work at night. After the explosion Ilme feared Taevasaar as much as the prison walls.

When Hilda milked the cows into the moss, Aadu looked at her as if she were doing the most stupid thing he ever saw in his life. He looked with big astonished eyes and then walked up to the girl, reproving her in his incomprehensible language. When that had no effect, he turned toward the village and started running—evidently to get the milk pails. But Tõmm was standing in his way, and refused to let him through. Aadu looked at the young man as if he were completely insane. Then Ilme, who had almost become a stranger, did the craziest thing under Aadu's own eyes that he had ever seen: she poured the milk from the pail into the bush.

The next pailful was handed to Aadu to drink. The old man dared not take it but when everybody else had drunk he held his beard with one hand and stuck his chin into the warm, fragrant milk. He drank, puffed and drank again. He licked his hairy lips and hummed happily, almost laughing. He sat down under a bush and lifted the milk pail to his mouth, holding it with both hands.

Tõmm walked under the trees, rifle in hand, and when he returned, he said: "I'll go to the village and check what's going on at home."

"No!" Hilda whispered, frightened.

"But we can't go on this way. We must know what they are up to. The hay must be stacked up in the meadow and if they should come, then. . . ."

"Don't go to the meadow any more! Go tell the men that. . . ."

"I don't know what to tell them," the youth muttered glumly.

Hilda ran up to the boy and begged him, her voice trembling with emotion: "Tõmm, please don't go! I could go myself. Permit me, listen . . . let me go."

Hilda went. Scared to death for Tõmm's sake, she forgot her own fears. When she returned after an hour she affirmed that everything was peaceful at Metsaoti. She had met Krõõt of Hiie and Linda of Piskujõe and both had regretted their recent panic. Soldiers had walked through all the farms, had looked around in the meadows near the houses and had walked up the river to the hayfields of Lepiku but had then turned around and walked across the fields of Kadapiku and Matsu, returning to Roosi. They had laughed and had seemed to be in high spirits.

"They are looking for their death," Tõmm muttered.

When the haystack was finished and Hilda had left, Tõmm had no time to sit down although his body tingled with pleasant exhaustion from the day's heavy work. The horse was turned loose in the meadow and the men began to erect a fence around the big haystack.

"I'll put it up by myself," Ignas said. "You should rest and catch your breath. You've swung the hayfork all day. Your fingers are still bent from holding the handle."

"Oh, that; it isn't the first time." "Tõmm was suddenly sorry for his father. Looking at the stooped figure of the old man and the thin grey hair above his high, tanned forehead that shone like brown leather he realized that the last two years had aged his father by ten. In a sudden impulse of tenderness Tõmm wanted his father to sit and rest while he fixed the fence. He knew beforehand that the old man would not consent to it and so he did not even suggest it. A painful, choking and embarrassed feeling ran through Tõmm. He had reached the age when one begins to appreciate one's parents.

Father and son sat on the grass in front of the hay barn and ate, taking turns in drinking milk from one cup and cutting a salted fish into strips with their pocket knives on a shingle from the roof. A short distance away the horse was chewing the grass between the willow bushes.

"We haven't eaten at the same table for God knows how long," Ignas said jokingly.

"No, we haven't," the son admitted. The father's joke was not funny.

"I thought I'd stay and spend the night in the barn. I couldn't get back from the moor before mid-morning and I want to help you with the fence." When he saw that his father's face was worried he added as an explanation: "It's impossible to sleep in the bunker. The men work and stay up all night through. And who would come here at night?"

"All right. You are a man. You should know what you are doing."

Ignas tied up the food parcel and they climbed into the barn. The fragrant hay rustled, still warm from the sun. It was delicious to sink into it, relaxing one's tired limbs. Tõmm placed his cartridge belt under his head and his rifle on his side. He did not fall asleep for some time, gazing at the pale sky that shone in the triangle formed by the eaves of the hay barn. Suddenly it struck him how little he had spoken with his father these last years, when there should have been more than enough to discuss and consider together.

Today, however, Father started the conversation.

"What is going to come of it?" he asked, lying on his back in the hay, his hands crossed under the nape of his neck. "Years go by, the pressure increases, opposition is smothered, the people are crippled. The end is probably quite close in our own district. But what will happen elsewhere? It seems that if this goes on, even accepting communism would not save the Estonian people from extinction. That's right. It's nothing but Russification, hidden in the rags of communism. Now that the new power has gained a firm foothold we can see it."

"What do you mean—that the end is close in our own district?"

The old man was silent for a moment before he answered: "I can see the end clearly. A stone that is rolling downhill will not stop halfway down the mountain. When Ilme came home, her dead child in her arms, then I knew that nothing could save us—us, the old people. You and Taavi and the others there—your hands and feet are still free; you can hold on. The winters are hard but the summers aren't too bad, and every day brings you closer to the solution."

Ignas stopped, his head heavy with restless thoughts, although his heart was now more at peace. Come what may, nothing further depended on him. When he heard that his son was asleep, he folded his rough, gnarled hands in prayer.

When Ignas awoke, he did not move for a moment, for he was sure that the child's crying he had just heard was part of his dream. The soft cover of the night had been torn by the pale light of dawn and the sleepy calls of the night owl had been superseded by the fresh cadences of the morning birds. The son at his side was deeply asleep. An armful of light hay had fallen over his head and his broad shoulders, moving in the rhythm of his breath.

Then Ignas sat up all of a sudden. There was no longer any doubt that a child was sobbing somewhere in the meadow. Sometimes it reached the old man's ears quite clearly; at other moments it came muffled, as if the wind had swept the sound away or the distance had covered it with its heavy blanket. As fast as his stiff limbs would allow, Ignas climbed to the opening of the barn and gazed into the pale mists between the willow bushes.

He was almost ready to jump down from the barn and hurry toward where he heard the sobbing when his ears caught a few quiet words from the opposite direction. His hand trembled on the rough logs of the barn. The words were in Russian. Then the horse neighed behind the barn. Ignas shook his son brusquely by the shoulder. The young man sprang up with the alertness of a forest dweller, looking at his father with sleepy eyes.

"Russians!" the old man said. "I think they have surrounded the barn."

Tõmm grabbed his rifle, still dazed with surprise.

"Where? How many? Let's get out of here!"

"Wait," the old man whispered, peering through a crack between the logs into the morning. The horse was coming toward the barn, looking around restlessly. "Wait, let's see where we can get through. Let's not run directly into their arms."

Tõmm waded through the hay from one wall to the other, straining his eyes, looking through the cracks. Ignas took the horse's harness and rushed out of the barn. The animal ran up to him and pressed his nose

393

under his master's armpit. Then the farmer of Hiie saw the feet of a man who was slowly approaching through the mist.

"Tōmm," the old man whispered.

When his son appeared in the opening of the barn the upper part of a man's body began to show through the grey wisps.

"Who's that? He doesn't even have a rifle," Tōmm mumbled, aiming at the stranger.

"Don't shoot." His father held him back.

The dark figure approached slowly, stumbling, arms stretched out to keep his balance. He dragged his feet over the wet grass and stopped sometimes with a jerk, as if he had been broken in half at his hips.

Tōmm retreated to the side of the barn. Taking aim through the cracks between the logs he trained his revolver at the man. It was August of Roosi, bareheaded, coat unbuttoned at the front. He was holding a grenade in his hand, and, each of his steps was accompanied by groans. At ten paces away he stopped on his trembling feet.

When Ignas took a few steps closer to August, he croaked: "Hiie, don't come." He moved his hands helplessly, as if this would help along the words that got stuck in his throat. "They sent me to kill you."

When Ignas did not know what to say, August continued: "Here I am—shot to pieces, but death won't take me. All of Metsaoti is full of Russians. Everywhere. The people of Kadapiku were taken last night. What are you waiting for, stupid. Jump on the horse and ride off. Maybe you'll get away," he hissed in agitation. "That's what I say, hurry up. You may make it across the meadow of Lepiku. Go. Quickly. Run." Then August turned around and began to retrace his steps. He stumbled, looked over his shoulder and croaked in desperation: "Hiie, damn it, jump on the horse. Go. Why don't you get going?" he shouted, falling to his knees on the meadow and raising his hands as if adjuring him.

"Tōmm," Ignas whispered. "Tōmm. . . ."

August had slumped down and his groans reached the hay barn. Then he suddenly straightened himself, although still on his knees, and shouted in a clear voice: "Old August was an Estonian too!"

The grenade exploded.

The frightened horse reared up so that Ignas could barely hold him. The little blue cloud of explosion gases mingled with the white mist among the bushes, under which a black figure now lay, motionless.

Father and son did not exchange a word. They both realized that their own lives could be lost in the next moment.

"Come," the old man said. "Give me the gun and jump on the horse. You heard him. You might make it over the meadows of Lepiku."

"You ride, I can run," Tōmm answered. His ears caught the sound of Russian voices from the meadow of Võllamäe. The explosion had disturbed them. Then he heard again the sobbing of the child coming from the same direction. They saw movements again in the fog. The attackers were coming closer. Tōmm sprang out of the hay barn.

"Father, they're coming."

"Jump on the horse," Ignas answered brusquely and seized the rifle from his son's hand. "You have a revolver. My hand has become unaccustomed to it. Well!"

"No! You, Father. Quickly!"

Then the old man got so angry that he grabbed his son roughly by his shirtfront: "Are you going to obey your father or not? Hurry on to the moor. Bring help."

The son jumped on the horse. When Ignas threw him the bridle, the attackers opened fire. The bullets whined by dangerously close, some of them hitting the wall of the barn with a loud clang.

"Go and . . . be a man," the father said.

When Tõmm did not direct his aimlessly prancing horse anywhere, Ignas emptied his gun in the direction of the attackers, startling the horse into a wild gallop. Tõmm looked back in desperation but when he saw that his father had stepped into the shadow of the hay barn he concentrated his attention on himself, for shots sounded from the bushes very near him.

Ignas squatted behind the corner of the barn and aimed at the figures that loomed up from the mist. He had to keep their attention until his son had escaped far enough. Suddenly his heart was strangely light and his senses calm. The fog began to lift. The attackers withdrew into the bushes.

Ignas knew that they were completing the circle around the barn. He had no time left to escape in the direction his son had taken. The strangest thing was that he could not bring himself to leave the barn. He had built it himself, filled it half full of fragrant fresh hay, and it was like a trusted companion whom it is a crime to abandon. The picture materialized before his eyes how they had once left their home at the last moment when the Russians were about to flood the country. They had left their home with heavy hearts and what good had come of it? No, to leave the barn now would be just as senseless.

The attackers had become ominously quiet. Ignas walked around the barn, rifle in hand and cartridge belt on his shoulder. He listened and looked in every direction. The mist was rising and the day was ready to burst forth like a bright flame from behind the forests. Ignas climbed up into the barn.

Then his eyes saw another frightening picture. A chain of little children was approaching through the lifting fog. There were six of them and the head of the tallest reached barely up to the fog that floated above them. They staggered under it, trying to get closer to each other, but an angry voice from behind them kept them apart.

Ignas raised his hand to his eyes for a moment. The children of Paavel and Sessi of Kadapiku were approaching the hay barn, the youngest taking its first toddling steps, the eldest just old enough to drive a herd of sheep. Russians were crawling close behind the children.

Ignas had seen much in his long life that had shaken him, paralysed his senses and robbed him of strength and power, but the sight that now opened before his eyes filled them with a sudden rush of angry tears. Although he could not move, his spirit rose with clenched fists directly up to God himself: Behold, and you let this happen!

When the old man looked again at the row of children they had come so close that he could make out the frightened features of each one of them, hear the piteous wail of the two youngest ones and the sobs of the others, see the wobbly, doll-like patter of their feet. But he also saw the guns of the Russians. He raised his rifle and aimed at the soldier crawling behind the smallest child. His hands quivered as if in a fever. The children stopped all of a sudden and all ran in the same direction, huddling together between the bushes, the smallest ones screaming wildly. They had reached August's shattered body. Ignas opened fire. The enemy was defenceless before him. Three of the six attackers remained on the ground; the others took cover in the bushes. Guns crackled now all around, and shots from automatic pistols burst forth in jerky flashes. The rat-tat-tat of a light machine gun sounded from behind one of the bushes closest to the hay barn. Ignas did not notice it. He had become a true fighter.

When Ignas felt the bitter smoke of burning hay in his nostrils, he looked back for the first time. The roof was burning and flames broke out from the hearts of smoke columns that wound their way up from the hay, until their rustling became a rushing blaze. It did not startle Ignas. On the contrary, he felt at peace at last.

Now everything would soon be over.

XVI

Aadu the old deaf-mute, could not understand what was going on at the Hiie farm. For years he had not been able to comprehend events. Too many strange things had forced their way between the peaceful forests by way of Kalgina and Harukurgu. He could get used to the fact that the work on the farm was done differently these last ten years, and even the machines that had replaced the horses were not as frightening as they had been at first. The times had passed beyond memory when Aadu had wandered down the road with his strong walking stick, hawking wooden spoons and butter kegs in the villages, at peace with the world and himself. Even when the cars had scared him off the footpaths and winter roads he had still been able to get around and observe how people lived. He had still been able to live himself.

Now Aadu had not dared leave Hiie for years. My goodness, the world had turned completely upside down. Now you could never tell when somebody went out through the yard gate where he was going, how long he would stay, or whether he would return at all. The faces of the people were squeezed narrow and stiff, their shoulders twitched for no reason at all, as if they were out stealing something, and their hands trembled even while at work. All this was caused by the topsy-turvy world which raced on the roads with terrible machines, by the red fire-glows on the horizon and the stinking soldiers who sneaked up to Aadu even when he was asleep.

Aadu had begun to fear darkness like a frightened child. Every night he closed and barred the trap door that led to his hayloft, and when he awoke at night he went to check whether the hook was still firmly in its place. One night he had found the trap door open. Blood had rushed to his head from the shock and he had shivered from fear on his bed until dawn, head wrapped in a sheepskin. Since that time he had been unable to trust himself. His nights turned into restless nightmares and his days became a feverish race from one corner of the farmyard to the other, accompanied by agitated guttural sounds. He felt he had to go somewhere, had to rush, but his weakened memory could not tell him where. Several times each day he stood at the gate of Hiie, stick in hand, eyes under the white bushy eyebrows turned toward Võllamäe, the estate of Kalgina, or the forests of Metsaoti. Sometimes he stood there for hours like a black scarecrow in the corner of the garden, and then turned quickly back to the farmyard, running as if to escape from something, and disappeared behind some outlying buildings.

Climbing down from the hayloft one morning Aadu felt sad and lonesome. The early autumn sun was gilding the tops of the trees with its faded, sticky rays. Chickens walked across the yard as they pleased. Surely some of them were under the rye shocks the farmer had set up. So what? Aadu was not a herder of chickens. He squatted near the corner of the barn, figuring out something, and suddenly he had the strange feeling that the earth had sunk lower during the night than it had been the evening before.

The gnawing restlessness that Aadu had felt upon awakening overcame him again. His stick took a quick step toward the yard gate, but the old man did not quite know what to do first. He drove off the chickens from the yard, as if they were trespassing, and hurried then to the gate. He stopped there for a brief moment and the tails of his loose coat began to tremble. He bent forward a little more and swept several times with his sleeve over his eyes. No, his eyes did not deceive him. Big throngs of people were milling around in the fields of Võllamäe, crowded together like herds of black rats, turning into grey soldiers as they reached the light of the sun.

Panting with fear, Aadu ran across the yard to the meadow and took cover behind the corner of the bathhouse, barely bold enough to look back. A new groan arose from his throat. He saw a red and black column of smoke rising over the farm buildings of Lepiku, just behind the corner of the stable, tall and menacing, covering the young sun that had risen above the horizon. Aadu shook his grey head, as if he were trying to shake off a bad dream that persisted even after he had opened his eyes. But the smoke writhed higher and higher and spread out in the windless morning air.

Aadu measured the distance and the direction. It must be a hay barn on the meadows of Metsaoti. It could only be an accident. Could it have been Hilda? Maybe she made a fire. But what would she be doing in the hay barn so early in the morning? Then he saw Krõõt standing on the threshold and Hilda running past him with her bare legs. The girl was not coming from the fields but from the forests of Verisoo. She ran directly to Krõõt and threw her arms around her neck. Old Aadu saw the mistress of the farm stroke Hilda's windblown hair with her hand as if trying to comfort her. He saw that Hilda was saying something, weeping and wringing her hands, and he saw Krõõt slump down on the stairs.

All this was too much for Aadu within a few short minutes. There was not a single ray of clear understanding in his brain to dispel the dazed gloom of the early autumn morning. He felt Hilda tugging at his hand. Exerting all their might, they dragged the unconscious Krõõt to her bed in the back chamber. Then Aadu felt his back. It was cold and wet.

Krõõt lay almost motionless. Her face was pale and her mouth twitched convulsively. Aadu did not hear her moans but he saw Hilda open her jacket with her shaking fingers and rub her hands, shoulders and face. Then a new groan of terror escaped from Aadu's throat. Blood was running from his mistress's hair—she had hurt her head falling on the threshold.

This broke the paralysed spell on Aadu's mind and made his body hot and alert. He remembered the herds of black rats approaching from the direction of Võllamäe. Blood and soldiers—they were an integral part of the fear that consumed him. Blood and soldiers and arms and engines on the highways—all of these reeked of death and Aadu could smell them from afar.

When Hilda ran out of the house Aadu did not realize from her terrified expression that danger might follow him even here, into the room that smelled of living human beings. But when he found himself alone in the house, terror seized him. More than ever before he felt the need of the presence of human beings. He had been left behind like a dog.

And then they were there. Aadu backed away from the window, beating the air with the stick in his hands until he hit the wall. The faces of the soldiers moved ever closer to the window. Aadu covered his eyes with his hand but this did not dispel the vision. In a paraxysm of fear he sprang to the kitchen, stumbling on the threshold and falling against the doorpost. As soon as his eye fell on the kitchen window, the same terrible vision greeted him.

Fleeing again through the living room, he saw living death masks behind every window. They jumped before his crazed eyes, smacked their lips, gnashed their teeth. Their brutal eyes were full of the ice-cold horror of death.

When Aadu ran into the room of his mistress, he saw that soldiers had entered behind him and were pointing their rifles at him. Aadu ran past Krõõt, who was crouching on the bed, toward the window, behind which he saw the apple orchard. Hands stretched out before him, he ran directly into the window glass.

Krõõt moved her buzzing head until she became aware of the cutting pain in her forehead. When she touched her face with her hand her fingers were bloody. What had happened?

She looked at Aadu, who was struggling in the window, hands and stick and head thrust through the broken panes, while his body and feet were kicking against the wall as if it should yield and open up for him. That fool! Why did he tear himself up with glass like that?

Then the Russians stood in the doorway. Their behaviour was rough, their voices were menacing and imperious. Some of them grabbed the old man and dragged him across the floor into the front room. Aadu's guttural shrieks sounded shrill above the thudding of blows with the rifle butts. His eyes rolled under his bushy eyebrows, about to explode with terror, unable to see anything. When he had been dragged away, the men seized Krōōt.

Grabbed by the brutal hands of the Russians, Krōōt felt clarity return to her mind. She was surprised that it left her indifferent and calm. The shock that had broken her down was still throbbing in her body. Her mouth was raw and the wound in her hair just above her temple pressed her down like a heavy cover.

"Burned alive," her lips repeated. Who? Ignas alone? Or Tōmm too? Anybody else? Burned alive?" She could not understand. She saw only the black column of smoke with its writhing snake-like neck beginning to spread apart in the sober light of the morning. Where was Hilda?

The voices of the Russians cut into her ears but passed them by at the same time. Krōōt looked at the farmyard of Hiie like a stranger. This was the end. She had pictured it to herself long ago. She had known it.

When Krōōt noticed a big truck at the gate she took her stick from beside the door. When the soldiers began to drag her across the yard toward the gate, the old woman suddenly shook off their hands. Her head was lifted high, proud and erect, as in her youth, and she began to walk slowly toward the waiting car. She did not look in any other direction, and noble dignity sustained her slowly moving body.

Krōōt of Hiie went. She knew only vaguely what had happened but she knew it was the end. She had prayed for strength and she was prepared for it.

When the soldiers began throwing a circle around the Hiie farmyard, Juhan of Matsu did not quite comprehend what was happening. He stood on the threshold, his limbs stiff and his head empty. He had seen the column of smoke rising from the hayfield. He had noticed Hilda hiding behind the shed and barn, then running toward the woods. Suddenly a grey mass of soldiers had risen from the ditches between the fields. Some of them, rifles ready to shoot, had gone on to the Lepiku yard, others forced the front door of the Hiie farmhouse.

Juhan had slept badly that night. His limbs ached. He awoke often, went outside, walked in the yard and felt restless. He knew that this was because of the shooting he had heard the night before from the direction of Kadapiku. He had gone out to listen but when everything remained quiet and even the dog did not bark, he had returned to the chamber.

Hearing about the death of Ebehard from Võllamäe and about the movements of the soldiers, Juhan had begun to breathe heavily through his nose and to sniffle audibly, as if he had caught a cold in his head from the hot sun of the summer's end. That was how it felt, anyway. No, Juhan of Matsu was not a coward. He was not afraid of that horde around the county house. He feared neither the militia nor the NKVD. He was as far above all those as he was above the helpless blind earthworm. He was capable of crossing his hands on his chest in front of each one of them, peacefully pushing forward his stomach, closing his eyes and—may the devil take them. He could even fall asleep, if he should feel like taking a nap. Juhan did not fear their weapons either. Gunpowder had been around for quite some time, and if the men behind the weapons were young jacks with runny noses, then a real man could not fear those weapons. A man's honour would not let him be afraid, even if death came on the spot.

All his life Juhan had respected men according to the strength of their bodies and characters and even more according to the state of their fields, horses and farm implements. He could not change his point of view. His sleeplessness these nights had been caused by his annoyance with himself. He could not keep his thoughts away from all those insignificant things that had no direct connection with either his fields, his threshing, or even the norms that he had to deliver. He had begun measuring in his mind the vastness of Russia, that enormous womb which had brought forth putrefaction and plague, which was now seething like a sea that has risen over its shores and which was pouring its stinking waters over the peaceful backlands of Kalgina. Even though Juhan was not afraid of a single Russian and although Communism for him meant only a licence to kill, all at once he found himself scared of the power that had brought about the violent surging of the east. Why had he no sons? he asked himself. Why had he no more children than these two daughters? Although they were capable to taking a man's place, women they were and would remain. All his doings would remain empty contention if his own wife could laugh at him, if the hoof-and-mouth diseased hordes from the east could come and trample over his house, his wife and daughters because he had no man-child to send to the fields or to set against the enemy.

When Juhan saw on that early morning the army of killers tramp into the Hiie house he was not really surprised. He had known all along that their peaceful days on their own fields would not last much longer. But what Juhan could not swallow and what made him catch his breath on the threshold was the fact that Hiie was considered more important than Matsu. When the stupid Russians passed by the Matsu gate as if it did not exist and turned in first at Hiie, Juhan felt that all his living and striving had been wholly in vain. Matsu had been marked inferior for ever, although Juhan could look down from his threshold into the Hiie farmyard as into a valley and almost spit into their well if provoked far enough. But if the Russians, who had less sense than animals, had not made a difference between the farms, how could Juhan legitimately feel envious of Ignas' sometime office as parish elder, of his now paralysed wife who had born him a strapping son and a daughter for good measure, or of the fact that old Anton of Lepiku still thought that Ignas, in spite of his snow-white hair, was more of a man than he, Matsu.

Juhan began to expect the Russians. He became nervous when the soldiers, with the red and blue caps of the NKVD, surged from the Hiie yard over to Lepiku, as if the Matsu farm up on the hill was not worth looking at. What the devil!

But when the heavy truck stopped right at the Matsu gate and the soldiers jumped into the yard, the farmer retreated into the house, his knees giving way, wiping his brow of the sudden heavy sweat.

To the laments of the womenfolk he gave the brief retort: "Get ready to go."

"What? Where?" asked Meeta.

This question seemed to Juhan so strange and stupid that he did not know what to answer. If his own knees had not been so weak and his throat parched as if crammed full of dry tow, he would have shouted just this one word against the infinite stupidity and idiocy of the whole world: to Siberia. Siberia—that word should have explained everything because it meant more than death. It meant death many times over. Only death in its old simple meaning could save a man from the journey to slavery, from the tortures of prison, from slow murder.

While the Russians swarmed over the living quarters Juhan stole into the adjoining barn where the rye was piled up and spread out to dry, and from there to the threshing floor, where in a crack in the wall stood his broad hog-killing knife. All his senses concentrated upon that broad shining blade in the wall, which literally seemed to draw him toward it. Juhan hurried toward the weapon, knowing nothing, planning nothing, only feeling instinctively that the sharp blade signified a solution.

When Juhan stretched out his hand for the knife in the dark, his knotty fingers touched empty wall beams. He searched for the knife with both hands, feverishly and worriedly, but he did not find anything. Hearing the voices of the Russians in the barn, he barred the door between the barn and the threshing floor and continued his search, more and more agitated and angry. His hands touched horses' harnesses, his nose smelled leather, varnish and animal sweat. His fingers got caught in knotted ropes, found the threshing rake, the flails and the handmill. The familiar smells—the drying rye, the clay floor, the moulding malt flour—clung to him and pressed close. Moving his hands mechanically, Juhan could not understand why he was unable to control his movements. After all, the voices and sounds in the barn or at the back door did not concern him. Nothing concerned him except the great hog-killing knife which—may the devil take them—he had stuck into the crack in the wall with his own hand. They could drive a man crazy with their wild beating! Tear it down, beasts. The first one that breaks the door open will get Juhan's first smack in his face. Is that how you

401

treat somebody's property, the home of an Estonian farmer! Meeta too—calling for him. That foolish woman. Once she let the Russians trample over their daughters. What's she calling him for now? A woman that can take the place of three men and can kill a pig all alone, if necessary, should now be able to take care of a few Russian fools.

Juhan struck a match, trying to locate the knife. Some stupid soul must have used it and, in his carelessness, must have left it lying somewhere. Then he remembered that he himself had repaired an old rake on the stairs of the granary and had used the knife to split off pegs from the ash log. So he was the one who was turning into a fool.

The match burned his fingers and he threw it on the floor. It fell directly into a heap of chaff. He rushed to put out the little flame, but its quiet burning amid the dusk of the threshing floor and the clamour and the shouting outside charmed him so that he stopped. Completely new thoughts flashed through his mind—obscure thoughts, broken into fragments, but somehow they calmed the heart that was pounding against his ribs. So what? he asked himself. Isn't it my own chaff heap? If everything belongs to the state, all the land, life and labour, let them leave him a little heap of chaff. A handful of dust for his whole life's work. Let them leave him his anger and a fistful of dry chaff and he would be able to meet the end like a man.

When the flame climbed higher and its shy trembling became greedy and assertive, Juhan suddenly realized that the whole farm might catch fire. Instead of thoughts of putting it out, the winding column of smoke that had risen from the hayfields materialized before his mind's eye and now a clear idea was hewn into his brain as with a chisel. So what? he asked pugnaciously. If Ignas of Hiie lights up a barn full of hay to greet the new gods, then Juhan of Matsu is that much ahead of his neighbour, that he lets the fire take what it will. There are the piles of dry sheaves of rye, there's the straw in the loft and the clover. At last Juhan is ahead of Ignas. Suddenly, his eyes full of fire reflections, he grabbed a sheaf of rye from the corner, dipped its end into the fire and threw the great flaming torch into the loft. At the same moment bursts from a submachine gun crashed through the plank door of the threshing floor. The golden rays of the sun broke through the cracks, cutting the darkness, the splinters and the dust like shining knives. Juhan withdrew through the back gate of the threshing floor, his limbs completely numb. Here, in the cool shade of the house, he sent his eyes roaming over the autumn-coloured fields, looking for help, but his feet got caught and fettered in the luxuriant garden grass and he did not attempt to run even a step. He raised his hands unemotionally when he saw the soldiers rushing at him out of the lilac bushes. Even threats did not make his hands rise very high and so he walked, eyes turned toward his fields, around the house to the front yard.

Without asking any questions he turned to the truck that was standing at the gate. His wife and daughters were already crouching between rifles. Lonni was holding the whimpering baby on her knees. Krõõt of Hiie was lying on the truck, too, her head covered with blood, and

Anton and Luise of Lepiku were just being brought by the soldiers.

What now? asked the eyes of old Anton, even though the answer was already deeply stamped into the lines of his face. Luise was carrying a little bundle in her hand.

"What about the stock?" she lamented. "Who'll take care of the animals?"

Juhan noticed that his beard was wet and heavy as if he had come from a steam bath. His forehead was dripping wet, the sun's rays fell into his eyes like thorns. He remembered suddenly the cool sour drink in the granary. He should have rolled that big barrel with its sour and invigorating contents on the truck to refresh body and soul!

When a loud uproar and Russian cursing started behind Juhan's back and the mouths of his wife and daughters opened in a silent scream, he turned his big body around. The sight startled him as if he had awakened from a dream. The gates of the threshing floor were gaping open and thick smoke curled out of them, in which soldiers seemed to be jumping up and down like unearthly beings. What did this mean? Juhan asked himself. That was Matsu burning. Through the dense smoke flamed the living fire, stretching its hungry tongue from the interior of the threshing floor to the eaves and up along the roof.

"Water! Put it out!" screamed Juhan.

He paid no attention to the blow with the rifle butt against his back that left him breathless for a while. He ran toward the well like one that has lost his mind and grabbed the full water bucket. He passed it to the nearest soldier, pulled up the milk cans from the well, handed those also to his guards and reached for the milking pail that was drying on the branch of a lilac bush. An NKVD lieutenant, his face distorted by anger, gave orders to the soldiers. Juhan overshouted them. Let them get moving. Let them carry water.

The guttural shrieks of Aadu sounded suddenly from the Hiie farmyard. The screams seemed to pierce Juhan's eardrums and the bucket fell from his hand. What did that mean? The prisoners on the truck had struggled to their feet. Their cheeks were sunken and grey in the sunshine, their eyes strange. The screaming of the deaf-mute, more terrible than the cry of an animal, yet coming from a human mouth, penetrated the shouting of the soldiers and the swelling rustle of the fire. Better if they'd shot him—a fragment of a thought flashed through Juhan's brain. Those beasts—they drive one completely out of one's mind.

However, when Juhan was standing on the truck and watching the flames, the women saw peace in his eyes. Juhan watched the unrestrained blaze which digested in its crimson stomach his home into embers and ashes, and felt that he had done well. That was a fitting end to his living. Let the Hiie people see. Let everybody in the Metsaoti village and the Kalgina district take notice. Juhan of Matsu, whom they have called ugly names all his life, is leaving his farm and going to Siberia.

But when the dying outcry of Aadu Mustkivi again pierced his eardrums and the truck suddenly started. Juhan fell on his knees and in-

403

voluntarily lifted his hands toward the flames. He was not sorry to leave anything but the fire. He felt that the fire that was being taken from him was life, the shining salvation he had been promised. He felt that he should run right into the flames, into the shelter of his burning home.

"Give the child to me!" he said to his daughter. "Don't you see how frightened it is? What are you scared of the Russian for? If he should happen to touch you, I'll pitch him backwards over the side."

Marta knew that she was fighting for her life. Her toughness surprised and pleased her. She had searched every square inch of her room—the walls, ceiling and floor. She had searched the attic and tried to guess where the wires led from the hidden microphone. The terror that had recently tormented her—fear of the forest, darkness, and Taavi Raudoja —had disappeared before a new, paralysing feeling that weakened her limbs and choked her throat. Revolver in one hand and flashlight in the other, she had sneaked around in the attic, but had found nothing but old archives, broken furniture and empty boxes. Only a couple of big rats had scared her. When she returned to her room she had not even dared to light the lamp. She closed the door and pressed her back to the wall, passing the beam of the flashlight hastily over the whole room until she convinced herself that there was nobody there. Then she turned on the light and stepped to the wall where the black ear of the microphone looked out from between the torn wallpaper.

An irrepressible urge arose in Marta to shoot all the bullets from her Browning directly into the microphone. Who knew for how many death sentences this lifeless ear had already absorbed damaging evidence? She touched the wallpaper, trying with moist fingers to stretch it back over the torn spot. Then, without realizing what she was doing, she grabbed the microphone and pulled. It came out of the wall without any resistance. The wires had been cut.

At first Marta was just as alarmed by her deed as she had been when she first discovered the microphone. She raised it to her ear, not knowing why she did so. But when morning came, she had carefully repaired the torn wallpaper, had hidden the microphone in her handbag, and had persuaded herself that the apparatus had been used to get evidence against the former chairman of the executive committee. Because Russian officers had been lodged in the county house, her room had been the bedroom of comrade Holde. Marta could not quite make herself believe that her assumption was correct. However, she fell asleep for a moment as dawn broke.

During the following days Marta strained every nerve. She suspected everyone she met. She listened, watched, and found hidden meaning in every casual glance, remark or act. She burned with enthusiasm and helpfulness, giving the NKVD as much information as she could muster. Her head was full of fiendish schemes for capturing the woodsmen, for she knew that only the most reckless activity could save her.

On the day of the great roundup Marta felt wooden, stiff and indifferent. The two smoke columns that rose above the rolling fields of Haru-kurgu reminded her of the past war years.

When the heavy truck carrying the people of Metsaoti and their guards roared past the county house, Marta staggered upstairs to her room. Leaving the office, she saw a question in the mask-like face of Captain Kasinski. But she did not stop. She would not have done so even if the man had ordered her. It was noontime and she had the right to go. Furthermore, they did not do any work in the office anyway and the wounded they expected from the forests had not yet arrived. Nobody came near the county house that day except soldiers and Communist youths with red ribbons tied around their arms. Even the fields around the village were empty, as if the people had fled to escape the plague.

Instead of preparing lunch, Marta threw herself down on the couch. She wanted to rest. But she knew that she would never sleep peacefully again.

When Marta saw Kasinski's stocky figure and two NKVD men in civilian clothes in her doorway, her eyes fell on a small woman between the men. It was Taavi's mother.

"I need your help," Kasinski grinned. He pushed the old woman into Marta's room and closed the door. "Interpret for us. The old bitch was caught in the woods. She is said to be the mother of the bandit leader. Is this so?"

Marta looked at Linda, whose tearful eyes, desperately searching for help, followed her with a faint spark of hope. Her hands had been tied with a rope.

"Yes. . . . I don't know. . . . Yes, she is," Marta muttered.

The air in the attic room was heavy and suffocating. The oppressive heat had been a curse which had plagued Marta all through the summer, except on days when it rained. Kasinski had been here before, quite often, too, but he had been different. He had had a bottle of liqueur, cognac or Crimean wine in his briefcase, and had thrown his gunbelt with the heavy revolver carelessly over the back of a chair. Now he held the revolver in his hand and a folder came forth from his briefcase, a writing pad and other things that filled Marta's mind with horror.

The two NKVD men forced Taavi's mother to sit on a chair in the corner. A table was placed in front of her, reaching from wall to wall, and Marta had to sit down at the table, ready to take notes. One of the NKVD men stood beside her, taking a flat bottle with yellowish liquid from his briefcase and placing it on the corner of the table. Kasinski had taken a bottle along after all.

The men asked their questions in a nervous hurry. Marta interpreted and wrote the answers down in Russian. Linda of Piskujõe was too shaken to talk.

"I don't know anything about my son. I haven't seen him for so long," was all she said.

"Speak," Marta mumbled. "You are accused of having been in contact with the bandits and of having gone to the woods to warn them today."

"No, I didn't. If you don't believe me—why should I keep on talking?

Hilda ran to tell me this morning that the Russians—that the hay barn of Hiie was on fire. When I began to hear the shots I didn't know what to do. I went to the place where my husband died and was there until the soldiers arrested me. That's all I know."

The old woman was small and helpless, crushed by what she had seen, coming through her home village with the soldiers who had seized her. The long farmhouse of Matsu was on fire, the threshing floor and the barns were burning. The whole village was empty and lifeless. The dog of Võllamäe was howling alone in the middle of the field near a wagon half loaded with sheaves of rye.

"Tell us where the bandits are hiding," Marta demanded. Kasinski hit her carelessly against her collarbone with his gun. Marta was not surprised at his action, for she felt as much a prisoner in her own room as the woman sitting opposite her.

Although Linda noticed that Marta got more and more excited, although she saw that Marta's hands trembled and that terror looked out from her eyes, she did not know what to say. She did not even know where the men camped. On Taevasaar, yes, but Marta knew that herself. Why did they keep on questioning her, when the battle was already going on in the woods? They were fighting over there somewhere and killing each other.

The Hiie farmyard rose again before the eyes of the old woman, and the bloody, mutilated corpse lying, face down, in the flower bed. A slight chill shook her in the overheated room.

Captain Kasinski shoved the bottle from the corner of the table in front of Marta.

"Try with that."

Marta saw a cruel, sadistic joy in his grinning eyes. Suddenly she had the feeling that the man had staged this for her sake. The information the old woman could give was not as important to the captain as Marta's behaviour, her submission to the NKVD.

"What is it?" the woman stuttered, touching the bottle.

"Do you want to try?"

Before Marta could think, the man in civilian clothes took the glass stopper from the bottle and passed it over the back of her hand.

Marta's scream turned into a husky groan. She jumped up, rubbing her hand against her skirt. The pain from her burning skin robbed her of her senses for an instant.

"Sit down and continue," the captain said, as if nothing had happened.

Marta sank on the chair. Everything whirled before her eyes. That meant her suspicion had been right.

"Make your protégée talk," the hard voice said.

Marta's hand slipped toward the bottle, fingers still trembling. Fear and pain made her weak, so she could barely control herself. She realized that what was now demanded of her was more than she could deliver. She saw the bound hands of the old woman in front of her, sinewy, gnarled, worn hands, tired with heavy work.

406

The eyes of Linda of Piskujõe looked wearily at Marta. She must have understood the situation in which Marta had been placed.

"Tell me, Marta, what do they want?" she asked with a tormented voice. "I don't know anything."

Marta raised her hand to her eyes. Her forehead was covered with perspiration. Somebody shook her shoulder brutally. Why didn't the prisoner confess?

"She doesn't have anything to say. Understand, she doesn't know anything," she moaned.

"Speak for yourself, then. Or if you don't want to speak here, we have other places, better places for you!"

"No! No! I'll do anything you want! I am a Communist. My father was a Communist."

"Your father was a traitor."

"My father was an old fool. He did not understand anything. He was scared, he. . . ." When nobody replied, Marta shouted: "I have always believed in Communism. I have spared no effort." She noticed her handbag on the couch. There was her Browning. Several new thoughts ran together in her brain. She was startled by them. Where could they be coming from, so clear and bold that their clarity dazzled her? All she needed to do was to fall to the floor, pretend that she was about to faint, or scream and throw herself on the couch over her handbag. If she could not kill all of them, what would follow would be faster and more tolerable than having this continue. In her imagination she saw herself already jumping out of the window, running down the stairs.

When she stirred herself, she realized that these desperate leaps of her imagination could never be carried out. She was barely capable of moving. The wildness of her imagination had always deceived her, until it had brought her here behind this little table where she had to play her last card.

When the commissar wanted to take the bottle, Marta held on to it with cramped fingers, quickly pulled out the stopper and ran it over the knuckles of the old woman.

Taavi's mother pressed her wrists hard against her breast and groaned. Her shackled hands began to writhe, while the acid left black traces on her skin.

"Marta, be merciful," she panted. "Don't do it! Please, don't do it!"

When the Russian stretched his hand out again, Marta's stupor vanished. The cruel battle of wills continued until Linda's hands and fingers were covered with black wounds and she could neither speak nor cry from the pain—only moan.

"What do you want?" Marta shouted. "You can see that she has nothing to say."

"Traitor! Speak yourself."

"I am no traitor," Marta shrieked. When she wanted to jump up she was forced down again. "I have done everything I . . . I am a Communist. I delivered fifty people into your hands. . . . How many do you want?"

Had Linda of Piskujõe, with her scant comprehension of Russian,

407

understood Marta's words, or did she burst out at random in her desperation, wildly guessing at the truth?

"Kill me, Marta! Kill me! A person who is used to killing should find it simple enough. What did you do with my grandson? What had the innocent child·done to you? Did you torture him too? And such a woman wanted to become my daughter-in-law. Marta. . . ."

Marta screamed and threw the contents of the bottle at the old woman's face. The bottle hit the hands Linda had instinctively raised to protect her eyes. The acid sprayed her face and hands. The bottle fell on the table and broke. One of the Russians tore angrily at Marta's hair, the other one cursed, while the third grabbed a pail of water from the corner near the stove and poured it over Linda's face and hands.

Nobody helped Marta, in whose lap had flowed most of the contents of the bottle, while she screamed and picked with her scorched hands at the shreds of her clothing that were smoking from the acid.

At the same moment rifles began to speak their angry, rough language near the county house.

XVII

The first clash was over. It had been short and violent. While Taavi attacked the enemy with his group near the burning hay barn of Hiie, Captain Jonnkoppel sprayed them with deadly fire from their flank. The open meadow did not offer any protection to the numerous groups of the enemy. Only a few machine guns hidden in the bushes continued their angry chatter, while the scattered main forces retreated, running toward the protective cover of the woods. Bodies of fallen Russians remained scattered all over the meadow.

Taavi and Tõmm were the first to run to the barn. The roar of the fire muffled all voices. The shots that sounded nearby seemed to come from behind a thick wall. Two soldiers of the NKVD were lying quite close to the flames, faces buried in the stubble.

"Where did you leave him?" Taavi asked his comrade, who was looking into the fire.

"In the barn."

Some of the men had stayed near the woods, some had chased the Russians across the meadow and were now returning from between the bushes with loads of captured weapons.

"Come on back," Taavi shouted at them. They did not know the number of the positions of the Russians. Who could guarantee that the numerically superior enemy would not outflank them in turn? Captain Jonnkoppel's men were still in contact with the retreating units. Those crazy fools! Had they ventured too close and got caught? "Come on back, men."

Osvald came through the smoke and the glittering sunshine with a strange burden. When he got closer, the men saw that it was a four- or five-year old boy, with dangling brown legs. Before anybody could ask anything, Osvald placed his burden on the soft moss under a fir tree.

"There," he said with a broken voice, straightening himself. The lines on his face were sharp and the whites of his eyes bloody as he looked at the sweaty faces of his comrades.

"Dead?"

"Say what you want, men," the hired man of Hiie spoke. "We have killed him. But who brought the children into the woods against us? It's Endel of Kadapiku. I cannot understand how the boy came to be among the Russians. Have they sent out the whole village of Metsaoti to destroy us?" He looked at the pale face of the child, his bloody shirt front and dirty hands. He cast a glance at the comrades around him, as if looking for help, and fell on his knees beside the little corpse.

The men called Taavi's attention to the village across the meadow where another column of smoke was rising to the sky.

"The devils, they are burning the village down."

"Let's go," Taavi growled. "We're in for some hard work before the day is over, and it's still morning."

Airplanes strafed the meadow at the same moment, aiming their fire at the edge of the woods. Near the burning hay barn some small bombs exploded in fountains of dust and fire. The ugly whine of splinters sounded through the smoke. Shell fragments crashed into the branches and trunks of the trees.

"Back! Farther back into the woods," Taavi shouted.

A wounded man groaned; the first of their number.

While the men ran farther into the thickets, dragging their wounded friend with them, Taavi rushed back to the burning hay barn. Tõmm was still standing in front of it, leaning on his rifle, face toward the flames. The crater of a bomb was quite near him on the other side of the barn. The grass, covered with steel-grey dew, was black from many footsteps.

"Come along, crazy," Taavi cried, grabbing the boy by his sleeve. "Come, there's nothing you can do. The village is burning. Your own mother is in there. There are the airplanes again!"

They rushed into the bushes, throwing themselves down between the protruding roots of old black alders. When the airplanes had passed over they heard the mine-thrower's short cough across the meadow—the bombs fell on Captain Jonnkoppel's position. In front of the hay barn, where Tõmm had just been standing, was a yawning black hole. The lips of the young man moved as if he wanted to spit out an angry mouthful.

Taavi's group had already joined Captain Jonnkoppel's men up on the heath. They had not suffered any more losses than the young man who had been wounded on the edge of the meadow by fire from the strafing plane. He was still alive, even conscious, but in spite of the bandages applied by Värdi it was obvious that he would die soon. He was lying under the pine trees, supported by his comrades, and bright red blood gushed forth from his mouth. He swallowed and panted for breath with short, jerky groans, until his mouth breathed nothing but blood and his head fell weakly on one shoulder. The men who were making a stretcher pulled the two smooth sticks out again from the sleeves of their overcoats.

"Take him under Your care, God Almighty!" Peeter of Valba said quietly. Nobody had time to linger further.

The barking voice of Jonnkoppel called for Taavi. His face was flushed and his black round beard, wet with perspiration, had caught crushed leaves, pine needles, and moss. The man limped on both feet.

"They rub me. The boots, damn them," he glowered at Taavi. "Just like a life-long curse. When life is peaceful the boots leave me alone but as soon as I get into battle condition they begin to gnaw at my heels. It was like that during the War of Independence and on the eastern front and now here—everywhere and always. Raudoja take your men and—on to the village!"

"Yes, sir!"

"Don't be funny. This is no war and no army. Kill the Russians but watch out they don't get you. Every man who lets the Russians knock him off—I'll see later what I'll do to that son of a bitch," he swore threateningly.

"I wouldn't dare go to hell with you," Leonard yelled.

"Nobody would let a milkbeard like you into hell. That's where the men go," was the captain's answer. Turning to Taavi, he continued quickly, stepping impatiently from one foot to the other. "I'll divide my men into small units. We must move quickly right now—a hit here, a slash there, and back again. We cannot give them a regular battle but the village is in flames. We must teach them a little lesson. We must kick their noses into a bloody mess so they'll remember. We have tried to keep out of it but there is no other way left. It would be good if you could get to the village without a shot. All right, get going! Listen, are they chopping faggots with their airplanes or what? Idiots!"

Taavi was taking his group to the west across the woods behind Päraluha in order to approach the village from the forest meadows and thickets. On the back pasture of Hiie they encountered the enemy again. They exchanged a few shots with the patrols and succeeded in disengaging themselves without any losses. The Russians, a regular army unit this time, kept out of their way.

The cows of Hiie were grazing calmly under the trees. Where was Ilme, Taavi wondered.

"Where could Ilme be?" Osvald was worried too.

"And Hilda?"

"Yes, both of them. I hope they didn't run to the village."

The men stood and listened. The sun had risen halfway up the sky. The open pasture and the smell of the cows was borne on the wind. Noise of fighting came again from the meadows.

The next people they met were Ilme and Hilda. They had left the herd and had climbed a tall fir tree with thick, dense branches, and when the men passed them they called down. Pontus was growling suspiciously under the tree.

Taavi would not let the men stop. The thinned-out file proceeded at its former tempo, with reconnaissance ahead and on the sides. He did not know what to do with the women. It would have been madness to send them alone through the woods to Taevasaar. According to their earlier information this attack was the beginning of a huge roundup comparable with those of the past summer in central Estonia. They knew only vaguely in which direction the enemy would strike. Their plans could be changed if they met resistance. The fact remained that about a regiment of the Red Army had been deployed in the woods of Kalgina, led by the terror squad and units of the NKVD.

Ilme was pale and serious. Her glance flew helplessly to Taavi but she did not dare say a word.

"Take my Browning. Here, take these cartridges."

Ilme took the revolver and walked at his side.

"Are you afraid?" Taavi asked.

"No, there is nothing to be afraid of any more," the woman answered quietly. "Is my father dead now?"

"Yes. He fell. How do you know?"

"Hilda. It was early in the morning when the Russians passed through here. Hilda ran to the meadow to warn the men, but she could not get through. She saw them set the hay barn on fire and. . . . Then Hilda ran to Hiie. Mother collapsed with the shock and then the Russians came to the village."

Taavi's eyes searched for Hilda. The girl was walking at Tõmm's side and the boy was holding her tenderly. Although it annoyed Taavi—any kind of tenderness annoyed him lately—he did not say anything. He was not pleased at all that the women were with them.

"Take the bag from Värdi!" he said to Ilme. "There are bandages. You and Hilda can use them if needed. You know how, don't you?"

Ilme threw the soldier's kitbag over her shoulder. Although she was pale, the man noticed the golden sheen of the summer sun on her cheeks.

"And you must not leave any wounded men in their hands," he added quietly.

"If I should . . . don't you leave me, Taavi. If I can't do it myself, then. . . . Taavi. . . ." She looked at the revolver in her hand.

When they reached the meadows of Lepiku the men could overlook the whole village. The farms were lying in peaceful silence, as if it were Sunday. Only the long farmhouse of Matsu was burning fiercely. Black smoke rolled toward the sky, as if it were gushing forth from the heart of the earth. The roar and crackle of the fire blended with the distant explosions and the barking of the machine guns.

"Osvald, move along the river bank with your men. Wait for us near Piskujõe. If there should be any Russians at Piskujõe, attack. Värdi, come along. Let's take a look at the village. Seems they have cleaned it out already. Let's begin at Kadapiku."

Ilme ran to Taavi.

"May I—Taavi, may I come with you?"

"You know what you have to do." Taavi's voice was sharp and cutting. While he was sorry as he saw his wife's hands sink helplessly and the disappointment register on her face, the cramp-like tension inside him made him suppress the tenderness he felt for her, as if it had been an unpleasant taste in his mouth. Was he really so weak that he could stand up only by supporting himself with brutality? He seized his wife's hands and squeezed them encouragingly. Although he did not smile, something like a smile flickered in his wife's eyes. It was a wordless pact between them—of mutual understanding that would leave its invisible binding tie for ever.

Taavi turned with Värdi toward Kadapiku. They hurried through the woods, not exchanging a single word, concentrating their attention ahead and around. The Russians were nowhere to be seen, not even in the farmyard of Kadapiku. They jumped from behind the woodpile into the wild raspberry bushes. The doors and windows of the farmhouse were open. Even the trap door to the attic was loose. Chickens were all over the vegetable garden. The dead dog was lying in the middle of the courtyard. Cows were lowing wistfully in their stalls, voices hoarse with thirst. As if divining the presence of people, their complaints got louder and more vehement. The men could hear the clanging of their chains and the crackling of the wood of the mangers.

They rushed from room to room, throwing quick glances at the woods through the the window.

"Seems as if they were shaken from their sleep," Värdi figured.

It certainly looked like it. The beds were unmade, bedclothes scattered on the floor. The toys of the children had been carelessly kicked around. A few books were lying there, too, folded backwards and torn apart. The kitchen showed the greatest effects of destruction: the concrete floor was covered with broken china and scraps of food were thrown out from the larder.

"Away from here," Taavi mumbled. The fate of the village suddenly caused him great anguish—and the fate of his own mother. Away from here and quickly. His mother might have succeeded in escaping to the woods. Hilda had said something like that. "Let's go directly along the ditch between the fields. If they should open fire from somewhere, they won't catch us. We'll get there faster."

Värdi only panted for an answer. His face was bluish from the strain and the coughing could barely be suppressed.

They ran along the dry, grass-grown bottom of the ditch between the fields of barley and oats that were shimmering in the sun.

The same picture awaited them at Lepiku. The windows of the old farmhouse had all been smashed. Great pieces of broken glass were scattered everywhere. The curtain had been torn out through one window and a chair was still caught in the frame of another, where it had been used to smash the panes. The old watchdog of Lepiku had been shot in front of the faggot pile.

"Go and see what you can find out at Matsu. I'll go to Hiie myself," Taavi said to his companions.

412

Growling angrily, with his submachine gun on his arm, Värdi turned toward the flames, whose rushing now damped any other noise. Ashes and sparks fell into the yards of the other farms. If there had been any wind from the direction of Kalgina both Hiie and Lepiku might have caught fire and the forests behind them, for there was nobody to check the red fury of the flames.

Hoping that things might be different in the house where his wife had been born, Taavi ran to the farmyard of Hiie and straight through the open door into the house, where he crashed into a man who was reaching for his rifle.

"Tõmm, damn it!" Taavi was startled. "Who gave you permission to come here?"

Tõmm did not answer. No words were necessary. His dark eyes, glowing with desperation, anger and pain, and his cramped lips spoke more than enough. He sat on the corner of the table and stared motionlessly into a corner. Taavi walked quickly through the whole house. The windows had been broken only in the back room. The rugs on the floor and the furniture had been turned over, the big clock in the front room had been smashed into the china cabinet, and the pictures had been torn from the walls. In the kitchen Taavi grabbed a loaf of bread and cut himself a thick slice. He even opened the kitchen cupboard to find some butter for his bread. When he did not find any he sprinkled salt on it. Swallowing mechanically, he remembered that this was the first bite he had eaten that day. None of them had had anything to eat. Without giving it any further thought, he took the whole loaf and returned to the front room.

Tõmm's broken voice sounded from his mother's bedroom. The young man was kneeling in front of his mother's empty bed and pressing the pillow slip against his forehead. His shoulders were shaking. He did not cry. A dry croaking came from his throat.

"Tõmm. . . ."

The young man did not move for some time. When Taavi called his name again he stood up, holding the pillow in his hand. His rifle fell crashing to the floor.

"Look here. This is my mother's blood." He held the pillow toward Taavi. "They have killed my mother," he screamed in a low voice, as if he had lost his power of speech.

"No, Hilda said she had had a fall. Look, this is hardly bloody at all."

"How do you know?" the young man shouted furiously. "Go outside. Aadu is out there. Then you'll see! What have they done to my mother?" Then he began to curse wildly, beating with his fists against the wall and at the broken window. "Father first, and now Mother too."

"Come along."

"Go. Go yourself. What business have you here. Tell me, what do you want here?" He sprang toward Taavi in a rage. "Everywhere it's nobody but you, damn it. There at the hay barn, and here, and. . . . Go where you came from or I'll. . . ."

"Wipe your eyes dry and take the rifle. I have regarded you as a man and counted you among the men," Taavi said. "Quickly now to the county house. The prisoners cannot be much farther. We may be able to save them. Listen, they may even be at Harukurgu!"

"Do you think so?"

"Let's go."

When they went out an airplane roared over the village. They withdrew again into the hallway. Tõmm was leaning against the doorpost, his rifle loosely at his side. Taavi cast a quick glance over the living room, as if he wanted to impress the sight of that shattered home forever on his memory. It had been his home too. Bright sunspots fell through the window on the woven rug on the floor, above which a handful of dust cast a golden shadow over the memories of life spent here in by-gone days. Then his look penetrated farther into the corner and he winced: there was his son's big wooden horse. A sudden pain bent him inside. He walked over to the wall, cautiously stepping closer to his son's toys.

The short, abrupt words exchanged by Tõmm and Värdi, who had returned from Matsu, forced him back into the present. Hurrying across the yard to the meadow, Tõmm pointed toward the flower bed near one end of the house.

"Aadu?" Taavi muttered.

They stopped for a moment. Taavi stepped up to the corpse. He handed the loaf of bread to Tõmm and moved the shattered body. The long black overcoat of the deaf-mute was lying not far away. That, too, was splattered with blood like the grass around them, trampled by many feet. Tõmm turned away with horror.

"What do you expect of the swine," Värdi mumbled in a tired, dull voice. Broad ash flakes fell slowly on the bloody grass and the shattered corpse. At the same moment the rafters of the long farmhouse of Matsu fell in with a great crash. The flames licked the beams with new crackling fury, reaching out for the calm blue sky that was covered with black smoke and soot. The smoke fell like a heavy veil over the fields and meadows, over the whole village, as if it wanted to cover up and hide from the sun the naked, bloody brutality of men.

The village of Harukurgu was swarming with Russians. The lanes of the large, open village were full of trucks that rolled toward the estate of Kalgina and the village of Metsaoti. Crossing the Koolu hills, the men had already noticed the Russians hustling back and forth in the farmyards of Võllamäe and Roosi. Observing them through field glasses from the hills, the men had not seen any prisoners or anybody dressed in civilian clothes. Jaak and Leena of Võllamäe must have shared the common fate of the people of Metsaoti and been arrested and deported from their farms. But where? The men rushed to find out as much as possible.

Taavi was worried about his mother's fate. The yard at Piskujõe had been empty, and Osvald, who had walked around the buildings waiting for Taavi, had not seen any trace of life. He had not noticed any traces of violence or destruction either, although the doors had been open. Taavi had no time to enter his home.

On to the county house. On to the heart of the red octopus, for it was a hopeless task to fight against its countless arms that were writhing through the woods. If you cut off one, ten new monsters stretched out after their prey.

Although they moved fast, the sweat on the men's brows was mostly caused by agitation. They did not know the numbers of the enemy but, considering the number of trucks they had seen on the roads and the units they had met in the woods, there must be many of them. When the distant noise of battle subsided for a few minutes the men halted. Had the enemy already become master of the forests? Had Jonnkoppel and his wolves been beaten down, engulfed by the masses of the Red Army? No, the former angry splutter began again, accentuated by grenade explosions like the furious spitting of an animal. The woodsmen were mobile and they kept their escape routes open, biting the enemy now here, now there.

"Listen, men, listen! That's the roar of cannon over there," Leonard shouted. He stumbled and swore. He was a little nervous and agitated, arranging continuously the belts of machine-gun ammunition he had wrapped around his body. True, the low roar had to come from heavy guns.

"I'm surprised they haven't called in an armoured division," Mart of Liiskaku said. He had turned up the sleeves from his hairy arms and loaded his belt and the wide shafts of his boots with hand grenades. "First the airplanes, now the cannon."

"Shut up and hurry," Taavi's icy eyes flashed. He hurried at the head of the group. His old, faded shirt under the rucksack, filled with submachine gun ammunition, clung to his body which was wet with perspiration. Crossing a ditch that flowed into the river, they swallowed some mouthfuls of water. Osvald distributed the loaf of bread they had brought from Hiie. Although they were all equally hungry, there were some whose share remained uneaten. Neither Ilme nor Hilda ate anything. Tõmm looked at the piece of bread but did not accept it.

Taavi's light hair kept disappearing behind the bushes. Tõmm had opened the buttons of his leather jacket. He was walking, leaning forward a little, his bayonetted rifle hanging indifferently from his hand, and he was not interested enough in his safety to look either left or right. Nothing existed for him at the moment—neither the pine grove, smelling of resin, nor the patch of bog where water splashed under their feet; neither the thicket, where the sharp twigs hit them in the face, nor the ditch, hidden by low bushes, where Leonard fell and cursed out loud, making Osvald so furious that he almost hit him in the face. Tõmm saw nothing. He walked and hurried, not remembering where or why. He did not even notice Hilda, who tried to keep near him.

Peeter of Valba, the old dried-out, sinewy stump of a man who took care of his clothes and often scratched the stubble of his grey beard from his chin, seemed to be tougher breaking through the thickets than anybody could have expected. His sunken cheeks were not even sweaty. He stayed close to Ilme, a little awkward and shy, as he had been last autumn when he had carried milk to the sick woman. He tried to comfort her with a few clumsy words but he did not really know how. He was a little dazed himself by it all. What a crazy dance of death he had been dragged into in his old age.

Strange as it may seem, the county house was the quietest place in the neighbourhood at noon on that restless day. By way of the pine grove of Harukurgu the group was able to approach without being noticed. The forest continued as a thicket of young fir trees below the sloping hillside, reaching almost to the fence around the building next to the county jail. Behind the house was a wall made of round field stones which had practically grown into the earth, and which seemed, with a few ancient pines, ash trees and bushes, an ideal defence position for the attackers. On the other side of the white-washed house the stone fence joined a live hedge of slim young pines, the trunks of which formed a steady, grey-red wall. Behind this wall was the crossroads with the cooperative store. Each branch of the road led to a village, then to single farms, fields and forests again, behind which was the hostile countryside filled with military bases, towns and cities swarming with Russians.

The sun glinted on the metal roof. A truck was idling in front of the county house. Except for two lounging NKVD soldiers not a soul was to be seen.

Taavi and Osvald were standing in a bush behind the fence taking counsel. Because of the truck with its engine still running it seemed quite probable that the people of Metsaoti had been hauled to the county house. Or had the truck brought more soldiers?

"If we could cut through the telephone wires. . . ."

"I'll try, once we get going."

"They might bear down on us like an avalanche from the direction of the store," Taavi hesitated.

"We can count on ten minutes. If we can get into the house in that time we'll surely be able to hold it for another ten minutes. Look, that's Marta's window. We might even get hold of her."

"I have a longer score to settle with her," Taavi said roughly.

Then they heard shots right at their side. One of the soldiers near the corner of the house crashed to the ground, the other threw himself down and crawled around the corner.

"Tõmm, damn him," Taavi shouted.

But by now the rifles of everybody else had spoken. Tõmm was the first to rush straight toward the county house, shooting as he ran. Värdi followed on his heels, firing his submachine gun from the hip. When Taavi managed to get from the bush across the stone fence the first hand grenades were already exploding inside the walls of the county house.

Although the attack had been sudden and violent the defenders reacted in the same way. Most of Taavi's men and Taavi himself were caught under fire on the wide open backyard. There was no other shelter than a few broad tree trunks. They were not very effective, for the enemy was firing from several windows.

"Osvald, the telephone wires," Taavi shouted. Nobody heard him. "Mart, run around the house. Keep your eyes open so that they don't surround us by surprise. Set up your machine gun. Quickly, damn it, don't let them kill you."

Tõmm and Värdi were the first to jump through the window into the house.

Angry bullets whined past Taavi from the window of Marta's room. He sprang blindly from behind the tree toward the black gaping hole of a window, scratching his wrist against the broken glass in his reckless jump. There was nobody in the little room. Even the large office was empty. A terrified stenographer crouched in one corner. A hand grenade exploded in the corridor. Somebody fell down the stairs with a loud crash. Värdi's submachine gun rattled again.

"Tõmm!" Taavi shouted. He suddenly felt a fatherly concern for the young man.

"They're driving away," the low voice of the girl came huskily from the corner.

Taavi sprang to the window of the office, breaking the glass with his automatic. Sure enough, damn them! The motor of the truck roared. NKVD soldiers hustled around it with a couple of civilians. Just as Taavi opened fire the truck began to move. He did not hit any of the soldiers, who retreated in the shelter of the truck. The men on the open top threw themselves down but several probably had a taste of his bullets. A woman among them—it was not Marta—spread out her hands as if she had wanted to fall on her back, but collapsed nevertheless on her face. Taavi did not like the picture that etched itself into his mind, as if an innocent person had fallen.

It was strangely quiet in the large building. The steps of the men, unused to even floors, sounded hesitant. No shots were heard from the outside. The heavy light of the day seemed to be hanging in the windless air, the shadows cutting sharply into the ground. The silence in the rooms that smelled of ink, papers and Russians pressed on the ears so that the men had to shake their heads for no apparent reason. The quiet had descended so suddenly. The momentary lull made them feel as if they had been caught on a flypaper.

"Where are the prisoners?"

"Taavi, Taavi," Tõmm called at the same moment from the waiting room. "Taavi, come quickly! Your mother. . . ."

Taavi's boots clattered on the floor of the waiting room. Tõmm's stunned face, covered with red spots from excitement, made him expect the worst. Hurrying into the hallway he stumbled over the corpse of a Russian who had been torn to pieces by a hand grenade. Another, dressed in civilian clothes, had fallen, head first, down the stairs, his arms wrenched apart and his bloody face crushed against the floor.

417

"He came crashing. I almost caught him on top of me," Tõmm spit out. "Your mother is upstairs—in Marta's room."

Taavi began to comprehend the meaning of those words when he ran up the flight of stairs. In Marta's room—and then his hands and feet became limp. He was standing on the threshold. In the small room, overheated by the sun, he saw a chair turned over in the middle of the floor. A bucket of water lay nearby. There was water on the floor. Taavi saw all that, even the curtain fluttering before the window, in his strange stupor. Yes, his eyes were even looking for Marta, before they stopped on the couch where his mother was lying. Värdi was busy in front of her, pouring water over her face from another bucket.

"Mother!" Taavi shouted. "Good Lord, what have they done to you?"

"Take me away from here, son," his mother whispered, breathing heavily.

"Värdi, tell me, Värdi, what is this? Has she been burned?" Taavi was staring at his mother's face and hands, eyes wide-open, hands trembling. His mother's eyes remained closed.

"What can you expect of the. . . . Some acid or something," Värdi panted.

"No," Taavi shouted, frightened. "Why? Was it Marta?"

"Marta. . . . They forced her. . . ," his mother whispered. There was more compassion in her voice than accusation.

Taavi could not say anything. He felt a strange weakness. His body might still have been able to do something but his mind was caught behind some kind of barrier and blood was pressing at his eyes and ears, covering the world with a filmy haze of unreality, rustling around him like sand that drifts down from a huge dune in the wind.

"We should take her away." A voice broke through the rustling. It was Tõmm. "The Russians. . . . We haven't much time—we might get caught."

"Mother, Mother. . . ." The son bent over the old woman, afraid to touch her. "Does it hurt very much? Can you see me at all? Look at me, can you see me?"

"Yes, yes, son, I can see. . . ." His mother got up, swaying on her feet. "You heard, they may come back. Help me, let's go. They may come back."

Carrying his mother to the door with Tõmm's help, Taavi's eyes searched the little room. He saw the purse that had slipped from the couch to the floor. The purse must have belonged to Marta. A Browning had fallen out of it. He went quickly back from the doorway and picked it up. Where was Marta? She must still be within the walls of the county house, for Taavi had not seen her among those who had escaped from the yard in the shelter of the truck. Or had she been there after all? Osvald and Mart must have caught her then or sent her to her Maker along with the day's abundant harvest of lives. Marta—that was a question Taavi could not leave unsolved any longer. When he and Tõmm had taken his mother to Ilme and Hilda behind the stone wall, when he had given orders to abandon the county house and retreat

418

quickly into the thickets, when he had turned the command over to Osvald, then he would return and look until he found Marta of Roosi. His limbs were trembling with exhaustion and rage.

"Check the attic," he shouted at Värdi.

When Taavi, Linda and Tõmm had left the room Värdi sank for a moment on the couch. A painful itch rose to his throat. It was from the kind of life he was leading and the cold on the moors. He had felt pain in his chest since last spring, and the heat of summer had not dispelled it but seemed to make it more and more intolerable. Sometimes he had fits of coughing that shook him up completely until he was exhausted and covered with perspiration, especially after great exertion. He spat out—this time it was blood.

Värdi was not particularly startled, for it was not the first time. His lungs had been weak all his life and the life he had been leading for so long—with the cold and rain, frustration and embitterment—was bound to take its toll. The reason why he had kept away from his companions recently was not his moodiness so much as his fear of infecting the others. His gloom was caused by the approaching winter and the realization that his strength was ebbing away daily.

Gnashing his teeth in his usual angry way, he straightened himself and stepped contemptuously on the blood on the floor. Feeling a chill run over his back, he touched his forehead with his hand. It was wet. Instead of fear and self-pity, the sharp flames of anger again cut through his dull resentment. What did it all mean—this destruction, this crazy inhumanity, that rose up against him everywhere? Why didn't it ever come to an end? The deportation of Värdi's parents to Siberia should have been enough tribulation for his family. The painful bloodletting to which the long war years had subjected the country should have been sufficient. It was cruel injustice that Värdi's home had been destroyed, that his wife and little daughter had been killed—these things robbed a man of his sanity. All right, he had suffered and borne the sacrifice. He had only slumped forward a little more, had closed his mouth to everything except vodka and curses, and had tried to wash his anger in the blood of the enemy. He had already found out that pain turned into scars and that blood washed away anger. But to be a human being again —he was not permitted that. Why? Ah, nonsense!

Värdi took a few steps in Marta's room. This was the room of the woman who had pulled the strings at the staging of today's deadly spectacle. Värdi was almost curious as he observed the details of this little sun-baked room. He had never seen the woman but he had heard too much about her and had seen the fruits of her actions.

Why was he still standing here? He had to find that woman, take her down from the attic. Where else could she be than in the attic of the county house? Her comrades had run down the stairs. Two had received their due, the third had escaped alive from their hands.

Värdi hurried to the attic. When he reached the dark space under the slanting roof he believed for a moment that he heard a quiet moan. It must have originated in his own mind. He tried to find his way among the dusty castaway furniture. When he lit a match he heard rustling again somewhere behind him. Rats, he realized. If somebody had been there he would already have been fired at.

When Värdi's feet got caught in something soft he bent down and pulled a bundle of cloth from between old boxes. The bundle unfolded in his hand by itself and something startlingly warm and tender welled up inside him, for in the weak light that barely penetrated the attic through the small triangular window he saw the clear colours of the national flag.

An enemy might have made him helpless now, even with his bare hands. Ferdinand Uba himself did not know that under his knotted anger, in his doomed little body, there lived a young idealist, twenty years younger than himself, who, seeing the colours of the national flag, would even forget his rifle leaning on a storage box.

The woman who could suppress her groans only with supreme effort saw it. But she saw also the flag which the man held in his hands like a precious treasure.

Ilme did not expect anybody to return, least of all Taavi and Tõmm. She had become used to giving, to renouncing herself, to accepting blows, to standing face to face with destruction and death. She was convinced she would have to sacrifice her last—her husband and her brother.

She pressed her forehead against the rough stone. She remained on her knees for some time, arms weakly hanging down. Her fingers were still cramped around the handle of the revolver, but the Browning had been emptied. Everything was so quiet that she could hear the rustling of a cornfield nearby.

There were only three of them left behind the stone wall; Ilme, Hilda and Peeter of Valba. Hilda and Peeter quietly explained the situation to Ilme, as much as the old man himself could see and understand of what was going on in the county house.

Although Hilda was so shaken by fear and terror that her face looked distorted, she seemed to have the clearest conception of the danger to which the men were exposed in the county house. Therefore the girl had climbed on the stone wall immediately after the shooting was over and was now looking around, full of apprehension. Destruction could overtake them from the roads, the forests, even from the open field behind them. The girl tried to force herself to be calm, and though worry about Tõmm tore her down from the wall, she remained at her post. She did not notice the group that returned from the building until Peeter uttered a startled cry.

They all ran to meet them. Nobody spoke. Glances asked questions and gave answers.

"Where is our mother?" Ilme asked.

"Where is our mother?" Tõmm repeated, as if waking up. "I don't know where our mother is. There's nobody else there."

"Ilme and Hilda, help her," Taavi begged. His voice sounded tired.

He wanted to return immediately, but stopped, because an Estonian flag appeared at a small attic window. A hand appeared with the flag, another hand emerged holding a submachine gun, and then the head and shoulders of a man.

"Värdi!"

Värdi climbed on to the roof and moved slowly up to the top, holding the unfurled flag in his hand. The roof creaked from his heavy boots and the automatic clanged against the metal.

When Värdi had reached the top he suddenly waved to the group on the ground.

"Wonder what he wants now?"

Gunfire began to rattle again at the same moment in front of the county house. Värdi hurried along the roof behind a chimney and took up his position.

"Ilme and Hilda, go with Mother! Quickly," Taavi ordered. "You, too, Peeter. You know the woods. We'll hold them for a while, then. . . . Come on, Tõmm."

The noise of the rifles became louder. Ilme opened her mouth but her husband had already gone. They withdrew hurriedly behind the bushes and the stone fence and on from there through a rain of whining and whistling bullets. In the middle of the field in front of them exploding grenades threw up earth, stones, ears of corn and whining metal.

Throwing a last glance at the county house, Ilme saw the clear afternoon sunlight falling like a broad, golden river on the blue, black and white flag, to which a man was clinging as if he wanted to hold it forever.

XVIII

The roundup in the forests lasted for weeks. The arrests and interrogations in the neighbouring villages seemed to have no end. Jonnkoppel withdrew with his remaining men farther and farther back into the forests. But so many units of the Russian army had been called out that not even Taevasaar was a safe enough hiding place.

When the fury died down in the thickets, the men took stock. Wounds were dressed with fresh bandages. The men stood at gravesides and levelled the sand over the resting places of their fallen comrades. The swell of past agitation subsided slowly in the survivors, turning joy at their escape into the wordless resignation of exhaustion.

Everyone was strangely busy with himself these days. The men felt the need to sit together but the support they instinctively expected from each other did not come. Answering brutality with brutality demoralized them, as did nightmarish thoughts of the approaching winter. They needed moral support from the free world. If somebody would only say: Hold out, men, we know of your plight. Hold out until the appointed hour. But no such message came from the free world. On the contrary, the voices that sounded through the ether declared that they had been abandoned, that they did not exist. Those of their fellow soldiers who had escaped to the West were held in prison camps, they were pilloried, treated like lepers and criminals by those for whose freedom they had fought.

Perhaps this was the greatest tragedy of all. Ilme had realized the fact when she awoke almost a year before in the cave on Taevasaar, and the knowledge had remained with her constantly since that day. It seemed incredible, but in spite of the destruction in her own soul there was still room in her for human compassion. She had observed the suffering of her husband and his struggle with himself. Although Ilme in her own desperation could only rarely understand it, this partial understanding grew into a feeling that paralysed her desperation. Stumbling along on this narrow path the woman realized that her personal ordeals were only a link in the chain of the suffering of the whole people. Thus the compassion she was strong enough to direct outside of herself became a shining string of pearls, the light of which strengthened her soul and body.

Strange—after the recent days of destruction she discovered to her own surprise that she had become stronger than she could ever have believed. Was she unable to suffer any more? she asked herself. Or did Ilme's strength derive from the warmheartedness and strength of character she observed around her, side by side with the cruelty?

There was Hilda, the half-grown orphan girl. How simple and compassionate had been her whole being when she tried to calm Tõmm, who had collapsed in a rage. The girl had done it almost without words, until the young man had lowered his head into her lap and cried like a child. Later Tõmm was ashamed of his weakness. If Hilda and the others could stand it, he was no weaker than they. He still had responsibilities and duties toward Hilda and his sister above all. And there were the empty fields of Hiie, the land of his forebears, around him, and people still living on that land.

There had been Paavel of Kadapiku, the tough-handed village smith, shivering with fear. What had fate intended, leaving Paavel lying in a bush during the battle until the Russians retreated and Paavel remained with the men in the woods? But when Captain Jonnkoppel had asked for information, his story had been quite incomprehensible. He had walked along with the men like a bear awakened from his winter sleep, frozen and alone. He could not rejoice in his escape, although he asked with a trembling voice: "Have I escaped now? Tell me, have I really escaped? Men, brothers, am I really still alive?"

Then he had sat for a long time at the edge of the moor, stiff and calm, and smoked. The noise of the battle did not concern him and nobody knew what he was thinking about.

When Osvald offered him a rifle, annoyed at his indifference when the lives of them all depended on the contribution of every fighter, Paavel stood up and asked: "Have you seen my children?"

That night Paavel of Kadapiku carried his fallen son Endel in his arms. The big man sat on an earth-clod, swaying quietly back and forth until next morning, his body stiff with the cold of the night, his face pale and sunken. At noon he had straightened himself up in the warm sun and begun to walk toward Kalgina without uttering a word.

The men stopped him and sent him back.

"I can't leave my wife and children with them," Paavel said quietly.

He was sternly ordered farther back into the woods.

Ilme observed him, while taking care of the wounded, and tried to think. She knew that Paavel was a coward. Was it merely insanity that made him act that way? Strange, it was Ilme who could clearly see the fate of the man returning to his family and the Russians. And stranger still—she was able to talk to Paavel. Her words came quietly.

"Paavel, I don't think you would be doing right if you went back. You will only sacrifice yourself without helping anybody. Your going will not help your wife and children but it will bring death or forced labour to yourself. Believe me, I know. They will make you trace down the men in the woods. Your going will even excite their anger against your family to new fury. Try to think, Paavel, for your own sake and for the sake of the others. I know. . . ." The voice of the woman broke and she did not know what else to say. With her tortured instinct she divined that the actions of a person often do not depend on himself.

Paavel said: "I am not strong enough to leave my children."

Who knows what is strength? Ilme considered her husband strong, many times stronger than herself. But when Paavel disappeared from amongst them under cover of night, taking the corpse of his little son with him, Ilme Raudoja could not hold him for a weakling. While Paavel of Kadapiku feared arms, blood and death, there was overpowering strength in his step and his heart when he knowingly went to his martyrdom. I am not strong enough to leave my children.

Ilme saw and realized the calm and serenity of others sharing the same fate—qualities conferring true humanity on beings swept away in the quicksand of time. It appeared in the silent suffering of the wounded and in the manly composure of those who died. Ilme found it now to a certain extent in the deeds everybody had done and on the faces of everyone, as far as there were any people left. Thank God, most of the men were still alive. But from the people of the village only Linda of Piskujõe remained with them. Peeter of Valba, Ilme's tireless helper, had managed to get some sweet butter for her facial wounds somewhere from Ilmaotsa. Taavi's mother kept her sight, contrary to all expectations and fears. Even her scars were not as terrible as they had seemed at first. Her mental suffering had probably been greater than anything but she did not complain, and when she recovered somewhat, she was the first from whom Ilme received a weak but grateful smile. Ilme knew that the smile was meant first of all to encourage and strengthen her.

It was almost a miracle. From that tired smile on the old woman's disfigured features even Ilme learned to smile again.

His back pressed firmly against the dry branches of their shelter, Taavi listened with a motionless face to the talk of the bearded men. The barking growl of Captain Jonnkoppel, which had replaced his normal voice because of a cold, had lasted far too long.

"I have said it clearly enough: No!" Taavi interrupted him again. "I am not fit for such tasks any more. In general, it is senseless, stupid. It is two years too late to leave the country."

"Everybody would leave at the first opportunity. Too late? We are still alive. It is not late. The people are still alive."

"But I—am I still alive?" Taavi exploded. "I do not live any more, and the dead cannot do anything for the living!" Taavi stared into the moss. "If I may, I should like to go now...," he muttered to the captain. When the latter did not answer, stepping from one sore foot to the other in front of him, he remained seated.

"I cannot compel you and I do not know much about the sea," Jonnkoppel continued. "But I thought that—then we would have done everything that is within our power. We are also sending a messenger south in a few days—to Latvia and as far as he can get. I thought you would be the man best fitted to make it across the sea. It is our duty to report these events to the free world."

"Who would listen to me?" Taavi interrupted him bitterly. "We know from the radio what the situation is like."

"At least our own people would understand you. And they are not a single voice in the wilderness but many thousands of mouths."

"I am no choirmaster that I could make them shout in unison about our plight, especially if their lips have perhaps . . . grown together from the comforts of the good life."

"If they don't know. . . ."

"Where did they get the divine inspiration to flee in time if they did not know anything?"

"Don't you begin to accuse anybody in your own ignorance and bitterness. Go and see for yourself. Speak up and demand. Point with your finger and call the things by their right names."

"Is that an order?"

"No. This is a request. Think about it and weigh it and we'll talk about it again more thoroughly when we have rested and when our heads are clearer."

Taavi rose to leave.

"We won't find any rest on this soil now, and when our physical resistance breaks down, so will our minds. My answer is simple, for I cannot leave my wife and aged mother again without knowing what will befall them." He gave the captain a look and turned brusquely around.

Although Taavi considered the talk of the old captain pure nonsense and held the idea of crossing the sea to be the twilight dream of one who has no knowledge of the facts, he could not free himself from it during the next few days. The idea kept coming back, perhaps because it was so different and new. When he began to gather up hazy memories of Finland, anger and disdain at himself surged in him. So it was life itself, most of all, that lured him across the sea. Then he smiled wearily at his own anger: This life was confined to little flashes of memory—no more.

When Taavi was not with his mother and Ilme, he walked alone through the woods, rifle on his arm. One evening he stood near the village of Metsaoti, where two years before he had climbed over the moss-covered fence and walked toward the inviting human dwellings.

He had time enough to stand there now, for nobody was expecting him in the village. Here, between the quiet wings of the forest, in the village that had been alive only recently, death had held a wild orgy. Although his eyes could see it and his nostrils could smell the burned ruins of the farmhouse of Matsu, it still seemed incredible. The crops had been beaten close to the ground by the rain, the potato plants had rotted, the black windows of the houses seemed like the gouged-out eyes of a living being.

There was no light behind any of the windows.

What had brought all this about? Whose fault was it that the flames had risen to the sky just here, that the wind had carried the ashes to the ripe fields, and that man, who had made his home in the forest village of Metsaoti for so long, suddenly stopped walking across the fields of his forefathers? Why had fate chosen this part of the land to mark with its branding iron?

Taavi fingered the moss-covered poles of the fence. Were they destined to mould now without purpose? Or would new people settle here who would bring in the harvest, fix up the fences, plough the fields again and throw new seed into the earth? They would probably be brought in from the east, foreign in custom, language and race. If years went by, would it be different anywhere else? The destruction of every village might not be as abrupt as that of Metsaoti. Some Estonians might succeed in staying near the land of their fathers, as slaves bound to the soil.

Taavi was tired and his thoughts were heavy but in spite of this he directed his steps right into the village and walked slowly through it.

"Go out into the world!" Captain Jonnkoppel had said. "Go out into the world, the Saviour had told His disciples. "Go out into the world and tell them that even the stones cry out here," the grey-bearded old man had told him in the prison cell of the NKVD a year and more ago. The captain demanded the same of him now, his comrades demanded it. A feverish request was in their eyes that were dulled by pain.

Speak to the world—how ridiculous! The world was not waiting for his words. The world did not want to hear about the tragedy of small nations. It would be much happier if these nations were dead already. The world wanted to be blind and deaf, to go on living under the shadow of a bloody sword until it fell.

Taavi walked across the Hiie farmyard. Not so long ago it had been a great, flourishing farm. There was nothing left for him; only his son's toys in a shattered living room and a grave on the meadow near the river where an unbaptized baby was at rest, whose face even its mother could not recall.

Feeling for the cross with his hand, his fingers stayed up for a moment in the moist, dark air and then fell helplessly. When his hand made new movements in the air, finding nothing, and his feet stumbled over the stones, he fell on his knees. His fingers ran quickly over the earth, the sharp stones, and the frozen, trampled autumn flowers. Hilja's carefully kept grave had been levelled. Taavi rose slowly, filled with helpless anger and pain. Chills ran through his body and his muddy hands cramped into hard fists. Some time ago Taavi's fingers had glided over the cross of his daughter, absent-mindedly and unemotionally, and he had not found contact with his dead child. Now, when the feet of the barbarians had desecrated her grave, Taavi felt a strong tie that united him with his daughter. The graves without crosses, the fate of his people, showed him his destiny and that of his children. Here flowed the heavy black waters of the river. Here was a pile of heavy granite boulders, from which his wife had stepped into the dark depths of the stream. Here was an open door, through which he could step calmly into the house of the dead. But Taavi could not use that door yet, for he had not reached the end of his trail. He felt it especially keenly now, when his hands were still covered with earth from his daughter's violated grave. A long road lay still ahead of him, although he had not much strength left.

How could he tell the world about it? How would the world understand the suffering that even God in heaven did not seem to understand? But the people here called out to the world, cried to God, turned to the dead in their desperation. Go, tell the free world so they may laugh at you or put you in an asylum.

Next morning, when the light of dawn tore the wet rags of the night from the fields, Taavi was walking across the Koolu hills toward Harukurgu. It was a routine reconnaissance trip, for there was no assurance that new forces were not being massed at Harukurgu, ready to penetrate again into the innermost thickets of the woods. In the pine grove behind the Võllamäe farm he smelled the sickening stench of death. He stopped and almost felt sick. But looking around, he could not find the decaying corpse anywhere in the bushes or under broken faggots. When he approached the Võllamäe farm against the wind, the sickening stench became stronger and stronger. His fingers around the handle of the revolver were wet and he felt a sudden sharp pain in his shoulder muscles, caused by lying on the wet ground night after night. It must be a fallen Russian. The men had thrown many of them into quickly dug graves after the roundups. One could often find traces of death in the neighbourhood now and nobody paid much attention to them.

The view that met Taavi's eyes in the little clearing in the wood rooted him to the ground. The momentary curiosity vanished from his ice-grey eyes, giving place to disgust. Fate itself answered some of his questions for him.

Three bodies were hanging from a strong pine branch. They were mutilated and they stank. The middle one was that of Marta of Roosi. To the right of her dangled the gigantic body of the militiaman, and to the left one of the woodsmen whose name Taavi could not recall.

426

He withdrew the way he had come. He suddenly felt that somebody was running at his heels, as if the eyes of the woman were still alive, although she had been shattered and violated beyond recognition.

Without noticing it himself, Taavi had started to run.

That day Taavi realized that he was unable to go on living in this land. Would he be able to do anything if the day of the final battle did not come? Hardly, for he had put everything without reservation into the battle that was not yet finished. He had no place to catch his breath and no warm back chamber where he could spend a peaceful old age. The poison of defeat and anger in his veins was too strong to be redeemed even by his own blood.

Very calmly he told Ilme about his task: to try to cross the sea. His wife listened even more calmly.

They had walked away from the campsite together. It was a beautiful autumn afternoon when nature is in one of her placid moods. The blue sky seemed to have descended low, and the warmth of the sun could no longer repel the coolness which emanated from the shadows and would grow soon into winter. Man and wife walked slowly, side by side, as if they were enjoying their walk—perhaps their last. Perhaps their eyes that were turned inside were wandering in distant memories. Perhaps they were saying good-bye within themselves. They were probably doing both, for thoughts have little logic in moments like these.

"I wanted to ask your opinion."

Ilme was silent. Ask her opinion—her husband had never asked for it in matters like this. What answer had she to give after all that had happened? She did not want him to leave; she wanted Taavi to stay with her. She knew she must kill this desire in her heart; it was just as futile as the hope to embrace again her children and her family. They would all stay with her in spirit, even her husband, for as long as she lived. No power would be strong enough to take her past from her. If her husband still had strength enough to look the future in the face and hew a path for them into tomorrow, then she, too, must be strong enough to follow in his footsteps. This meant that her own path, too, would go on.

"I'll wait," Ilme said with a broken voice.

"You will wait," Taavi repeated. "You. . . ." His voice, too, broke into a whisper with emotion. "I won't go. I'll never leave you any more! Never!"

When Taavi stroked his wife's hair, Ilme's eyes filled with tears. How old and thin Taavi seemed. Ilme looked at her husband like one who takes leave for ever, for she felt and knew more about his future than he did himself.

The following days passed like a dream for Taavi. Somehow whatever happened did not touch him, although he participated in it: the activities of the men who caught some stray cattle in the woods, or the trip at night to bury the three hanging corpses. Taavi had selected the men for this task and had asked them to keep quiet about it. When they returned, their grim faces spoke more than words.

In the evening Taavi sat with his mother under a great pine tree

427

where they had built a crude shelter against the wind and rain, and where they were planning to spend the night. Ilme and some women from Tenise were caring for the wounded a short distance away. Most of them were recovering, except for two whose wounds had become inflamed. Osvald and a few others hid their bandages under their coats and did not count themselves among the disabled but helped the others with lighter work—herded the cattle or gathered firewood.

The sun had gone to rest and the great bogs began to breed hoarfrost for the morning.

"What are you looking at, Mother?" the son asked suddenly.

"Nothing. I was thinking that . . . you'll be going your way again soon. . . ."

"How? Who told you that?" Taavi was startled.

"Ilme told me several days ago."

So Mother knew about it and yet she was so serene, with the black wounds on her face covered with ointment, her hands in white bandages.

"I don't know yet. . . ."

"You have to know, son. Don't let me stand in your way. It is good if you know your way. Go! I told Ilme, too, that if we can keep calm it will be best. What should we have to say about it? You still know your way and that is good for us to know too."

Taavi looked in admiration at his mother, who was talking quietly and calmly.

"But how . . . how are you going to stay behind like this?"

"What about us. . . ?" his mother whispered. She wiped once over her cheek with her bandaged hand and smiled. "These silly eyes! We'll manage somehow. Our feet are still good—and Ilme's hand, too. We won't bother the men much. We'll be waiting—for you and the others who will come back. A person must have something to wait for in life and we have so much to wait for. We are still rich."

Ilme's decision was the same. Both women had learned to be silent and to deny themselves.

When Taavi looked at those people who had suffered so much—his wife and mother and many others, whose suffering and anguish he could compare only to those of the Saviour bearing His cross—he had no more doubts. He only asked defiantly: Cannot these nameless thousands, tens of thousands, millions of innocent people really redeem the world? Shall these people who remain here in the grey evening at the mercy of the night really never see even the faintest glow of the dawn? Are these people really lost? If that is so, then truly humanity itself is at the threshold of its ultimate end.

Taavi Raudoja cannot believe it, for he is still alive. These doomed people do not believe it for they, too, are still living. They are living their lives for future generations, for a new day, and, when it arrives, they will be those who have redeemed humanity in their graves without crosses.

England, December 1951